Firesong

Born in London, brought up and educated in Ireland, Joseph Hone is a well-known writer and broadcaster and bestselling novelist. He lives in Oxfordshire.

Also by Joseph Hone

Fiction

The Private Sector
The Sixth Directorate
The Paris Trap
The Flowers of the Forest
The Valley of the Fox
Summer Hill
Return to Summer Hill

Travel

The Dancing Waiters
Gone Tomorrow
Children of the Country: Coast to Coast Across Africa
Duck Soup in the Black Sea

Firesong

A NOVEL OF RUSSIA

JOSEPH HONE

PAN BOOKS

First published 1997 by Sinclair-Stevenson, an imprint of Reed International Books

This edition published 2004 by Pan Books
an imprint of Pan Macmillan Ltd
Pan Macmillan, 20 New Wharf Road, London N1 9RR
Basingstoke and Oxford
Associated companies throughout the world
www.panmacmillan.com

ISBN 0 330 32150 1

3 5 7 9 8 6 4 2

A CIP catalogue record for this book is available from
the British Library.

Printed and bound in Great Britain by
Mackays of Chatham plc, Chatham, Kent

For Susie

Now therefore ye are no more strangers
and foreigners, but fellow citizens with
the saints, and of the household of God.

St Paul, Epistle to the Ephesians, 2, 19

BOOK ONE

1906–1915

1

The wolves increased their pace behind them.

The sun dipped towards the horizon of the frozen lake, strange hues emerging in the pure air, the snow turning carmine, dusky scarlet, blood red. The two *troikas* remained one behind the other. Their drivers, long experienced *yamshchiks*, and the two armed guards with them, were not overconcerned. Wolves, at this deep midwinter season, sometimes followed traffic at a respectful distance across this vast expanse of frozen water. So that now, glancing behind them, the drivers merely flicked their reins over the horses' rumps, setting the two loosely harnessed outside animals into a faster canter, each central horse, under its wooden arched *duga*, breaking into a faster trot.

The presence of these wolves on the huge lake was not surprising. This winter of 1906, in these immense northern spaces of Karelia some hundreds of miles north of St Petersburg, had been the hardest for years. So the wolves, finding less and less to sustain them in the surrounding forests, had ventured out and about the lake and its shoreline settlements – famished, voracious, indiscriminate in their prey.

The two children in the second *troika*, the twins Alexander and Yelena Rumovsky, in their identical squirrel-tail hats and fur *shubas* – thrilled in any case by this annual new year sleigh ride over Lake Ladoga to their grandfather's island castle at the northern end – saw these wolves simply as an additional excitement in their journey.

Yelena, thrusting her little black pug dog Samson into the arms of their governess Miss Harriet, half stood on the seat. 'Look!' she yelled across at her brother, speaking English, which was the language they spoke best between themselves.

'They're getting closer! They'll have us all – at the heel of the hunt.'

The twins, at just eleven, were bright and precocious, especially with words. Yelena was particularly intrigued by the curious Irish phrases which Miss Harriet sometimes used, repeating them to herself, even when she didn't understand these expressions, until they became magic incantations, added to her store of such spells, which she treasured for future use.

'They're racing us!' Sasha shouted back. 'But they won't get us.'

'No, Sasha. Because we'll throw you out to them!'

'They'd far sooner eat you, Linochka. Wolves like little girls. Everyone knows that. Remember "Little Red Riding Hood", you great stupid!'

'We'll throw you out first, and they'll eat you and then I won't have to practise with you any more. There'll be no more music lessons, and that'll be even better!'

'Oh yes there will. Miss Harriet will make you go on playing on your own – *twice* as much! – you silly cow.'

The twins either loved or hated each other. There was little if any middle way between them. They were inseparable in their affection or else hoped for the other's death. Yelena turned her eyes on her brother fiercely – so that, just about to embark on some further taunt, he fell silent – literally, as it seemed, struck dumb by this ultimate rebuke.

Yelena's eyes were an astonishing feature. Even in repose, they glittered with intensity, as if kept alight by some other power outside her life. In anger they blazed, as they did now, transfixing Sasha, silenced by this hypnotic quality in her gaze.

He remained silent, turning to watch the wolves. He thought they were gaining on them. Soon, surely, when they were within range, the guards would unsling their carbines, swing round on their high seats and shoot them. That was what wolves were for: to be shot and killed.

This was what the *yamshchiks* thought, too, when, five minutes later, they looked behind them and saw how the pack had divided, a leading group of half a dozen running faster, starting to overtake the second *troika*, as outriders now, but with the clear intention of coming between the two *troikas* and separating them, the better to make a kill. The armed guard on the second *troika* unslung his carbine, readying himself.

Yelena looked around her at the wolves. She had no fear of them, despite what Sasha had said about Little Red Riding Hood, or all that she knew of them in their huffing and puffing the little pigs' houses down. For her these wolves had no wicked reputation. They were creatures of an enchanted kingdom. Therefore they would not harm her, for she thought herself part of all that wondrous company of wolves, firebirds, hobgoblins, witches, fairies. She shared their magic. She jumped up and down again. 'They'll eat you, Sasha – at the heel of the hunt!'

The twins' governess, Miss Harriet Emily Boulting, of Ardmore House, Durrus, West Cork, did her best to restrain the two children, with little success. She, too, had made this long midwinter *troika* journey across Lake Ladoga from the railhead at Ladenpohja on the western shore half a dozen times. She, too, like the twins, was without fear now – both by natural temperament, and from her confidence in these bearded *yamshchiks* in their great padded coats.

None the lesss she was forced now by the conventions of her position to display concern. And she did so with conviction, for she was a woman of frustrated histrionic ability and romantic inclination, qualities which, if she rarely showed them in public, she allowed full play in her mind and in her dealings alone with the twins. 'Sit down,' she shouted at them. 'And behave yourselves . . .'

Now, turning her pale blue eyes over the ice, Miss Harriet saw how the beasts behind were gaining on them, while the ones at their side, increasing pace, were about to cut in ahead, separating the leading *troika* from their own. She saw the leading pack clearly now: big animals, ears pricked, yellow slanting eyes, at ease in their run, biding their time, as if certain of their eventual meal. And she was incensed at the presumption of the wolves in so reversing, as she saw it, the natural order of things. As a keen huntswoman in Ireland, out in every weather with the Carberry and West Cork pack, she thought it an outrage to see the fast-advancing muzzles of such beasts, rather than disappearing brushes.

Now the guard above her fired, twice. She saw the blue flash from the muzzle of the carbine, the resounding crack, echoing over the ice. One of the wolves fell. But the others simply continued their run.

In the first *troika*, some hundred yards ahead, the occupants jumped in their seats at the shots and turned, alarmed. The twins' parents, Prince Pyotr Mikhailovich Rumovsky, his wife the Princess Sofia, with their thirteen-year-old son Ivan, were less disposed by nature or knowledge to take a relaxed view of these wolves.

Ivan was an unhappy-looking boy, his face wedge-like, unnaturally thin, undernourished. His expression was usually aggressive or set in a sulk – masks which hid his real torture, which was that he felt unloved by his parents. This was largely true so far as his mother was concerned, while his father, who cared for him greatly, was unable, by an inhibited temperament, to show him this.

So the boy lived alone with his pain – set at a distance from his parents, sensing the chill separation between them, and separated from the twins, knowing equally well how they both survived by supporting each other, with Miss Harriet as a mother, in their own private world of music, books, games and codes. Now he secretly feared these wolves, seeing in their approach some sort of nightmare punishment for his unhappiness.

His mother, the Princess Sofia, in her late thirties, seeing the leading pack closing on them, trembled. These wolves to her were the essence of everything she hated and feared in Russia: a land where the unpleasant and uncouth, the malign and the malodorous, singly or all together, were ever-present. She turned to her husband, hiding her fear, looking at him disdainfully with her chill blue eyes. 'Wolves . . . a whole vicious pack. What more may we expect? To be eaten alive before we even reach this barbaric castle?'

'No.' The Prince didn't look at her. 'They are only harrying us. After those shots, they'll keep their distance, come no closer.'

The Prince was not certain of this. Trained as a zoologist, and now, in his mid-forties, one of the 160 constitutional Democrats in the first Duma in St Petersburg, he knew how tireless and persistent these animals were, when hungry and once joined in the chase; knew what havoc they could wreak if they managed to close with them.

Both packs of wolves, seen against the setting sun, took on a monstrous air, appearing in grim silhouette, dark undulating beasts riding out of an apocalyptic sunset, creatures of nightmare.

They lengthened their stride now. They were hungry, impatient. No longer distant followers or outriders to this transport of sweating, sweet-smelling flesh they were determined to kill, to eat. The chase began in earnest.

In the first *troika* Prince Pyotr saw the leading pack of wolves approach. The *yamshchik* above him saw them, too, whipping the horses on furiously, while the armed guard started firing at them over the passengers' heads. In the fading light with the violent action of the sledge, he missed, and missed again. The wolves increased their pace, soon running on either side of the *troika*, dark shapes closing on their prey. In a moment they were alongside the horses, snapping at their legs.

The horses panicked. The wolves set upon the two outside animals, jumping, snatching at their hindquarters, the horses terrified, neighing wildly. In a minute, with this harrying, the horses stumbled, wild with fear. The driver lost all control of them. The *troika* slowed to a stop. The horses reared and kicked, fighting to escape these vicious predators. The two outriding animals broke free of their loose traces and galloped away. The one at the centre, more firmly harnessed under its wooden *duga*, could not so readily escape.

The wolves fell upon it, half a dozen of them, bringing it down, strong jaws ripping into the stomach, starting to devour it. The passengers, only a few yards away, watched, horrified. The armed guard, down from the seat with the driver, started to fire at the beasts. Two were hit. Two others, lying low behind the belly of the fallen horse, had cover. The last pair, seeing the position, chose other cover. They moved out of the guards' firing line, behind the *troika*, uncertain for a moment, before they turned. Their yellow eyes gazed at the three passengers, huddled together beneath their rugs on the back seat. Princess Sofia screamed. The guard could do nothing now. He was fumbling with the carbine, reloading.

Meanwhile the driver of the second *troika* behind, with Miss

Harriet and the twins, seeing the fate of the first, sought to throw off the pack pursuing them by veering suddenly to the left, off the ice track, setting the horses at a gallop out over the snow of the frozen lake, while the guard let off a fusillade, hitting one of the wolves. The pack broke formation, uncertain, falling back, some hundreds of yards behind them now. The *troika* sped on, before the wolves regrouped and resumed the chase.

In the fading light the driver didn't see the sudden obstacles rearing up ahead – windblown snow banks, each increasingly high, which lay diagonally across their path – waves of hard frozen snow which had formed off the beaten track. The horses jumped through them. The *troika*'s runners hit them at an angle. The big sledge was suddenly bucking up and down, over ever-higher crests, a ship caught in a wild storm, tipping about violently before hitting a larger frozen drift.

The *troika* sheared over viciously. Sasha and Yelena, half up on their knees on the seat, were flung out, together with the little pug dog Samson, straight in the path of the pursuing wolves, before the *troika*, righting itself on the far side of the drift, sped on.

Miss Harriet, who had managed to hold her seat, screamed at the *yamshchik* and the guard. Turning, they saw what had happened, but could not immediately restrain the horses, careering away madly now over the snow.

Yelena picked herself up, unhurt, having landed in softer snow on the far side of the frozen drift. With Samson at her heels, she ran to the top of the hardened crest. Sasha was lying on the other side, motionless, one arm twisted beneath him. The wolves were less than a hundred yards away, approaching fast.

She stood on top of the crest, looking across the lake to where the sun was setting, a huge orange ball right behind the pack, so that the wolves, their paws dipping into the snow, hidden at each pace, appeared to be levitating in their run, suspended over a carpet of cobalt tinted gold.

The pack, seeing their quarry immobile ahead of them, slowed. Only the large she-wolf, who headed the others, ambled on ahead.

Yelena screamed. Filling her lungs, she let out a succession of piercing screams – an expression of fury and command, not of fear – following these with a series of equally imperious orders.

'Back! Back. Go away. You're not going to eat either of us.' Then she suddenly thought of something more effective to say, and the strange words rose on the chill air. 'Oo goggery bag-wag! Goggery bag-wag! Go away – away!'

The she-wolf, hearing the screams, paused some thirty yards from her – then came forward, more circumspectly, only to stop once more when these last strange threats were hurled at her.

The whole pack came to a halt, looking curiously at the little girl and the fearlessly barking dog. Yelena could see the slanting yellow eyes of the wolves, their pricked ears, their great muzzles, see the storms of panting breath rising from their nostrils, heads shifting quizzically from side to side as they watched her. Encouraged by the success of this magic incantation, Yelena repeated it, varying the pitch of her voice up and down. 'Oo goggery bag-wag! Goggery bag-wag! . . .' The words rose over the snow like a song, notes of victory, a triumphant music in her voice now.

The wolves, put off by these fearful screams, began to circle the two children, seeking to attack them in a flanking movement or from behind.

Several minutes passed as Yelena and the little dog watched the pack circling them in the violet light. Then the armed guard ran up behind Yelena with his carbine. The shots came in a furious volley, the muzzle flashes bright in the fading light, with sounds of vast tree trunks cracking, reverberating over the lake. Several wolves fell. The remainder turned on their heels.

The passengers in the first *troika* escaped the attentions of the wolves, if only just. The guard, finally reloading his carbine, had rounded the sledge, and shot most of them. It had been a close-run thing. The Princess Sofia remained hysterical. The boy Ivan had lost his nerve completely. The normally phlegmatic Prince Pyotr was badly shaken. The *troika*, without horses, had to be abandoned. Walking back over the ice, with the *yamshchik* carrying their baggage, they eventually joined the other party, crammed into the remaining *troika*, and resumed their journey.

Only Yelena remained quite calm, a core of warmth and

certainty expanding all about inside her. Their own escape from the wolves, and her means of achieving it by the magic incantation, seemed quite natural to her. Good spells like this always worked.

Yelena was crushed in next to Miss Harriet, who was nursing Sasha on her lap. She was warm again under the great fur rugs, the *troika*'s lanterns lit as they continued across the lake towards the fire which they could see flickering on the horizon, the great timber fire always lit at night on the castle's ramparts.

She looked up at Miss Harriet. 'It was the spell from the story that really frightened those wolves away,' she said.

'Which story?'

'*The Phoenix and the Carpet* – that chapter you read us last night on the train, when the children take Cook with them on the magic carpet to the island with the savages. And the cannibals shout "Oo goggery bag-wag". And the children and Cook run for their lives. That's where I got the magic spell from. And it worked.'

'Yes. Yes, of course!' Harriet looked at Yelena, hiding her astonishment. An unlikely idea, she thought, that such spells from a child's book would stop a pack of hungry wolves. Yet something had stopped them. She had seen them stop as she'd run up towards Yelena with the *yamshchik*. And she'd heard the last of Yelena's shouted imprecations, the strange oaths from Miss Nesbit's book. Perhaps it was the truth.

Good books could have such practical magic, she knew, giving you ease from the hurts of real life. So, she supposed, the situation could be reversed. Such stories could give you weapons against your enemies, as they had perhaps in this instance with Yelena. She had simply extracted this magic power and used it for her own protection. Why not? All Yelena had done was to turn the story of Little Red Riding Hood and the Big Bad Wolf on its head.

Yelena looked at Sasha then, taking the hand of his good arm in hers, squeezing it beneath the rug, reassuring, loving him now, whereas half an hour before she had hated and scorned him.

The twins, having shared the same womb, had shared almost everything ever since: the same Russian wet-nurse, nannies, same governess, tutors, bedrooms, nurseries, meals, games, music lessons on piano and violin. And books. As much as their music they shared books, in reading alone themselves and in the readings aloud, every day, by Miss Harriet. Nursery rhymes and fairy tales, poems, adventure stories, the Russian fables of Baba Yaga the witch and the Firebird; and latterly *Treasure Island*, *Little Women*, Henty's Tales for Boys and E. Nesbit – and on to the latest stories from America, *The Wizard of Oz* read several times the year before and then the same writer's *John Dough and the Cherub*, which they thought even better.

From all these books and their magically endowed or heroic characters, the twins took a life often more real to them than their own. From this cornucopia of fantasy they drew grist for their own personal battles and affections, using these stories – their titles, characters, phrases – as weapons, or forms of endearment, as a shorthand communication, a secret coded language between them, so that the stories came to dictate the shape and direction of their lives, enabling them to survive the hazards and disappointments there.

The twins were not identical. They had little of the same build or feature. Both were smaller than average for their age. But Yelena was more robust, a stocky girl, already strong, boyish in form. But nothing in this chunky, competent physique was unbalanced or overdone. She was not fat or thin, too light or too heavy. All was of a piece, all cohered.

Sasha on the other hand, as if the fates in their shared womb had mixed up the design, had a face and form which his sister might rather have had. He was slim for a boy, taller than Yelena, small-boned and muscled, with pale almost translucent skin; eyes that were deep set and slightly hooded like his mother's, with her thin firm lips and straight nose. His temperament was quieter, more contained than his sister's. Yet he was just as firm in having his own way.

They had the same big blackberry eyes and short dark hair. But the almond ovals of Yelena's eyes stood proud, were less widely spaced, with narrow tightly knit dark eyebrows, almost coming together over the bridge of her nose. Her mouth might have seemed ungenerous, with the thin upper lip, until one noticed how the lower lip was one of sensuous rebellion, folding out and down in an inviting perfect bow. Beneath lay a decisive chin; she had small ears with pointed lobes, and overall a peach complexion that flushed easily, in enthusiasm or anger.

They were twins only in having been born ten minutes apart, and in that intuitive understanding and closeness found in such couples. They were opposites in every other way. And there was a tension between them in this. They were separate, yet each complemented the other's character. Each lacked what the other possessed. So, though so often openly hating or scorning each other, they unconsciously sought for union.

Sasha's features were less striking. But these, too, were all of a piece: everything in the right proportion. One day he would be handsome. Yelena, on the other hand, in her face at least, was never likely to achieve any mere conventional beauty. For she had one flaw in her features which was at odds with all the other great promise there: a nose which turned up at the end, which didn't quite belong, didn't fit with the rest of her face. A nose which increasingly tormented her as she grew older. She looked up at Miss Harriet then, envying her long straight nose.

Miss Harriet, indeed, had a perfect nose, with eyes of morning-glory blue set in an attractively freckled-skinned, pre-Raphaelite face; long and thin, distinguished, a face topped by a fine fluffy toss of usually quite uncontrolled red-streaked auburn hair.

Her limbs were angular and sinewy, the skin tightly drawn over the bones, so that some of them protruded, seeming brittle. In fact she was a strong woman. She was too tall and wiry in form to be thought willowy, though this description she sometimes allowed herself – just as, at twenty-three, she saw herself as a happily unmarried woman, in no way a spinster. Indeed, there had been ample confirmation of her allure already. There had been several serious proposals of marriage, from admirable, sensible men, from neighbouring Anglo-Irish families in West Cork. But all these men had been too sensible, she had persuaded herself, had lacked qualities which she felt she must have in a man to find him really attractive.

She hardly dared admit it, but she looked for something wayward here; something irresponsibly gallant. Rascally even. She knew it was ridiculous. But there it was. She longed, whenever she dared think of it, for some sort of crushing, voracious, negligent power in a lover. In short, the qualities she sought here would have made a marriage to any man who possessed them unsatisfactory, if not disastrous. So, since she thought herself more wise than passionate, she remained unattached, while yet living with the secret hope that one day she might meet such a man.

Attracted by the unreliable in this way, she hid this fact and withheld her heart, giving expression to these wild impulses only in daydreams, in her bizarre use of words, her vivid idioms and Irish turns of phrase, her taste for the dramatic, in books and games, and in the enthusiasm with which she handled her music lessons with the twins.

Music was an even greater passion of Miss Harriet's than books. But it was one which she had not so successfully encompassed. Its glories, she knew now, she was best able to appreciate and teach rather than perform. Once she had hoped to interpret them professionally. And the auguries here had been good. As a child, and then at the Dame school in Cork, she had been taught music, and had discovered a natural gift for both the piano and the violin. Afterwards, at Alexandra College in Dublin, she had improved on both instruments, finding how she had a perfect ear, pitch, tone. Later, in London, she had concentrated on the piano, studying at the Royal College of Music.

Here she had partnered another student, a Scotsman with the settled name of Duncan, a reliable youth who had played the violin and accompanied her beautifully in duets: a man she had come to love in many ways, but who had not that animal edge to him, so that she had turned him down when he had asked her to marry him.

It was perhaps the greatest regret of her life that they had not continued playing together, and more especially that they had not made an even closer partnership in marriage. Yet she could not have married him. That was the crucial point. She had so clearly felt that with Duncan, as with her other suitors, their general worthiness disqualified them. They lacked that dangerous element in their natures which was what she wanted of a man in her heart of hearts, but knew she must not have.

So, when she had arrived as governess for the twins in St

Petersburg three years before, she had set out to make good all her own lost opportunities, in music at least, teaching them the piano and violin, launching them along the same paths she had taken herself and where she had lost her way. She was sure they would not do the same. Though they squabbled in their playing and resented the hours of practice she imposed on them, it was clear almost from the start that they had extraordinary gifts.

They had, when they wanted it, something which she and Duncan had never quite managed, an astonishing instinctual accord in their playing, drawn from both loathing and love for each other, which gave their music together a cruel sharpness and beauty. Music flowed from them with an indolent, impudent ease, as if all the necessary gifts and skills for this, which others had so to labour over, had been imprinted on them, long before, in their shared womb.

Their mother, Princess Sofia, on the other hand, had betrayed her gifts and nourished instincts which were not at all creative. She was now a frivolous – but had never been a stupid – woman. This was her misfortune, that she had come to promote her shallow appetites with a good mind, so that her flaws had come to outweigh the virtues her husband had first loved her for. So, in time, in prospering her weaknesses by her reason, she found value in her frivolities and infidelities, seeing them as a keystone to her life rather than, as they had become, millstones round her neck. The Princess Sofia, knowing she was intelligent, had come to believe equally in the value of her shallow feelings. She thought, in these, that she swam in deep waters. In fact she had sunk in them. This might not have been altogether her fault.

Her family, the Panevežys, were Lithuanian nobles, originally Prussians who had long before plundered and settled that Baltic nation, with a castle and large estates near Vilnius, the capital. They were a dull and narrow-minded *Junker* family, vital only in the arrogance of their race, who saw themselves as superior to every other, so that Sofia had been brought up in a world she wished to escape from before she was twenty, but whose values she had unconsciously retained.

Prince Pyotr had met and married her in her first mode of liberation and reaction against her background, when she appeared both engaging and open-minded. But after some years marooned, as she came to see it, in Russia, the doors had closed on the happier parts of her soul and she had reverted to the unamiable and illiberal nature of her family, most particularly as regards anything Russian, which drew her scorn and hatred. Her husband, inevitably, came to be included among the objects of her disgust.

So, in time, she had taken revenge against him for bringing her to this savage land by first criticizing him and denying him, then by flirting with other men, and finally by spending little more than the winter season at her husband's palace on the quays of St Petersburg.

She contrived to spend the rest of the year at the Panevežys' castle, in Berlin where they had a town house, at the Rumovsky villa in Nice or at one or other of the fashionable spas, Marienbad or Baden-Baden. She moved from pillar to post, persuading herself that she had familial or other hygienic duties at each. In fact her constant peregrinations were simply intended to refresh her indulgences, a change of site to whet her appetites.

Her beauty encouraged this trivial life. High-cheeked and browed, straight-nosed, lips kept invitingly ajar; huge, deep-set, dark eyes; a creamy skin and a crown of glossy black hair, curled on top and running over her delicate ears to a variety of fashionable ties at the back – the Princess Sofia offered an image of proud sensuality. She was in truth an ice maiden.

This essential coldness was something she successfully hid from others, offering instead clear hints of pain and neglect in her marriage, of a passionate nature unfulfilled thereby, so that many men, married and single, had taken to her, several of whom she had betrayed her husband with. Latterly she had indulged herself with a German count living in Berlin, a middle-aged widower with whom she believed she had found the true love of her life: a man who, did she but know it, trembled in his boots each time they met, for the Princess, beneath her apparently vulnerable surface of a wife misused, was a shrew, intent on dominating and dictating to her paramours, as she had long done with her husband.

Prince Pyotr, mild-mannered, with two spiky tufts of hair rising to either side of his head and a neat moustache, was a good man. Except with his wife, who had drawn out all his few bad qualities and created fresh faults in him as well. Her callously unfaithful behaviour over the years had given him good reason to hate her. Which he did. But with his natural restraint and indecisiveness, he had never properly come to grips with her about this, when he could have shown her the door. Instead his criticisms of her were always made in small measure, went off at half-cock. And he was ashamed of this. So, in time, to avoid this feeling, the Prince had taken to near silence with his wife, conducting their affairs with a curt formality in private, a chill affability in public.

The Princess, knowing her husband's weaknesses here, and long certain of her power over him thereby, dallied with her distaste for her husband now.

She looked at him close to, crushed together in the overloaded *troika*, his face illuminated by the *troika* lanterns, speaking in an angry whisper. 'That we should risk our lives like this! Simply in order to spend the new year with your ogreish father and his ridiculous retinue of boyars. An unholy alliance if ever there was.'

The Prince, without looking at her, grunted mildly. 'Even so, it brings you a wealth – his and mine – which you have never been slow to draw on, for your frivolities, fripperies – and infidelities.'

'Nor you, in your pursuit of extinct animals, old bones and fossils, all over the world. Or in promoting your dangerous liberal views in the Duma with your dreadful friend Mykulov. What is all that if not extremely foolish?'

'If you thought about it at all, you would see such liberal attitudes differently: how only through them can we have freedom, knowledge. And these are all that really matter in life.'

'And human emotion? Love?' She looked at him coldly.

'Yes, they matter greatly as well. But in their corrupt forms–' Now at last he turned to her, looking at her dismissively. 'They mean less than nothing.'

The *troika* approached the huge pile of shimmering logs high on the ramparts of old Prince Mikhail's castle. A fire which was a beacon for travellers everywhere on the lake, which would guide them unerringly over the ice, from darkness to light, to a world which Yelena knew contained just as much magic as any of her books.

But now she felt a twinge of fear. Wolves she understood. She could control them. But not the castle. In all its mysterious doings, its unexpected excitements and terrors, the castle was beyond her control. Here was a different sort of magic. Not the magic of a book, which however frightening you could close at the end of a chapter, when Miss Harriet would kiss her and Sasha, snuggling them both down in bed, taking the big lamp away, leaving only the faint comforting glow beneath the icon on the far wall, when you fell asleep.

At the castle Yelena knew you couldn't stop things. And nothing ever stopped. There was never complete stillness or quiet. There were different noises all night, the heavy footsteps of the watchmen on the ramparts below their bedroom window in the tower; softer footsteps, stopping, then gliding past their nursery door; the sudden baying of the borzoi hunting dogs in their kennels by the boathouse; equally sudden shouts, singing and laughter from the great hall. And on summer nights – the menacing 'clack-clack' sound, like some vicious snapping animal, echoing from the deep woods on the shore: the gamekeepers with their strange wooden clappers, keeping in touch with each other and warning off poachers.

The castle was a book that never closed, a story never completed. It was a tale that went on and on, like Scheherazade's endless stories to the fierce sultan, facing death if once she failed in her invention. All this Yelena knew from her copy of *A Thousand and One Nights*, with its magic pictures of turbanned courtiers, castles and minarets in Baghdad. But this castle was real, and had its own fierce sultan and its strange court as well, in the shape of her grandfather and his friends, dressed in their old-fashioned clothes: all waiting for them in the great hall, her grandfather on his high throne, when she would quake at the sight of him – when, like Scheherazade herself, she felt she would have to defend herself with every invention, every spell and incantation that she knew. The castle thrilled her. But she also feared it.

2

The old Prince sat on a slightly raised dais at one end of the great hall. Around him stood his bastard son Dmitri Mikhailovich, his chief steward Stephan Vassilievich, together with a number of cronies and retainers. Dmitri stood next to his father, looking over his shoulder. The others in this retinue, standing in a respectful semicircle, were like medieval courtiers, for all were dressed in the fashion of years before – boyars in rich silk kaftans, embroidered peaked caps, jewel-studded belts and high leather boots. And all were intent now, gazing at the floor beneath the Prince's feet.

Prince Mikhail leant forward from a carved, high-backed chair, a throne of sorts set on the dais, which allowed him free play with one foot, dangling a few inches above the flagstones at that point – his bared right foot, a thick pencil forced between big and second toe.

His foot stabbed adroitly, decisively, over a large map set beneath his toes, showing the top of Lake Ladoga and then a huge territory which lay beyond to the north: the Rumovsky estates in Karelia, uncountable acres of lake water and chill wilderness, some of it arable land, much of it forested, most, still farther north, under permanent frost or snow for eight months of the year: an estate dotted with a few towns, many villages, and many more smaller settlements of Karelian peasants and Lapp tribes – a cruel but lovely wilderness which was all Rumovsky land, theirs in great swathes and in various separated pockets of smaller *volosts* or estates, a land which in such large and small stepping-stones ran all the way from the lake, hundreds of miles north, almost to the White Sea.

Though the air was warmed in the great hall by a huge log fire set beneath a conical stone canopy at its centre – warmed and smoked, too, by the rush flares set all along, high up, on the boulder walls – the Prince kept a sable cloak securely wrapped about his narrow shoulders, tucked in beneath his beard, his arms invisible; a cloak richly embroidered with lake pearls and precious stones, with a long, white Shantung silk shirt beneath, running down over his immense thighs, his left foot encased in a high boot. A fur *koshniki*, ringed at the bottom with gold and silk thread with a crust of glittering opal and turquoise stones above that, sat on his head like a crown. Prince Mikhail Andreivich Rumovsky – wrapped in his gleaming sable, with his sombre, powerful features, his quick darting dark eyes beneath even darker bushy eyebrows – sat now on his throne atop the dais with all the air and dress of a Tsar from another age.

Which indeed, so far as this huge territory went, he was. The Prince was absolute master here, as his Rumovsky ancestors before him had been – the land given to the founder of the dynasty, Prince Pyotr Alexei Rumovsky, by his cousin Tsar Mikhail, first of the Romanov Tsars, early in the seventeenth century – as a gift but also as a means of ensuring that his formidable cousin and rival would live out his life fully occupied beyond the barrier of the great lake, far distant from the Kremlin.

And the Rumovskys, though they remained absolutely in the blood line of the Romanovs, had stayed away, becoming, over the centuries, ever more isolated from the centres of power in Moscow and then St Petersburg, content with their own vast lot which, given its unpromising nature and distance from the capitals, they soon came to run as a private fiefdom, as Tsars of an almost separate country.

The writ of Empire, though formally posted, was not the law that mattered here. This was Rumovsky law, law reflecting the circumstances of each defendant or petitioner and adapted to local conditions, so that it was generally fair. But since these were unwritten decrees, composed at the whim of each successive Prince, they were enforced in a quite arbitrary manner. And if the present Prince was often unduly tolerant, he was, on other occasions, quite unjustifiably severe.

He loved his Karelian people, for their songs and laughter, their lightness of heart, not typically Russian. He dealt and spoke with them, in his archaic Church Slavonic, after the manner of an Old Testament patriarch. But this passion made him blind at times, allowed no room for any consistent justice in his land. Of course, in this love, the Prince thought himself a just man, a Solomon, and this was often so. It was the exceptions to his rule here and his wicked temper and abrupt changes of mind which made him a despot, a Tamburlaine of the snows.

The orders and regulations he made for the running of his vast estates, with his one foot scribbling over parchment paper, were edicts which he often enforced himself on horseback with his retinue of boyars, travelling with them for days on end over his domains, his great thighs and legs locking him onto his horse, closing like a vice over saddle and flanks. For these fierce limbs were his only means of reach and command.

The Prince was without arms, and had been from birth. Two shrivelled, deformed stumps, a tapering of withered flesh, was all that nature had allowed him here, a disadvantage which he had dealt with and usually overcome with stoic forbearance – but one which, when crossed or in anger, made him a tyrant.

Now, with his foot, the Prince stabbed at the map again. 'Yes, we shall hunt towards this *volost* of Yanisyarvi, with our birds. And then go north to the Skolt settlement by Suoyarvi.'

He spoke to Stephan Vassilievich, a fair-haired Lett, tall, with a leather waistcoat, coarse cloth shirt and high boots. 'My son, Prince Pyotr and his entourage – some of them may accompany us. Though I doubt the Prince will himself. The animals he hunts, they are all dead! Dead as that bird he described for us on his last visit, the Dodo bird, do you remember?' There was laughter among his retinue. 'Can you imagine? A bird of that sort and size, without wings, a giant duck it seemed, from some island in the south seas, where he had sought for it; long months, among the savages there. Like the Firebird – mythical!'

There was more laughter in the great hall. But the Prince, with a glance, stilled it, concern on his face now. He turned. On a table nearby stood a large hourglass, sand running slowly through the narrow waist. 'The dark is on us,' the Prince observed. 'They were to have been here by sunset.' He turned and spoke to Dmitri. 'Send out a search party. There have been wolves about.'

His son, obeying him at once, moved away into the body of the great hall, directing men, sending them hither and thither, in a voice that was soft and accommodating, but which, in this, did not in the least reflect his real character.

Dmitri was short, small-limbed, stunted, with a puffy, thinly bearded face, but almost totally bald. The product of a liaison nearly forty years before between the Prince and a Lapp woman, one of the Skolt tribe who inhabited a part of the Prince's estates to the north, he had inherited the stature and features of his mother. More than this he had taken from her mongol ancestors the yellow-skinned tinge of her race and the perceptibly slanted eyes, so that his expression, covert and wary in any case, was made the more so by this colouring, in this slight deviation of the eyes. Aware of all these physical departures from the Russian norm, Dmitri, by way of recompense, kept his face set in a faint smile, an effect which made his expression all the more unfortunate.

The Prince neither liked nor disliked his son. He could not afford either emotion. Instead, knowing him to be a sly, unattractive, generally unpleasant man, and not caring to be reminded of this, he cultivated a studious neutrality in their relationship. In his guilt at his origins, and feeling so little warmth towards him, the Prince gave Dmitri the benefit of his many doubts.

His son, by no fault of his own, had been put at a disadvantage, the Prince always reminded himself. And so he owed him a blood loyalty, then and ever since. He had taken him away from the Skolt settlement shortly after his birth, bringing him up at the castle with a wet-nurse, giving him, if little or no formal education, every other advantage there. Thus his son, he knew, bonded to him in this way, remained faithful to him in one vital manner at least: Dmitri put his slyness, all his eavesdropping, his secret schemes and manoeuvres, almost entirely at his father's service. 'Almost' was the key word – the Prince was well aware of that, too.

The Prince's other legitimate children – there were two sons and a daughter from his marriage to a Karelian beauty from the Duchy of Finland who had died three years before – had long since left and rarely returned to this medieval fortress, which they had never enjoyed. They were modern people, who had gone out into the new commercial world of Russia, to St Petersburg, Moscow and Odessa – cities which the old Prince despised, and which he had long before ceased to visit, perfectly content to remain a bizarre anachronism, a patrician set on maintaining every old Russian tradition to the letter: an ageing man who had always been happy with his own still vigorously pursued affairs, the wellbeing of his tenantry and his estates, the hunting there, all the daily miracles which he experienced in this wild and lovely northland.

Dmitri alone had stayed with him at the castle, had never wanted to leave and was never likely to marry, so was at his father's side day and night, for he slept in a small dressing-chamber next to the Prince's bedroom. Dmitri was, literally, his father's left- and right-hand man. He fed and gave him drink, cut his hair, trimmed his beard, washed and dressed him – did everything which the Prince, without arms, could not do himself: Dmitri, his father's ever-willing helpmeet, obeyed at once his least command.

Yet the Prince knew well what was dangerous in his son, what seethed in him beneath all this ready compliance, knew of his secret ambitions, which Dmitri thought he hid so well. Dmitri longed for legitimacy in the family, so that beneath his accommodating surface he schemed for power behind a throne which he thought he could one day obtain. But knowing this, the Prince watched Dmitri just as carefully as his son watched him. So that Dmitri's power, which he thought almost absolute, in fact hung by a thread.

A high full moon shimmered in a dome of clearest sky. The bells of the monastery church behind the castle rang out and the pack of borzoi hunting dogs barked and ran on their leashes from the kennels on the ice, all giving tongue as the *troika* drew near. Yelena could see the great fire on the ramparts clearly now, sparks streaming up, little starry cinders flying towards the greater stars in the velvet arc above. Now the book opens, she thought: here the real fairy story begins, with all its good and evil. Sitting next to Sasha she took his hand in hers and felt her heart beat faster.

A series of heavy holm-oak tables were set in a large circle right round the central fire with its stone canopy in the great hall. And now, with the arrival of Prince Pyotr and his family an hour before, a company of some sixty people – courtiers and their wives, senior retainers, the Abbot from the monastery and some of his favoured priests – feasted upon these tables, gorging from red wooden platters on a banquet brought in relays from the kitchens across the courtyard behind the castle.

The dishes, all in the old Russian fashion, were rich and varied, endless, substantial, served in a leisurely manner, and eaten with great gusto by all present, with the exception of Prince Pyotr and his party, who, apart from the children, had no taste for these rough manners and picked awkwardly at their food.

There was fresh caviar and cured fillet of sturgeon; stuffed pike and the small powan fish from the lake, which the company ate with their fingers, by the mouthful. Roast fowl came next, duck, ptarmigan, geese, cranes, and then the *pièce de résistance*: a dozen large capercaillie birds stuffed with minced pork and mushrooms and served with a sauce of arctic bilberry. Sizzling haunches of reindeer, cut directly from two turning spits on either side of the fire, came later. And after that there was fruit from the ice cellars, pears, apples, plums and enormous sweetly perfumed melons, which were grown all year round in dark, heated rooms, from Crimean seeds, softened in milk and planted in horse-manure and straw. For drink there was only cranberry kvass or vodka, in various flavours and colours, both brewed and distilled on the islands, for the old Prince would serve almost no food or drink which had not been produced from his own estates.

The Prince and his retinue were robed more elaborately now, in finer silk shirts and fur-trimmed kaftans, celebratory clothes, again in the fashion of days long before. Their dress was in stark contrast to that of Prince Pyotr and his family, the Prince in a tail-coated evening suit, with a starched shirt, high winged collar and bow tie, while the two women of his party, the Princess and Miss Harriet, wore silk and chiffon evening dresses, both in the latest Paris fashion. The three children, sitting between and to either side of the women, were clothed equally *à la mode*, the boys in green velveteen knickerbockers and coats, Yelena in a blue velvet smock dress.

Prince Pyotr sat next to his father, with Dmitri feeding him on the other side, so that the sartorial contrast between the two men could not have been more marked: as wide as the difference in character between them. Prince Pyotr had been educated at the Tishenev Academy in St Petersburg and then at Oxford, where he had read natural history, before doing nominal military service with the Tsar's Preobrazhensky Guards. Now, apart from his zoological interests, his pursuit of rare or extinct flora and fauna all over the world, he filled most of his time representing the Constitutional Democratic party in the new Duma.

Prince Pyotr, though his real passion was set in the past, among what was dead, also believed in every sort of lively social and political change for his country. His father, of course, believed in none of this. For him progress could only lie – a fact proven through Russian history and long endorsed by every Tsar – by the strong leading the weak, an autocratic paternalism which his son hated in his father, endorsing as he did the full rights of men – and of women.

Though in this last the younger Prince had become soured. To his mind, by cuckolding him so publicly and painfully, his wife had betrayed his views and those rights, so that he had offered her little of his liberal ethic for many years. His father, who had long known of the real situation between them, despised his son for this craven weakness towards his wife. Now he alluded indirectly to all this, looking over towards his grandchildren. 'Wonderful children . . .' Then he turned to his son. 'It is a sad thing not to have more of them.'

'How lucky, in the circumstances.' His son was curt.

'You should either have been firm with her, got rid of her, or been more tolerant. Instead you have made the worst of everything by your indecision. Women, given their nature, given the opportunity, are all alike. Yes, even Russian women. You should have kept a tighter rein.'

'I gave her no opportunity, nor any excuse for her behaviour. What can you mean?'

'The old Adam, older Eve. And indeed, in your animal studies, you must have been long aware of this – as I am here, so close to the real nature of things – of how in matters of regeneration, inconstancy is the norm – apart from swans, polar bears, the whooping crane – a matter of survival.'

'Of the fittest, as in Darwin. Of course. But such has no relevance now among civilized people. We are more than the animals. We are not here on earth now merely to survive. We have developed. There are higher considerations, of law and Christian morality.'

His father grunted. 'They have done little to add to our sum of happiness. Rather the opposite. Truth lies in following the natural order.'

'I cannot agree. We have moved far beyond those base instincts – in our intelligence, our knowledge of right and wrong. That is our distinction as human beings, just as it is our obligation to fulfil that intelligence, these moral laws. We have adapted in this manner – from the beasts.'

'But it is clear you have not adapted – to your circumstances with the Princess. You are troubled. And that, for a man, should not be. Why do you not divorce? You may petition our cousin the Tsar. He would grant you such. Or if not, take a mistress? There is that matter of things, a natural urge, which pains for lack of expression.'

His son was embarrassed by this suggestion, picking at his wing collar in the heat, lighting another of his Russian cigarettes, the cardboard-tubed *papirosy* he always smoked. 'That is not my way.

'It has been mine, at times.'

Prince Pyotr knew this well. It had been his father's way from the beginning, with that Skolt woman, which had produced the malign Dmitri, his half-brother – his way as well, he was sure, with some of his courtiers' wives and serving girls, about them at that very moment.

Prince Pyotr hated his father's easy sensuality as much as his feudal paternalism, while the old Prince despised his son's beliefs and laughed at his pursuits. Where had they led him? A Jezebel wife and mythical birds. Of course it was to be expected. His son was weak, and the weak went astray once they denied the leadership of the strong; something which his son was proposing for all Russians with his ridiculous democratic notions in the Duma.

But much worse were the implications of this for him

personally. Having just had this further confirmation of his son's liberal principles he was now more than ever concerned about his inheritance, the future of the castle, all the Rumovsky land and its people. In Pyotr's hands these would soon disintegrate and disappear, the people becoming infected, as his son had been, by such destructive views, taken by disaffection and revolt. He could not allow this to happen, could not let all his own efforts here, and those of his Rumovsky forebears, the work of centuries, be dissipated in the hands of a misguided weakling. He would have to consider alternatives.

After the feast a group of half a dozen Georgian dancers ran into the hall, skipping and shouting in their entrance, before linking hands and starting an ever more vigorous dance round the fire, moving one way, then back, feet flying, heels thundering, keeping time and singing to the galloping swells of two vividly fingered concertinas. Then came the jesters, minstrels, jugglers, singers and a small troupe of actors, giving a lively commentary on affairs and people within the castle, before miming the incident with the wolves on the lake, where Yelena became the heroine.

These boisterous gypsy *skomorokhi*, some score of whom the old Prince kept permanently in the castle throughout the winter, excelled themselves, the men in short, flamboyantly coloured silk kaftans and high felt boots, the women in vivid kerchiefs, bright dresses and red shawls draped over one shoulder. At the end, the embers of the great fire glowing behind her, a fair-haired Karelian girl, tall, austere, motionless, her head cast down, sang a Karelian lament accompanied on a balalaika, a lament for that lost country, divided now between the Duchy of Finland and Russia, a song which the old Prince particularly appreciated, for he saw the Rumovsky family as more Karelian than Russian, inheritors, and himself now protector, of what was left of that brighter way of life.

For Yelena the song evoked an echo, a meaning which she couldn't understand, some music remembered. A lullaby sung by Marusya, her mother's old maid, who had looked after them when they were younger? Or by one of the other servants, for they were always singing, in their palace in St Petersburg? She was half asleep already, her eyes closing as the music ended . . .

Yelena woke with a start. The woman, pausing at the end of her dying fall in the song, now let out a great cry, then threw a glass of vodka over the bright embers, so that flames leapt up with a roar. Then she continued, but in quite another mode, shouting the words exultantly, vehemently, while the balalaika followed her, the man's fingers dancing over the strings, ever faster, until both of them reached a crescendo of triumphant sound, a long held, high note soaring up to the rafters, which suddenly ceased, leaving an instant's total silence before the wild shouts of applause.

'What is it?' Yelena heard Miss Harriet speak to her mother.

'Oh, some local piece of Karelian folklore,' she said dismissively. 'About a kingdom taken over by a tyrant usurper, holding the true prince captive in the castle, until his princess returns years later and rescues him – that's when she throws the vodka on the fire. It's called "Firesong".'

The midday sun, at its apex now, halfway up the pale blue dome of sky, slanted on the castle walls, its towers and ramparts, and glinted on the star-sprinkled, turquoise blue and green cupolas of the monastery church beyond, giving the stone a crystal sheen, so that the buildings emerged from the snowy canvas of the lake like a pile of jewels – emeralds, opals, diamonds rising from a gilded box.

Now, in the crisp bright morning light, where the night's deep frost made the ice glitter and crackle, the spectacular situation of the castle and its attendant island settlements was revealed. There were three islands here, close together, each of almost equal size: three crowns of granite outrock, rising sometimes almost sheer from the water, with jagged teeth rising above that, but with spaces of flat land on each island where the various buildings had been set, on the thin soil, among groves of fir and silver birch trees.

The islands ran out in a line from an equally rocky shore, separated from this by several hundred yards of water, but linked together by narrow wooden bridges, each with its own drawbridge at one end, while the longer distance from the first of the islands to the mainland was traversed over a pontoon bridge in the summer and by a track set across the thick ice in winter.

This access to the first island from the shore ended at a heavily fortified boulder wall, with an arched gateway in the centre, protected by a portcullis and two great oak doors beyond. Behind lay a cobbled courtyard, flanked by store-houses, corn and hay lofts, stable and carriage houses.

The bridge across to the second and largest island led to the monastery buildings, with its blue domed church, dedicated to the Blessed Virgin of Smolensk at the centre, its refectory and other offices set along one side overlooking the lake. Here a score of monks lived under the care of the old Abbot Theodosius, amidst the regular tolling bells, at prayer or at work in the extensive vegetable gardens or tending their animals.

The last bridge led to the highest but smallest spur in this chain – to the almost totally sheer-sided Castle Island where the Rumovsky fortress, extended from an earlier medieval castle, had been built nearly 300 years before. Since then it had been extended still further, so that it and its numerous outbuildings, its arsenal, servants' quarters, kitchens and store-rooms, now covered almost the entire surface of the rock.

It was a well-nigh impregnable stronghold shaped like a huge letter V, jutting out into the lake, with a tall conically hatted tower at its lower point and long battlemented walls running away to either side, ending in two smaller, squatter towers. Arrow slits and narrow windows, set high up, punctuated these towers and walls. The great hall lay behind the boulder stone to one side of the central tower, the armoury, the Prince's chambers and a long gallery to the other.

Beneath these walls, circling the bole of the main tower, lay a wide terrace, where the great fire burned at night – a terrace protected by ramparts with half a dozen gun ports, old Krupp assault cannons protruding, some still in working order, the central and largest gun booming out over the lake at sunrise and sunset, to mark the beginning and end of the day's work.

The ramparts fell almost sheer down to the lake, from where the only access up to the castle lay in a zigzag of narrow steps, cut into the stone, or through a great archway at the water's level, the entrance to the boathouse, a long high cavern blasted from the solid rock, closed now by two great iron doors, firmly embedded in the ice.

In front of this bastion the skaters frolicked on the following morning in a space beneath the ramparts cleared of snow, where Prince Pyotr and his family, in furs and flowing red scarves, disported themselves in graceful swirls, or with sudden falls, over the clear, greeny deep ice.

Yelena, skating recklessly, crashed into her elder brother Ivan. 'You slowcoach!' she spat up at him, lying spreadeagled on the ice, kicking at him fruitlessly in her high-buttoned boots. 'Why can't you steer clear when you see me coming?'

Ivan sniffed. 'You little brute – I'd box your ears, if you weren't a girl.'

'I'm *not* a girl. I'm *not*.'

'You are – and a little liar as well.' He skated away.

'Not really,' she shouted after him. 'I can do all the skating things you can do. And I'm far better than Sasha – at everything.'

Sasha was standing with his grandfather by the ramparts, his arm in a sling, watching the skaters, but without envy. Unsure of his balance, he had never quite mastered the art. But his grandfather, believing that he might feel left out of things, commiserated with him. 'You must not fret, Alexander. I cannot skate either. Besides, it is a modern thing – to no real purpose.'

In response, Sasha, who was normally frightened of this great bearded man without arms, suddenly took courage, speaking out in candid annoyance. 'It's not the skating I mind, grandpapa. It's Yelena. Did you hear her? Not a girl, she said.' He spoke in Russian, looking up at the old man, fascinated by the droplets of ice which, in his breathing, had come to infest his beard. Several of them fell then as he moved his jaw to speak.

'Of course she's a girl, Alexander Pyotrovich.' He looked at Yelena, racing away over the ice again now, boisterous and pushy once more. 'But some girls are born with a man's soul.'

'Oh?' Sasha was suddenly interested in this. 'Is that why she's so plain and ugly, for a girl – with her turned-up nose?'

The hunting party, in their reversed sheepskin coats and fur hats, the horses in their dark caparisons, moved over the lake ice, black on white, approaching the frozen forest and wilderness ahead under a bright sun and blue sky. Yelena, insisting on this outing as much as her grandfather had encouraged her, sat forward, high up in the saddle with the old Prince, held securely against the pommel in front and by the Prince's great thighs gripping her to either side, so that she felt absolutely confident with him. The stallion's reins, much shortened, were attached to metal hooks sewn into the trouser leather above the Prince's knees, a method which, together with the fierce grip he kept against the horse's flanks, enabled the Prince to manoeuvre, even to gallop the horse, almost as well as any in his retinue.

But now the cavalcade trotted easily over the snowy ice, taking a short cut from the castle across the bay towards the Rumovsky lands to the north. The Prince led the way, his two lieutenants to either side, Dmitri and his chief steward Stephan. Behind them rode a dozen men in line, the other hunters with slung rifles, but led by the real hunters of the day: two great tawny Imperial eagles, hooded, with feather-topped leather cockades, swaying gently on their perches, set on top of a small sleigh attached by traces to a horse ridden by the falconer: the birds with their hooked beaks thrust forth questingly, blind now, but sensing well how they were moving forth towards some kill.

Yelena gazed over the vast flat expanse of snowy ice, then looked up at the Prince. 'It's beautiful. But will it be like this all the way?'

'No, child. Soon we will reach the shore – hills, forests, lakes and rushing rivers, land of the white fox and the lynx. My land, Karelia, Lapland.' The Prince, in his harsh-soft voice, seemed to Yelena, in these flowing words, to be speaking a poem. Then, breaking into a language she had heard him speak sometimes before, she knew by the rhythm of his words that he was definitely talking poetry, for the words came out in just the same 'dum-ti-ti-dum-ti, dum-ti-ti-dum' fashion as they did in the bouncy lines from 'Hiawatha', the long poem which Miss Harriet often read to them.

Gukken darren dawgai vuolde
Sabma suolgai Samedednom . . .

'What language is that?' she asked.

'Lapp language.' Then the Prince recited the poem in Russian.

North beneath the Great Bear's stars
Lapland looms, our silent land:
Hills of purple, uplands gleaming,
Lake on lake with shores in flood:
Summits glisten, grey fells lowering
Gently rise to heaven's high vault;
Rivers rush and forests sigh
Dark cliffs pierce the foaming surf.

That's what the land here means to me, Linochka – everything, the whole of life. All my love. This wild land. This is the old Russia, where people still live like they used to do. The old virtues, the old truths.'

'Is that why you wear your strange old clothes and funny things?' Yelena ventured.

The Prince smiled. 'Partly. But also because they are more comfortable, more suited to the climate here – and the life I lead.'

'I *love* your old clothes!' She glanced up at him. 'And I love the land here. It'll be really exciting, when we get to it.'

'We are in it now. There is no end to it.' The Prince looked ahead into the empty frozen distances. 'Day or night the land is always here, without the count or stay of hours, without limits.'

'Not like St Petersburg, then. The days there are all cut up into starts and stops by Miss Harriet. A "timetable" she calls it – for everything. Getting up, then music lessons, then school lessons, meals, walks, play, then more music lessons, dancing class, reading, bedtime. It's so boring – she cuts everything up like that into little bits and pieces.'

'She is English.' The Prince felt no need to elaborate. But Yelena did.

'She's not, Grandpapa!' She looked up at him, triumphantly. 'She's Irish. Another island, called Ireland. Near England. They're always fighting each other.'

'Ireland?' The Prince was mystified. 'Anyway, there are no "timetables" here. Only the difference of day and night. And not even that farther north, where, in winter and summer, there is either no day or no night, all light or all darkness.'

'But that can't be. That would be magic.'

'It is. One day I'll show you the land far north, where the sun lives all the time in summer, and disappears for most of the winter.'

'Will you, Grandpapa? But is it really true?'

'I would never lie to you,' he chided her.

Yelena, hearing this, and without fear of the old man now, turned and looked up at him intently. 'Will you tell me then, Grandpapa, why am I so plain? I've heard people – my Mama and Sasha – heard them say it. I'm not beautiful. I've got a terrible turned-up nose. And no one will ever marry me then, will they?' She ran on, over other real and imagined disadvantages, in fits and starts, until the Prince quietened her.

'I will tell you the truth, Linochka, for I have watched you carefully ever since you first came here and have loved what I have seen. Beauty will come to you. And many will love you for it. But greater than that is another beauty which you have in you now, of soul and spirit, of courage – and love for this wide world here. You have said so. But I have seen it long ago – you go towards that magic world, so that in time it will all come to you. You will be the bride of every spring. I see all this in you, for you are like me. A girl will suffer the wound of thinking herself plain. A boy, born and growing to manhood without arms, suffers in the same way – that God should hand out such punishment . . . But He gives great recompense, in hidden gifts, which have grown in me, which will grow in you. Gifts which others, for all their beauty or full-armed strength, will never have.'

'Gifts? But what? What are they, for us?'

'I have said to you – courage of heart, and a great love for all created things, and the gift of seeing into life's secrets, while others can only look in mirrors.'

They came to the northern shoreline, a steep, rocky coast, heavily forested beyond, but with an inlet between two great granite spurs, where a track wound up from the ice into the thick woods above, great stands of snow-laden fir and silver birch. The eagles, smelling these woods, and sensing prey there, became restless on their perches, pulling at their jesses, ruffling their tail feathers, twitching their feathery cockades and great beaks.

The company, following the twisting track beneath the thick canopy of trees, emerged on a high bluff of open land. The tops of a few dwarf birches and some outcrops of bare dark rock were the only things visible across the long white sward, with its rolling waves, snowdrifts whipped up into regular crests by the wind, a sharp, stinging breeze blowing the snowy crystals into the eyes of the horsemen so that they shaded their faces, allowing them clear vision across the wide panorama.

Yelena could see nothing. But the sharper-eyed hunters could. 'There!' Stephan cried out. 'To the left, less than a *verst*, on that long rock below the hill.'

Yelena saw the animal now, an arctic fox, appearing clear for an instant against the dark rock before disappearing behind it. Then, before she had time to turn, she heard the sudden thunderous wing-beats, as the great bird, released from its hood and jesses on the sleigh behind her, flew straight up over her head.

Craning her neck she watched the eagle gain height, then hover for a moment before it spotted the fox, when it flew forward. The horsemen followed its flight, cantering up the track. Coming to the top of the rise, they looked down a long open valley, ending in a line of trees.

The fox, in its white coat, was barely visible. But its track over the snow as it made for the trees was clearly seen by the eagle as the bird followed it, gaining fast on the animal. The eagle rose a fraction, then glided, before setting its talons well forward, making a final swoop when it took the fox, clawing into its neck, its whole weight crashing into the animal so that the fox somersaulted in the snow, the bird collapsing over it, hiding the prey completely with its great wings.

When the Prince's party arrived minutes later the only evidence of death lay in the smear of blood seeping into the snow behind the bird's tail feathers.

Stephan dismounted with the falconer who, with a piece of meat held between thumb and forefinger of his leather glove, offered this to the bird while Stephan, on the other side, pulled the fox from beneath the wings. The bird, thus tempted and deprived at the same time, was coaxed back to its perch on the sleigh, but unwillingly, for even with its jesses attached now by a leather thong to the perch it fretted and strutted about, attempting to rise again, as if it sensed some further prey in the nearby trees.

Stephan, seeing this, looked questioningly towards the woods himself. Then, with the Prince and Dmitri following, they walked into the treeline. Some way inside the forest, just to the side of the track, they saw the body.

There was little left of the man. His fur *shuba*, his shirt, high boots and trousers, all had been torn from him and lay in shreds scattered about. The body was half skeleton now, where the wolves had eaten at him: thighs torn away, entrails gouged out. The voracious pack had stripped half his flesh before being disturbed, leaving just a bloody butchered mess on the circle of trampled red snow which the animals had struggled over, contesting their prey, not long before.

But the wolves had not killed the man. Dmitri pointed out the neat hole in one side of his skull: a rifle bullet which, on its exit, had blown half of the man's head away on the other side. But his features, where the wolves had found no meat, were clearly recognizable.

'Boris Andreivich, our gamekeeper for this Yanisyarvi estate. Poachers – before the wolves got him.'

The Prince stood up, his feet slipping on the trampled ground, where the blood had not yet frozen. 'They cannot be far away. The wounds are fresh, the wolves just scattered. And see.' The Prince had moved forward along the track into the forest. 'The snowshoes here. Two sets of them. Two men here, before the wolves.'

The company made haste now, following these tracks through the forest, until again they emerged on top of another high bluff, with an open run of land sloping down to a wide lake in the distance below them, several *versts* away, with low forested hills beyond that.

Dmitri, thinking he saw something move, took a pair of army fieldglasses from his saddlebag. 'Yes,' he spoke after a minute. 'It's them, in snowshoes, sheepskin coats but with the fleece outside, and white fox caps. Camouflaged. Making fast for the tree cover on the other side of the lake.'

'They will be in the woods then in a few minutes.' The Prince spoke hurriedly. 'Too far to shoot or to cut them off.' He turned to the falconer. 'The birds – would they take them? It's our only chance.'

The man nodded. 'One of them, Katyuskaya here.' He pointed to the big female. 'She might. Especially if they are wearing fox-fur hats.'

'Try her, then. Set her up.'

The falconer, returning to the perches on the sleigh, released the second larger bird now, held her aloft on his leathered arm and, with a quick swing upwards, set the eagle into the sky. At first, rising up ahead of the party, the bird was undecided, circling about, beginning to quarter the land below. But then, at the end of a run down towards the lake, she spotted the white figures on the far side. The bird soared upwards, gaining height, aligning herself right behind the two men before starting a long glide towards them. The company at once set off in hot pursuit down the slope.

The poachers saw or heard nothing of the great bird falling from the sky behind them, approaching them on their blind side in a long, gently angled dive. The second of the two, trailing his companion, only sensed something at the last moment. He turned suddenly, to confront the huge dark shape making straight for his head. He ducked, but could do nothing else, so that the outstretched talons slashed into his shoulder. The rest of the bird crashed into him, its speed and weight knocking him over, leaving him stunned on the ice.

The eagle crouched over him, raking his chest with her talons, wings forming a canopy over the body. The poacher struggled with the bird, twisting over the ice, wrestling furiously with it as it pecked and tore at him.

His companion ahead turned with his rifle. But he could take no sure aim at the swirling mass of sheepskin and feather. He ran towards the mêleé. But then, seeing the Prince's party, out on the lake ice now and galloping fast towards them, he turned back and fled into the forest ahead of him.

Stephan and the falconer, dismounting, quickly disengaged the bird from its prey. The man's face was bleeding, his sheepskin coat in tatters across his chest. But when he rose to his feet he was calm, almost insolent as he looked up at the

Prince. Dmitri, pulling at the dozen pine-marten and fox pelts tied to his belt, detached them one by one.

'These are not your property, I think.'

'No. They belong to the land here – which is for all of us.'

Dmitri slapped his face viciously with one of the pelts. But the Prince reprimanded him with a shout.

'No, you fool! We have care of the man now, as a prisoner.' He turned to the poacher. 'This land is mine by long title – and all life thereon, man and beast, all equally under my protection. And you have killed these animals under my care. And the man who cared for them.'

'I did not kill that man.'

'Your companion then. It matters not. When one man murders, with another, both are equally in the blood.' He turned to Dmitri. 'Bind him, hands and feet, and set him across a horse. The Skolt settlement is not far.'

Yelena, watching all this spellbound, looked up at her grandfather. 'Will you kill him now as well?'

'No. Certainly not. He must come to court first and be sentenced. Then executed. That is the law.'

3

By the time they reached the Skolt settlement it had started to snow – a thin persistent drift from a grey sky. The small tribe lived in a dozen conical reindeer-skin tents set along the bank of a frozen river at the centre of a narrow valley, the tents huddled amidst a sheltering grove of silver birch and low willow, with heavily wooded hills rising to either side. For these were forest, not mountain, Lapps: woodcutters, carpenters and trappers, who continued to live in this hidden valley, under the Prince's protection, when most of their kind had been pushed ever farther north over the years.

However, the Prince had never allowed these Skolts to be disturbed. He commissioned his throne and the other rough-carved furniture in his castle from them, bought their furs and coloured cloth. But more, he had a closer personal association here, for it was from this tribe that Dmitri's mother came, and he continued to see her when he visited the settlement every year, just before the new year, for the old woman had strange gifts.

Dmitri would not see his mother. He stood apart now, with the other men and their horses, at the edge of the settlement. The Prince, with Yelena, walked through a double line of welcoming Skolts in reindeer smocks, leather leggings and brightly coloured woollen caps – small, wiry men with brown eyes and faces and high cheekbones, who dipped their heads gently forward as the Prince passed, the woolly bobbles of their caps falling over their eyes.

Ahead, just outside the main circle of tents, lay a smaller tent. The Prince stopped before it. Then, using his head as a butt, he bent down and pushed through the door flap. Yelena hesitated behind him.

'Come, Linochka. She will see you as well.'

She followed him inside but immediately wished she hadn't. The space was dark, lit only by the smoky flames of a slow fire, set on stones in the middle, with an opening in the forked poles high above. The floor was covered with reindeer hides above a thick layer of birch twigs. There were no chairs or tables, no furniture of any kind, but for two big wooden chests, on the far side of the tent, and it was in front of one of these that Yelena, her eyes stinging but becoming accustomed to the smoky light, saw the strange figure, completely wrapped in furs, sitting cross-legged on top of a cushion of reindeer skins: a small, elderly woman, her face creased with innumerable wrinkles. She leant half forward now, over a drum in front of her.

But it was not so much this witch-like figure that disturbed Yelena. It was the series of white, flat-faced masks which she suddenly noticed, set on posts in a semicircle behind the old lady: masks with huge dark staring eyes, painted black, with round, white wooden noses, like carrots, sticking straight out above square mouth slits. Yelena drew back with a gasp.

'Have no fear, little one.' The Prince turned to her. 'They are good faces, not evil. They ward off the evil powers – before the bear hunt and to celebrate the kill. The *noaide* keeps them here, to preserve their strength –'

The Prince was interrupted then by the voice of the old woman, speaking for the first time. But she was looking at her, Yelena saw, not at the Prince. And her voice was stranger than her face: a man's voice, low and harsh, keeping the same regular tone, the same rhythm. Yelena, though she knew she was being addressed, could make no reply, for she understood not a word of the strange tongue.

'She asks for you, little one. Go to her. Go to the magic drum. To the frog. And the bone.'

A frog? A bone? No, Yelena thought, recoiling again. These were the tools of witches. 'No, Grandpapa. I can't. I won't. She's a witch!'

'Not a witch. Just the opposite. She fights the evil spirits. She is the *noaide* here, the wise one, the soothsayer – living with the spirits of the past, bringing messages from them, and foretelling the future, with her magic drum. Go to her. There is no fear, no evil.'

Yelena came slowly forward towards the fire and stood in front of the old woman. The drum lay at her feet.

A large oval of reindeer skin, pulled taut by rivets of bone over a shallow wooden bowl, it was decorated by a score of strange figures and symbols, blood-coloured, each isolated from the next. Some were clear pictures of hunters on skis, bears, wolves, reindeer packs on the move, of tents and sleighs, of fish and elk. Others were mysterious designs, circles, crosses, squiggles.

The old woman leant farther forward now, placing a small brass charm in the centre of the drum. Then she held out a hammer-shaped bone, gesturing with it, showing how Yelena should beat the skin with it. Yelena took the hammer doubtfully. But then, urged by sudden confidence, she brought it down with a thump on the skin. The brass charm jumped sharply from the taut surface, landing some distance away, right on top of one of the symbols, a match-like human figure holding up two strange poles in either hand, with triangular tops to them. They must be spades, Yelena thought, or boat paddles.

But whatever they were, this turn of events didn't please the old woman at all. She leant forward intently, gazing for a long time at where the charm had fallen. She seemed puzzled. She was certainly annoyed. Then she spat three times into the fire, the globules sizzling briefly in the flames.

The Prince spoke to her. After she had replied, her hoarse voice clearly agitated now, the Prince turned to Yelena, translating. 'The "frog" – it landed first on the sign of the great wind god, Bieggolmai. And because it landed there first, on this your first telling of the magic drum, it means the wind god is your guiding sign, the sign that has your fate and will order it.'

Yelena didn't understand. 'Is that good? Or bad? It must be bad, else why should she be so annoyed?'

It was the Prince's turn to look surprised, gazing at Yelena. 'It's . . .' He paused. 'It's because she knows you now to be a rival, in her own secret gifts. That displeases her.'

'Me? That I am a witch, too?'

'No, but that you seem to have the gifts of a *noaide*, a soothsayer like her. The great wind god Bieggolmai, you see, he has the power to go anywhere, be anywhere, in the past or the future. He can blow where he will, into every secret place, across all the world – and bring back messages from his journeys, to the person whose earthly body he inhabits.' The old woman interrupted the Prince again, still annoyed, restless. 'She says there is nothing she can tell you of your fortune. That one *noaide* does not talk to another, that you yourself will come to know all things, of yourself and in others.'

Yelena felt a thrill in hearing this. Yet she was disappointed as well. She would like to have heard about her future. It was an exciting idea. But the Prince, bending down with his stumpy arm, led her away, and she sat down near the opening of the tent while he took her place in front of the old woman. Using one foot against the other he pulled his high boot off, then sat down, when the old woman placed the bone hammer between his toes. He started to hit the drum with it, and the little 'frog' leapt about, the old woman murmuring to him betweentimes, telling his fortune for the coming year.

Yelena meanwhile gazed about her, seeing again the wicked white masks. How could this old witch – so exactly like Baba Yaga, the worst witch of all – be *good*? And how could she be like her in any way? The idea frightened her. Had she really this power, to see into the future? She thought furiously, about her future and then Sasha's. But nothing particular came to mind, other than the certain fact that they would soon be back in St Petersburg, caught up in Miss Harriet's boring 'time-tables'. That was all. She knew nothing more of the future, hers or anyone else's. The old woman must be a witch, or a liar.

But the Prince, before the telling of his own fortune, had enquired further about his granddaughter. Was it really so – that she had the gifts of a *noaide*? The old woman had refused to elaborate. 'It is not wise,' was all she would say, 'to speak of such people to others. For they have the power of revenge, from whatever distance, on you, on me. They are their own law.'

The following morning the old Prince began to question the poacher – Dmitri and Stephan at his side – in the estate office, a large semicircular room in the great tower giving out onto the terrace through a heavy oak doorway, with small square windows to either side. Again the Prince sat on a slightly raised dais, allowing him free movement of his bared foot, suspended languidly then over the flagstones.

'I did not kill your gamekeeper.' The poacher spoke firmly.

'As I told you, you are equally guilty, even if you could prove you did not fire the shot. Who is your companion? His name? Where does he come from?' The man said nothing. 'It is a most serious matter,' the Prince said at last. 'My keeper had a wife and children. You and your companion have killed their lives, too. And you have killed my life a little as well. For I am their protector. They are my life and I am theirs. Will you say nothing?'

'Nothing. Nothing – but to the court of the Tsar.'

'There is no such here, not for many *versts*. I am the law here.' Again there was silence. 'Take him away.' The Prince turned to Dmitri. 'Let him cool his heels and consider things below. He will talk then perhaps.'

'He will surely talk,' Dmitri said with sudden enthusiasm. 'He will talk down there. I will have him talk.'

'You see my hourglass here?' The Prince glanced towards this, the sands running smoothly through the waist. 'You have an hour.'

A steeply falling spiral staircase led down from the Prince's chambers through a succession of lower floors to the dungeons beneath: small rooms, lit by a rush flare in Dmitri's hand, hewn from the solid rock. From the last of these rooms, through an iron doorway, another stairway led down to a railed platform set above the great boathouse beneath. Flares along the rails illuminated one end of the dark cavern. The white prow of the Prince's steam yacht, the *Prince Onegin*, loomed up out of the shadows, the boat frozen hard into the ice. Between the bow of the boat and the end of the cavern an iron portcullis fell from the roof, securely fixed in the frozen water beneath.

The poacher, escorted along the platform, was led down to the ice on a ladder, which Dmitri then pulled up so that the man was left there, imprisoned now between the portcullis and the sheer granite walls at the end of the cavern. He seemed puzzled as to why he should have been put here. The reason was soon apparent.

In the shadows, beneath the ice-bound hull of the boat, halfway along its flank, something stirred. There was a rustling. And then the first of the wolves came forward into the flarelight. It stopped beneath the prow of the boat, yawned and stretched itself. But then, seeing the poacher beyond the portcullis, the half-starved animal trotted eagerly towards the grille, coming right up to it, gazing at the man with its yellow eyes, unblinking, sniffing the air, uttering a low growl. A few moments later it was joined by its companion, a larger beast, equally hungry.

Dmitri, moving along to the end of the platform, grasped a chain leading to a pulley high above, which then ran down to the top of a small iron barred gate set in the middle of the portcullis. He pulled the chain so that the gate rose a few inches from the ice. The two beasts at once pushed their grey muzzles into the narrow opening, whimpering excitedly before Dmitri released the chain, the doorway falling on their muzzles, so that they howled in pain.

'You see how it is,' Dmitri shouted down to the man. 'You have an hour, by the *Barin*'s hourglass.'

The hour passed and Dmitri returned alone, standing by the rails, looking down on the poacher, who talked now in a fast babble, giving Dmitri the name and likely whereabouts of his companion. After he had finished he thought himself saved. But this was not the case. Dmitri, looking down on him, spoke dismissively. 'Now, as my *Barin*'s gamekeeper was devoured, so will you be.'

Dmitri grasped the chain and pulled it quickly this time, so that the little gateway rose all the way up. The wolves came through fast, making straight for the prisoner. He ran back to the sheer walls behind, clawed at them, then turned, then tried to beat the animals off. But it was hopeless. The wolves, jumping up and about his body, tore at his arms, his shoulders, then his neck, so that soon he was down on the ice, struggling with the beasts, wrestling with one successfully for a moment, before the second, coming at him from behind, drove its teeth deep into his neck. The man was gone then, his struggles dying as the two beasts set about their long delayed meal, fangs ripping into his clothes before they started tearing him limb from limb.

Prince Pyotr was unaware of the poacher's demise until,

visiting his father in his chambers that afternoon, he brought the subject up. 'He will be officially charged, I assume. You will send him over the lake to Ladenpohja?'

The old Prince shivered an instant, drawing closer to the small fire. It was *sommerki* now, the short minutes of twilight, an indigo tint in the air over the snowy lake beyond the windows, a hazy gauze of sunset orange creeping up the sky. He turned to his son. 'The rogue is dead. There is no further business with him. We shall scour the land for his companion now. We have his name.' He spoke calmly. But his son was astonished.

'*Dead*? Without a trial?'

'Trial? He had just such this morning. Though it was no more than a formality. It was plain beyond dispute that he and his companion murdered my keeper and left his body to be picked clean by the wolves. What would you?' The old Prince looked at his son in surprise. '"An eye for an eye". You believe in the gospel, do you not? Despite your "liberal" principles?'

'Yes, the gospel of the New, not the Old, Testament, whose message is one of forgiveness, of charity. Not vengeance, not of taking the law into your own hands.'

The old Prince gave a smile of feigned astonishment. 'Who but I – in this vast lost land – can hold the law? That is exactly my duty.'

'There is only one law, throughout all the empire, the Tsar's law. You know that very well.'

'Yes, indeed!' The old man smiled again – ironic, triumphant this time. 'But you know equally well yourself, it is an entirely corrupt law, based on police spies and bribery in every quarter. And you yourself, from what I hear, have made it your life's work in the Duma to expose all such corruption and injustice of the state. But my law here is already just and incorrupt. And all in my domains know this and therefore do not fear the law, knowing that I cannot be bribed and will have no truck with informers or police spies. My way is the true way – of the land and the people. Mother Russia was ever thus. She draws her very being from a strong father, and can never do so from half a dozen "leaders" – weak and foolish "politicians", squabbling and disagreeing in the Duma. That will bring nothing but the destruction of the Empire, in riot, revolution, war. I rule in peace here – you know it well. There is no unrest in my domains, except that which outsiders bring.' He looked at his son.

'Father, you are living in the distant past. The serfs were freed over forty years ago.'

The old Prince laughed. 'Yes, and how many of them wished they hadn't been – losing, as they have, the protection I at least still provide for them! The freed serfs are at the mercy of a corrupt and distant "government" now, which they fear above all things. Here I am directly concerned with their lives, their wellbeing. You should see, Pyotr Mikhailovich, as I have done long years ago, how if you want to help people you can only do so in your own local world, not in the smoking rooms of St Petersburg. Nothing of any worth can come from that distance to here – nothing but foolishness. And pain, ignorance. I *know* my people. I share their lives. We help each other. Ask any of them – are they not happy with my dispensations?'

'They have been in the main, I will grant you. But that is not –'

'Indeed they are! And they would not be if any of your liberal principles came to pass here.'

'None the less, justice must be commonly agreed upon, arrived at democratically. It cannot lie in one man's hand. That is anarchy.'

The old Prince gazed over the broad expanse of lake, the sun sinking fast, casting a brilliant orange glow over the ice. 'Anarchy? There is none here, nor will there be as long as I live. I fear only what will happen after me.' He looked at his son pointedly. 'If you inherit, what will happen here? With your ridiculous "principles" – it will all collapse.' Warming to his theme now, he pursued it passionately, incautiously. 'How could you not but see this from your own life? How it is strength without compromise that must rule all our affairs, public and private. Had you but seen this you would not be in the shaming position you now suffer with your wife, a woman who sees fit – by the same "liberal" principles as your own, no doubt – to fornicate with other men. Can you not see the shame you have brought on yourself, and on the house of Rumovsky, by these modern beliefs? "Principles" you call them. They are evidence simply of your weakness as a man.'

His son, though stung by these remarks, remained calm. 'I am not here to punish my wife, to take revenge. She must find her own way. That is her fate.'

'And your destruction,' the Prince added fiercely.

'No, my freedom, to express my beliefs, to put them into action.'

'Well, you will not put them into action here when I am gone!' The old Prince was forthright. 'For I have given it much thought and have decided: I shall leave all this, my castle and my lands, to my granddaughter Yelena –'

'Yelena – a mere girl! It's impossible –'

'Not at all. I may leave my estate to whom I will.'

'If not to me, then what about my brothers Anton and Leonti, who would normally share in it?'

'They have no interest in the place here, the land or the people. They are interested simply in making money – from these new industries and factories that have come to infest and ruin Russia. Yelena alone among my descendants loves this land. I have seen it in her: loves it with a passion like mine. This I know. She will inherit it.'

'A girl? How could she run such vast estates?'

'A girl who will soon be a woman, with power, my son, which you lack and are not aware of in her. Extraordinary powers . . .'

'I have seen nothing particular.'

'You are blind then. The wolves, for example, when you travelled over the lake, how she stopped them in their tracks.'

'Mere chance, or that she screamed at them.'

'You have seen nothing!' The Prince was angry now. 'It is clear from your dealings with your Baltic wife. You have seen and know nothing of women, particularly Russian women – and their power. Russian men . . .' The Prince shifted restlessly in his chair, then got up and paced the room. 'Russian men – drunken, lazy, incompetent oafs for the most part, who use their women cruelly. Your daughter will never suffer men that way. I know it. She will lead them. She has power, a great power . . .'

The old Prince nodded his head, looking away over the lake to where the sun had just set, so that it was almost dark in the room, but for the low flames in the fire. He went over to the big grate and kicked the logs viciously into life again, so that they sparked and flared. 'Yelena will inherit all that I have. I will make my will accordingly. She will rule this little empire, like Catherine the Great . . .'

'Father, you have lost yourself here. You don't see that, whether you like it or not, things have changed everywhere in Russia – and greater, faster change is still to come: industry, increasing migration from the land, real money in people's pockets now, beholden to no one.' Prince Pyotr shook his head and lit another *papirosy*, the smoke rising in circles above his domed head. 'Your talk of Catherine the Great – it's the same as your clothes and your boyars' court here. You've intentionally set yourself up in a Russia that's been lost for years. It's perverse of you, all these fantasies – the idea of Yelena inheriting. It can come to nothing. You are like King Canute trying to hold back the tide.'

'Who?'

'Canute – an English king, long ago.'

The old Prince smiled. 'There are no tides on this lake. I have nothing to hold back, nothing holds me back. I shall do as I say.'

Prince Pyotr said nothing. It was obvious: the old man had entered his dotage. But just outside the door, Dmitri, eavesdropping as usual, thought otherwise. He knew well how firm a man of his word his father was. There was no question. Quite soon Yelena would be the legal inheritor of the castle and these vast lands, of all that he had for so long coveted for himself. Well, he thought, he too had certain powers. But he had not much time. His stepbrother and his family were due to return to St Petersburg immediately after the new year. Little time – and less opportunity, he thought, as he stole away down the corridor. On his way he saw the great fire being lit against the night out on the terrace. He paused, thinking, at a loss. But he would have to do something, at any cost.

Upstairs, from her nursery bedroom high in the tower, Yelena watched the sparks fly straight up past her window. Her uncle Dmitri, she saw, was out there on the terrace talking to the men tending the flames. Sasha was downstairs with Miss Harriet and the doctor who had come to inspect his sprained arm. She was alone. There was time to prowl before nursery supper, time to explore all the nooks and crannies, hidden corridors and stairways in the castle, some only glimpsed on previous visits.

'Come on, Samson, let's explore.' She picked up the ever-present little pug dog and hugged him, this dog that she talked to, shared secrets with, even more than she did with Sasha. Together they left the room.

She walked round the curved landing to where the main spiral stone stairway rose from the great hall and wound on to the next floor. Taking this, she circled upwards – and, before she reached the higher floor, saw the narrow corridor leading away at a right angle into the castle's great boulder walls. She had seen it before, but had never been along it. Now she turned into it.

It was darker here, leaving the main flare-lit arteries of the castle. The stone wall to one side ran with icy damp, the passageway itself not much more than her own height, lit only by a single rush flare at one end, a flickering beacon disturbed by some wind which she felt nothing of herself.

Coming to the end of the corridor she saw two doorways, facing each other. The one on the lake side was partly open. Peering through it she saw how it gave out onto a small stone platform with a hole in the middle, and a sheer drop down to the terrace far beneath. She felt the bitter chill of the night and the wind which ruffled the rush flare. She drew back quickly from the bright moonlight outside which lay over the snowy lake in a glittery frozen sheen.

The door behind her suddenly creaked, so that she jumped and turned, watching it swing open until it stopped halfway. Now she was petrified, seeing all the little round faces staring out at her – the dolls.

There were more than a dozen of them, clearly illuminated by the shaft of moonlight, all lined up on shelves, right across the far wall of the windowless chamber: big china dolls with round innocent faces, perfectly dressed, in white socks and neat button boots and shoes, ribbons in their glossy hair – all staring out wide-eyed at her.

She ventured over the threshold. They were the biggest, best-dressed dolls she had ever seen. Well, no, she had seen dolls like this, at the toyshop in Karavania Street in St Petersburg –

German dolls, which she'd coveted, but far too expensive. And the clothes of these dolls – all so smart and different. One dressed in fussy frou-frou silk, a ballgown with a long train, another in a starched pinny with a red cross, a nurse; a third dressed in a tartan skirt with a shawl, a fourth in a long lacy nightdress. And some of the dolls were almost undressed, just in their underclothes, she saw, as she walked along the shelves. She looked into their unblinking, wistful eyes, at their half-open rosebud mouths, their cheery faces. Whose could they be? And why hidden away like this? She wanted to touch, to play with them. She reached out a hand, touching the lips of the doll dressed as a nurse for an instant. Then Samson whined at her feet. She turned and saw the short, stooped figure of Dmitri standing in the doorway, his body, his bald head, silhouetted against the moonlight.

'Little one . . .' His voice, as always, soothing, confiding. She loathed it. His face, though she could not see it then with the moonlight behind him, would be set in that awful half smile. She hated that even more. But she was trapped. 'So, you have found my little nursery room, Linochka. You have come to play with the dolls at last. I'll show them to you. We can play with them together.' He came towards her, coming closer, blocking out all the light with his squat bulk, coming so close that she could smell him now, a horrid, bitter animal smell.

Almost immediately then – and for years afterwards – she blotted it all out – what had happened, what he had done to her that night. Offering her one of the dolls first, pretending to play with it, then playing with her, holding her. Then grasping her more firmly, running his hands about, groping over her body, under her dress. Then trying to undress her, half succeeding, his cold fingers probing. A hardness somewhere then, as he pressed himself to her. The awful smell, his open icy flesh on her warm skin. His wriggling against her, groaning, then a suffocating feeling. His hands, fingers tightening about her neck, so that she screamed . . . She blotted it all out.

Samson saved her. She heard the little dog barking as Dmitri pressed against her. He'd turned away from her, kicking out at the dog, letting her go for an instant, so that she'd run from the room and raced down the corridor, back into her own bedroom, slamming the door and hiding under the bed. After ten minutes she had come out and straightened her clothes. Crying. Then not crying. It was over. It had never happened. A nightmare. She would tell no one.

But Miss Harriet, at their nursery supper an hour later, knew at once that something terrible had happened to Yelena. Pale as death, red-eyed, shivering and unable to eat her supper; would only pick at her favourite food, white bread and butter spread with coils of golden syrup from the tins bought from the English Shop on Nevsky Prospekt. Something dreadful had happened to her. Miss Harriet made a mild enquiry. She had to be very careful – she would never hear the truth otherwise. But no, nothing had happened, nothing, Yelena said. She was cold, that was all. That was why she was jumpy and shivery.

'Well then,' Miss Harriet said. 'A good hot tub for you. And bed. And a story. We'll go on with *The Phoenix and the Carpet.*'

The two nurserymaids brought up cans of hot water and Miss Harriet gave Yelena her bath that night by the fire, in the collapsible English rubber tub they'd brought with them. And it was then that she saw the beginnings of the bruises, around Yelena's shoulders and neck and the same on hidden parts of her body, lower down. Now Miss Harriet knew what had happened to her and was aghast. But she showed nothing of this, and said nothing about it, turning away, frisking the towel warming on the fireguard, getting the talcum powder ready.

Then, without turning, she said offhandedly, 'You've hurt yourself?'

'No.' Yelena sat in the tub, her legs firmly closed. She couldn't see the bruises on her neck.

'Those bruises.' Miss Harriet turned back, smiling. 'On your neck.'

'Oh that – that's nothing. I was playing.'

'Fell, did you?' Miss Harriet said casually, turning away again, opening the towel out, before Yelena stepped into it, wrapping herself in it. 'Must have taken a bad bump.' She knew the girl hadn't been playing with Sasha or with Ivan, because both of them had been downstairs with her for the last hour before supper. And neither of them, nor any of the castle servants, would have done these terrible things. Who could it have been? She had a suspicion. She took the chance. 'He pushed you, did he? Uncle Dmitri?'

'Yes,' Yelena replied brightly, before she knew what she was saying. 'But it was an accident. He didn't mean to.'

'No, of course not. But sometimes, grown-ups – they can be a bit rough. Doesn't matter – I've got some wych-hazel in my bag. Just the thing for bruises. Remember, you like the smell of it, don't you?'

'Yes, I love it. Let's have some wych-hazel.'

Miss Harriet went over to her carpet-bag, a great treasure trove inside: a first-aid kit, eau de cologne and other toiletries, chocolates, digestive biscuits, books, string, hairgrips, needles, pins, candles and a score of other bits and pieces. She rummaged about in it, head bent, biting her lip. Good God, she thought: Dmitri. And quite apart from whatever he'd done between the girl's legs, those marks on her neck. He must have tried to strangle her. There was no question, she would have to speak to Prince Pyotr at once. And he would speak to the old Prince. Something would have to be done about Dmitri. He was a dangerous maniac.

That night, when Miss Harriet had left them, and there was just the faint light beneath the icon, Sasha sat by Yelena on her bed. She was facing the wall, head buried in the blankets. There were snuffles. She was crying.

'What happened? You can tell me if you want.'

'I was just pushed. That's all.'

He knew she was lying. But he would do nothing to insist with her over a secret she wanted to keep. He never had. Instead he just stroked her hair for a minute. Then suddenly she poked her head up out of the blankets and turned to him.

'He pushed me. And then touched me all over, and hurt me everywhere, down there . . .' Just because he had not insisted she felt a great need now to tell him the truth. That was why she loved and trusted Sasha above all people. He often scoffed at her. They argued and fought. But he never tried to dig into her secrets. And if she told him secrets, he never ever told anyone else. So she felt utterly secure with him – alone with herself when she wanted to be, and close to him, closer than to anyone else, when she wanted that. So she said to him now,

'*Kill* Uncle Dmitri! Let him die, soon, tomorrow or the day after. I want him *dead*.'

The old Prince, as was his regular custom and according to the Karelian traditions which he favoured, took a *savu-sauna* every day in the wooden bath house on the other side of the courtyard behind the castle, sometimes with Dmitri discussing business. He sat there, a few days after Prince Pyotr and his family returned to St Petersburg, on one of the upper benches inside.

The hut was without windows or chimney, a smoke-blackened room where a pinewood fire, lit beneath a central pile of porous stone, had been left to burn overnight, before the door was opened in the morning, the smoke extracted and the red-hot stones doused with water, filling the room with steam.

The Prince inhaled deeply, a biting resinous smell of charred pine entering his lungs, the boiling moisture quickly opening his pores, his naked body a glistening flood of water trickling from his stunted arms, flowing down his hirsute chest to his powerful thighs.

Dmitri sat to one side on the bench beneath him. They talked casually in the steam-filled half-light before Dmitri got up and, taking a wooden ladle to a bucket of ice-cold water, doused the hot stones again. It was an easy matter then, when the steam rose everywhere in a great sizzling burst, filling the room with a thick vapour, for the old Prince to move along the top bench and open his thighs. When Dmitri returned through the cloudy steam he saw nothing of this move nor, when he sat down again, anything of the great muscular vice which had opened up above him. As he leant back, the old Prince's thighs snapped round his neck viciously, holding him rigid, so that he started to choke.

Struggling violently, Dmitri twisted about on the bench, attempting to rise and turn, using his arms, trying to prise open the fierce grip that held him. But the more he struggled, the more the old Prince closed his great thighs about his son's neck. Retching and choking, Dmitri felt his strength begin to fade.

'Now, Dmitri Mikhailovich – you will tell me. What you were doing with my granddaughter Yelena –'

Dmitri struggled again, half rising in another determined

effort to release himself. He managed to twist round, so that he faced his father now. But he got no further. Again the Prince increased the pressure round his neck. Dmitri stopped moving completely, his tongue out, eyes popping from their sockets – his puffy face no longer with its faint smile, but a red mask, coursing with sweat, where the water seemed to be being squeezed out of it, the features set in a rictus of pain.

'Admit it to me – this foul deed!' The old Prince, suddenly enraged by his own words, tightened his grip without realizing it. 'Yes,' he roared. 'And apart from that – all the years of your schemes here, to inherit. You may be sure I have known of them all along. But that you should think to violate and kill my granddaughter to further your foul ambitions. This foul act! Admit your sin!'

The Prince, swinging his thighs to and fro, began to shake his son like a dog with a rat. 'Admit your foul sin!' he roared again. Dmitri's face was arched back away from him now, his eyes open but unmoving – his tongue out, but motionless.

Dmitri could admit nothing then, for he was dead. When the Prince released his grip the body fell away, slithering over the moist bench, falling to the ground with a thump. It was only then that the Prince became aware of what his fierce temper had done. Stepping down from the bench, kneeling over his son, he frantically sought to revive him. He tried to cradle him, to lift him up. But he could get no grip on the moist body with his stunted arms.

'My son, my son!' he cried out now. 'Wake! For I have done thee wrong.'

But nothing stirred in the inert body. The Prince became quite still then, kneeling over his son, head bowed. Nothing moved but the swirls of cloudy steam – and rivulets of water, coursing down the old Prince's face, with his tears, into his great beard.

4

Yelena, as she grew older, came to hate Russia. *Troikas*, wolves, gypsy balalaikas, the tolling bells from blue-domed churches, snowy visions, holy men and monsters, peasants in red kerchiefs. All that had seemed natural and happy to her before now became hateful.

Russia . . . She came to think she'd known it right back through the centuries. Her grandfather's Russia, with its despotic boyars' court, barbaric cruelties, deformities – it was medieval, she realized. She'd been thrilled and intrigued by the castle during holidays there, thought it all a fairy tale, *A Thousand and One Nights* come to life.

Later she saw how the book was more a history of Ivan the Terrible, a story in which she had been a minor character, victim in that awful tale. A child with no voice. Afterwards she was more determined than ever to control every aspect of her life, to have a voice, her own way in every matter.

Russia, the foul Dmitri, all that had happened to her that night at the castle – it stained her soul. She wanted to escape from everything, the horrors of that new year, the unhappiness, the nightmares it brought. She wanted to disappear, to go away to Europe, to leave Russia for ever.

There was a whole world to the west, beyond the frontier station at Wirballen, which she knew about from holidays to Paris, Berlin, Nice, Biarritz. A *modern* world. Sensible, organized, reliable. That was it, she felt. A world where everything was quite different. Countries without fear or shadows.

Russia wasn't modern and never would be, she felt. And since she wanted to be modern she therefore couldn't be Russian. She'd change her name, her country, run away from everything, parents, relations, home, for a life anywhere else on earth. And that world elsewhere would be with Sasha, of course.

As a child then, after the terrible events at the castle, she naturally assumed the world over the border in the future would be with Sasha. It would have to be, wouldn't it? They were twins, quite apart from the fact that he was the only person she really loved and trusted. So it was natural: they would spend the rest of their lives together.

But later she realized there was a big difficulty here. Brothers and sisters, even twins, didn't live together all their lives. They came to love other people, absolute strangers, with a different sort of love which gave them children, a love which took brothers and sisters apart, because you couldn't love close relations in that way. Realizing this, she was quite desolate. It seemed there could be no future for her and Sasha together.

But then a few years later everything changed, settled itself. It suddenly became perfectly clear to her that she also loved Sasha in that way, the way you love outsiders, strangers. So all would be well with them. There was no difficulty now. They'd be together all their lives.

She remembered the moment perfectly – the first time this feeling came to her, that she loved Sasha like this – and how happy she was.

He had been watching her over his violin bow. A difficult passage in Tchaikovsky's *Valse-Scherzo*. She was hunched over the keys – it was midsummer – out on the wide first-floor balcony of their granduncle's house at Orlov in the Ukraine, her hair bobbing up and down after the new cut she'd had in Nice – hearing the sudden sharpness in his music, as she paused in her part and he took up the string crescendo which heralded the end of the piece. When she took up the piano's response again she saw in the huge sky across the ravine a flight of migrating geese. At the same moment a dark plume of smoke ran in a widening, lengthening wash along the bottom of the picture – the Moscow–Kiev express moving in the opposite direction, the train itself invisible, hidden in a fold of the great wheatlands which ran away in a golden haze all the way to the horizon. This view of real life distracted her. She lost her place and stopped.

'Difficult?' Sasha, ironic, arched his dark eyebrows.

'No.' She pointed over the landscape. 'Distracted. The Moscow train. And a flight of geese.'

Sasha went to the edge of the balcony and lowered the awning so that the view was almost entirely shut out.

A summer evening. The day had cooled. A vague breeze from the river. The dog Samson stirred at her feet. The summer of 1912. The twins were nearly seventeen. Every summer, for the latter part of the holidays, when they came back from Nice or Biarritz, they went to their granduncle Sergei's estate, the big house at Orlov near Kiev. They never went to the castle on Lake Ladoga now. Moving the grand piano out from the ballroom behind, they practised on the open terrace in the cool mornings and evenings. This deep, shady balcony, with its sheet music strewn about, its regiments of potted plants and wicker chairs, was the centre of their world at Orlov.

The groves of oak, willow, poplar and hornbeam trees in the English parkland, with its shrubs and winding paths and ponds, small wildernesses and surprising vistas; the intentionally haphazard vision which sloped gently down to the ravine where the river lay and then rose up beyond that to an infinity of flat land and huge skies; they distanced, protected themselves from this distracting world, making one of their own on the balcony, equally infinite, but inviolate; a world of their music where everything was directed towards a precisely intended interpretation, where nothing was haphazard – all within their control, they thought.

'Let's try his *Sérénade mélancolique*.' Sasha rested his bow on the piano. 'Misha's bound to ask for it tomorrow.'

'Let's not. *Trop mélancolique*.'

'His *Souvenir d'un lieu cher*, then?'

'All right.'

Samson got up and went over to Sasha, reaching his paws up to his knees. 'No, Samson. Down. We're not finished yet. Down!' The dog obeyed at once. Yelena liked Sasha's firmness. She was just as firm, herself, of course, if not more so. Everything was simply a matter of will between them.

She watched Sasha's hands as he clenched and stretched his fingers, easing the tension there. Why did she so like his hands, for example? She suddenly wanted to inspect them closely. She went over and took one of them, gazing at it. The fingers were longer and thinner than hers, narrow, taut, the skin very smooth between them, little half-moons at the bottom of each nail. There was a graceful arched length to his string hand, with a fine gossamer of dark hair along the back. She turned it over: a high thumb mound, a long life line, deeply indented, but broken here and there.

'What's wrong?'

'Just wanted to look at your hand.'

'You've seen it before.'

She had seen his hands before, but simply as the instruments of their shared music. Now she felt something quite different about them. Open, visible, touchable, they were the final extensions of his body, evidence of everything else untouchable, invisible there. His hand was exciting.

Sasha picked her hand up and gazed at it. That was more exciting still, she felt. Of course he was the only person she'd ever let touch her like this. There was always that absolute trust and confidence between them, even when they were having one of their screaming or sullen rows together. What arguments, what tantrums! Why did these rows never take them apart for long? She supposed they were just evidence of how close they were in one way, as twins. And wanted to be in another, like quite separate, unrelated people.

She let her hand lie easily in his. And that's when she had the clear feeling, how she felt that sort of love for him – a love which came fully formed then, all in a rush, so that a choking sensation rose in her throat. She loved him then, in every way. But all she said was, 'I wish my finger span was longer.'

'If it was, you wouldn't have the power, the attack you have. Fingers all over the place. Temptation just to be showy. Misha said it the other day. You play like Medtner, not Scriabin. "Taut, rhythmic, accurate." None of those romantic, mystic effects Scriabin goes in for. Like me, you're businesslike.'

'Medtner doesn't leave his audience truly excited though.'

'Does better. Unresolved tension. Leaves them wanting more.' He stroked the minute hairs on the back of her hand so that she felt a prickle running down her spine. He let her hand fall suddenly, as if he'd got an electric shock from it – taking his bow up, settling the violin beneath his chin.

'Right. The *Meditation* first. *Da capo . . . A piacere* – please ourselves over the pace.'

Suddenly she was angry, frustrated. 'Why not *appassionata* while we're at it? For God's sake, Sasha, all this boring "businesslike" thing of yours. I can play like Scriabin any time I please.'

'Yes, by imitation. Not nature.'

'How do you know, you great cold fish.' She flared then. 'You don't know everything about me. We're not Siamese twins.'

'I know enough about you to know your nature is pretty much the same as mine. Not cold fish. But we're . . .' He hesitated. 'We're disciplined.'

'My God, you're so schoolteachery! And hypocritical. If you were so disciplined you shouldn't suggest doing this *a piacere* but the way Tchaikovsky marked it. You know what? You can go to blazes and I'll play on my own. I can play just as well that way. And just like Scriabin.'

She started straight away, playing Chopin's *Fantasie impromptu*, very much in the Scriabin manner, with all his soulful excess and romantic finish. He watched her hands intently, as they spanned, narrowed, caressed, chipped, clipped and paused in their rhythms over the keys.

Yelena noticed how he watched, proud of her own free hands, unencumbered by having to share the music with him. Just me, myself, she thought, my hands, no longer part of him. She could see the admiration in his face. He didn't hide it. As honest as she was. Or was he? she wondered.

'There,' she said when she'd finished, still annoyed. 'You and your self-control and unresolved tension. *That's* resolved.'

For answer he immediately played an equally romantic solo violin piece by Paganini, in just the same utterly fulfilled, emotional manner. Quite unlike his normal very controlled style. When he'd done they looked at each other. The anger between them had dissolved. But both were still trembling with another passionate emotion which their separate music had exactly expressed for them. An adult emotion. But they were not yet quite adult.

Sasha had outgrown Yelena now. He was handsome in a farouche, leonine manner, shanks of dark hair radiating out from the top of his skull like the thick strands of a mop. A broad forehead narrowing down over dark eyes, pale cheeks, a firm straight nose, the shadow of a moustache, to a sharp chin. His expression was usually intense or preoccupied, the broader top half of his face other-worldly, the sense of impossible dreams churning about just behind the eyelids. But the lower half, with his thin lips, narrowing jawline, his sharp chin, suggested someone calculating, prosaic, hard-hearted even – at least someone who knew exactly what he wanted and would get it by patient stealth, by 'hook or by crook' as Miss Harriet used to say of him. Yelena got what she wanted much more openly.

Sasha's body, strengthening and filling out his height, had lost all its earlier girlish attributes. Though he was still slim, more thin-boned and less fleshed out than Yelena, with an inward smile sometimes, full of calm certainties, indecipherable, almost smug. A smile that made Yelena furious – Yelena who wished she'd been a man, and couldn't be doing with any sort of silent, enigmatic, womanish business.

She too had changed in looks and build. A mop-cloche of glistening black almost straight hair, a compact face, a little square-jawed, eyes deep set, like Sasha's, but with a usually bright, questing, thrusting expression – which some people thought was simply aggressive. An unattractive face, they then decided. Perky and impertinent. Lantern-jawed, *jolie laide*, monkey-faced – they added their further silent criticisms. But Yelena liked her face. Apart from the nose.

Certainly her body had changed. It was quite clear now – she was a woman. She had filled out in all the right places, narrowing suitably at the waist. A neat, competent body. Competent hands. Somewhat chunky in parts, with the puppy fat not all gone, particularly round her thighs. She was certainly a woman. But the way she behaved and viewed the world was masculine. Like her aggressively turned-up nose. Her dreadful nose.

But she made the best of it, this nose, as an imperious weapon to cock a snook at people, just as she used her penetrating eyes to glare at them, subduing them, and curled her lips in arrogance or scorn. Self-possessed, controlled, shrewd. Like Sasha. Both of them were criticized for the private, superior world they'd created around themselves, a fortress which they left only on forays to attack. Or rather Yelena did. Sasha usually stayed behind, using silent well-aimed arrows against his foes, avoiding close contact.

They were both strong-willed and keen to promote this – to win, against each other and the world. A will that required that they no longer just defend themselves, as they did as children, but actively vanquish their opponents now. An imperious, unpleasant couple, some thought.

The early nineteenth-century house at Orlov – with its copper dome above the big hall, its white pillars, porticos, pediments, tall sash windows and wide balcony running along the garden side – was as classic a building as the castle on Lake Ladoga was barbarous. And their granduncle here, Sergei Mikhailovich Rumovsky, their grandfather's younger brother, was as civilized a man as the other was despotic. He and his wife Tatyana – their three children had long since left home and married – were people of a liberal and very practical outlook, always vigorously implementing their ideals.

Sergei loved England. He admired everything there from its constitutional monarchy to its plum puddings. Now he managed his estate along English lines, importing prize bulls and rams, together with all the latest agricultural ideas and equipment from that country which he had visited only once – a visit which had resulted in his pride and joy, the centrepiece of his rural life at Orlov: a model dairy, equipped with all things British, from oak churns to new cream separators; spick and span throughout, just in the manner of Prince Albert's dairy at Windsor Castle which, as he loved to recount, through the good offices of the Royal Horticultural Society, he had inspected and so admired. So that now, at Orlov, from a herd of Jersey cows he produced big rounds of creamy Gruyère cheese, packing them in straw and chipboard boxes before sending them off to the Kiev and Moscow markets on the train.

Sergei, now in his mid fifties, had reacted long before, as a child in the castle on Lake Ladoga, to the tantrums and excesses of his elder brother, Prince Mikhail. He had wanted no part of these, deciding as soon as he came into his patrimony to distance himself from his brother – indeed to reverse the feudal attitudes of this monstrous scion of the family by showing how an estate could be run successfully in an exactly opposite manner, by following every sort of progressive principle. And so, on marrying thirty years before, he had bought the house and lands at Orlov, far from the frozen wastes of Karelia, in the warm southern heartlands of Little Russia, with its fertile black earth, pretty women, bright colours, its feel of the Black Sea and the Mediterranean not too far away, if one turned left outside the big wrought-iron gates and carried straight on down the road.

In fact this would have taken him along the single street of the estate village, between two rows of neat wooden houses, past the yellow church with its white picket fence and the priest's house, to the estate shop, then the vodka distillery with its nearby fields of pink potatoes, to the sawmill and on to a dead end at the great forest of Orlov: old oak and beech at the centre with an ever-widening periphery of more recently planted conifers, carefully culled each year and taken to the sawmill.

Turning right outside the gates, along the dusty carriage road, brought you to the town of Varitsa, fifteen miles away, where three miles beyond the trains between Moscow and Kiev stopped. So that although Orlov itself lay at the end of this road, in splendid isolation, it was not really isolated at all. An hour's journey south took one to Kiev, the old capital of Rus, while from the north, the post-chaise, meeting the train from Moscow every day, brought Sergei all the friends and news he wanted from the wider world: academicians, professors of agriculture, visiting English landowners, distant neighbours in that vast steppe land, holy men and pilgrims on their way to Odessa and thence to Jerusalem, liberal members of the Duma, and a host of Sergei's other cronies from Moscow and St Petersburg who stayed in the house in droves, or, like the pilgrims and itinerants, camped in the gardens, sometimes for weeks on end, at all seasons, entertaining and being entertained; the train which, as well as this human cargo, brought pamphlets on bee-keeping, the latest memoranda on the use of copper sulphate potato spray from the Royal Horticultural Society in London and copies of the London *Times* no more than a week out of date.

Orlov in that summer of 1912, with its new McCormick reapers from America, the wheat harvest about to be brought in, its early Worcester apples reddening in the big orchard, huge bunches of purple grapes, melons, peaches, quinces, apricots, greengages, all equally ripening in the many glass-houses, its wonderful cheeses stacked up in the cool dairy – Orlov was a model universe, from which only the twins held aloof, distant wraiths in the household, given over entirely to what they saw as even higher ideals: their music and themselves.

Sergei, in the long, first-floor drawing-room with the rubicund Tatyana doing needlepoint by the open window, taking the evening breeze on her rosy cheeks, went over to the big samovar, poured tea and passed it round, before settling down to his regular early evening game of beggar-my-neighbour with Miss Harriet. The music drifted from the balcony farther along as they cut the pack.

'Delightful, don't you think?' Sergei cocked his head, seeming wistful, though he almost entirely lacked any real musical appreciation. A small, dapper man, thinning grey hair, brilliantined, combed severely sideways, clipped moustache, a round, bluff weather-reddened face above a generally rotund body, he was dressed impeccably *à l'Anglaise* that summer evening, in a white linen suit, silk shirt, striped cravat and polished brown shoes. He looked up at Miss Harriet, in her loose-fitting tea dress, a quizzical twinkle in his eyes, for she had not replied. 'Don't you think?'

'What?' Miss Harriet had been thinking of something else.

'The music. The twins.'

'Oh yes. Beautiful.' She listened to it now. 'Tchaikovsky's "Memories of a Dear Place". How apt!' She paused. She had been thinking about the ever greater separation she felt between herself and the twins. Having been more or less a mother to them for so long, their closest confidante, teacher, friend, she was now a distant appendage to their lives.

Of course, children grew up and went away into their own worlds naturally. But in this instance she had been hurt, because the break the twins had made with her had been so complete, and was quite without cause on her part. It had been sheer bad manners and insensitivity on theirs. As a result, having seen mainly virtues before, Miss Harriet was now more aware of their faults. They had become smug, opinionated, overcritical, particularly Yelena. A real shrew. She was devious as well, deceiving herself as much as others. She made such a point of seeming forthright, open and honest about everything. But honesty for her was more a way of hurting people. And when not doing this she was trying to turn them to her own purposes, wanting to be liked at any cost, all false smiles and compliments, telling them how wonderful they were. And then the opposite of this, the way she came to slash people with her telling words, in Russian or English: the vivid phrase with which she wounded them. And finally the aggressive way she tried simply to browbeat others, glaring at them with her flashing, hypnotic eyes. She was a bundle of contradictory, unpleasant impulses.

Of course, as Miss Harriet supposed, these unhappy characteristics were largely a result of what had happened to her that night at the castle. Yelena, so hurt in body and mind then, had had to grow up with this deep wound. Yet she had kept it hidden, denied it, replacing her own hurt by hurting others.

Thus Miss Harriet explained Yelena's behaviour. So, too, she understood the girl's great need for Sasha, her twin and therefore her closest helpmeet and companion. But they were too close now. It was unhealthy, Miss Harriet thought, looking up at Sergei, brightening.

'Yes, I've heard so much of their music over the years, sometimes I'm not aware of it,' she said. Then she paused and listened again. 'I hear it even when they're not playing. Like a gramophone in my mind. It's always there.'

'Ah, yes . . .' Sergei leant back in his chair, pretending to savour the notes, hands clasped pensively under his chin.

'You are an old fraud, Sergei. You know as much about music as I know about . . . about leaf curl on the nectarines.'

'You are right, my dear. I am tone deaf. I think only of how much you have brought the twins, with your love of music, your own abilities there, your teaching them in the first place.'

Miss Harriet took the compliment graciously. 'The truth is I wanted for them what I could not quite have myself. I'm no second-rate musician – no false modesty. But they are more than first-rate. That's the point. They've shut the door behind them on mere good playing now. How can one describe it?' She tapped her fingers on the green baize table. 'Except by saying one can't describe it in words at all. Soul on soul coming together perfectly in their music? But that I'd had their gifts!' She picked up the pack suddenly and started to cut it vehemently. 'But what nonsense! One should never try and define what one loves – start digging into it, like a worrier over the tomato plants, disturbing the roots. Just eat the tomatoes!' She twinkled back at him now.

'Indeed, Miss Harriet, well said. You Irish, of course – so quick and apt with words. That construction you use, by the way – "*But* that I'd had their gifts" . . . Archaic surely? Are you teasing me again, Miss Harriet?'

She smiled at him. She did tease Sergei over his Anglophilia, but more often she promoted it, informing him of its less obvious aspects, correcting him as to fact, bringing him up to date on English matters. But teasing him as well. She adored him. She well understood Sergei's love of England and things English. It was an affair of the heart for him, a romantic honour which he did for that distant, unknown country. She understood because in all this his feelings, his love for what was essentially unknown to him, were just the same as hers for Russia.

She had come to Russia originally because, through books and music – Pushkin's verse, Tolstoy's novels, Tchaikovsky, Borodin, Rimsky-Korsakov, Mussorgsky – she had fallen in love with the whole idea of this startling land: taken originally by all that she sensed so exotic there, and now equally set at ease by these greatly hospitable, original, highly emotional people.

The Russians were like the Irish, she thought, in their wayward, romantic character. They were moody, extravagant, uncompromising. Ecstatic or glum. They laughed or cried. They took life by the scruff of the neck or were beaten into the dust. People of spirit. They gambled with their lives, their thoughts. They were vastly penitent or unrepentant, saved or damned spectacularly. All this she loved in them: that their souls were uppermost in their lives.

Sergei returned Miss Harriet's smile, very much one of her

teasing smiles, he thought: a smile of long friendship, ease in his company, admiration. But how he wished it were a deeper look, that quite different unmistakable expression signifying love. For he loved her, and had done so for years, with a silent, unrequited passion.

Prince Pyotr arrived then and took tea from the pot on top of the samovar. There was a jar of raspberry jam to the side. He ladled a well-filled teaspoon of it into his glass.

'You peasant, Pyotr Mikhailovich.' Sergei looked up at his nephew in mock distaste. 'For all your sophisticated ideals, my dear fellow, you have the soul of a *moujik*.'

The Prince grunted amiably but made no response other than helping himself to another spoonful of jam. The two tufty rises of hair set halfway back to either side of his scalp were flattened and sleek now. He had just come from a swim at the deep-water pool on the river.

'Or else you are a "toady" – that's the word, Miss Harriet, isn't it? – trying to ingratiate yourself, to ape the manners of the peasants for some political advantage. It will do you no good. You must face and deal with them fair and square as I do, as equals, when we can respect each other. Your ethic must be *practical*, not political.'

They had started to play the cards now, Sergei snapping them down apace, against Miss Harriet's almost equal pace, in this daily joust.

'Uncle, I am very practical in this matter at least: I have a passion for raspberry jam. And my ambition is to satisfy it at every opportunity.'

'You will get fat – even more so – about the belly.' Sergei snapped another two cards over. He was winning.

'It will increase the girth of my happiness, too – and the more so with this particular raspberry jam. Wonderful flavour.'

'Yes, those new canes I put in a few years ago – "Ruby Cascade". I had them from Suttons in Reading.' Playing faster now, Sergei lost the next two hands in a row. 'Do you know Reading, Miss Harriet? I loved the town myself. Stopped there two nights, at The Royal George, when I visited the new Agricultural College there.'

'You are simply trying to distract me, Sergei.'

'No! I have a real interest in the place.'

'My knowledge of that town is practically non-existent,' she told him firmly. 'Other than that they do seeds, and biscuits, and that poor Oscar Wilde was imprisoned there, so it would seem a place of rather limited, not to say reactionary, attributes. And now, my dear Sergei, you have not been keeping your mind on the game. I see an end here – your end!' Miss Harriet, while she was speaking, had won another two hands in quick succession. She was about to win the whole game, which she did in another minute. 'There!' she said triumphantly. 'Three nights in a row, Sergei. Oscar would certainly have described that as *great* carelessness.'

'Ah, Miss Harriet, it is that . . .' He stopped. '*But* that I am blinded by you! Your skills, your charm, your intellect – you ravish me. I am "all of a dither" with you. That's the phrase, isn't it? What's a poor man to do but lose, in face of such?'

He smiled hugely, got up and took some more tea from the samovar. 'But look at these,' he said on his return, taking an envelope from his pocket. 'Here *I* have won! Arrived on the post-chaise today.' He put the set of cigarette cards down on the table in front of her. 'See, at last, from my suppliers in Fleet Street, the one cricket set I didn't have: The Surrey Eleven. Including Mr Hobbs!'

He spoke with such love, such naïve joy, that tears pricked Miss Harriet's eyes as she bent her head, observing these mysterious flannelled figures with their bats and beards, striped cravats and tiny caps – figures and a game almost as meaningless to her as she knew they were to Sergei. Oh, yes, she thought, the Russians, even so seemingly sensible a person as Sergei, were children. And she loved them most of all for that – for this quality of impromptu honesty, in their flirting, their fervour for an arcane English game, their belief that Reading was some sort of Babylon.

She loved them for their innocent wonder at the world, their reckless appetite for, and happy misconstruction of it. They brought to this a passion which, as she often regretted, she was always just too wise to give to the world herself.

Tatyana joined them from the window then, sitting down, with Prince Pyotr, for their regular game of *Vint*, auction bridge of a strange sort, Miss Harriet thought, but which none the less she had become adept at and which they usually played before supper every evening.

They were happy. All the Rumovsky family were happy, for the Princess Sofia was away in Baden just then, taking the 'Kur'. Even the youth Ivan was happy just then, his hurts and resentments temporarily forgotten, upstairs in his room cleaning his new 16-bore shotgun, which Sergei had given him for his birthday. He would be out in the forest in half an hour. The place was thick with game. But what had happened to his shooting cap, the smart black leather cap, with the snap peak and feather to the side, in the German mode, which he'd bought with his Christmas money earlier that year?

The twins walked up between the raspberry canes, Sasha carrying a chip basket. It was early morning, the sun just up in a sky of hazy, mackerel-ribbed clouds, and they were picking their breakfast, which would go with cream from the dairy before they practised.

'Ivan, did you hear him last night? Banging away till after it was quite dark. What could he have seen to shoot at?' Yelena was eating almost as many raspberries as she put in the basket.

'Ivan just wants to shoot, even if there's nothing there. You'll be fatter than ever if you gorge on them now.'

'I won't have any cream with them this morning, to make up for it.' Moving up the row, they rustled the bushes, so that even at this cool hour a luscious sweet raspberry smell rose on the still air.

'I can't make him out,' she said.

'You don't like him, you mean.'

'He's so cocky and shows off. All this talk of joining the *Gardes Chevaliers*.'

'He will. He'll have to anyway. Military service. Me too.'

'Misha said you won't have to if we get a gold medal at the Conservatoire.'

'Yes.' Sasha was pensive. 'All the more reason – more practice.'

'I hope you don't do it – get sent off to Tashkent or somewhere wild. Let them send Ivan to Tashkent.'

'Just because he mocks us.'

'He hates us, for our music together. And I hate him.'

They moved on up the line, Samson following Yelena. He never left her heels. Sasha ate a raspberry then. 'I don't hate him. He just bores me. That's worse, I suppose.'

'Yes.' She studied a grub on a leaf carefully. 'Hate at least means something.'

They went back and into the dairy. It was cool and shadowy, light filtering down from the high clerestory windows. Sasha lifted the beaded muslin cover from a big earthenware crock. The cream was thick and yellow. He started to ladle it out into a jug.

'Those blue tiles, Dutch tiles, with boys playing marbles beneath windmills and so on . . .' Yelena looked round the walls. 'I *love* them. How can one be indifferent?'

'No. Just more self-controlled, about what you love and what you don't like.'

'We'll travel, Sasha – won't we?' She walked down the line of earthenware crocks. 'To Holland and places. Do our music there, when we're good enough.'

'*If* we're good enough. With a bit more discipline . . .'

'Goodness, you're so boring.'

They had another row then, so that when Misha, their summer music teacher, came out from Kiev that morning he sensed these disagreements almost at once in their playing. Their *Sérénade mélancolique* was ragged, tense, uncooperative, dull. He stroked his goatee beard, then took off his pince-nez: a fussy, dictatorial man with a small head and watery blue eyes which he dabbed at constantly with a handkerchief reeking of eau-de-cologne. He should have been altogether a small man, yet the rest of his physique was imposing, his clothes those of a dandy.

'Stop!' Picking up his silver-topped cane he walked away across the verandah and leant over the balustrade, his back towards them. Silence. The twins started to fidget. Misha seemed totally absorbed in the view. They rather feared this contrary figure, who had won a gold medal himself, on the violin, at the Kiev Conservatoire years before. 'Play your part alone in that *Sérénade*, will you please, Yelena.' He didn't turn round.

'Alone?'

'Yes, just by yourself.'

'But, it won't mean –'

'Just do as I say.'

She started out well enough, keeping the tempo, leaving the right spaces for the non-existent violin. But soon the music became hesitant, rhythm and tone were lost, and then it became a shambles. She stopped. Another silence.

'Now you, Sasha. Alone.'

Sasha repeated the exercise, with just the same results. So that he, too, soon stopped.

'Well?' Misha inspected his nails, blinked, got out his hanky again.

'Well, it's composed for two instruments,' Sasha spoke finally.

'Which is not to say that one can't play each part alone. Indeed, you could both have finished your parts solo. But you didn't, did you? That's the point.'

'No. No, I couldn't.'

'No, because you've got more sense. Had either of you continued to the bitter end I should have given you both up, here and now.' He left the balustrade and returned, swinging his stick like a *boulevardier*, in a lighter mood. 'It would have shown me that you two would never have done more than bark up the wrong tree. The niceties of technique rather than feeling. A concern with simply completing things, willy-nilly. Well, you have the technique, I don't doubt that. But feeling – that's quite another matter. And when you played that *Sérénade* together there was only a feeling of division between you. You both know perfectly well that any duet depends for its success on a sympathetic accord between the partners. Some coolness between you today? Well, that simply won't do. If you want to succeed you must put your own tempers and tensions and all that rubbish right aside. *Good* feelings for each other, positive feelings.' Misha relaxed now, swinging his stick, doing a little dance with his gangly legs over the boards.

'There are several points here, my dear Yelena, dear Alexander: first of all you are frightened of your own feelings, and then you're frightened of the feelings in the music itself. No good. You must give yourselves to each other in the music.' He circled his hands out from his chest. 'Then give yourselves to the feelings in the music. *Promote* the feelings. Music is pure emotion. It's not passing the time of day with chat about the weather and the crops. It's love and hate and everything in between. And at your level, and if you're to make a career out of it, you have to go out of your depth with it, every time. For as long as you hold back your feelings, or deny them – well, you'll do fine entertaining the *nouveau riche* in their over-stuffed drawing-rooms. But you won't be making real music. That's like making love. Try it again together now.'

He went back to the balustrade and leaned right over the edge, as if something of particular interest had caught his eye in the garden beneath. They played the *Sérénade* once more. Afterwards they went straight on with the *Souvenir d'un lieu cher*.

At the end Misha turned to them. 'Good.' He dabbed at his eyes again. 'Very good.' He shook his head. 'In fact, from the ridiculous to the sublime, in the space of ten minutes. If you can go on playing like that together, you'll do. You'll do very well.'

Later, when they were alone, Yelena said to Sasha, 'I'm sorry, let's try and not row any more.' She didn't look at him. She was trying to compose herself, trying to swear, by an act of pure will, not to have rows with him again.

The yellow prairie of rye and buckwheat, stretching away to the horizon beyond the ravine, was pock-marked everywhere with blotches of red – of poppies and red shirts and smocks, of the men and women starting to scythe the harvest, which had begun that day, as it always did, on 26 July, the feast day of St Ilya, patron saint of the harvest.

Thunderstorms were expected, for that was the tradition, too. So that Sergei, as usual, had tents set up at intervals down the lanes which wound through the steppe, where there were barrels of fresh water, bread, tomatoes, and large rounds of cheese.

The twins had been there that morning outside the largest of the tents, at the launching of the harvest, when the village priest had offered prayers to St Ilya, and had blessed the hundreds of harvesters, who had then dispersed like a red tide, before separating out in lines, their scythes swishing in unison, the keen blades cutting into the wheat, felling it in great swathes.

The day was hot and humid as the twins took their horses, riding away down the lane from the big tent, the vision ahead silent until they heard the strange clatter of the two new mechanical reapers. Soon, coming to where they were being used for the first time, they saw the peasants scything in an adjoining block, their faces sullen, disturbed, as they watched these new American machines at work, the wheat falling out neatly, cut and bound quickly in a never-ending stream behind the blades, women following, putting it into stooks.

'Work still for the women. But not the men,' Sasha said.

'But the machines do it all much quicker, don't they? So they can get back to their own plots of land. They're mostly paid in kind in any case, not money, aren't they?'

'They see a day when they won't be needed here at all. When they'll get nothing, in kind or cash.'

Spurring their horses, the twins cantered away, then galloped along the endless dusty lanes through the wheat, riding out towards the featureless horizon, always receding, no matter how fast they rode. Far out on this yellow sea, where there was nothing and no sound but the corncrakes' cry, they stopped and dismounted. Yelena took a cloth from the saddlebag and wiped the foam from the mare's neck and from between her haunches. Then, with another clean cloth, she mopped her brow. Sweating and sunburnt, in a short-sleeved shirt, her arms, face and neck were all the colour of the wheat. Sasha was the same, both of them bronze toasted. He took off his new wristwatch and shook it gently.

'Slow. Or it's stopped.'

She noticed the band of white skin round his wrist where the sun had not reached: quite white, like a bracelet. She found herself staring at the mark. She couldn't take her eyes off it. It was like gazing at something in a shop window, she thought, something she longed for.

Finally, dragging her eyes away, she looked round over the huge land. 'How many acres Sergei has . . .'

'Not as many as you.' Sasha put his watch back on. 'From Ladoga almost to the White Sea. Millions of acres.'

'I don't want anything at Ladoga. It's all – foul. And you know it. And why.'

On the way back, underneath the overhanging willows by the deep water creek on the river, they stopped and let the horses drink. Everyone bathed naked here, the men and women separated by a spur of thick willows, which jutted out, dividing the creek. But the twins had their smart new bathing costumes with them, bought earlier that summer when they'd gone to the Rumovsky villa in Nice. So they swam together now in the same inlet. They didn't delay, just dived straight in, making for the deep water, swimming up and down there, some distance apart, concentrating, gliding under water, dipping into the black depths, rising again, dipping again, like porpoises.

The water enveloped Yelena, supported her deliciously – like chilled mercury, she thought. Her legs and thighs were stiff from the long ride. She turned on her back and stretched her calves, turning up her toes, wiggling her ankles, so that the tension leaked away. She lay with her head right back in the water, staring up through the willows at the approaching thunder clouds and thought of God suddenly, so that she righted herself and shouted, 'I don't need him.'

'Who?' Sasha was over on the far side of the pool.

'There's no need – for God.' She felt all powerful then, as she did sometimes, just as she'd done with the wolves six years before out on the frozen lake. She thought of her sign in the great wind god Bieggolmai and what the old Lapp woman had said in the foul-smelling tent, how she was a *noaide*, a soothsayer, had the gift of communicating with spirits in the past, of having visions, of seeing into the future. She hadn't believed the old witch then and had had no reason to believe her since, for she'd neither seen nor foretold anything in the meantime.

'God,' she said again, treading water now. 'What does he mean?'

Then her legs seized up, with a paralysing pain. She started to flounder, sinking, gasping, rising, then sank right down, then up again for a moment.

'Linochka!' Sasha swam towards her. But he was some distance away.

As she sank again, deep into the black water, a vision came to her, absolutely clear, flooded with light: Sasha, bronzed and naked, floating in some balmy, golden-moted air, smiling, beckoning to her to join him – which she couldn't. She couldn't move, so that she snatched at him, where he was always tantalizingly out of reach, moving away from her then, receding into dark clouds, before he disappeared, quite lost to her. Then there was blackness everywhere. She was drowning.

'Cramp,' Sasha said, when he'd managed to drag her back onto the bank under the willows. 'Lucky you weren't alone.' He massaged her legs.

'Sasha . . .' She saw his body glistening above her, water dripping from the point of his chin, his shoulders. 'Sasha, I was drowning. And I saw you.' She couldn't tell him exactly what she'd seen.

'Yes, I was there. And you didn't drown.'

'No, I meant – I saw you in another way, underwater.' Still she couldn't explain it to him. For what could it mean, she wondered. This spiralling, gravity-free, golden-limbed body, forever eluding her, so perfect in its elusiveness, offering such happiness, if only she'd been able to reach it. Then, as she lay under the willows, she knew what it all meant. It was obvious. What she had seen had been a forecast of the rest of her life. It was the gift of Sasha in the future, which she would always have to move towards now, to reach, attain, be one with him. He had just saved her life. So it was doubly clear now: her life must be given to him. She closed her eyes.

A first faint rumble of thunder sounded away in the distance. When she opened her eyes, she expected still to see Sasha. But he had gone over to the horses, starting to loosen their halters. If, when she'd opened her eyes, he'd still been there above her, she knew exactly what would have happened. She would have reached up for him, joined him in that golden, free-floating vision.

Soon after they left the creek, the thunderstorm exploded above them in all its fury.

Yelena saw Ivan's silly German cap on the tray which the great stuffed bear in the hall held out in its paws for visiting cards. She put it on, laughing, looking in the small mirror by the hatstand. Then she ran upstairs and out onto the balcony where Sasha was fingering the sheet music on the piano.

'Such a terrible cap, isn't it?' She tipped it back over her head and stood arms akimbo, glaring at Sasha. 'A revolutionary?'

'No. You look more of a fool in it than Ivan does. Don't tease him.'

She left the cap on the piano and they started to play. Ivan appeared soon afterwards in his hunting clothes. Seeing the cap, he exploded. 'You thieving curs! I've been looking for that cap everywhere.' He snatched it.

'I took it. Not Sasha. Just trying it on. No need to get in such a temper. Sorry.'

'Sorry indeed – just "trying it on"! Just trying to make a fool of me!'

'No! I thought I looked quite the revolutionary in it.'

'You brat, you. Just laughing at me. Always your line, while all you two do is play your cissy music. Why don't you do some real work in your lives?' He stomped away, his heavy hunting boots clattering over the parquet floor.

'I wish he was dead,' Yelena said.

That evening in the forest Ivan shot nothing. The rabbits, the pheasants, were strangely absent. He sat on a fallen tree trunk in the twilight and smoked a *papirosy*. He was still annoyed about the cap. He took it off and preened the feather at the side. It was such a good cap. He was really grown-up in it. Then something stirred in the bushes behind him, a faint crackling over the dead leaves in the undergrowth. He got up, turned and raised his gun.

The poacher, with several rabbits and pheasants at his belt, stopped and listened behind the bushes. Something had stirred ahead of him. He had set several snares out in the glade, beyond the bushes, near the fallen tree trunk. He peered through the branches now. A figure was standing by the trunk, in a peaked cap, his gun raised, pointing straight towards him. The poacher retreated. He hadn't gone far before he heard the shot, so that he ran now, as fast as he could, back into the forest.

Ivan lay flat out, on his stomach, his foot caught in a snare, the shotgun beneath him. In his fall, with the gun held out straight in front, he'd collapsed right over it, his hip bone ramming into one of the twin hammers over the breech, the end of the barrel under his chin at that point, so that the charge had blown most of the front of his face away, his German cap lying in shreds on the other side of the glade.

'It wasn't your fault, Linochka.'

'It was. It must have been. I wished him dead, just before he left. Just as I wished Dmitri dead, you remember – and he was, a few days after we left the castle, dying somehow in that bath house.'

Yelena was too shocked to cry. Her mind, like her legs a few days before, had seized up. All she knew was that what the old Lapp woman had said was true. She could see visions now – of Sasha. She could see into the future. Equally she could will people's death. There was no doubt of it. Ivan's death confirmed this. And it terrified her. These strange powers, which before she had rather liked the idea of, she now knew to be evil. She had hated the foul Dmitri. Ivan had always just annoyed or bored her. But she'd not meant to kill either of them. She'd just *wished* them dead. She tried to blot out the idea that some other being lived in her, a demon, an evil genie who, at her least command, could rise up and cause such mayhem.

Her father was inconsolable. And her pain was so much worse in that she had caused his. And her Mama's anguish, when she quickly returned from Baden. Though Yelena cared less about that, caring as she did so little for her Mama, who had cared so little for Ivan. She was just a frivolous woman. But Yelena knew now that some part of her was worse than anything in her mother. Part of her was monstrous, and she had only to have a thought and then give voice to this element in her soul for that monster to rampage and maraud however she willed: a malign power which could spread disruption, like a plague, among the innocent.

The day after Ivan's funeral, his death being the fuse, the whole estate exploded in violence, becoming as barbarous as that frozen world far to the north on Lake Ladoga ruled over by the old Prince. The police, investigating the accident in the poacher's snare, had questioned the local men too vigorously.

One of the harvesters, since he'd been caught poaching before, was arrested. And despite the fact that he'd spent that evening with friends at the village vodka shop, he'd been beaten up and dragged off to the jail in Varitsa.

As a result, the following day, the harvest not yet ended, his friends, angry and frustrated, used the man's arrest as an excuse for what they'd wanted to do all week. Running into the distant wheatfields – soon joined by a crowd of other discontented men with scythes, in another red-smocked but this time violent tide – they unhitched the horses, clobbered the drivers and destroyed the two McCormick reapers.

The revolt spread. Others with real or imagined grievances joined in. Two under-gardeners, dismissed the year before for stealing fruit on a commercial scale, returned and smashed up the glasshouses. Three women, who before had worked in the model dairy, responsible for laboriously separating the cream from the milk by hand, took advantage of the situation by upending and breaking the new Alfa-Laval separators. Then, with the wooden butter rollers, they smashed the Dutch tiles round the walls and broke all the earthenware crocks, so that the dairy soon became a milky lake. Some men not concerned with the estate at all raided the vodka distillery, plundering the stock before crossing the road with broken bottles in a drunken foray towards the big house. Shots were fired. People were injured. The police arrived. By midday, with reinforcements on the way, the great hall at Orlov was strewn with casualties. The local doctor, with Sergei and the others, did the rounds, with bandages blankets, pillows, administering first aid, the twins helping where they could.

'There,' Miss Harriet shouted to Yelena. 'Oleg – over there.' She pointed to a corner of the hall. 'Bring these blankets and a pillow.'

Oleg, the chief coachman, a heavy, bearded, normally jovial man, had just been helped in by two stable-boys and lay now on the flagstones, writhing in pain, his leg seemingly broken. Yelena had struck up a friendship with Oleg long before. He sang soulful Ukrainian ballads and love songs and she'd sometimes persuaded him to sing while she accompanied him on the piano, extemporizing the music, following his deep bass voice. Now, kneeling down with the two stable-boys, she moved him carefully onto the blanket, putting a pillow behind his head. She comforted him, while he tried to reach his knee, groaning in pain.

'There,' he said, his eyes clenched tight shut, breathing and sweating heavily.

'Where?'

'Just below the knee. I can't reach –'

She put her hand very gently on his shin bone, keeping it there for a moment. She would have taken it away but for the sudden ease she saw in Oleg's face. He opened his eyes, nodding his head. 'Yes, yes – just there,' he said enthusiastically. 'Keep your hand . . .'

She kept her hand where it was – for a minute, two minutes. And as she rested it there all the pain in Oleg's face drained away. His eyes cleared, a thin smile emerged. 'Thank you, thank you, little one. But what did you do? I felt your hand – what have you in it, that took away the pain? It was like ice at first and then very warm, your touch.' He looked at her curiously. And, equally mystified, she looked at her hand.

'No, nothing,' she said. 'I have nothing in my hand.'

This was the first time she realized it. She could cure as well as kill.

5

Yelena called these strange gifts 'tricks'. But they were more than that, she realized. There was no accounting for them. Was it to do with her sign in the wind god, Bieggolmai? Well, perhaps, she thought – if you believed in that sort of thing. But as she grew older, she didn't. She didn't want these powers. They became an affliction, a curse. They were so completely at odds with what she saw as her real nature – controlled, reasoning, disciplined – that she could only think of them as something quite outside herself, not part of her. She'd simply become a medium through which a bizarre force, some spirit, sought release. An evil spirit in the main, taking temporary possession of her. That was perfectly clear.

So that over the next few years, and usually quite against her will (for she kept that severely in check after what she'd willed for Dmitri and Ivan), she found herself, willy-nilly, the instrument of some supernatural agency. It was nothing to do with her. So that what had frightened her at Orlov that summer now just made her furious – or embarrassed – for she kept the whole business hidden, except from Sasha.

The only good part of it was that, if she really wanted to and concentrated or was lucky enough, she sometimes found she could see Sasha when he wasn't with her. The first time this happened he'd gone to Moscow with Leopold Auer, the Hungarian violin maestro who had been his tutor in Petersburg, to take part in a concert with him there. She was in her bedroom, on the top floor of the Rumovsky palace in St Petersburg, their huge red *palazzo* on the Naberezhnaya Quay looking over the river: a small room, painted in light yellow, with darker apricot curtains, her collection of little musical-boxes on a shelf beside her, Samson on the end of the bed asleep. She was lying down reading a score, a piece by

Debussy, which she and Sasha were doing together. Closing her eyes and thinking of him, she suddenly wanted to be with him. And just as suddenly she saw him.

It was all quite clear: he was in a heavy, over-furnished suite at the National Hotel on Manege Square in Moscow; the elderly bearded Auer, in a floppy bow tie and frock coat, sitting in a high-backed chair by the window, Sasha, a little flustered and stalled in his playing, rehearsing by a music stand, with a bad oil painting behind him of some Cossack horsemen caught in a snowstorm – and the rain lashing down outside on the square. Auer, the maestro, was speaking, in his thickly accented Russian. She could hear him briefly. '. . . less *attack* on that last passage. *Legato*, remember. And you'll get that simply by taking it a little slower.'

When Sasha came back he confirmed that everything she'd seen and heard of them both in the suite was true. This was astonishing, that she could see Sasha in this way. Then she found she could see future events in his life: that a string, the D string in his violin, would break during a concert they were going to take part in at the Conservatoire. And it did. That was funny.

But the other manifestations of this power, which came quite unbidden or stemmed from the merest vague thought of hers, were not so amusing. Once she was thrown out of bed in the middle of the night. She'd been fast asleep and had woken up thinking a violent storm was coursing through her room. There was a roaring cold wind; the bedside table with its commode inside rattling next to her. Then it seemed as if she had been lifted sheer into the air and was hovering above the bed for several seconds, held up by this bitter cold wind, before being thrown aside, landing with a crash on the floor.

Sasha, when she told him, said it must have been a nightmare and that she'd simply fallen out of bed. 'Or a poltergeist got at you. That's what they do. Mischievous. Puckish spirits!' He laughed it all off.

A few weeks later something of the same inexplicable sort happened, but this time in public, so that Sasha couldn't deny it. The Rumovskys were giving one of their rare dinner parties, just a dozen guests, stuffy people, in the small first-floor dining-salon leading out of the ballroom. Princess Sofia, very elegantly dressed at one end of the table, was wearing a new pearl necklace she said she'd just bought in Paris, telling everyone of her recent stay there. Yelena found herself staring at the necklace, certain that some new lover had given it to her, and hating her.

As she glared at her, the Princess's shoulders started to wobble. Yelena didn't at once realize the cause of this, so that before she could look away and think of something else, her mother's whole body started to shake violently, the chair beneath her tilting this way and that. She jumped up with a shriek. Then the necklace snapped viciously, as if some invisible hand had torn it from her throat, the pearls flying all over the table and floor.

'My God! What was it?' the Princess screamed.

One of the guests next to her got up to retrieve the pearls, crawling about on all fours.

'Princess! Are you all right? What on earth –'

'My chair – you saw it. Shaking, started to rock.'

But clearly the guests hadn't really noticed this, had simply seen the Princess rocking, standing up, the string of pearls – in her violent movement – breaking. She had had a turn, they thought, or too much wine, or was in some way overwrought. Thus everyone chose to make little or light of the incident. Certainly no one looked to Yelena as the cause of it, except Sasha, who, knowing of his sister's strange gifts, realized she must have brought it all about. He looked at her in astonishment.

Then there were the nightmares. Yelena had had these on and off ever since the Dmitri business. Now they were more frequent – and upsetting. A mix of extreme pleasure and horror, which made the dreams the more disturbing still. The sequence of events was nearly always the same, the settings different. She was being caressed, fondled, undressed, then more or less forcibly made love to by an unknown man: always in public, in streets and parks and theatres, in full view of other people who took not the slightest notice, either when they were coupling together or when she was shouting for help, which she did to begin with, but never wholeheartedly, soon acquiescing in the man's desire, sharing in it, the men themselves never properly undressing; so that she became frustrated in the dream, anxious to be fulfilled, ripping their clothes off and hugely enjoying the rest of it.

But the real horror for her in retrospect was that the men had no proper faces. Just blurred features, blobs, no identity. They were just bodies. And the worse horror, when she woke, was to remember, to realize how she'd enjoyed it all; had been quite wanton in collaborating in what was really rape, the sort of half-rape she'd gone through with Dmitri. Worse still was the thought of how she could enjoy something so much in a dream which had so terrified and hurt her in reality. And worst of all was that Sasha never appeared, was never thought of, was totally absent from these nightmares. As if he didn't exist. She seemed to have completely lost his protection.

All this came to depress Yelena badly, these midnight disturbances, erotic dreams, inexplicable powers, not being in control of herself. And the unfairness of it all, she thought. Why had she been chosen as a medium? Had she not strange power enough in her music? Why should these other bizarre 'gifts' – these curses – be added? Some bad fairy at her birth? Of course, she'd thought this as a child, believing how her misshapen nose was the result of just such a curse. Was she to believe this now? – and in addition that the curse laid on her then had resulted in some awful flaw in her soul, as well as her body? These dreadful dreams, inexplicable powers – she wanted none of them. She just wanted to be herself, fully in control, cool, calm and collected, in charge of her destiny, which was playing music with Sasha, minding his and their and her own business.

So she did everything she could to suppress these powers, not to allow them space in her mind or heart. She fought them. But they were stronger, she discovered. They wanted her. She couldn't resist them. For how, she thought, could you resist some spirit that came inside you, unbidden, by stealth, like the sudden presence of a robber, a murderer, in the house of your soul?

She became tired and depressed. She feared to go to bed and couldn't sleep when she did, feared to look at anyone with the least unkind thought, started to behave like a fugitive. Everything in her life began to go wrong. Her music suffered.

She couldn't concentrate, so that Sasha had to take the whole thing seriously then.

She cursed her fate, because there was so much happiness waiting for her in those years, with Sasha, all about her in the city. And she was crippled by these demons, unable to give herself to the real world, to all the joy there. She didn't hate the old Russia then, in St Petersburg at least, during those early months of 1914. 'The glories of those frosty days, our secret promenades in sleighs,' she thought. Pushkin's wonderful winter weather.

Yet even during those brilliant white-earthed, blue-skied months after Christmas, Sasha had to force her out, force her to do anything.

It was March. *Maslenitsa*, Butterweek, the week before Lent. They were upstairs in the small gilded music salon, practising for an important charity concert that evening at the Conservatoire. But the rehearsal had gone badly. Yelena stood by the double-glazed window, looking out at the frozen river; big chunks of ice, caught in the stream the previous autumn, were covered in snow now and rearing up like little icebergs. Between the two large panes of glass, the edges of the window, against the frames, had been sealed with putty, leaving only a tiny window at the bottom. She opened this, sticking her hand out into the chilly air.

'It's *freezing*. I'm not going out.'

'Oh, come on, Linochka. Let's go sliding. The big ice hill in Mikhailovsky Gardens. The engineering students – they've built a tremendous slide. Best I've ever seen, steep as a cliff, with a Chinese pagoda on top and coloured flags along it and little fir trees and running almost right across the gardens. It's huge. No point in our struggling on here.'

'I'm *not* struggling. I'm playing Rachmaninov's *Romance*, opus six, number one. Or trying to.'

'Only get worse, if we persist with it.'

'Yes, Maestro . . .' The irony in her voice was cutting. She shut the little window, turned and glowered at Sasha. Cold, affronted, immobile, she was verging on one of her bitter, antagonistic depressions.

'Linochka . . .' He spoke slowly, advancing towards her in a stilted gait, arms and legs swinging stiffly, head moving jerkily.

She knew what he was up to – about to play The Game, started in childhood, when they took on the roles of characters from books, from history, family, friends or enemies, miming or speaking for them. 'Linochka, can you smell how delicious I am? The Gingerbread Man. Just out of the oven, all stiff, but made with the magic elixir the Arab left with the baker's wife. I'm John Dough the Gingerbread Man. And you're the Cherub.' He strutted across the salon.

'No! I won't play the game. And I won't go out.'

'Oh, come on –'

'Why don't you go out with your pal Kyril?'

'Because you're more of a pal. And Kyril's gone to Moscow, spending Butterweek with his uncle. So come on.'

'I can't.' She lost her temper. 'I *can't* because we've got this final rehearsal with Savonov at six this evening. And we – or I – can't get this damned piece right.'

Sasha took no notice of her tantrum. 'It's the best day ever out. The brightest blue. And glittery. But freezing hard, so all the slides are perfect.' He mopped his brow. The salon, its tall porcelain stove roaring away in the corner, was baking. She went back to the piano. 'Here, I got you a jam *kalachie* from one of the stalls when I was out – stalls everywhere with all sorts of good things. He unwrapped the sugary bun and offered it to her. She took it without thinking, taking a great bite out of it – she couldn't resist it – and then found her fingers all a sticky mess.

'Hanky?' She licked her thumb.

'No, I haven't.' Sasha was delighted. 'Now you can't play. Jam all over your fingers. So you'll have to come out.'

He grabbed her, a bear hug from behind, pulling her up from the piano stool, turning her round, gazing at her, lifting her chin, so that she was forced to look at him. 'Not today, Linochka. No dumps today. Not now, not *ever* – or not with me at least. We both of us have more or less a free week. It's Carnival! So we can go out and slide and have fun and be back and practise in the afternoon and the Rachmaninov will go fine tonight. It will. You'll see. Because we're good. We're *both* good.'

He shook her shoulders gently, with that brightly confident look of his, so that she capitulated. Sasha's look. She knew it so well, the slightly beetled eyebrows, so straight a nose that she wished it was hers. The small curls, like scimitar moons, that ran down before his ears, so good to kiss. The lips that were like hers, the fine bristle along the jawline, the slightly clefted chin. Oh yes, my dearest Sasha, she thought, as she gazed at him: this face discovered, travelled and remembered better than any other; grave yet smiling, indeterminate, chameleon, beyond description. This face and no other. Their two faces – a double-headed coin. Twinned, inseparable.

They soared then, rushing out of the overheated salon, flowing like a joyous wind through the ballroom, out onto the main staircase, tearing past startled retainers and cleaners, helter-skelter, down to the big hall with its pillars and double doors leading out onto the quay.

'Money. For more *kalachies* and things. I've none.' Yelena was vibrant now, shouting from the back of the hall, putting her tall buttoned boots on, her *shuba* and fur hat.

'I've only a few kopeks left.'

'Ask Papa. He's in his study.'

'I asked him yesterday.'

'Well, ask him again!'

Sasha moaned, pushed his red-banded cadet's cap up at an angle, and sloped away to his father's study beyond the hall. She followed, peeking through the open door.

'Papa, Linochka and me, we're going out sliding. And for *kalachies*. And I'm right out of cash again . . .'

Prince Pyotr sat at the end of a long committee table littered with books and papers, a roaring stove at his back, a picture of a dodo bird on the wall to one side and his pet brown bear Ivan, fretfully sucking a paw, at his feet. The Prince had rescued him as an orphaned cub on a fossil-hunting expedition to the Urals the year before. And Ivan had since completely taken to him, was inseparable, sitting contentedly on his haunches while the Prince worked in his study, sucking his paws or eating fruit, following him all over the Palace when he was allowed in, or when he wasn't out in his 'Swiss Cabin', a log hut specially built for him in the back courtyard. A tame, loving Russian bear, but growing fast, so that he demanded all the more human attention now, as if he knew that with his increasing size, strength and appetite, he would soon have to be sent off to the zoo.

Seeing Sasha, and no doubt smelling the remnants of sugar and jam on his fingers, Ivan ambled over and, standing up, started snuffling into his pockets and coat sleeves. Sasha, raising his hands, turned and tried to bump the bear away with his backside. 'Get down, Ivan!'

But Ivan had no mind for this at all. He embraced Sasha, leaning against him unsteadily, like a drunk, the two of them beginning a ragged little dance. 'Just a rouble or two, Papa?' Sasha, trying to release himself, had to shout through Ivan's furry neck. The Prince came over and tried to disentangle the two of them, only to get embroiled himself in these furry embraces, so that all three of them were soon embarked on a manic dance round the table. Yelena came into the room then. She roared with laughter. She surprised herself. She'd forgotten what pure happiness was like.

Coming out of the study she almost bumped straight into her Mama. Delicately touching up her new swept-back hairstyle, the Princess was coming down the wide stairway in a long sable cloak, about to go shopping. Yelena was suddenly back in cold reality.

'You won't forget, Linochka, your final fitting at Frau Behrens tomorrow. At three. For the ball on Saturday.'

She had forgotten. She hated these seasonal balls. 'No, Mama, I've not forgotten.'

'Would you like me to come with you? Or would you like to come out shopping with me now? We could have a pastry at Bormann's.' She smiled. In one of her most amiable moods, Yelena thought. She supposed it was because her mother was going away soon, leaving for Europe, renewing her amorous adventures, as she always did the moment the season finished in St Petersburg, when Lent began.

Yelena's relationship with Mama was politely formal at best. A situation which neither of them had any wish to improve. So Yelena was surprised when her mother took her arm, walking with her to the big hall doors, opened by Boris, the chief *dvornik*, with her sleigh waiting for her outside.

'My dear Linochka, I do want you to look your best. I told

Frau Behrens – no expense spared.' Sasha was trailing behind them. Yelena felt alone, exposed.

'Of course. Yes . . .'

'We're making a party up for the ball with the Buchanans next door. And Meriel: you like her. With Mr O'Beirne and some of the other staff. Important it all goes well. Your father and I, we're very fond of the Buchanans.'

'Yes, of course.'

Next door was the British Embassy, housed in the front part of the Soltikov Palace, leased from the family, who continued to live in the back – another much larger building next to the Rumovskys, looking over the wide river. So they were immediate neighbours. The Rumovskys knew the Buchanans well – Sir George, a willowy, silver-haired man with a droopy moustache, was the Ambassador; Lady Georgina his wife, and Meriel his daughter, a girl the same age as Yelena with whom she got on well. But why should her Mama think this impending arrangement so especially important? They'd been with the Buchanans for parties, dinners and shared summer outings on many previous occasions.

Mikhailovsky Gardens, the trees heavy with encrusted frost. Drooping branches. But the bright midday sun melting the icicles, dripping translucent crystals. Hundreds of people milling about, their breath rising in cloudy spumes. Shouts and laughs and gasps and shrieks coming from the long slide. The twins pushing their way towards it. Climbing the steps, a queue above them. Yelena on top of the slide in the little pagoda, the icy slope falling away almost sheer in front of her. Swaying with an instant's vertigo as she looked down and beyond, to how the slide levelled out flat, way above the ground, then fell steeply again and snaked back in a hairpin bend to a final dip a hundred yards away by the huge oak tree at the end of the gardens, where there were half a dozen *blini* stalls, smoke rising from the tall stovepipe chimneys above the ovens. And above the oak, on the horizon, the slim gold steeple on top of the Peter and Paul fortress clearly visible against the pale blue sky on the far side of the river.

Getting the long wooden tray with its foot-rest, sitting for a moment on the edge, Sasha behind her with his arms on her shoulders, waiting for the two men just in front of them to get going. And when they did the twins were suddenly off after them, down the cliff of ice, stomachs somersaulting, the little fir trees and coloured flags racing past them. Quicker, faster, the freezing air cutting into their faces, like a thousand tiny pinpricks, until Sasha's red scarf, pulled from his collar in the wind, flapped across Yelena's face, temporarily blinding her as she shrieked. On the level then, still going fast, gaining on the pair in front, dipping again, banking into the turn, close to the others now – they seemed complete fools at the business, Yelena thought – until, on the last run in, they were right behind them, unable to stop themselves, crashing into the two men at the very end of the slide, all four ending up in a heap on the big mat beneath the oak tree.

'Sorry. We couldn't stop.'

Sasha picked himself up. The shorter of the two men remained stretched out on the mat, his astrakhan hat gone, his dark formal greatcoat covered in dirt, smart black shoes filthy now in the slush. Neither of the men were dressed for sliding at all. And now the shorter one, lying there, crossing his legs, putting his hands behind his head, was just laughing. Roaring with laughter. Crinkly fair hair, a plumpish face, and a short nose and eyes dripping with tears from the icy rush of wind, lying there like a madman.

'Sorry,' Sasha said again.

'Godamnit,' the short man said, finally picking himself up, taking out a large handkerchief, shaking it like a duster before wiping his eyes. 'Say, what are you two up to? Trying to kill us? We were going fast enough.' He shook his head, looking at Yelena with a reproachful smile. Fools indeed, she thought. And not even Russian. Speaking English.

'It's a fast slide,' she told him at once, in English, suddenly feeling cheeky. 'You should have tried an easier one first.' She was exuberant, tingling all over.

The shorter man picked up his astrakhan hat. And then Yelena's hat, which had fallen off in the mêlée. 'This yours?' He came over and plonked it on her head, pulling it firmly down over her ears with both hands. Equally cheeky. 'There! Now we're quits. It suits you like that, right down over your ears. Say, you two English?'

'No.'
'You speak just like Britishers.'
'Why not? We all learn English here. Not savages, you know.'
'Sure, I know that . . .' He smiled. Then that laugh again. 'We're the savages, we Americans. Aren't we, Matty?' He turned to his companion, a taller, thin-faced man, the same age, late twenties, who was still brushing himself down, looking bruised and affronted. He was shivering. He said nothing. 'This is Matthew Walsh, my quantity surveyor. And I'm Johnny Quince. John William Michael Quince,' he continued more formally now, 'from Charlottesville, Virginia,' as if the twins should know the place well. He dipped his head minutely, then took off one of his smart leather gloves, offering his hand. They made things up, with introductions all round, by having *blini* smothered in butter under the frozen oak tree. Mr Walsh didn't seem to like his, fingering it gingerly, taking an unwilling bite. But the snub-nosed Mr Quince ate his dripping pancake in a flash.
'Let's all have another.' He didn't ask any of them first, just held up four fingers to the stall owner. Then he said 'Four' very clearly and loudly in English. Dictatorial. 'See?' He turned to them. 'I always find if you just speak English *loud* enough – they'll understand you. Anywhere in the world!' The huge smile then, his round face crinkling up like his crinkly hair. He wolfed the second *blini*, then looked at his morose companion. 'Yes, we're the savages, aren't we, Matty?' Without waiting for a reply he turned to Yelena. 'Well, so long. And thanks for nearly killing us.' He took out his big white handkerchief, making a fuss with it again, flapping it about, before wiping his fingers, and shaking hands very formally. Then he turned smartly on his heels and was gone, pushing through the crowds. Gone before Yelena had had a chance of – she didn't know quite what. But she wished him back suddenly. Then just as suddenly he *was* back, there, right in front of her. 'Hey, I was a bit abrupt. My turn to apologize.' He looked at Yelena intently. 'Come and have dinner with me tonight. At the Astoria. Both of you.'
'We can't.' She was abrupt now. 'We're playing in a concert tonight. At the Conservatoire.'

'Oh, great. On Theatre Street. I know it. I'll see you both there then. After the show. We can all go on to Cubat's or somewhere afterwards.'

He swung round on his neat little feet once more and this time he was finally gone. If he hadn't come back then, Yelena thought – well, she'd have forgotten all about him. Why had he come back? Because she had wished him back, of course. That roguish face, the brash good humour. She'd felt a pang at his leaving so abruptly and so had simply pulled him back, like a doll on a string. Her strange powers were sometimes useful.

As John Quince walked away through the crowds a second time he wondered why on earth he'd gone back to the couple. His friend Matty wondered the same thing.

'What was your thought in going back there? Sassy little vixen.'

'I don't know.' Quince shook his head in genuine surprise. 'I'd quite forgotten about the two of them. Then the thought came to me out of the blue: "Go back. You have to go back."'

'For what? She's only a kid. And you've enough on your hands back home with women.'

'Yes. But not one like this.'

'Johnny, don't. She's only a kid. It's your not knowing what you want with women that's put you – and them – in the soup.'

'I know. But something took me back, so strongly . . .'

'That's just romantic horseshit. Like your making us go down that crazy slide on a goddamned tea-tray. You nearly had us killed.'

Johnny turned, putting an arm round his friend, smiling hugely. 'But that's just it. I *am* a romantic, Matty. That's what I love about Russia. The exotic! All this!' He gestured round the gardens. 'And that's what I'm looking for in a woman. Why not? Same wonderful notions that I have. And she has it, that girl. I *know* it. Her eyes – didn't you see her eyes?'

Sasha grabbed Yelena. After the *blini* and the meeting with the two intriguing Americans, the day seemed even more inviting to her. They left the gardens, crossed the Moika canal and went out onto the Marzovo Pole, the vast cobbled military parade ground behind the Rumovsky Palace. And there it was

– the carnival town, specially built for Butterweek by the city authorities. A whole town, with dozens of little streets running between rows of elaborately carved and decorated wooden buildings and flag-draped tents. Shops, stalls, theatres, puppet shows, merry-go-rounds, swings, skating rinks. And coursing through this fantasy town an endless succession of *Skormorokhi*: street players, jugglers, clowns, ventriloquists, bear tamers, comedians, singers, musicians with balalaikas and concertinas, dancers.

At every street corner the *kacheli*, long sets of beribboned swings, whole families soaring up and down on them, two to a seat often, rising high in the glittery air, petticoats aloft, scarves trailing, shrieking, before toppling off and running to the food stalls. The nut vendors, with their huge *funduki* – hazelnuts as big as eggs. Then the sweets and gingerbread stalls, others with oranges in huge pyramids. And everywhere the bright log braziers and tea stalls, huge brass samovars boiling away, dozens of different-sized teapots – and sleighs sweeping by between the booths with tinkling bells and red ribbons flying from the harness. Music everywhere, laughter, the smell of smoking birch and pine, tart orange peel, burning butter from the *blini* booths.

They went on the swings. They watched the Punchinello show and saw clowns on stilts having a boxing match on high. They took a 'dozen of tea' with a group of droshky drivers, sharing twelve small cups in a row, sucking the tea through big lumps of sugar like the cabbies did. They went to the mime theatre and saw the ventriloquist and spun on the English merry-go-round, astride the gilded horses. And then, just about to go and see the Cossack dancers in another tent, they found they'd run out of money.

There was a small booth next door with a circular table and an arrow spinning over the dozen segments, each with a different fruit painted on it. Fifty kopeks if you guessed which fruit the arrow stopped over. They had ten kopeks left between them. Sasha looked at her.

'Can you tell? In advance?'

'No. I can't. I'm not in that mood.' She was annoyed with him. Being happy, she'd forgotten all about that side of things.

'Go on, Linochka. Let some good come of it all. If we win, we can get in to the Cossack dancers.'

Well, why not, she thought. They wanted to see the dancers. She looked at the table. The arrow, spinning, finally stopped over an apple. Then the clear thought of the pineapple, right next to it, came to her mind. 'The pineapple,' she told Sasha. And they both put their last two five-kopek pieces on the segment. The arrow stopped just over the pineapple on the next turn. They had won a rouble between them. Sasha wanted her to do it again. But she wouldn't.

'No point in tempting fate.'

'Fate? But this is a good part of your powers. They're not all bad.'

'Everything is bad, if you can't control it.'

'You could make a fortune in that casino in Nice. Or the one in Biarritz. Guessing the numbers.'

'I couldn't. I wouldn't. Don't you see? They're all a curse, these powers.'

In the Cossack dancers' tent. The sudden flooding music from a small orchestra, concertinas and balalaikas. Then the dancers charging in. The girls in long, swirling, vividly coloured dresses. The men in red and gold tunics, high boots. Sword dances, swinging round in great swoops and jumps. The men facing the girls in wild, feet-stammering fandangos. Yelena was happy forgetting all her good and bad powers.

John Quince came to the concert at the Conservatoire that evening. His presence was very clear to the twins, since he had the cheek to wave at them when they came onto the platform to do their piece. He was sitting alone, near the front, in a shiny dress suit and an unsuitable frilly silk shirt, sitting on the little gilded chair, clapping excessively and shouting 'Bravo! Bravo!' when they'd finished. He overdid the huzzahs, Yelena thought, bounding to his feet, an odd figure among all the other more formally dressed men and their sober women, the *haute monde* of St Petersburg.

After the concert, when they were all out in the foyer, she saw him over by the *vestiaire*. Here he'd picked up a flowing opera cloak, lined in red silk, white silk scarf, top hat and cane. He'd really overdone things all round, Yelena felt. They were surrounded by people – their parents, Miss Harriet, some friends. He came over, hovering on the outskirts of their group, the pudding face, the flashy clothes – a real stage-door Johnny. But she had to rescue him.

Before she could do so another couple came up behind him, friends of the Rumovskys – the von Mecks, Nicholas and his wife Anna. Baron von Meck owned the Moscow–Kazan railway, the largest private railway in the country. He was one of the richest and most prominent men in the capital, while his mother, a passionate music lover, had been Tchaikovsky's great patron.

'Good evening, Mr Quince.' The Baron spoke nearly perfect English. 'I did not know you were interested in classical music. You should have told me this morning at our meeting. I would have asked you to come with us. My wife, the Baroness Anna . . .'

Yelena was astonished. John Quince had friends in the highest places. He turned away from their group then, talking with the von Mecks, and she thought he wouldn't bother with them any more. But a minute later he was back, making for her, the von Mecks in tow.

'Hi!' He beamed. 'Miss Rumovsky, Mr Rumovsky. I'm no expert, but I could tell from the applause you were both *wonderful*! Congratulations. It was great. Really great.' There was a surprised silence among the Rumovsky group at this brash intrusion. Quince took no notice, turning, gesturing towards the Baron and his wife. 'Say, meet my friends the von Mecks. I'm building a new railroad for Nicholas.' At this news the silence was more pronounced. But the Baron, in high good humour, eased matters at once, continuing to speak in English. 'Their Excellencies, Princess Sofia and Prince Mikhail Rumovsky – Princess Yelena, Prince Alexander, they are old friends of mine, Mr Quince. But thank you all the same! Good evening, Princess, Prince Pyotr, Miss Harriet.' He bowed all round. 'Allow me to introduce my friend, Mr John Quince, who is indeed building a new railroad for us, our mining extension up in the Urals beyond Perm. And supplying the rolling-stock.'

'Prince? Princess?' Johnny looked at Yelena in ironic surprise. 'You never told me – *Miss* Rumovsky! – that you are a princess . . .'

Yelena nodded briefly, returning his smile. It all became easy then. Johnny Quince and the von Mecks, with the Rumovskys and their friends, made a party of it that evening, taking *troikas* to Cubat's restaurant, way out over the Neva bridges on Kameno Ostrovsky island.

In the big sleigh, with a fur rug up to his chin, Johnny sat opposite the twins, with Miss Harriet next to him. 'Why, Miss Boulting,' he told her, hearing she was from Ireland. 'You must meet my quantity surveyor, Mr Walsh. His family hails originally from your country.'

'Indeed. What part?'

'Do you know, I don't know. He's not the most communicative of men, unusually for his race. It's a problem. Because I love talking.'

'You should be Irish then,' Miss Harriet said nicely. 'We're great talkers indeed.'

'Unfortunately not. Quince, like the fruit. Hard and tart . . .' He smiled. 'We were a British family originally. From Yorkshire. Came over to Virginia on one of the earliest ships, helped make the first colony. Literally. The first Quince, Ebenezer – he was a master carpenter, came up the James river in 1607 with John Smith – Smith and the Indian girl Pocahontas and all that, you know the story? – and built the first settlement there at Jamestown. Prospered, till a few years later when he got gold fever, went up-country and the Indians got him. But by then he'd had four children. All boys. And the Quinces never looked back. The hard-working, canny, evangelical Quinces. The Wesleyan persuasion, in fact. John Wesley, Methodists, you know. We became Methodists in the States. Great builders. You know what they said of John Wesley? "He builded better than he knew."'

How he did talk, Yelena thought. No stopping him. Until the *troika* gathered speed up the English and then the Admiralty quay, and they crossed over the Troitzky bridge, the icy wind starting to whip over her ears, so that she couldn't hear him properly, just the odd sentence, as he continued to regale everyone with his own and his family's history.

'. . . an aunt now, my father's elder sister, Mrs Chauncey Phillips . . . big gingerbread mansion set on the ramparts looking right over the James river, further down at Lynchburg

. . . leather-tanning business, wasn't doing too well, until she took over . . . husband was a drunk. Then she made a real fortune out of it – after she'd pushed him down the ramparts one night . . . drowned him in the river, rumour had it. She's a fanatic Methodist!'

Gales of laughter. There was a sharp wind now. A night almost without stars, hidden in thin layers of cloud over the Neva. A moon somewhere behind, which finally emerged halfway along the Kameno-Ostrovsky Prospekt, a big sharp orb which bathed everything in silver light, the snowy roofs and trees glinting with diamond crystals as they raced ahead on the long straight *chaussé*, their heavily padded *yamshchik*, reins tied round both wrists, whipping the horses up, attempting, as usual, to outrun all the sleighs and *troikas* in front of them.

She didn't bother trying to hear everything Johnny was saying then. She just enjoyed looking at his gleeful face, ducking every so often as bits of icy snow, kicked up by the horses' feet, hit the net pulled over the top of the *troika*. The exuberant face of a truant schoolboy, she thought. Yes, he was 'filled with the exuberance of his own verbosity', as Miss Harriet used to say of her – she who could 'talk the hind leg off a donkey', as her governess had usually added.

But that evening, Yelena was just content to watch Johnny's face, vivacious in the moonlight; this happy, *outré*, childlike man, who must have been nearly thirty and built railways. How prosaic, she thought. But that certainly didn't seem his age and wasn't his mood then. He was her age, Yelena felt, and his gift was for making her and everyone else amused and happy with his bizarre tales, his family gossip, his so openly sharing every stray thought, offering everything of himself in his every moment. He had that trick of immediate intimacy, but without threat, presumption, intrusion. A free spirit brushing close, so that you could feel the thrill of his flight, his elation as he soared and swooped, without being seduced, taken away by him.

'Why, it's all just wonderful here!' he shouted across to Yelena. 'We don't have that much snow in Virginia. Except up on the Blue Ridge mountains, west of Charlottesville, where we have our castle – yes, it's a real English castle, turrets, battlements, the lot. Phony, of course, copied from one in Yorkshire. Quince's Folly, we call it. Now up there one year it really snowed when we were kids, we were snowed up for a week. So that the firewood ran out, then the food and we *froze*. So what did my father do? Upped bags and baggage and we all slid down the mountainside, on old timber boards and trays and children's sledges, anything we could get – to the railhead, the little private station at the bottom where father had a special line built out from Charlottesville . . .'

Yes, she liked this gadfly chatterbox. She wanted to tease and please and talk the hind legs off this man. To joust with him. Friendly combat. To *play* – that was what he so invited. Not love. Love was Sasha, sitting beside her. She reached for his arm then under the fur rug and squeezed it. Turning to him, looking at his thin face, cadaverously shadowed in the moonlight. He turned to her with a half smile, as Quince embarked on another astonishing tale, with Miss Harriet, shouting in her ear: '. . . the thing about a good railroad is what we call the "permanent way", the foundations. Well, in the States, it's sometimes not so permanent. When we were building out west in the 'nineties, with the gangers in tented camps, there were still great herds of bison out there. And this time, one morning at first light, well, there just wasn't any railroad there . . . Or permanent way. Bison had trampled and rooted it all up during the night. I saw it. I was there as a kid. Nothing but bison all round, far as you could see, stampeding, pushing, shoving, right round the camp . . .'

Yelena saw how Sasha was aware of her interest in this man. But there was no hint of worry or jealousy in his face. She saw that as well. There couldn't have been, because Sasha had no rivals with her. He knew that. She knew it of him. They were absolutely secure in their love. Complete trust, together or apart.

6

Sasha saw her watching the American over the long table at Cubat's, saw her amusement, interest, as she exchanged snatches of conversation with him, above the vivid music of Goulesko's gypsy orchestra. He wasn't jealous. No, of course not. Because he didn't love her in that way. The way he knew she loved him.

He realized how she wanted him in love, ever since she'd nearly drowned in the creek at Orlov – the way she'd looked at him then, lying back, closing her eyes. It had all been quite clear. And he'd had some difficulty in resisting the temptation.

And if he'd felt that temptation? Well, there was a problem. What did that bode? Nothing, he'd decided. It was simply a matter of continuing to resist. The real problem was that Yelena was so un-Russian in her complete lack of restraint in this – like their adulterous Baltic mother, he thought – in that she had so obviously, guilelessly, wanted them to love in that way, there and then, at the creek, and on other occasions since . . .

They were out in the small rowing boat, one hot afternoon, the following summer at Orlov, way up river, when they'd pulled into the bank halfway beneath a clump of overhanging willows. Since they'd brought no bathing costumes, she'd stripped off her clothes and jumped from the stern, naked. He'd done the same. And she'd frolicked about, swimming close, then ducking right under and coming up behind him, happy, her mouth full of water, a stammered bubbly shout of laughter. A look of longing supplication later, back in the boat under the trees, as he got dressed and she remained naked.

It was clear what she longed for. 'Why not?' she'd said suddenly, coming towards him from the stern, on her knees, the muddy water in the bilges squelching up as she moved, dirtying her glistening thighs, the sun-shadow through the leaves patterning her body, her breasts. He could have said, 'Why not what?' but he would never openly lie to her.

'Because . . .'

'We love, don't we? So why not that way too?'

'Lots of reasons. Brother, sister –'

'The Pharaohs did it – all the time.'

He'd laughed at this sudden unexpected historical justification. 'We don't have a royal dynasty to maintain. Against usurpers, outsiders. That's the main reason they did it.'

'They must have loved, though, too.'

'Not necessarily. It was a duty.'

'Yes, I suppose so.' She dressed, silent, preoccupied. But not sad. She'd kissed him on the forehead and said simply, but with great emphasis and certainty, 'Later'.

He hadn't asked what she meant. It was obvious, just as his own desire was equally clear. No matter – both their desires would have to be suppressed. That was all there was to it. But not quite. The problem had remained hanging over him, if not her, like the sword of Damocles.

The whole business remained disturbing – the more so since it was clear that Yelena herself was disturbed, obviously, after her experience with Dmitri. Which introduced a real puzzle. Why should any girl, related to him or not, who had gone through such a terrible experience, want to repeat it, compound the offence with, in his case, an even closer relative?

After leaving Cubat's, at two in the morning, Johnny Quince hired a droshky and took the twins to the rail sidings beyond the Nicholas station, where he was testing one of his engines.

'At two in the morning?' Yelena asked.

'Hell, yes. We always run them then. The best time, if we can get the dozy engineers up. Not much traffic on the line then, you see. Come on!'

It was well below freezing and pitch dark. An official led them down ramps and over rails with a big acetylene torch, past grimy banks of snow, between long lines of silent carriages and freight wagons, all capped in white with long icicles. Quince, his red-lined opera cape flowing behind him, with his top hat and cane, strode ahead. Part magician, part schoolboy anxious to play with his trains, Yelena thought. What a sight! His face a rosy glitter as they passed the orange-punctured coal braziers by signal boxes, leading towards a big engine shed, half lit, with a dozen slumberous, vaguely hissing steel monsters on the lines. To one side stood an even bigger engine, sighing and steaming.

A man emerged from a little cabin, in smart overalls, with pince-nez and a goatee beard, speaking English, not at all surprised to see the American.

'Good day, Mr Quince –'

'This is Vitaly,' Quince introduced him. 'Our Chief Engineer for the Perm mining line. Prince and Princess – Rumovsky! How do you like that, Vitaly? We'll give them a spin.' Vitaly bowed minutely, saying nothing.

'How is it, Vitaly?'

'Steam is up and we are ready to go,' he said punctiliously. 'We are fixed with the port low-pressure cylinder – I think.'

'Okay! Well done. Let's go then, Vitaly. Let's ride the iron monster!'

They all moved to the engine. It wasn't like a Russian engine, Yelena thought. A very long boiler part, with a tall, straight chimney and a 'cow-catcher' in the front, as Johnny explained.

'No, not Russian. One of ours, though adapted to the five-foot rail gauge here. A 4–4–2 Atlantic type, with added high- and low-pressure cylinders – a very large firebox and a special double braking system – for holding back on steep gradients. "Mother Hubbards", we call them back home. Very powerful. And fast, in the passenger version we run on the Philly–Reading Railroad. So come on up!' The twins scrambled up into the cab, crushing in behind the driver, fireman, Vitaly and Johnny Quince.

The great dense dark plume of smoke shooting up against the white night as they pulled slowly out of the shed. A sudden change of tempo, the wheels churning round, the chimney bellowing in quick successive gasps, the huge wheels skidding on the icy lines outside, two big bright beams of light piercing the darkness as Yelena leaned out over the edge of the cab window. Gathering speed, clattering over points, green signal lights ahead, leaving the yards, joining the main line to their left. The colour of the smoke changing to twirly, belching spirals of white. 'Give her more juice, Vitaly, now that we're out on the straight'. Charging forward then along the line, the fireman shovelling coal into the great gaping orange mouth of the firebox.

The engine beginning to sway and rattle, pushed to its limit out in open country, the pistons forcing their way to and fro, faster and faster, the sulphurous stench of burning coal. The noise was tremendous. But wonderful! – Yelena thought.

'Can you feel it?' Johnny shouted back to them.

'Feel what?'

'Like an *animal*!'

'Yes, yes!' she shouted back. 'Alive. A live animal. Yes!'

The freezing wind ripped across one side of her face from the cab window, a blazing heat from the open firebox burning the other. Chilled and burnt, the engine rocking, quivering, jolting every bone in her body. Her body being pummelled, slapped and forced about in the grip of some thrilling, unstoppable energy, faster, faster, charging into the black hole of the night.

'Okay, Vitaly – that cylinder's fine. Take the steam off a bit. Let her glide.'

And then the glide. The smoothness of that – she revelled in it. The engine with another sort of life now, relaxed, easy, a beautiful oiled smooth sensation beneath her then, gliding along, steady, the firebox closed, chinks of gold spilling out from cracks. She had never felt anything as exciting as this, until – 'Brake her, Vitaly. Cut her right out, then try the brakes again' – and when this happened she lost her balance and surged forward, thrown into Quince's bulky body, when he held her up as they slowed to a stop.

'Godammit! You again. Just like that ice slide, trying to do me in.'

His face, close to her now, was all begrimed and sweaty in the gold light from the open firebox. He smelt sulphurous to Yelena as he set her straight again, holding her shoulders. He was all a mess, his bow tie gone, collar open, cape and coat discarded, just in his smart trousers and soiled silk shirt, the engine gasping and hissing now, exhausted. Yes, just like an animal, she thought, that had run its course. As he had, holding her motionless then.

Ciniselli's circus on the Fontanka. The twins had front seats. A special Gala matinée for Butterweek. The sweet and sour smell, of sweat and cheap perfume, a musky attar of roses, with the odour of sawdust and straw. And behind this the rank air, the clear whiff from beyond the curtains, the dung and urine of wild beasts. The music from the blary little orchestra, right up to date with 'Alexander's Ragtime Band'. The house going dark, the drums rolling, the limelights spinning round.

Yelena watched the tiny, slender girl, glittering in sequins, high on the trapeze, holding the bar with a great Imperial eagle perched above her. Swaying into space, girl and bird, wings outstretched, huge scimitar beak and talons, a piercing limelight following them as they swung to and fro, ever faster, the bird seeming to carry the girl as she started a series of dazzling aerobatics, twisting and turning as if trying to escape its talons, until finally they soared away into the darkness. Then the clowns, the bareback Cossack riders, the jugglers, the tigers. Yelena, heart in her mouth, tears in her eyes, gripped Sasha's arm fiercely.

The clowns. And one particular clown. Tall, gangly, in a tailcoat, baggy trousers and oversized shoes. But his face was not that of a clown. It was a mask. He did a mime with a variety of different papier-maché masks, exchanging one for another, to the thumping music and drums. A Chinese dragon mask, Phantom of the Opera, a Shylock mask, pastrycook and country bumpkin. Enacting each role, advancing on the children next to the twins in the front row, striking terror or laughter.

And terrifying Yelena. For the point of his act was that this clown could be everyone except himself, for he had no face, as was clear each time he changed masks. A silk stocking pulled tight over his features. A blank face. Just a blob. Like the men who seduced her in her nightmares.

He approached the twins for his finale, in a bulbous mask, puffing himself out, a fat man laughing. Then, in quick succession, he peeled off this mask to display another beneath it, then a third, a fourth, until he got down to the stocking; when finally he pulled the silk off and Yelena saw his real face.

A wistful young man, with puffy cheeks, and extraordinarily mobile features. Dank, dark wispy hair, sweat coursing down his face. Wide, alarmed eyes, a tense innocence about him, his loose limbs flopping about now as he set off round the ring, taking an encore, pretending to canter on a horse, miming it all expertly, until he'd come back round the ring, stopping in front of the twins.

He reached a baggy-sleeved arm out to Yelena's throat – plucking a white dove from her collar, then a rabbit, a carrot and a handful of corn, letting them feed then in the ring, to renewed applause, before he leant over to her for a moment, miming the words 'Thank you' before cantering away again on his imaginary steed through the curtains.

Yelena wondered about this strange young man. So gifted, yet worried-looking. 'Who is he?' she asked one of the doormen on the way out. 'Oh, that's Ostrovsky. Mikhail Ostrovsky. From Moscow.' That was strange because she knew the Ostrovskys vaguely. She'd been to parties with some of the Ostrovskys years before, at their Arbat Street house in Moscow. But not with this Ostrovsky. She had no memory of him.

The great ball on Saturday at Countess Shouvalov's sumptuous palace near the Foundling Hospital on the Moika Canal, climax of the Butterweek festivities, grandest social event of the season. It would be all stuffed shirts and silly women, Yelena knew, and she was dreading it. But no family in the *haute monde* of St Petersburg could refuse an invitation, nor any member of the family. Their mother had insisted the twins come.

After Yelena had dressed, she went to see Sasha in his bedroom along the landing from hers. Frau Behrens's new ball gown, a dramatic affair in crimson satin, trimmed in black with a black silk embroidered bodice, was itching round her shoulders and her pointed satin shoes pinched. Sasha stood by the long tailor's mirror, dressed but for his tailcoat, trying to subdue his unruly hair, which he'd just washed and dried by the porcelain stove, so that it crackled each time he wrenched the comb through.

'It's awful,' he said.

'Well, don't put brilliantine on. Make it worse.' She sat

down on his bed, took her shoe off, stuffed a fist in it, trying to make it bigger.

'Thanks. You're such a brick.'

She hobbled over to him, with one shoe on. 'At least your dandruff's gone.'

'Thanks again.' He was surly now, trying to do up his bow tie in the mirror. She put her hands round his neck and did it for him. 'You're like a fussy wife.'

'No, just your unfussy loving sister. You can't tie a bow tie properly if you're looking at it in a mirror.' She kept her hands on his shoulders. She could feel the warmth of his back through his silk shirt.

'So infuriatingly competent, aren't you?'

'Yes. But come on, there'll be *some* fun, at least. Colombo's orchestra. Strauss and Lehar. "Blue Danube" and "The Merry Widow".'

He turned. 'Having to cheer *me* up now. How you've improved.'

'Yes! It's been a wonderful week and I'm better. And it was all *you* who started it off, on the slide that morning. As long as I'm with you . . .' She let the rest go. There was a small shaving cut on his jawline. She kissed him on it, getting a sudden whiff of some sort of cologne. 'Oh God, so you *have* doused yourself in that awful stuff from London again. What is it now?'

'West Indian Lime. A whole new lot of new things in from London in the English shop.'

'Ugh!'

'Yes, why not? And I'll use the brilliantine, too. Hair'll never lie down otherwise.' He moved to the dressing-table where he kept his collection of bottles.

'You are a card –'

'Just because you don't like the smell doesn't –'

'No, it's not so much that. Just I like *your* smell.'

Sasha, she knew it so well, had a natural, crushed wheat-and-honey smell. She could smell it now, on his warm skin. She wanted to go to the ball, and dance with him and smell that smell, close to, that smell and no other. And no West Indian Lime.

Countess Shouvalov's palace was very grand. A vast marble

staircase circling up to the ballroom. Everyone pushing and shoving in the great hall, getting rid of coats and hats and capes when they arrived – late, since there'd been a long queue of lantern-lit sleighs and *troikas* ahead of them, pulling up behind the covered porch.

Colombo's orchestra already playing upstairs. A bouncy waltz. 'Gold and Silver'. Strauss. Excitement. Warmth. Yelena's cheeks were blue with cold after the sleigh ride. The Buchanans and their party were waiting for them. Sir George, Lady Georgina, Meriel their daughter. Introductions to the others. The charming asthmatic Counsellor – the Irishman, Mr O'Beirne – she knew him. Then the naval and junior military attachés, Commander Jackson and Captain Woodrow, who were both new to her. Then three assorted English women whose names she didn't properly catch. Her mother was all over the place with greetings – in a turquoise crêpe dress with a short lace cape and long gloves, everything embroidered with silk flowers and heart-shaped sequins. Miss Harriet wore a simple outfit of very fine black silk chiffon trimmed in royal blue. Her father looking awkward. Sasha even more so.

'You didn't bring your bear then, as a *chasseur* to clear the way in all this crowd?' Sir George joked with her Papa.

'No. I might well have done.'

They all went upstairs, moving towards the widowed Countess at the top, who was standing by the double doors, with her Master of Ceremonies bellowing out everyone's name as they went through into the vast, brightly lit ballroom beyond. Meriel turned to Yelena. 'Our *chasseur*, we gave him the night off. He really is too much, pushing and walloping people out of our way every time we go out to something grand. Embarrassing.' She took Yelena's arm. 'So nice you're here. I loved your concert on Monday. Really. So did Sandy. He knows about music.'

'Sandy?'

'Yes, behind us. Our new assistant military attaché.'

Yelena turned briefly. A tallish, earnest-looking figure, ramrod-straight, with a clipped moustache and rust-coloured hair, was following them, a nondescript woman on his arm, with a frightful piled-up brush of straw-like hair decorated with organza roses. The woman was talking to him animatedly, while he nodded his head repeatedly, saying nothing.

'Oh,' Yelena said. 'Musical, is he?' He looked pretty dull to her. The tone-deaf sort. Typical British bore.

'Yes!' Meriel was very bright. 'Splendid, in an army man. Usually they're so dull. No talk of anything other than guns and things. But not Sandy. He looks a bit of a stick-in-the-mud, with that regulation moustache. But not at all stuffy behind that. *Quite* other! Even reads novels – and plays the piano! Classical music. But all the latest things as well. Ragtime, Everything. Didn't you hear him at our Xmas party?'

'No. I don't think –'

'After you left, perhaps. We had a tremendous time later. You must meet him properly.'

Meriel was clearly taken by this Sandy. But Yelena hoped not to meet him, properly or otherwise.

The Master of Ceremonies, his boomy voice ahead of them now. A cadaverous gloomy figure in ridiculous eighteenth-century court dress, with a gold chain round his neck, lace-trimmed frock coat, tight cream pantaloons and blue stockings: 'Their Imperial Highnesses, the Grand Duke and Duchess Vladimir . . . Count and Countess Kleinmichel . . . Count and Countess Nostitz . . . Madame Serebriakov . . .'

Then he was ushering them in: 'Their Excellencies Prince Pyotr and the Princess Sofia Rumovsky; the Prince Alexander, Princess Yelena, Mademoiselle Harriet Boulting . . .' Yelena was facing the Countess Betsy, who looked like the Queen of Spades on a playing card. Great locks of rich dark hair, certainly dyed, bunched round her ears and topped by a magnificent tiara, heavily blacked eyebrows over dark imperious orbs, a magnificent royal-blue silk dress, the organdie bodice embroidered with lake pearls and garnets, a double-stringed diamond and emerald necklace falling nearly to her broad waist.

A smile, a brief curtsey, a regal word. 'Yelena, my dear one. Your concert, superb . . .'

Then the vast gilded ballroom, overwarm already, heavily scented, hot-house flowers everywhere, mignonette and winter roses, with ferns and vine leaves intertwined, garlanding the marble pillars. Three great pear-shaped chandeliers glittering above. The company sitting on flocks of gilded chairs or promenading. Colombo's orchestra at the far end, on the Countess's private theatre stage, fiddling away beneath the blue velvet curtains draped artistically above them, studded with flowers and hanging ribbons.

Colour everywhere. And lights, always moving, glinting from the crystal chandeliers, striking the women's dresses and the uniforms of the Guards officers. The Imperial Guard in scarlet tunics. Hussars in white and gold with crimson-trimmed dolmans. The *Gardes Chevaliers*, white-tunicked, silver-trimmed. The women swirling, in olive, ruby, crimson, navy blue. All light and colour – and Yelena dancing with Sasha. Two-steps, polkas, waltzes. Then dancing with her father. And with Sir George and some of the others in their party. With Mr O'Beirne and Commander Jackson. But not with Captain Woodrow.

It was her mother who did this, did her best to monopolize him, on the floor and chatting together, sipping flutes of champagne at the buffet. And Yelena thought she saw the reason now for her wanting to put on such a show that evening. She was lining up another conquest. And seemed to be succeeding. Captain Woodrow, all smiles and interest in her. This surprised Yelena. What could her mother see in this so correct-looking Englishman? What could he offer her? In his late twenties, he was surely too young for her. And not much of a catch in any case, a minor official at the Embassy, no sort of likely paramour or frequenter of the spa resorts, unlikely to be rich – less likely still, in his official position, to take up any dalliance with her. No real prospects for her there. Yelena was curious.

She told Sasha of her thoughts – she'd seen him talking with the man earlier. 'Oh, he's nice enough. And obviously quite musical, yes. He was telling me of a concert he'd been to in London, the Queen's Hall. Some good new English violinist – a Mr Catterall who plays in a string quartet. And Captain Woodrow's Russian is surprisingly good.'

'Well, it would be, wouldn't it? That's why he's here, surely? A sort of spy, no doubt.'

'Possibly.'

'God, it's hot. Let's get some air on the stairs.'

They left the ballroom and leant over the balustrade, looking down into the hall. And there, a moment afterwards, they saw Mr Quince rushing up towards them, in his stage-door-johnny's outfit again. 'Hi!' he shouted as soon as he saw them, bounding up the steps now three at a time. 'I'm late. Got held up in the marshalling yards, some cockamamie Inspector wouldn't let us out on the tracks –'

'You?' Yelena said, surprised at his appearance here and feeling cheeky again.

'Why not?' He stopped pumping Sasha's hand and looked at her, aggrieved for a moment. 'The von Mecks arranged it, with the Countess. Are they here yet?'

'Yes, but –'

'What's all this "Yes, but" business for, Princess? We *can* dance in America, you know. I've been to balls as grand as this – and better – in Richmond, Virginia. And not all of us use spittoons. Here, I'll show you how we dance!' He pulled Yelena away then, into the ballroom, and spun with her vigorously, but gracefully, given his bulk, in a waltz which the orchestra had just begun. He held her too close for Russian propriety. But she liked it. There was a whiff of woodsmoke about him now. She liked that and told him so, as they whirled round. 'You smell of your engines again. Not coal, but all woody!'

'Yes. Wood-fired tonight. And here am I trying my best to get them to burn coal in my locomotives.'

'That trip – it was wonderful. Really.'

He bowed happily. 'Any time. Why don't you come out with us to the Urals next week? We have a special carriage, Matty and me. Put another on for you – and Sasha – give a concert out in Perm.'

'Can't. Sasha and I have concerts here, half a dozen through Lent. It's the only public entertainment allowed.' She grinned at him. She loved teasing him. Then, over his shoulder, she suddenly saw Ostrovsky, the clown, the conjurer, from Ciniselli's circus. He was alone, over by the stage. She was surprised, since she'd seen nothing of him before, or of any of the other Ostrovskys. They lived in Moscow. What was he doing here? Why wasn't he at the circus? With a sudden now-or-never feeling, she went straight over to him after she'd finished dancing with Johnny, and introduced herself.

'We met – sort of – at the circus, that matinée, remember?'

'Yes.' He looked around nervously. 'Yes, of course.' His eyes returned to her and she willed them to stay there. Fine eyes, she saw. Bright, liquid, chestnut brown, flecked with darker notes. Skittery, blinking eyes that hovered and darted about, like a moth about a light, unless you trapped it, trapped him.

'What are you doing here? Not at the circus?'

'Oh,' he said vaguely. 'The Countess, she asked me to do my turn here, on the stage, in the supper interval.'

'Would you like to dance meanwhile?' She wanted to dance with this elastic-limbed, indiarubber-faced man.

'I don't know . . .' He hesitated, looking so put-upon and nervous that the now-or-never feeling swept over her again and she dragged him out onto the floor.

'I loved your circus mime,' she shouted, as they set about a brisk two-step. As she'd suspected, he danced superbly. An inspired Daddy-Long-Legs. Perfect balance, tempo, control. And she liked all that, appreciated it. He was like a good piano-player. But playing with his whole body, not just his fingers. And he must have read her thoughts, for he said, 'And I loved your concert on Monday. I recognized you at the circus.'

He smiled, a funny, but exaggerated smile, opening his eyes wide, staring madly at her. Relaxing. So that she came a bit closer to him then, sniffing under his chin. He was startled. 'Do I smell?'

'I'd hoped so. Of sawdust and dung and straw and fierce wild animals. I love that circus smell.'

'Sorry. I bathed. And I don't work at Ciniselli's full time. Only matinées, in Butterweek. I'm just a beginner, you see.' And now his expression changed completely again: wan, gauche, lost, so that she burst out laughing.

'You live in Moscow' – he nodded – 'because we went to children's parties with you Ostrovskys, years ago, when we spent several Christmases there. But I didn't meet you, did I?'

'Don't think so. You must have known my younger brothers and sisters. There's Elizaveta, she's rather prim and simpers . . .' And now, releasing her, stopping the dance, he started to impersonate his sister, lengthening his face, simpering, pursing his lips, batting his eyelids coquettishly. 'And there's Vladimir. He's tough and struts about. He wants to be in the Hussars . . .' Now he strutted, marking time, presenting arms, being very military. 'And then there's little Nina. All curly ringlets with rosy cheeks. She wants to be a milkmaid.' And he mimed that idea, crouching down, picking up two milk pails and then, with a beatific smile, face tilted, took dainty steps across the floor – until people started to stare in shocked surprise at these antics and she pulled him back into the dance.

'Oh, what does it matter?' he asked defiantly then, glaring round at the formal assembly, changing his mood suddenly from the gauche to the confident and derisory. 'All these frightful "booboisie" –'

'Who?'

'Bourgeois, for that's all they are. Filled with inhibitions, obsessed with being correct. They need to be shocked.'

'Do they?'

'Yes, shocked by something *new*. They're doomed, you know, for want of the new. Now in Moscow, there's so much that's really new. The Studio Theatre – have you seen it?' – he rushed on, saving her the reply that she hadn't – 'and Shetkels' wonderful new Kinematograph Theatre in Arbat Square. And talking of the Kinema, I've just been making a Kinema film – well, helping a bit – with Mayakovsky and the painters, Natalya Goncharova and Larionov, *Drama in Cabaret 13*. Incredible! What did they do? They just filmed their ordinary everyday behaviour. Now *that's* interesting! Though in one scene I do a conjuring trick, taking endless garbage, tin cans and things, out of a rich old dowager's mouth. And in another we had Larionov coming out onto the street, his eyes painted with green tears, carrying Natalya in his arms, wearing an indecent mask – I made it for her – and one breast bared. Can you imagine! Nearly caused a riot on the street. We're Futurists, you see.'

He ran on about how full of life the 'new' Moscow was, about the Futurists' manifesto – 'A Slap in the Face of Public Taste' – which rejected all previous art forms, and how they intended to throw Pushkin, Turgenev, Tolstoy and all the other old fools overboard from the 'Ship of Modernity'.

Eventually Yelena got a word in. 'Well, it's not all happening in Moscow, you know. We had Mayakovsky's Futurist play, *A Tragedy*, and an opera, *Victory Over the Sun*, at Luna Park only a month ago. Terrible fuss. People roared and hissed and fainted. The police were called –'

'Did you *see* it?'

'Well, no. But I heard all about it. And I saw the opera, by one of your Futurist composers – what was his name? Matyushin, yes – and it was really awful. And besides, we have Vera Komissarzhevskayas's Dramatic Theatre here. And Blok's symbolist plays. And Bakst's wonderful designs and costumes. And Meyerhold's incredible production of *Hedda Gabler* – huge, misty, blue-green tapestries and white furniture and white furs strewn over an extraordinary white sofa, with Hedda laid back on it in a sensational shimmery dress. I bet you didn't see *that* –'

'No, I didn't.'

'So you see, you don't have everything in Moscow.'

'Well, we have the Bat Theatre. And The Wandering Dog. You've nothing like that here. Cabaret-Theatre. Satire. Popular songs from Berlin and Paris! Really *cruel* satire. And all so daring! So new!'

He was bubbling over, almost levitating with enthusiasm. And she shared in it then, because she wanted the new – though they had a good argument about it all while they danced, and he was surprised by her knowledge of what was modern. 'I thought you were just a stuffy concert pianist,' he said. 'Classical music and so on. That's what you said.'

'No. I didn't say I was stuffy. Or that the music was. Tchaikovsky, César Franck, they're not stuffy. They're – melodious.'

'It's all practically in tune, though. "Tum, ti, ti; tum, ti, ti; tum, ti, ti, tum".'

'Nonsense, it's not. You're thinking of Strauss. What they're playing now.'

'Well, it's all so *predictable*, that sort of music. Surprise in every art. Astonishment. Outrage. *That's* what one needs. Have to shake people up. Especially we Russians. *Shock* them! That's the key to it all.'

Then, to demonstrate his point, he contorted his face into a fearful rubbery smile again, eyes wide open, glaring at her, quite manic.

'No, not that!' she shouted at him above the music. 'Not that!' She released herself. 'I won't dance with anyone with a face like that! It's horrible.' They were standing motionless again while everyone else waltzed round them, staring critically, until they both laughed wildly, and he took her in his long lanky arms once more and they waltzed away defiantly among all the old boobies in their stuffed shirts and silk finery. 'That horse you mimed, at the circus,' she said to him later, close to his ear. 'That canter you did. That was wonderful.'

'So – I'll do it for you now.' And he began to lurch up and down with her, in a bizarre sort of waltz-canter.

'No!' she shouted. 'You've done enough damage to my reputation! No! You idiot!' She was bouncing violently now in his arms, going up and down like a madwoman with this mad, runaway horse.

'Yes! Yes!' he cried. They were the scandal of the ball.

Mikhail Nicolaivich Ostrovsky. Miki, as he'd asked to be called. He had brought her the 'new' that evening, in himself, in his crazy ideas and enthusiasms, the wild shapes of his face, his so fluent body. The new and the modern, which she longed for then, longing to escape the horrors, the memories of the old Russia: all the dull, doomed people who surrounded them then at the ball. Yes, how she enjoyed dancing with him. And what dread she felt an hour later, when she looked into another face, grave and immobile, and found herself partnered with Captain Woodrow for the cotillion.

Oh, God, Yelena thought – not Captain Woodrow. She nearly turned away in horror. The Master of Ceremonies, some minutes before, had wheeled on the ridiculous cotillion hedge covered with roses and ribbon favours, men and women to either side, invisible to each other, so that the dancers had to reach up on tiptoe, groping for a hand on the other side, find one, then move on down the hedge before rounding on their surprise partner. And there, in front of Yelena, was Captain Woodrow, in his dress uniform and neat moustache, just as startled and speechless as she was.

'Princess . . .' he murmured, bowing stiffly, so that she saw the crown of his head, the thinning crinkly rust-coloured hair, almost a bald patch. Strange in a young man, she thought. Losing his hair so early. Already old, this fuddy-duddy. What damned bad luck picking him out for the cotillion. However, she was determined not to let any gloom descend on her evening, so she took him in hand at once, in her best bright cheeky manner.

'Oh, don't call me that, Captain Woodrow. Hardly more than a courtesy title in Russia. If some boyar ancestor was made a prince *all* his descendants, not just the eldest sons, can use the title, prince or princess. It doesn't mean much here. Not like your royal family in England. We're not royal.'

'Oh?' He showed surprise, putting his head to one side in a quizzical gesture, angularly emphatic, like a cockerel studying a worm. His eyes – his grey-green eyes – were full of sudden interest. 'I understood you *were* royal. Your ancestor, Prince Pyotr Rumovsky, was a younger brother of the first Romanov Tsar, Tsar Michael, was he not?'

Goodness me, the man had done his homework, Yelena thought. But of course – he was a spy. 'How clever of you.' She rounded on him, adding pointedly. 'How *good* of you to take such an interest in our family.'

'No, I didn't. It was our Counsellor, Mr O'Beirne, actually. He told me. He makes a study of all that sort of thing here. Knows all about everyone in St Petersburg.'

It was she who felt put down now. 'Why, so he does. Dear Mr O'Beirne . . .' Suddenly, as they walked away, waiting for the cotillion to start, he took her arm, steering her clear of a couple she'd been just about to bump into. And now, keeping his hand gently on her arm, he patted it and smiled.

'So you see, you must surely remain in the Romanov bloodline.'

'Yes –'

'And if the present Tsar and half a dozen Grand Dukes and all their children,' he interrupted, running on with quick enthusiasm, 'if they were all to drown together on the royal yacht, say, then your father would be Tsar.'

'That's a nice idea.' She turned to him, smiling, expecting to see a similar smile. But instead he had a curiously sympathetic expression, as if in mourning for this imagined tragedy; a deeply concerned look for her, as if she were a last bereft remnant of the Romanov dynasty: a sudden, alertly caring face, emerging from behind the stern façade, grey eyes melting.

Then in a flash the expression changed, to one of amused irony. 'Yes, an accident like that – and you'd be moving into the Winter Palace. And you'd be a real princess then right enough. Like Cinderella and the glass slipper . . .' he mused, lost in a sudden vagary, another characteristic of his which she noticed then. 'The pumpkin coach and the prince,' he went on. 'The fairy tale. I wonder if you know –'

'Yes, of course I know it! Not savages in Russia. Miss Harriet – you've met her, our Irish governess – she read all those tales to us as children. Not as good as our Russian fairy tales, though. Baba Yaga, the witch who lives in a hut made of human bones set on chicken's feet, and so on. But I don't suppose you would know any of those.' She smiled rather sniffily at him.

'Well, I do actually.' His smile was deprecating in return. 'I have a wicked uncle.'

'That's just like a fairy tale.'

'Yes – yes, he is rather. Uncle Cedric. Lives in London. Travelled a great deal in Russia. Traveller and scholar. Speaks Russian fluently, of course. Well, he stayed with us, at home where we live in the Cotswolds, when we were children – and read us many of those Russian folk tales, from Afanasiev's collection. He'd translated a lot of them – "The Little Daughter of the Snow", "The Firebird", "Alenoushka and Her Brother" – I remember them all very well.'

Yelena was surprised and rather put in her place. But he took no advantage, just went on nicely. 'Well, that's good. Fairy tales . . . Something in common to talk about. Always a problem, isn't it? These grand balls, meeting someone new – what on earth to talk about?' Then he put his head on one side, like a cockerel again, and she began to think she'd misjudged Captain Woodrow. He was nice. Behind the formal military exterior there was something easy and secure, something careful and caring and unusual about him.

'Why was he wicked? Your uncle?'

'Oh, he still is. A great womanizer, you see. He has mistresses all over the place. In Paris, Tashkent . . . In London he keeps one of them in a villa residence up in St John's Wood . . .'

'I see. That *is* wicked, isn't it!'

'Well, it is rather – in our family. Because my father is the rector – the priest – of our local church in Gloucestershire. We live in the rectory, it's our family home as well – next door to the church.'

'Oh, is it haunted?'

'As a matter of fact it is. Or supposed to be. How did you know?'

'Aren't all rectories haunted in England? And Ireland? Miss Harriet told us. And ghost stories I've read.'

'Not all, I think. But ours is. Usual sort of story. Ghost of a serving girl. Walks up and down the top landing furiously now and then. Made pregnant by some ancestor of ours – so it's rumoured. Killed herself. I love ghost stories. And fairy tales,' he added, rather wistfully. She was surprised to hear such from this down-to-earth-seeming young officer.

'Why?' Yelena was suddenly interested.

'I suppose it was being brought up in the rectory. And hearing all Uncle Cedric's wonderful Russian tales, which made me want to learn Russian – as I did in London – and come to Russia. As I have!' He was naïvely pleased at this neat equation. She began to take to him then. 'Yes, all that sort of thing rather interests me. Ghosts, strange powers in people, things beyond the normal, that can't be explained in any rational way. And fairy tales have their origins there, don't you think? In people's sense of the supernatural.'

Hearing him say all this, something moved in Yelena then, a *frisson* of fear, of fascination. Captain Woodrow was interested in what plagued her – she who was a medium for these malign spirits. 'Oh, do you think them real?' she asked lightly. 'These ghosts and strange powers and other things beyond the normal, that can't be scientifically explained. Levitation, for example.'

'I don't know. I've never experienced anything of the sort. Never heard the serving girl tramping about the top landing. Though my mother has. I'm sure if I did hear or see these things, well, I'd believe in them. I'd have to, wouldn't I? Have to trust the clear evidence of one's senses. If you were to levitate just now, and go spiralling up to that chandelier – well, I'd believe it! Everyone here would have to believe it – and what a pretty sight that would be, if I may say so! Pity, really . . .' He went back into his vague mode. 'Pity – that I'm not receptive to spirits and suchlike. And a pity you can't levitate!'

Little did he know, she thought. 'Oh, but I *can*!' she said at once. 'I can!' And they laughed and she thought indeed how she'd misjudged the man. He was delightful.

'Well, I hope to see that one day,' he said. 'I hope you'll show me!'

Yelena danced last with Sasha that night, holding him as close as she dared, when his lotions had worn off and she smelt that real crushed wheat-and-honey smell of his.

'Well, the belle of the ball,' he said as they spun round the floor. 'And all this week,' he added, 'with these new men in your life.'

'Nonsense.' She smiled up at him, holding him a bit closer.

'Oh, you deserve it. I'm not jealous.'

It was his use of that word, which he'd never used before, which told her he was. And she felt a tenseness in him then, as if he knew he'd lied, as he never had to her before either.

7

'Dear Sergei, I really find it rather difficult –' Miss Harriet crossed this out and wrote instead 'Dear Sergei, I really don't know what to say!' – adding the exclamation mark with a flourish. That was better. She must keep it light-hearted. But then she was faint-hearted once more, about writing in such openly admitted terms at all. She gazed glumly from her bedroom window. All the white and gold midwinter beauty of the city had disappeared in these first weeks of Lent, replaced by grey skies, driving snow, sleet, bitter winds, the streets awash with slushy mud, the river – now that the ice had started to break – an ashen lead colour, filled with dirty little ice floes drifting by.

Drifting . . . As she was drifting in her thoughts about Prince Sergei, quite unable to decide how to respond to those embarrassing parts of his otherwise friendly letters in which he had made it clear – for over six months, since their last visit to Orlov the previous summer – that he loved her. The whole thing was very difficult. How could she respond without making things worse? In acknowledging his feelings she would then immediately have to tactfully rebuff them and thus hurt him. How could she bring to an end what, for her – in fact and in her earlier replies – had never begun?

She tore the letter up. It was hopeless. She would have to go on pretending that their correspondence was no more than a continuation of what they enjoyed during their summer visits to Orlov: exchanging news and views, educating or correcting him in the more arcane manners and mores of the English, sharing things with him in every companionable, intellectual way, but in no other.

She fiddled with her fountain pen. The letter, she acknowledged, the letter she would really like to have been writing then, would have begun 'Dearest Sasha . . .'

It was a terrible thought. She tried to dismiss it at once, getting up from the little *escritoire* by the window, walking aimlessly about the room, rootling about in her carpet-bag, taking a book from her bureau, Trollope's *Irish Sketches*, glancing at a page, then going over to her dressing-table, using the silver-backed hairbrushes there, trying to settle her unruly hair, gazing at herself in the mirror: a windblown, freckled face, once happy, outgoing, now wan and inward-looking. Piteous.

Yes, these thoughts of Sasha were not just pathetic, they were unthinkable. And yet at that moment, looking at herself – her face, her unused body – she could not but think of him. So she gave herself to the thought, drawing a deep breath, feeling her breasts, her whole being, expand at the idea. Sasha, yes, ever since he'd grown up, thoughts about him had gradually impinged on her consciousness; until suddenly one day watching him play a violin solo the blow had come with terrible force. She longed to be his other half: in music – piano to his violin – and in love; to have with him all that she had so stupidly thrown away with the young Scotsman at the Royal Academy of Music in London years before.

She longed for all that she knew Yelena had with him. And she was jealous, and so had come sometimes to hate Yelena, thus increasing the guilt and horror of her feelings, digging herself ever deeper into the mire. And this was why she had rebuffed those other men in Ireland and had remained in Russia. It was this quite appalling weakness, like a disease, which kept her there.

And worst of all was watching Yelena, having everything she would like to have had with Sasha – the shared music, mutual love. And recognizing something else: that what Yelena shared with him was quite unnatural. Yes, perhaps they shared everything together, even that ultimate thing? The horror of this idea – until she had to recognize that her own desire for him was almost as perverse, as indeed was Sergei's love for her, that of a supposedly happily married man more than twice her age. Love, which she had thought so simple and clear-cut, was preposterous. She lay down on her bed and wept.

'Of course it's obvious!'

'Nonsense!'

'Miss Harriet has a crush on you, and she hates me and –' Yelena turned away. Samson had disappeared, barking furiously, rabbiting again. And since there weren't rabbits anywhere near the meticulously kept lawns of the Krestovsky Club out on the island, he was starting to dig up the privet hedge next to the tennis courts looking over the Gulf. 'Samson! Come back here, you bad dog.'

Sasha meanwhile had become petulant. 'One of your "seeing" into things again, is it? Into other people's secrets.'

'No. It's quite clear in the way she looks at you, these last months. And then doesn't look at you suddenly, turns away. Like a child, suddenly joyous. Then downcast. I know the look. I know the feeling.' She looked at Sasha, and kept her gaze on him, smiling.

'Miss Harriet? She's just frustrated. And not because of me. It's Captain Woodrow she's after. That's obvious. She's playing tennis with him back there right now.'

'Only a ploy. A decoy. It's Mama who's keen on Sandy. We know that. And of course it's great-uncle Sergei who has his eye on Miss Harriet. We know that, too, from the way he looks at her in Orlov and all the letters she has from him now. He has a soft spot for her. And getting nowhere!' She laughed, a little cruelly.

'No laughing matter.'

'No. Uncle Sergei is happily married, isn't he? Or supposed to be.'

'Exactly.'

They looked at each other. Sasha undecided, Yelena more blatant in her smile now. She was smiling at the idea of Sergei's getting nowhere with Miss Harriet. This already seemed to her the norm in love.

'What a roundabout,' Sasha said wearily. 'And what nonsense. Because none of these ridiculous suits have any chance of working out. Life's not like that, not for people like us at any rate. It's proper and controlled. No matter what goes on under the surface.'

There was no trace of irony in Sasha's voice, so that Yelena said, 'Well, that idea's the greatest nonsense. When you love, you love, suitably or not!' She laughed then, in a happy way, taking Sasha's arm, walking on, looking out over the white-flecked waves in the Gulf. 'You can't hold back the tide – or the spring!'

Easter was late that year. But spring had come, a week before, the short hectic Russian spring, a great bubbling up out of the snow, in the parks and gardens, of snowdrops, tiny violets, a few anemones. There would only be a fortnight or so of this before the first heat of summer, when it would be difficult to remember what spring had been like, Yelena thought, when it was so suddenly over. But it had begun, and nothing could hold it back, she knew, just as nothing could hold the ice on the river, when a few weeks before it had begun to crack like pistol shots, ice-breakers pushing their way upstream, blundering through, trying to release the waters – when a week later the real guns had thundered from the Peter and Paul fortress and the city Governor, in his great painted barge, went out to meet the Governor of the fortress, stopping together in mid-stream, solemnly declaring the river open.

How decent of them, Yelena always thought, formally allowing the inevitable. Which Sasha was so unwilling to do. It seemed as if in his heart he hoped to rely on a permanent idea of winter. But spring always came. And sooner or later Sasha would have to acknowledge this, in his life, in hers – in *their* life – just as the city Governors did, finding union in the middle of the river, the waters flowing freely then, rushing in a tumult to the sea.

It was Easter week. Climax of the Russian year. 'The Festival'. The ultimate festivity. The Rumovskys' great red *palazzo* cleaned and scrubbed from top to bottom. Endless preparations. Everything becoming gradually more intense and *agitato*. A slow *crescendo*. Yelena spent a lot of the time in the kitchens. Her favourite place then, helping the cooks, Irina and Nana, making the Easter bread and cakes and pastries, the chef Nikolai dealing with the savouries – the meats, great hams and roast fowl and whole lambs, waiting to be stuffed with bunches of dried sage and thyme. The wonderful smells everywhere, as she moved from one kitchen to another. The almondy, buttery smells of one; crushed herbs, rosemary and basil and onion filling the other. Huge piles of fruit, imported pineapples, oranges and lemons being cut and peeled in a third. A cornucopia of tart-sweet smells. She loved it all.

And everywhere eggs. Eggs. And more eggs. Helping to dye them blue and green and gold – and decorate them. Some of the food prepared in egg shapes, or served in egg shells that opened cunningly, or in egg-shaped pastry crusts. Irina over her treacly *babas* and *muzurkis*. Nana, knowing herself to be the star of the show, preparing the special Easter food. *Kulich*, the luscious sweet bread, in long cylinders, filled with crystallized plums and candied peel. And *pashka*, the thick creamy white pudding made of eggs and cream, curds and sugar, which went with it. And on each coloured egg, each loaf and pie, on any bit of food which would take the raised crust or imprint, the letters 'XB'. 'Christ is Risen' in the old Cyrillic script.

Flowers everywhere in the palace, from the hothouses in the courtyard. Great pots of blue lilac and white hyacinths. The footmen travelling the endless corridors, dousing them with swinging censers filled with violet-smelling 'Court water'. Workmen digging the putty out from the frames of the double windows. But many of the big porcelain stoves still burning. Warmth. And warm smells. Enclosed. All waiting. The palace filled with everything. Food and flowers. All waiting to burst.

She wandered the streets with Sasha on Good Friday. Going from church to church. All the churches dark. But the doors wide open, people endlessly standing. Waiting. Fasting. Famished. The air tense with expectation. Frustration.

Kazan Cathedral towards midnight before Easter Sunday, packed to overflowing. The Tsar, his family and courtiers gathered in the Court Chapel. Everyone with unlit candles. All dark, with strange stirrings. Suddenly a candle was lit, the flame passing from one to another, the gloom lifting across the great nave. A surge, a wave of brightness spreading. Still waiting.

Then midnight.

The vergers with long tapers, reaching up to the huge candelabra. Setting one fuse alight on each, a fire running round the circle of braided wicks. A wonderful crackle as the flames ran, setting each candle alight, thousands of candles, so that the nave was flooded in gold. The golden doors of the iconostasis thrown open. The priests in procession, leading everyone out of the Cathedral, circling three times in the great semicircular space in front. Chanting, then turning to the crowd.

'*Khristos Voskrese*!' Christ is risen! Three times. And three times the vast echoing response. '*Voistinu Voskrese*!' He is risen indeed! The whole cathedral illuminated then, the bells ringing, taken up by other bells all over the city. And turning, she saw the rockets and fireworks exploding above the Winter Palace. The sky ablaze with light, cannons from the Fortress firing.

Standing next to Sasha, with Miss Harriet just beyond him, her parents in front, friends, relations, retainers, all round her. She looked at Sasha, his face lit up in the spurts of light everywhere. His face calm and still, composed in brightness. Listening to the Metropolitan Patriarch in his splendid cloth-of-gold vestments, moving through the crowd, followed by the priests with crosses, icons and censers, intoning the words 'The goodness hidden in the hearts of the holy shall be revealed in their risen bodies just as the bare trees put on their leaves in the spring.'

Their risen bodies, she thought.

She put her arm through Sasha's and felt the pressure there in return. Then glanced across at Miss Harriet, who looked at her for an instant, with an expression of barely concealed dislike, frustration.

'Come!' The Prince turned towards his family, his retainers, arms wide, smiling. 'Christ is risen – come!' And they all kissed one another, each and everyone, family, servants, coachmen, cooks, doormen. 'Christ is risen indeed,' they replied. And kissed. And kissed. The whole vast semicircle in front of the cathedral colonades was filled with kissing. Yet a kiss so cold and quick when Yelena came to Miss Harriet . . . A brush of chilled skin. A vapour of horror between them. But Yelena felt such a sense of sadness and abandonment emanating from this woman – so strong a feeling that, as if touched by the holy risen spirit itself, without wanting to, she embraced her. Quickly, fiercely.

The summer started well. A succession of puffy cotton-wool

clouds sliding in over the Gulf, with airy-bright May days. Things boded well generally, for everyone it seemed. The twins gave part of a concert – the whole second half of the programme – at the Conservatoire. A French critic, from *Le Monde*, wrote an article about the musical scene in St Petersburg in which he described them as 'very gifted, with a seamless technique, giving a sense of quite fresh emotion to the Kreutzer Sonata'. Yelena was pleased, though she knew they were good already, because they'd just won the gold medal for piano and violin at the end of that summer term.

Yelena and Sasha were pretty full of themselves that summer. Yelena didn't miss the men in her life, as Sasha now jokingly referred to them. Johnny Quince had gone back to America and Miki Ostrovsky had gone away with Ciniselli's circus for their summer tour. But before they had left they'd all met regularly, becoming quite a little group. Johnny and Miki had come round to the palace for small suppers together. Better still, she and Sasha had gone out with them, once to the Astoria restaurant – and more often, and much better fun, for lunch at Dominique's on the Nevsky, with its billiard table in a back room. Johnny had shown them all how to play the game here. '*No*, Princess. You have to pocket the balls, by colour, in *order*. Not just take any ball you fancy.' Then he'd leant over her, showing her how to pot a difficult shot. He didn't smell of woody cinders any more. He'd stopped testing his engines then. Pity, she thought.

Miki, with his natural deftness, took to the game at once. And that manic smile, when he potted a difficult shot, then lifted his eyes to her in an exaggerated stary-glare. She came to enjoy that. 'Easy,' he would say then. 'It's easy.' Yet he was not quite at ease, she thought. Only on stage, acting, doing his tricks, in costume, wearing a mask. Then he was at ease, in his gift. But without these props, disguises – always those shadows behind the eyes. Something tense, unfulfilled. A performer, only really happy in performance. He was like her and Sasha. Except that, outside their music, they were so happy with each other.

Sasha, with the precision of his bow arm, soon became good at the game, too. Only Yelena remained incompetent. 'You're hopeless, Linochka,' Sasha told her. 'You must be cross-eyed to miss that easy shot.' And she'd run round the table and tried to beat him over the head with her cue, before swaying with him, caught in his arms, still trying to biff him one, in a boisterous fight which ended in an embrace. It couldn't have been clearer who Yelena was 'with', whom she loved.

Sandy Woodrow came to supper quite often at the palace that spring as well, largely at Princess Sofia's promptings when she returned from Europe after Lent. But soon it was clear how Sandy had eyes for Miss Harriet, not the Princess Sofia. He gazed at Harriet over the dinner table, clearly taken by her, and afterwards invited her to the Krestovsky Club on the island, where they played tennis, and out to Murino for nine holes of golf.

This came to annoy Princess Sofia, who had no athletic abilities whatsoever, and to please Yelena, since it took Miss Harriet out of Sasha's hair.

'Ah, Miss Boulting,' Sandy said to Miss Harriet one evening at dinner, looking at her mischievously, 'I'd not realized you were the *complete* sportswoman. Shooting as well!'

'Oh, indeed, yes. I used a 16-bore at home in Ireland.'

'Perhaps –' There was that caring hesitancy of his – 'Perhaps you might like to come with me to the rifle range, out at Krasnoye Selo? Just half an hour on the train. I go there sometimes.'

'Thank you! I'd be delighted.'

Yelena said to Sasha later, talking of Harriet and Sandy, 'Things *are* turning out differently.'

'Yes,' he said abruptly. 'Things change.'

'For the better, you mean?'

'Not necessarily. One can't tell. But that they change. That's all. Only you'd know how – in advance . . .' And he looked at her quizzically.

'No, not these days. It's funny, isn't it? How all that side of me – seeing things in advance, all those strange powers – they only come to me when I'm unhappy. And I'm not any more. I can't see anything in the future. Except you and me. And that won't change.'

The only blight for Yelena in that summer of 1914 was the matter of inheriting her grandfather's castle and estate at Lake

Ladoga. Her father asked to talk to her in his committee room one day. They sat at the long mahogany table, more formally arranged now, chairs set all round, with notepaper neatly piled and freshly sharpened pencils, for the Prince had recently been appointed deputy Minister for Education at the Duma and used the room for meetings in the evenings.

'I'd forgotten about all that,' Yelena said. 'Grandfather can't still mean it.'

'He does. His "scribe" has just written to me.'

'But I can't take it over, couldn't run the place. I have a career with Sasha, our music. You know all that.'

'Yes.'

'And besides, I've not been up there for years. I've no interest now. I – don't like the place. I don't . . .' She hesitated. She'd never spoken to Papa, or to anyone besides Sasha, about Dmitri.

'Yes. I know that . . .' Her father was equally hesitant, lighting a *papirosy*. He was uneasy suddenly. 'None the less –'

'And there are plenty of others in the family. Uncle Anton and Uncle Leonti. And you, Papa. Above all it should go to you.'

The Prince sighed. 'Yes, but it seems he's determined. There's his letter. And a note for you.'

She read the first letter, written by a secretary, a lot of detailed legal matters. His note to herself, on the other hand, was very much stamped with his own unique imprimatur: written from his wound, his soul, written with his foot on a large sheet of paper in his clumsy but still incisive writing:

> You remember what I told you, Linochka, when you rode with me that day to hunt? When you thought yourself plain, hating your upturned nose: that you had another and greater beauty of soul and spirit, a great love of this north world of ours. That you would go towards this world, be the bride of every spring, that God had made up for what irked us in our bodies with gifts which others, for all their beauty or full-armed strength, could never have: courage of heart, a love for all created things, the gift of seeing into life's secrets. This is what I saw in you then and know you must possess in greater measure now. So I hand on this trust to you, confirming my gift of this land, certain that you will guard and keep

it secure in my, in our family's, and in God's name.

'It's all really – impossible.' Yelena looked up at her father, who returned her glance, trails of smoke drifting up past his two spiky tufts of hair.

'Yes . . .' He thought a moment. 'Those "gifts" he speaks of – he must mean for your music. But that's hardly a gift – in running a huge estate!'

'No, indeed.'

'Yet he feels you have other gifts as well. I remember his saying to me how you'd be another Catherine the Great up there . . .' He blew a smoke ring, smiling.

But Yelena wasn't going to confirm anything. No one knew of her strange gifts, except Sasha and her grandfather. 'No,' she said firmly. 'I don't really have any other sort of gifts. Only with music.'

Then just after she'd spoken, something strange happened. The door out to the great hall suddenly swung open. But there was no one there, just a cold wind coursing through the room, slapping the letter from her grandfather into Yelena's face and blowing all the other stacks of notepaper along the table up in the air. An icy wind, buffeting things, until it died out just as quickly as it had come.

'It's Boris,' the Prince said, speaking of their head *dvornik*. 'He must have left the hall doors open.' He got up and shut the door of his study. But Yelena knew that it hadn't been Boris leaving the hall doors open. That wind, that sudden fierce wind, had surely been the wind god, Bieggolmai. Her sign in the world. The sign that linked her to that other world of the spirits. And she had just denied those spirits, those gifts the god had given her. And she had denied her grandfather, too; had already broken faith with him in what she'd just been saying to her father.

In these last months of happiness she'd thought herself free from these strange powers. But it wasn't so. They were ever to hand, she realized, waiting. To remind her forcibly of her betrayal in this case. To punish her, no doubt, if she continued to deny them. Happiness had not made her free. Or rather, she could only be free and happy in so far as she did not deny or betray these gifts, this god. That seemed to be the clear message to her here.

So she changed course with her father when they settled down again. 'On the other hand,' she said easily, 'perhaps I'm wrong. Perhaps I could run the estate . . .' She hesitated, treading carefully with her thoughts and words, making sure they matched, were both honest, 'With your advice, Papa?'

'I doubt it! My way of running things up there would not be your grandfather's.'

'With Stephan, the steward, running things when I wasn't there. That might work.'

'Would you follow your grandfather's lines? They're rather – old-fashioned, outdated. Reactionary, to say the least.'

'Yes, I know. And I don't know – how I would manage things up there.' And indeed she was puzzled about this. She'd loved the castle in the old days, before Dmitri – feared it, yes, but been thrilled by it. The vast snowy wilderness, that old Russian way of life. But she'd come to hate all this afterwards.

Having read her grandfather's letter, and sensed the clear message of the spirits in the great wind backing him up, she was caught now between the demands of these powers – that she should sustain what she knew to be a barbaric world, and her real need to get right away from it, with Sasha, to move into the 'new', wherever and whatever that was.

'What will happen here, Papa? Will grandfather's world go on in Russia? Or will there be another?'

'Another.' He lit a *papirosy*. 'There's no doubt. The Tsar is completely discredited now. The Tsarina and that awful evil monk Rasputin who dominate him with their nonsense – they have both torn away the last vestiges of belief in the Tsar, for most people. He's no longer seen as the "Great Father". And soon your grandfather won't be seen in that way either. There'll be big changes here. A constitutional monarch, a democracy, along British lines. That's what I hope for. But I fear the worst.'

'What?'

'Most of the present ministers, those who are not vicious and corrupt, are lazy incompetents. Time-servers or men who have given up hope. And the few optimists, like me, have no real voice, can no longer mediate between the other parties, with the Tsar or with the public. So we are simply drifting. And of course the great likelihood is that we'll go on the rocks.'

Smoke drifted into the air above the twin peaks of his tufty head, which sank for a moment then. The Prince looked sad, exhausted.

'The rocks?'

'Of revolution. But a successful one this time. Not like 1905. Always the extremes with us. Only there do we see answers. Not in stages, in compromise. It's our flawed nature, that we either love or hate too much. We hope to jump from this degenerate autocracy straight into a free democracy, which can't be done. Instead we shall jump into the mire between. A bloody mire. So what your grandfather or you or I would like to happen up on the lake may soon become irrelevant, taken out of our hands.'

'Yes, we Russians . . . Only love or hatred . . .'

'But for you, Linochka, surely you already have all that you want and love, in your music, with Sasha?' He tapped a pencil in the silence, for she didn't reply at once.

'Yes, Papa,' she said at last.

'So you have no need to be Catherine the Great – up at Ladoga?'

'No. But if what you say comes about in Russia, then we'd lose everything, wouldn't we? No more music then.' And possibly no Sasha, no all of us then, either, she thought.

'I only feel it, Linochka. It may not happen. Who knows exactly what the future holds? If we had that gift of foresight . . .' He smiled. 'Then it would be easy. But we don't, do we?' He looked at her steadily now. 'Not even you, who see into "life's secrets" according to your grandfather. Or do you see things there?'

'What should I see?'

'I suppose you might see the Four Horsemen of the Apocalypse?' He smiled wanly. 'Death, famine, pestilence and war coming to ravage the land.'

'No, I see nothing of that,' she said truthfully, smiling back.

'Good!' He stood up, walking round the table. Then he stopped suddenly. 'Because I think I sensed something of them here.' He turned to her. 'Traditionally – the Four Horsemen – they come with a great wind, a bitter icy wind, just such as we felt in the room here, not five minutes ago.'

She was astonished. 'But Papa – you said it was Boris, that he'd left the hall doors open.'

'No. No, I don't think he had. When I got up to close the door here, I had a clear view right out into the hall. Both the front doors were shut.'

Forebodings. Her father's sense of impending doom in this mysterious wind surprised Yelena, first because she'd no idea he was receptive to such strange intimations and then because there was nothing in the air of that early summer of 1914 to suggest any such apocalypse. Rather the opposite. Apart from the usual strikes among workers in the suburbs, all seemed peaceful in the city – with peace even more accentuated between the nations.

In late June a British battlecruiser under Admiral Sir David Beatty's command paid a state visit to St Petersburg, anchoring off Kronstadt. A week of enthusiastic Anglo-Russian celebrations followed. Dinners and dances in the Town Hall, at the British Embassy, a garden party at Tsarskoe Selo, a great ball aboard two of the cruisers roped together for the occasion, and a Gala Day and grand luncheon on board HMS *Lion*, out in the Gulf, with the Tsar, the Tsarina and their children as guests of honour, to which all the Rumovskys were invited.

A balmy day, cloudless sunshine, the huge grey battleship, brightly spotted and dotted everywhere now with colour, with flowers, flags and bunting, long dining-tables set beneath the big guns, with an awning on the foredeck.

Yelena was placed next to Sandy at the lunch, on one of the higher tables, with the Tsar and his family, the Admiral, Sir George Buchanan, Count Tolstoy, the Mayor of Petersburg and other bigwigs at a table beyond them.

Sandy . . . That was good, she thought, for she'd had little opportunity to talk to him alone since the ball. The food was awful, though. But that started them off well, as had the talk of ghosts and haunted rectories before.

'Sorry about the soup,' he whispered to her after a bowl of thick, sludgy brown liquid had been placed in front of them. 'It's called Brown Windsor. *Not* quite the thing for a hot day.'

'I don't mind! A thrill to be here anyway.'

A band of Royal Marines, the men all in white, with white

pith helmets and a pompous moustachioed bandmaster conducting, was playing beyond them, grouped in the bows. Marvellous jaunty music, Yelena thought, with a lot of brass blowing, drums thumping, cymbals clashing.

'Gilbert and Sullivan,' Sandy told her. 'And very suitably naval – the overture to *HMS Pinafore*.' He nodded his head to the tempo for a moment. 'Though in fact – since Sullivan was a rather lazy fellow – it was most probably written by one of his musical assistants.'

'I love it! I've not heard it before.'

'You've heard of them, though?'

'Do you know, I haven't. Awful of me.'

He was downcast for a moment, so that she felt ashamed of her ignorance and suddenly wanted to please him, to touch him, which she did, on his arm, quickly. 'Oh, no – I *do* like other sorts of music. Popular music. Ballads, operetta. At the Arcade Theatre here – I go there. They do Russian operettas. But not Gilbert Sullivan

'Gilbert *and* Sullivan. Two of them.'

In her general enthusiasm and excitement, she was forgetting herself, not paying attention. 'Sorry, I should have heard of them.'

'Yes, well, they are rather a national institution. At home.'

This idea seemed to depress him further. He looked at Yelena as if searching for something in her face which would cheer him up, a half-smiling, quizzical expression, grey eyes staring at her for just a moment too long, so that he turned away quickly.

She was suddenly aware now, for the first time, how he had looked at her as a woman, not a musician, when she had showed herself to be fallible, not always knowing, in control. He had briefly, she realized, ceased to be in awe of her. And certainly she saw him then as very human, behind his smart dress uniform, his spick-and-span military polish – a man back 'at home' now, in one way, on his British battleship, but thinking of his real home, she sensed then, so that she said, 'I long to go to England. Your home. Do tell me of it.'

'Where to begin?'

She shrugged. 'Anywhere. What's your best "thing" about home? What do you like best to remember?'

He paused, thinking, eyes way off over the Gulf – then started off suddenly, in his clipped manner, in gradually more enthusiastic staccato sentences. 'The big lilac tree at the end of our avenue into the village of Saunderton . . . Between the front gates and the lych-gate into the churchyard. It would have been in full bloom a month ago. Dripping purple clusters. And the smell . . . On hot Sundays in the late spring, with the church doors and windows open. Well, the lilac absolutely wafts right in over all the pews so that the dozy farmers almost drop off asleep. As a child, and ever since – that smell, so rich, mixed with the rather musty, mousy smell of the church after winter. Mouldy hassocks and cassocks!'

She laughed at the end of his account. 'That's wonderful! What a cosy life. Everything together in one place. Church, rectory, lilacs, village. You've made me feel it all!'

'Well, thank you! Yes . . . A cosy life. I suppose so. Way up there, the village lost in the wolds. But the countryside beyond isn't cosy. Just behind the rectory – the long meadow running up the hill, a beech wood on top and nothing but high sheep pasture for miles beyond that. Until you get down to the tiny hamlet in the valley on the far side, where the brewery is. My father's younger brother, my uncle Willie, runs that! And on a hot day it's a wonderful walk over there. My brother Jonathan and I used to do it. Up so high on the land in summer, with cotton-wool clouds. And then to drink the beer. "Saunderton's Best". In the cool cellar taproom straight from the barrel. Or swim in the small lake, where the water for the beer comes from. Or fish the stream that feeds it, rushing white water, circling down the hill beyond. Small trout.'

He was so pleased and happy in speaking of these memories, smells, that she longed to see this idyllic-sounding countryside, this home, this church and landscape which he had so lovingly filled with people. She wanted to walk with him, as his brother Jonathan had, over these high hills.

'Your brother Jonathan, what does he –'

'I'm afraid he died, two years ago.'

'Oh, I am –'

'Yes. Older than me. And something of a mountaineer, too. As I was. He slipped. In Scotland. We were climbing a rockface in the Cairngorms. Rope wasn't properly secured.'

'I am sorry.'

'Yes, well, there you are.' He paused, looking at her, frowning. 'I understand . . . your own elder brother – the same thing. A shooting accident.'

'Yes. Yes, at my grand-uncle's estate in the Ukraine. Just two years ago as well.'

'Neither of us strangers, then. To such tragedy.'

'No,' she said warmly. But her reassurance didn't seem to help him. He took on a haunted look that she'd noticed before.

'May I tell you something?' He turned to her quickly and without waiting for a reply went on. 'I've not been honest with you. You see, Jonathan died because I was at the top of the rockface at that point – and I hadn't quite secured the rope properly – I'm sure of it, though no one held me to blame.'

Everything froze between them. Sandy's face . . . she was riveted to it. The band music suddenly cut out. And the laughing chatter. And she heard nothing any more. A concentrated silence, a drumming in her ears. His face seemed to shimmer and shake in the heat beneath the awning. Or was she shaking? She was filled with some great emotion, as if she'd contracted it, like an illness, just then, from him. Guilt. He felt responsible for his brother's death just as she felt she had been for Ivan's. They were suddenly companions of quite a different sort. Disarmed. But why her, she wondered? Why tell her? And then with a quick intuitive sympathy, he answered the question which she could not have asked.

'You see,' he was almost irritable now, looking down at the table, fiddling with his cutlery, 'it's just that – I always tell people, when the subject comes up, that he died in an accident. But not that I was part of it. Because one can't go into that with most people. But with you, since I knew you'd lost your own elder brother as well, it seemed different, that I should be honest with you.' He kept his head turned away, avoiding her eyes. 'It's a hateful thing to be dishonest. As I nearly always have to be about this. That's all. Do forgive me.'

'Nothing – nothing to forgive. But particularly so far as I'm concerned, since I've felt what you feel – guilt, at my own brother's death.'

He looked at her, surprised. 'That you were – in some way – involved?'

'No, not directly. But – I didn't like him. And the day he died, just before the shooting accident, I willed him dead.'

'A childish wish, though, surely? A whim?'

'No. I was adult enough. I knew what I was doing. I *willed* it.'

In saying this, having gone thus far, could she go farther and explain the whole truth about her strange powers? He had been honest with her. Could she be the same with him?

He waited, saying nothing, giving her time to elaborate, if she wanted to, on this statement. But again, as if he sensed her quandary, he solved it for her, absolved her from a direct answer, by saying, 'We can will things very strongly, good things or bad. Sometimes they come about, or not. But no rhyme or reason really. Unless you mean . . .' His face lightened in a smile. 'The casting of spells and suchlike, witches, sticking pins in wax figures of your enemies!'

There was silence between them then, each of them trying to determine something in the other: he wondering if she was pulling his leg, Yelena wondering if he believed her.

'No, it's true,' she said at last. 'You may not believe me, but I have these inexplicable powers. Not gifts, for they're a curse.'

He nodded his head and said simply, 'I believe you.' Nothing more. No further enquiries. He was like Sasha, she thought. He didn't push or pry. Like Sasha he told you the truth himself – and waited for your truths, if you wanted to tell them. So that, recognizing this, she was put entirely at ease with him in the whole matter. He trusted her. It was as simple as that. 'Thank you, Captain.'

'Oh no, I've stopped calling you Princess! It's Sandy – why not?'

'Sandy, then. A nickname? The colour of your hair?'

'No, actually. Sandy's a pet name in England, for Alexander.'

'Is it?' She was surprised. 'Same name as my brother. Sandy – as in Sasha?'

He nodded. 'Yes. Coincidence.'

They laughed then and he tapped his fingers to the music for a moment. 'This is a lovely bit in *Pinafore*. A trio singing at the end of Act Two: "Never mind the why and wherefore".' He sang the words then – suddenly in as joyous a mood as the music, erasing all their previously glum thoughts. 'One day, if you come to England, we'll go to the Savoy Theatre, the D'Oyly Carte Company there. See *Pinafore* itself. Your "Gilbert Sullivan"!'

'I'd love that! Yes, I will come to England. Sasha and I – we want to tour, give concerts.'

'Of course – both of you come. I'm sure your brother . . .' He hesitated then, disconcerted for an instant. 'I'm sure he'd like it just as much as you would.'

But that wasn't really what he meant, she thought. For a moment he had forgotten her brother. He wanted her to come to the Savoy Theatre alone with him.

8

Forebodings? There had been none that afternoon as they sat in the brilliant sunshine under the huge guns listening to the jaunty music. And none next day at Elysieff's café on the Nevsky, where Yelena ate cream pastries with Sasha, telling him of her talk with Sandy, about 'Gilbert Sullivan', and how he'd asked them to see the real thing with him if they came to England.

'So, you think him a good man, this Sandy?' Sasha smiled, distant, ironic. He might have been encouraging her with him.

'Yes! He could help us when we start giving concerts abroad. We will, won't we? We're good enough now?' She'd lifted a pastry halfway to her mouth, when the cream started to slide off, and she gulped at it, so that a great blob got hooked on the tip of her turned-up nose.

Sasha leant across with a napkin and wiped it off. 'You are a piggy eater. Yes, almost good enough.'

'But you don't really *want* to go abroad!' She was exasperated.

'I'm in no hurry. I like it here.' He leant back, licking his fingers. 'I like Russia. My friends here. I'm seeing Kyril and Leonti tomorrow, in fact – out at the *dacha*. We were going to play some music, swim.'

'Can I come?'

'Can if you want.'

'Not if you *don't* want.'

'It's not that.' He looked at her more intently now. 'Just, we don't have to do everything together, do we? Not Siamese twins, as you've said yourself.'

'No. All right, I won't come. Plenty of things I can do by myself.' She glared at him. They were quarrelling for the first time in months. 'Yes, you can go and do what you want with your pals. But you know perfectly well it's *our* music that really counts. And we need to give more concerts now. And why not *abroad*, for goodness sake! Some fresh air. That French critic, from *Le Monde*, he said we'd be sure to get concert offers in Paris.'

'Too soon. Need more experience here. Next year.'

'You are a bore, Sasha. No spirit of adventure.'

He laughed. 'Go abroad on your own then! You play, we both play – pretty well on our own.'

She scowled at him again.

Finally he relented. 'Do stop making a drama of things, Linochka. Since we play together, of course we have to *be* together . . .'

Sandy had hit the inner circle three times in his last five shots with the Winchester target rifle. Miss Harriet had scored two, at the edge of the outer circle – the rest wild, off the card, the bullets raking into the great straw bolsters behind the row of targets at the Krasnoye Selo shooting range. Retrieving the cards, he showed them to her.

'Terrible!'

'No. Your best yet.'

'I'd be better with a shotgun. I'd hit it then all right!'

He smiled at her, very much liking this lanky, freckle-faced woman in her long white muslin dress and floppy straw hat tied round her chin with a Paisley scarf, her hair tails blowing in the wind – an acrid, smoky wind coming from Finland across the Gulf, from forest fires which had started there in the blazing dry summer weather. A dust-laden, somehow sinister breeze. Harriet started to cough.

'Foul, isn't it?' he said.

'Yes. Gets in your eyes, everywhere.'

She started to pick at her eye then, something caught in it, so that he peered at her more closely. 'Can I help?'

Angling her face up a fraction, she allowed him access. Putting a moist point on one corner of his clean handkerchief, and using it as a probe, he extracted a bit of grass.

'Thank you.' She laughed. 'So like a cheap novelette! People get to know each other that way – a speck of dirt in the eye, the other takes it out and –'

'They live happily ever after!' They laughed. Then she jumped involuntarily as the man in the next bay started to fire rapidly.

'Will you ever go back and live in Ireland, do you think, Miss Boulting?' he asked, when there was some silence again.

She turned to him, her face flushed in the hot wind. 'Oh, I wonder. Sometimes, yes. But all this . . .' She looked round the spaciously elegant club grounds. 'Russia – above all Petersburg – I've come to love it.'

'I too. But I couldn't live here permanently.'

'I think I could. I'd feel so isolated back in the wilds of West Cork, beautiful as it is. I adore the bustle of big cities. It's over ten years since I came here.' She pushed a strand of hair away from her freckled cheek, listening nervously now to the haphazard crack of rifles down the line. 'And the Rumovskys. I've grown very fond of them. They're my "family",' she added with both pride and irony. 'More than my own family, whom I don't get on with. Especially the two children – when they were children. I've looked after them, taught them, practically brought them up.'

'Indeed. And so successfully, too, if I may say so. Their music – quite wonderful.'

'Yes . . .' She pondered this, then took to a fit of coughing, before saying, rather abruptly, 'Almost too good in a way. Too confident now. And spoilt because of this. Arrogant. Especially Yelena.'

'Well, with such gifts – bound to be "temperament", no?'

'Yes, perhaps. In their music, though. Not in their lives. They're too close there.'

'I suppose that's the nature of the bond, though. Twins, inseparable. Act of nature –'

'It's *not* natural, though, Captain. That's the point. How can it be?' She was suddenly upset.

'Indeed, Miss Boulting. Yes . . . Yes indeed.' He temporized. Then he coughed, the dry, burnt wind tickling his throat. 'What do you say? Shall we have some iced tea back at the pavilion?'

They walked back, up a winding path towards the ring of pine trees, with the white pavilion at the centre. He took the rifles back inside before they sat at a table on the verandah. She undid her scarf, taking the straw hat off, when her bouncy, unruly hair at once flew up about her ears.

'Oh, my hair . . .' She sighed. 'Difficult to manage at the best of times. And in this dry weather with all the dirt in the air I must look a fright.'

'Far from it, Miss Boulting.' He was decisive, looking at her even more decisively. 'Most appealing,' he added, with sufficient irony in his voice to mitigate the hint of presumption there as well.

She smiled back.

Oh, he liked her, no doubt about that at all. Her present abstracted expression particularly appealed. She was flustery, excited, vulnerable. He very much wanted to do something for her. Or with her. He wanted her.

'Could you – would you like to have dinner with me tonight?' he asked as they left the Club. 'We could go to Cubat's out on the island. Or the garden at Contant's –'

'I'd love to – but tonight I promised to go and see old Mrs Boyd, at the Home for Governesses. She's a little infirm – asked me to take her to evensong at All Saints.'

'Tomorrow then, perhaps?'

'Yes!' She nodded happily.

'We could eat. And I'd love to show you round the Jews' Market beforehand. Have you been there?'

She hesitated a moment.

'Tomorrow night then?'

'Yes, that would be lovely. Thank you!'

He held her arm a moment, helping her into the cab returning to the station – her sinewy arm, feeling the long bone down to her wrist. Taking her seat, she turned and looked at him with a radiant smile. Yes, he thought, tomorrow they would meet, away from the palace, the embassy, at The Jews' Market. Yes . . .

The Jews' Market beyond the Sadovaya. A warren of covered alleyways, long arcades with little wooden shops and stalls, selling everything under the sun. Miss Harriet hurried on, not to be late, pushing through the densely packed crowd: dirty, voluble, singing, shouting. People of every race and creed. Jew and Tartar, Moslem and Christian moving through the fetid, dust-clogged, spice-filled air, yellow motes of smoky summer light glinting on old brass pots, shabby ikons, jewels, silver-threaded shawls and gold-tasselled patchwork Tartar waistcoats. Bumping into people, not to be late. Raucous itinerants and pedlars, drunks who leered at her, ill-dressed *moujiks* and peasants, 'Holy Men' in rags declaiming the gospel to the infidel. Debauched old men who stared at her, inviting her with their eyes. Huge, open-breasted women who called to her, beckoning. This world, this whole secret city, appalled yet excited her with its coarseness, its so vigorous admission of basic commerce, exchange, need, its blatant sensuality. But hurry, she thought, not to be late. A desperate running walk. Not to be seen to run.

There at last was the Azerbaijani's spice stall, the young man in the embroidered skullcap standing behind the raked shelves, the scores of little sack bags filled with every sort of exotic spice and herb, the hot air trapped beneath the awning reeking of cinnamon, cloves, pepper. Where they had arranged to meet. But he wasn't there. They had said seven o'clock. It was ten minutes past. He must have come and gone.

She couldn't hang around the stall, the man looking at her enquiringly now. She walked on, into the glitter of the jeweller's arcade, then left into an alleyway selling old clothes, then left again, making a long detour, a complete circle back into the spice alley and the Azerbaijani's stall. Still he wasn't there.

There was still time, of course. She could abandon the whole arrangement. Then, hearing the flap of pigeons overhead, she looked up at the pale blue evening sky between the awnings. The endless twilight of midsummer – leading to the White Nights. It was now or never, she thought. White nights . . . She had known them so often in St Petersburg. Empty nights, sleepless, wishing, wanting. Looking from her bedroom window in the palace at four in the morning. The silver river in the brighter light of dawn beneath her, flowing, flowing. No, she would abandon nothing, on this white night.

She stopped again by the stall, fingering a stick of cinnamon, then the dry leaves in a bag of tarragon, the Azerbaijani looking at her again, smiling, inviting. She could stay no longer. Until, suddenly, a touch on her shoulder, so that she jumped and turned, confronting Sasha.

'Hello.' Sasha spoke first. She could say nothing, her heart in her mouth, quite breathless. He was dressed *à l'Anglaise* in a light blazer, flannels, an open-necked shirt with a cravat. He looked at her easily. 'Sorry, I'm late.'

'No. No, I was too. The train back from Krasnoye Selo was delayed. And then Sandy – he wanted to take me to dinner.' The words tumbled from her lips.

'Doesn't matter.' Sasha was abrupt. 'We're here. Come on, we'll take a *likhatchi* to the island. Quicker that way.'

They sat in the expensive horse cab, with its pneumatic tyres, saying nothing. They crossed over the main stream of the Neva on the Nicholas bridge and saw the sun, a great orange dipping in the sky to their left. Cutting down the long boulevards of Ostrov Island the white apartment blocks still radiating heat like cooling stoves. Turning over the Little Neva, on Tuchkov bridge, coming into Petrovsky Park. The trees, the willow and ash, green in the hazy blue twilight. Windless and hot. They said nothing. Driving, clip-clop, in silence, down Petrovsky Prospekt, almost to the point at the end of the island, where the cab stopped outside a high wooden fence, with an arched gateway, big double doors.

She stayed in her seat.

'It's all right.' He looked up at her from the roadway. 'It's empty. I told you, my friends have gone to Imatra for the weekend. Gave me the keys, to rehearse there if I needed.'

She got down from the cab a little unsteadily. He opened the double doors, slammed them shut. Ahead lay a weedy stone path, winding between two patches of dry summer grass. At the end of the garden lay a decrepit wooden *dacha*, set right over the water. Up some rickety steps then, across a small porch. Another key and they were in the big salon, a row of French windows on the river side with the late sun streaming in now, illuminating the large room in a rosy glow. Clusters of cushions on the floor, haphazard furniture, a violin lying out of its case, half a dozen music stands, one fallen over, a rust-coloured samovar on a table, catching the bright red rays of the sun.

The room was hot, stuffy, dust-moted as they moved across

it. A dry, papery, cindery smell everywhere, trapped in the air, from the forest fires across the bay. He opened one of the French windows. They went out onto a wide verandah giving over the water, filled with wicker chairs, card tables, a big cushioned swing-seat. And still the silence between them as they moved instinctively to the edge of the verandah, leaning on the balustrade, looking out over the pale blue water, streaked with pearly crimson, towards Volny Island a few hundred yards away, with its big bushy clumps of trees, the sun still visible, a great red ball across the bay, just dipping into the roofs of the city, glinting on the gold spire of the Peter and Paul fortness.

Turning the other way they gazed at the calm sea out in the Gulf to their right. A number of rowing-boats on the gleaming swell, a steam yacht, returning from Sunday outings. The echo of distant voices, a song far out on the water. The clank of a tram behind them in the distance running down Petrovsky Prospekt. A sudden small breeze. The dry grass rustling a moment on the steep verge beneath them. The rushes by the boathouse, bending. A green willow tree, its weeping branches stirring. And still they said nothing, taken up completely, as it seemed, stunned by the beauty of the view. Silence.

'What are we doing here?'

Harriet was startled by the sound of her own voice, thinking aloud, without realizing it. It was a perfectly pointless question, of course. It was obvious what they had come here for – to this conveniently empty *dacha*. Obvious, too, in their almost complete silence ever since they'd met that evening: conspirators who dared not speak of their conspiracy – in case, by so doing, the deed be seen for what it was, as something rash beyond belief, and so abandoned. Yet they had to say something now, she thought.

'Let's go back. Let's drop it all.' She turned decisively and was halfway across the verandah before she heard his voice.

'No! We'll stay.'

She rushed on – through the French windows, into the salon, making for the hall door, quick-footed, her muslin skirt rustling furiously – until he caught up with her, taking her by the shoulders, turning her round.

'No, Sasha. We made – I made a mistake. I –'

But trapped in his arms now, feeling the touch, the whole length of his body against her own, it was too late, she thought – as he held her, embracing, kissing her clumsily.

God, how *clumsy* it all was, she thought. And what nonsense. It wasn't too late. She must stop it. Stop him. This alternative thought, rushing into her mind, was perfectly clear to her. All she need do was act upon it. But she couldn't. Another part of her absolutely refused to do this. She couldn't and wouldn't stop him now, all her thoughts destroyed by the quite extraordinary sense of their bodies pressed together, the sudden exhilaration of his rising – something rising, pressing into her, lower down beneath her waist.

They seemed to stagger about the room for an age. Drunken dancers, she thought. Kissing, kissing each other with ridiculous ferocity and lack of aim. Lips, neck, ears. Savages. What an appalling show they must make, that other sensible side of her mind told her. What a scandalous business! How wrong. Yet irresistible. Was this what they meant, in the Shilling Shockers, by being 'carried away'? No doubt . . . All the suggestions of physical love, all the euphemistic descriptions she had ever read, all her own thoughts of it, over years, rose in her mind.

Well, here it was, at last. And it was ridiculous. Yet astonishingly delicious and overwhelming as well. The whole business *demanded* an answer. And it was then that her clumsy ferocity left her, and she was calm, knowing her goal, sure and clear, and she set out for it, as she put her hands beneath his lapels, opening his coat out, slipping it off his shoulders, pulling up his shirt, unbuttoning it carefully, doing the same with her own blouse, calmly and surely, before loosening his trousers, when they were suddenly both half naked, standing in a tangle of clothes.

With Sasha, she felt then, she held in her arms, possessed and was possessed by, the whole voracious, negligent body of Russia. All that she had longed for in this way over the years – soul and spirit, of the people and place, and all that she had wanted for her own body – was hers now. All together. So that she gave herself to him without reserve, released herself completely, letting go, saying goodbye to all the pent-up longing of the years.

This was it. This was how things should be. Here she was, lying spreadeagled on the tattered old cushions in this decrepit *dacha*, among the fallen music stands and the old fiddle, naked and so open to him. Here she was, where she ought to be. Nor did this feeling of total, quite guiltless abandonment surprise her. This was what she had always expected, hoped for. And whatever happened afterwards she would never regret it. A great joy had come into her life, giving her control of it, releasing her into power. No question of guilt.

But the guilt was there on Sasha's face, she saw, as he moved from her, saying nothing once more. She turned, not holding on to him, but stroking his stubbly chin, his face, smiling.

'Sasha, don't be sad. It's a happy thing –'

'Yes, yes . . .'

But he lied, she knew. And that was sadder still. He stood up, glistening, sweaty, caught in a streak of crimson sun from the Gulf, a strangely bronzed, naked figure for a moment, before he dressed quickly. He picked up the fallen music stand and put the abandoned fiddle back in its case. And she knew why he was sad, how he felt about what they had just done: he had betrayed Yelena.

Sasha was not his usual commanding, superior self the next morning in the little music salon in the palace, going through the Beethoven piece they were to play that afternoon, out at Pavlovsk, a grand picnic in the English Park there, celebrating the Dowager Duchess Marie Pavlovna's birthday.

'What's the matter?' Yelena asked. 'That's surely an E flat on the last legato passage?'

'Nothing. The heat.'

It was certainly hot in the little gilded salon, even with the windows open, the heat burning up from the wide river. And the air was filled with a smell of hot tar, and sooty cinders from the forest fires. But something else seemed to be worrying him, she thought.

'Your pals last night, Kyril and Leonti, did you see them?'

'No. I went out to the *dacha*. But they'd gone to Imatra. Left me a note.'

'Inconsiderate of them.' She got up from the piano. 'Still, we are at least having a life of our own now, separately!'

'What do you mean?'

'Guess who called round just after you'd left? Sandy! He'd been out at the shooting-range with Miss Harriet. She'd left her scarf in the cab. Bringing it back. Just an excuse to see her again, of course. He seemed in quite a tizzy about her. But she wasn't here.'

'Gone to church, I suppose. That evening service at the English Church.'

'Yes, I told him that. So guess what? He asked me out instead. Took a carriage, drove out to the Yacht Club and had lemon ices on the terrace and listened to the gramophone. It was fun. He was nice.'

Sasha put his violin down, mopping his brow, taking an interest now. 'Oh, was he?'

'Yes, he was.' She smiled like the Cheshire cat. Sasha started to bite his nails, preoccupied. Then he surprised her. Coming over he kissed her, rather severely, almost on the mouth. She liked it. 'It's all right,' she went on. 'He wasn't trying to make love to me. That's what he wants to do with Miss Harriet. And that's a relief, isn't it?'

'Why?'

She laughed. 'Take her mind off wanting to make love to you!' She kissed him in return, but it didn't improve his humour much. 'Come on, I'll buy *you* a lemon ice at Elysieff's,' she said.

The Rumovskys went out to Pavlovsk in a special train that hot afternoon. A hundred or more guests. A selection of the nobility, the highest of the *haute monde*, court dignitaries, some ambassadors, a few acceptable Ministers, a bevy of superannuated army and naval officers. A hotch-potch, patrician hoi-polloi, a gruesome pot-pourri of largely enfeebled old men and their rouge-faced women. The curdled *crème de la crème* of the decadent regime, most variously but uncertainly dressed. Uncertain how to dress for this '*Pique-nique*', this *fête champêtre* which the Dowager Duchess had decided to hold, unaccountably and so inconveniently, in the middle of some woods apparently, way beyond the formal English park at Pavlovsk, a good mile or more, it was said, from the palace itself.

Some few, like the Rumovskys, making up a party with the Buchanans from the Embassy again, were in suitable summery dresses, flowery hats, blazers, linen suits. But many in formal court wear, stiff frock coats, grey morning trousers, top hats. The women in heavy satin robes with preposterous confectioner's hats, carrying parasols and cumbersome wicker baskets.

Crushing, with much unsuitable pushing and shoving, into the specially decorated train. Carriages garlanded with streamers of paper roses. Vases of real roses inside. A sultry-sweet stuffy smell, the heat overwhelming, so that the carriage windows had to be opened, which made things worse when they set off, as bits of soot and burnt grass from the forest fires – which had spread over to the Petersburg side of the Gulf – blew in. A dusty, fiery dragon's breath which soiled people's clothes, tickled their throats, made them cough and their eyes smart, so that Countess Tolstoy, the Mayor's wife in the Rumovskys' carriage, swooned in a half-faint, to be revived by Miss Harriet with smelling salts, luckily to hand in her carpet-bag. A nightmare journey.

Droshkies to take the guests from the station. But some, including the twins, walked, to take the air, past the yellow palace, into the formal English parkland, with its grottoes and pavilions suddenly emerging in the view. Artificial ruins, broken Greek temples, columns and miniature fortresses springing up in vistas through artfully planted trees. Then beyond this artificial Arcadia moving into real countryside along the river. Cooler there, by the water. On up through groves of old oak and chestnut, rising through a meadow filled with poppies and cornflowers, towards a forest-clad hill, a circular space cleared between the fir trees, and a wooden pavilon specially built, with a small stage in front and a long awning jutting out, above cushions carefully scattered.

A *Pavillon des Roses*, part of a theme that was continued and exaggerated everywhere. Formal tubs and terracotta urns of real roses. Rose garlands hanging from a crystal chandelier above the little stage, entwining the barley-sugar columns that supported the awning, all the tapestry cushions embroidered with the flowers.

Behind them a trail of carriages still lumbering up the hill. The guests climbing down stiffly, being escorted into the clearing by liveried court footmen, bowing, making curtseys to the Grand Duchess together with the Grand Duke Cyril, his wife and their retinue. The royal group wobbling uncertainly, sitting on high piles of cushions, more or less seated, nodding gracefully to their guests from semi-recumbent positions.

The Rumovsky and Buchanan party were allocated a pile of cushions near the stage. A string quartet fiddling through Vivaldi's 'Four Seasons'; Sasha and Yelena would play later. The food then, every sort of excessive, unsuitable picnic fare from ortolan's eggs to Beluga caviar, served on Sèvres china, on beds of crushed ice in silver platters, by footmen in powdered wigs, blue jackets, cream pantaloons and tight stockings. A group of peasants from some nearby village peering out from between the trees, goggling with astonishment and envy. The Dowager Duchess's string of little Pekinese dogs, tied now to one of the awning columns, barking constantly. A sense of uneasy merriment.

A *pique-nique* at which the Rumovsky and Buchanan group were as awkward as everyone else. Princess Sofia, dressed in a low-cut, candy-striped outfit and floppy hat, making eyes at Sandy, but getting nothing in return. Sandy trying to engage Miss Harriet, who took little notice of him, while covertly glancing at Sasha, Yelena noticed. Sasha, in a pale blue blazer and cream trousers, paying no attention to Miss Harriet, but more to his sister – though simply as a means of keeping clear of Miss Harriet, Yelena felt. A frustrating *ronde d'amour* as the baking afternoon dragged on, a Mad Hatter's tea party, with odd disjointed conversation heard here and there, from their group and others nearby. Frivolous, illogical, inconsequential chatter.

Lady Buchanan complimented Princess Sofia on her new dress from Paris. 'Thank you! Not *exactly* what I wanted. The fashion there this summer is for black-and-white stripes.'

Sir George, looking droopy and under the weather, trying valiantly to maintain a lively conversation with the Prince about the Embassy drains. '. . . having them all renewed. Had to. Made of wood – at the time of Catherine the Great, I'm sure. All quite decayed. Cesspools under the building. No wonder I've felt seedy lately.'

A mincing woman, to their right, in a feather boa, addressing another. 'I looked him straight in the eye – Oh, he had such wonderful eyebrows . . .'

An irate General on the other side, twisting and turning on his hard cushion like a bed of nails, his dress sword caught between his feet, growling at his more comfortable wife. 'I enjoy eating out of doors as well as the next man, my dear. But with tables. And *chairs*.'

And other febrile voices, lost sentences, drifting in the air. 'Nibbling at your *elbow*? Were you hurt?' 'Sergei, nothing is the matter with the *man* from Kiev – it was his *wife* . . .' 'Irina, it's far too hot. Mushrooms, we must remember the preserved mushrooms . . .'

Enervated, idle voices. Only Sandy was alert, intent on pursuing his suit with Miss Harriet. 'I've eaten plover's eggs, yes, delicious. But not ortolan's. Never had them. A kind of garden bunting, isn't it, Miss Boulting?'

'Yes, I think so. Though I don't believe I've ever seen the bird.' She would not be further drawn on this ornithological discussion. Had Miss Harriet and Sandy fallen out at the shooting range the day before, Yelena wondered? The thought gave her an entrée.

'How did your shooting go yesterday at the club?' she called across to Miss Harriet.

'Great fun!' She was very definite, confident now. 'Though I was rather hopeless.'

'And church?' Yelena decided to interfere properly now. 'You missed Sandy last night. Came round later with your scarf. He and I went round to the Yacht Club.'

'Yes, he's told me. We were late back from Krasnoye Selo. And I went straight on to the evening service. And late back from that, too. The Reverend Lombard – went on and on in his address.'

'Did he?' Sandy interjected. 'Thought he was on leave.'

'No.' Miss Harriet looked puzzled. 'Unless I'm going blind. Or senile.' She laughed nicely.

Sasha started to crack his knuckles. 'Don't eat too much,' he told Yelena. 'Else we'll never get through our piece, in this heat.'

'Not eating too much.' Though she was. It was hot and she was irritable. The whole afternoon was fraught. An air of pent-up frustration. Everything hanging by a thread somehow. She turned then, for distraction, to Meriel Buchanan who was sitting just behind her. 'Ghastly, isn't it?' Yelena whispered. 'Awful,' said Meriel. 'I think I'm going to faint. Nearly fainted yesterday evening in church. We had that long-winded American clergyman, the Reverend Orr, from their Congregational Church, giving the address. Droned on and on. Daniel in the den of lions. I could have thrown *him* to them . . .'

'Oh? I thought you had your own English priest there yesterday. Called Lombard, isn't he?'

'No, worse luck. He's all right. Boozy Lombard. Ten-minute sermons.' She smiled. 'But he's away on leave.'

The thread of the afternoon snapped for Yelena. And it was she who nearly fainted then, starting to shake, beads of sweat coursing down her cheeks. It was all suddenly clear to her. How rash of Miss Harriet to so embroider her lie, she thought. Certainly she would never have been any the wiser if Miss Harriet had omitted that detail about Lombard being there. As it was, by giving this clerical hostage to fortune, she had betrayed herself. What had possessed her, Yelena wondered? In any case, Miss Harriet had lied. She had not been at church: she had been with Sasha, out at the *dacha*, conveniently empty then with his pals gone to Imatra. Miss Harriet had caught her prey. Sasha had betrayed her. She was certain of it.

She turned to Sasha, but couldn't speak. Rage, fear, a feeling of bottomless horror, of total loss, overwhelmed her. She simply couldn't open her mouth, sitting on the sticky cushion, trembling. Sasha, unaware of anything wrong, looked at her with a superior expression. 'What's the matter now?' he asked.

Tears welled in her eyes and a great lump rose in her throat; she would have burst out howling and run away but for the sudden commotion just then beyond the stage. A policeman and two park *gardiens* had come into the glade, the former talking urgently to the Dowager Duchess's major-domo, the other two urging the reclining guests to their feet.

'Those peasants over there, about to run amok, are they?' the General next to them enquired, with heavy irony. They weren't. The danger was coming from the other direction, to their right, beyond the ring of fir trees from which the *gardiens* had just appeared. The major-domo, bending low, spoke to the

Dowager Duchess. Easing herself on the deep cushions, she glared at the messenger, ignoring the message. Her brood of nasty little pekes, on seeing the police officer, had jumped up and were barking furiously, straining on their leashes, attempting to bite the ankles of this uniformed interloper. Instead, unable to make headway in this, they fell to fighting among themselves, so that a mêleé ensued, among the dogs and the Duchess's retinue – the men in her party trying to separate the animals, but managing only to infuriate them still further, so that, straining on their cords, they dislodged the column and the awning collapsed at one corner, enveloping the Grand Duke Cyril and his wife who had been standing at that point, attempting to get the portly Dowager Duchess to her feet.

With the arrival of more policemen and *gardiens* it was clear that something serious was afoot. Yet for what seemed an age no one moved: the guests stuck firmly to their rose-embroidered cushions, gripping fiercely the silken thread that still held up the afternoon. No one budged until the *gardiens*, out among the company now, waving their arms and sticks, started to shout, 'Your Excellencies, ladies and gentlemen – please – raise yourselves. Fire! Fire!'

Then everyone moved, very quickly, and more or less at once. At the same time, the wind changing direction, a great searing gust of dusky smoke blew across the clearing. Now, clearly heard, there was the hungry crackle of flames in the undergrowth behind the wooden pavilion – and then, clearly seen, a scorching yellow fire leapt up from the trees beyond, spreading rapidly through the circle of dry fir and birch that enclosed the little glade.

Throwing aside their precious platters, leaping from the cushions, the guests panicked, running this way and that like animals in different directions, pushing and shoving, tripping and trampling over one another, sprawling headlong on the cushions, smashing the card tables, upsetting the samovar stands, all intent on saving their skins, making for the one exit to the glade, the narrow corridor breaking the ring of trees which led down the hill to the open parkland.

Panic and pandemonium as they all crushed together, fighting, pushing through the gap, funnelling into it in a wild farrago, clawing and tearing at each other. The General, cockaded hat awry, struggling with a liveried footman for advantage. A heavy woman, her face livid and elaborate coiffure all tipsy over one ear, battling with another in the same dishevelled state, both apoplectic, like fishwives. A bearded, black-uniformed Cossack officer, a member of the royal guard, attempting to make passage for the Dowager Duchess and her party, whacking a top-hatted ambassador in their path with his white *bashlik* hood. An agile couple, unable to make headway through the gap, down on all fours, in their party finery, pushing their way like dogs through the thick undergrowth to one side.

Behind, as Yelena turned, she saw the wooden pavilion engulfed, the awning catching fire in a long rising wave of flame, the barley-sugar columns and entwined garlands of paper roses igniting skywards like rockets. In front of this the peasants, out from the woods and taking their chances, were looting as much of the precious plate and food as they could, fighting among themselves and with the *gardiens*, a maddened *tableau vivant*, staggering, fighting groups, their bodies shimmering against the great curtain of fire behind them.

'Come on, keep together.' Sandy had taken charge of the Rumovsky party, with the Buchanans. 'In order. Don't push!' They were all together then, stuck in the narrow corridor between the trees. But they had no choice but to push, pushed as they were from behind, by other shrieking groups closer to the fire, their backsides singed by the approaching flames. So that, with this force behind them, they were finally expelled through the gap, exploding out into the open like a champagne cork, all of them rushing and stumbling pell-mell down into the open parkland. When Yelena turned once more, the whole top of the hill above her was a fiery crown, a diadem consumed by great forked tongues of flame.

The next morning there was an account of the fire on the front page of the St Petersburg *Gazette*. Most of the guests had escaped unharmed. But two of the villagers had been badly burnt and half a dozen more arrested. They must certainly, the paper commented, suffer the fullest penalty the law allowed for this looting of precious royal plate and provisions. To one side of this shocking report with its clearly most serious implications, leading the international news, Yelena noticed the column headed in large letters: 'Archduke Ferdinand and his consort assassinated at Sarajevo.' But she thought nothing of it, distraught – obsessed as she was – by her new understanding of Sasha and Miss Harriet.

9

In a calmer mood Yelena saw that the way to retrieve the situation – and to regain Sasha – was to suppress her real feelings of hurt and fury at this betrayal and play the part of bruised friend to her brother – then, as she hoped, that of confidante and counsellor. She who could see into life's secrets, the *noaide*, the soothsayer, who could see already the disaster he was headed for if he continued with Miss Harriet. She who, as was obvious now, was more sensible, stronger than him, who would forgive him his folly – but see an end to it, one way or another.

They were upstairs after breakfast in the music salon about to play a Debussy sonata. She didn't corner or browbeat him. She was quite calm, smiling even, sitting at the piano, giving him an A to tune his violin.

He adjusted the string. 'Again?' She gave him the note once more, then said casually 'I hope you enjoyed yourself with Miss Harriet out at the *dacha*?'

He didn't pause, tuning the strings meticulously until all the notes came true. Then he settled the violin beneath his chin. 'So, you *can* still see what I'm up to when I'm not with you.' He was equally composed.

'No. Miss Harriet let the cat out of the bag at the picnic.' She told him what she'd heard.

'Yes.' He sniffed, looking out over the sun-burnished river, vast and calm in the hazy summer light, a faded blue with streaks of oily silver. 'I wasn't going to tell you in advance, was I? But there's really nothing to hide.'

She laughed. 'People always say that when they've everything to hide. Nothing to hide? – except that you love me. Or so you've said. What are you *doing*, Sasha? Running away from me. *I* love you. And *we* can do all that –'

'No, we can't.'

'Who says so? Just a lot of fuddy-duddy priests and people. They were doing it in the Old Testament and in ancient Egypt and Japan and all over the place. Then along came the Church and said it was wrong. Which it isn't – not if you love the person. Nothing's wrong then.'

'You and your Pharaohs again. We're not living in ancient Egypt or Japan. Things – laws and our knowing what's right and wrong – have all moved on since then.'

'You're just like Papa. So keen on the letter of the law, rather than the spirit.'

'And you're like Mama, in your far too free and easy feelings. The thing is – one can't always control such things –'

'I've controlled such feelings – that I have for you.'

'Good.' He sighed. 'Well, we'd best just forget it all then.'

'Forget it?'

'Forget it. We must.' He didn't turn round.

'And Miss Harriet? We're all just to forget about that as well? As if it never happened. That'll be no easier. Even if it is just a passing fancy. How can you be so shallow?'

'I'm not.'

'You're lying, Sasha. You're not in love with her. Why don't you admit it? You've got yourself into a jam – and don't know how to get out of it.'

He turned from the window, looking at her with a studied gaze, a half smile. 'We'll see,' he said. Temporizing. Enigmatic. She couldn't stand it. She started to play the opening of the Debussy piece, the soft compelling legato introduction. And went on playing, willing him to join her, until finally he left the window, settled the violin beneath his chin, and did just that.

Wordlessly then they came together in their music. Almost like making love, she felt. They both felt it, she was sure, could hear the need in the searching, intertwining strands of the shared melody, could see it when they glanced at each other. She'd won him back. He was hers again. They belonged to each other inextricably. Miss Harriet didn't count. Or at least, Yelena would see to it that she didn't.

Yelena thought Miss Harriet wouldn't be able to look her in the eye after this. She was wrong. The whole business roused

Harriet, fuelled her romantic, melodramatic temperament, her red-headed Irish high spirits, her insistence on the forthright in life, her tenacious pursuit of anything she thought right and worthy. Her fearlessness. She was like Yelena in this. Yelena should have known.

Certainly, from the moment Miss Harriet came into her bedroom that afternoon – Sasha had obviously told her that his sister had found out about them – it was clear she thought her amorous adventure entirely right and worthy. She didn't quite flounce into the room, but her jaunty walk was more pronounced. Spring-heeled, full of gestures, with that head-tossing mannerism of hers.

'It's no use glaring at me like that, Yelena.' Hands on hips, head to one side as she spoke in that amused, chaffing tone of hers. Yet resolute. 'Always glaring at people!' She smiled nicely at the idea. 'Willing them your way. Well, that'll do no good with me, because I've nothing to account for with you, nothing to explain or justify.'

Just like Sasha, Yelena thought – when, if she was to talk of it at all, she had a good deal to explain and justify. Another one in a jam. Another hypocrite. Yelena had been on her bed, moping in the heat, half-asleep. Now she got up, the better to do battle.

'Explain? Justify?' Yelena said, ironic, but cool. 'Not to me. To yourself perhaps.'

'Nor to myself either.' Miss Harriet turned then. 'I'm glad you see it that way. I know how close you are to Sasha. But adult now. Both of you. And not his keeper. All the same . . .' She hesitated, looking at her with a little less assurance. 'If your parents knew, they'd ask me to leave. I hope you'll keep the matter to yourself.'

'No, no need to tell them. Because whatever you're up to with Sasha won't affect him and me. He's told me that already. What we feel for each other won't alter.' She looked at Harriet carefully. 'We're inseparable. In our music. And every other way. So we're all right,' she said nicely. 'Your future with him on the other hand would seem much less certain . . .'

Honours even, Yelena supposed.

Yelena didn't tell her parents. Miss Harriet stayed on, which meant that things had to hang fire, which didn't suit Yelena at all. But there was little she could do about it. Her hope was that the two of them, without any interference from her, would see the folly of their ways, and that Miss Harriet, realizing she had no future with Sasha, would leave the family of her own accord. Or that, with the start of the war with Germany that August, she would return home to Ireland. But she didn't. Instead she soon took up war work with the British community, making mittens and woollies for the troops at great knitting parties presided over by Lady Georgina Buchanan in the ballroom of the Embassy next door.

Why didn't she leave, Yelena wondered? Though Sasha was increasingly distracted and morose, full of Russian *toska*, that awful depression that she had so suffered until a few months before, Miss Harriet's mood, during those tense, hot, July days which led up to the various declarations of war, was one of happy self-satisfaction. What made her so confident? Was she still making love with Sasha? Yelena couldn't tell. And though she was unhappy enough now, none of her 'gifts' returned. She couldn't 'see' anything of what was going on between them, could forecast nothing.

Meanwhile the twins made things up, after a fashion. They played together again. But the attack, the sense of intimacy, the fun was gone from their music now. They simply went through the motions, without any real soul or verve.

'Not much use, going on playing like this,' Yelena said to him one day in early October, stopping halfway through the second movement of the Franck sonata in A major. 'No real point. We have to do something, Sasha.'

'What?' He was petulant.

'Settle your business with Miss Harriet, I should think.'

'Yes, I shall have to settle it.' He plucked the strings in a nervous pizzicato.

'Finish with it?'

'No, it's only just beginning.'

'Oh? Then why are you so in the dumps these days? And she so head in air?'

He went on picking the strings for a moment, then looked up at her. The brightness had gone from his eyes, along with all his old confidence. He was grimly fatalistic.

'I should think she's happy,' he said, 'because she's going to have a child.'

Yelena should have been really disturbed by this startling news. But instead, after the initial shock, she felt almost light-headed. It was clear to her – she was completely in control now. In this pickle Sasha was going to need her more than ever.

'Sasha, dearest . . .' She stood up, came to him, touching his arm. 'It's all right then, isn't it? She'll *have* to go home to Ireland. Or get rid of it. Or both.'

'Yes.' He made a movement towards her, as if about to touch her as well. But at the last moment he turned away. 'Yes, but she says she'll do neither – that she'll have it here. And stay here.'

'But she can't.' Yelena was incredulous. 'She must be mad. Who is she going to say the father is?'

'I'm the father of course. But she's not going to hold me to that.'

'She'll have to say someone's the father.'

'Yes.' He turned to the window now. 'She will. And since it's me, I'll marry her.'

At this news Yelena was truly shocked. This was worse than a pickle. But she retained her composure. 'Well, that's nonsense, Sasha. You're not in love with her. Sheer disaster to marry. You *can't* marry her, Sasha,' she said firmly. 'We'll see to it that you don't.'

'How?' He turned from the window, picking up his bow and violin again, despondently. 'What other way is there?'

'Lots of other ways. Don't be a fool, Sasha. You're just as able as I am to get what you – what we – want. What's best. You're just down in the dumps, punishing yourself and being boringly Russian. So stop it!' She gazed at him fiercely. 'Stop all this dreary business – and let's finish the allegro.'

She willed him then to come to her, in spirit, in the music. He brightened, settled his violin, and they picked up where they'd left off in the sonata, soon getting into the turbulent cannonade, in this musical picture of a marriage.

They made a world together again in their music, where they were inviolate, all-powerful, with a shared destiny once more – to win out over all the follies of others, the imperfections and compromises of ordinary life. She dragged him back from that ridiculous, self-indulgent Slav sorrow, forced him to their music, to its rhythms and its brio, giving it the tension, daring, the provocative vivacity and explosive resolution which it had quite lacked in these last months. As the tempo gathered pace – the two instruments merging, fighting, separating, finally coupled inextricably – she thought neither of them could ever have another as they possessed each other then.

Subsequently Yelena had a different worry about Sasha. She could well lose him in another way. Though before Sasha had been exempt from military service, with the start of the war he was now due to enlist, when he would be packed off to the Prussian front. She had to try and keep him in Petrograd now – as the city had been renamed at the start of the war, to the discontent of its citizens, who thought it an omen of bad luck – as well as try to get him out of Miss Harriet's clutches.

In the event her first problem, solved out of the blue, would now more or less certainly lead to the resolution of the second. Savonov, the director of the Conservatoire, called the twins in one morning to tell them that the Army Ministry had asked him to get together a group of musicians and singers to entertain the troops at the Front, where they would travel later that month in a special train. Savonov had smiled. 'The Army Minister especially asks that you both join the group. He believes your playing together would be a particular inspiration to the men.'

Sasha was at first doubtful. But since, if he refused, he would likely be sent to the Front anyway, he finally accepted. However, their leaving Petrograd so soon raised another possible problem in her mind. Sasha might think to marry Miss Harriet at once, before they left. Though surely, faced with the marital and the patriotic, he would come to see how the latter duty absolved him from the former. Yelena encouraged this belief. 'Well, you can't marry her now, in just the few weeks we have left.'

'I can't just leave her here either, to face everything alone.'

He had given her the cue she needed. 'You won't be leaving her here alone. Sandy's staying on as well.'

'So?'

'It's obvious! You know as well as I do he's mad about her. I bet you anything when he finds out about her condition, as he will when she starts to show, he'll do the honourable thing. The English are like that. Damsel in distress. He'll jump at the opportunity.'

'You're mad, Linochka. I can't just rely on Sandy to take up with her. And I can't just run out on her either.'

'But you wouldn't be running out on her. You're going to have to go away in any case whether you like it or not and whatever Harriet wants. So she'll *have* to do something on her own then. Either go home. Or take up with Sandy. Or both. So be firm when you tell her we're going. It'll be perfectly clear to her then – that you've no alternative but to leave her. There's a war on. *Force majeure* . . .'

That settled it, she thought. She'd contrived nothing, done or suggested nothing untoward. The war had taken everything out of their hands. But a moment later it was clear that nothing had been settled.

'The war,' Sasha said, heavily ironic. 'All so very convenient, isn't it? There has to be some other way. If I go away she and the child will have to be cared for –'

'*If* you go away? But you *are* going away. You forget –'

'I've forgotten nothing. Don't tell me how to run my life.' He turned on her, angry now. He'd lost all the confidence she'd given him in the whole wretched business, she saw. Cornered. Panicking. 'This bossy attitude of yours,' he went on. 'Always knowing what's best, telling me I'm a humbug. Well, you're just smug. And unfeeling. And having me do things to suit your ends, not Harriet's. You and your sweet reason, when in fact you're encouraging me to do everything that's wrong!'

Yelena was furious herself then. He was attacking her for all the sensible support and advice she'd given him, betraying her again, and the solidarity she'd built up between them. 'That's so unfair of you!' She lost her temper, shouting. 'Blaming me for the jam you've got yourself into – when all I've done is show you perfectly reasonable ways out of it. You are a fool, Sasha – you and Miss Harriet. I wish she was dead –'

The words escaped her before she knew what she was saying.

The following morning, perched on a small gilt chair so that she felt larger and more awkward than usual, Miss Harriet looked at herself in the mirror of the hairdressers on the Morskaya. Irina, the fair-haired Lettish girl who usually did her hair, had trimmed it all round and was tidying and titivating it now. But the new effect was not greatly pleasing, she thought. More manageable, but not more attractive.

She longed for some obvious, incontestable beauty of feature or body then. Did not pregnancy make you beautiful? Where was that velvety skin she had seen on other women in the same condition? Where was the glowing aura, that expectant repose?

She did not have it. She had nothing now. Sasha had told her so coldly the previous day of his imminent departure – and the full enormity of her predicament had finally come home to her. Before she had been confident in the outcome – in herself, because there seemed several sensible courses of action open to her, and because Sasha had been so reassuring, concerned not only for her future and that of the child, but also to marry her – a course she had gently dissuaded him from.

'No, Sasha, you have a life of your own to lead and this is my responsibility,' she had told him, up in one of the small attic rooms of the palace where they met, among the old cabin trunks, tailor's dummies, bric-a-brac. '*I* have money enough of my own to support myself and the child – anywhere I want.'

'But how? How could you survive, if you don't marry? Who is the father supposed to be?'

'You, of course! But no one need know.'

'But you couldn't lead such a life here indefinitely – alone, unmarried, with a child. How could you survive, face people?'

'I don't fear people's opinion – as long as I know I'm doing the right thing. And I would be.'

'But I have a responsibility, too. We should either marry. Or you should get rid of the child. Or have it adopted.'

She had smiled. 'No, I shall keep the child. I could never think of getting rid of it. Or giving it away. That would be truly immoral. I told you from the start, out at the *dacha* – it was all a good thing. I took the risk – and accept the consequences. And they'll be happy. I'm determined on that.'

She had felt and spoken so confidently then. In control of things – optimistic, sensible, loving.

When he had told her so offhandedly, so distant and cold, that he was not enlisting but leaving for the front with Yelena, all her control, her confidence, had evaporated. With *Yelena*! The two of them, away for months together, where she could not reach him, see him, touch him. The thought opened an aching pit in her stomach.

'But Sasha – with *Yelena*?'

'I've no alternative. Don't you see?' He'd been cross and embarrassed. 'We have no future, Harriet. It's all been a fantasy. Our loving, marrying, everything. Pretending, deceiving ourselves. We've simply made a terrible mistake. Don't you see?' He'd turned and glared at her, scraping a hand violently through his hair.

'No –'

'*Yes.* You won't marry me. Or get rid of the child – or have it adopted. I've offered, suggested all these things.'

'And I won't do any of those things, Sasha. Because they'd all be wrong. Look at me, Sasha,' she'd said softly, reasonably.

He had turned, unwillingly, glancing at her hopelessly for a moment. She saw it then, in his coldness, awkward embarrassment, frustration and temper. Of course he didn't love her. He'd thought he ought to love her. She saw it all in a flash – how he had played the role of lover and she had been willingly deceived by his performance. He was right, they had deceived themselves and each other. It was a horrifying realization. Of course she should have come to it before – should have seen how, in his wanting her to get rid of the child or have it adopted, he was anxious not to take responsibility for her, but to avoid it. She should have seen how, in these suggestions, there was not care or love for her but mere expediency – while his offer of marriage had been simply his grasping at the straw of honour.

She left the hairdressers that morning feeling sick and unsteady. She didn't want the child now, because she no longer wanted herself, no longer wanted to be joined to that other infatuated, lascivious woman whose needs had so betrayed her better self. She had certainly given herself to her romantic dream of Russia, of Russians – all that negligent passion. She was part of it now, and its awful consequences.

She laughed drily at the idea as she walked along the street, then almost cried, being jostled by the crowds, importuned by flag sellers offering little cameo pictures of the Grand Duchess Olga in aid of her fund for the war effort. Grand Duchesses and *troikas* and snowy visions! Romantic Russia! What terrible nonsense. The reality was quite different, she saw – for herself, for Russia. A moist wind whipped off the river, scattering the yellow leaves from the dishevelled linden trees above her, a wind with the smell of winter. The reality was war, the gloomy people all about her, numbed by the disastrous news coming every day from the Front, an end to the happiness she had known in Russia. For her there was only a future where she would be reminded daily, by the child she carried, of nothing but her folly, of the appalling mistakes she had made, with Sasha and in all her absurd beliefs about the country and its people – from the very beginning.

She saw the crowded tram coming towards her, up the Morskaya, its bell clanging, travelling fast, people waiting for it to pass, then skipping across the street behind it. It would only take a moment, she thought – for her to cross right in front of the tram, before it passed over her.

10

'Damn you, God – you've taken Sasha – and I'll pay you back. I promise.' Distraught, Yelena watched the crowded troop train pull out of Petrograd's Warsaw station two days later.

No one heard her. There was pandemonium. Young conscripts filled every carriage window and doorway, singing and waving, while from the platform, among the throng of abandoned parents and friends, a terrible discord arose, a mix of bitter tears and happy exhortation. Proud fathers shouted patriotic encouragement, while sobbing women ran along beside the train, grasping a son's arm, a lover's hand, clutching at a finger and finally at empty space as the train slid away into the night. After the overwhelming disasters suffered by the army on the Prussian front in the last month, at Tannenberg and in the swamps of the Masurian Lakes, it was clear to many on the platform, including Yelena, that few of these men would return alive.

But Yelena didn't move. She would show no outward sign of grief, no conventional emotion. She was, she conveniently believed, the victim of a malign fate, a cruel God. Sasha's sudden departure must be ascribed to this, not to her or Miss Harriet. So she repeated the malediction, to confirm her outrage at this theft – part of herself, torn away from her – hoping as well by these evil words to unearth those strange powers of hers with which she could smite God.

But an hour later, when she saw Miss Harriet in the hospital, all these angry resolutions evaporated. Two candles flickered by the bed where Miss Harriet lay, quite still, as if on a bier. She was dead. She must be. Miss Harriet had died before she could reach her – she had lost her way among the confusing corridors of the Pokrovsky Hospital, walking down passages reeking of cabbage soup where bandages had been hung out to dry, running through a ward filled with wounded soldiers, before she finally came into the wing of the British Hospital beyond, finding the room at the end where Miss Harriet lay on the narrow bed, still as a corpse.

The weather had changed. The blustery, unsettled conditions of the last few September days had given way to an oppressive calm, an unseasonable humidity. Great plum-blue thunder clouds had gathered out over the Gulf that afternoon and now a violent storm was moving over the city, disrupting the electricity, approaching the hospital on Vasily Island with sudden flashes of lightning, followed by vicious thunderclaps which rattled the windows of Miss Harriet's small room.

Harriet lay straight out on her back, rigid, pallid-faced, a bandage round her forehead, eyes closed, sheet drawn right up under her chin, strands of wavy reddish hair, gold-streaked in the candle flames, tossed across one side of the pillow. Beside her, on a cane chair, lay her capacious bag – still filled, Yelena thought, with all that it had contained when she and Sasha had been children: the salves and lotions, the treats and tortures of childhood – digestive biscuits and bon-bons, wych-hazel and eucalyptus oil, hairgrips, nail scissors and tweezers. A bag which seemed the sum of Miss Harriet's worldly possessions then; the sum, too, she thought, of all her own happy years in the care of this woman whose life she had destroyed. So that suddenly, having called on those strange gifts of hers at the station, Yelena wanted no part of them now.

For, of course, she had killed Miss Harriet. Just as with Dmitri and her brother Ivan, she had wished her dead only two days before. Now she had the wild hope that somehow she might make her live again.

Kneeling by the bed she put her hand across the body, resting it on Miss Harriet's stomach. 'Please,' she murmured, 'Wind God or whatever other spirit gave me those powers, give them to me again now and make this person live. Do what you want with me – damn me – but spare her.'

The body stirred. Miss Harriet opened one eye, then the other – then the faint drowsy word 'Hello . . .' Yelena, astonished, stayed on her knees. Then, overcome with emotion, she buried her head in the blanket and wept. 'Oh, God, I've been such an evil fool,' she said at last, looking up.

'Why? Why evil and foolish?' Miss Harriet's tone was inquisitive, interested.

'Because I wished you dead.' Yelena started to sob again.

'No, Linochka, you've got it wrong.' Miss Harriet was almost brusque. 'It was I who wished myself dead.'

Yelena looked up at her, incredulous. 'But the tram, they said it was going too fast, it ran into you.'

'No, no. I ran into it.' There was irony in her slight Irish tones. 'I tried to kill myself.'

'But before the accident. I wished it –'

'So did I, even more than you, I dare say. But it doesn't matter now. We both failed. I've survived.' A small smile crossed Miss Harriet's face. 'Do get up, Linochka. I can't see you there, kneeling like a penitent. Come and sit over here by the candles where I can see you and tell me the news. I feel I've been asleep for months! Your news? And Sasha's?'

The window rattled suddenly in the approaching storm. Yelena got up, wiping her nose with a hanky.

'Sasha's left Petrograd,' Yelena said evenly, trying to control her voice, the surge of bitter emotion she felt rising in her throat. 'He's going to enlist in the army. He left for the Gatchina barracks earlier this evening. I've just seen him off.'

Miss Harriet was strangely composed when she spoke. 'Ah, so the bird has flown. It's a pity he's gone away – that he can't see me now, hear me, know how I've changed since the accident. As if that tram knocked sense into me at last. And gave me something more. When I finally woke up this morning and thought about everything, I realized – not that I'd made a perfect fool of myself with Sasha, I knew that already – but that perhaps I'd been spared for some reason. I didn't know what – not the child, I suppose, which he must have told you about, because I must certainly have lost that. But I think I know now . . .'

'What?'

'One's really meant to love easily. "As leaves grow on the tree." If it isn't that it's disastrous, perverse. I can't think how I came to have all those ridiculous feelings. But there it is – I did. Quite preposterous! When love has to be just the opposite.'

'Yes,' Yelena said. 'Yes, perhaps.' But she would not confirm this idea in her heart.

Miss Harriet sighed briefly. She put out her arm, grasping Yelena's hand for an instant, then let it fall. Her eyes closed. 'I'm tired.'

'Yes. Yes, of course. I shouldn't have stayed so long. I'll go.'

'No, we'll both go . . .' Miss Harriet's voice was confused, drowsy, as if she were already asleep and voicing thoughts in a dream. 'A long way to go, not to drown, that's the main thing . . .'

Yelena left the room, walking away down the long corridors. 'Not to drown', she thought. What did she mean? She remembered so nearly drowning in the river creek at Orlov two years before. The sudden cramp in both legs that had taken her under water, right down into the black depths, when she'd had that extraordinary picture of Sasha, naked and bronzed, floating in some balmy golden moted air above her, beckoning to her, always tantalizingly out of reach.

The message had been so clear – that it must be her life's work to reach him, to be and stay with him. She had been given a miraculous vision of her fate then, which was to share her life with Sasha, their music, their love for each other. How could it be perverse, she thought, to remain true to this vision?

Despite what Miss Harriet had said the issue was quite simple. Yelena confirmed the thoughts she'd had back at the station. She would find Sasha, bring him home, see him returned to her, so that they could continue their lives together, their love and their music. That was the essence of the whole matter. It was her responsibility to bring him back. She would remain true to her vision. Out of the hospital now, on the dark unlit street, she stepped confidently forward, promptly missed her footing on the kerb and fell headlong into the rain-filled gutter.

She was stunned for half a minute, before she felt someone's arms about her, trying to lift her up. She saw the vague shape of a man's head, an army cap, in the stormy gloom above her. Then the words 'Are you all right?' in Russian, but not a native speaker. 'Here, let me help you up.' The voice continued in Russian. Of course, she thought, coming back into full consciousness. It was Sandy, Sandy Woodrow.

'Yes, I think. I'm fine,' she told him in English, as he pulled her up, the two of them swaying, buffeted by the wind, the fierce thunderstorm, barely visible to each other, but recognizing their voices.

'It's Sandy, isn't it? It's me, Yelena!'

'Good God, so it is. I thought some drunken woman had keeled over.' He had to shout above the weather. His hands clutched her shoulders, her sodden cape. 'Dear me, you're soaked. Here, let me –' But there wasn't much he could do. They were getting even more drenched. He fussed about her impotently. 'There are no droshkies. But there's my umbrella. I was just on my way to see Miss Boulting at the hospital. Only heard today –'

'I've just come from seeing her. She's all right. Asleep now, so no point in your going. See her tomorrow. She's out of danger.'

'What happened?' There was a note of urgency in his voice.

'I'll tell you about it later. Let's get out of the rain!'

'My flat. We can take a short cut across University Gardens. There's a fire.'

'Yes. Let's go – anywhere out of this weather.'

He held her arm as they ran down the street, huddled together, heads lowered into the wind, like a couple in a frantic three-legged race, a flash of lightning over their heads followed by a fearful clap of thunder. They reached the main gateway leading into the University Gardens. Normally the long gravel avenue here, bordered on either side by huge trees, would have been lit by ornate, white-globed lamps. The formal beech alley was dark and deserted. Sporadic gusts battered the trees. Pools of water lay ahead of them, reflecting the jagged flashes from over the river. But the avenue was quite straight. Their way was clear. They had only the fierce rain to contend with. Sandy gave her the umbrella. 'Here, you take it.' They moved on, a few paces apart.

Halfway down the avenue the gardens were suddenly illuminated by a brilliant white light. The lightning, immediately overhead, flashed down, finding the iron tip of the umbrella. Yelena felt a ferocious stab of pain running down her arm, a fizzing shock that snatched the brolly out of her hand, sent it spinning away from her. A stupendous thunderclap detonated right above her, sent her sprawling to the gravel, punching all the air out of her lungs. She couldn't breathe, seemed to be suffocating in a vacuum. A moment later a wind hit her, reverberating waves of air that pushed her along, rolling her over and over like a doll, with such force that she thought she was going to roll right down the avenue and out into the river. Then she fell unconscious.

It was Sandy, a dozen yards away then and running after her, who saw the second flash, heard the crack of splintering wood, turned, and watched the great branch fall over the gravel, right across the spot where Yelena had been lying.

Half conscious now, she took a shallow breath. Then another. She was alive. Sandy was leaning over her. She could move her arm. It ached. But she could move it. She wasn't dead. Nor even badly hurt, she thought. In fact, as she gathered consciousness she felt strangely elated, exultant even, filled with a buoyancy, a fierce jubilation, as if the lightning which had grazed her had invested her with some astonishing new spirit, a powerful elixir seeping into her every vein, transforming her.

'Yelena! Are you all right?'

'Yes. Yes, I don't know what happened but –'

A sudden flash illuminated the avenue again and she saw the black dog for an instant, a little pug dog just like Samson – who had died years before – a few paces in front of her. It stood there motionless, glitter-eyed, gazing up at her quizzically, as if waiting to do her bidding. 'Why, it's Samson,' she cried. 'But it can't be. He's dead.'

'What dog?'

'There – right in front of us.'

Sandy looked about in the stormy gloom. 'Can't see anything.'

Another flash, farther away, confirmed there was nothing there, no animal, in front of them or among the trees or anywhere along the avenue.

'It's a miracle you weren't badly hurt.'

'Killed, you mean?'

'Well, yes . . . If not by the lightning, then by that great branch. It fell right across where you were lying.'

'The wind – I felt a great wind.'

'I felt it, too. It rolled you out of the way just in time.'

'The wind god, Bieggolmai,' she said almost to herself. 'He saved me.'

Ten minutes later, leaving the gardens, moving down the Prospekt towards the river and turning onto the embankment on Universitetskaya opposite the Admiralty and the Winter Palace, they stopped in front of a large town house, an ornate building with big double doors and tall windows, illuminated in a brilliant flare of light from across the river.

An old *dvornik* let them in, half the big door sweeping open in a gust of wind, propelling them past the baggy-coated man into a sudden calm. She stood there, water dripping from her cape onto the parquet floor. The hall, illuminated by several tall standard oil lamps, rose up two floors to a vaulted ceiling decorated with gilded cherubs and cornucopias high above. At ground level there was an equally opulent air. Classical statues towered on pedestals, interspersed with urns of potted plants, pampas grass and dry bullrushes. An intricately carved mahogany staircase in the centre led up to a minstrel's gallery which ran right round the first floor.

'How very grand! A flat, you said. This is a whole house.'

'Yes. But divided up into four flats. The Embassy bought it a few years ago. Extra accommodation for menials like me. Place was built by a British businessman. You'll see, there are real fireplaces, not stoves.' Sandy gazed about him, then turned back to Yelena. 'I say, you've cut yourself.' He came over. 'Let me look. Hold on, I've got a handkerchief.' He took his army cap and greatcoat off, got a handkerchief out and started to dab carefully at the cut. The *dvornik* looked on curiously, a small bearded man, dodging around them like a gnome, offering advice in a slurred voice. He was drunk, perhaps, Yelena thought, on some foul home-brewed spirit which people made now, since the Tsar's decree at the start of the war prohibiting the sale of all alcohol. And she was shivering, water running down the small of her back.

'Sandy, can't we go upstairs? I'm soaked. You needn't worry, I have been alone with a man before!'

'Yes. Yes, of course.'

They went up the grand staircase, Yelena, with her new vim and vigour, running ahead of Sandy as if they were making for her flat, not his.

As soon as he opened the door, leading her down a short passage, pushing through a heavy curtain at the end, Yelena smelt the oranges. Not exactly oranges, she thought. A faint essence of orange. It was delicious. The large room was in shadow, vaguely lit by a sluggish fire in a big grate and by two Aladdin lamps to either side, turned low, which, when Sandy brightened them, showed a conventionally furnished space, much in the English manner: chintz-covered armchairs by the fire, a long Chesterfield sofa, a big dining-table covered with books and papers in the middle, an upright piano, a roll-top desk by the heavily draped window. A large map of the Western Front, stuck to a board, was held on an artist's easel by the desk, pins and ribbons attached to it. By the fireplace, on the floor, stood an ornate Turkish hookah. On the other side of the grate, next to the armchair, there was a church lectern, with a heavy dictionary open across it. Comfortable bachelor quarters, Yelena thought. Everything to hand, neat and tidy. And Sandy, reflecting this order, most businesslike himself.

'Take your cape off. And I'll frisk the fire up.' He knelt by the grate with bellows and a poker. 'Wet birch. No decent wood this autumn. And it cost a fortune. Every sort of profiteering.'

'But that isn't the smell, is it? The strange smell. It's wonderful.'

'Smell? Just damp birch.'

'No, oranges. A faint orangy smell everywhere.'

He shook his head, sniffed. 'I can't smell it. But here, you're bleeding again.' He stood up and inspected the small cut above her temple more carefully now. 'I'll get some cotton wool. Have to wash my hands. Won't be a moment.' But he turned back. 'Your clothes first, sorry. Here, you can use the bedroom. I'll show you.' He picked up one of the Aladdin lamps and she followed him, through another curtained doorway into a smaller room with just a single bed in it, but with a vast clothes cupboard all along one wall. He opened one of the mirrored doors. Inside were rows of drawers. He pulled several out. Clothes of every sort were neatly stacked inside. 'Here, choose what you want. Shirts, pyjamas. And towels – up there. Then we can dry your own things by the fire when it gets going.'

He was so matter-of-fact about everything. She wasn't in the least embarrassed by the situation. She undressed and towelled herself, standing naked by the bed, seeing herself reflected in the long mirror, the bright rays of the lamp behind her sharply defining her figure in the glass – her breasts, her waist, her bottom. Naked, alone with a man in his flat, by his bed, she thought, about to step into his pyjamas. She should have felt uneasy. But not the slightest. Rather the opposite. There was a piquancy in the situation. She was pleasantly provoked by it all. Yes, safe of course. That was perfectly obvious. Sandy, with his clipped moustache and very diplomatic manners. Sandy, so obviously an officer and a gentleman. He would take no advantage of her. She found herself regretting this for an instant.

The logs had brightened when she returned to the drawing-room, her damp clothes under one arm, holding the lamp with the other. Sandy had put three dining chairs in a row, backs to the fire. She laid her clothes along the top of them. The cape, her dress, her underclothes and stockings. Sandy emerged from another doorway, with a first-aid box, and a faint smile.

'Very smart. The khaki jersey goes well with the striped trousers.'

'A bit baggy!' She drew the sides of the pyjama legs out, flattening the material against the front of her thighs, her stomach, pulling the cloth into tented points with the tips of her fingers, making a small curtsey. 'I'm too thin.'

'You mean – I'm too fat.' A wan smile again. 'Yes, I've become a real office-wallah lately. Fatter . . .'

He let his clear grey eyes roam over her shapeless body for a moment. Their eyes met. His head to one side, that worried cockerel stance. Lower jaw moving, unconsciously clenching his teeth. His eyes moved upwards, towards her forehead, her temple. He pulled a wad of cotton wool from the first-aid box, searching for her wound. He was close to her. And now she smelt the slightly tart essence of bitter oranges again.

'That orangy smell,' she said. 'In the room everywhere. It's you!'

'Me?' He drew away, surprised.

'Your smell. Everyone has a particular smell. Nobody has quite the same. Their skin, their sweat. They breathe it out, too. It's special. And it gets everywhere, in the rooms they live in.' She sniffed the air. 'It's nice! Don't worry – if it hadn't been I'd not have mentioned it.'

'You must have a very sensitive nose,' he said politely.

'What do I smell of? When you were close then – nothing?'

'Nothing I noticed. Just the iodine!' He looked at her from across the room. He was keeping his distance, she thought, where another man might have taken her hint and approached her again, close to, smelling her. She saw now how she'd given him this clear hint, this invitation. And this surprised her, for she'd not meant to.

'I've a telephone,' he said, bending down to prod the fire. 'You may like to call the Palace, say you've been held up?'

'I told Papa I'd be at the hospital. But, yes, perhaps. He's worried. So is Mama. It's been an awful few days.'

'Of course: Miss Boulting. Poor Harriet . . .' His tone was much more concerned now, which annoyed Yelena. 'You must tell me –'

'Well, that as well. But she's better. She'll recover. No, the really worrying thing now is that Sasha has gone. He just upped and left.'

'Disappeared?' Sandy stood up from the grate, worried.

'No, but he might as well have done. He's joining the army.'

'Oh, I see.' He was relieved. 'I'm sorry. But should I be? Everyone's been enlisting. Off to the war, here, at home. Wish I could go.'

He was so calm and unenquiring, Yelena thought. So bland, polite, uninvolved. She was even more annoyed with him now. Did he not know? Did he sense nothing? He loved Miss Harriet, she knew that. So she suddenly wanted to upbraid him then for this innocent, fatuous loving – of a woman who loved another, her brother, and was pregnant by him. She wanted to tell this worthy but foolish man the truth of things; this good man who, for months past, had attended them, courtier-like, on the periphery of their lives – hers, Sasha's, Miss Harriet's; this trusting man, left in ignorance of the reality behind his friendships; the lies, the deviousness there. She would tell him now. It was her duty.

The fire started to blaze at last. Her clothes steamed on the chairs. The storm passed by overhead. The windows ceased to rattle. She tried to telephone the Palace, but the lines were down on Sandy's side of the river. There was no tea, he told her, since the gas in the kitchen stove had gone as well. Would she like some vodka, to warm her? Opening a bottle, he gave her a small glass. 'Ah,' she said, 'it's nice to do something illegal . . .'

'It's an old bottle,' he informed her with mock severity, denying her this lawlessness, 'bought before the Tsar's decree. Besides, his writ doesn't run here. This is British territory.'

They sat opposite each other on the chintz armchairs. The Aladdin lamps cast a steady, golden glow.

'Will they let you go to the war soon?' she asked, hoping to find some natural entry to her real topic via such small talk.

'I don't know. General Knox is the Military Attaché here. I'm only a junior. But my Russian is perhaps better than his, so they'll want to keep me here as long as possible, I suppose. I so wanted to be with my regiment in Flanders. They were at Mons.' He stood up impatiently, went over to the map of the Western Front on the easel by his desk and gazed at the pins and ribbons there.

'But you like it here, don't you?'

He moved a pin on the map, then a ribbon, stared at the changed positions, lost in a dream of battles which had been denied him. 'Yes . . . Yes, I like it here well enough,' he said at last.

'And there's Miss Harriet – the good you can do there. Now.' She added the word, to avoid a too obvious reference to his affection for her.

'The good? Yes, of course. I'd like to help. Tell me, what exactly happened, with the tram?'

The vodka had warmed Yelena, made her slightly light-headed. She dived straight in. 'She tried to kill herself under it. She is, or at least she was, going to have a child. Sasha's child – which is one reason he's disappeared.'

Sandy was startled. He paced back over the floor, then poured himself another glass of vodka. 'But – it never crossed my mind, that she and Sasha –' He drank the vodka, starting to pace the room again. 'One simply wouldn't have thought – Miss Boulting, his governess.' He shook his head in disbelief.

'You shouldn't be surprised.' Yelena was pleased with herself. She had at last made a dent in his sang-froid. 'There are thousands of foreign governesses in Russia. It's long been the fashion here to seduce them. Fathers or sons. Though they should have known.'

'What should they have known?'

'To look before they leaped. Sasha isn't in love with Miss Harriet. Nor she with him. Just thought she was. She simply had a bad crush on him. So when she found she was going to have a child – well, they both lost their nerve. She tried to kill herself and he's run away to the wars.' She finished her vodka, getting into her stride.

Sandy was uncertain, lighting a cigarette to cover his indecision. Finally he said, 'Yes, but one has to be very careful. Miss Harriet and Sasha, they're not children. And one really can't set oneself up as God, over other people's affairs.'

'So you find nothing wrong in their behaviour?' she asked him innocently, changing her tone now, assuming one of reason and genuine enquiry. He said nothing. 'Are you not hurt, as I am? Since we love – or are at least fond of – both of them.'

'Just because I'm fond . . .' He flapped his hands uselessly, turning away. 'I'm all the more loath to judge. That's the very point I made. I . . . I can't be entirely objective.'

'I'd have had more spirit,' she said firmly. 'Which I thought they had. And then done something practical, not run away.'

'Perhaps Harriet did want to do the practical thing,' he retorted, even more firmly. 'You can't be so cut and dried about such things. You're not them. You'd feel differently if you were directly involved, either way,' he ended sharply.

'You're lecturing me!' She glared at him.

Not to be put down, he gazed at her challengingly in return. The small head, wide blackberry eyes, the slightly pouting lower lip, turned-up nose, the short, cropped, damp-dark hair, falling untidily over her small ears, the slightly plump jawline and chin. Her features were still those of an adolescent. And yet this bird-like creature was so sure of herself and her beliefs, exuded such a sense of adult power: her eyes especially, demanding, willing him to agree with her, to do her bidding.

'So, how do you intend helping – either of them – practically?' he asked, rather clipped now, in his most military manner.

'Sasha and I were going up to the front anyway, to entertain the troops. So I'll go on my own. I'll find Sasha myself.'

'Among several million men, over a five-hundred-mile front?'

'I'll find out his regiment. Besides, I can sometimes "see" him, see where he is, in my mind. I have these strange gifts – remember? I told you about them, on the battleship.'

'Yes, I remember. But even if you do find him, and persuade him back, he's likely to be shot for desertion. And as for Miss Harriet, she'll just have to recover in hospital, in her own time.'

'You love her. Like I love Sasha.'

'That's neither here nor there. You – we were to be practical.'

They glared at each other, on the verge of a real row. Then, seeing the pointlessness of their dispute, in that they were never going to agree, the tension snapped between them and they burst out laughing.

Suddenly it was perfectly clear to her. They were fighting each other. Simply because both had lost, been betrayed by, people they loved. And they had covered their loss in aimless chatter about Sasha's behaviour, and Miss Harriet's, and their own differing views. They had talked too much of others. What they really wanted was each other.

Or at least she wanted him.

11

In a surge of vindictive desire, sensuous malice, sheer amusement, Yelena wanted an end to thought, reason, duty, virtue. She wanted instead to actively confirm the huge irrational power she felt – wanted to regain an incontestable ascendancy in her life, to do more than even the score with Sasha, who had betrayed her, in his affair with Miss Harriet and by leaving her that evening. She wanted an outright, brazen victory over both their meagre spirits – and sought this now by domination over Sandy, by seducing him, by destroying his bourgeois inhibitions, his dull morality.

'My clothes are dry,' she said casually, her back towards him. Then she simply pulled the cord of his pyjama trousers, stepped out of them, took off the jacket and, turning, stood naked in front of him.

He thought she was about to get dressed. But she made no move to do so. He saw her body framed against the firelight, the narrowing but still immature waist, the puppy-fat cladding her thighs, the small dark triangle beneath the rounded stomach. Now that it had happened he couldn't believe it; this girl was offering herself to him.

'You can't think . . . ?' He tried to hide his shock.

'No, I'm not thinking. At last!'

She came towards him, walking easily, without the least hint of provocation. She just kept her eyes fixed on his, a steady gaze, moving to where he was standing by the open gramophone on the big table.

'Yelena,' he said very firmly. 'We like each other. But that's no grounds for –'

She stopped by the table, putting the gramophone on suddenly. A jaunty march burst on the air. She recognized it at once. 'It's that march we heard on the battleship! Gilbert Sullivan.'

'Gilbert *and* Sullivan.'

She sat up on the edge of the big table, confronting him. She gazed at him, willing his complicity. She looked at him unwaveringly, her eyes alight with easy invitation. Sandy was transfixed, dumbfounded by the hypnotic quality in her stare. She said, 'Come and take me, do everything to me – whatever men do.'

He didn't move. He stood there bemused, immobile, an officer faced with some astonishing manoeuvre by the enemy which he simply couldn't fathom.

So, pushing herself off the edge of the table, she took him herself. She went to him quickly, grasping his shoulders, twining a leg round his, struggling then against his struggle, a battle he soon lost as she tugged him over to the table. She leant back, pulling him down, feeling his uniform scratch and prickle all the way up her thighs, her stomach, her breasts. She opened her legs as he moved between them. He was kissing her now, aimlessly, fiercely, on her chin, shoulders, a nipple, her midriff, as she leant further back, squashing his books and papers.

'Sandy!' She fell right back on the table, moving her head from side to side as he kissed her farther down her body. Then, craning up at him and seeing him so far away, she reached for his lapels and tugged herself up, clutching him round the shoulders, wrapping her legs about him, so that he carried her off the table, like a limpet, stuck to him, towards the fire, pushing the chairs away with one foot, letting her cape and dress and underclothes fall to the floor, then putting her down on top of them, undressing quickly above her, so she lay there watching him, seeing how huge he was between his legs, rising as he knelt over her.

She opened her legs, then moved her whole body towards him, along the floor. But when he pushed, he was unable to make headway inside her – until, adjusting his angle, he forced himself into her, pushing gently then, just at the entrance, so that something, all round the doorway, started to pulse with pleasure, sending messages shooting up to her nipples. The soles of her feet started to tingle. She clutched at him as he searched and manoeuvred, hands on his buttocks, helping.

Then the pain, so that she gasped, grasping him viciously, scratching her nails round his hips, wanting to tear him apart, as the great soft-hard log began to burrow into her, feeling the sloping top cleaving her open, the strange indentations and ridges following, rippling up through the entrance, scorching her there with pleasure, with pain, as he started to see-saw above her, easing, with each small retreat and greater advance, ever farther inside her.

And it was then, at this onset of real fever in their coupling, that she felt herself spinning away from her normal self, from the whole earthbound cage of her life, rising into another mode of existence, one of pure instinct. It was something which before she had only experienced at the height of some shared music with Sasha, when they had come together so completely – the two instruments, both sounds, seamlessly joined – that there were no notes to follow, the score was lost and they were playing not even from memory but by sheer intuition, seeming to create the music, rather than interpret it, as they went along. Now this same feeling came to her, but with greater force; a sense of living way above herself, beyond all her previous knowledge, experience and capabilities, inspired towards feats of purely sensuous artistry now, possessed by something quite outside her, which had taken her over, so that she was no longer responsible for her actions, was another person: ravenous, predatory, abandoned.

From then on she made the running, gripping him firmly, moving beneath him, egging him on, taking him way beyond the bounds of any retreat, far from the shore, out of his depth. So that now he swam with her, lost to all doubt and restraint, adept and forceful as she in promoting their pleasure, as she pulled him into the depths of herself, far underwater, both of them gasping for breath, battling with each other for survival – until suddenly she went quite still, every muscle taut, suspended above some vast deep-sea abyss for a moment. Then her stomach wrenched apart. An agonizing joy exploded everywhere inside her. Her mind went dark and her body seemed to disintegrate, the debris scattering everywhere behind her tightly shut eyes in brilliant points of light.

Sandy said nothing afterwards. He was dazed, dead, as if in this brutal runaway love-making he had not only lost his head, but his soul as well.

He went to his bedroom at once, taking his uniform, returning eventually in flannels and a shirt. Yelena meanwhile had half dressed. Sitting in her underclothes on the edge of the armchair, she looked up at him, smiling. She had won. But she was grateful, thankful, as well. Her face, soft and pliant. She had taken the great hurdle, proved herself in love-making. She basked in her success.

But she saw how Sandy was clearly horrified by it all. She didn't care. There was nothing for either of them to apologize about. Regret, guilt, shame – everything in Sandy's drear face – they were irrelevant, and worse, an insult, a smear on something quite natural, something freely willed, on her part certainly, which in any case, in the event, ought to have been enjoyed by both of them, two people who liked each other at the very least; more than enough, she thought.

So she would not question his dumbfounded air, his dead look, would not ease his conscience with any reassurances or sweet nothings. A man who regretted such pleasure was a traitor to himself, and that was truly immoral. Instead she said simply, 'That was incredibly happy. Thank you.'

Sandy didn't know what to say. He was not only appalled, he was astonished by his behaviour. He sought no excuses for it. But he saw in hers – in her having so lasciviously provoked and seduced him – something worse, something you couldn't love in a woman. She was possessed by some devil in the flesh. She was wanton.

'Sandy? Do cheer up. It was *happy*! I've never felt so alive, so full of energy. I could do it all over again!'

Fiddling with his papers on the table, he said nothing.

She laughed outright. 'Sandy, you misery! What's the matter? Why didn't you want it?'

'We simply shouldn't have done it,' he said at last, turning into the firelight, his face still a mask of distaste.

'Well, you *did* it – pretty well in the end!'

'We don't love each other. Just a physical reaction, like savages.'

'It's *natural*, not savage. I bet you wanted to do it with Miss

Harriet, for example. Well, she wouldn't. So why not me? – who would. And wanted to.'

'Not the point. I wouldn't have done it with her –'

'Why not? You *love* her after all.'

'She's not like that –'

'Oh yes she is! She did it with Sasha.'

Sandy flapped his arms about for an instant, turning away, frustrated once more in these arguments. Then he faced her suddenly. 'She was in love –'

'No, she wasn't! I told you. She only thought she was. Just a crush on her part. And sex – on both their parts, which should have made it all perfectly all right, if they hadn't had to *think* they were in love before they did it. And get all tied up in ideas of "honour" afterwards. So they made a complete mess of it all.'

'That's just perverse of you. Those ideas –'

'Perverse? As if the way you people love isn't perverse!' Yelena was equally roused and critical now. 'Mama, for example, with a new lover every six months – isn't that perverse? And Sergei, my great-uncle Sergei down at Orlov, he's mad about Miss Harriet, you know –'

'No, I didn't –'

'Isn't that perverse, too? Supposed to be happily married and twice her age. And what about you and Miss Harriet?' she stormed on. 'All unrequited. And Miss Harriet and Sasha? – the awful mess they've got themselves into. Isn't that pretty perverse, your kind of loving, and theirs? Because it's all quite hopeless – a dead end for all of you. And isn't that worse? I'd sooner the so-called "perverse" that worked, than something ordinary that didn't – and never could. But Sasha and me – that "works".'

'That's certainly perverse. Think sensibly and seriously about it, Yelena. There's a world of love out there. You have to live with someone, make a home, with children, to see the whole picture of love. And if you never try and paint that larger canvas, well, you're just going to be buying lots of rather grubby little picture postcards.'

She saw nothing valid in what he had just said, replying very firmly, 'I don't want the big canvas. I want the grubby little picture postcards. What I can see and hear and hold, *now*.

That's what I want. You talk of a world of love. But you live in one of guilt and shame and saying "No" to making love. So how are you ever going to get that ideal world? I'd prefer to have what I have already, with Sasha, or what's in front of me right now, as you are. I don't want some idealistic future with someone, which may never happen. I want what's good and happy with them – now. Anyway, we're not going to agree about it. Why can't we find something we *can* agree about?'

She jumped up, stretching her arms out wide, then clasped them about her, snuggling herself. 'Sandy, it was *good*, with you, just now. And here we are picking it all apart. "Never mind the why and wherefore". That's the point, isn't it? We've *done* it. And we're still here. Not struck dead. But better. Better than ever! Can you play it? Now, on the piano – "Never mind the why and wherefore"?'

'No, not really.' He made no move.

'Oh, go on. Of course you can. Meriel said how well you played at their Christmas party. I'd love to hear it. Or I'll play it. Do you have the music?'

'No. It's hardly –'

'Don't be an ass! I bet you have the music. Your favourite composer.' She went over and started to rifle through the sheet music on top of the upright piano. She soon found what she wanted. 'Here it is.' She flicked through the pages. 'And here's *HMS Pinafore*.'

She sat down in her petticoat at the upright piano, set the book in front of her, studied the key, tempo and notation for a moment, then started to play.

She was just rather surprised at first, that her playing was so forced, awkward. It must have been the effect of the lightning, she thought, the dull ache in her arm. The score was easy; the key of C Major, in two/four time, *vivace*. Yet she found it difficult to hit the right notes, so that nothing finished emerged, only a ragged, inconsistent melody; the chords hesitant, unlinked, the flow muddy, the effect pretentious.

She stopped, wrung her fingers out, stretched them, started again. Her playing was no better. Though she entirely grasped the music and knew in her mind exactly what should emerge by way of sound and rhythm, knew so clearly how it all should go, she could no longer transfer this knowledge to the keyboard. Her fingers would not obey her. She was suddenly fearful, desperate to get it right. But the more she tried, the worse it became – a dissonant, hopeless reflection of the happy music.

She was appalled. It was as if some malign spirit had taken away her great gift – as if, in return for her body's vast excitement ten minutes before, she had bartered her soul.

But then suddenly she saw it otherwise. No demon had touched her. The malign spirit was God. God had punished her – for damning him earlier that evening at Warsaw station, for her independent judgements with Sandy, her wild couplings with him.

'I can't play any more.' She turned to Sandy, glaring at him as if he were responsible for this.

'How do you mean?'

'It's gone! My playing. I know how it should go perfectly well. But it doesn't come out in my fingers, on the keyboard.'

'Must be all the knocks you've taken this evening.'

'It's not that.' She clenched and unclenched her fists. 'I told you, I've never felt better in my life. It's something else. I've been punished by that dreary old God of yours, for being clear-sighted and happy – and for cursing him at Warsaw station.'

'God? But if you don't believe in him, he can't exist for you. So how could he do anything to you?'

She looked up at him dismissively. 'He exists for others, though – you and all the others – doesn't he? So he's there, waiting, to punish people like me.'

'That's nonsense. You can't have it both ways, can't be a non-believer and still think he could punish you.'

'Oh yes he could.' She held her hands up, gazing at her fingers. 'It's a battle, don't you see – you should, being such a Christian – for those who've escaped the fold. To hurt, to punish them, to get them back, I suppose. That's all part of your belief, isn't it? A cruel God. Well, he is. But he won't have me.'

She got up, finished dressing quickly – then, curt with him, and refusing to be seen even to the door, she left the flat.

Sandy looked around, viewing his comfortable bachelor quarters with distaste. The room had been defiled. He sensed something malevolent in the atmosphere and in himself, a feeling of having been brushed by some evil, sullied, poisoned even.

Yet what real evil could there be in this girl, he thought? Someone able to draw out such beauty in her music must have an essential beauty of soul herself, surely? But there was something malignant about her. What was it? What had overcome her, changed her, in the last hour or so, from elfin sprite to witch?

She had reminded him that evening of her strange gifts. And he had told her before that he believed she had such gifts. Yet in truth he had thought them no more than a childish fancy, or part of her artistry, of a temperament vastly sensitive, intuitive.

Was he now to believe in the actual existence of these powers? Was he to believe that she had, in fact, willed her older brother dead? Then, too, as evidence for the reality of her gifts – her curse or whatever it was – there were the unexplained incidents earlier that evening. How had she survived the lightning strike? And how had the cut in her temple healed, almost completely, when he had come to tend it? And what of the black pug dog she had seen in the park? He had seen no dog.

No, he was rational, logical. He couldn't really believe in anything of all this. And he said so then, out loud, shaking his head. 'What nonsense! There are sensible explanations to it all.'

Leaning on the mantelpiece then, looking down into the fire, he saw one of her garters, a blue velvet elasticated band, by the fender. He picked it up, this intimate evidence of their coupling, and threw it on the low flames in disgust, waiting to see it burn. But it didn't. After a minute he took it out with the tongs. It was barely singed. Mystified, he looked at it. Then, taking it in his hand, kneading it an instant in his fingers, he felt the warmth of it, as though it had just left her thigh. In the same instant – as if, in rubbing it in this sensuous way he had released a genie from a magic lamp – he heard Yelena's voice behind him.

'Sandy, you *are* a misery! Do cheer up. It was *happy*' . . . He spun round. There was no one there. But the voice continued. 'Go on, Sandy, you can play it. Go on, of *course* you can!'

She must be back in the flat. She had returned, without his

hearing her, and was in the hall corridor behind the curtained opening. He went over and pulled the curtain aside. The corridor was empty, the hall door securely locked. She wasn't in the flat. Yet her voice had been there.

He didn't know what to make of it, her words still ringing in his ears – 'Go on, Sandy, you can play it – of course you can!' Suddenly angry at this clear taunt again from her, he went over to the piano and, looking at the *Pinafore* score, started to play the 'Why and Wherefore' music. Once more he was astonished. Instead of his usual amateur tinklings he found himself playing with an almost professional competence and fluency – playing as he'd only ever dreamt he could, with great brio, perfect control, tone, tempo, harmony, just like the pianist in the pit with the D'Oyly Carte orchestra at the Savoy Theatre in London. He couldn't understand it. This was how Yelena had played the piano before. Was that what had happened? Some further magic coming from her, as if, in their frenzied couplings, the sexual exchange had been reversed, and he had absorbed her gift, as she had lost it. Had she fertilized him?

He stopped, looking at his fingers, and said, 'Well, I'll be damned!' And then he wondered – had he been, in fact?

Yelena confirmed her distaste for Sandy as she walked home. His talk she had enjoyed, even his moralizing, since she'd clearly had the better of him there. But his niggardliness of spirit over what really mattered, his dishonesty towards her and himself in the business of their lovemaking – this she scorned in him. True, he hadn't wanted it and she'd had to force him. But in the event he'd taken to it more than willingly. So why hadn't he been happy about it afterwards? And worst of all was his sour gloom afterwards, refusing even to play that favourite music on the piano.

'Sandy, you *are* a misery!' she said out loud as she turned into University Gardens, taking this short cut again back to the river. 'Go on, Sandy, you can play it. Of course you can play it!' She taunted him out loud as she moved down between the long avenue of beech trees.

Halfway through the park, as she started round the great branch which had fallen across the avenue, she heard the sound of clicking feet trotting behind her on the gravel. Turning, she saw the black dog, which had appeared and disappeared so suddenly during the storm. It was the same dog, a snub-nosed pug, a bit larger than Samson and without a collar. The dog stopped, as she stopped, and they considered each other. She wasn't surprised to see it. 'Of course you were real! I knew you were!' She crouched down, held her arm out, twitching her fingers gently. But the dog made no move towards her. 'What's your name, I wonder?' She stood up. The dog sat down, looking up at her easily. 'Thunder? Or Lightning? Either would suit. Do you want to stay here? Or come home with me?' The dog remained on its haunches. But when she turned and walked on it followed her immediately. She looked back at it now and then, confirming its presence. The dog kept a precise distance behind her, stopping when she stopped, moving when she moved on, like a tactful servant, her familiar.

Yes, she thought, with this new companion she was inviolate. She ran towards the Rumovsky Palace, the little dog behind, feeling there was nothing she couldn't do and no one, not even God Himself, who could touch her now or set her back.

12

The electricity had just come on again in the Rumovsky Palace, so that Prince Pyotr could see his wife clearly, the frenzy in her face, the malice, the wild anger in her normally calm and calculating features, watching her, hearing the quick swish of her dress as she stormed round the temporary oil-lamp on the end of the long table in his study at the back of the hall. She bounced up and down in her stride. She seemed to be levitating with anger.

'And you can simply *sit* there!' she shouted at him.

'Indeed. I have no need to race round the table as I talk.'

'The situation is a disaster. It's preposterous – can't you see?'

'It's difficult. Not a disaster, nor preposterous.'

'You must get in touch with the Minister, that fool Sukhomlinov, at once and get him to apprehend Sasha, before he registers at the barracks in Gatchina. He is supposed, after all, to be entertaining the men at the front, not fighting with them.'

'Yes. Sasha would be better employed in that fashion. I will speak to the Minister and see what may be done.'

'And you will speak to the Ambassador, too?'

'No. That's another matter altogether. There's no actual proof at all that Captain Woodrow is the father.'

'Proof enough.' The Princess Sofia, having rounded the end of the table, now bore down on him along the other side of it. 'Who other than Captain Woodrow – who has been paying elaborate court to her all this year?'

'I should first have to speak to Captain Woodrow himself,' the Prince said sharply.

'To what purpose? He will deny it. The doctor believes she is at least three months pregnant. Captain Woodrow must have known this. Were he honourable he would have already taken

Miss Harriet in hand, set a marriage in train. But he hasn't. So obviously he will deny his paternity now.'

'That's pure surmise. From all I know of him it's clear to me that Captain Woodrow is a most honourable man.'

'Who then? Do you think Miss Harriet a woman who would have bestowed her favours lightly, on some casual friend or stranger?'

'No.' He looked up at his wife pointedly. 'No, indeed. She is not a woman of that sort. But nor is the Captain a man of that sort either. There is some other factor, something we don't know about. We – you perhaps – will have to speak to Miss Harriet herself, when she is better. She may tell us.'

'Why should she, if she has not told us already, after three months? She will continue to keep silent, to protect her lover – a misguided loyalty. Meanwhile we cannot let things slide, the scandal. I shall speak to the Ambassador myself, if you will not.'

The Prince lit a *papirosy*, inhaling delicately before he let the smoke spiral up about his tufty hair. He gazed at his wife. What a hypocrite she was. This talk of scandal, when she herself and her behaviour with successive paramours were the subjects of such real scandal. 'You will not speak to Sir George before we have made our own enquiries.'

'You!' she interrupted with venom. 'Always the same. Temporizing, delaying. We must act *now*, about Sasha. And about Miss Harriet. They are both of them our most particular and immediate responsibility. And if you will do nothing about it all, then I will.' She moved away to the door, but then swung back. 'And I shall speak with Yelena, too.'

'On what matter?'

'About Sasha, of course. Do you not ask yourself why he should so suddenly have left?'

'Indeed I have. A fit of patriotism.'

'No.' She looked at him scornfully. 'It undoubtedly had to do with Yelena.'

'How? That's nonsense. They've always been the best and closest of companions.'

'And there's the reason why.'

She left the room. The Prince was mystified.

*

Yelena, on returning to the Palace, had gone straightway to her own and then to Sasha's bedroom, the dog following her upstairs. She thought Sasha might have left a letter or a note for her. And if not this, then she wanted to be among his things, to touch and handle them, as if, in this intimacy with his personal possessions, she might the better come to 'see' him, as she had before when he had gone away. She was determined now not to suppress these strange powers of hers, which she had before seen as a curse, but to promote them in every way she could.

There was no note or letter in her room or in Sasha's. She fingered hungrily instead among his things – finding, resurrecting him here and there about the room, in the smell of his hair from his silver-backed hairbrushes, and his skin – that faint honey-and-oatmeal odour – on a shirt; and another vivid sense of him, more formal and sharply tangy, from the colognes on his dressing table. It pained her, savouring these aromatic essences and memories of a body she could no longer touch.

Just as she was about to leave the room she saw a book on the floor, half hidden by the trailing covers of his bed. She picked it up – a gilt-stamped copy, from a set: Trollope's *Irish Sketches*. Opening it she saw Miss Harriet's signature inside the cover. Then, flicking through the pages, she found the letter. But it was not to her. She recognized Miss Harriet's hurried, flowing handwriting at once, on two sides of a thick card, the letter dated three days previously, the day before her accident.

Dear Sasha,

I can't think now that we were entirely mistaken in our feelings for each other. There must have been something to begin with there which allowed us to experience the happy things we did. Wrong to have done these things, perhaps. But that's another matter. Not wrong in the feelings we brought to the doing of them. That at least we shouldn't deny.

I write this because you said yesterday in the attic how it – 'us' – had all been a 'terrible mistake' and that we had 'no future'. Well, the second point is true, perhaps, but not the first. I can understand your anger now, your feelings about it's all having been a disaster. Indeed, after you rushed out of the attic I felt the same thing.

But on reflection I don't feel this. The essence of 'us' was, and ought to remain, real. It can't be destroyed by the knowledge that it was wrong or by subsequent anger – by regrets, recriminations or by anything else. We came together in love. And the child will be born out of that same feeling. And will live in that same love, be a continuation of it.

So we shouldn't speak of any 'terrible mistake' or, indeed, that we have 'no future'. These are surely hasty words, thoughts – brought on by anger, hurt, despondency. Because there will be a future for 'us', you see, without any mistakes. I'm carrying it with me. It's waiting to be born.

Harriet

Yelena was furious. She had come to rely on the idea that, for Miss Harriet, her relationship with Sasha had all the time been nothing more than a crush, a ridiculous infatuation, a purely sexual passion – and on his part something driven by simple animal instinct, an animal trapped in her clutches, who had reacted in the only way open to it, without his having any other feeling for her. Now, with the evidence of this letter, Yelena was inclined to see their liaison as something truly felt – that they had come to share, through physical passion, a real love; had achieved in this exactly what she herself had wanted with Sasha.

These thoughts came to infuriate her, so that she started to tear the letter up. But the thick card resisted her attempts to destroy it. She looked at her hands, her fingers. Was she somehow losing her strength there? Was that why she was unable to play the piano properly, the onset of some creeping muscular disease?

She decided to burn the letter instead. Finding some matches and a metal bowl on the windowsill, she set the card alight in the middle of the room. But again it resisted destruction, refusing to ignite properly. She found some old newspapers in the log box next to the porcelain stove and added them to the half-charred remains. The whole lot took fire, the flames shooting up so suddenly that they engulfed her hand, when she discovered something else. The flames had no effect on her. She passed her hand through the bright fire intentionally now, quickly at first, then more slowly. Apart from a tingling of the skin, there was no pain at all. She looked at her hand carefully afterwards. There was a sooty discolouration on the underside of her fingers, a slight singeing of the skin, but no sign of any real burns. She tried the other hand then, moving it slowly into the dancing flames.

At that moment her mother came into the room. She saw the fire, and her daughter on her knees before it, with her hand suspended in the yellow flames, the black pug dog next to her.

The Princess Sofia screamed, 'Why, it's Samson!' She stared at the strange scene in horror, where all that she saw had the aspect of some evil rite conducted by her daughter, sorcery which defied the laws of nature, a dead pet dog reborn, like a phoenix from the gathering ashes, her daughter's hand impervious to fire.

Her mother stood in the doorway transfixed as Yelena looked up at her venomously, a piercing gaze.

'Yes, Mama? What is it you want to say?'

The Princess Sofia stopped in her tracks, put a hand to her throat, as if trying to ease some fierce constriction there, craning her neck backwards, grimacing. She had been struck dumb. Her mother turned and fled from the room.

Rain set in the next day, falling over the city in squally intermittent downpours. The Ambassador, in his smaller private office beyond the Chancery on the first floor of the British Embassy, murmured something which neither General Knox, a big incisive man with a Roman nose, nor Sandy quite heard.

'I beg your pardon, sir?' The General, who had curled-up moustaches and his hair parted right in the middle, leant forward, his arm on Sir George's desk for a moment. Sandy sat to the other side.

Sir George cleared his throat. His thin face was haggard with overwork. And though the drains at the Embassy had at last been replaced he still suffered from bouts of some mysterious stomach upset – quite apart from a general lowering of the spirit which he always felt with the damp onset of winter in Petrograd.

'I said "What nonsense", Knox.' He turned a more sympathetic eye on Sandy then. 'Of course it is. And I take your word for it, Captain, that you are not the father of this child.' He rubbed his long fingers together judiciously. 'You are simply the victim of the Princess Sofia's flirtatious discontent. It has long been known. As regards the opposite sex she is a scheming woman. And prone to sheer malicious invention, no doubt, when her schemes are thwarted there. For, indeed, I take your point, Captain, that it was you whom she earlier had designs on – and in your quite rightly failing her there, she is taking her revenge for this. I realized as much when she spoke to me yesterday – that there could be no grounds whatsoever for her accusation.'

Sir George fiddled with his moustache, remaining silent then, as did the General, both of them looking at Sandy expectantly, so that he felt the need to fill the silence firmly. 'No, sir, none whatsoever.'

The Ambassador cleared his throat once more. 'The real problem, you see, Captain,' he went on in a vaguely apologetic tone, 'the further problem, is that the Princess has powerful friends, at Court and among the Ministers, particularly Sukhomlinov, that incompetent War Minister. She will put this fictional scandal about. She will seriously impugn your and our reputation here at the Embassy, and hence that of our country, which is something we can ill afford with the Russians at this juncture. So that General Knox and I are of the opinion that it would be wise for you to leave Petrograd for the moment.'

'Sir?' Sandy, leaning forward suddenly, was perturbed.

'Yes. It was something which the General has had in mind for you in any case, before this other matter cropped up. General? Perhaps you would care to explain.'

'Captain Woodrow, I want you, as an observer, to join the Russian 65th Division, on this second front they've opened in the south, in Galicia, against the Austrians – a foolish decision by their Army Command, when they should be concentrating all their efforts on the Prussian front. None the less –'

'But sir –' Sandy could no longer contain himself. 'It will seem as if I were simply running away, that the Princess Sofia's accusations are true.'

'We will have to disregard all that, Captain.' The General

was brusque. 'There's a war on. And we must – as an ally with the Russians – we must have first-hand and reliable information on what is going on there down in Galicia. There is no question . . .'

'None at all, Captain.' Sir George lent firm support. 'I am badgered every day by the Foreign Office on this matter of the second front in the south. At the moment we can give them only the barest details, and those likely to be exaggerated, or false. You know what the Army Command here is like.'

'Unquestionably a matter of urgency, Captain. And something which, as Sir George says, I'd in mind for you in any case, before all this business with the Princess cropped up. I shall make arrangements with the appropriate authorities at once. You should be able to leave by the end of the week.'

The Ambassador stood up, followed by the General, so that Sandy had to get to his feet, too. The interview was over. He was furious. One way or another, whether they believed him or not, for the sake of the Embassy's reputation they were selling him down the river. He fumed inwardly at the injustice of it all – especially since he knew who the father was. He was suddenly tempted to tell them.

'Sir,' he addressed the Ambassador. 'I wonder if – if it were known who exactly the father was, whether this would put a very different complexion on things.'

Sir George looked at him, surprised. 'If we knew? But how should we? Unless . . . you know?'

'No.' Sandy weakened at the last moment.

'Through your friendship with Miss Harriet, do you mean? You have some inkling, suspicion?'

'No. Not really. There are people here, one might think of . . .' He left the idea hanging in the air.

'Indeed, I know such people myself. Yet I know Miss Boulting even better. It's inconceivable that she would have . . . taken up in this manner with any of them.' Sir George got up and went over to the window; gazed out on the wide river, rising now, in a muddy flow, pock-marked with rain. He turned back to Sandy. 'In any case, thank you, Captain, for your co-operation. As the General says, we must put it all aside now. There's a war on.'

Sandy, returning to his office, was increasingly furious. He had much wanted to join his regiment in France, to fight with them on the Western Front. He was quite prepared to die for his country, but not to wrongfully suffer disgrace for it, by being effectively banished, as a mere observer, to this minor theatre of war, lost in the Carpathians down in Galicia.

'The bitch,' he said out loud. Then he wondered which of the three women he was condemning: the Princess Sofia, for having so monstrously interfered in his life; Miss Harriet, of whom he'd had such high hopes but who had given herself to Sasha – or Yelena, for her lewd seduction and for so generally unnerving him. He wished he'd never set eyes on any of them. 'Bloody women,' he went on, aggressively sorting through his papers – before he found the letter which the clerk had put on his desk in his absence. Opening it he saw the signature at the end – 'Harriet'. He nearly tore it up without reading it. Then he relented.

The English Hospital
30 September 1914

Dear Sandy,

You'll have heard, I imagine, how I walked into a number 11 tram on the Morskaya. Stupid of me! Daydreaming. Still, lucky to be alive and fat little Dr Bazevich (he's always laughing, like roly-poly little men are supposed to do, but don't always) says I should be out and about in a week or so. Meanwhile, I'm getting better. Able to write, at least. And read a little. Light material anyway, which Mrs Bryant brings me from the British Library. Wodehouse – *The Man Upstairs* I'm reading – and an Oppenheim thriller. But not Elinor Glyn! – whom I think I'd rather prefer! Perhaps you could bring me one of those 'shilling shockers' we talked about? – if you're not too tied up with the war effort. (Mrs Bryant is threatening me with wool and knitting needles at any moment. Socks and mittens for the troops at the front. Ugh! How I hate knitting.) Yes, do come and have tea, and eat chocolate mint creams with me. Mrs Bryant has brought me a box of those too!

Yours affectionately,
Harriet

The cheek of it, Sandy thought. This woman, making provocative overtures to him again, with her talk of shilling shockers and mint creams, when before, while going out with him, she had been expressing all that side of her erotic nature with Sasha. He did tear the letter up then, disgusted – angry now by the whole business of her affair with Sasha, its full implications finally striking home.

She had betrayed a close friendship. Or worse, she had led him to believe it was this, and that it might well lead to something even more intimate – by pretending they had so much in common and faking enjoyment of these things. For most of that year she had used him as a convenient consort in public, as a front to hide her secret liaison with Sasha. Her affair with Sasha had been foolish to a degree. She had lost her head, no doubt. But her deceit towards him was monstrous.

Thinking of this betrayal, he thought of Yelena in the same context. Yelena, though equally driven and foolish in the same lascivious ways, as well as in her naïve and intemperate opinions, was entirely open and forthright about it all. Misguided but never two-faced. Besides one might excuse such hotheaded faults in a girl – for she was hardly more than that – and perhaps he'd been over-critical of her in this. Whereas Miss Harriet, a grown woman and Sasha's governess to boot, should have known very much better. So that now he wanted Yelena again, the memory of what they had done together that evening flooding back to him.

Yes, he felt determined on some action with Yelena now. The idea of his impending banishment appalled him. She could save him from that fate. And much more importantly she might, in herself, add immeasurably to his life, and he to hers, in that sort of appropriate and fully reciprocated union with a woman which he longed for. Recognizing his crass stupidity with her that evening, feeling the logic of his suit now and the strength of his emotions for her, he saw every good chance of renewing their relationship and making a lasting thing of it. He had looked a gift horse in the mouth. It all boiled down to that.

But how to see her? They could not meet at the Palace next door, where he would be *persona non grata* now. Nor was she likely to want to come to his apartment again. Still, since they were literally next-door neighbours a meeting could surely be contrived in some other way.

An opportunity for this arose sooner than he expected. Several windows at the top of the Embassy, among them those of the old map room now made over as a War Operations office, gave directly out over the porch of the Rumovsky Palace. And it was while working in this office that afternoon that he saw Yelena emerge from the front door, open an umbrella against the squally rain and, accompanied, he saw to his surprise, by a little black pug dog, walk away down the Quay. Dropping everything, without even stopping to put on his army greatcoat or cap, he rushed downstairs and out onto the Quay, following her at a run.

He saw her umbrella for an instant as she turned the corner that led into Marzove Pole, the great military parade ground that lay behind the Palace. By the time he rounded the corner himself she had extended the distance between them, moving fast, but without giving him any indication which direction she was taking into the centre of the city, for she zigzagged across the huge open square, avoiding the deep puddles, skipping from one island of raised cobbles to another, doing it exaggeratedly, the little dog dancing behind her, as if they were playing an elaborate game of hopscotch together, the pair of them dancing to and fro against the backdrop of the city, the yellow and ochre colours of the Engineering Institute on the far side of the square becoming bright, spotlit in sunburst rays of clouded autumn light that had suddenly emerged from the bruised skies above.

In following her, in keeping her in sight without her seeing him, Sandy was forced to twist and turn himself – in a much less competent manner, splashing about, drenching his boots and trousers, as she led him he knew not where, in a will-o'-the-wisp career over the vast space. Yet he didn't mind. Oblivious of the wet and rain he skipped clumsily after her, certain he was pursuing a happy destiny.

Finally, having tacked this way and that, she made towards the corner of the Mikhailovsky Gardens, where he made an easier pursuit, following her beneath the dripping trees and out the gates at the far side. There she turned onto the Moika canal, arriving some minutes later among the crowds and fashionable shops on the Morskaya. Halfway along, folding her umbrella and dragging the little dog with her, she strode into Watkins's English Bookshop.

Giving her time to establish herself inside he gazed at the latest books from England displayed in the arched windows – new novels by Galsworthy, Bennett, Walpole – with a large pile of H. G. Wells's latest offering in the centre window. In a side window, his eye was caught by a display of second-hand illustrated books, which included a set of *The Yellow Book*, one volume opened at a Beardsley picture of Salome, fierce-faced, frizzy-haired and practically naked, flourishing a tray with the head of John the Baptist on it. The stylized line drawing, emphasizing her long thighs and midriff, her small saucer-like breasts and sinewy arms – the cruel sensuality here – triggered an itch in his body, a nerve of desire. Pulling himself together, he opened the shop door briskly and went in.

The customers inside were largely women from the British community, some of whom he knew and greeted quickly, including Betty Pankhurst, the busybody chief assistant there, with her prominent teeth and froth of white hair, standing behind the counter talking with Mrs Miller, the commercial attaché's wife. But since Yelena was nowhere to be seen he didn't delay, giving himself an air of hurried purpose elsewhere in the shop, this shop which he knew well, smelling of leather and glue and paper of every sort, and of damp clothes now, warmed by a tall stove in the centre.

Wiping the rain from his face and hair he went down the long room. It ran far back, display counters in the middle and high shelves to either side, ladders set against them at intervals, with other shelves partitioning the shop farther down, at right angles, beyond which lay a warren of passages housing the second-hand books. Yelena must be there among these old volumes, sold, given away or thrown out by several generations of British residents in the capital.

Ahead of him a young Red Cross nurse was perched on the upper steps of a ladder, her ankles on display at eye level. Pausing here, since he had to squeeze between the ladder and a portly Russian, he was once more stirred, this time by the view of unexpected parts of a real body, the young woman's legs sheathed in the starched folds of her gently rustling tunic, the neat ankles, six inches of pale flesh linking boots and hem. The intimate vision disturbed him more than Beardsley's illustration in the window. A floodgate of repressed sensuality opened briefly in him, waters from that deep well which Yelena had so successfully tapped a few days before: Yelena, whom he had spurned, but whom he now longed for. Yelena, somewhere in the shop ahead of him. He hurried forward, unable to subdue his excitement.

He found her at the back, in one of the gloomy, deserted passages of the second-hand department, picking through the children's book section, the black pug dog at her heels as she bent down, taking a large quarto volume from one of the lower shelves.

'Hello – just saw you come down here.' He spoke casually, glancing at the books himself as he moved towards her.

'Oh, it's you.' She spoke less easily, inspecting him briefly, dark eyes glistening beneath a sable hat, matching a long sable coat which ran down over her high buttoned brown boots. 'You look like a drowned rat.' Then she opened the book in her hand, fingering through the illustrations, stopping at one, gazing at it intently, as if she were quite alone.

'Yes. *I* need a change of clothes now, and a towel, and a warm fire.' His tone remained easy, confident, friendly.

'So you do . . .' Keeping her head down in the book she acknowledged his reference to her own state two nights before, but only in the most perfunctory way. 'What are you looking for here? *The Water Babies*?'

'No. Never liked it. Wishy-washy, sentimental. More my reverend father's style.' He smiled at her but she wasn't looking at him.

'This might suit you better. *Undine*, with Rackham's wonderful illustrations.' She looked up at him then, a quick and rather sour glance. 'More appropriate, with her being carried away – into the depths of the sea.' She emphasized the last words in a deeper, ironically dismissive tone. Then she showed him the book, opened at a full-page illustration of Undine, the naked water sprite, hair swirling round her breasts and waist in the weed-filled current, falling away into the depths.

'Yes, I love Rackham.' He looked at the picture – seeing, again, the sexual provocation here, hers and Rackham's. But now he decided to relax, to run with these sensuous images that had plagued him ever since he'd stopped outside the bookshop, and to provoke her in the same way, if need be. 'Yes, he's – it's very evocative.'

'I wouldn't have thought you'd have cared for that sort of thing.'

They stared at each other.

'I'm sorry,' he said at last, changing his tone – serious without being over-apologetic. 'I was rather unnerved the other night, after what you told me about Miss Harriet. Over-critical of your opinions. And grudging and ungrateful about what we did later. I'm sorry.'

'You English . . .' She dismissed his efforts here. 'Apologizing now for making love with me. That's as bad as the way you behaved about it all at the time.'

'We all have things we're not good at facing, for one reason or another. We're mortal, flawed. We have souls. We're not like Undine here.' He flourished the book at her. 'You know her story?'

'Not exactly –'

'She was born without a soul. But she had one privilege. She had to marry a mortal and bear him a child, when she could obtain a soul – and with it all the pleasures and pains of the human race.'

'So? What's that got to do with us – and making love?'

'Quite a lot.' He fingered through the book. 'Undine was one of the elemental spirits, of water. And you – of wind. Remember? Your telling me how you lived under the protection of the great wind god, the Lapp god Bieggolmai or some such name – how he'd saved you that night in the thunderstorm.'

'So? All just a myth. I don't really believe in it.' She had moved away, down the bookshelf, looking at other books – backtracking now, seeking to deny any supernatural influences in her life.

He paused, thinking. 'No, I suppose you don't have to believe in it. Because you're living it all. A fairy story yourself – like all these other myths and fairy stories here. Except that it's real with you.'

'Well, what of it?' She turned on him now, angry. 'It's

largely a curse. And nothing to do – with us.' She took out another book then, Caldecott's illustrated *John Gilpin*, and started to finger through the pages.

'If it's such a curse – why not exorcise it? By living in the real human world. You'd have that privilege, like Undine.' She moved away again, taking the book with her, round a corner to another bookshelf. 'Do stop galloping away again all the time, like John Gilpin!' he called after her, following her once more, down shelves filled with books on English topography, travel, estate management, cookery books, when she turned and confronted him.

'What *are* you going on about?'

'John Gilpin – at the moment.'

He laughed and she looked down at the book she was carrying, surprised by it now. 'John Gilpin?'

'Yes, in your hand – Gilpin, trying to celebrate his wedding anniversary, with his "frugal" wife on pleasure bent, when the horse runs away with him.'

'Yes. Yes, I know it. Of course.' Yelena woke from her cold dream, smiling for the first time, opening the book and looking at the illustrations properly. 'Of course I know it – this very edition. Miss Harriet read it to us – Caldecott, he's such a happy illustrator. So English – I can *smell* England when I look at his pictures. We had quite a few of his books.'

'Yes, we did too. This very same illustrated edition. As a child at home in the Cotswolds –'

'Did you? Your "cosy Cotswolds", I remember, with the church and the lilacs and the place where they made beer over the hill.'

'Yes – all that. And Caldecott!'

They looked at the book together, becoming engrossed, commenting on it, quite forgetting their arguments and animosities. Yelena glancing up at him enthusiastically – relenting, forgetting, warming to him, as they poured over this ballad of a London linen draper – his marital harmony, its brief upset on his wedding anniversary in his loving but farcical attempts to celebrate this.

'It's lovely! I'd forgotten how good it is. This picture! – with the bottles exploding at his waist. And look at the rump of him – and the horse! I'll buy it –'

'No, let me get it for you.'

'No –'

They pulled the book to and fro between them, jostling. He saw her smile, the laughter of an unaffected girl playing, of someone no longer touched by genius or plagued by the supernatural.

And it suddenly seemed to him that this book, which they had both loved as children, and had found again together, had given him the key to Yelena; that it was this robust ballad with its sturdy illustrations which would truly cement things between them, which would lead to that balance in love which he wanted with her, an appropriate love and a seemly life which he felt she could be readily turned towards then – a good life, like John Gilpin and his wife, with him.

So that he said, when they'd finally agreed to pay half each, 'Yelena, why not come down to earth with me?'

'How?'

'Marry me.'

Breathless after their struggles, she froze. '*Marry* you?'

'Yes.'

'You must be mad.'

'No. Not at all. I mean it. Absolutely. Come home with me after the war, to where all these good books are.' He gestured round the shelves, the books on English topography, on estate and domestic management next to them, the children's books farther back. 'Look – Mrs Beeton's cookery book here –' He pulled a fat volume out beside him. 'Caldecott and Kate Greenaway and Rackham over there. Dickens and all the other English novelists beyond. And all of them at home. And all my Russian books, too. Pushkin and Gogol and Afanasiev's fairy tales. You'd never be too far from Russia. We could translate things together. I've got lots of dictionaries.'

He rushed on, quickly overwhelmed by thoughts of his Cotswold life, his family home in the old vicarage, which he would inherit. 'Come with me! You'd like the place. The house has latticed shutters on the outside, looks French almost, more than Cotswold. Especially in slanting sunlight. The stone goes yellow. The lilac and the long meadow and the brewery over the hill. And we've got a good piano, too, a Blüthner grand.'

She had looked at him wide-eyed, astonished, throughout

this rendering of English rural and literary delights, this evocation of a distant land which she knew of only through books, but which he was offering her now, in reality, all of it, lock, stock and barrel, on a plate. She was tempted by it – and by Sandy as well once more, as she focused her eyes on him, seeing him again, as she had earlier in their association, as a good and attractive man, an officer and a gentleman, who had in his gift all these happy things, and was offering them to her, there and then, at that very instant.

She hesitated. But then she said, 'No, I couldn't. Couldn't marry, even if I wanted to. And I might with you, yes. But I can't. There's Sasha, you see. You forget.'

'But for God's sake, you can't marry him!' He was roused.

'No. But no one else either, because I have to be with him.'

Taut now, his mind tantalized with both sensuous and domestic images, seeing this prize slipping away from his grasp – and all for the sake of her ridiculous feelings for her brother – he lost control, lunging out, taking her in his arms, putting a hand through the open folds of her coat, gripping her round the waist, pulling her to him, searching out her lips as she struggled, the two of them swaying down between the bookshelves towards the main shop, until finally the little pug dog, worrying at his trousers, bit him sharply on the ankle, when Sandy and the dog both yelped and Yelena broke free, flushed and angry.

'It's no use, you idiot! Forcing things –'

'No more than you did with me, stripping off like that, in my pyjamas.' He was breathless with anger, a sort of crazy joy, agony, frustration.

'Yes, but that's all over.'

'Why? If we did it once, we can do it again just as well – and better.'

'It's too late. I wanted you then. Not now.'

Now she was quite changed. Her voice was harsh and strange, in just the way it had been when she'd demanded that he take her that night in his flat. Eyes blazing, adamant, full of a cold and dismissive enmity, she embarked on a litany of spiteful comment. 'Why should I want to take up with you – here or in England? Old children's books! And dull dictionaries or cookery books. And who wants your terrible English food anyway? Dreadful rice puddings . . . Who wants your cosy Cotswolds, full of stupid farmers, all shut away in some dreary country backwater, miles from anywhere!' She continued her tirade.

He listened to her as she backed away from him, mocking him, denigrating, destroying all the hope he had for her, every happily imagined detail. And he felt again that something truly malignant, a spirit other than her own, had taken possession of her, giving her insight into exactly how and where he could be most hurt, an evil wisdom way beyond her years.

He could bear it no more. Before she could continue, and without either of them realizing where they had moved to in the shop, he slapped her sharply on the cheek.

They had in fact by this time, and during most of Yelena's last furious comments, moved back into the shop proper. So, for the last minute, they'd had a fascinated audience. Sandy turned. Betty Pankhurst, to the side of projecting shelves, was looking at him astonished. On the other side two women he knew, the Reverend Orr's wife and her friend Mrs Crowther, wife to the secretary of the English Club, were peering round the edge, wide-eyed.

Yelena took it all in her stride. Rubbing her cheek she glared back at them. 'What do you all want? What's none of your business, as usual. You boring, nosy-parker English. Nothing better to do than interfere and gossip and spy on other people's lives.'

Swinging her head round she addressed these last words directly to Sandy, before calling the dog to heel, stepping arrogantly down the long aisle and out of the shop.

But Sandy was not to be put out either. Attack was the best form of defence here, he thought, suddenly remembering Miss Harriet's letter.

'Ah, there you are, Miss Pankhurst. I was looking for some shilling shockers. Or something by Elinor Glyn. Even better. *Three Weeks* would suit well. I'm sure you have copies. Or do you keep them under the counter?'

'Captain Woodrow!' She began to remonstrate with him but, thinking better of it, said no more.

13

Miss Harriet's letter to Sandy had been written in a surge of joy the previous evening. Dr Bazevich, who had examined her half an hour before, had been astonished to find that the child she carried was now certainly alive, and had told her so, putting away his stethoscope.

'No!' Miss Harriet was incredulous.

'Yes. I was sure, when I first examined you, that it was not so, that you had lost it. But there is no doubt it is alive. After your accident, something of a miracle,' he added, his round red face creased into a smile.

Now, the following afternoon, sitting up against her pillows, listening to the rain, Harriet delved into her capacious bag, took out her hairbrush and mirror and tried to tame her unruly hair. She ran a finger over her cheek, and smiled, looking at herself in the glass. She had, she thought, something of that velvety skin now, the glowing colour, that happy aura of pregnancy which she had expected and missed before. Yes, by some miracle, the child was alive inside her. She put her hand down, moving it over her stomach, then left it there, letting it lie gently below her navel.

Lulled by the monotonous sound of rain on the window she fell asleep. She had a dream of swimming, a watery dream, in some big river at home in Ireland – the Blackwater it must have been, for there was a tree-topped cliff, a high dark bluff above her which she remembered from times when she had fished the river with her father, though he was not with her then. She was swimming naked, alone. But she was conscious of something following behind her in her wake. Turning, she was horrified to see it was a wolf, its grey muzzle snouting up out of the water, swimming strongly, pursuing, gaining on her.

She woke with a start, sweating, terrified. Sandy was

standing in the doorway, watching her. He was carrying some books and a bunch of hothouse red roses.

'Thank goodness you've come.' Her whole face lightened in a smile. 'I just had the most awful dream.'

'I'm sorry' He came forward rather awkwardly, army cap under his arm, both hands full.

'Of wolves, an awful beast, pursuing me.'

'Dear me. Rather a Russian dream.'

'Do dreams mean anything?'

'I don't know. An unhappy dream like that –'

'But I'm *not* unhappy! Just the opposite – especially to see you, Sandy! Those roses, they're beautiful, thank you so much.' She took them from him, smelling them hungrily. 'And the scent. Oh, you are kind. And the books. What have you brought? Some "shilling shockers"?' She looked up at him mischievously – she was sure he wouldn't have done. But then, handing her the books, she saw the first title. It was *Three Weeks* by Elinor Glyn.

'Sandy!' she whooped, waving the book in the air.

'Well, you said you wanted her.'

'But as a joke.'

'We talked of it, remember?' he interrupted her enthusiastically. 'The nonsense of such books –'

They would have rushed on with this risqué subject if they had not suddenly realized how close to the bone they were, of their own lives, their earlier association and her affair with Sasha. They looked at each other, serious now, in the silence. They had been getting on too well together. They had surprised themselves with this larky chitter-chatter, forgetting their secret knowledge, the things each withheld from the other – Harriet her pregnancy, Sandy's knowing of her affair with Sasha. But now, in Sandy's wan and disappointed expression, Harriet was aware that Sandy knew all about her predicament, and then saw how only Yelena could have told him – Yelena, jealous and spiteful once more.

'So,' she said evenly. 'You know all about me, don't you? About Sasha and me and the child. Yelena must have told you.'

'Yes.' He nodded. There was another awkward silence. The rain had stopped. People, evening visitors, walked to and fro along the corridor outside. Someone, a woman, passed by sobbing.

'I'm sorry. I should have told you myself. Anyway, it's all over with him now. And not because he's gone – you know that too?'

'Yes.'

'But because I've come out of it myself. After the accident, I suddenly came to my senses.'

'The accident, yes . . .' He couldn't avoid the touch of doubt in his voice. He ran a hand quickly over the small balding patch at the back of his head, wondering if, in his equivocal tone, she'd also sensed that he knew she'd tried to kill herself. She had.

'So she told you that as well, did she, the little wretch, that I'd meant to kill myself? Never mind,' she ran on. 'That's all done with, too. It's you I'm thinking of now. I owe you an apology. I was underhand with you. I was deceitful with you – and behaved very foolishly with Sasha. I'm sorry.' She flapped her long hands on the sheet, then grasped the hem, wringing it viciously in her fingers.

'We all behave stupidly, at times –'

'Not that stupidly . . .' She spoke quietly, looking away, so that he saw her fine profile, the straight nose, the long thin neck, the vague freckles on her pale skin, the tousled reddish wavy hair falling to her shoulders, touched with gold in the lamplight. A face the Pre-Raphaelite painters would have taken to, he thought, Rossetti or Burne-Jones. And he saw then, in her delicate colouring, in these fine bones that formed the sharp elegance of her features, the sensuous lines and length of her body, exactly why he'd been so quickly attracted to her.

Her sudden fit of bitter self-recrimination gone, she turned back to him. There was an aura of calm and confident repose about her now. And Sandy, though no longer smitten by her, was moved by her honesty and sanity. He saw how, in her reasoned reflections on her behaviour, she had quite regained control of herself. She had behaved foolishly. But she saw this, admitted it, where Yelena, given to the same unsuitable passions, never would. Yelena, driven in her perverse morality, her sexual rapaciousness, seeing no fault in this, either indulging it with those she didn't love, or with her brother. Oh yes, he'd been seduced by Yelena, taken by her in that way, to the heights. But it was perfectly clear now – they had little else in common.

About Miss Harriet on the other hand he had already changed his mind. Though he no longer desired her, it was obvious they had a natural affinity: a shared mother tongue, same sort of a class and rural background; a love of outdoor pursuits, as well as music, books; an equal sensitivity – to each other's moods, unspoken thoughts and feelings, a ready picking up of nuances, so that they could sense hidden changes and intents in advance, so skipping *longueurs*, dull explanations and avoiding *faux pas* in their responses. They had a happy shorthand in this. But especially they had a comparable wit. They liked each other's jokes, could appreciate the other's verbal sallies – run with them, piling one conceit upon another, trading idiocies about shilling shockers. To share such things was of the essence in any lasting love.

There was no doubt. They were two of a kind.

'It's all such damned bad luck,' he said at last, with vehemence, looking at her forcefully. It was all he could think to say in the end. It seemed to cover everything he felt then – the disaster with Yelena in the bookshop, the loss of his passion for Harriet, the future they might have had together, her 'accident', her present predicament, his departure as a non-combatant for an unimportant war front.

'Yes.' She returned his gaze candidly. 'Especially you and me.'

'Yes,' he admitted, showing his surprise at this latest intuition.

'That was probably the stupidest thing I did, ruining our chances together. I hope you never have the sort of illness I had, these obsessive, preposterous feelings for someone that I had for Sasha. It ruins everything.' She turned away from him again.

'Yes,' Sandy agreed again – but hiding his astonishment now at this revelation of her equally strong feelings for him, which he had not suspected before.

Perhaps he'd been wrong in his talk with Yelena, he thought, as he walked down the crowded corridors into the Russian section of the hospital, through wards of bandaged and crippled soldiers – perhaps every sort of love, the ordinary as much as the perverse, was, in the end, preposterous, in its misdirections, its gathering confusions and misunderstandings, its sudden, quite illogical turnabouts of feeling, its jealousy and pain, its high hopes but more abject falls and painful failures. Whatever good feelings, whatever passion, sense or reason you brought to loving – it was always going to end up bloody well out of kilter.

Putting on his cap and greatcoat outside the hospital, he saw the military ambulances, just arrived from the Warsaw station – the bloodied, the unconscious, the heavily bandaged being taken out on stretchers. He watched the grisly parade as it went past him. Yet it somehow pleased him. He wished he could have gone to the war and fought himself then, and so rid himself of these harrowing, intractable emotions – on the field of battle where, with only life or death to consider, there could be no such complications.

Prince Pyotr wanted to speak to Yelena alone, so in order to avoid any possible interference or interruption from the presently almost demented Princess Sofia, he suggested Yelena come with him next morning to the Natural History Museum halfway down Tamozhenny Pereulok. The Prince had business to conduct with Count Nikolai Nasónov, the curator, and wanted to see as well a new exhibit, a display of native Russian animals, not shown individually but seen all together, grouped in their natural surroundings.

Now, having run from their carriage in the chill rain through the entrance of the large grey building, they walked through the first big room, past glass display cases of smaller animals – rodents of one sort or another – before moving into rooms containing larger, more exotic beasts. Finally, they stopped in front of the new exhibit.

It was a very large rectangular glass display case, where the animals, in their winter colouring – a great elk, polar bear, a wolf, hares, arctic foxes, a pair of capercaillie birds – were all seen in a wide panoramic view, hunting, eating or hiding, set on a rising snowy waste of land, with nooks and crevices for the smaller animals, with silver birch rising through the snow, bare outcrops of lichened rock here and there and birds of prey, an Imperial eagle, a bustard and peregrine falcon, hovering in the chill blue sky above, each detail of the landscape rendered exactly in perspective, a perfect reproduction of those frozen northlands of Russia which Yelena had known so well, so that in looking at it for a minute she had the feeling of leaving the warm and drowsy hall and being drawn right inside the display, into those northlands which she had loved and which she realized now she had missed.

'It's wonderful,' she said quietly.

'Yes.'

'Ladoga – it's just like the land there north of the lake – the animals, all of them, so real.'

'Yes. Your inheritance, which you've always been so scathing about!' He smiled at her easily, so that she suddenly responded with enthusiasm.

'You know, just now, I don't feel that any more. I'd love to go back. It's years since – I've forgotten when – forgotten all about it. I didn't like it then . . .'

'No. I remember.'

'But now I feel quite differently about it.' She turned back to the display. 'You see! There, that Imperial eagle – Grandfather took me hunting with a pair of them once. There were poachers. The birds attacked them: the poachers had killed one of the gamekeepers . . .' Her voice trailed off. Gazing steadily into the glass, so that her eyes finally became unfocused, she let herself be drawn back in time and space, to that magic north world which she had revelled in as a child, but had fled in such pain and horror.

'Yes, the poachers . . .' The Prince remembered, too – the barbarity of it all. He shuddered at the thought. 'But, yes,' he went on. 'We will go back. Your grandfather always asks for you. I've told you. He still wants you as another Catherine the Great up there. But the war will change things, for him, for all of us. We should go before it's too late, perhaps . . .'

They wandered away from the display into a farther hall, where the Prince took up his real theme. 'You see, it's Sasha I wanted to talk to you about, to tell you about. He's disappeared again.'

'Again? How –'

'Yes, we heard last night. You remember, I spoke to

Souhomlinov, the War Minister. Well, he made arrangements with the recruiting people in Gatchina barracks, to stop Sasha enlisting. They sent some officer down, who knew what Sasha looked like from your concerts, so that when Sasha got to the recruiting desk, enlisting under an assumed name, they stopped him. But while taking him to the station – they were going to escort him back home – he gave them the slip, jumped out of the motor and ran off across the big park there. That was twenty-four hours ago. Well, of course he hasn't come home.' He looked at her closely. 'Yelena, what is the matter with him? You're closer to him than anyone. Why did he run away like this? What is going on?'

'I . . .' She hesitated. She hated lying to her father, but saw no alternative. 'I don't know.'

She was not convincing and her father didn't believe her. 'Have you had a row with him or something?'

'No,' she lied.

'But he must have told you something more, about why he was going to leave so suddenly.'

'Yes, and I told you – that he felt he had to do something more positive for the war effort than play the violin for the soldiers at the front. And if he's run away again, well, I suppose he's hoping to enlist somewhere else, at another barracks.'

'But it still doesn't make sense.' The Prince shook his head. They had stopped by a case containing a rather moth-eaten African lion. 'His going off like that. Never had the remotest interest in joining the army. And knew he didn't have to enlist anyway, that he was exempt. So I don't really believe in this fit of patriotism of his.' They moved on, stopping again in front of a huge Russian brown bear, up on its hind legs, towering above them, front paws rampant, as if about to pounce on them. 'And you don't believe in it either,' her father said, looking at her pointedly. 'Why don't you tell me, Linochka? You can trust me. It won't go beyond me, I promise. Tell me. Though I think I know.'

'Know what?'

'Miss Harriet's going to have a baby.'

'Yes, she told me, when I first went to the hospital.'

'But I think you knew that before, because it's Sasha, isn't it?

He's the father. And he must have told you. You've always been so close. He must have done. And that's why he's run away.'

Yelena nodded. She could no longer maintain the deceit. 'Yes,' she said resignedly. 'Yes, he is the father – and that's why he felt he had to get away. I did all I could to stop him, told him there was no need, because Miss Harriet didn't want him to marry her or anything.'

'But if that's the case, why did he feel he had to get away?'

Yelena wasn't going to tell her father the other reason – the fact that he was running away from her as well – so she simply shrugged her shoulders. 'I don't know. Except that he felt he'd had enough of everything, here in Petrograd.'

'Well, at least we know now. Though I wonder how your mother will take it when she discovers this, as she's bound to. She's certain Captain Woodrow is the father, made trouble already about it, with Sir George next door.'

'But the baby, she's not likely to have it now, is she, after the accident. So surely it'll be all right – Sasha could come back?'

'Oh yes, she's very likely to have it. We heard yesterday from Dr Bazevich. Against all the odds the child is still alive, when he thought it was dead and they'd have to operate –'

'Alive? Are they sure?' Yelena was put out.

'Yes, by some miracle.'

And then she remembered – of course – how, on first seeing Miss Harriet, apparently dead or dying on the hospital bed, she had knelt down, put a hand on her stomach, and had prayed that she should live. But Miss Harriet had been alive all the time. It was the child in her womb that her touch had resurrected.

They arrived at the curator's office. The Prince left, and Yelena wandered off on her own, along corridors, round corners, moving through rooms that became progressively more empty as she went farther back into the museum. She came across a few students, in these distant recesses, singly or in groups, coming out of the chill rain for the warmth, reading textbooks alone or whispering together on benches.

And then, in one of the smaller rooms, walking quickly towards a big partition doubling on one side as a display case for a collection of dazzlingly coloured butterflies, and moving round the edge of it, she surprised a pair of lovers, caught in an embrace. When they broke free she was astonished to see that the tall young man, with an expressive mobile face and chestnut-brown eyes, was Miki – Miki Ostrovsky, her friend from the spring, clown and mimic, met earlier that year at Ciniselli's Circus; Miki, whom she thought was still away, on tour with the circus, or that he'd been conscripted.

'Miki!' She greeted him. She had to, though it was clearly an embarrassing situation for all of them. She looked at the woman. She was a striking figure, older and almost as tall as Miki, with long raven hair, a thin but very determined face, a face which – in its drawn skin, its lines of taut anxiety – had suffered, Yelena thought, and was clearly unhappy then – the lips puckered, her expression fraught, a silk cravat round her neck which, in settling it, revealed for a moment a long scar, running up from the side of her throat, confirming Yelena's feelings of pain inflicted here.

Miki was as she remembered him, nervous, abstracted, but more than usually ill at ease now. He seemed hardly to recognize her, or didn't want to do so. 'Miki, you remember? It's me, Yelena!'

'Of course, Yelena. And this is . . .' He stopped, hesitant again.

'It's all right, I'm not going to tell anyone!'

'It's just that . . .' He looked at the woman uncertainly.

'It's all right! You don't have to explain. Are you back at Ciniselli's, already? I thought you'd have gone to the war.'

'No. I – I've been exempted. And I'm not sure about the circus. I've not heard.'

'Perhaps you'll come and see me, both of you, and we'll have lunch at Dominique's and play billiards there again.'

'Yes. Yes, I'll – we'll – do that.'

They parted awkwardly. And when she turned back, thinking to wave at them, they had disappeared, like one of Miki's conjuring tricks. Of course, it must have been the girl, Yelena thought – being caught with her like that. Someone else's girl? Or a married woman even. For she was clearly older than Miki.

Some minutes later, wandering on, Yelena was startled by a sudden violent commotion in the hall ahead of her. The sound of glass shattering, of running feet, of shouted commands and exclamations, the echoing blast of a gunshot. And then another.

She ran to the entrance of the hall and peered round the doorway. The scene was confused. In front of her, in the middle of the room, crouching behind a huge elephant, she saw the raven-haired woman and two young men – students, whom she'd seen together on a bench earlier – all of them with their heads down beneath the big wooden display stand, the woman with a revolver, keeping a group of armed policemen at bay, plain-clothes police obviously, at the far end of the gallery, peering round the other doorway at that moment, heads emerging suddenly, but as quickly disappearing when the girl aimed the revolver and fired another shot.

Yelena's father, with the curator, was suddenly behind her then. 'Linochka! Don't stand there. Come away.' He managed to get her out of the firing line. As he did so, the students, deciding to retreat, rushed past them through the doorway. One, two, then the woman. Yelena had somehow expected to see Miki there as well. But he wasn't. She peered round the door again. There was no one else in the hall, except the police at the far doorway, standing there for an instant before charging down towards and past them, pursuing the three students.

Arriving at the entrance hall a few minutes later they found a mêlée of people – museum staff, with plain-clothes and uniformed police attempting to handcuff the two struggling young men, a burly plain-clothes man sitting astride the girl's back, pummelling her, then trying to turn her round, while she resisted fiercely.

The Prince, incensed at this brutal treatment, shouted at the man. 'Get off her. She's a woman, a student. Get up and deal with her appropriately.'

The man looked up at him briefly. 'You mind your own business. The brute was armed.'

'She's not now. Get up or I shall see you suspended from your duties.'

The man took no notice, until the curator intervened. 'Prince Pyotr Mikhailovich Rumovsky, Minister at the Imperial Duma, is speaking to you. I advise you to do as he says.'

The man grudgingly acceded, pulling the girl roughly to her feet. She stood there, defiantly, her mouth bleeding, a flow of blood from one corner streaming down over the livid scar exposed at her throat. She was formidable-looking, more so in defeat, the black hair wild about her long face, the dark eyes blazing, thin fingers at her mouth trying to staunch the flow of blood that was dripping down about her smart, grey serge coat and tall button boots, onto the marble floor.

Yelena was suddenly filled with an intense sympathy and admiration for this woman. She went to her, offering her a handkerchief. The woman refused until, moving closer to her, Yelena said softly, 'Take it. Don't worry about Miki. I won't say that you were with him, or that I know him. I promise.' The woman took the handkerchief with a tiny gesture of assent, of thanks.

A senior police officer approached her father. 'Your Excellency, I appreciate your concern. But these "students" are in fact Bolshevik terrorists. We've been following them. They came in here singly, at intervals, for a meeting of some sort. They are armed and dangerous Bolsheviks. Look, we found this on one of them, and half a dozen copies on another. Quite apart from anything else, they've been distributing seditious literature.' He held up a small newspaper, the title *Northern Pravda* blazoned across the top.

'None the less, you must treat them correctly, whoever they are.'

The officer said nothing, merely bowed stiffly. He turned to one of his lieutenants. 'That's all of them, then?'

'Yes, sir. As far as we know. We're making a search of the museum now. One of the officers says he thinks there was a fourth man, that they came to meet in here. But he can't be sure. He didn't get a proper view. We're rounding up everyone in the museum now in any case, and will be questioning them.'

The police led the three prisoners away. Some minutes later all the other visitors in the museum were brought into the hall. Yelena held her breath, waiting to see Miki among them. But he wasn't. He had somehow escaped once more.

But escaped from what, she wondered? Not, by some clever trick, from a sealed box in front of an admiring circus audience, but from the clutches of the secret police, the dreaded Okhrana. Miki, clown and conjurer, must be involved in some political sleight of hand as well – hidden business, secrets with these revolutionaries. He must be a Bolshevik himself.

This idea immediately appealed to Yelena, as the raven-haired woman had done. Bolshevism. It was just what Russia needed, what she needed then – the 'new' – just as she had years before when she'd left the barbaric castle on Lake Ladoga, and that spring after Miki had told her of his enthusiasm for the revolution in Russian art. But this time, by seeing Miki with this woman in the museum, he had differently defined it for her, as political not artistic change: Miki, somehow involved in bringing this, as she saw it now, much more essential transformation about.

But there was still Sasha to think of.

If Yelena was surprised by Miki's likely revolutionary activities, she was equally bemused by Sasha's further disappearance, now completely into the blue. He hadn't taken much money with him – he didn't have any real money – nor clothes. If he failed to enlist at some other barracks, how would he survive? Why hadn't he come home? What on earth was he up to? Where was he? She had no idea, had no 'sight' of him now. But she still had to find him. And for some reason she couldn't quite identify then, she had to find Miki too.

Yelena confirmed all these feelings the following morning, in the little music salon at the Palace, where she read news of the fracas in the museum in *Novoye Vremya*. Of the three people who had been apprehended, one of them – the young woman – was Vera Komichevskya, a young actress and singer in Russian operetta and farce, at the Arcade theatre and the Palace. The other two younger men were history students at the University. They were part of an underground Bolshevik 'cell', the report said, a terrorist group supported and financed by Bolshevik exiles, wanted men living in Germany and elsewhere abroad, who in turn were financed by the German government, intent on fomenting revolution as well as creating chaos in the capital, to undermine the war effort and the morale of the citizens by sabotage, bomb outrages, assassinations and the like, which was just what this group had met to plan in the museum.

There was no doubt of all this, the report went on. Copies of *Northern Pravda*, the Bolsheviks' newspaper, edited by Lenin, the Bolsheviks' exiled leader, printed in Germany and smuggled into the country, had been found on two of the students, while the leader of the group, Vera Komichevskya, scarred at the throat, had obviously been involved in some earlier terrorist outrage which had backfired on her. 'In these times of great national peril,' a leading article on another page commented, 'this sort of activity is treason of the worst sort. All three must suffer the full penalty which the law allows . . .'

Yelena put down the paper. There was no mention of any other student being associated with this group, either at the museum or discovered later. No mention of Mikhail Ostrovsky. Yet Miki must be involved with it, as he certainly was with this Vera Komichevskya, involved as her lover obviously, so that he must surely know of her terrorist activities.

It surprised her, this. Miki, with his other worldly airs, his apparent wistful innocence, seemed an unlikely person to be brandishing revolvers or throwing plum-pudding bombs about the place. And yet, seen in another light – with his skill as a mimic, in disguising himself, his ability to take on so many other character roles, his general audacity of temperament – she supposed it was possible. And she knew from all her talk with him, at the Countess Shouvalov's ball and later that spring, how he despised the 'booboisie', the corrupt and doomed bourgeoisie and nobility, at Court and in government, all who ran and dominated the country so cruelly and stupidly. But would he attack these people with revolvers and bombs? She was intrigued. What was Miki? Clown or revolutionary? Or both? Where was he? She must find him, talk to him, help him if need be.

Yes, now she knew why she'd felt the vague need to find him the previous day, why she felt impelled to do so now. Quite apart from bringing her this vision of a new order of things in Russia, she was attracted by this equally fresh view of him as man of illegal action. She was attracted by the aura of risk and bravery, of danger and lawlessness, which he had for her now. These were attributes which she possessed herself. And she wanted to share them with Miki now, who could well be her equal in these qualities, as Sasha had failed to be.

Miki was not just an artist, she realized then. And nor was she now, having lost her gift. They could both involve themselves in something more important than art, which was to help create a new order in Russia, an end to the obscene privileges and hypocritical morality of the 'booboisie', the ignorance, superstition and squalor of the poor – an end to everything that stemmed from the cruel and corrupt rule of the Tsar, of these Romanovs whom she despised, though she was part of the same family, a cousin to the Tsar himself.

Then, too, there was the woman, Miki's woman, Vera Komichevskya, an actress and singer – an artist, as she had been. If Vera Komichevskya could forsake her art and risk her life in the cause of a greater good for the Russian people rather than just entertaining them, then so could she.

And besides, with the memory of the strikingly beautiful woman still fresh in her mind, Yelena wondered why Vera Komichevskya had taken up with Miki. She herself had not before found him attractive in that way. Now she did – acknowledging in this another desire, which was to emulate this woman, perhaps match her charm and revolutionary prowess for Miki, replace her, in short, as Miki's companion in arms – in every way.

But where was Miki? Where could she even start to look for him? Though there had been no mention of him in the paper, this meant nothing. The Okhrana could well by now have learnt of his identity as part of this Bolshevik 'cell' by having forced it out of the others, and be searching for him everywhere. So he would not have returned to Ciniselli's circus. Nor could she make any enquiries about him at the Palace or Arcade theatres. The Okhrana would be there as well, inside and out, waiting, listening.

But there was a new theatre she had heard about. 'The Drunken Boat', set on an old barge apparently, moored way up river, beyond the Peter the Great bridge, outside the city's limits – a cabaret theatre like the ones in Moscow, 'The Wandering Dog' and 'The Bat', which Miki had appeared in and frequented with his Bohemian friends – the 'futurist' poet Mayakovsky, and the other singers and actors with their 'wickedly satiric' songs and verses. She might look for him or hear something of him at 'The Drunken Boat'.

In any case she must *do* something now. She was determined on action, of any sort, reckless or sensible – it didn't matter. She had nothing to lose, nothing else in her life then. Sasha had been the key to her life. But he was gone. And without him she could no longer go to the front and entertain the troops, could no longer even play the piano properly.

So, while she looked for Sasha, she must find another life: a new cause which she felt was waiting for her, somewhere out in the rain-drenched city. The river below her window was rising every hour, coming to flood. She must rise with it, fill herself with all that she felt unexpressed.

She turned back from the torrential view and went to the piano. She picked out the beginning of Beethoven's Fifth Symphony.

The little black pug dog, whom she called Thunder, looked up at her as she played, his eyes bright and eager, as if he too was encouraging her in some prospect of rash adventure.

14

'Hi, Princess!'

Yelena and the little pug dog spun round in surprise.

Just as she'd left the Palace that same morning a large green automobile had drawn up behind her, a brand-new four-seater of a kind she'd never seen before, open at the sides, with a high black hood, shiny brass fittings, huge headlights and strange white-sided tyres, the rain spattering on the gleaming paintwork of the gracefully curved mudguards and long bonnet.

A man in a high-collared leather coat leant out. She could see little of his face, hidden by goggles, a floppy check cap and flowing red scarf, which he loosened now, taking out a white handkerchief, blowing his nose like a trumpet, then squeezing the klaxon, so that an even louder squawk filled the air, like a goose being murdered, startling the pedestrians on the pavement. The man laughed uproariously, then got out of the motor. Yelena gazed questioningly at this rather manic figure – just like Toad in *The Wind in the Willows*, she thought.

'So, you've forgotten me?'

'No –'

'Yes, you have. It's me, John William Michael Quince, of Charlottesville, Virginia.'

He took off the goggles and cap, loosened his scarf, and she saw the crinkly fair hair, cherubic face, bright blue eyes and pudgy chin – a chin once covered in butter from the *blini* he'd scoffed during the *Maslenitsa* fair when they'd first met. And she knew him then.

'Johnny!' she shouted.

'Of course!' He smiled hugely, the cherub face creased from tiny ear to ear. 'Johnny Quince!' He put the bulbous cap back on the top of his unruly hair, setting it impudently there like some strange, wide-beaked bird on a flourishing nest.

'Johnny! Where have you been?' She came towards him, lifting her umbrella.

'I'm back, that's all that matters. Back to win the war for you darned people. Come round – hop in.' He gestured to the seat on the far side. 'And I'll take you for a spin in my new Caddy.' He burped the klaxon loudly again.

'New what? Do stop doing that –'

'My new Cadillac. Had it shipped over here months ago. But it only arrived yesterday, by way of Vladivostok and the Trans-Siberian, can you imagine. Get in, you and the little dog, and I'll take you –'

'No, I can walk. I want to exercise the dog, and I'm only going up to the Nevsky.'

'Goddamnit, Princess! – stop arguing, as usual. I'm going that way, too. Or near enough. To the Astoria, our new offices there. Get in. And tell me all the news, of you and Sasha and Miki and Miss Boulting – and my beloved Russia!' He shook his head in wonderment at this idea. 'Yes, beloved Mother Russia,' he added with heavy emphasis, opening his arms wide, lifting them, gesturing over the glistening quay, the flooding river, the gold spire of the Peter and Paul fortress on the far bank shrouded in low grey cloud, raising his arms on high, blessing the whole rain-sodden city.

Beloved Mother Russia indeed, Yelena thought. What a rogue. Yet there he was, right in front of her: not Miki whom she'd gone out to start looking for, but Johnny, a sudden harbinger of some altogether different kind of hope, in this gloomy weather, a happy animal who had swooped up on her, taking her by surprise, with his blue eyes and snorting klaxon. He went round the gleaming motor and opened the door for her. The invitation was irresistible. Lifting her skirts, she followed, climbing into the deep leather seat next to him, the dog jumping in after her, settling at her feet.

He didn't take her towards the Nevsky. 'Not this way!' she shouted, as they turned left, about to cross over the river on the Troitzky bridge.

'No, we'll go the other way first, won't take a moment, out onto the islands. I want to let her have her head, on the long straight.'

He'd jammed the cap down over his curls, and the goggles

over his eyes, and was flexing his arms against the wheel now, adjusting his backside on the leather seat, like a jockey before a race. Or like Toad, she thought anxiously, Toad setting off on that first blissfully indulgent, untutored, calamitous journey. What had she let herself in for?

Gathering speed, rushing over the muddy, foam-flecked river onto the Kammeno Prospekt, they drove like fury along the dead-straight avenue. The rain bit into Yelena's cheeks from the open side. They lurched from the smooth paving onto the cobbles in the middle, swerving past a tram in front of them on the wrong side, Johnny's scarf flying out behind, while she gripped the door fiercely, her other hand jammed against the brass edging on top of the dashboard.

'Too fast!' she yelled. 'You're not driving a train now. We'll have an accident!'

'Thirty miles per hour – thirty-five – I'd like to try it to its limit. It's the new model, with an eight-cylinder engine – the earlier ones had only four.'

'I thought you wanted to hear my news!' she yelled back at him.

'I do – I do! But I want to see if I can get her to do fifty . . .'

'You're mad – slow down.'

But she could do nothing with him. No possibility of controlling the man. In just the same mood as he'd been that spring, after they'd dined at Cubat's, listening to the gypsy orchestra, when he'd taken Sasha and her out to test the locomotive afterwards. Gripped now by the same mechanical frenzy. But he was no Toad, she soon realized. He could drive, was expert, alert to every movement among the oncoming trams and motors and droshkies. Deftly guiding the huge vehicle, overtaking, speeding in and out of the traffic with easy grace. So that she resigned herself to the pleasure of it all, of riding and rising, up and down, the deep springs taking the bumps out of the road. Skimming along in a cloud of spray, the bright green bonnet surging forward, a thrilling hum of power from beneath it, thrusting into the watery gloom.

A mile farther on, at the end of the Prospekt, they stopped by the Kammeno Ostrov bridge over the Little Neva. He switched off the engine. She wiped the rain from her eyes, thinking they'd reached their destination and could talk now. But almost immediately, pulling a lever beneath the wheel, Johnny started the motor again. Yelena was mystified.

'How did it start? You have to turn the handle in the front, don't you?'

'Not with this one, you don't. Starts by electricity. There's an electric battery. It's the latest thing – only the Caddy has it. And electric lights, too!' He moved another switch on the board behind the wheel. 'There, see?' She couldn't see, but she took his word for it. 'All the latest developments in automobile design. The Caddy has them. And the best. We Americans, we're good at these things. We'll win the war for you!' he added boisterously. 'Hey, Princess, let me show you – it's not far – show you what we're doing over here, for the war effort. Our railroad company . . . Matty – you remember Matty? – and me and half a dozen others. We're all over here now. But since America is neutral it's something of a secret. So keep it to yourself. It's really quite something we're organizing here at the Astoria and out of town. Just a little way. But not far in this Caddy.' He looked at her, wide-eyed. He was just as she remembered him that night driving in the sleigh to the Nicholas station, childlike, a schoolboy, incredibly eager, impatient, about to play with his trains.

'Well . . .' she said doubtfully.

'Princess, it's really something. I'd like to show you.'

She nodded, gazing back at him, taken by his spell, the rocket-like exuberance of the man.

'Come on then!' He turned the car round, opened the throttle, the motor skidding again as he fought to control it briefly, twirling the wheel, fighting with it, before they drove all the way back the Kammeno Ostrov Prospekt, at even greater speeds. 'Forty, forty-five, fifty!' he shouted out, before they slackened speed approaching the Troitzky bridge again, crossing over onto Admiralty Quay.

'How are you going to win the war for us?' Yelena asked, in the relative quiet as they drove down the Quay. 'Not by selling huge autos like this to us?'

'No. But even bigger steam locomotives, with proper freight and ammunition wagons. To move troops, guns and ammo, out to the front. Right now the whole damn railroad network here is all clogged up, practically useless. Can't handle the increased war traffic. And the traffic yards are all shot to hell, can't get trains in or out. Chaos, so your poor bloody Russian soldiers have hardly anything to fight with. Why, half the men at the front don't have rifles. Or even boots, some of them, can you imagine? So the Baron – Nicky von Meck – he's called us in to try and sort things out for the Transport and Army Ministries.' He turned onto the Nevsky Prospekt, overtaking a tram on the wrong side again. 'No, Princess, not automobiles. But *know-how*. American get-up-and-go know-how. That's what it's all about.'

At the end of the Nevsky they speeded up again – down Izmailovsky Prospekt, past Warsaw station, driving out of the city. They took the main road south to Krasnoye Selo and Gatchina, following the Petrograd–Warsaw railway to their left. The line appeared and disappeared as the road veered towards and then away from it.

A troop train came into view. Opening the throttle, Johnny drew level with it – waving and hooting the klaxon at the soldiers leaning out of the windows, packed into every compartment, before overtaking it. 'See?' he shouted. 'Easy. Eight cylinders. Get you past anything.'

They sped on, through the town of Krasnoye Selo and twenty minutes later arrived at Gatchina, driving past the ornate gingerbread villas, through the parkland of this summer resort of the nobility, which was also an army town, headquarters of the Northern Command, with a large barracks. Driving past the yellow ochre station buildings, they left the town by the main road, following a high wall to their right.

'This is it!' Johnny was impatient. 'Gatchina Junction. And that's the marshalling yard, beyond that wall, where everything gets fouled up. You'll see.'

They drove up to an arched gateway in the high wall, manned by two soldiers, where Johnny showed an army pass – and Yelena was met by an astonishing sight beyond. Her whole vision was suddenly filled by trains, locomotives of all sorts. Passenger carriages, freight wagons, horse-box cars, flatbed cars, heavy artillery transporters. All of them moving to and fro, seemingly to no purpose. Shunting, pushing, pulling. Great spurts of dark smoke and white geysers of steam thundering up into the sky, with the piercing shrieks of whistles, the vicious clang of buffers. The sounds seen first and heard half a second later across the vast expanse. Wafts of acrid smoke, held in suspension beneath the moist grey sky, swirled in the air above her head, tickling her throat. It seemed to her as if all the trains in Russia had been gathered together in this one vast yard, set on a score of tracks spread right across the view. Yelena was mystified by it all.

'So – what happens?' she asked.

'What shouldn't happen.' Johnny sneezed suddenly, getting out his huge white handkerchief again, bellowing into it. 'I'll show you. See that big signal box there, in the middle of the yard? That's where it's all *supposed* to happen. Come on.'

They walked across a dozen rails, pushing between wagons, before reaching the big signal box, raised on brick with a wooden superstructure high above them. On climbing the steps and opening the door at the top, they were met with a blast of warm, tobacco-filled air. Ahead was a long space, windows all round, a shimmering metal stove at one end, with signal levers, scores of them, in rows to either side.

The cabin, giving out over the whole vast space, was filled with people, uniformed railway staff, others in shirtsleeves manipulating the signal levers, men shouting instructions down field telephones. Another man with binoculars, gazing intently up to the top of the yard, giving orders to a colleague immediately behind him. Bells rang. Telegraph machinery whirred and clattered. The cabin reeked of sweat and cheap tobacco. A sense of barely controlled pandemonium everywhere. Several men were clustered by an open window, shouting furiously, in both Russian and English, down at some others standing by a wagon. Johnny moved away to join them.

'What's up, Matty?' He spoke to a thin-faced man in shirtsleeves, gaunt, like an undertaker. Yelena recognized him – Johnny's assistant, met that morning at the Butterweek fair.

Matty turned, glancing at Yelena disapprovingly for an instant before answering Johnny in exasperation. 'The usual foul-up. That ammunition train up there, on the westbound line. Should have been all ammunition. But they've hitched two flat cars to the end of it, with two damned great howitzers on them, so the tank loco can't get the wagons up the gradient. Have to unhitch.'

'Or get another locomotive,' Johnny said immediately. 'Two could do it. If they have to unhitch and move those two flat cars it'll take all day.'

'Take all day anyway, Johnny. Sure, put another loco on it. But where to find one? With steam up?'

'We'll find one. Here, give me that telephone. Is Vitaly up there, at his post, like I told him?'

'Yes. Well, he *was* leastways –'

Johnny was already on the field telephone, turning the handle, then yelling into it. 'Hi, Vitaly?' he shouted. 'No, goddamn it – Vitaly – *da*, Vitaly, my chief engineer. Where the hell is he then? No, don't tell me in Russian – it's Vitaly I want. Should be there. Speaks *English* . . . *Da*, *da*, . . .' He dropped the handset in frustration, turning back to Yelena. 'Princess, come here a minute, would you? This Russian guy I've got can't speak English – tell him, will you? Tell him I want Chief Engineer Vitaly Simonov, quickly. Or get this guy to tell you where he is – urgently. Okay?'

Yelena took the telephone, translating the instructions, listening, before turning to Johnny. 'The man says engineer Simonov has already gone to get another locomotive . . . to help push the ammunition train that's stopped up there –'

'Great, Princess, that's just what I wanted to know. Vitaly's got his head screwed on at least.' He got out his big hanky again and mopped his brow. 'Thanks, Princess.' He smiled at her with real thanks in his eyes. 'Say, could you translate a bit for Matty and me? With this crisis on right now. I'd appreciate it.'

So she worked with them, helping the two men in their various commands, interpreting for them on the field telephones, for the next hour or so. She soon came to enjoy it, being at this centre of power, in the middle of this vast web of rail lines, with Johnny as the spider, she as his aide-de-camp.

She watched Johnny, expert, quick, decisive, Johnny, finding chaos and setting it all to rights. Johnny, in his true element now, lord of all he surveyed from this high perch above the yard. Johnny, once more the gleeful truant playing with this huge train set, sorting out the wagons and locomotives, sending them hither and thither, putting huge armoured flat cars through their paces, propelling them, by sheer force of will it sometimes seemed, to all the right places.

'Can you take this message, Princess, translate it to the signal box up at the main junction: the troop train from Petrograd, due at midday – hold it in a siding. We have a more urgent ammunition train to make up and send down the westbound line in advance of it. Got it? Great!' She noted the message, then went to the telephone.

Becoming so involved in the work, she forgot about Sasha and about Miki, too. Miki, whom she'd set out to find that morning. So that when she thought about them again a few hours later – when they stopped, and Johnny thanked her, and even Matty unbent a bit and acknowledged her help, and Johnny said, 'Hey, if we're quick, we could get back for lunch at Dominique's, and you can tell me all your news then' – she realized she'd come across quite another cause and creed in this traffic yard, with Johnny and his railways, with Johnny himself.

Over *zakuski*, meat *piroshki* and pre-war champagne at Dominique's on the Nevsky, Yelena told Johnny most of what had happened, with her and Sasha and with Miss Harriet, in the six months since they'd last met. Though about Miki she said very little, other than that she'd not seen him, assuming he was back in Moscow – and she barely mentioned Sandy since Johnny had only met him once.

After she'd finished, Johnny, who had listened without interruption, leant back, savouring the bubbles breaking in his glass. 'Well, I'll be darned. What a catalogue.' He raised the glass, then hesitated. 'Nothing really to celebrate, I suppose. Your losing your gift for the piano – why, that's the worst thing. That's terrible. How could it happen so suddenly?'

'It just went. My fingers, I don't –'

He reached across quickly, taking her hand in his, examining it carefully, then the other one. 'I can't see anything . . .' The intimacy raced up her arm, through her body, running up her spine, ending up as a prickling sensation round the back of her neck. 'Except these blisters.'

'That was a candle – I burnt myself. But that was after I found I couldn't play.'

'Nasty burns.'

'Oh no, didn't hurt at all,' she told him truthfully, though she wasn't going to tell him why it hadn't hurt, was not going to embark with him on anything about her strange gifts, her powers. 'Anyway, it doesn't make much difference, because I can't really play properly in any case without Sasha.'

'Hell, even if he's disappeared again at Gatchina like you say, he'll get in touch – once he *has* joined up, somewhere else. And, besides, if you give me all the details, I could probably locate him for you. We have a whole network of contacts, including two Americans, down at the railheads, on the front.'

'Could you? Help find him?'

'Why, sure I could.'

She looked at him carefully. He didn't know about her real feelings for Sasha, how, and in what ways, she loved and wanted him. And she wouldn't tell him, just as she hadn't told him everything about Miss Harriet. She was starting something quite fresh with Johnny.

'Tell you what.' Johnny leant forward suddenly. 'If you're not playing the piano now, why not help me out, do your part for the war effort? You could really help me, in the office at the Astoria, in the yards. Translating, interpreting. Would you? I'd really appreciate that,' he said earnestly, taking her hand briefly again.

She was silent for a moment. Then she lifted her glass to him. 'Well, now we *do* have something to celebrate – I'd love to!'

Their glasses met and clinked over the table and they nodded at each other, both smiling, without saying anything, without adding any more words which might break the spell of what seemed to both of them then to be the start of a happy conspiracy. Only the little pug dog seemed unhappy, fidgeting at Yelena's feet, looking up at Johnny unamiably.

The Ambassador turned to General Knox in his private office at the Embassy. 'I can hardly believe it of the Captain, even though Mackie confirms your account of it all. His wife was in the bookshop at the time. Saw everything apparently.'

'Indeed. As did the Reverend Orr's wife. And Miss Pankhurst.'

'All over town by now.'

'I fear so. He practically assaulted the Princess Yelena, having earlier tried to "come to grips" with her, shall we say, behind one of the bookshelves. Our young Captain would appear to be a man of ungovernable appetites in that direction: first the governess, then her charge. Who next, one may well ask?'

'Not a question we need ask at all, General. There won't be a next time.' Sir George got up irritably, rubbing his hip joint. His arthritis had come on again, in the foully damp weather. He scratched his ear, perplexed. 'If he'd been at the war, well, one might understand it – that he was suffering from nerves.'

'Simply a matter of unbridled appetite, sir. And not yet satisfied by all accounts. He subsequently demanded of Miss Pankhurst that she furnish him with a copy of *Three Weeks* – by Elinor Glyn,' he added gravely. 'And then had the further impertinence to suggest that she kept such books under the counter.'

Sir George was now further perplexed. 'Did he, indeed? *Three Weeks* – I shouldn't have thought it of him. His father is a man of the cloth – and Captain Woodrow himself is very much the scholar, you know.'

'Indeed I do know, sir. But then in matters of this sort, with women, it's been my experience – I don't mean mine personally – with young chaps, that once they get the bit firmly between the teeth, in this area, well, there's no stopping them. Capable of every excess –'

'Yes, Knox, I think we need not dwell on it. No doubt you'll be sending him off to the Galician front at the earliest opportunity.'

'The very earliest, sir.'

The two men gazed out silently at the rain-sodden view. '*Three Weeks*,' Sir George murmured at last. 'Never read it myself.'

'Nor I, sir. Wouldn't have it in the house.'

'Very popular, though, wasn't it?'

'Oh, very. Very popular – among, shall we say, the less fastidious sort of woman.'

'Yes . . .'

Silent again they considered this literary matter, before Sir

George turned to the General. 'Do you suppose that Miss Pankhurst actually does keep such books under the counter?'

'Oh, there I couldn't help you I'm afraid, sir.' General Knox moved uneasily on his feet.

The Ambassador pulled himself together. 'Come, Knox, to business – we have this telegram to send to the FO. There's a war on.'

The Philadelphia and Reading Railroad Company had taken over three interconnecting bedrooms on the top floor of the Astoria, and were halfway through turning these fussy, over-decorated quarters into a suite of offices. When Johnny got back there later that afternoon he found Matty in the room they shared at the end of the suite, hidden behind a drawing board, squeezed between a huge Louis XVI-style bed and an equally vast, mirrored *armoire*, both dripping with gilt excrescences, encrusted with ormolu.

Johnny stood by his desk at the window looking out at the rainy view: the bronze dome of St Isaac's Cathedral, the great square which surrounded it, with the even greater open spaces of Alexander Gardens and Admiralty Square beyond. The room was overheated and overstuffed. The city outside, cold and drear, was becoming swamped. He felt a dislike for everything Russian then: the mud, the squalor, the feckless incompetence and arrogant stupidity of those in power – the whole rag-bag Russian soul with its endless, purposeless talk, its glittering dreams and almost total inability to make anything useful out of them.

He thought of this until he thought of Yelena. She made it all different. With her there was a different Russian soul, slumbering now, which could be set on fire; a warmth, a blaze then which would propel anything, herself and anyone, to heights unknown. He sensed the secret energy, the power of the woman – admired there what he so openly possessed himself – so that he wanted to release all this in Yelena and to share in it. He leant forward pensively, stroking the boiler of a model locomotive on the windowsill, a 'Mother Hubbard', 4–4–2 Atlantic, painted in the silver and blue livery of the line with the company's name set in white along the side of the coal tender.

'So, what are you up to with your Princess this time?' Matty spoke, invisible from behind the drawing board.

'She's going to work for us – that's what I'm up to. Translation. Interpreter.'

'We have two already.'

'And not much damn good. She's absolutely fluent in English.'

'Interpreter . . . And what else, Johnny?' The voice was resigned. Johnny ran a hand through his corrugated straw hair, moving to a map on the wall of the Russian rail network to the south and west of the capital.

'What else?' he said at last. 'Her company, to start with. I like her. She's special.'

'Special trouble.'

'Sure, I see that too. That's what makes her special. But I can handle that.' He gazed at the map. 'She's lost that twin brother of hers, Sasha.' He told Matty what had happened. 'She wants him back. I said we'd help. She thinks he's somewhere down at one of the fronts.'

'Needle in a haystack, then. Besides, why should she want him back, if he's managed to enlist somewhere else and wants to fight?'

'She wants him back because she's nuts about him.'

'You mean nuts about him – in *that* way?'

'Yes. That way.'

'She told you that?'

'No. But I know it.'

'Well, there's one *really* good reason for not getting mixed up with her.'

'Yes. But an obvious reason.' Johnny turned away from the map and went back to the window. 'If you want something – especially with women – don't do the obvious. Or show your hand. I never do either. That's what's got me where I am.'

'That's what's got you nowhere with women, at least. It's not worth it, Johnny.' Matty came out from behind his drawing board, wire garters drawing up his sleeves, a clutch of pencils in one hand, scratching a sallow cheek with the other. 'She'll screw you up. She'll use you, Johnny, one way or the other. Or just to get her brother back. And you won't get him back anyway, with two or three million Russian troops on the various fronts. Where would you begin to look?'

'I don't know. But I don't want a fling with her, Matty. This is the real thing. I want her seriously. Marry her –'

Matty was exasperated. 'You're nuts, Johnny.'

'Well, maybe one reason why it'd work. Two of a kind.'

'You hardly know her. You're kidding yourself –'

'No. I feel it. You feel it when it's the real thing.'

'Horseshit, Johnny.'

'No. Matty, why don't you look at it reasonably? I'm nearly thirty. You found the right woman from the start with Clara – and the two kids back in Philly. You were lucky. I just want the same thing. But it's taking me longer. Okay, you're right. The Princess is a real handful. She's got this thing for her brother – and a lot else that's crazy. All fouled up. Lost him, lost her gift for the piano, burns her fingers in candles. But there's a wonderful woman behind all that. I can free her.'

'Prince Charming and the Sleeping Beauty. Come on, Johnny.' Matty's tone was quite flat, without irony.

Johnny turned to him quickly. 'Yes!' he almost shouted. 'And why not, goddamn it? "Trust in the vision, true to the end".'

'Trust in the Weights and Measures, Johnny. True to the Schedules.'

Yelena, having decided to involve herself with Johnny, saw no reason in this to abandon her search for Miki. She wasn't hiding anything from Johnny, she argued, since she could never have told him of her meeting with Miki in the museum, given the clearly dangerous implications of his having been there with his terrorist girlfriend.

So, leaving the dog behind, she took the steam tramway that evening, via the Nevsky and the Schüsselburg Prospekt, a journey in the rainy gloom, the windows of the tram all steamed up, which brought her out of the city, along the river bank, past the Imperial Porcelain Factory, through the village of Murzinka and into the country beyond. Somewhere out here, she had learnt from friends at the Conservatoire, 'The Drunken Boat' was moored, the cabaret-theatre set on an old barge, well beyond the city limits and the eyes or interference of the authorities.

The barge, she saw when she got there, was literally drunken, straining on the flooding waters, swaying to and fro against the wooden quay. She went on board, up a rickety gang-plank, contributing 50 kopeks to a long-haired youth holding out a collection box, and then went down into the smoky theatre in the covered hold. She had to watch her step on the pitching floor, already slippery with *kvaas* and tea spilled from the rows of long tables, with benches that made up the small auditorium.

She took a seat on a bench at the back. Students, still exempt from conscription, filled all the benches, with some older people, bearded anarchists, Yelena thought – wild eyed ne'er-do-wells, a few workers from the nearby woollen mills, and simple tramps come in out of the cold for a glass of tea. All of them were cat-calling, whistling, applauding the act that had just finished.

The air reeked of cheap tobacco, sweat, unwashed feet. There was ribald pandemonium everywhere as the curtains closed across the small stage, the oil footlights and swinging lanterns with their flickering orange glow casting fantastic shapes and shadows over the heads of the babbling, bibulous spectators. They must have got hold of some illegally distilled spirits, Yelena thought.

The curtains opened again. A singer came on playing an accordion. He wasn't dressed in the Russian fashion, wearing a short, check jacket, collarless striped shirt, a thin cravat, baggy fawn trousers, and he didn't sing in Russian either but in French, heavily accented, so that Yelena couldn't follow the song, except to gather that it was about exile from some rural part of France to the slums of Paris. The tails of a dark moustache curled down to either side of his mouth. A powerfully compact body, something of a gypsy about him. Yelena watched his fingers deftly skimming over the keys of the accordion. She liked the music. It was new to her, full of running trills and darting arpeggios, lightning-quick changes of tempo.

He sang another song, and then a third, in different tempos, waltz, polka, then a *paso doble* – at which point, in the middle of the song, an astonishing woman jumped from the wings onto the stage, with such sudden *éclat* and a stamping of steel-tipped shoes that the audience visibly jumped in their seats: a tall woman, garishly made up, with exaggerated rouge, heavily pencilled eyebrows and an atrocious wig, a splay of mop-like black hair; a real harridan, a woman of the streets, in a flimsy, tattered silk dress, which she lifted up over her knee, displaying the top of a stocking and a red garter, as she started a provocative *paso doble* about the accordionist, a foot-stammering Spanish clatter over the boards, like a mad thing, silently clicking her fingers, trying to tempt the man away from his music, pursuing him round the stage with all sorts of indecent nods and winks and gestures, yet without saying anything, not a word, not a single 'Olé!' It was all mimed.

And it was this so skilled and wordless imitation of a Spanish hussy which gave Yelena the clue. The mime. Of course. She had seen such splendid mime before, seen the gangly legs, the exaggerated puckering of the lips, the ever-mobile expression. Behind the dreadful wig and squalid dress was Miki.

At the end there was wild applause, fierce cat-calls and whistling, a crashing of mugs and glasses on the tables. Nobody heard the crack of the aft mooring rope as it broke from its bollard. And no one was aware for half a minute of the movement of the barge as, caught in the flood, it swung out into the river, gathering pace in the flow, swinging right round, stern first now, so that the forward rope, with the whole weight of the boat on it, snapped as well. Now the barge was left free, moving out into the middle of the dark, swirling waters, no longer attached, setting off, a drunken boat with a drunken crew, stern first, without power or direction – on an unknown voyage down the great river.

'Quick! We've come adrift. Get out and swim for your lives! We're all going to drown.'

This contradictory advice, shouted from the stairway, came from the long-haired young man who had collected Yelena's money. He was drunk and had panicked. The audience beneath him in the hold, mostly in the same tipsy state, and aware now of the movement of the barge, quickly lost their heads as well, jumping up and making a tumbling, chaotic rush for the stairway that led up to the aft deck.

Yelena, one of the last in, was among the first to get out onto the little rear deck, which now faced downstream, the barge, caught in the surging flow, having swung round. The night was dark and wild. Wind and rain thrashed in her face. Apart from the lights of Thornton's huge woollen mill way downstream to the left, she could see nothing, not even the water a few feet away. But she could sense it, smell and hear it all about her: a stale, sulphurous breath of risen mud, a quietly threatening presence, as they rode the top of this undulating flood, all hidden muscle, this voracious animal, waiting to strike, playing with them meanwhile – searching, licking round the hull, shouldering it, then suddenly smacking the timbers viciously, slapping the sides and the blunt stern, as if, opening its great mouth, it was about to swallow them all whole.

They were bound to capsize, Yelena thought – or crash into the bank, or the pier of a bridge lower down, or even be swept out to sea: to drown one way or another. But turning, she saw a more immediate peril – the increasing panic on the barge. The small aft deck was crowded now, shadowy figures pushing and shouting everywhere, with others doing the same, trying to force their way up the stairway, seeking a place in the open. If she stayed where she was she'd be shoved into the raging torrent.

She clambered up onto the wooden roof covering the hold, and moved along it on all fours towards the bow end. There, dropping down onto the small bow deck, where another stairway led up from the back of the stage, she found herself among the performers, huddled at the top of the companionway, their faces just visible in the light of a swinging lantern.

A voice was shouting in French. '*Non! – saut pas. Pas nagez! Ça sera pire. Restez au bord surtout.*' It was the accordionist, the gypsy-faced man, addressing Miki, the other players standing next to him.

'Miki!' She came forward, yelling above the wind. He turned. He still had the terrible wig on, with an army greatcoat over his flimsy dress now, his stockinged feet showing beneath the hem, so that he looked an even more bizarre figure than he had on the stage a few minutes before.

'Who?'

'Me! Yelena.'

'You, indeed.' He was quite cool. 'We always seem to meet in the most awkward circumstances.'

'Yes. You got yourself out of the last corner, though. Can you conjure us out of this one?'

'No.' She saw his faint smile, acknowledging his escape from the museum. 'No, not this corner. Hands of God here. And since I've no belief in that quarter, God knows!' He laughed. 'There are sandbanks farther down, below Thornton's Mill. And several islands. If we're lucky we may run aground on one of them. Meanwhile we should all go below and lie down, else we'll be just pitched overboard if we hit anything.'

They peered over the roof to the other deck, now filled with people swarming about in terrified confusion. So that the barge, so much heavier at that end, began to swing round in the current, Yelena and the others facing into the wind now, looking ahead. But still they could see nothing.

'Come on!'

They clambered down the stairway to the stage where the footlights still glowed, and then stretched themselves out in the hold, buttressing themselves as best they could, against the wooden ribs of the hull or against upturned tables, joined by the audience, prevailed upon to do the same – all of them lying flat out, awaiting their fate, petrified, in silence, some few with prayers and moaned invocations, until the Frenchman, to take their minds off things, started to sing The Internationale in rousing tones.

Soon he was joined by others, singing in Russian, then by the rest of the company, who hummed the tune, until finally they were all gathered together in one loud, triumphant chorus.

First there was a violent rending sound, a cracking and splintering of wood up by the bows. The barge reared up like a charger. There was a long grating, grinding moan, a vicious shuddering, a more fearful cracking of timbers, like cannons going off, inside and out. Finally the barge slewed to a halt, bodies rolling into one another, spinning towards the bow before the boat tipped over to one side and everyone rolled in another direction, into the side of the hull, shrieking and shouting.

There was silence, before Miki and Yelena, lying next to each other, released themselves from each other's arms, unaware how they had come to hold onto each other like this, clinging for dear life.

By morning the weather had changed completely. The weeks of scouring wind, the damp gales and flooding autumn rain had gone. The day was windless. The sun climbed in a shallow arc, into a pale blue sky without a cloud. A day of absolute stillness after the storms, with a touch of ice in it, a chill from the north, presaging winter.

The barge, careering down a narrowing channel between a group of islands, and crashing through the trunks and tops of submerged willow and birch trees, had come to an angular halt on the higher ground of one of the islands, among half a dozen others, near the right bank of the wide river. So that the passengers, emerging at first light, saw themselves saved, but marooned, without any access to the mainland.

But Yelena, with Miki, the Frenchman and some of the others, climbing through the trees to the highest ground of the island, saw how it was still linked, at the end, to a larger spur of land, itself inundated but next the shore, where a ruined mill stood just above the risen waters, surrounded by treetops. Beyond they saw a great flood plain to the north over the land proper, a vast expanse of blue water, shimmering delicately in the chill blue morning light. Smoke emerged in an unwavering vertical plume from inside the four walls of the roofless mill.

'I know where we are.' Miki, grasping his army greatcoat about him in the chill air, shivered, turning to Yelena. 'That's one of the camps – army deserters, down-and-outs, runaways of one sort or another.'

'How do you know?'

'I've been in the camp. That's why. Come on, we'll get the others. Take all the tea and food and drink we have on the barge and join them.'

The bedraggled passengers, some forty of them, with the Frenchman carrying his precious accordion strapped to his back, trooped down to the end of the island and then across the lip of land, now almost submerged in the rush of water coming down the channel, so that the more able-bodied men, forming a perilous chain, up to their thighs in water, had to help the others across. Finally, moving along a ridge, on a sodden path with the tops of birch trees level with their feet to either side, they reached the higher ground where the big granite, three-storey mill stood, with broken, gaping windows and a large arched doorway in front of them. Picking their way over a tide wrack of muddy sticks and other debris, they went inside.

The large ground-floor space, with piles of broken masonry, lath and plaster scattered about, but with a ceiling high above largely intact, sheltered a score of people – in an even more haggard and dishevelled state than the passengers: men and a few women of every age, every sort of shape and size and decrepit condition, bizarrely dressed in an equal variety of dirty, tatty clothes, from ruined military and even court uniforms to sackcloth. Grouped round a fire, dunes of ash spilling away all round it, and only sluggishly alight, they sipped tea, tore at hunks of black bread, on makeshift stools, on their haunches, and some still asleep by it, their toes keeping warm stuck into the mountains of ash. Beyond, by the wall, some goats were tethered and a number of mongrel dogs rambled about, enjoying the morning, barking then, as the two groups confronted each other coldly, silently, until a tall bearded man in long felt boots and a cloak got up and came to Miki, greeting him.

'Comrade! It's good to see you.'

'Nikolai Vasilievich – how are you?'

'We are well. Though you people . . .' He looked over Miki's shoulder. 'You are not so well.'

'No. But we are lucky to be here at all.' Miki explained what had happened.

'Come then, join us.' The bearded man put a hand on Miki's shoulder.

'We brought tea and a little food – and some vodka – from the barge.'

'No, indeed! You will be our guests. We have tea and food – and vodka, too – for such special occasions.'

He led Miki forward and the shipwrecked passengers followed, joining the others round the fire, grateful for the warmth, and soon for the tea, brewed up in a rickety samovar, and then the vodka, several bottles of it, which were passed from hand to hand round the assembly. The fire was stoked up with dry wood, old lath and rafters from the floors above. So that soon there was a blaze, the heat spreading into the wide spaces, with a bright sun streaming through the ruined windows – an air of mounting conviviality among all the dishevelled people – tramps and misfits, students and runaway soldiers, petty criminals, revolutionaries of one sort or another who had taken refuge here, ten miles upstream from the capital, fleeing home, prison or barracks, finding sanctuary in this mill, now set in the middle of a vast expanse of water, this flood which had taken the barge, like an ark with its motley collection of artists and their supporters, to safety among these others of their revolutionary kind.

As the drink began to go to their heads, one of the men picked up a balalaika and started to sing a folk song in a cracked voice. '"Ah, Nastasya, my heart is chilled without love. Come, open the door!"'

Others joined in the song. Soon there was ragged dancing round the blazing fire, people linking hands, arms, a stuttering of feet over the old flagstones. The Frenchman joined in on his accordion. Soon, with the sun barely up, there was raucous merriment.

Yelena was enchanted by it all. She would have danced herself, but Miki advised caution. 'That sable-lined *shuba* you're wearing, your general air – be careful. Among these people – they may think you're an *agent provocateur*. You'd better say you stole it!' he told her lightly. 'And better get back to Petrograd, too. Your parents, they'll be worried, out looking for you. The police . . .'

'Yes. And searching for you, too. After the museum . . .' They looked at each other carefully, standing well apart from the others, sipping tea laced with vodka, savouring the drink and the warm, wood-smoky air. 'But don't worry. I told nobody. Nobody knows I saw you in the museum. With her,' she added.

'No.' He gulped his tea, his mobile features creasing deeply as he swallowed the hot mixture. 'No, I wasn't certain.'

'You can trust me, absolutely. Something of a surprise,

though.' She smiled easily. 'I thought you were just a – revolutionary artist.'

'Yes. But as well as that, I'm with these people.' He nodded towards the circle of dancing, singing, gesticulating figures round the fire. 'Them, and all the other downtrodden masses in Russia. You know what I feel about those in power in this country.'

'Yes. I didn't know you actively supported them, though.'

'One must. There has to be change. Everybody knows that – known it for years.'

'Me, too. I'm on the same side.'

'Yes . . .' Again the careful glance. 'Yes, I was pretty sure you wouldn't tell anyone. But the others, caught at the museum – a different matter. Torture. One of them could well have told the Okhrana about me. So I've been on the move ever since. In the city. And here, where I have friends.'

He was awkward, unsettled in his speech. They moved away from the fire, standing by one of the gaping windows looking out over the flood plain, where the sun, rising in the sky, had turned the vast sheet of water into a still blue mirror, studded, here and there, with seagulls and the tops of silver birch.

In the distance a small rowing boat, with half a dozen people in it, its bow cutting a long V in the water, oars making regular pools in the mirror, was coming towards them.

'It's the old boat they have here, since the floods came,' Miki said. 'Some come, some leave. We'll take it back to the higher ground over there. They can take us all back in relays.'

'Yes.' She turned to Miki. 'Yes, you don't really trust me. Why should you . . .'

'There's a strict policy to speak to no one, not even one's best friends, if they're not involved.'

'Of course.'

'And yet . . .' He hesitated, blinking in the strong light. 'I need friends like you just now.' He looked at her intently. 'You could help.'

'Yes!' Yelena turned to him with enthusiasm. 'That's why I wanted to find you, after the museum. Why I came up to the barge last night. I thought I could help. I want to.'

He nodded, believing her. 'I'll explain then. And you can tell me all your news as well.'

She nodded. They lifted their glasses and toasted each other – the start of another happy conspiracy, Yelena thought, as the dazzling silver light, reflecting off the water, freckled their faces at the window, the songs and music flooding the warm space behind them.

Afterwards, going down to the other side of the mill by the flood plain, they watched as the rowing boat arrived, running up over the submerged earth onto the bank. The passengers clambered past the oarsman, a youth in a dirty cap and greatcoat who, shipping his oars, still had his back to them. The boat secured, he stood up and turned. Yelena saw his face – the dark curly hair, the deep-set, slightly hooded eyes, the firm, straight nose, the cleft in the chin.

'Sasha!' she yelled. 'Sasha – it's you!'

She ran past the new arrivals and waded into the shallow water, almost falling into the boat in her eagerness to embrace him. But he didn't help her. He didn't smile or return the greeting. He stood there glowering at her, resisting all her happy advances, ignoring her.

15

Something wonderful had happened to the city. The first snow came the following afternoon, quite suddenly, out of a chill pale sky, small stinging flakes at first in a bitter wind, and then, with the dusk, falling from leaden clouds, thickly and slowly, all night – and all next day, in swirling gauze curtains, and for most of the second night.

But early next morning it stopped as quickly as it had begun. The sun came out, the air cleared and it froze hard, leaving a city transformed: a new metropolis, cleansed and pristine, sugared everywhere with curling meringues and crystal drifts, the gold spires and coloured cupolas set off against a bright blue sky, a world of dazzling white.

The temperature stayed well below zero. Winter was confirmed. The inhabitants revelled in this second seasonal magic of the city – as they had six months before with the equally sudden arrival of spring – taking cheer and every sort of new life in the tingling air, throwing off their coughs and sneezes, the damp *cafard* of autumn. The *izvosthchiks* exchanged their droshkies for sleighs, bundling themselves up in grotesquely padded, full-skirted coats. The municipality prepared to lay tracks across the freezing river. Log-burning braziers had been lit at street corners, making little circles of warmth all down the main thoroughfares.

The *izvosthchik* taking Yelena up the Nevsky Prospekt was jubilant in his new role as sleigh master, cracking his whip so that they skimmed along in the keen air, the runners hammering on the impacted snow, racing past the white-dusted dome and porticos of Kazan Cathedral, and over the Fontanka canal bridge where the hot-chestnut sellers had congregated.

But Yelena was not part of this joyous renewal. She cursed God once more for having so tantalizingly brought Sasha back into her orbit, only to withdraw him again. She was furious, just as she had been when Sasha had left her at Warsaw station, and sought now, with renewed determination, to take revenge in any way she could – to outdo, to set herself above this malign fate which had dispossessed her for a second time.

So she sat huddled morosely in the back of the sleigh, cradling the black pug dog, Thunder, in her arms, astrakhan hat pulled down over her brow, fur collar up about her nose, only her eyes showing, darkly angry, not seeing anything, oblivious to the glittering world around her. Even now, three days later, she could think of little but the cruelty and indignity of her meeting with Sasha. He had barely recognized her as she'd waded out towards him. Then he had left her behind, refusing to take her with him, rowing straight back across the flood plain with a group of other passengers from the mill.

His words, their shouted, increasingly angry conversation, still rang in her ears.

'No, I don't want to see you –'

'But Sasha, I've not been following you. It's quite by chance I'm here. The boat, the barge – it ran aground on the island last night, Miki will tell you.'

'Just leave me alone.'

'But you can come back. Miss Harriet *isn't* dead. You can't be so stupid! What have I done? What's she done? What are you running away for? What *from*?'

'I'm running away from nothing. Because there's nothing for me, with either of you. I want my own life now.'

The other passengers had started to clamber into the boat then, pushing past her, Sasha barring the way to her, sitting down, taking up the oars, pulling the boat out onto the shallow water, when she'd shouted after him then, in tears of frustration and anger. 'Don't! Don't go! Please. Or let me know at least where I can write to you.'

But Sasha had said nothing, rowing away across the chilly blue flood plain. Miki had stayed with her, consoling her. Later they made arrangements to meet again. Now, Miki having given her the address of the clockmaker's shop up by Nicholas station, and sworn her to secrecy, she was on her way to meet him.

When the sleigh drew up at the end of the lane she saw the

painted timber sign of a clock halfway down, one of several signs hanging in front of these artisans' two-storey houses that ran along both sides of this alley off Ligavsky Pereulok in one of the shabbier parts of the Moskovskaya quarter near the railway station.

The white drifts, which had blown up along both sides of the narrow lane, were too deep for the sleigh to pass through. Yelena had to struggle along a narrow corridor of trampled snow on foot, until she came to a small window with clocks and mechanical toys in it. She opened the door.

A bell sounded as she went in – a sudden sharp tinkle above her which made her jump – followed by silence, apart from the irregular ticking of clocks of every sort and size which stood on shelves all about her. The small interior, bright where she stood at the doorway from the reflected snowy light but gloomy further in, was empty. Empty of human form at least. Beyond her, by the counter, she was startled to see a brown bear, up on its hind legs, gazing at her. When it spoke in a deep growl and slowly lifted its front paws, holding up a visiting-card tray, she nearly jumped out of her skin.

'Good morning, young lady! The password, please.'

The little dog barked furiously and Yelena started back in astonishment. Then she turned in further alarm as a second voice spoke from the other end of the counter, a shrill, girl's voice. It came from a small ballerina in a gauze skirt and crimson bodice, perched on a bronze stand who, with a whirring noise and the tinkly notes of a mazurka, began to turn delicately, elongating one leg, raising an arm. 'You mustn't be afraid of the big bad bear! He just wants the password.'

Yelena was dumbfounded. Then she swung round once again, hearing other voices now, this time from two brilliantly coloured songbirds in a gilded cage on the middle of the counter, who started to flap their wings and open their tiny beaks. 'Yes! Yes! The password, the password. You must have the password!' they chattered at her in petulant twittery voices.

'Well, go on, stupid. Have you forgotten it?' It was the bear again, growling at her now, still lifting his paws up and down.

Yelena, dizzy in her turnings, with the dog yapping this way and that, was finally annoyed by these impertinent voices, so that, glaring round at her persecutors, she shouted: 'No, I haven't got the password. I wasn't given any. I came to meet –' At which point Miki emerged from behind the counter where he'd been hiding. 'Miki!' She scolded him. 'What are you doing? How? It was you, all those voices?'

'Of course! "To speak . . ."' he touched his lips '"from the stomach."' He touched his belly, his wide chestnut eyes darting about, unwilling to come down to earth, be still, to look at her. He was just as he'd been when she'd first seen him at Ciniselli's Circus, she thought. Clown, conjurer, magician. 'Ventriloquism,' he went on. '"Speaking from the stomach."'

But she wasn't going to forgive him so quickly. 'Circus acts now? I thought all this was serious – my coming here, meeting the owner.'

'Yes: Vasily. But he's gone out. There's only me,' he added, blinking, looking down at the floor, bemused, as if wondering which of many people he was, before he began to detach the threads tied to the clockwork mechanisms of the automata with which he had set them in motion. Then he looked up at her brightly. 'Besides, I wanted to cheer you up. You were so down, after Sasha left you.'

'All the same, to be *quite* so jolly.' Yelena was snappish. 'Sasha hasn't just left me. I've lost him again, completely. Like you've lost Vera,' she added pointedly.

'Vera . . . Yes,' he said flatly, before his skittery eyes settled on her at last. 'On the other hand, one has to stay sane. And work is the best way for that. And all these games and toys and voices and things –' He gestured round the shop. 'Well, it's part of my work.'

'What work? To bring about the revolution?'

'Yes, in a way – I'll show you later – because the revolution isn't just about bringing political change but everything new in the arts as well, in theatre, literature, poetry, painting, music, the circus – everything! It's the happiness we can give as artists that is as important as anything else for the revolution.'

'Yes,' she said unwillingly. 'Except that I can't give that sort of joy any more. I told you I've lost my gift for the piano, losing Sasha.'

'They're connected?'

'Yes. We always played together.'

'And can't play apart?'

'No. We've always done everything together,' she said with sudden bitter force.

'Yes.'

Miki hadn't been concerned by her passion for her brother, which had been apparent to him earlier that year. Unconventional feelings and relationships were common among the Bohemian crowd he moved in. But it annoyed him now and he didn't quite know why. He suddenly wanted to dispossess her, to cut this link, this umbilical cord, she had with Sasha. It stood in the way of something. He didn't quite know what. He turned to her. 'Come on.' He locked the door of the shop. 'Vasily won't be back for some time. We can go upstairs and talk there.'

Climbing a twisting staircase and walking along a narrow corridor, she followed him into a cluttered room immediately above the shop. It was filled with clothes of every sort and size, for men and women, hanging from racks, with hats and caps and boots and shoes, walking sticks, umbrellas, bags and suitcases scattered in corners and on the floor. A dressing-table with a mirror stood near the single window, a skylight immediately above it, the table covered with a debris of theatrical make-up, pots of rouge and kohl and old burnt corks. To either side of the window, on shelves, were a number of wigs set on bald, sightless heads, together with moustaches, spectacles, jewellery and a variety of other personal knick-knacks. The room smelt of greasepaint and glue. Apart from a narrow unmade bed in one corner it might have been a dressing room in a theatre.

Yelena, taking all this in, was surprised. 'Where's the theatre, then?'

'Everywhere out there.' Miki nodded towards the small window, where the light, reflecting off the banks of snow outside, gave the room an unearthly sheen. 'The city and beyond. I live here usually. But this is where I disguise people as well. New faces, clothes, hair, a whole different personality. People in our Petrograd group, other Bolsheviks on the run. That's what I do for the revolution.'

'You lived here with Vera?'

'We did. But she's gone.'

'Like Sasha.'

They were silent for a moment, Yelena with her back to him now, before she turned, saying sharply, 'I couldn't believe it, when he wouldn't have anything to do with me that morning, wouldn't take me back with him, just left me.' There was desolation in her voice, then anger.

'Tell me about him. What's it all about?'

'Tell me about Vera.'

'Later. You first.'

She sat on the bed, with the dog at her feet, Miki sitting at the dressing-table. She told him most if not all about what had happened between the two of them that summer, how they had fallen out for one unimportant reason and another, and he had run away to the war. She told him about Sasha and Miss Harriet – of Miss Harriet's attempt at suicide, and the impending child, with Sasha as the father. She told him everything – except, as with Johnny, of her own meddlings and dealings with her brother that summer, her attempt to break up his affair with Miss Harriet, her unrequited passion for him. She told Miki everything, in short, except the real truth of things.

Her story was punctuated by the intermittent melody of various chiming clocks downstairs, the sounds from the lane, of boots crunching through the hard drifts of snow, of cries from the street vendors outside the railway station, of steam engines belching smoke. But all these noises were strangely muffled, absorbed by the snow, swallowed by the general stillness that had fallen over the city. Only the cluttered room and her own voice seemed real, yet both suspended now, isolated from the city, divorced from the reality of her life, and Sasha's, in that world.

So that Yelena, as she talked of Sasha, felt she was speaking of someone dead, whom she had loved and who had betrayed her when they had both occupied that other world, which had disappeared as well, covered now in a white shroud. The snow had dispossessed her of everything she valued. Reflecting this she said, 'It's all so unreal, that he should behave like this with me.'

Miki, picking up a wispy moustache, put it against his upper lip, studying his face in the mirror.

'Well?' Yelena asked. 'What do you think?'

'I was thinking how I might disguise myself today.'
'About Sasha, I meant.'
'Perhaps it's just as well he's gone again.'
'How can you say that?' She was suddenly roused. 'He's my brother, my twin!'
'Well,' Miki went on. 'You'd be entirely occupied with Sasha, if he was here. That's the point I'm making. Not with me, with us. And if you'd gone off with him that morning in the boat I wouldn't have told you about this place. You wouldn't be here. Because all this . . .' he gestured round the racks of clothes, the theatrical make-up '. . . this is real theatre. People's lives depend on what I can do for them here. And since you know about it all now, well, you can't really go back to your old life now, can you?'
'I can't? But I must, I have to. I live at the Palace.'
'Well, yes, go back physically, because that's where you can help. Your father, at the Duma. He's a deputy Minister, so he sits on the Council of State as well. You'll hear things, perhaps get a look at his papers, minutes of Council meetings and suchlike. We need all that sort of information. That, and money of course.'
'Money? I haven't got any real money.'
'Not necessarily money. But things we could sell. Vasily downstairs, he deals with that. Small *objets d'art* about the Palace. Clocks, jewellery, cut glass, fine porcelain. You could help us there.'
'Yes. Yes . . .' Yelena was not so sure about all this.
'You want to help. Don't you?'
'Yes. Just, I hadn't expected –'
'What?'
'I suppose it's you. I'd not seen you in this role.' She looked at him curiously. 'So efficient now. You don't dance about on gangly legs any more, in that innocent wistful way you had, with jokes, and that face – like indiarubber!'
'Oh, that's still me,' he said brightly. 'The real me. But I changed – a part of me did – when I met Vera, being with her.' He picked up another moustache, a luxuriously curled affair, and tried it on, putting his head to one side, making faces in the mirror in his old funny way. Then he was serious and efficient again, putting down the moustache. 'She taught me, changed

me, told me what I could do in a practical way for the revolution, these disguises and so on. And loved me,' he added flatly.

'Yes.' Yelena was touched by this account. 'Vera. It's your turn.'

He shrugged. 'One can't really put a love affair into words. You could mime it. Or in poetry. Or sculpt or paint it – or set it to music. But not conversationally. At least I can't.'

'Show it to me then!' she said quickly, urgently. 'Show me how it was.'

'I met her at the Palace theatre. She was singing there, some of those French songs one evening, with Gerard on the accordion. There was a party backstage afterwards, dancing to the same sort of music. We both knew there was going to be something special between us. Even if it didn't work out in the end.'

'No?'

'No. Not at all. When you discovered us in the museum that morning I was really kissing her goodbye. She'd been involved before, with bombs and so on, accidents, that scar on her neck – she was lucky there. But I knew she'd be killed or caught one day, and I asked her to stop the violence. But she wouldn't. Fanatic in that way. And besides . . .' He hesitated. 'Well, I don't really believe in violence for the revolution. Not now, while the war is on anyway. We'd started arguments about this, which got worse. Things were dying between us. And now they're dead. Literally, since she's likely to be sentenced to death. So you see, it was going to end badly, one way or another. But the beginning – and the middle – was wonderful.'

'Yes . . . I'm sorry.'

The sun, climbing over the roofs, had come to reflect more directly on the banks of snow outside so that the room was even brighter now, with this backdrop of flat white light, while from the skylight a single beam shone down on the floor – a clutter of boots and shoes spotlit there, like vital props in a drama at curtain-up. A pie-seller, stopping at the end of the lane, started to shout his wares, of hot *piroshkis* and jam *kalachies*.

Miki, as if taking these off-stage cries as a cue, jumped up, stuck the droopy moustache on his lip, grasped an astrakhan hat, took a silver-topped cane and, humming one of Gerard's tunes, started a skipping waltz, like a suave boulevardier, about the room. Yelena laughed. Miki, clown and magician once more, had changed the sad mood in an instant.

'Come on!' Pulling her off the bed suddenly, he took her in his arms and waltzed round the room with her. 'You see,' he told her urgently, 'revolution isn't just about freeing the people politically. It's releasing everything else in them too. The sort of things you and I have, clowning and music and happiness for everyone, not just the silly booboisie, the fools and stuffed shirts like the lot we were dancing with at the Countess Shouvalov's ball last spring. They'll all be gone soon. And then it'll be the people who'll be dancing like this with us in the streets!'

They swirled round, silent then, in and out of the sunbeam, raising the dust, kicking old clothes and boots about. And Yelena realized how, apart from taking these revolutionary points out of this sudden dance, Miki was showing her what his affair with Vera had been like, the happy unspoken essence of it: his holding Vera like this, when they had first danced together at the party, as he held her now. And just as they had apparently known almost at once that something vital and life-changing was going to happen to them, so Yelena sensed this same feeling with Miki, quite taken by the fluid dash, the sensuously happy fun in dancing with this man. She had expected talk of revolutionary plots with guns and bombs in coming to see him that morning. Instead, as she danced, she felt a quite different explosive force in his arms, the stirrings of another sort of revolution altogether.

Miki felt the same. He knew now what had annoyed him about her feelings for Sasha a few minutes before. He wanted her – and wanted rid of that ghostly other who had betrayed her, her brother, yet who still possessed her.

They both wanted each other suddenly, wanted to expunge the memory of their unhappy love affairs, to throw off the dead weights here by possessing each other.

Miki was an inept lover – too nervous and loving – while for Yelena, seductive as ever, the whole thing hardly mattered, since she was not so much aiming to please Miki as to please herself and punish Sasha. So she made light of it all, as if in performance, like an old stager, while Miki behaved like a tyro, forgetting his lines. The two of them lay half undressed on the unmade bed while he took to her like a clumsy feeder. Yelena relished his lack of experience.

'You smell of – of almonds!' she told him lightly, at one point, burying her face on his shoulder, beneath his ear.

He nuzzled her longingly. 'Attar of roses . . .'

'Come on,' she said, suddenly getting up from the bed, disappointing him momentarily. 'Let's go out and get some hot *kalachies* from that man at the end of the lane. Some sticky jam *kalachies*!' She looked up, shading her eyes in the beam of sun from the skylight. 'How bright it is! How bright.' She was happy now with the snow, the beginning of winter in the glittering city. She could celebrate it. Sasha had left her once more. But she had paid him out again, by taking a second man. She looked at Miki. Revolution had gone from his thoughts, his eyes, which were only for her now. Yes, she had gained another man and would take him out for hot *kalachies*, just as Sasha had done for her, getting her out of the dumps six months before at the start of Butterweek. Two could play at Sasha's game.

Outside, as they stamped about in the snow at the end of the lane, eating their jam rolls, Miki suddenly felt irrepressibly happy, exalted by the sparkling day and by what he took to be this true loving from Yelena.

'Hey!' He turned and gazed at her, his skittery brown eyes at rest, absorbing every part of her, his face absolutely his own at last, and said without hint of guile or performance, 'Hey, if you're not going to be doing music with Sasha, do things with me! Now – and when the revolution comes. In cabaret-theatre or the kinema. You could act. You've a wonderful face. That turned-up nose of yours is perfect. Or the circus. We could make up an act together. I could teach you all the conjuring, the magic tricks and so on. And there's some I can't do without a partner. Maskelyne's "Levitation Extraordinary" and Buatier's "Vanishing Lady". And the clairvoyant trick where you take things out of people's pockets in the audience and I'm on stage blindfolded, telling everyone exactly what you have in your hand. We could get a real act together,' he ran on, chestnut eyes ablaze. 'What do you say?'

'Yes! To levitate, see what's hidden.' She was completely taken by this idea momentarily, astonished by its aptness seeing how well it might work given the extraordinary gifts she already possessed in those directions. Then she came down to earth. 'But what about the revolution?'

'I don't care a damn about the revolution – if you'd do this with me.'

'Acting. Do you think I could? It might be fun . . .'

'Of course you could. And it would be fun!' He was bubbling over. 'Will you come to the Paris Kinema tonight? There's a new film –'

'Yes. Let's do that. You'll have to disguise yourself though, won't you?'

'Not in the dark.' He made a face, with glaring eyes, and they laughed.

Miki was wonderful, she thought. She liked him a lot. It troubled her not at all that she didn't love him. She was furious with Sasha, but her love was still bespoken there. And he would come back. She would get him back. Meanwhile she and Miki could do all sorts of happy things together, for the revolution, for art, in bed or whatever.

That same day, having had jam *kalachies* in the shabby workers quarter with Miki, Yelena had caviar and *filet mignon* for lunch with Johnny, served by innumerable obsequious waiters in the warm and expansive luxury of the Astoria dining-room.

She took the stark contrast for granted. She was living in two worlds now, quite opposed, the illicit and the open, one of revolutionaries, the other of the rich 'booboisie' – a spy in the latter, which was corrupt and doomed and which she inhabited only to help undermine and destroy.

Yet she had not really forsaken that old world or its values. She had kept more than a foothold in it, a stance she chose to think insignificant, by not telling Miki of her renewed association with Johnny. So, too, by reason of the secrecy now imposed on her, she told Johnny nothing of her most recent encounter with Miki, the Bolshevik revolutionary.

In any case, she argued, the clear separation of the two men was inevitable now. She couldn't include them openly, together in her life. They wouldn't mix. The vast differences between them, in their beliefs, their view of Russian life generally and the answer to her problems, was confirmed for her that day in the Astoria.

At lunch, Johnny had spoken – no, he had gabbled in his vast enthusiasm – of how Russia could be saved in ways which she only vaguely understood but which it was clear differed entirely from the plans which Miki and his friends had in mind.

It was a matter, Johnny told her, of 'harnessing the engine of wealth' to all the Russian people, of 'increased capital investment' from outside as a means of 'liberating the oppressed masses'.

'You see,' he told her boisterously, 'as everyone knows, if things are left to go on as they are, Russia is headed for revolution, whether she wins the war or not. And the only way to prevent it is to give the vote and start sharing out the wealth of this country among everyone, not just keeping it in the hands of the rich. You have to put *real* money in the people's pockets, so they can all buy the good things of life. *That*'s the only way to stop revolution,' he added, stabbing his finger at her.

'And to do this you need a change of direction at the top here, with the Tsar, in the Finance and Trade Ministries – with greater investment from outside *dependent* on their changing their economic policies. And you need the get-up-and-go know-how to set a rocket under Russian industrial practices, which are in the Stone Age. And all these things – why, this is what we aim to supply – my railroad company and other companies in America, banks, J. P. Morgan, a group of us there, all ready to supply the money and skills when the situation is right. Our countries are much the same – two vast continents filled with every sort of natural wealth, which we're tapping and sharing in America, but you people aren't. And that's the answer. Democratic capitalism! Not Bolshevik revolution.'

He ended with a flourish, signalling the waiter for the bill. Afterwards they took a sleigh out to the ice rink at the Aquarium on the island, hired skates, and skimmed round the ice. Again, as he moved about her, skating towards and away from her in provocative sallies, he elaborated on these themes, in snatches of shouted comment, his face alight with certainty, cheeks glowing pink in the cold.

'You see,' he said, skating up to her, taking her by the shoulders, 'there's still time to save the place – this way, the American way, my way. Will you help?'

'How do you mean help? I know nothing about money or "capitalism".'

'No. But you have the right contacts. You – and your father obviously. He's a Deputy Minister, sits on the Council of State. I want to meet him properly and the other Ministers. And I want to meet the Tsar himself. I have to meet him – because that's where the real power begins and ends in this country – and tell him about us and these other American investors. About the money and know-how we have available if he could get to see things differently, politically speaking. And who better than your father to help me on this? Why, you Rumovskys – you're part of the Blood Royal, related to the Tsar.'

'Only distantly –'

'Hell, don't you and your father want to help save this goddamn country?'

'Yes. Yes, we do. But can you save it this way? You alone? You talk like God. How are you so certain you're right?'

'I don't care if I'm right or not. That doesn't interest me. I know my ideas will *work*. That's all that counts. And as for playing God – well, why not? – if I can give the people here a decent life. All it takes is vision. And playing hunches.'

Yelena knew as little about Bolshevism as she did about capitalism. Yet she could see the very different means they would take to their shared destination – one violent, the other not, Miki involved with the former course, Johnny with the latter. She was briefly torn between the two, not as a matter of moral choice, but simply because she was equally drawn to the two men.

'So?' Johnny asked her easily as they sipped coffee on the terrace above the rink, watching the skaters circle and dawdle beneath them. 'What's it to be? You'll help me?'

'Yes. Yes, I will.' She had thought about it. She was quite definite. Why not? Both men had asked for her help. So she would give it. The conflict of interest in her doing this was quite clear to her: in helping one she would be hindering, if not betraying, the other. But the implications of this didn't worry her now. She liked the idea of being poacher and gamekeeper at the same time. In any case, neither man would know of her involvement with the other. Miki and Johnny inhabited utterly different worlds. She was the only common factor between them. Only she held all the strings. And this idea pleased her even more.

'What about Sasha?' she asked innocently before they left. 'What can we do about Sasha?'

Johnny had expected this enquiry, and had prepared his response. 'Give me all the details. We'll do our best to find him.'

'Your best?'

'Well, it's in the needle-and-hayrick department, isn't it?'

'Yes.'

'Maybe if you came down with me, to the front, you could help. I'm going down end of the week, overnight, to test a new engine, to Dvinsk, the junction for the Prussian and Galician fronts. We could make enquiries there together.'

'Yes. Yes, we could,' she said at once, though she was almost certain that Sasha wasn't at any of the war fronts now. He was somewhere in or about the city, hiding out with some other group of deserters and down-and-outs. But she would accept Johnny's suggestion. She had committed herself with him to finding Sasha. Besides, she liked the idea of a train trip away with him.

Johnny smiled at her, a cherubic, innocent smile. Of course she was using him to find her brother. She was crazy about him. But that was okay. Her needs here had given him the opportunity of taking her to Dvinsk. And she had agreed, had agreed to a journey on which he could play things with her to his advantage. The cards they held against each other were just about even.

16

Johnny and Yelena, with Thunder in tow, walked along the duck-boards between the tracks towards the locomotive sheds in the marshalling yards outside Warsaw station. Snow had fallen again, so that the roofs of the stalled carriages and box-cars to either side were draped in a doubly thick white canopy, frozen hard overnight, but thawing now in the bright morning sun, crystal rivulets of water dripping everywhere onto the slushy ground between the rails. Locomotives shrieked and belched ahead of them. A train rattled past on the mainline tracks to their left. The dog got under Johnny's feet, where it tangled with the flaps of his ankle-length bearskin coat and nearly sent him flying into the slush.

'You could have left him behind, couldn't you?' He looked down at the animal unhappily.

'No, I couldn't. Thunder's my lucky talisman. But he won't get in the way.'

'Yes, well, you'd best keep him in your compartment. We have one of the railroad director's carriages for the trip. And another for the engineers. Vitaly Semonov's coming with us, along with two other Russian engineers, while Matty holds the fort at the Astoria. We'll be hitched to this new engine we're testing, with a long line of ballast wagons behind us. Hey, Princess, I want to show you this engine. It's really quite something.' He took her arm, suddenly enthusiastic again, striding forward, and she felt the whole vigour of the man once more, the set intent on whatever was in hand, where nothing else mattered.

It was hot and noisy inside the vast locomotive shed, with sulphurous fumes and fire everywhere, from boilers raising steam all about them. They stopped next to a locomotive larger than any of the others, a monster with six huge driving wheels on either side, a funnel-shaped smokestack and a strange red-painted conical nose. Johnny met Vitaly with a group of engineers, talking with them animatedly before turning back to Yelena.

'You see,' – Johnny had to shout above the roar and hiss of steam – 'the big problem with Russian passenger locos is that they're all too small for the work offered, especially right now, when they need the longest possible troop trains. Yet they can't use heavier and stronger locos because the rails are too light and half the bridges are still made of wood. Crazy. So what we've done here is adapt this twelve-wheeled freight loco – the most powerful they have here, the Baron uses it on his Moscow–Kazan line – for passenger use. The trick I've come up with is to convert it from coal to an oil-fired boiler, take off a lot of the iron cladding – all of which'll make it lighter – streamline it with a cone nose and increase the superheating process, which should give it better acceleration and speed. So we're testing it to Dvinsk and back with this ballast train.'

He ran on happily, before turning back to Vitaly, the air thick with grime and soot. The two of them climbed up into the driver's cabin high above her. She stood beneath the great monster, cradling Thunder in her arms. The dog was quite calm, entirely at home in this inferno of heat and noise.

Half an hour later they sat opposite each other, a table between them, in red-upholstered armchairs in the forward saloon of the director's carriage.

Yelena settled herself. 'The moment of silence,' she said. She had taken off her sable coat and hat and the silk scarf from her throat. 'In Russia, before we go on a journey –' she went on knowingly.

'Yes, Princess,' Johnny interrupted, equally knowing. 'You Russians, you compose yourselves, silently, before a journey.'

He eased himself in the high-backed chair, smiling sweetly at this small victory. They were silent. She looked at the chess set on the green baize table, the unopened packs of playing cards, the collection of Tauschnitz novels, the cut-glass decanter and rows of mineral-water bottles set to one side of the table, beneath the tulip-shaped reading lamp. At the head of the saloon a doorway led through to a small galley. To one side of the doorway was an ornate samovar, on the other a table with cutlery, napkins, tea glasses, biscuit boxes and a pile of chocolate bars. The floor was thickly carpeted, the walls panelled with gilt-embossed leather and polished cherrywood, both patterned with the fleur-de-lys emblem of the Baron's private railway company. There were inset mirrors and wide picture windows, clerestory lanterns above, mahogany and brass fittings, and a pianola set along one side of the carriage. Behind were four sleeping compartments, in one of which Yelena's luggage had been put and where she'd left the little dog. Johnny's things, she'd noticed, had been put in the compartment farthest from hers.

'You play chess?' Johnny stirred himself after a minute.

'Yes.'

He moved the board to the centre of the table, pondering the pieces. 'Maybe we'll have a game.' He picked up the Queen, fondling it. 'But right now I'm going forward to the loco. Ring Josef, the steward. He'll bring you anything you need, get the samovar going, and have lunch for us all at twelve, before we get to Pskov. Then Dvinsk tonight, where we can start making enquiries about Sasha in the morning.'

'Yes,' she said. 'Yes.'

He got to his feet, a touch of irony in his smile, she thought, so that she had the distinct impression he knew, as well as she did, how they were off on a wild goose chase as far as finding Sasha was concerned. To cover the moment's awkwardness, she sniffed the air and said, 'That lovely chocolaty smell – what is it?'

'Borman's chocolate factory. It's just up the line from here, beyond the yards. The cocoa-processing plant.'

'You do know about Russia.'

He nodded. 'You want some chocolate? Plenty of it up on the table there.' He went over and brought her back a selection of bars wrapped in silver foil and exotic coloured paper – Cailler, Kohler, Borman's chocolate.

'Thank you.' She undid one delicately. 'Like some?'

'Later.'

Then he was gone and the train lurched forward, a great billow of steam curling down over the window, obliterating the pointsmen on the track beside her. The engine bellowed repeatedly. The great wheels skidded on the rails before they took a grip, and the train, with surprising acceleration, moved out of the yards. She gorged on the chocolate then, excited.

After a substantial lunch which they all ate together in the engineers' carriage, Johnny stayed on with the men, poring over graphs and stop watches, while she returned to the saloon, and fed Thunder some scraps. Afterwards she curled up in the armchair, gazing out the window. The flat, snowy landscape rolled by. Desolate scrub and marshland, undulating gently, interrupted by groves of birch and windswept fir, sunk in snowdrifts, half bent over frozen ponds, seagulls motionless on the cold ice: a muffled empty country under a pale blue sky, thin and fine as glass, where there was no war.

It was only when they got to Pskov in early afternoon, and she walked Thunder up and down the main platform, that she came into the war. A troop train, on its way to the front, had stopped on the next platform. Soldiers stormed the buffet, gulped glasses of tea. Officers shouted at orderlies for the same. Other troops, having changed trains at a farther platform, staggered by with their kitbags and blankets, each man with his blue tea-kettle. Two priests with tall black hats, long hair and beards and soiled grey gowns made imperious progress through the mêlée. A group of Austrian prisoners in their blue-grey uniforms at one end of the platform were quietly drinking tea, glad to be out of the war. Two soldiers, one with a balalaika, started to sing outside the buffet.

The snow came on again as she pushed her way forward. It fell in icy motes, a snow as thin as dust drifting over the throng. Then, to her astonishment, she saw Sandy coming straight towards her. They weren't going to be able to avoid each other. He was in full uniform, holding an attaché case, an orderly behind carrying his luggage.

'Hello!' She smiled. 'What on earth are you doing here?' He couldn't have seen her, she thought, his eyes blinded by the stinging snow. 'Sandy?' she asked again. He pushed past her. 'Sandy, I'm sorry, last time we met –'

But he had walked right past her now, moving on down the platform, soon swallowed by the crowds, lost to sight in the slanting flakes. He might have been a ghost, she thought, for all that he had said, with those glazed, unseeing eyes.

Sandy must be off to fight at the front, she thought. What

had happened that had made him leave Petrograd in this manner? Back in the heated saloon by the window she suddenly felt a pang for him, an irrational surge of emotion, and wanted to rush after him. But it was too late. Their own train was moving.

The sun, dipping into the horizon ahead of them, cast a pale crimson film over the snowy marshland as the engine picked up speed out of Pskov. Johnny joined her in the saloon as dusk fell. He was in overalls, dirtied now, His hands were grimy and he smelt of oil.

'Princess! The new oil adaptor works.' He was in high spirits. 'We made Pskov in just under five hours. A hundred and seventy-one miles from Petersburg. That's an average speed of thirty-five miles an hour, including stops at Gatchina and Luga. Almost as fast as the Nord Express. Adapt more of these locomotives and we can halve the time to the front and double the passenger load!'

'Great. We'll win the war then?'

'I doubt it. But at least I'll have fixed up some decent locos and wagons for the soldiers. Give me ten minutes for a shower, and I'll be back with you for dinner. And a game of chess?'

Later, with the heat on, the train rushing into the night and the little tulip-shaped globes lit up all down the saloon, Johnny came back in a smoking jacket and they played chess. They moved initial pawns about innocuously for five minutes, before Johnny made a daring move with a bishop, backed by his Queen, so that Yelena had to avoid an impending check.

'You're quite good.' She moved a pawn out, protecting her King.

'We used to play at home. My brothers and I. Father taught us. Always said it was the best training for a business career.'

'I didn't know you had brothers.'

'Two. Harry and Jimmy. Younger than me. And a younger sister, Ida. I love her. She's crazy about Russia. She wants to come out here. But the war – and she's in her last year, doing English, at a new girls' college, Sweetbriar, down the road from us at Charlottesville. She plays the piano too. Not quite as good as you.' He brought his other Bishop out, making another foray across the board, attacking her King from the other direction.

'I don't play the piano now.'

'Heck, you will again. It's temporary.'

The train suddenly rattled, the wheels echoing over space, as they crossed a bridge.

'Not without Sasha.' She moved a Knight out, hesitated, then brought it back again, moving another pawn instead.

'He'll come back.'

She looked up at him quickly. 'You don't want him back though.'

'Don't I?' He gazed down at the board, then moved his Queen into another threatening position.

'No.' She moved her other Knight out in a second protective move. 'Why should you? When you want me. Me on my own.'

'Yes. I do want you, on your own.' He was equally off-hand, intent on the board, moving a Knight. 'Check.' He'd cornered her now, attacking her King from both sides, so that she had to move it, out of cover, into dangerous open space.

'That's all right, then,' she said, leaning back comfortably, contemplating her move with unjustified satisfaction. 'That's good. But I want Sasha too.'

'Sure. I know that. And that's fine by me as well,' he added, still looking at the game. He moved his Castle along the base line so that it faced her King. 'Your turn, Princess. But that's checkmate, I think.' He sat back. The train swayed, rounding a curve. The mineral-water bottles rattled beside them.

She leant forward quickly, bringing her Queen across, to the square ahead of her King, so that it blocked his check, while at the same time checking his King. 'Not quite mate,' she said quietly.

Thereafter Yelena counter-attacked skilfully, hounding his King, taking one piece of his after another. He watched his destruction silently. Finally she cornered his King, with her Queen and a Bishop on a long diagonal, before administering the *coup de grace* with a simple pawn, moving it up a space so that it checked the regal ivory which couldn't take it in return and now had no other place to go. 'Check,' she said. Johnny surveyed the ruin of his bright game. There was no way out. 'And mate,' she added.

They gazed across the table at each other – not as victor and vanquished but as people contemplating a return match in quite a different sort of game. They were silent and serious for a moment. Then he suddenly burst out laughing. 'You and your brother,' he said. 'What does it matter, for Godsakes? Why – I love my sister, Ida, too.'

He rubbed her hand lightly, his fingers moving up, smoothing the fine hair on her wrist, so that suddenly she wanted to be properly touched and taken by this good-humoured roly-poly man. Making love with Johnny would be a witty business, a thing of convulsive laughter, a bouncy romp – something entirely frivolous which would make it nothing but a pleasure.

Back in his compartment they couldn't take their clothes off quickly enough. Blouse, skirt, shirt and trousers; silk bodice, camiknickers, socks, stockings, shoes and garters. They stripped each other in high good humour. They laughed and gulped in gleeful expectation, before they fell back together on the lower bunk in a tangle of intertwined legs and arms.

They played then, in dainty feints and snatches, up and down each other's body, cheerfully probing, with lips and fingers, touching and tasting sensitive morsels, making brisk frolics over open spaces, light-hearted forays into hidden places – so that soon they lost their good manners and gorged on each other.

He took her sharply and furiously, see-sawing, finding a rhythm, giving and taking, a wonderful flowing, his pace quickening, running a race, both of them uncontrolled, wrenching and clawing.

Suddenly she went quite still, suspended above an abyss for a long second. Then she fell. Her body gave way, disintegrated. Her limbs shuddered viciously, exploding in violent ecstasy. Eyes clenched shut, teeth clamped, her neck arching away from him, a hot dark tide overwhelmed her.

Afterwards – so different from her experiences with Sandy and Miki – there was no possibility of any recriminations, accusations or sentimental proposals for a shared future. Just an exhausted warmth, a huge gratefulness. This was what making love should be like, she thought. A thing of itself alone, which needed no other commitment, no emotional hopes or tangles, no necessary future, something free of everything except its own physical imperatives.

Johnny, unlike the others, didn't mind a bit about Sasha and didn't want to marry her. He had simply wanted her, as she had him, free of all such emotional or moral baggage. So, rid of these dull encumbrances, they had properly given themselves to each other, their bodies freely coming together, without a past or future. Yes, this was what true loving was like, she thought, hearing the little dog bark suddenly back in her compartment, as if agreeing.

'Thank you, dear Johnny. Thank you.'

The train rattled over some points and he moved away from her, looking at his watch. 'Just coming into Dvinsk.' The train slowed. Looking upwards she saw slivers of light compassing the ceiling, platform lamps slowly passing, shining through a chink in the curtain, before the train stopped with a long sigh of brakes.

He dressed so quickly, with such practised speed and efficiency, that she wondered if he might have learnt the skill in deserting many other women in bed. This idea, and his leaving her so abruptly, left her with a feeling of disappointment, a sudden sharp emotional ache which she had felt before only with Sasha. So, just as she had once before with him, when they'd first met during Butterweek, she summoned him up in her mind, concentrating on him, *willing* him back to her.

Striding briskly up the saloon, Johnny was elated at having so successfully negotiated this first hurdle. Of course he wanted a great deal more of Yelena than just making love with her. He wanted everything of her – to see her disentangled from Sasha, to bring her back to America and marry her. But he would tell her nothing of this for the moment. He had learnt not to rush fences with women. Just the opposite. You laid out the bait and waited.

Then, just before he went through the doorway forward into the engineers' carriage, he suddenly thought how calculating this attitude was. Yelena was no ordinary woman. She was quite unlike the others he had had. He had just made love to her, and that had been part of the calculated bait. But since he wanted all those other things of her, he was not playing fair in promoting himself as just a casual lover. He turned, hurrying back. She was still lying on the bunk when he opened the compartment door.

'Hey, Princess, I forgot to tell you. I love you! Will you come back with me to the States? And marry me?'

He saw his mistake at once. Having smiled happily at him when he'd come in, she frowned now. 'Marry you? We hardly know each other.'

'Oh, come on, Yelena – we just made love.'

'That's different. That's separate.'

'Is it? Goddamnit! I wouldn't have said so. Not in my book it isn't. Did you think I just wanted to screw you and nothing else?'

'Yes. Why not? It was wonderful.'

He shook his head in astonishment. 'You're crazy –'

'I'm not!' She was roused. 'Just why should you want to tie me – us – down in this dull way? Why can't we just enjoy what we have *now*? I'm not yet nineteen. I have my own life to find – or regain – before I think about marriage. There's my music. And there is Sasha . . .' She hesitated, seeing his look of fierce annoyance. 'Anyway, we can talk about it.'

'No we won't. I've asked you. And I won't ask you again,' he added coldly, leaving her abruptly once more.

She sighed. Why did every man she came across ruin things by wanting to marry her? The reality of that would be no fun at all: rice pudding and old children's books lost in some rural vastness in England with Sandy, or being a subsidiary partner in a lot of conjuring and circus tricks with Miki, or finding herself marooned in some American wilderness, stuck in a phoney castle on top of a mountain, playing second fiddle as a railroad magnate's wife with Johnny.

All the three men appealed to her, but none of the permanent roles they wanted her to play with them. Why couldn't they see that? That she liked them all a lot and wanted them, to do things with and make love, but not to be committed to them throughout some indefinite future, not be tied to them.

'The bitch,' Johnny said, as he walked back up the saloon a second time. He had quite misjudged Yelena. She had used him, as Matty had said she would, not as a means of finding her brother, but just as a casual sexual partner. He had done all he could. He had laid out the bait, and had then come out into the open and committed himself to her. And she wouldn't change either way. He was finished with Yelena.

But change did come for Yelena a month later, just before Christmas: first when news came from Lake Ladoga that the old Prince Mikhail, her grandfather, had died in his sleep at the castle, so that she was now the owner of this and of all that vast land and water; and then when she discovered she was pregnant. She had no doubts about taking over the huge estate. But she wondered who the father was.

17

They followed the open coffin, in *troikas* and sleighs, over the lake ice, going north to the Rumovsky lands across the bay.

'Why this way? Why not direct to the Monastery church?' Sasha asked.

'Grandfather wanted it, to be taken on a last tour of his domains. He left me instructions.'

Yelena spoke already with the authority of ownership, command – and of victory. It seemed to her that in losing her grandfather she had won more or less everything else. True, through their own faults – their prudish moralizing, possessiveness or unwarranted hopes – she had probably lost three other men. And she was certainly pregnant by one of them: Sandy, she thought, given the dates. But what was this by comparison with what she had gained: the spectacular castle they had just left, these wonderful frozen northlands ahead of them.

Above all, at her grandfather's death, she had regained Sasha – Sasha, who had turned up at the last moment that morning for the funeral, sitting beside her now, with Miss Harriet in front of them, their parents and uncles ahead in two other *troikas*, driving behind the sleigh which carried the old Prince, his favourite hunting eagle set on a perch above him, driven by his steward Stephan.

She had known Sasha would come back. She was certain of it. She had told Miss Harriet early that morning. 'You'll see, he'll be here any moment now, from the night train.'

'How do you know?' Miss Harriet, fully recovered and glowing in her pregnancy, tried not to show the mix of excitement and disturbance she felt at this news.

'I know. I just know it.'

The two of them had stood waiting on the castle ramparts, shivering in the dawn, by the ashes of the great fire which, on the old Prince's death, had been allowed to go out. 'There's nothing to worry about,' Yelena had continued. 'We can get things sorted out at last. We can run our lives properly now. Start again.'

Ten minutes later, far out on the ice to the west, the sun rising behind them, casting a pale orange light over the snowy ice, they saw the sleigh in the distance, a hired sleigh, two horses, one with a *duga*, coming in a direct line towards them – and then the heavily padded *yamshchik*, with his whip and rifle, and Sasha behind him, when the borzoi hunting dogs in their kennels down by the boathouse had begun to bark at the prodigal's return.

Now, in their own sleigh some hours later, she turned to her brother, her eyes triumphant, glittering, reflecting the snow and the bright blue sky, tears seeping down her cheeks as they trotted along in the freezing air. Sasha's eyes were tired. He had a stubble of beard. But otherwise he looked well. Composed and at ease. Where had he been? What had he been up to all this time? There had been no opportunity to talk before they had set off and he seemed in no mood to confide anything just then. Yelena was somewhat surprised – he wasn't in the least contrite or awkward in this sudden enforced company with two women he had run away from, one of them carrying his child.

'I knew you'd come back.' Yelena broke the silence.

'Your second sight?' He was vaguely ironic.

'Yes, as it happens. But then I thought you'd be back for the funeral in any case – would have read about his death. He was your grandfather as well. And the place belongs to all of us now, doesn't it?' She looked across at Miss Harriet.

Neither of them made any comment until Sasha said acidly, 'Yours alone. Not mine, certainly. I'm surprised you're so cock-a-hoop about it all. You hated the place.'

'I've changed my mind about it. Since you left,' she added pointedly, hinting at many things that he had missed in his absence.

'Good,' he said. But he said no more.

She longed to erase this awkwardness between them, longed to take Sasha's arm, to hold his hand, as she had so often before, as children, racing over this same ice from Ladenpojha, the two of them tucked up under a mound of fur rugs, as they were now, with Miss Harriet on the seat opposite, as now.

Suddenly Yelena was exasperated. 'Sasha, why this coldness?' She looked at both of them, smiling, shaking her head for emphasis. 'Sasha, you're home. And we're all still friends – much more than friends. And everything can be sorted out. You'll see! We can all live here now, if we want, now that I have the place. Do things together, *everything*! Boating and hunting and picnics in the summer. And music. It'll be wonderful.' She looked from one to the other. But they made no comment. 'God, you're both so dreary! Can't you see, Sasha?' She turned to him, her eyes, her whole expression, filled with energy, hope.

He looked at her non-committally. 'I can only see that we're going to my grandfather's funeral at the moment.' He leant back, with the resigned air of a sober relation, abroad for a long time, returned to find the usual folly among his family at home.

The cavalcade stopped at the northern shoreline of the bay. The hooded eagle, ruffling its feathers, thrust its beak out, sensing prey in the heavily wooded slopes above them. The coffin was raised up at an angle and turned in a circle, so that the old Prince's bearded face, gone blue and dusted with frost, made a complete survey of the lake and his lands. His eyes were closed, hooded like his eagle. Yet like the bird as he turned, and even in the repose of death, it seemed as if, in his own hawk-like features, he sensed everything about him: the carmine tints on the snowy lake ice, the thick birch woods where the lynx and the arctic fox lurked and the capercaillie, the old Prince absorbing all the marvels of these happy hunting grounds for the last time, before they returned across the bay to the church on Monastery Island.

The Abbot Theodosius, a tremulous old figure with palsied features and an unkempt beard to his waist, met them in the forecourt, a score of monks ranked beside and behind him. The chanting started, 'Eternal Memory'. Inside the church, under the great starry domed cupola, the monks flicked their censers, the air already misty blue with incense, warmed by hundreds of flickering candles and by as many people, from all over the Prince's estates, crushed together.

The chant continued. The coffin was laid, sloping upwards, facing the congregation, below the steps in front of the gilded iconostasis. The patriarch turned towards the vast array of supplicant, tearful faces, speaking in a quavery voice: 'For a man walketh in a vain shadow, and disquieteth himself in vain: he heapeth up riches, and cannot tell who shall gather them.' Then the choir responded, the words, in their soaring music, coming from their bellies, as if gathered from the depths of the Russian earth, the body and soul of Russia herself. 'Hear my prayer, O Lord, for I am a stranger with thee: and a sojourner, as all my fathers were . . .'

The eyes of the mourners were fixed on the armless body of the old Prince: cronies, friends, retainers, tenantry, remembering their years of friendship, their pride and security in his service, confidence in his prowess and justice – and fearing what might come.

All knew how Yelena was mistress here now and were alarmed at this, doubtful of their future in the hands of this puny woman. They glanced at her dismissively, now and then, as she stood at the foot of the coffin with her parents. They crossed themselves more often and more vigorously, as the candles guttered before the miraculous ikons, prostrating themselves in front of these as the service progressed, as if, in this beseeching abnegation, they could turn the tables on death and restore this man as their lord and master and so postpone the succession of his frail and surely incompetent granddaughter.

Yelena became aware of this mistrust and distaste all about her. She became restless, angry, as the monks, nearing the end of the service, held triple candles over the coffin. The abbot, at the foot of the coffin, now held up the precious glass ikon of the Blessed Virgin of Smolensk towards the old Prince; 'Spare me my strength, before I go hence and be seen no more.' The mourners started to wail, 'In the name of the father, the son . . .' The abbot turned, displaying to the multitude the ikon in his shaking hands. Then he presented it to the Rumovsky family, so that they might take a blessing, come forward to kiss it.

But before they had the opportunity, just as the abbot confronted Yelena with the holy picture, the glass shattered from side to side, exploding with a sharp crack, as if it had been hit by a stone, disintegrating, falling out of the frame onto the steps in a clatter of shards and tiny pieces.

There was a moment of incredulous silence. Then the cries erupted all over the church, an uproar of fearful lamentation. This inexplicable destruction, this defamation of the holy image, at the height of the ceremonies, was an omen of the most terrible sort, a condemnation on the mourners, their future, above all a curse on the head of this woman and her impending rule. The funeral broke up in disorder. People rushed the coffin, surrounding it, crying out, touching the wood, attempting to restrain its passage along the church towards the Rumovsky family vaults, where at last, amidst scenes of wild fear and anguish, the old Prince was laid to rest.

However, on the family's return to the castle, it was not so much the breaking of the ikon which absorbed their attention – this was put down to the frailty of the abbot and his shaking hands or the excessive heat in the church at the time. It was the return of the prodigal which was of more concern, and whether or not the fatted calf should be slaughtered.

Sasha, realizing this, decided to divide the opposition by dealing with each person separately, in turn. So it was that he bore the initial brunt of criticism from his father alone, speaking to him in the old Prince's chamber next to the armoury in the tower, overlooking the lake.

'No, Papa, I am a grown man and do not have to account for my behaviour while I was away.'

'Indeed, and I do not ask for that. But I have responsibility for Miss Harriet, and of course to her parents in Ireland, who cannot visit her with the war on, and it's this I speak of: I realized soon after you left – and Linochka confirmed it – that you must be the father of Miss Harriet's child. Well, something has to be done about that. We neither of us can evade our responsibilities there.'

'The child?' Sasha's deepset, slightly hooded eyes flickered. 'I had thought, after her accident, that it would not have survived.'

'It has survived. As she has. She expects it next spring. Miss Harriet and the child – they remain a responsibility – for both of us.'

Prince Pyotr had moved to one of the narrow windows, lighting a *papirosy*. Now he returned anxiously to the fire set in the great chimneypiece.

'Yes, I see that, obviously.'

'Why, then, did you run away so suddenly?' The Prince was abrupt, with dismay, anger even, in his voice.

'I tried to enlist.'

'Indeed, and we successfully stopped you, since you were exempt, had no need –'

'I wish you hadn't, because there was need. You don't know all the facts.'

'All the facts? What are they? – other than that you embarked on a most foolish and improper affair with your governess? You wish we speak of that? The obvious irresponsibility and immorality of your so doing – quite aside from the cowardice of your then running away from the mess you had created?'

'Yes!' Sasha was roused now. 'But I tried to avoid the mess, as you put it, at the time. I offered to marry Harriet. But she quite decidedly refused. I then suggested that the child might be adopted. But she refused this as well. She told me she was quite determined to have the child and to bring it up herself, that she had the will and the means to do this, and that I should not feel tied to or responsible for her in any way. So I did not avoid my responsibilities in the matter. I offered her marriage, then suggested other ways out of her – our – predicament. But she refused every suggestion.'

'Then why did you disappear without telling me all this? I'm a liberal man. We could have talked it over, come to some sensible arrangements about it all. Why run away? And so allow all of us, quite aside from the great worry you caused, to put the worst possible construction on your behaviour?'

'"Run away" . . .' Sasha was further put out, biting back his anger. 'Well, if you put it like that, let me explain something which should make it clear why I had to leave. I don't want to be disloyal, but I shall have to be blunt. You know I've always had the closest and most affectionate feelings for Linochka, and she for me. But latterly, indeed for several years now, she's wanted to extend this in – in an unsuitable manner. She has had it that we should "marry" in effect, live together in an entirely intimate mode. She had pressed for this, in argument and literally, which has caused great difficulties for me. And it was this problem, which came to a head at the same time as I learnt Miss Harriet was pregnant, which made me "run away", as you put it. I think, given this fact, you may see that it was the best course open to me at the time.'

'I see.' The Prince only half saw. He was very shocked. 'I had no idea.' He was silent. 'Though now I think of it, your mother hinted at something of this, just after you left.'

'It's quite true.'

'She may take it from her mother, these irresponsible feelings.'

'Possibly . . .'

'Like her, she is of a generally unsettled, impulsive disposition. And especially since you left. Out all hours of the day and night in Petrograd. We don't know what she's been up to. Disturbed by your disappearance, as we all were. But what can be done now?' Prince Pyotr looked at his son man to man.

'I will do what I can.' Sasha, having made his excuses and explanations, changed his tone. He was forthright – and critical. 'But I will not be living here. Linochka can run things as she wants. But as I told her before I left, she cannot rely on me for her every support, emotional or otherwise. She must find her own supports. As must Miss Harriet. And I must go on living my own life now, in Petrograd or elsewhere.'

'Yes, Yes . . .'

'I'll talk to them both, of course. One must have these things out in the open. I must make clear decisions about them now, once and for all – not go on compromising or letting things fester.'

'Yes, I agree, as a general principle. But in this instance your attitude seems too cut and dried. It will hurt them.'

'What else can it be? I was too emotional about it all before. And look what that's brought. It will only lead to worse hurt if I let things go on as they were.'

'Yes.' The Prince reminded himself then how he had ruined his own life with his wife through compromise, so that he added more confidently, 'Yes, I should have had the same sort of firmer views about such matters myself. All the same,' he went on, 'Linochka's rather a particular case. Look at her now.'

Sasha joined his father at the window. Beneath them on the ramparts, by the ashes of the great fire, they saw Yelena giving instructions. Men were carrying big logs, setting them up in a pyramid. The fire was to be lit again. 'She's so happy with your return – involved, taking control of herself. But if you go away again I'm sure she will deteriorate, as she's done in your absence. Become depressed, do foolish things.'

'Yes, I know. She's done it before.'

'She relies on you.'

'Too much.'

'But Sasha, she had grounds for it. You are her other half, as twins. And in your music together. She told me she can't play now, without you.'

'Did she?' It was Sasha's turn now to be indecisive.

'I fear for her generally,' his father went on. 'The people here were already against her. Now, with that unfortunate business with the ikon, they will be doubly so. She will have difficulties here in any case. Without you she may find them insurmountable.'

'Yes.' Sasha, looking out the window, was suddenly concerned with something else. 'That little black dog, I'd not seen it before. Just like Samson. Where did she get it from?'

'A stray. She found it in University Gardens, that night of the great thunderstorm, just after you left.'

'Strange, to find an identical dog.'

'Your mother said the same. Very put out by it all. She found her in her bedroom with it that same night. She was burning some papers, apparently holding her hand in the flame without flinching. Nonsense, of course. Your mother has the idea that she's mad, touched by evil in some way. Of course your grandfather had the same idea, though for him she had been given great gifts.'

'It's true,' Sasha said suddenly. 'Mama is right – they're both right. She has these gifts, good and bad. I know of them.'

Prince Pyotr was surprised. 'You mean other than just natural gifts?'

'Yes. Inexplicable things she can do – and things that have happened to her.'

'Inexplicable? You mean supernatural?'

'I suppose so, yes. That ikon this morning, for example. I'm sure she broke it herself.'

'How? She didn't touch it.'

'Just by glowering, by looking at it.'

'Surely not? It was old Theodosius's hands, shaking like a leaf. Or the heat.'

'No. I don't think so. She broke Mama's string of pearls – you remember? – at that dinner party years ago, in just the same way. And she can see things, in the future. And other people, what they're doing, when they're miles away.'

'You never told me.'

'I didn't want to be disloyal. But now, you should know – she has these strange powers, for good and ill. A curse, she's felt them to be, by and large.'

'A curse? But that's in the realm of fairy tales!'

'You and I are literal-minded, Papa. But I promise you, it's true with Linochka. There are such people, here in Russia especially. Rasputin, for example.'

'You're not comparing –'

'No. Well, yes, possibly I am. Linochka has something of the same powers.'

'Well, I can hardly credit it.' Prince Pyotr moved away from the window. 'But in any case, these powers, or whatever, are not the immediate issue. We have to think of Miss Harriet.'

'I'll see her. Talk to her. Though I don't know what's to be done now. She will not have changed her mind.'

'And you have no wish to marry her, I take it?'

'No. Not now. Nor she me, as I told you. We've both realized. It was all a very foolish mistake.'

They walked down the long gallery, once the armoury, which was now hung with medieval swords and halberds and portraits of Rumovsky ancestors. Harriet's skirts rustled as she moved. She was still wearing a dark satin mourning dress. The high lace collar accentuated her long neck, just as the buckled sash did her waist. But her waist was not half so narrow now. She had filled out generally, above and below the waist. She was no longer the wiry, taut-skinned, rather ungathered woman Sasha remembered. Everything cohered about her now, was held together and blossomed from a secret centre.

Sasha was struck by the beauty which this pregnancy had brought her: the wavy reddish hair no longer dry and frazzled but gleaming; her colour less delicate, a cherry tinge on her freckled skin, her high cheekbones sharply defined by the dazzling afternoon sun that streamed off the snowy lake through the mullioned windows. He was suddenly moved by her velvety radiance, her rounded body, her repose and confidence, stirred by these changes which he, in part, had brought about.

'You look beautiful,' he told her simply.

She turned her cornflower eyes on him. 'Thank you. Yes, I feel so, at least. I learnt so much after you left. To be calmer. Not so fool-headed, impetuous.' She spoke almost distantly as they stopped in front of a full-length portrait of a Rumovsky ancestor, a severely bearded man with a fierce nose, eyes too close together, in a jewelled sable tunic, hunting boots and a goshawk perched on his arm. She gazed at the stern features. 'Will he look like that? If it's a boy?'

'Harriet!' Sasha was urgent now. 'That's the whole point. My running away – not only from you and Linochka, but from him. Or her. What are we to do?'

'What should we do?' She looked at him with surprise. 'But wait. For him. Or her. That's all that counts. Though I do rather hope, if it's a boy, that he doesn't look anything like that gloomy fellow up there!' She laughed, walking down the gallery ahead of him, light-footed, unconcerned.

Shasha, seeing her go like that, the free and generous spirit she was now, so transformed from the fraught and obsessive woman she had been with him – seeing this he was suddenly overwhelmed, with guilt and with love, and with the feeling that he was now making a terrible mistake in abandoning their child, in losing a future with this beautiful woman.

Hearing his quick footsteps behind her, Miss Harriet turned. Before she could do anything about it he had taken her in his arms and was hugging her, holding her fiercely.

'Harriet, Harriet! I've been such an idiot.'

Her head forced over his shoulder, she couldn't see his face.

But she felt everything of his body, felt the love there. And she loved it and him, in return.

'No,' she said, looking over his shoulder into the far distances of the gallery, the bright snowy light flooding the room. 'We were both fools. But perhaps now we can be easy, love easily, "As leaves grow on a tree".'

'And marry?' he asked.

'Yes, we'll marry,' she said quite simply, as if there had never been any question of this.

He held her again, gripping her with such vehemence that she was reassured about this. There were risks of course. It might not work out this time between them either. But love was a rare gift. Equally, there were risks in properly developing it. So when it was offered one should pursue the gift and take the risk and so she would go with him. Of course there was still a rival to be reckoned with.

'And Linochka?' she asked.

'I'll speak to her. She'll understand about us this time. She's much happier now, calmer. And in the sleigh this morning she was so hopeful about everything, saying how she wanted us *all* to live up here. This time everything will be all right.'

'Dear Sasha, what have you been up to?' Yelena spoke lightly, putting her arm through his. The huge orange ball had dipped just below the distant edge of the lake. The air was freezing hard, the sky streaked with crimson, rising into flights of pearl and pale blue far above them as they walked with the black pug dog along the ramparts, past the Krupp cannon, towards the great fire, lit below the tower once more.

'I came back for the funeral.'

'Yes, of course. But before that, all these months.' She turned to him, squeezing his arm, her face alight with happiness, her dark hair sparkling as they neared the yellow flames dancing up from the huge pile of logs. 'Oh, Sasha,' she rushed on, overcome with a confiding spirit. 'I've so much to tell you! How things have changed with me. My feelings for you especially. I don't have that stupid need of you any more. But you, tell me about you. Where have you been? How did you survive? Why didn't you send me the least message, you wretch!' She spoke in a teasing voice, anxious not to spoil their reunion by making too much of things.

'I . . .' He hesitated, so that she jumped in.

'You spent all this time among those down-and-outs?'

'No. Well, yes and no, some of the time, with some of them –'

'What does it matter!' Again she interrupted. 'What does it matter where you were, now you're back. That's everything.' She looked at him tenderly, shaking her head in happy disbelief. 'Sasha, I've missed you. And I've done such stupid things myself when you were away, so I've no grounds for criticizing you.' She went up to him and laid her chin on his shoulder, cheek against his, feeling the heat of the fire on her face now, seeing the big yellow sparks fly up into the darkening sky as the huge logs crackled and blazed. 'But all that's over now, that nonsense. For me. For both of us. Isn't it?'

'I hope so. That's good. I hope so.'

He spoke in a distant, staccato manner. She couldn't understand it. 'Sasha, what's the matter? We can all of us just get on easily now. You and me – and Harriet. And do our music together again – I'll get the Steinway up here for us! . . . Sasha, why don't you relax, speak to me properly?'

'I am relaxed,' he lied.

'You're worried about Miss Harriet – and the child. Papa's told you, obviously. Well, she's going to have it. But she's entirely happy about that. She's told me. So there isn't anything to worry about. She can have the child up here, if she wants to, out of the way of all those nosy parkers in Petrograd. So you see, my taking over here, it'll make things easier all round. You and I and she – we can do what we want up here, as friends. You don't have to marry her. Or worry about me, in the old way I was. We can just get on with everything else. Oh, Sasha, don't you see? We can all be happy now!'

'You make it sound so easy –'

'But it is! It will be.' She saw his strained features in the firelight. 'You must believe it.'

He looked at her carefully. She had spoken in the most heartfelt tones certainly. But could he believe her? Had she changed? Had she really lost those obsessive feelings for him?

She had, he decided, so that, brightening now, he relaxed at last.

'I'm sorry to have been so distant, Linochka. I wasn't certain – about your changing. But that *is* wonderful! Because I've got everything to tell you. Things that happened while I was away, but mostly what's happened since I got back – something that will certainly make life easier for all of us. Harriet and I . . . we've made things up. I was a fool to behave the way I did with her. And with you, to run away from you both. I'm going to stay with Harriet now as well. We're going to marry.'

Yelena froze. She couldn't believe her ears. Despite the heat she began to shiver. Her head began to throb. She started to gasp, to choke. She tried to be sick, feeling something poisonous in the depths of her stomach which she had to expel. But nothing came. The sickness inside her refused to emerge. She began to whimper. Then, sinking to her knees, she started to cry.

Seeing her on her knees like this seemed to confirm Yelena's change for Sasha. She was upset at his news. But she seemed to have taken it without any of her previous anger and dictatorial bluster. She would come to accept this new situation, he thought, when indeed they could all live together, up here on the lake, in happiness and peace. Yelena was suddenly just as dear to him as Harriet had become an hour before. He was committed to both of them, he saw now, both of them equally in duty and in love.

He bent down, starting to help her up. 'Linochka, don't cry. Because you were right. And surely you can see it now? We can all three of us live together here, just as you said, with our music, running the estate, the child –'

But before he could say any more she reached up and took him by the throat, both hands around his neck, in a fierce grip, a woman transformed in an instant from tearful penitent to savage virago. On her feet then, they struggled about the great fire. He saw the look of convulsive frenzy in her face, exaggerated by the flames, an unearthly, terrifying expression of sheer hatred.

She cursed him, screaming, in a voice not hers, harsh and deep – 'You cheat! You liar. You damned betrayer!' – heaping curses and obscenities on him, raving, spitting in his face. He tried to release her hands from his neck, pulling with all his might, but to no effect. It was unreal, he thought. No woman could have such strength. It was as if some outside force had taken possession of her. He felt himself lifted almost off his feet in the fury of her hold, being tossed about, as the little black dog barked furiously round her ankles, encouraging her in this murderous assault.

They swayed to and fro, her hands locked around his neck. She was manoeuvring him towards the fire. He saw the blazing logs, coming nearer, before his vision began to blur. Her curses and screams were fainter in his ears. But his mind was still clear. He thought he knew what had happened. Those powers of hers – her gifts for good and evil – had broken out in her again with vengeance at this news, with evil in complete ascendancy. And he realized he was struggling then, not with his sister, but with some demonic spirit which had overwhelmed her. He was fighting for his life with the devil.

18

Though it took all their strength, the two burly watchmen at the end of the ramparts, hearing the commotion, managed to separate sister from brother, so that Sasha was saved from the fire. But thereafter no one could save Yelena.

Sasha, fearing to provoke a repetition of her insensate violence, did not confront her again. Her parents and Miss Harriet tried to reason with her, but with no success. Yelena seemed inhuman now, behaving in the strangest, most irrational manner, presenting a grim silence or else berating them with shouts and curses, making vicious criticisms of their 'virtue' and assumed good sense, both of which, she told them, were a sham. Underneath they were mean and calculating, simply set on betraying and destroying her. She would not be so destroyed, she told them, would not be taken in by their devious arguments. They were corrupt. She would live her own life now, up on the lake, free from the odour of their sanctimonious hypocrisy. They were surprised by this attack on their morality. This issue seemed to have nothing to do with her trying to incinerate her brother.

With their precipitate departure – for she told them to quit the castle the following day – Yelena's personality dissolved and separated into savage islands which had no connection with the civilized main, so that she presented to the world a persistent but ever-varying mania, swinging between brooding, malign silences and explosive, dictatorial frenzies as she took on her role as chatelaine of the castle.

With Stephan Vasilievich, the chief steward, as her increasingly bemused and unwilling aide-de-camp, she set about running the place in a way her grandfather might first have admired but would have soon seen to be careless, irresponsible and simply vindictive, a manner least calculated to further the interests and welfare of all those who depended on her and drew their livelihoods from the vast estate. So it was that everything these people feared, with the accession of this woman and the breaking of the miraculous ikon, came to pass.

In these dangerously varying moods, Yelena followed her grandfather's precepts faithfully in one way at least. She decided, as an extension of her vicious criticisms of her family, that the world outside the castle was entirely misdirected and corrupt. So that, like the old Prince Mikhail, she came to despise everything that was new or progressive in Russia – all that she had previously espoused with Miki and Johnny – choosing instead to promote an older Russian way of life, exaggerating this, just as her grandfather had, but without any of his sure command and innate gifts, by living in an almost medieval manner.

She took out her grandfather's boyar clothes, cutting or adapting these to fit her, dressing as a man, seeking to recreate his boyar 'court', shaping her dark hair under his gold-threaded *koshniki* with its crust of glittering opal and turquoise stones, wearing his sable cloak embroidered with lake pearls, over a crimson tunic, with a broad gold belt and long felt boots beneath.

In this regal attire she sat on her grandfather's roughly carved Lapp throne in the great hall every morning, with Stephan beside her, dictating orders or dispensing casual justice to retainers, petitioners or defendants. And she took the same seat there almost every evening, in more elaborate dress, picking at her dinner at the head of the long table by the huge fire, surrounded by a diminished band of her grandfather's more venal and wily neighbours and retainers, the remnants of his 'courtiers', who placated or fawned on her, hiding their dislike and derision – but also their uncertainty and fear.

For here was a woman, they saw, who held real power, but quite irresponsibly, and who implemented it recklessly, by feminine guile or with a wicked temper, so that they could never be certain if they were to be beneficiaries or victims. A woman of such unstable moods and whims that they knew not how best to approach her, by way of gaining or keeping her favour, or to influence her to their own advantage, which was what they wanted most of all, hoping now, with the loss of her grandfather's iron and consistent control, to take rights and divide spoils about the great estate.

The Princess Yelena, they saw, was no Tamburlaine or Catherine the Great, but simply a madwoman of the snows, a woman unhinged who, if they waited their chance, played their cards suitably or gave her enough rope, would fall into their hands or hang herself. All these things they saw in and sought of the Princess. So that the castle became a cockpit of intrigue, a nest of vipers, a place of evil schemes and shadows.

But these wily 'courtiers' and neighbours largely failed in their purposes. As the winter deepened, the lake and castle locked hard into the ice, marooned by darkness and by freezing blizzards, other attributes emerged in the Princess which they had not bargained for, qualities they had first dismissed as fantasy but which the superstitious retainers and the other local people had believed in from the beginning, from the moment the miraculous ikon had smashed in front of Yelena at the funeral: the Princess's madness was not just malign, it was supernatural. It was the work of the devil. And it was this factor which everyone at the castle and on the estate came truly to fear, so that they restrained their greed, postponed their schemes, fearing no earthly but some hellish retribution.

The incident which finally confirmed these beliefs, among courtiers and servants alike, occurred one evening at the end of a lavish dinner in the great hall. A rich *moujik*, red-faced and portly, whose land marched with the Rumovsky estate to the south, had put his case forcibly, that he should buy several hundred *desyatinas* from the Princess, at a price which even she knew to be derisory. She told him so. But the red-faced man, fired by drink and standing up, had continued his bullying offer, increasing it by a pittance. The Princess, tiring of his impertinence, had turned on him with a withering look – whereupon the *muzhik*, gasping in pain and clutching his chest, had slumped forward and fallen to the floor amidst a clatter of dishes and glasses, dead.

After this it was agreed by nearly everyone that the Princess was undoubtedly one of the *vedmy*, a wicked sorcerer endowed with every sort of evil magic – one of those who, with her black dog which was obviously an agent of the devil, travelled by night on a broomstick, casting murderous spells over cabins and farms, landing in the forest, where she was in league with the dreaded *leshii*, the wood demon with decaying bluish flesh, long hair and protruding eyes; a woman also at one with Baba-Yaga, even more feared, the foul, hook-nosed creature who moved about in a windowless cabin set on chicken's feet, with her fearsome black cat, devouring humans, thatching her *izba* with their bones.

Once these beliefs took root in the minds of the credulous local people, rumours of the Princess's witch-like behaviour spread far and wide, about the whole estate and across the lake to the railhead at Ladenpohja. Yes, the *yamshchiks* and fur traders said when their sleigh teams arrived, taking tea at the station buffet with engineers and conductors, the Princess Rumovsky was a *vedmy* of the worst and most potent sort. She could indeed fly, if not exactly on a broomstick, then feet above the ground. She had been seen actually doing this, levitating in anger, one morning in the estate office, rebuking a servant. A woman of the bedchamber had witnessed her flailing about the floor, raving and screaming, shouting in some unknown tongue, her face twisted in a fearful grimace, while a nightwatchman, in the light of the great fire, had seen her running like the wind, her legs unnaturally supple, but *backwards*, up the zigzag steps that led from the lake to the ramparts.

Then, too, in the middle of winter, people's fears increased when, her stomach swelling, it became clear that the Princess was with child. And since she went with no man in the castle or estate it was obvious that she had been consorting with some other evil spirit – the *vodyanoi* probably, the hideous green-bearded man, evil spirit of the waters. This would account, they thought, for the inexplicable thaw in the new year, which cracked some of the lake ice prematurely, sending a trader's sleigh team to their doom as they crossed. Wolves rampaged as well, with unaccustomed ferocity, coming out of the forests, marauding about the lake settlements and attacking fishermen bent over their holes in the ice. The *leshii* of the forest, in league with the *vodyanoi*, were both joined in some unholy union with the Princess, they said, intent on destroying them. Some great doom was implicit in this mating between a spirit and a mortal: the progeny would be more evil still. The people came to avoid the castle whenever they could, blessed themselves repeatedly in sight of it and only entered its precincts under extreme duress.

So Yelena came to create a far more barbaric world on the lake than any her grandfather had sustained there – a barbarism from which she had suffered there herself years before, with her uncle Dmitri, and which she had loathed and left, but which now she recreated and extended, for others and in herself, for she came to suffer every sort of horrifying thought and hallucinatory vision – thoughts of persecution, visions of foul and threatening figures.

She was mad. And she was ill as well, from lack of food and sleep, her small body becoming grotesque, swelling out about her stomach, but thinning, wasting away everywhere else, bloated like a diseased animal.

Meanwhile, having been back in Petrograd for nearly three months and with their child due in the spring, Sasha and Harriet had not married. Harriet, having had second thoughts, refused him once more – much to his annoyance. She did this, she explained, because – though she loved him – she could not take away his young life, bind him to her in this way. It would be wrong. She had in fact other more important reasons for refusing him again, but she withheld these from him at that point. Anxious to avoid embarrassing the Rumovsky household, and wanting independence in any case, she had moved out of the Palace on their return from Lake Ladoga, renting a small apartment where she would have their child, on the first floor of an old house next to the Imperial stables overlooking the Moika canal.

Sasha had resumed his musical career alone, playing in the string section of the Petrograd Symphony Orchestra and giving some solo performances. He was thought to be a coming virtuoso, though audiences who remembered the inspired effects, the sensuous cohesion and uncanny unison, when his twin sister had accompanied him on the piano, found his solo playing somehow less exciting.

Sasha became aware of this, and was annoyed that he should be any the less a musician without Yelena. And his irritation here matched that which he came to feel for Harriet. As a result he became generally uneasy and childish – felt unanchored, indecisive, spiteful, aggressive. So that by way – as he hoped – of making Harriet more amenable, he became moody and unreliable towards her, erratic in his movements, spending some nights at the Palace, some at her apartment and others, without warning, away altogether. In this unbalanced mode he was over-attentive in her company, or ignored her.

Harriet, since from the outset she had never expected anything of Sasha, was not put out by these slights and vagaries. She was moved, yes, but not in the way Sasha had intended. Instead of being upset that they weren't together more often, she came to love him in a heightened, though not now obsessive, manner. She saw a virtue in his absences, the uncertainties of his visits, by recognizing how this increased the pleasure of them.

She was quite aware of the equation here, of absence making the heart grow fonder, and became aware of another, this time a chemical formula, less creditable but irresistible, whereby she saw them as two inert elements which, in sexual tandem, ignited brilliantly together, suggesting a natural affinity, a rightness for each other.

Yet she knew they were not entirely right. She knew how her passion, as it had before, had suppressed her better judgement – how, despite all these happy immediacies, they were not, by background and character, suited to a permanent life together. So she saw, too, how she was carrying on the relationship under false pretences; how, while full of rational concern for Sasha, she was in thrall to a greater imperative with him, caught again in the toils of what she had rejected with him before – his voracious, negligent passion and the excitement this released in her. She knew well how, in any longer term, she needed a more reasoned love, a more constant lover, which it was not in Sasha's nature to give her or to be.

Yet she couldn't tell him any of this, couldn't, for what were largely selfish, sensuous reasons, relinquish him. So, recognizing her bad faith in this, but unable to end the affair herself, she gave Sasha the opportunity of ending it, by telling him one truth at least, that she would never marry him.

But he didn't end it. Instead he simply took it badly. He stormed and fretted and became morose by turns. He sulked and fumed, filled with a typically contradictory Russian mix of gloom and excited anger. He would have what he wanted. And so intent was he on getting this that, with equal Slav perversity, it never crossed his mind to end their relationship. He insisted on his assumptions, on the necessity of marriage, seeing this as both socially appropriate and a guarantee of love.

Harriet tactfully pointed out that she was more than ten years older, that he had his youth to live, a time to find his own right ways in life. But he would not be persuaded. Had he been he might well have left her, for she would have destroyed all his romantic and social notions about love. Instead he held hard to these, believing that by persisting in his inconsistencies, by withholding and then giving himself to her with such ardour, she would come to want a more secure tenure with him. So he stayed, accepting his unhappy situation with her.

However, with regard to Yelena neither of them could do the same. Both became increasingly disturbed by news of her behaviour at the castle, which arrived in letters from Stephan to Prince Pyotr at the Palace every week. It was clear from these that Yelena had lost control, lost all touch with reality, was mad.

Sasha felt guilt and regret, thoughts which particularly assailed him as he walked along the canal to Harriet's apartment through the snowbound city at night after a concert: a feeling that he had betrayed his other half in the solo violin music he had just played, that he had abandoned his twin sister in every personal way as well, leaving her to languish alone in that gloomy northern castle across the frozen lake.

Harriet's attitude, though sympathetic, was more practical. 'What can you or any of us do? We've talked to her. And you and I and your father have all written since – to no avail. The only thing now is for your father to go up there and bring her back, forcibly if necessary, before she does any more harm to herself or the estate.'

'Yes. Though she would resist it, more forcibly, just as she attacked me. I've told you, she's got these extraordinary powers, now obviously in full flow. They think her a witch, a *vedmy*, Stephan says. Well, she is!'

'Do you – do we – really believe that?' Harriet had asked, uncertain of her own feelings about this.

'Yes, I do. She's possessed by some demon, some evil spirit.'

When Prince Pyotr heard from the steward that Yelena was very obviously pregnant, and told Sasha, Sasha was appalled, so that his father assumed the worst.

'You?' he asked.

'No! Not at all.' He started to walk agitatedly round the long table in the Prince's study. 'It's just as you said. I should have stayed with her – we should have stayed with her up there.'

'What difference if we had? This is something which obviously happened before she went up to the lake. Who of her friends might be the father? Last year, for example, when there was a group of you going about together?'

'There's Johnny Quince, the American; you met him. She liked him.'

'Yes, and indeed they went off together now I come to think of it, while you were away, to Dvinsk overnight to test a locomotive.'

'And there's Miki Ostrovsky,' Sasha broke in. 'Another close friend of ours you met here – who worked at Ciniselli's Circus. But he went away to tour with them last summer.'

'So how could it be him?'

'Because I saw them both together again, by chance, on the river, when I was living rough last autumn. A barge they'd been on had run aground. They were marooned, very much together then. So she'd obviously been seeing him as well as John Quince. It could be him.'

'She did it out of spite,' Sasha told Harriet that afternoon. 'Because I left her.' In some deep, secret place inside him he felt annoyed, outraged even, at this betrayal by Yelena.

'But that was *why* you left her. Or one reason why,' Harriet went on. 'Just as you left me.'

Harriet stood by the first-floor window, fiddling with the new floral curtains she had bought at the English shop, looking out at the Konvush bridge, where the hot-chestnut sellers had congregated, surrounded by customers anxious for any hot food, since, with the war, bread had become increasingly scarce in the city.

'Yes . . .' Sasha, looking furious, lifted his tea glass from the small drum table brought from Harriet's room at the Palace. A decorative brass samovar burbled in the middle.

'She did it out of spite, whoever she did it with. Certainly not love. You're the only one she loves. She's always been the dependent one, despite all her bluster. Clutching, trying to hold on to you, with you wanting to be free of her. So she fights all the more to get you back, because you are two sides of the same coin. And she feels she has no real existence without you, so that everything you do alone, and with me especially – for her that's a terrible betrayal.'

'But I don't feel that I'm part of her in that way.'

'No. But you are. You've simply chosen not to feel it.'

Sasha stood up, roused. 'Well, I'm *not* going to be pulled back –'

As he spoke he put his hand suddenly to his head. He felt a stab of violent pain, as if someone was pushing a needle into his skull.

'Sasha?' Harriet came to him, putting a hand to his brow.

'It's all right. It'll go away. It has before.'

'Sasha, you must see Dr Ivanov.'

'What good will that do?' They gazed at each other. 'You know perfectly well what I think. I've told you, but you won't believe it. It's her, not anything physical. She can reach out with those powers, and hurt me like this, no matter that she's hundreds of miles away.' He looked at Harriet resentfully, then sat down, putting his hands to his head, rocking slowly to and fro.

Harriet was upset. She knelt in front of him, clasping him. 'Sasha dearest,' she said. 'Even if you are right, we can still *do* something –'

'What?' He pushed her away, glowering. 'What can we do? She has this devil in her now – and the only way to be rid of that would be for her to die.'

Johnny Quince had already heard the news of Yelena's strange behaviour at the castle, and then of her pregnancy. Rumours had come down the line, from Ladenpohja to Vyburg and then to the Finland station in Petrograd. He had overheard the stories, and these had been more exactly retailed to him when he had made direct enquiries, of conductors and engineers who travelled to and fro between Ladoga and the capital. Yes, they told him, there was a mad woman, the Princess Rumovsky, over at the northern end of the great lake, a *vedmy*, a real witch, who rose in the air setting curses on all and sundry, who could turn base metal into gold and much else, a woman now with child by some evil spirit!

Johnny had pretended amusement at these preposterous stories. But with Matty, when he told him all this, he was more serious. They spoke one morning in their office on the top floor of the Astoria.

'Your child?' Matty asked bluntly.

'It could be.'

'Well, you got what you wanted from her, that way, at least.'

'I wanted much more than that, and you know it.'

'You're well rid of her, Johnny. I told you all along.'

'Well rid of her? If it's my child?'

'You told me you asked her to marry you, that night on the train, and she gave you the brush-off. So it's her funeral, isn't it?'

'It's not as simple as that. She liked me, Matty. We had something special – that thing you feel – okay!' He held his hand up against Matty's ironic sigh. 'But this time it was real. We both felt it. And you can't invent it or disguise it. And it's nothing to do with the other person's money or talent, or being good in bed. It's two people finding that secret part of each other, that no one else'll ever find. And there it is, out of the blue – you both have this secret of the other, and you don't have to talk about it, not ever, because you know it's there, and it's the heart of the whole thing, and it'll keep you well together ever after. We had that. So why did she turn me down?'

Matty, coming to listen to this with more respect, said, 'I don't know, Johnny. Except, like you've been telling me about these stories of her up at the castle, she's certainly nuts. That's why she turned you down.'

'Yes . . . It's a pity all the same.' Johnny went to his desk and picked up the telephone. Then, just before he asked for the number, cupping his hand over the mouthpiece, he turned to

Matty. 'You know something, though? I told her I'd never ask her again, to marry me. And I won't.'

Matty looked up. 'Good. You're not quite as nuts as she is.'

'Oh, I am. That's the real reason why it would have worked.'

Miki Ostrovsky had heard nothing of Yelena's pregnancy, or any other news of her. Busy with his disguises and other underground activities with the Bolsheviks, he missed her now and then, when he thought about her, running over in his mind, with a mix of regret, anger and puzzlement, her changed moods and the inconclusive talk they had had during their last meetings.

He had seen her several times before she had disappeared up to Lake Ladoga. She had come round to the watchmaker's shop with small *objets d'art* she had taken from the Palace – crystal paperweights, an ormolu vase, a Meissen figurine, things of no great value but which made it clear she was still willing to help his cause. In other ways, though, she had lost her enthusiasm – for him, and for life in general. That happy, imaginative spark which had ignited and given shape to all her daring instincts and fired her singular vision – this had disappeared. Her heart wasn't in things any more.

They had talked one afternoon up in his small room, sitting on the narrow bed together, the snow falling silently outside, hearing the chiming clocks downstairs. He would have liked to have taken her to bed again, and would have said as much but for her dulled expression. Instead, holding up the little Meissen shepherdess which she had brought, he said, 'Linochka, why don't we do things more permanently? This sort of thing' – he held up the figurine – 'Things for the revolution. Or things just together, as partners after the revolution. Go back to the circus then, my tricks. Or the kinema, all that. We could make a life together. We've things in common.'

She turned, and it seemed from her expression that she was going to say something happy and positive. But instead, like a horse refusing a fence, she said, 'I can't. I wish I could, because you're a fine and gifted person. And you deserve all those things in return. But I can't give them now. I haven't any goodness or gifts any more.' She looked down at her knees, brow furrowed, twisting her fingers together viciously, as if battling with some great problem. 'I'm bad,' she said vehemently at last. 'Bad with myself, with everyone else. I know it – but can't do anything about it.'

'It'll change for you, though. It's temporary. Things will change.'

'How? When?' she asked viciously.

'I could change them for you,' he told her firmly. 'If you let me. I won't always be stuck up here hidden in this room, on the run, giving people false moustaches. The revolution will come, one way or another, and sooner rather than later. And afterwards I'll be involved with running things – in the arts, theatre. You could be, too. You could be with me on all this from the start, now, because we've been making plans for it already. I've talked with some of the Bolshevik leaders – even Lenin, yes! There'll be a big Commissariat of the Arts, with a Chief Commissar. Well, you could be involved with the musical side of this, organizing things at the Conservatoire. Don't you see, there's a whole new life coming for the people. And for us.' He gazed at her, breathless. 'Yes, your life, too, Linochka, when there'll be so much excitement and things to do, you won't feel bad with yourself or anyone else. When we'll be free, and free together. Why not?'

Again, she looked at him as if about to agree with all this, and join him. But at the last moment she retreated. 'I can't. I can't, not now –'

'Linochka!' He took her by the shoulders, gazing at her intently. 'You *can*. It's all waiting for you. It's here, the start, right now. And me, because I love you. A whole new world. You can't – you mustn't – run away.'

But she had. He had walked back with her, between the banks of snow along the lane, when she had told him how her grandfather had just died and she had inherited the estate up on Lake Ladoga and was going there at once. He had held her momentarily, and kissed her in the falling snow before she moved away, taking a few steps, and had then returned, kissing him quickly again, her fur hat and *shuba* dusted white, looking at him, her blackberry eyes empty, saying nothing, leaving him nothing but the kiss. Then she was gone and he was desolate.

But later he was annoyed as well. Why had she not taken up with him – personally and professionally? They had everything to offer each other. And the future he had offered her in the new Russia was no distant unlikely ideal either. It was real. It was just round the corner. He consoled himself with the thought that she was unaccountably perverse, flawed beyond repair, no fit woman for him or any man. And yet . . .

'Even if I could easily get there, I don't want to go back and vegetate in England. I can be of use here, in the office, translating documents, cyphering, decoding.'

Sandy spoke to the Ambassador in his private office beyond the Chancellery, and Sir George replied, writing another message on a sheet of paper and passing it over. 'Well, if you insist. But you should at least take a spell of sick leave before returning to work here.'

Sandy was nearly deaf. He could hear quite well sometimes in one ear, but with a ringing, tinny noise if anyone spoke too loudly. His other ear took in almost nothing.

A week before, as an observer with the 65th Division of the Russian Ninth Army in Galicia, he had been going up country in the Carpathians, early one morning, sitting at the back of a wagon carrying a platoon of soldiers. They were moving along a rutted track through a forest of old oak, towards the Russian forward positions at the edge of the wood. He could hear their two artillery batteries, hidden to either side, banging away every few minutes, opening a barrage against the Austrian line a mile ahead of them, in the foothills of the mountains. The Austrians, allowing the Russians to exhaust their meagre daily ration of ammunition, had made no reply with their heavier guns.

Suddenly, some minutes after the Russian barrage had ended, the Austrians opened fire. He heard the whistle of a shell going overhead, followed by another, with two tremendous explosions just behind them in the wood. A third shell, crashing through the trees, landed on the track just in front of the two horses. Sitting at the end of the truck with his back to the driver, he was briefly aware of a fierce ball of light sweeping over him, a rush of air like a fist – then oblivion.

When he regained consciousness he smelt the sappy odour of freshly sundered timber all about him, mixed with cordite fumes, and tasted blood on his lips. Looking up he saw the big oak tree, branches and part of the trunk split in pieces. He was lying in the undergrowth some yards from the track. Turning, he saw the remains of the wagon, one wheel in the air, the rest in smithereens, with a dozen wounded or dead soldiers lying about. Of the two horses there was no sign whatsoever.

He could see and smell and taste all these things. But he couldn't hear a thing. It didn't surprise him at first. It was to be expected, this eerie silence after sudden, brutal carnage. It wasn't until the Red Cross unit picked him up and a medical orderly spoke to him that he realized it was he who was almost deaf and not the world that was silent.

The Russian doctor at the field hospital thought the deafness temporary. But Dr Webb, the Embassy physician, when he had visited him for tests at the Alexander Hospital on his return to Petrograd, told him that both ears had been damaged, the ear drum in one slightly ruptured, which should heal naturally in time, but, more seriously, a part of the inner ear, the cochlea, was damaged in the other and that he should return to London to have the condition properly appraised and dealt with.

Sandy had ignored this advice. He had stayed on in Petrograd, through the deepening winter, over Christmas and into the new year of 1915, working in the war operations room at the top of the Embassy, where the side windows gave out over the Palace next door, so that he was forced to think of the Rumovskys now and then. Not that he wanted to see any of them – and indeed, apart from Prince Pyotr and his wife, neither the twins nor Miss Harriet were to be seen leaving or entering the Palace. He would like to have seen Miss Harriet at least. He was tempted to make enquiries of her, but did nothing about this until the letter arrived from Prince Pyotr a few days after he had returned.

My dear Captain Woodrow,

I have heard of your accident and write with my apologies to you. I know that it was as a result of quite unfounded rumours, coming from my household and concerning Miss Boulting and yourself, that you were encouraged to leave for the Front. I must say that I myself never believed for a moment that your association with Miss Boulting was other than entirely proper – a belief which was confirmed when I subsequently learnt who was the father of her child. I can only renew my apologies and assure you of my good thoughts for a full recovery. If there is any way in which I personally can help to this end I hope you will let me know.

Sandy put down the letter. So, the family had discovered the real culprit – Sasha. But where was he? And Miss Harriet? Brother, sister and governess, all three had disappeared. He was curious. Had Miss Harriet left Petrograd? Returned home to Ireland to have the child? He thought he might at least take the Prince up on his offer to find out.

Prince Pyotr was embarrassed when he met Sandy the next day, both in having to write notes to this nearly deaf man, whose condition his wife had indirectly brought about, and in having so formally to admit that his son was now living with Miss Harriet in an apartment on the Moika Canal. He gave Sandy the address.

'I am sorry for this,' the Prince wrote. 'It is not what I hoped for in my son, or for Miss Boulting. All most unfortunate. I am glad that you will visit her. She is determined to have the child here. You may perhaps persuade her to return home – with your influence at the Embassy this might be arranged?'

'Indeed, I can try to persuade her.' Sandy stood up. 'And Yelena?' he asked easily, making it seem an afterthought, simply a gesture of social goodwill. 'I have not seen her about. She is well?

The Prince paused before writing his reply, uneasy again. Then he wrote, 'Her grandfather died some months ago. She has inherited our family castle and estate on Lake Ladoga. She lives alone there now. We don't hear much of her. I believe she is well.'

Sandy, seeing the Prince's awkward expression, thought he was lying. All was not well with Yelena. She was estranged from the family for some reason. He supposed Miss Harriet might tell him. He would write her a note and hope to see her alone. He was somewhat upset – more so than he had expected – to hear that she was living with but not married to Sasha. Though this last fact gave him a twinge of hope, so that, having said goodbye to the Prince, he suddenly felt impatient. He was more knocked about by his experiences in Galicia than he cared to admit. He was desperate now, in fact, to reclaim his life in some fashion. He longed for some sympathetic talk and companionship with someone absolutely of his own world. He decided he would go round and see Miss Harriet there and then.

'Sandy! What a surprise. What a lovely surprise!'

Harriet's voice rang out in real welcome when she opened the door of her apartment. But he heard little of this, could only assume the words of surprised greeting, that very slight Irish brogue of hers which he had always liked. She came forward and embraced him quickly, so that having seen her swelling stomach, he now felt it briefly against his own. She took him through the narrow hallway into the front room. 'Sandy, you might have written!'

He heard her voice only as a distant warble. He took out the note pad and pencil he always carried now, and said, 'I was deafened at the Front, a shell exploded. I'm afraid you'll have to write things down – and tell me if I'm talking too loud!'

'Sandy – oh, my dear Sandy, how terrible! Come, sit down here.'

He looked around the cosy drawing-room. There was no one else there. They took chairs together at the round table, a cold samovar in the middle, and, sitting next to her so that he could see what she wrote, they started a long, rather disjointed and frustrating communication. He told her of his experiences at the Front. They swapped news about the war, news from England and Ireland. They were happy and excited in each other's company, as they had been before, when he had last seen her in hospital – until, just as had happened there, they came to more personal matters, which Harriet introduced quite casually, but in a less excited style.

'I'm here with Sasha,' she wrote, having reached a fourth sheet of paper. 'He came back from his wanderings. I'll be having the baby. About two months.'

'Not going home? Would that not be better? I think I could arrange something through the Embassy. One of the British warships that sometimes come to Archangel or Murmansk.'

'I'm staying here. Why risk the journey home? All these U-boats?'

'It won't be easy, surely, on your own. Especially since, as I understand it, you're not expecting to marry Sasha?'

'No. I love him –' she wrote emphatically. But then she paused, with a slightly pained air, gazing out at the frozen view along the canal, so that it seemed to Sandy that her emphasis, even her words here, had led her too far forward, beyond her emotional means – had left her stranded with the idea of having a great love for Sasha, which was something which her better judgement could not entirely support.

'You needn't go on.'

But then, as if she had squared her conscience about this, she rushed on in her writing. 'Loving someone doesn't mean you have to marry them. Not for me.' She turned, seeing his perplexed expression. 'It started with a mistake – the child – and that's no reason to tie someone down for a lifetime.' She saw the doubt in his eyes. 'You find that strange,' she wrote on. 'But why? Marriage is a convention – good if it works, but it wouldn't with Sasha. We're very different. Background and character. And I've told him I won't marry him.'

'Forgive me for saying so, but if you're not going to marry him, and have told him this, why stay on with him now? Or perhaps you're not going to stay on with him?'

'Yes, I will. For as long as he wants.'

'But why? If there's to be no security for you in the matter? Or for him?'

Harriet was uneasy again before she replied. 'Because I love him. Enjoy his company, day by day. And he mine. There is a life of love in the here and now, as much as in some future.'

Sandy tried to restrain his annoyance, his jealousy indeed, looking at this woman, voluptuous in her impending motherhood, seeing the velvety peach bloom of her skin. Her sensuous nature, which before had largely been hidden, was now starkly evident. 'Yes, a love in the here and now, of course,' he said. 'But, if Sasha wants to marry you, and you refuse him, is that not – in the longer term – perhaps unfair to him?'

Harriet showed her unease again. For a moment it seemed as if she was going to curtail these lines of enquiry. Then, as if she saw Sandy as a useful sounding board, even a moral confessor, she wrote on quickly, justifying herself. 'He's free to leave whenever he chooses. That's perfectly clear, as well – to both of us. Because it's an honest, open relationship. You may see immorality in our situation. I see the honesty of it.'

Sandy couldn't argue with this. Instead he made a flanking movement in his next sally. 'Indeed. Though I know if, for example, I wanted to marry someone and they refused, I should find it hard – no, I simply couldn't live with them. I would find that intolerable. And I'm surprised that Sasha doesn't feel the same.'

At this point Harriet recognized that Sandy had cornered her. Sasha, she very well knew, did find living with her in this unsecured manner very difficult, if not quite intolerable. Then she decided that, having gone this far, she should maintain her honest approach. 'Yes, he does find it difficult,' she wrote. 'But the fact remains that a marriage between us wouldn't work.'

'But what of the child in all this? He, or she – you are denying it a father. And what of the future practicalities – yours and the child's?'

'I have the means to bring up the child myself. Ideally I should wish for marriage, both for myself and for the child. But with Sasha, that can't, or shouldn't, happen. Sasha's a young man. To tie him into marriage would be to have an unhappy marriage. Honesty and foresight are far better. I know that now.' She paused in her writing and looked up at him, smiling a little wanly, then continued, 'So what I've decided is, for as long as he wants it, to make the best of Sasha's company now. And yes, the child may not have a legal father. But at least we know who the father is, unlike Yelena.'

'Unlike Yelena?' Sandy felt a prickle running up his spine as he read this last sentence.

'Yelena is having a baby as well.' Harriet, looking up, almost smiled at Sandy's exaggerated expression of surprise. His pale grey eyes showed unwarranted alarm, she thought. Harriet then wrote a brief account of all that she knew about Yelena at the castle – of how, possessed of a quite unnatural strength, she had attacked Sasha, intending to incinerate him, and had then told them all to leave and was now running the place with arrogant irrationality – and fearful supernatural powers as well, if Stephan's reports were to be believed. It sounded indeed as if Yelena had gone mad.

Sandy, on his feet now in his agitation, and the better to see what she wrote, leant over her shoulder. 'So you see,' Harriet ended, 'Yelena's the worry now, in real trouble, a child on the way and no known father. Though we think it may be one of her friends she was going round with last year – John Quince, the American, or Miki Ostrovsky, the clown –'

Harriet stopped writing, realizing that Sandy had moved away from her, over to the window. He turned suddenly. 'No, no!' He shook his head vehemently. 'Not them. Don't blame them, as I was blamed for being the father of your child. It was me. I'm the father.'

'You?' It was Harriet's turn to be amazed, so that she forgot to write anything down.

But Sandy could read the word on her lips. He was beginning to lip-read now. 'Yes, me.'

Harriet came to him at once, not censorious for a moment, so full of sympathy and concern that, taking his hand, she forgot herself and said, 'Oh, Sandy, dear Sandy – and I thought it was only people like me, and the twins, who made mistakes like that!' Then, in a hurried scrawl, she had to repeat herself in writing.

Later, when he said he would go up to the lake and try and help Yelena, Harriet was taken aback. 'Why?' she wrote. 'I told you, Yelena was with the other two men towards the end of last year. So you can't be certain it's your child at all.'

'It's very likely to be, given the state of her pregnancy, as I understand it, and since I was with her earlier in the year.'

She looked up at him, frowning, then wrote: 'But even if it is your child, in her present mood she would dismiss you out of hand, or do you some injury.'

'Injury?'

'Yes. Yelena is not just ill or dotty. She's thought to have supernatural powers. Sasha thinks so. And a *muzhik* who angered her, she just looked at him and he died at her feet. It sounds ridiculous, but –'

'No, no!' He interrupted her as she wrote. 'I can believe it. She told me of these powers almost the first time we met. I didn't believe it then. But afterwards I did, when she came to my flat that night of the great thunderstorm last autumn. Believed it then because I experienced it myself. She talked to me – I heard her voice – when she wasn't there, after she'd left the flat. And other things. She was struck by lightning that night and came to no harm. And that black dog of hers – after the lightning struck her she saw it in front of her, in University Park, but I never saw it. Yet it was real, she had it with her the next time we met. In myth the devil's familiar is often a black dog.'

'The local people at Ladoga say that too, that the dog is the devil's agent.' They looked at each other. 'But Sandy,' she wrote on hurriedly, 'surely you and I can't sensibly believe any of this?'

'Are you and I that sensible?' he asked quickly, running a hand through his thinning hair, then flapping his arms about in frustration. 'We like to think so. But look what we've both done – with the twins. Was that sensible? No. It was madness. Everyone – we all live on the brink of lunacy, obsession. Just underneath the surface there's all sorts of madness, in us and outside us. We control it, take the harm out of it, by rational thought or by turning it into fairy tales or grand opera. But the evil itself is still there, behind all the good sense and the fables. I used to believe all this just as theory, when I studied folk tales and legends, when I first learnt Russian and read Afanasiev's fairy tales. But after my experiences with Yelena I'm inclined to see it as fact – the *reality* of such personal evil. So I'm not surprised to hear of her doings, these strange tales about her at the castle.'

'Well, if that's so,' Harriet wrote angrily now, with furious pace, 'why are you going up there, to risk yourself? And you would be. That's not just quixotic, you're being lunatic now. *Why*?' She underlined the word vigorously.

'I owe it to her, if it's my child. And I feel I owe it to her in any case. Evil she may be. But there's something equally good hidden in her, which perhaps I could help her to recover.'

'You're half in love with her!' she wrote, looking up at him, almost spitefully.

'Yes. Yes, I was. And you're right, that was exactly the proportion, because I despised her just as much. But in the end – I'd do the same for any woman who was carrying my child. I'd have done the same for you – long before you tried to kill yourself under that tram,' he added pointedly, his face flushed now.

She nodded. Then she wrote '*Touché*' and looked up at him. Her eyes were moist. Before he left she gave him a little envelope. Inside was a four-leafed clover. 'Keep it,' she wrote. 'I had it from a man in west Cork, years ago. The "little people" grew them he said –'

'In a crock of gold at the end of the rainbow, no doubt. Yes, those Irish fairy stories. I know all about them, too!'

They laughed and he embraced her quickly before he left; and when he'd gone she thought once more what a terrible mess she'd made. Sandy was right. Everyone lived on the brink of lunacy, mindless obsession. If it weren't so, she would have been living with him now, not Sasha.

Sandy, after he left her, felt something of the same thing. But it was more a feeling of petulant animosity applied directly to Harriet and not to fate, a searing, sexual bitterness that she had given herself to Sasha, and not to him.

19

At Ladenpohja Sandy had great difficulty in persuading any of the *yamshchiks* with their sleighs for hire to take him across the ice to the castle. In the station buffet, with one of the more literate waiters writing out their replies, he'd had to bargain with them. It was a dangerous trip now – in every way, they told him. There were many more wolves about than usual, voracious beasts; they would have to take another man with a rifle. But it was his destination that was the worst of it. Did he not know of the mad princess at the castle? A *vedmy* there, with her black dog, in league with the devil, who walked the ramparts raining curses down? It was madness for anyone to go to such a place. In the end he had to pay them more than double the usual fare.

And indeed it seemed mad to Sandy as well when he eventually set off across the ice next morning, sitting behind the two heavily padded *yamshchiks*, the sun just a pale smudge low down on the horizon, with a sharp wind and snow clouds threatening from the north. To be attacked by wolves, to have curses rained on him – why? To help an evil madwoman who, even in her sensible times, had dismissed him cruelly, out of hand, and who might do him some further, material injury now. He could only reassure himself with the idea that it was the right thing to do. It was his duty, his responsibility.

As the sleigh gathered pace he pulled the fur rugs more closely up about his neck against the biting cold, tears already freezing on his cheeks. He wrapped his scarf about the lower part of his face. Finally he drew the rim of his astrakhan hat right down over his forehead, and closed his eyes, so that he saw nothing.

He thought of Harriet and the good-luck charm she had given him. Did he really believe in such things? Or were there only realistic ways of combating evil? With the small Smith and Wesson revolver, for example, which, when he was in civilian clothes, he always took with him on his trips about Russia, carrying it in a special holster strapped to the inside of his leg.

Later, when the wolves came, as the *yamshchiks* had forecast – a small pack of hungry, white-dusted grey beasts, loping along behind them – it seemed as if his latter thought was confirmed. The men used their rifles, killing or dispersing them. And it struck Sandy then that evil, that what was brute or malign in man or beast, could only be overcome by rational and, if necessary, violent means.

But when, in the early twilight, hours later, the snow falling now in sharp flurries, he saw the speck of light in the distance, which grew into the great fire on the castle ramparts Harriet had told him about – when he saw the all-engulfing flames, sparks streaming up into the night sky like an apocalyptic vision of fiery hell – he had doubts again. Sasha had nearly been burnt alive in this great fire. Would either gun or good-luck charm protect him from the same possible fate?

The *yamshchiks* would not approach the castle. They left him in the snow some distance away, so that he had to walk with his bag towards the steps that led up from the lake.

A few minutes later, having climbed the narrow steps to the ramparts, he was confronted by two watchmen with rifles, and moments after that he was being marched between them into the great hall. A fire blazed in the centre. Yelena sat at the head of a long table, a group of scruffy, uneasy-looking men to either side of her, including a tall, fair-haired Lett, quite different from the others, whom Sandy took to be the steward, Stephan.

He barely recognized Yelena, in her rich vestments, her gaunt face, hair pushed beneath a heavy fur *koshniki*, looking like a man. The black pug dog lay at her feet. There was a musky unpleasant smell in the air. Servants cowered about as she picked at her food, while watching a group of wary *skomorohki*, some dancers and musicians with balalaikas entertaining her round the fire.

The musicians stopped playing with his entry, and standing in front of Yelena in his snow-dusted *shuba*, Sandy shook himself free of the two watchmen. The whole situation was preposterous, he saw – this shabby, dissolute group in medieval clothes. It was a charade, some elaborate game which Yelena was playing, which but required a sensible response from him for her to abandon it.

He approached her easily, speaking in English. 'Yelena, these theatricals! It's not your Russian new year is it? Or a party?' But before he got any further the dog growled and Yelena, speaking to the watchmen, had them take his arms again. 'Yelena, this is nonsense –' He tried to shake himself free. 'I've come up from Petrograd to speak to you. But I can't hear. A shell exploded almost on top of me at the Front. I'm nearly deaf. So you'll have to write down your replies. I've got a pencil and notebook here. If you'll tell these men to let me go.'

Yelena stood up and came towards him – a more bird-like figure than ever, he thought. But a wounded bird now, weighed down by her fancy dress. He saw her swollen stomach between the folds of the gilded sable cloak, a small dagger at her waist, the spindly feet encased in long black boots. These ridiculous props – a child playing games. 'Do tell them to let go of me. So that we can talk.'

He saw her lips move. The men released him. She took the notebook and pencil he passed to her. 'Talk about what?' she wrote in Russian, and passed the book back.

'About us. Your child. It could be mine,' he continued in English. She looked at him curiously, as if he were a total stranger. 'Whoever the father is, we must do something about it. I've seen Harriet and your father. You should come back to Petrograd with me, make things up with everyone. And we can arrange something sensible about the child.' He gestured round the hall. 'All this, it's not getting you anywhere.'

He waited for her reply. The rush flares, high up on the boulder walls, flickered in a sudden draught. The black dog looked up at him malevolently.

Servants and musicians shifted uneasily on their feet. A puff of dark smoke, belching down the huge chimney, invaded the space with a sulphurous smell, a dark pall hanging in the air between them now. Yelena finally started to write in Russian.

'I don't know you. Or the people you talk of. A deaf stranger, speaking in a foreign tongue – who turns up here saying he is the father of my child – and expects me to write to him? Sheer impertinence. You will cool your heels downstairs, until I deal with you in the morning.' She gestured to the guards. They gripped him again. He started to struggle.

'Yelena! Of course you know me.' He shouted in Russian now. 'Sandy. Sandy Woodrow.' The men were pulling him away. 'Tell them to let me go! Of course you know me. And you speak English just as well as you speak Russian –'

They dragged him struggling out of the great hall, along a corridor and down a circular stone stairway, through a succession of ill-lit rooms to another dank and freezing corridor below. Opening a heavy door, the men pushed him inside and locked the door behind, leaving him in darkness. This was no charade, he thought.

Lighting a match he found himself in a small, arched room without any windows, some old straw on the floor, with chains attached to the wall running to leg irons beneath. He was incarcerated in a medieval dungeon. It was preposterous. He was furious. He fumed and fretted, unstrapped the revolver from his leg. But there was no escape.

Some hours later – nearly midnight by his watch – the big door opened and Stephan came in holding a lantern. He handed him a note in Russian. 'You should leave at once. If you follow me I can get you out of the castle and onto the mainland.'

Sandy nodded in agreement. Then, showing Stephan his revolver, he followed him out of the cell.

But he never got to the mainland.

At the top of the winding stairs, as they were moving along to the end of the vaulted corridor that led into the great hall, Stephan heard footsteps beyond and quickly pulled Sandy behind a curtain that hung by the entrance way. Peering through into the hall they saw Yelena, with the dog and the two armed watchmen, making towards them. It was clear, with their hurried steps and air of purpose, that either they knew of or suspected his escape and were making for the dungeons. But it was equally clear that the dog would smell them out and start barking as the group neared the curtains, when they would be immediately unmasked. Sandy, raising his revolver, prepared to take the initiative.

A moment later, just as he had expected, the dog, smelling their presence and starting to bark, ran towards them. In the same instant Sandy, whipping the curtain aside, levelled his revolver at the group as they came towards him, not five yards away.

'Stop! Don't move,' he shouted in Russian. A moment later the dog arrived at his feet, biting his ankle viciously, forcing him to kick out at it, taking his eyes off the two watchmen, so that one of them had the opportunity to unsling his rifle and had half aimed it at him before Sandy was able to fire – a quick precise shot, which hit the man in the shoulder. He spun round like a top, dropping his rifle, yelping in pain.

As Sandy turned the revolver on the other watchman, the dog renewed his attack, biting fiercely into his ankle again, finding the flesh above the boot. He gasped in pain. Infuriated now by this malign animal and by all that it might well stand for as an agent of evil in Yelena's life, he lowered his gun and shot it, firing at close range, hitting it somewhere behind the neck. It fell over at his feet.

Yelena ran forward, screaming at him so loudly that he could hear her in his half-good ear. She started to grapple with him before Stephan pulled her away, holding her firmly, while Sandy confronted the second watchman with his revolver, disarming him. His colleague lay on the flagstones, groaning. But now that the dog was dead and Yelena a captive, there was no more fight in either of them. Indeed, with the dog gone, the second watchman looked relieved, as if this event presaged a return to normality in the castle. The whole atmosphere seemed lighter.

Sandy took both the rifles, slung them over his shoulder, and approached Yelena. Her face was livid with fury. She was still screaming at him, though he couldn't make out her words. Instead he noticed her glazed eyes. She was sweating, feverish – her hair, without the regal *koshniki*, damp and straggly. Sandy had never seen anyone looking both so ill and so venomous. His ankle stung with pain. Suddenly he was equally furious with her.

'Why don't you just shut up!' he shouted at her in English. 'And stop your screaming and the rest of your childish behaviour. We've all had enough of it. Just shut up, for once, and start to see some sense.' Hearing this, and understanding it, Yelena screamed the more, gesturing down at the black dog, dead at her feet. 'And yes, that dog of yours, that evil dog – you are well rid of it.'

Sandy looked down. The dog was moving. It wasn't dead. It had risen on its front feet, growling throatily, flecks of foam on its muzzle. It was trying to make for him now. He shot it again. It collapsed once more, lying out inertly, blood coming from its mouth, this time certainly dead.

At the same moment, Yelena went quite still, as if the life had gone out of her as well. Eyes closed, she fell forward, so that Stephan had to hold her up, a dead weight in his arms.

Some other servants, hearing the commotion, had arrived in the hall. They stood in doorways, wary, astonished at the scene, but relieved, as the watchmen had been, by the demise of this witch, this *vedmy* and her evil cohort, the black dog. Sandy took Yelena from Stephan, and held her swollen body in his arms. 'Her bedroom?' Stephan gestured upwards. Sandy followed him.

Taking a winding stairway, they climbed the tower to a small room near the top, with a single window, a waning oil-lamp and two large, white-painted iron cots to either side. The place was in complete disorder. Toys and dolls, with English children's books of all sorts, were strewn about. It was clear to Sandy that this had been the twins' nursery, when they had come here years before. One cot, holding a teddy bear, part of a tin train set and a kite, was undisturbed, its iron side rail drawn up. The other, nearby, with its rail down, the net blankets all tossed about, was obviously Yelena's and still used. Sandy laid her down in it.

He turned to Stephan. 'Can we get a doctor?'

Stephan took the notebook and wrote, 'Doctor at Salmi. I will go. He would not come for anybody else.'

When he'd gone Sandy felt her pulse. It was weak. Her breathing was shallow. He covered her up completely, using extra blankets from the other cot, then stoked up the stove behind him, brought the oil-lamp over and sat down next to her on a small nursery chair.

Her face was calm and pale. But after ten minutes, regaining consciousness, her expression changed. She became agitated, her face creasing in pain. Her eyes closed, she began to twist and turn in the cot, clutching at the iron rails, as if she was drowning and trying to reach the sides of a boat. He took one of her hands firmly in his. 'Sasha!' she called out in relief. 'Sasha.'

He thought she spoke his name. 'Yes, it's me, Sandy,' he replied in English. 'There's nothing to worry about. The doctor's coming. I'm here. I'll stay with you.'

She relaxed and seemed to sleep. He kept her hand in his, resting just above her swollen belly. The children's books in the cot had fallen to the side, caught against the lowered side rail. He saw the titles: Kate Greenaway's Nursery Rhymes, E. Nesbit's *The Phoenix and the Carpet*, *The Tailor of Gloucester* by Beatrix Potter. The blizzard, which had started with his arrival at the castle, seemed to be dying outside the narrow window.

With his free hand he eased out the small copy of *The Tailor of Gloucester* from behind the bars, and opened it.

Inside he saw the neat handwriting. 'For Linochka, on her sixth birthday, with love from Miss Harriet.' With his other hand, lying just above Yelena's stomach, he felt something move, a minute stirring from beneath the folds. My God, he thought, this child-mother, with all her fancy theatrical costumes and props downstairs, found her only real succour up here with Beatrix Potter.

As she slept he turned to the first pages and started to read out loud. He couldn't hear his words but he saw them on the page as a sort of benediction, letting them flow over her sleeping face, she as deaf to the story as he was. 'In the time of swords and periwigs and full-skirted coats with flowered lappets – when gentlemen wore ruffles and gold-laced waistcoats of paduasoy and taffeta – there lived a tailor in Gloucester . . .'

He let the words die at the end of the page – of this tale of mice who had saved the life and fortune of the old tailor. Nesbit and Greenaway and Potter, happy icons of a nursery world so far removed from the malign aura of this gloomy, evil castle. And it was to this world, of familial reassurances, of children's rhymes and fables where things turned out happily ever after, that Yelena had been trying to return.

She wasn't possessed by the devil, he decided now. What nonsense all that was. Made ill by her obsession with, and loss of, Sasha, she had simply fallen into that other underworld which he had not spoken to Harriet about – a netherworld not of Satan but of common human aberration, of mania and depression, that despair and darkness which also lay just beneath the thin ice of sense and civilization.

Sandy reassured himself with these thoughts of the rational. He didn't want to believe in the devil, or that it was the influence of that foul dog, the devil's familiar, that had made her ill and brought her evil.

But what if that had been the case? He was suddenly assailed by doubt again. Could it be so? As a reality, beyond all common sense, beyond myth and fable, and as a cause of human disruption, could one find the influence of the supernatural? Had the dog somehow been the agent of all this in Yelena? Was it conceivable that in killing the dog, he had released Yelena from the toils of the devil? Either way, whether he had slain the dragon or not, it didn't matter. What Yelena needed now was human care and affection.

As soon as Stephan came back and she had seen the doctor, when she was better, he would take her back to Petrograd, where she could have her child in safety and be cured at home on the Neva. He would sit with her meanwhile, keep guard, until dawn. Releasing her hand gently, he pulled his *shuba* more closely about him and, hunched in the little chair, drifted off to sleep.

He had a nightmare then, intensely vivid. Surrounded by half a dozen very provocatively dressed young women, he was sitting in the front pew of his local village church at home in the Cotswolds. But the church was ruined now, the stained-glass windows broken, with a bitter wind coursing through. The women to either side and behind him – prostitutes, he saw them to be – were ogling him lasciviously, trying to seduce him, while his father was ranting away, delivering a hell-fire sermon from the pulpit. 'For the devil is as a roaring lion seeking out whom he may devour. Be ye therefore ever vigilant –'

His father stopped suddenly, looking towards the doorway of the church with an expression of incredulity and fear. All the half-naked women turned round as well. And as he turned in the dream he woke with a start and found himself looking at the door of the nursery.

It was open. There was something there, some form, waiting, looking at him from the shadows – a pair of eyes, large and yellow, reflecting the lamplight. The form approached him.

It was the black pug dog.

But it was not in the same form. It was twice the size and quite monstrous now, misshapen and filthy, covered in slime, dripping blood, its squashed pug features exaggerated and distorted in deep slobbering folds, its mouth half open, foaming.

He must still be dreaming. But the longer he looked at it the more real this horrendous vision became. He waited, transfixed. He couldn't move. He was tied to the chair as if suffering from a terrible cramp. And there was a loathsome smell now, of musky excrement. He felt in the presence of something overwhelmingly evil, which he could do nothing to combat. He was certain that he would be swallowed up and annihilated at any moment.

The dog slouched towards him, slowly, awkwardly, dragging itself across the floor in a trail of blood. He tried to get his revolver out from the pocket of his *shuba*. But still he couldn't move. His heart pounded. He was going to faint. He remembered no more, falling forward off the chair, into blackness.

The screams woke him, they were so loud. Yelena was sitting up in the cot screaming. 'The dog!' she shouted, so that he could just hear the words. 'The black dog – get it away! Save me!'

He got to his feet. There was no sign of the dog now. 'Where?' he shouted at her.

'There!' she pointed to the end of the cot.

'There's nothing there, Yelena. The dog was here. I saw it, too. But it's gone –'

'No!' She shook her head vigorously. 'It hasn't! I can see it at the end of the bed! It's coming for me. Get it, save me –'

She fell back, flailing her arms, struggling fiercely as if trying to repulse this animal which was savaging her now.

Then her movements took a different form. She seemed to be doing battle with herself. She stretched her body this way and that, sweating, frightened, her eyes screwed up in pain, clutching at the iron bars of the cot as if she was trying to release, get rid of, something poisonous inside her.

The child, Sandy thought. Her child – his child. She was trying to give birth to it, lifting her knees up, spreading her legs wide, her whole body racked with pain as she swayed about, moving up and down, caught in fearful spasms, convulsing, contracting.

The intervals between her spasms shortened. The contractions in her body, as she strained to and fro, became more rapid and forceful. He could hear her agonized screams. He took her hand – took both her hands, standing at the end of the cot and leaning over her, so that, arms above her head, she held onto him like the bar of a trapeze, pulling against him each time the pain came, coming more quickly now, when she launched herself away from him, the blankets all tossed aside. Below her rolled-up tunic, he looked down on her naked stomach and thighs, legs splayed apart, knees swinging wide, as her nails bit into his hands and she almost dragged him over the end of the cot. He had to take her by the wrists, to maintain a grip, as she pushed and retreated in a furious rhythm.

Suddenly he saw something damp and wine-red, round and squashed like a bloodied grapefruit, emerge from between her thighs, followed by what might have been a skinned rabbit, a slippery, purplish-blue form, with tiny arms and legs and starfish fingers, and a jelly-like cord after that, until finally the whole small macerated body lay between her legs, silent, without a breath of life in it.

Yelena, too, seemed in the same state, lying back, eyes closed, unstirring, dead. He put his hand underneath her red tunic, settling on her swollen breast, feeling for a heartbeat. He felt nothing.

Horrified, he looked at the ugly pain stamped like a seal on her frozen features, the gutted, emaciated body of this once beautiful, gifted woman. All this had been taken away in giving birth to her child – his child surely – so that he had caused her death. He picked up her hand. He held it for a minute. Then he said, 'Let her live, dear God. Let her live and I'll do anything for her afterwards, so that she never falls into these depths again.'

He didn't hear the footsteps running along the passageway outside and only turned round when Stephan and the doctor were right behind him. 'I think she's dead,' he told the elderly man in a snow-dusted *shuba*.

The doctor, observing the gory scene, was businesslike. 'No, not quite dead. Though she's certainly just had a miscarriage.' He turned to Stephan. 'Water, boiling water, and towels, as quickly as you can.' He took off his *shuba* and gloves and opened his bag. Stephan and Sandy left the room.

Stephan went downstairs, while Sandy went upwards, round the circular staircase and out onto the battlements at the top of the tower. The storm had gone. Dawn was breaking. The sun rose, a faint pink rim at first, invading an indigo gauze on the far horizon, vibrating through the chilled haze before it emerged fully grown, a huge orange ball, climbing into a cloudless sky, transforming all the night-blue colours, streaks of bright umber running across the lake, the broad beams of light making a ripple of endless shadows in the small valleys of fresh snow, over the ice where the crests of these waves shimmered in silver crystals.

It was one of those miraculous passages in the northern Russian winter, the first of those clear days which come in late February or March, when the storms and blizzards die away and the earth, rubbed clean, is set in a frozen, sun-struck, blue-skied world of pristine colour.

He sat on the battlements, smoking a cigarette. What had he done in that promise to God about staying with and helping Yelena? He didn't love her. He had committed himself to her out of duty and guilt, not love. Why should God let her survive for such cold ministrations from him? And what an arrogant presumption on his part to offer them. If they'd loved each other, that would have been a different matter. God might have made efforts, on behalf of both of them. But they shared no such feeling. In truth, he had come up to the castle largely under false pretences, to spite Harriet more than to help Yelena. He had been dishonest with himself and with Harriet, and before that brutish with Yelena, succumbing to sheer animal instinct in giving her this child, which she had died in giving birth to. He was a monster. His guilt and hypocrisy were unbearable.

He took out his revolver, slipped the safety catch, put it to his temple. But he did nothing more. He did not even have the courage to kill himself.

The rising sun glinted on the turquoise-blue and gold domes of the monastery church on the next island, shone on the whitewashed buildings giving them a patina of gold. The whole monastic settlement rose from the snowy canvas of the lake like a pile of jewels. He heard the sound, faintly repeated, reverberating in his good ear – the bell for matins. He put the revolver back in his pocket. 'When the day breaks, and the shadows flee away,' he said to himself. He turned and went back down the narrow stone staircase.

Ten minutes later the doctor emerged from the nursery. Sandy was in the corridor outside, pacing up and down, waiting with Stephan.

'Dead?' he asked.

The doctor shook his head. 'No, she'll be all right. She'll live.'

Sandy explained his deafness. They went downstairs to the estate office next to the old armoury where the doctor could write replies and explanations. 'She's lucky,' he wrote on a sheet of paper. 'The child's dead. And so should she be. I'll arrange for a woman – a sensible enough woman in Salmi – to come up here and look after her. The Princess needs complete rest, proper nourishing food, proper attention. Her family are all in Petrograd?' He looked up at Sandy, who nodded. 'You'll be staying on here with her, I assume?' he wrote. Sandy nodded again. 'It's surprising,' the doctor added to his note. 'She must have great resilience. Or luck.'

'Luck?'

'She ought to have died. The child was dead in her womb for some hours beforehand. And deformed as well, its head grossly enlarged. It's surprising she was able to expel it down the birth canal at all.' The doctor stood up. Then, thinking of something, he wrote again. 'She must be moved down from that nursery to a proper bedroom. The room is quite unsuitable and far too isolated. Some animal – a dog – has been up there, worrying at her in the cot – trying to get at the remains of the child, I suppose. Paw marks all over the floor. Do you know anything of that?'

Sandy didn't reply directly, saying simply that he would see that the Princess was moved downstairs. He hadn't noticed any footprints. He had come to think that his vision of the frightful dog, and Yelena's, had been some sort of auto-suggestion, or a continuation of his nightmare set in the village church at home. He didn't want to believe that this foul dog, after its death, had been somehow resurrected, and had climbed all those stairs to terrorize them both. But now, with the doctor's completely objective evidence, he had to believe it. Or did he? When the doctor had gone he spoke to Stephan.

'That black dog of hers, did you see it, after I shot it?'

'No,' Stephan wrote. 'I was surprised, when I got back with the doctor, not to see it where we'd left it in the hall. But it couldn't have been dead. It must have gone upstairs later to the nursery.'

'That's impossible! It was quite clearly dead, that second time, after I shot it.'

'I thought so too.'

'Well, where is it now, then? Did one of the servants take it, pick it up?'

'None of them would have gone near it. They believed it was the agent of the devil.'

'Do you believe that?'

'No.'

'Well, if you don't believe in the supernatural, and you confirm that the dog was certainly dead after we'd left it in the hall, how did its footprints get onto the nursery floor? And where is it now?'

'I don't know.'

They looked at each other. Both were rational men. Neither wanted to admit to the other that in this instance there seemed no explanation but the supernatural.

'What does it matter? The Princess is better,' Stephan wrote with a final flourish.

'Yes,' Sandy said slowly, thinking. 'When the doctor said she should have died. Instead the dog it was that died . . .' he ran on, talking more to himself than to Stephan. 'And saved her.'

Stephan looked at him, perplexed. But they left it at that.

Sandy, extending his sick leave, stayed on at the castle. The days lengthened. The sun shone. The ice beyond the ramparts began to groan and whisper, then to crack like pistol shots. There were stirrings everywhere, warming currents, in the air and underwater. The wolves disappeared, and birds flew again in the unaccustomed light, the brief midday hours of almost balmy weather, opening parliaments in trees with a cacophony of chatter. Spring came and then Easter, when the Monastery bells rang out at midnight and the braided wicks were lit beneath the huge candelabra, a crackle of flame running round the hundreds of candles, the nave flooding in gold. The iconostasis doors were opened. The old Abbot emerged and with the monks led everyone out of the church in procession, chanting '*Khristos Voskrese*! – 'Christ is risen!' Circling the church three times then, to the responses from the congregation, '*Voistinu Voskrese*!' – 'He is risen indeed!'

Sandy, having exchanged kisses with all and sundry, returned with Stephan and the other servants over the wooden bridge to Castle Island. Overhead a star-speckled sky enfolded them, the moon upended on its back just above the horizon as the Krupp cannon boomed from the ramparts over the silent lake, while great sheets of broken ice, and miniature icebergs, ghostly white, glided slowly by, drifting south to the river and the sea.

It was nearly a month now since Yelena's miscarriage, the horrors and nightmares of Sandy's arrival and the days and nights when Sandy and Olga, the widowed Karelian woman from Salmi, had watched over and ministered to Yelena. Though still weak and spending much of the time in bed, she was almost entirely recovered.

They had brought her downstairs from the tower and put her in the old Prince's large bedchamber in the south wing, above the estate office and armoury. Here the old woman slept near her, while Sandy took a bed in the small dressing-room next door. He had written of events to Prince Pyotr every week, who had replied, thanking him, saying he would come up to the castle after Easter, when he would take over and make more permanent arrangements about the running of the estate. He had also written to the Ambassador, telling him how his hearing had improved, as it had, and that he would soon be returning to the Embassy.

As soon as Prince Pyotr arrived there would be nothing to hold him, Sandy thought. He would be leaving, his duty done. It should all have been so simple. But it wasn't, and wouldn't be, because everything had changed completely now between him and Yelena.

Taking a tray of Easter food from Olga, *kulich* and *pashka*, he had gone into Yelena's room early that morning as he had promised her. She lay to one side of the huge, Lapp-carved, crimson-canopied bed, propped up by pillows, a large oil-lamp beside her, waiting for him impatiently.

'Sandy!' He put a bowl and a plate in front of her, then started to cut slices of the sticky sweet bread and spoon out the thick creamy *pashka*. 'Sandy!' she shouted again in his good ear. 'Happy Easter!' She held out her arms to him. He kissed her chastely. She gazed up at him intently. He saw her eyes sparkle, her slightly turned out lower lip pucker, the ends of her dark black mop of hair shiver, over her high lace collar. Then he bent down quickly and kissed her properly, and said 'Happy Easter! Happy happy Easter, dear Linochka.' It had all happened so quickly. Was he really doing this – loving and kissing this woman who, a few weeks before, had nearly died herself, and had been quite dead to him?

To begin with Yelena had made no progress at all. For almost a week after her miscarriage she hadn't recognized or properly spoken to him. After the old woman had tended her, changing her night clothes and trying to get her to eat, he'd sat by her bed for long stretches, morning and evening, when she either slept or was restless, her eyes, when they came his way, looking at him vacantly. Now and then he saw her lips open briefly in some sort of speech, making an effort at communication. But she would almost immediately abandon the effort, as if overwhelmed by the whole idea of expression.

She seemed to be trying to struggle up from some deep pit – to remember, to regain something, a foothold in a previous reality, trying to identify the shapes and colours and contours of a world she had abandoned long before.

With nothing else to do he'd thought to read to her again, from some book she'd once been familiar with, in the hopes that this might give her a life-line back to sanity. There were only her English children's books in the castle. He chose a more substantial example than the Beatrix Potter story: E. Nesbit's *The Phoenix and the Carpet*.

Soon Yelena began to make vague responses, her eyes lighting up at some incident in the story, or at one of the illustrations which he showed her. But it wasn't until he'd got well into the book that she suddenly and properly responded, as if the images in the passage he was reading had some special meaning for her, had finally brought her back to reality.

'"The savage looked at the children. Concealment was impossible. He uttered a shout that was more like 'Oo goggery bag-wag' than anything else the children had ever heard, and at once brown, coppery people –"' Sandy had looked up. Yelena's lips were moving. She was speaking whole sentences. Though his hearing was much better he still couldn't hear her properly. But he let her finish before he said, 'I'm still a bit deaf, Yelena. What did you say? Can you write in this notebook.' She'd said something else then, looking at him quizzically, but had then sat forward, taking the notebook.

'That story you're reading,' she wrote hesitantly at first, but then with more vigour. 'I know it – *The Phoenix and the Carpet*. Miss Harriet was reading it aloud to us on the train up here years ago, before we took the *troika* across the lake and the wolves attacked us, and I frightened them away, with those same words – "Oo goggery bag-waggery".'

He'd stood up and was looking over her shoulder as she wrote. 'Good,' he'd said, when she'd finished. 'And me? Do you know me?' and she'd looked up at him, and had written, 'Yes, I know you. Sandy Woodrow. But why are you here? Weren't we in your flat in St Petersburg last time we met? After a great thunderstorm.'

'That was seven or eight months ago. Don't you remember anything else in between?'

'Only a few awful things. All jumbled up. How long have I been here?' She'd looked up hesitantly at him, frowning. 'I remember some things, but I can't put them in any order. Tell me. Do you know?'

'Yes, a little.'

And he'd told her then, talking that day and the next, when she'd left her bed and they'd sat at a table together, Yelena filling his notebook when she replied. He'd told her most of what he knew of her behaviour, ending with the events of the terrible night a month before – his killing the dog, her miscarriage.

'Yes. That nightmare. All that, I remember now,' she wrote. 'But the father?'

'Me, I think.'

'There were others. Johnny and Miki.' He'd nodded. 'It's all becoming clear now. There was my grandfather's funeral. And Sasha and Miss Harriet were up here. And I tried to kill Sasha in the big fire.'

'So I heard.'

'Sasha –' She wrote, then stopped, looking up at him intently. 'How is he?' she went on. 'Where is he?'

'He's all right. He's living with Miss Harriet, in a flat in Petrograd.'

'They're not married?'

'No.'

He saw a look of relief in Yelena's eyes, and assumed this was because she was still in love with him. But in the next sentences she wrote she seemed to dispel any idea of this. 'That's good. It won't work with her – just as it wouldn't have done with me. Mad things never work out in the end.' She'd looked at him quizzically then, before continuing. 'Except I don't feel I did all those wild things. Someone else did them. Why is that?'

'Perhaps because there are two people in you. Or there were. Do you remember seeing that black dog of yours, at the end of the cot that night?'

'Yes!'

'You really saw it?'

'Yes! It terrified me. It was coming for me.'

'Just as it came for me. Because I saw it as well, before you did, standing at the nursery door. But was it really there at all? How could it have been? It was clearly dead when Stephan and I left it. Anyway, the point is the dog may somehow have been responsible for that other bad part of you.'

She'd looked up at him then intently, then wrote, 'The dog? But surely one can't believe that sort of thing?'

'Exactly. That's what I've thought. But so many things have

happened with you – things you've told me about and which I've experienced with you – that can have no possible rational explanation, which quite clearly suggest the supernatural. So one must believe in them. Just as one has to believe in your gifts, your strange powers.'

'But I haven't got them any more.'

'No?' He'd put both hands behind his back. 'How many fingers am I holding up in my hands now?'

'Seven,' she'd written. And after he'd confirmed this, he did it again.

'And now?'

'Three.'

Again she was right – and she was aghast. 'I don't understand it.'

'Nor I. But you haven't quite lost your strange gifts.'

She'd started to write furiously then, a succession of short sentences, before she handed him the notebook. 'No. But I want to lose them. They're a curse. But can I lose them? I was born with them. An old Lapp woman here, years ago, a soothsayer, told me. Yet I have to lose them. Look at the trouble they've caused. The evil. But how? *How*?' She'd underlined the word viciously.

He'd picked up the notebook and wandered round the big room, thinking, looking out of the mullioned window, bright sunlight glinting on the ice floes drifting down the lake. He turned to her. 'I don't know. If one believes in the supernatural, in the existence of the devil or whatever, well, this evil may be dead in you already, with the death of the dog. If one doesn't believe in any of that, then it has to be human intervention.' He came back towards her. 'And I don't know which it is for you, what has or will let you lose these evil things and free you completely. I'd like to believe in the human principle, of course.' He'd looked at her slightly downcast. 'Anyway!' He'd turned away briskly, speaking in his old clipped manner. 'You've got over your illness. And your father will be up here soon to set things in order. And I'll have to get back to Petrograd then, and London if I can, to have these ears seen to. Can't spend the rest of my life as a deaf man, can I?' He smiled, then went over to the window. A group of men were cleaning the old Krupp cannon on the ramparts, and some others were out on the lake just below him, on board the big steam yacht, the *Prince Onegin*, painting it, preparing it for the summer.

Yelena wrote again, then came up behind him, handing him a sheet from the notebook. 'London, you told me about the theatre there where they played those operettas, by Gilbert Sullivan. You can go and see him.'

'Gilbert *and* Sullivan,' he replied rather pedantically. 'At the Savoy Theatre. Though the D'Oyly Carte season doesn't start until Christmas.'

'You promised to take me with you, remember?' she wrote again, her expression almost impudent when she handed him the page.

'Yes, so I did. You – and Sasha.'

'Could you just take me? Sasha's got Miss Harriet now.'

It was then that things began to change between them, when she hurriedly went on writing. 'Dear Sandy, don't go back to Petrograd at once. Stay till the better weather comes and we can take the *Prince Onegin* out and have picnics and do things. Stay here a bit longer, so that we can share a bit more of the "human principle".'

When he had read the message he'd turned to her and nodded.

And so it happened. Sandy stayed over Easter, when he'd brought her *kulich* and *pashka*, and had kissed her properly in the big four-poster. And he'd stayed on afterwards, going out with her in the *Prince Onegin*, the top-heavy, two-decked lake steamer, with its gleaming brass and mahogany fittings, pushing through the ice floes in the sharp sunlight, a dark plume of woodsmoke trailing up into the chilly blue sky above them, anchoring off a small island on the northern shore, taking a hurried picnic in their *shubas* – and the next day out with Stephan, leading the pack of borzoi hunting dogs onto the mainland, where they coursed through the thick woods, chasing arctic hares and foxes.

Spring rushed in everywhere, the short northern spring, snowdrops and cyclamen piercing the blanket of winter. Sandy's and Yelena's spirits rose with the weather. No longer the feared *vedmy*, nor he the stranger to her, they toured the estate together, day by brighter day. Yelena, abandoning her grandfather's boyar clothes, a woman again, in bright-coloured, Lapp woven coats and tunics and long felt boots, the two of them out riding, along tracks in the birch woods, hooves shattering the crystal puddles.

The thought inevitably struck Sandy, one morning, watching Yelena so transformed, this happy woman riding ahead of him, was she, this time at last, the woman with whom he could share his life, with purpose, reason and passion? Was this what he had been spared for – by the Austrian shell and his failure to kill himself? – spared, not for Miss Harriet, but Yelena?

Harriet, for her own bad reasons, had chosen to continue her irregular situation with Sasha. Why should he not once more try and create a life with Yelena? He had come to help her at the castle in guilt and duty – and pique with Harriet – but had stayed to see Yelena transformed and thus find himself once more fascinated by her. In nine months they had gone through thick and thin, had coupled with and spurned each other, experienced much more horror than pleasure. Yet they had finally come together again, in mutual affection and a balanced manner, in a relationship which seemed secure at last and suggested a future.

But was she for him? Had she really got rid of her obsession with Sasha? She had dismissed him cruelly twice before. She might well do so again. Well, there was little time to ponder or prevaricate. Prince Pyotr would be arriving next day. He would then be returning to the Embassy in Petrograd. He had to make his mind up almost at once – to love or to leave her, to marry her, if she accepted him, or to finally abandon her.

Oh, yes, he wanted a life with her. Watching this now so composed figure riding through the mottled arcade of the birch alley . . . Well, he loved her. They had condemned each other before, he for her juvenile philosophy and loose morality; she for his over-conscientiousness, his niggardly spirit. But these criticisms seemed pale shadows to him then – her faults and his – all part of one long nightmare which was over now.

Quite objectively there was still a risk in his suit, of course. A nearly deaf man, possibly about to be invalided out of his profession – he didn't offer much by way of a future. And in offering such to Yelena he might, with some justification this time, be refused and dismissed once more – or be accepted and committed then to something which might still quite possibly turn out disastrously. Or he could seize the day, embark, in this place, in these impending minutes, on a lifetime's happiness.

He was stricken, yet urged on by the moment, this instant of spring, filled with the menace of irrevocable decision: the sun filtering through the branches, glittering on the icy puddles – this moment, or the next, but no others; moments which could not be repeated, where the prize was just ahead of him, waiting, when one either went forward to glory or retreated.

The track gave out at the end of a narrowing promontory, in a tiny shingle beach, hedged by dry bulrushes and overhung by stunted firs. They dismounted. They could go no farther. The lake lay in front of them in all its immensity, big chunks of ice blown south in a strong wind, chopping the water dangerously. An unknown sea, forbidding, beckoning. Waves lapped fiercely over his boots. The wind raked through his thin hair. He had to shade his eyes against the glitter. The elements taunted him with power. He knew he'd come to the moment of decision. But he was tongue-tied, rooted. He couldn't move or speak.

Yelena took out the field-glasses they had brought and focused on something far out in the water.

'Can you see anything?' he shouted, glad of this diversion.

'No.' She shook her head. Then she shouted back, in his better ear. 'Just the white crests of the waves.'

'They're called "white horses" in English.'

'What a teacher you are!' She shouted back at him. But he couldn't hear her now in the wind. She took up the notebook and pencil which she kept permanently tied by a cord round her neck, writing out her last words, showing them to him.

He nodded. 'Yes, that's what's called being a pedant. Too full of book learning.'

'Yes, I remember!' she shouted. Then she went on writing, tearing off the page, handing it to him, excited now.

'In Watkins's bookshop,' he read. 'When you told me how many Russian books and dictionaries you had at home. How we'd translate things together. Pushkin and Gogol and Chekhov. And how we'd read all your famous English books – Mrs Beeton and John Gilpin. And I'd play on your Blüthner piano. And I was so rude afterwards – about English rice pudding!'

'Yes, I remember that – and got slapped for it, too. English rice puddings are wonderful!' He was excited himself now, coming to stand by her shoulder, reading as she wrote.

'And your home in the Cotswolds, with latticed shutters and stone that went yellow . . .' She rushed on in her writing, looking round at him every so often, wide-eyed. 'And lilac outside the church and beer over the hill beyond some long meadow –'

'Yes, that's all true as well –'

Such was her enthusiasm that she stopped writing, gazing at him, breathless with excitement. 'And "come home with me" you said, to where all these good things are. Well, I will! I will!'

She shouted all this so loudly, in his good ear, that Sandy heard almost every word. He was so startled that he just shook his head, saying nothing in return. Struck dumb now, he thought, as well as deaf – so that all he did was laugh at this idea of her coming home with him. A bubbly, gasping laugh as it became when she started to kiss him repeatedly.

BOOK TWO

1918

1

Three years later, in the hot midsummer of 1918, Sasha and Yelena were playing their music together at the end of the long gallery in the castle on Lake Ladoga.

Sandy had gone back to England, separated from Yelena over two years before, while Sasha, at the castle, where Harriet lived in the north wing with their little daughter Holly – Sasha now had only the most distant relations with the girl's mother. So the twins, cooped up for the last six months on the island, had come together again – in their music at least.

The melody flowed through the open windows out over the still water. It was early morning, puffy white clouds high up in the already hot July sky. There was silence, but for the music and the voice of the corncrake in the tall, untended meadow grass on Monastery island. The sounds of peace everywhere about the great Rumovsky stronghold.

Yet the Rumovskys had lost everything, in fire and terror, nine months before with the October revolution in Petrograd. The family had escaped to Ladoga – where now, as most of them thought, they had simply been given a stay of execution, marooned far north on the lake in the castle, which the Bolsheviks, in control almost everywhere to the south, had not yet managed to take.

Everything had changed. Only the twins seemed oblivious to this – now that they had regained their music together, Yelena playing the steel-framed upright piano, Sasha using his fine Amati violin.

He had taken the violin with him, among little else, when they had fled the Palace on the quays in Petrograd, very early on the first day of the revolution. It had become quite clear to Prince Pyotr at least, when the Bolsheviks had stormed the Winter Palace the previous night, that they would soon gain control of the whole capital. The Prince had increasingly feared just such a Bolshevik *coup* throughout the summer. Kerensky's Provisional Government had become fatally divided and incompetent. Lenin and his Bolsheviks were single-minded, well organized and ruthless. Lenin, the Prince saw, once he made a move, would come to power almost unopposed. With most of the Russian army in disarray or deserting from the German Front there was almost no one in Petrograd to stop him.

So that when the cruiser *Aurora*, moored on the river, had fired the first shot at the Winter Palace, the Prince had already made arrangements for his family, with Harriet and Holly, to leave the city for the castle on Lake Ladoga.

The Prince, as a Deputy Minister, had insisted on staying on at the Duma. But the others had escaped at first light, dressed in old clothes, in two shabby but well-provisioned droshkies. They had made their way north out of the city, taking side streets, avoiding skirmishes on the main thoroughfares, past smouldering buildings and others still on fire, with Bolshevik shells from the quays and the river whistling over their heads.

At that point the depleted City Garrison and the officer cadets from the Military Academy were still holding off the Bolshevik sailors and hurriedly armed Red militia in most sections of the city. As a result by midday they were out of the fighting, beyond the city limits, on the river road moving north, among thousands of others, on foot, in carts, carriages and a few motor cars.

Unlike most of these refugees the Rumovsky entourage had a secure and certain destination – and gold coin to ease their passage. Making good pace that day and the next they reached the ferry which crossed the Neva on its passage out of Lake Ladoga, taking it over the river, the droshkies and horses firmly secured on deck against the choppy water.

Three days later they arrived at the railhead town of Ladenpohja halfway up the western shore of the lake. Here they were well known. The lake had not yet completely frozen over. They hired a small steam launch which took them across the water to the island castle on the northern shores.

They were without Prince Pyotr. They thought him dead in

the subsequent fighting in Petrograd. But the Prince survived. He had taken refuge first, with Kerensky and some other Ministers, in the American Embassy. Afterwards they had gone their separate ways. Kerensky had been driven in one of the Embassy cars over the border to Vyburg in Finland. The Prince, in the tattered old clothes of a tramp, had made his way north on foot, following the river road as his family had, then taking the ferry over the river at the bottom of the lake and making his way north to Ladenpohja.

The town was not yet in Bolshevik hands. But there was no boat for him now. The lake was nearly frozen. He had to wait a further week until the ice would bear traffic. Then, taking a horse-drawn sledge, he crossed over to the castle. He had arrived at nightfall, the driver directed by the great fire on the ramparts, a beacon of safety. Then all the Rumovskys, with Harriet and the child, were secured in the island fortress.

Now, eight months later, the twins were playing Tchaikovsky's *Souvenir d'un lieu cher*. Sasha looked at Yelena affectionately. Yelena was less sure, less involved either with him or the music. Her face was pallid, the colour and vivacity washed out of it. She was bad-tempered, eyebrows furrowed, biting her sensuous lower lip as if to deny any suggestion of relish in her life. Her dark eyes no longer flashed, had lost their imperative command, their invitations to pleasure.

It was Sasha, more often now, whose same dark eyes suggested adventure. But she couldn't share this with him now, so that once more there was tension between them, frustration, which showed in their music.

At the end of the piece Sasha put his violin and bow dispiritedly on the piano. 'What's the matter, Linochka?' She looked up at him sourly. He came and touched her on the shoulder. She withdrew instinctively. 'Dear Linochka, what's to be done? If only . . .'

'If only what?' She looked up at him crossly. 'You know it's not me, not my will, that makes me cold towards you, everyone. It's something else that's taken hold of me. Powers only for good now,' she added with harsh irony. 'Gifts that chill me.'

As if to confirm the problem Stephan, the chief steward, came in then, walking down the long gallery through the shafts of brilliant sunlight. 'Excuse me, Princess. Some people have arrived – a young boy, badly burnt. His father asks for you.'

Yelena was put out by Stephan's news. 'I did ask you not to let these "pilgrims" onto the island. You know they've nearly trampled me to death in the past.'

'There was nothing I could do to stop them, Princess. And they are not pilgrims, but local peasants. A little boy with his father and uncle. They're in the kitchen annexe. The child – about two – he was burnt in a fire at their *izba*. His mother died. The side of his head and arms . . .' Stephan made a hopeless gesture. 'Shall I bring them?'

Yelena shook her head a fraction, as if about to refuse. Then she said, 'Yes. Yes, I'll go to them.'

The child, when she saw him, with Sasha, in the long flagstoned annexe, was screaming. Held in a bundle of rags by his distracted father, a dull, red-bearded man in a tattered blouse and trousers, the little boy squirmed in pain. The father, on his knees now, offered the child up to Yelena. 'Holy mother, help us! Help me and my son Dmitri Nikolaievich who was burnt in the fire. Help him, O holy mother.' The boy's uncle, another red-haired man, held up a small icon, blessing himself, intoning the same words.

Half the child's hair had been burnt away, great blisters risen on his neck and shoulder. The boy needed medical attention, but there was none of that to be had these days, and she could surely do nothing for him, Yelena thought.

She had thought this often during the past six months, when people had come from all over – the halt and the lame, the sick and war-wounded – bringing all their ills to her, congregating outside the castle gates; these imploring crowds, crying out for her attention, the gift they knew she had, news of which had spread far and wide about the lake, the miraculous gift of laying on of hands, and curing.

Each time, confronted by such pains and ills, Yelena doubted the power in her hands. Yet when she put them on the open flesh and kept them there, where it hurt or where there was a wound or a broken bone beneath, or put a hand on their forehead where there was some fevered sickness – almost every time something inexplicable happened, sometimes immediately, sometimes later: the pain went, the condition improved.

So she took the boy now and, cradling him with one arm, brushed her hand very lightly over the charred hair, the burnt and blistered skin. Then she held her hand lightly on his forehead, keeping it there for several minutes, hiding his weeping, bloodshot eyes but feeling the great heat of his skin and his warm tears on her palm.

The child's shrieks died to a whimper. She felt his brow becoming cooler. When she took her hand away the boy's eyes stared up at her, dulled and unmoving, as if he'd been stunned by a blow or some other force, like electricity, which had coursed through him.

The father and uncle, giving thanks, tried to prostrate themselves on the stone floor of the corridor, before Stephan helped them to their feet. Meanwhile the few kitchen staff remaining at the castle – for nearly all the servants, given the choice, had left for the mainland months before – watched from the end of the passageway and blessed themselves.

Yelena walked hurriedly away with Sasha behind her, the servants bowing, genuflecting as she passed them, surprised only by the unhappy, frowning face of this holy woman.

Yelena felt maimed by this sainthood, which had changed her whole nature and character. Before, in her thoughts and actions, she had been incapable of thinking or doing any good. Now she could barely contemplate, let alone act upon, the least evil thought. Goodness had paralysed her. Someone or something – God or the devil, it hardly mattered, for the results had been equally dire – had punished her again; first with an apparently infinite capacity for evil and now with an equal burden of grace which she could neither deny nor dispose of, some miraculous flame within her which she couldn't extinguish.

Evil – and good. Both had brought her disaster. The first attribute had lost her Sasha. And Sandy, whose curing affection had seemed to inspire her present sanctity, had been lost to her as well, because of this awful piety, she was sure – the frigidity which had overwhelmed her nearly three years before. So that now, in every loving, warm and human way, she was alone again, left, like a nun, a most unwilling bride of Christ.

*

The next morning Sasha, with Prince Pyotr and Princess Sofia, Harriet and Harriet's child, the little girl, Holly, who had been born over three years before, all watched from the back of the castle ramparts as Stephan, with Yelena, secured the four-inch cast-iron shell in the breech of the Krupp assault cannon. They stood back and turned away as Stephan pulled the detonator cord. The loud explosion was followed by a gust of white smoke from the muzzle – and then, way out on the lake, beyond the target raft, by a fountain of water.

'The shells still work.' Stephan turned to Yelena. 'And they're not shrapnel, but top percussion for use against fortifications. Explode on impact, so you have to make a direct hit with them. We must lay the range better. And we can't risk trying the other guns. Corroded barrels. The shell might explode in the breech. But this one is fine.'

'It'll be enough.' Yelena gazed out at the rippling blue waters of the lake. 'Only needs one direct hit. These shells will sink any boat of the size the Red Navy can get up here. And as for their Red Army, with the pontoon bridge to the mainland gone and the machine-gun at the main gate, we could hold back a brigade of Bolsheviks until the White armies regain Petrograd.'

Stephan nodded agreement. He didn't want to contradict her. He knew there was no guarantee of a White victory – and that if the Whites lost, they couldn't defend the place for very long against the Reds. They needed other plans for escape. He had proposed alternatives already. The Princess hadn't agreed with them. He would have to persuade her. This play with the cannon was like a game with toy soldiers. No more than a useful exercise in keeping up everyone's morale.

Meanwhile, quite losing her gloom of the previous day, Yelena was triumphant in the bright summer light. She shaded her eyes, gazing about, the sun glinting on the blue and gold domes of the monastery church on the next island, the trees in fluttery, full summer leaf along the shoreline beyond: Yelena, mistress of all she surveyed, determined to defend the three islands against the Bolsheviks, that misguided mob of soldiers, sailors and workers who, led astray by Lenin and Trotsky, had usurped the power of the legally constituted Provisional Government and taken control of Petrograd and Moscow.

Yet the Bolsheviks, she knew – or at least so far as rumour

went – controlled little else in Russia, where civil war raged, the Reds against the Whites, the White armies largely in the ascendant now, everywhere regrouping and counter-attacking, from all points of the compass, preparing for a final assault on Moscow and the capital.

So, too, at the castle over the past months, Yelena, with Stephan, had been making their own preparations for battle, reactivating the old cannon, drilling the score of servants and estate workers who had stayed on with them, out every morning in the castle courtyard, practising their marksmanship with sporting rifles and shotguns, against swinging nets of straw and targets set on the inner walls.

'We've enough food and ammunition to withstand a siege of six months or more!' Yelena turned to Stephan quizzically, raking long fingers through her mop of dark hair, pianist's fingers now incongruously given over to handling explosive metal. She had changed in these last months of military activity, and never more so than that morning, seeing the gun finally working. Having so failed in her human affairs, she took to the role of soldier now with enthusiasm as a means of escape from what she could no longer bear or control in her own life.

'Yes, Princess. We have plenty of these big shells left.'

'And we have the machine-gun.' She referred to the Vickers machine-gun, and belts of ammunition which a castle raiding party had seized from the police station at Salmi, farther down the lake, some months before.

'Except that we cannot have it in two places at once, the main gates and the ramparts here. The Reds will surely attack from both sides, by land and by water, when they come.'

'They won't come.' Yelena gazed up at the castle tower where the old Imperial flag, with its double-headed eagle, barely stirred in the windless heat. 'By all accounts the Reds are too thinly spread, fighting on a dozen different fronts, to bother about us. We'll be safe if we just keep our heads down, stay put here, until the White armies get to Petrograd. Besides, we've really no alternative. We can't go anywhere.'

This was obvious, she thought, refusing at that point to accept Stephan's other plans. The Bolsheviks controlled the road leading south along the eastern shore of the lake, to Petrograd, just as they did the area around Ladenpohja, the railhead on the other side of the vast expanse of water. And it was too late to surrender. They had refused that in February, when early one morning the new Soviet Commissar in Ladenpohja, with a small group of Red Guards, had travelled across the ice in sleighs, and stopped beneath the ramparts. The Commissar had shouted up to them. He had come to requisition the castle, the monastery, all the islands, in the name of the new Soviet government, in which, as he patiently explained, all private property had been abolished and now belonged to the people. Stephan, taking cover behind one of the gunports, had shouted back, refusing them entry.

Nor would they make any entry by force, as they soon discovered – either up the almost sheer steps leading to the ramparts from the ice, or across to the main gates on the landward side, heavily defended by the castle riflemen. All three islands, and certainly the outermost, Castle Island, as intended by their medieval and later fortifications, were well-nigh impregnable.

None the less the Reds had been expected to come again in greater force in the spring, when the lake ice melted. So as soon as this happened the Abbot and the dozen monks had left, abandoning the monastery, taking all their precious chalices and ikons, and travelling in the *Prince Onegin* to join their brother monks at the other much larger monastery on Valamo Island at the northern end of the lake. But nearly three months had passed since then, with no sign of the Reds. They wouldn't come now, Yelena thought. According to every rumour from the mainland they had far more important fights to win elsewhere, but which the Bolshevik's raggle-taggle army were apparently losing in pitched battles and skirmishes all over Russia – retreating from Generals Denikin and Wrangel in the south, with the Germans in control of the Ukraine and the Crimean peninsula; retreating, too, in the east beyond the Urals in face of the Czech legions, who now controlled most of the Trans-Siberian railway – and likely to be attacked at any moment from the north by a British force, known to have arrived at Archangel a month before. Yelena was sure of it: the country would be free of this Red scourge before winter set in.

The others in the Rumovsky party were not so certain. In public they looked on the brighter side of things, pretending agreement with Yelena's optimism. But privately, and between themselves, they were beset with all sorts of fears and doubts. They had good grounds for these. With their aristocratic status and their earlier refusal to surrender, they would certainly be murdered or executed if they fell into Bolshevik hands. Even if spared this fate, they would hardly survive under the new regime; and their chances of escaping it now, surrounded as they were by water in this inhospitable northern vastness, seemed equally remote.

But in public they made the best of things, coming to promote, especially with the advent of the fine weather, almost a holiday atmosphere in the castle and among the islands. They played badminton in the long gallery, skittles on the ramparts and endless games of whist and auction bridge long into the white nights. Outside, in the hot sunshine, they picnicked among the fir and birch trees in the meadow, with the animals, behind the refectory buildings on Monastery Island, or took small boats out to the crescent of island reefs at the mouth of the bay – more wary here, while swimming among the clumps of water lilies, or fishing for perch or trawling a spinner for the big pike which lurked in the lily beds beneath them.

They played with Holly, or read to her, or drove her helter-skelter across the two small drawbridges, from one island to another, in the wooden wheelchair which old Prince Mikhail had used in his declining years. Holly, three and a half now, bouncing about in a frenzy, shouting, 'Faster! Faster!' The little girl with cornflower-blue eyes like her mother and a mop of curly dark hair like Sasha.

In these co-operative activities the Rumovskys, with Harriet – in face of the terrible events of the past year – appeared to have buried their past differences, forgotten their mistakes, their earlier deceits and deceptions, in making common cause against the Bolsheviks in the remote sanctuary of the castle.

When not brooding privately on their future, they were able to congratulate themselves. Among few of their kind in Russia they had so far survived everything: the war – for there was peace now, albeit a shaming one, with Germany – and the two revolutions of 1917, the first in February which had liberated them from the total incompetence and corruption of the Tsarist government, and the second in October when the Bolsheviks had taken power by default, more or less without a struggle, which had put them in toils again.

Now, marooned in this balmy world of rock and water, in the eerie silence of the three islands, depleted of almost all the servants and estate workers, they waited on events, for their future to be decided, on the outcome of a hundred battles, large and small, far and near, raging all over Russia.

Isolated in this deceptive calm, in the burning light, the humid afternoon heat, the windless evenings and long white nights, the women took fretful siestas or fanned themselves on chairs under a wide canopy set up on the terrace, flicking the evening mosquitoes away; or entertained Holly or arranged elaborate meals, drawing on the vast larders and cellar storerooms in the castle, lacking for nothing in this way, eating preserved or smoked provisions: meat, fish and fowl, pickled vegetables, bottled fruits and dried mushrooms; Yelena and Stephan meanwhile, at arms, securing the defences, organizing target practice, guard duties, secret forays and patrols on the mainland.

Yet for all this apparent ease they lived now with false hopes or with deep forebodings, suspended between past and future, waiting on the shores of the tranquil, tideless lake for the tide to turn elsewhere, where news of this movement was all uncertain rumour, and where they could only with any certainty contemplate the recent past, the vast changes which had taken place, in Russia, in themselves and their relationships; relationships which were secured now only by their shared peril, and which beneath that remained unfulfilled and contradictory – as precarious and as much in the balance as the political situation all about them.

In three years everything had changed for all the Rumovskys and for Harriet. Yet nothing had been resolved amongst any of them.

Yelena's relationship with Sandy had died over two years before, in the winter of 1915. Despite their loving affection and commitment, after that spring day by the lake shore, Yelena, when it afterwards came to the point, found she had no physical feeling for Sandy at all. She was numb to him – as soon as he touched her. Sandy reacted calmly, making little of it. It was a temporary feeling, they both thought, to be expected given the recent terrible events in her life. It would pass.

But it didn't. By the autumn of 1915, on their return to Petrograd, the matter seemed to Yelena at least to have a supernatural cause. They spoke of it one day – or in Yelena's case mostly wrote of it, for Sandy's hearing had got only a little better – when she had come to his apartment after a visit to the Russian war-wounded at the Pokrovsky hospital.

Sandy, in his uniform and long boots, had been standing at his easel, studying a map of the Eastern Front, moving pins and coloured tapes on it, showing the Russian army everywhere in retreat. Yelena, by the fireplace, still in her sable cloak, with a poker in hand, was trying to coax the dull logs into life. Earlier in the day they had been circling their problem, inconclusively, so that there was a tension in the air, of things not yet properly spoken of, unresolved.

Suddenly Yelena, getting up and taking a pencil, had written on top of the map on the easel, 'It's no use – us – is it? I feel so hopeless.'

Sandy had turned to her, brow furrowing, seemingly still preoccupied with his dispositions on the map. Then, with Yelena sitting down at the big, cloth-covered table with its piles of books and magazines, they had talked and written to each other.

'It happened again this afternoon,' Yelena wrote, with Sandy looking over her shoulder. 'A young artillery officer – most of his stomach shot away, dying. But when I touched him, kept my hand there, he rallied. He'd had morphia, but that was earlier. It was my hands. Yet nothing to do with my *mind*, what I really think or want there.' She'd looked at him despairingly. 'I'd do *anything*,' she wrote on vehemently, 'not to feel like this about you. Not to be numb that way.'

'Perhaps it'll go, in time. Or if we tried once more?' he added without conviction. He put his hand on her shoulder. Without looking up at him she reached round and clasped it, then continued to write with the other hand. 'Time? We've had months of that – and "trying again". Why can't I cure *me*? Or you, for that matter, of your deafness? Why can I only help strangers? Why have I been punished like this?' She'd stood up then, distraught, shouting, so that he could hear most of what she said. 'I've been punished for all the wrong I did before. By God or the devil – to stop me being happy, in the one way I want, in my body, with you.'

'It's not God or the devil, Linochka.' Sandy was resigned. 'It's medical. Or something, some block in your mind. There are doctors – you could talk to Dr Morton here at the English hospital. Or there are others who specialize in this sort of problem.'

'Yes!' She was still shouting. 'I'll talk to him, to them. I'll do anything to be cured.' She gazed at him, jaws clenched, with an expression of desperation.

Yet Sandy suddenly wasn't convinced by it, or by her words. She had said something, he felt, which ran right against the grain of her heart. She didn't really want to be cured of this coldness – at least not with him.

She was so like her brother just then – the dark, tousled hair, the same slightly pointed ear lobes, the sharply defined bow of the upper lip. She resembled him – and wanted to be one with him. The second thought immediately followed the first. Sandy had this sure intuition then – confirming what he had always known and feared in Yelena, and what he had suppressed in these last months of almost complete happiness with her. Yelena wanted, still wanted, Sasha.

Yelena meanwhile had returned to her writing on the table. 'I'll see anyone. There must be a cure. Then we can be properly together. And my music – I can have that properly again with Sasha.'

She had given him his cue. 'Yes, without Sasha your music doesn't make any sense. Or your life,' he added, unable to keep the bitterness out of his voice.

'Sasha?' she wrote questioningly. 'I don't need him for my life. Just our music together.'

'No, Yelena. You need him lock, stock and barrel. This nonsense about God or the devil again – punishing you, by giving you these new gifts for curing people, which makes you cold – all these are excuses, which you've built up as a reason for being cold with me. The real reason is that you want him in that way, not me.'

'No . . .' she said, looking up at him horrified. Then she

wrote: 'All that's long over. I don't want him that way at all now.'

'You do. But since he's continued this ridiculous affair with Harriet, and completely removed himself from you – you can't have him. So you took up with me instead, to try and blot him out of your mind.'

'No!' she said again, standing up now, looking at him aghast.

'It's true. It was true that first time we made love, here on the floor, by the fire. It was him you wanted then, not me. And it's true now. Oh, we've come to love each other in a lot of other good ways, which are just as important. But not a love for life. One needs the other thing as well for that.'

Then, regretting his own huge loss in the matter, and relenting suddenly, he'd taken her in his arms. She started to cry. He couldn't hear her stifled sobs. But he felt her tears on his neck as she leant over his shoulder, seeing the piles of books on the table beneath him, amongst them Caldecott's illustrated *John Gilpin* which they had bought together in Watkins's English bookshop eighteen months before. The book which had prompted him to ask her to marry him.

The life that he had imagined with her in England – the ballad had partly inspired it; a world of bare Cotswold beeches and horses and Russian dictionaries over big log fires in winter; of Pushkin and Gogol, Mrs Beeton and a Blüthner piano; of 'beer over the hill in summer and stone that went yellow and latticed shutters and lilac outside the church and some long meadow.'

This content with her would never be his now. And worse than this loss of the expected things in what they might have done together was the loss of what could not be imagined between them in the future, the unknowable forms and directions their lives would have taken had they lived together through that fullness of time. He had lost that united voice and presence with her in the future where two people can push back the dark, can shout and crowd out the empty ether. It was strange, because holding her then he felt as close to her as he had ever done – and she, it seemed, with him, as she nuzzled into his shoulder.

Yet no blood rose between them.

Sandy, after this fraught occasion, unable to face the slow death of things between them, had made preparations to return to England at the next opportunity. He had good reasons. As well as his life with Yelena, his work at the Embassy was not prospering. He should have gone back to London long before to have his deafness seen to. The rupture in his left ear drum had healed naturally, as Dr Morton had hoped. He could hear quite well with it. But the damage to the cochlea in the other inner ear was no better.

He'd thought to visit Harriet before he left. It would be polite at least; a continuation of that purely social mode which now characterized their relationship, for they were no longer close. He had seen her with Sasha now and then, and sometimes with Yelena, all four of them together. But this was rare. There had been an akwardness in these occasions, an imbalance, an air of doubts and criticisms, of vital things left unsaid.

For Sandy, Holly's birth six months before had seemed to compound Harriet's folly, lending her affair with Sasha a spurious authenticity, when there should now, he thought, for the sake of the child, be all the more need for formal bonds with the father, or a clean break with him. For Harriet to continue the affair in what was now a familial context seemed to him both morally wrong and, in practical terms, bad for all three of them. The child highlighted the essential falseness of Harriet's relationship with Sasha, which was surely not one which any feeling, intelligent woman – as he knew Harriet to be – could maintain with good conscience.

Why, then, had Harriet continued with Sasha? Was it simply, as he had long thought, a matter of physical attraction? Then, too, was she quite unaware, as he certainly now suspected, that Sasha had taken up with her not because he really loved her but because he loved Yelena and wanted to avoid this issue with his sister? Did Harriet not see that, like him, she was a substitute love?

He had for so long recognized and then avoided this essential fact himself, hoping against hope that he could release Yelena from her fixation on her brother. But now at last he had to face the matter with Yelena squarely. He had failed and it was time finally to quit the field of this long emotional battle. And

Harriet should do the same with Sasha. It was all so demeaning. They had both of them been caught and used in the cross-fire of a larger tussle for possession and should now, both of them, release themselves from the perverse and intractable contest between this bizarre pair, brother and sister.

All this he would like to have told Harriet. And ask her, just possibly, to come back with him, and the child, to England? The idea struck him, for there were still the embers there, he knew, of his once passionate feelings for her. Yes, he thought, as he started to pack up things in his apartment – perhaps at this last moment they could both turn the tables on Sasha and Yelena, rescue something vital from these emotional débâcles by rescuing each other?

Then he thought – no. He was beyond it now, too tired of fighting for love with these two women. In her way Harriet was as perverse as the brother and sister. All three were birds of a feather. Let them stew in their own murky juice. He had done his best to help clarify things, for both women, with conventional wisdom, orthodox love and affection, and had got nowhere. There could be no winning for him in this business. In maintaining these preposterous emotions both women were set on destruction. And love didn't have to follow this calamitous course. The game wasn't worth the candle then, when it became the sport of the devil. 'Let me be done with them all!' he said out loud as he packed a suitcase. 'Lock, stock and barrel.'

He'd decided not to try and see Harriet again. But just before he left Petrograd – waiting for the call to go north to Archangel where he would take passage on the next British supply ship or submarine back home – he wrote to Yelena. A few brief, to the point, and, he hoped, unemotional paragraphs.

My dear Yelena,

I am going home now. It's been difficult. Much more so for you than for me. We haven't, in the end, made a go of it with each other. We have to accept that now, and remember all the good – and sometimes extraordinary – things we've shared, from Gilbert *and* Sullivan, through *Undine*, *John Gilpin* to *The Tailor of Gloucester* – and having shared these things will keep something indestructible between us.

You'll remember our interest in myth, in legends and fairy tales. And how I said to you at the Countess Shouvalov's ball that I thought these things had started out as an attempt by simple people to explain and control the supernatural. To take the fear out of that. Well, I think I may be right. For it was surely in reading you *The Tailor of Gloucester* that terrible night at the castle which put you on the road to recovery – that took the sting out of your 'devil' if you want. Some books can have that magic. So we won't forget this either.

My dear Yelena – Yours affectionately,
Sandy.

He'd gone out to post the letter as soon as he had written it, fearing that, if he didn't, he would have second thoughts, tear the letter up, stay in Petrograd, and return to her. When he got back to his apartment in mid-afternoon, with a heavy mist coming on, he found another letter waiting for him, from Harriet.

My dear Sandy,

I hear from Mrs Bryant that you are leaving the Embassy and returning soon to England. I must assume from this that things have broken up between you and Yelena. I am so sorry. I know how strongly you have felt for her, and helped her – so obviously up at Ladoga earlier in the year, where it's certain your care and affection was the reason for her recovery.

I know you both hoped properly to take up together, and marry. That's not to be now, I imagine. Sasha has told me of her subsequent decline again, not into madness but, as I gather, into a sort of bemused coldness – towards life, towards everyone, which I assume must include you.

I hope I don't assume too much in saying this – and I have no wish to pry; simply to say that, knowing something of the situation allows me to feel all the more sympathy for you. I can only say that, knowing Yelena myself, so well – knowing of her great gifts but her so volatile and difficult nature – you would probably not have had an easy life together. I know this, too, through Sasha, who shares much the same unsatisfied, mercuric, hot-and-cold temperament. Which is why, as I told you, I've always felt that he and I could never set up permanently together.

I know, too, how you think it wrong of me to continue the relationship under such conditions. Well, I now know this to be quite wrong myself – bad for all three of us. But I've not yet been able to bring myself to end things with him. I make excuses for not doing so – he is obviously fond of Holly. He would miss her. Or I selfishly postpone the issue, since I know in some vital ways we would miss each other, or I delay things, hoping for his, or some other, intervention which would take us apart – his deciding to leave me, or a blazing row which would lead to the same thing. My weakness and general indecision is so demeaning . . .

The fact is I feel paralysed, unable to bring anything to a head at the moment, with Sasha or about my situation here in general. I should go home, of course. I would like to go home – to England, not to Ireland, where my parents have still not come to terms with my having Holly, and not marrying. Go to London, where I have good friends in Chiswick where I could live temporarily with Holly.

But I simply can't go home at the moment – couldn't risk it with the U-boats and so on, not with Holly. So I shall stay here in Petrograd with her, if not with Sasha (for that must come to an end sooner or later), until the war is over.

We make mistakes. And I've managed to make mine worse with Sasha! You, on the other hand, have decided, it seems, to cut your losses with Yelena. You are right, since I don't think that anyone, not even you and I with our very strong feelings for both of them, can make any sensible impact or change on the twins. I have to say – what I think we've both known all along – that they are really only bound up with each other, and that we could never be more than outsiders there. We might have acted on this knowledge sooner, of course. But some of us don't, or can't or won't – swept off one's feet, just like the 'shilling shockers'! How clouded one's judgement becomes in loving. I long for sanity there. It isn't impossible. Of course it isn't. I just haven't managed it yet!

Perhaps we may keep in touch? I do hope so. Come round and see me before you go? Meanwhile, every affectionate good wish.

Yours,
Harriet.

*

He'd been astonished at this turn-about, this finally so honest appraisal of her situation with Sasha in the letter. At last Harriet had seen how wrong it was of her to go on living with him in this manner, realized how the twins still maintained an obsessive bond together, while she could never be more than a diversionary figure in Sasha's life. Harriet had come to her senses at last. And just as he had an hour before in his letter to Yelena, she planned to set things right by ending her relationship with Sasha. More important still, it seemed that, reading between the lines, she was holding out her hand to him.

He changed his mind about her. He would go and see her, first thing in the morning, when Sasha was likely to be out at the Conservatoire. They would talk and, yes, if in her mood he confirmed the hints he felt she had made to him, he would suggest that she and the child come back with him to England. He would delay his departure. He could fix a safer passage for her – and later possibly offer her and Holly a life together, with him.

Just then the porter, his *dvornik*, had knocked loudly on his door and come in with another letter. It was a note from the duty officer at the Embassy. A British supply ship was arriving at Archangel in the next few days. An army freight train was leaving Petrograd for the northern port at eight o'clock that evening. He had just a few hours left to see Harriet, and possibly save everything; their mistakes with the twins and with each other. Putting on his army greatcoat he rushed out of the room.

The mist floated low over the city, rising thickly from the river and the Moika canal, partially obscuring the line of old town houses where Harriet had her apartment. When he arrived at her house he rushed past the *dvornik*, up the stairs and knocked urgently on her door.

After a considerable delay it was opened by a total stranger, an irascible, elderly man in a tasselled velvet smoking jacket, who berated him. Of course – in the mist he had mistaken her house. He ran to the one next door, knocking again at the first-floor apartment. There was no answer. The *dvornik* shouted up the stairway at him. He couldn't hear. He joined the man, who shouted in his good ear this time.

'Madame Boulting has gone out. You have just missed her.'

'With her – husband? And the child?'

'No, her . . .' The doorman hesitated. 'The Prince is away,' he continued. 'Only Madame Boulting and the child. They left just a minute ago.'

'How? How did they go? A car, a carriage?'

'They walked – the little girl in her child's carriage, which Madame keeps in the hall here. They go out most afternoons at this time for a walk.'

Sandy rushed out into the street. The mist was thickening, swirling round him in billowing folds. He stopped, looking wildly both ways, undecided. He might have heard her footsteps if he hadn't been half deaf. Cursing his disability, he turned left, towards the Nevsky Prospekt, running in the middle of the street before he saw the headlights of a car suddenly right in front of him and had to jump for his life. He changed his mind then and retraced his footsteps, going back down the canal past the looming porticos of the Imperial riding stables to his left, towards the little Konvush bridge, with the corner entrance to the Mikhailovsky Gardens opposite. She might have gone in there for her walk.

Sure enough, when he got to the corner and looked across to the big entrance gates, he saw the vague shape of a cloaked figure, a woman, passing the gateway, wheeling something in front of her. A perambulator! 'Harriet,' he shouted as he ran towards her.

But it was an old woman in a shawl, going home, wheeling away her hot-chestnut barrow. She looked up at him in frightened surprise, a pinched and withered face, shaking her head before scuttling off.

He went into the big gardens. The nearer trees were shrouded in a faintly luminous pall from the street lights, the various paths disappearing in a murky gloom. She could have gone anywhere in the gardens. He wasn't likely to find her there now. He want back to her house on the canal, and waited for her. Fifteen, twenty minutes. But she didn't return. Lost in the mists herself? Or perhaps she'd walked over to the Rumovsky Palace, across Marsove Pole, the great parade ground. The Embassy driver would be collecting him in an hour. He could delay no longer. He would go home. He couldn't telephone the Palace, for he couldn't hear on the telephone. He would write her a letter.

There'd been no droshkies about, so that by the time he'd walked back over the river to his own flat, he was later than ever. He started to write her – he would give the letter to the Embassy driver. 'My dear Harriet . . .' What could he say? How could he put it all into the short time left to him? 'Thank you so much for your letter. I have to leave for Archangel at once. I tried to see you this afternoon. But you'd gone out with Holly – lost in the mists! Like me. I much wanted to see you. I have ideas –'

There was a knock on the door, which he didn't hear. His *dvornik* came in anyway, pointing downstairs, picking up one of the several large suitcases. The Embassy driver had arrived early, because of the mist. The mist, he thought. The bloody Petrograd mists. But for that he would easily have found the right house and caught Harriet long before she had left for her walk with Holly. It wasn't meant that they should meet again, or take up together. He had to leave then. He tore up the letter. He had lost her.

2

As Harriet had said in her letter to Sandy, her relationship with Sasha was doomed. It would come to an end, one way or another, sooner or later. They were both to blame for what became an increasingly uneasy emotional situation: he for his naïve and romantic attitude, his brooding silences – more and more often interspersed by explosive complaints; she for her bad faith in continuing the affair largely by reason of the physical pleasure it afforded them both, but which she well knew was only a part of what Sasha wanted of it – albeit that what he also wanted, to her mind, was quite unrealistic.

The final crisis between them had occurred in Petrograd in the early spring of 1917, after the February revolution but just before the Tsar's abdication a few weeks later, when the whole city, having already endured nearly a fortnight of food riots and mob rule, was on tenterhooks, awaiting the likely arrival of troops from the Front still loyal to the Tsar. At that early point they might well have unseated the Emergency Committee of Government which had just been set up under Milyukov, leader of the Progressive parties, and Rodzianko, President of the Duma.

Sasha had been out and about all morning, gathering news, tramping through the snowdrifts which, in the chaos of the city, had been allowed to pile up on the streets and pavements. And later, with Holly at the window between them in Harriet's apartment overlooking the Moika Canal, they had watched subsequent events – the scurrying crowds, the hot-chestnut sellers shutting up shop, replaced by a platoon of ill-kempt people's militia setting up a machine-gun on the bridge opposite. Harriet had picked up Holly, cradling her protectively, in advance, as it were, of what seemed the certain and much greater violence to come.

Sasha had turned to them both in an equally protective and concerned manner. 'The Tsar, with some of the loyal generals down at Mogilev – the news is that they've certainly sent troops up from the Front. The only thing that can stop them are the railwaymen. But if they fail, there'll be serious fighting, with artillery, all over the city. Come to the Palace, Harriet. The back courtyard, the cellars – much safer there.'

'No. There are back rooms here. I want to stay here, where I live, where Holly lives.'

As well as being adamant, Harriet's tone was unfriendly. And she was unwise, too, in her choice of uncompromising words, which seemed to exclude Sasha from any say in the matter. And what he'd said was perfectly reasonable, so that now, feeling excluded, he became abrupt himself.

'Harriet, the child is mine as well as yours. I have as much a right as you in matters concerning her – and your – safety. And it's obvious the Palace is a much safer place.'

She wouldn't discuss it. '*I* feel safe here. And Holly and I will stay here. Accept it or not, I have sole responsibility for the child. You and I are not married.'

This last riposte was unwiser still. The vast upheavals and tensions of the last few weeks had let it slip. She wished she had not said it. But it was too late. By bringing up this old bone of contention she had initiated another crisis.

It didn't explode until later that evening when, with the child in bed, Sasha confronted her in the small back dining-room, away from the front windows, Harriet at the table, sewing buttons onto one of Holly's velvet smock dresses. Sasha, who had been out on the streets again, threw his astrakhan hat in a corner. Scowling, eyes wide, he paced the room. Almost immediately he picked up on her last point of a few hours before. 'That we aren't married and that therefore I have no rights with Holly – in saying that you add insult to injury, for it's you who've refused to marry me, as I've long wanted. Instead, and what's worse, you've encouraged me to stay with you for – for quite other reasons.'

'That's not true,' she lied, for she knew exactly what he meant. 'And even if it were, those "other reasons" – they've suited you as much as me. And if they hadn't suited you, you could have left.'

'Half a loaf is better than no bread,' he said bitterly. 'But I've stayed on increasingly unwillingly, since I feel those other considerations are the only reason you want my company now. We do almost nothing else. Evenings out together, theatres, concerts, trips to the country – all these you've refused or avoided doing with me this last year and more, giving one petty excuse or another. I've always had to propose everything, latterly to almost drag you out to do anything with me.'

'Can't you see that I've been very busy these last few years, with Holly. She takes up most of my time and energy.'

'Yes, of course I've seen that. But all the same you might sometimes have taken advantage of all the ready help available at the Palace, retired wet-nurses and *babushkas* there, absolutely reliable, who'd have been more than willing to come over for the day, or an evening or longer, and look after Holly. Instead, exhausting yourself with the child, you've barely had the energy even to talk to me.'

'Talk . . .' she said dully. 'Except for the sounds of your violin you've spent your day in silence, on your own, while I've been talking and wrestling with the squealing and demanding Holly. So that when she's finally in bed, my mind is numb. Or reeling. I'm exhausted with talk. I can't deal with both your needs and the child's. And you are not a child.'

Sasha had relented at this, seeing her crestfallen, tired expression which so amply confirmed what she had just said. It was probably the last moment when, by changing course and accepting things as they were, he could have saved their relationship. Instead, breathing hard, he took the other course, to destruction, by continuing his bitter recriminations.

'No, not a child,' he said vehemently. 'But a man, and father of the child, and part of you both in that way, who therefore might reasonably expect to have some share of your company and interests. I am not some moonstruck admirer who should have to plead for your company. To all intents and purposes I am your husband.'

Harriet, who herself at that point could have saved things by a conciliatory move, failed to do so. 'But it is exactly that which you are not! You know in your heart, Sasha, that it wouldn't work between us. You're just pig-headedly set on playing the *role* of husband, for some reason – '

'No!' His eyes were blazing. 'No, it could have worked. Simply you've never allowed it to *begin* to work. And you've snubbed every effort, every hope of mine in that direction ever since I've tried to share things with you, to adapt and compromise –'

'But I don't *want* you to change or compromise yourself because of me. People mustn't do that in order to love. Love should come as easily as leaves on a tree, or not at all.'

'That's nonsense. You have to make an effort over it. It's like music: even if you have a great natural gift for it, you have to work at it.'

'I did work at things . . .' Harriet frowned painfully. She saw that they had gone too far now for either of them to retreat, that the truth, so long avoided, would now have to be squarely faced and voiced. 'I've considered so much about us, Sasha. Things I've not told you – for both our sakes – but you shouldn't doubt it. Considered, for example, that both of us took to the other by default – in my refusing to get involved with Sandy, and your refusing to do so with Yelena, when it was more than clear they both wanted us. Have you thought of this?' Sasha had pretended astonishment at this point. 'It's true,' she continued. 'Though this didn't mean we failed to make a go of things in our own special way. Ways I never could have had with Sandy, and you never should have with Yelena.'

'But I don't ever want to have Linochka in that way,' he said brusquely.

'Are you sure?' She waited a moment, giving him opportunity for a reply which she knew he would not make, before she continued. 'In any case, that's exactly the point. I was able to release you from that frustration – and was only too willing to do that.'

Sasha relapsed into silence. He saw how, in so doggedly proposing and having her confirm these truths, he had rushed them both towards a point of no return. So that suddenly he wanted to take back everything he had said, make amends, start afresh, as they'd done often before after such crises, by taking her, embracing her, going to bed.

But when he did so, suddenly hugging her, holding her, she could not respond, remaining quite inert in his arms, like a dying animal, hardly breathing. She wasn't angry. Without emotion or force she could not repulse him. She felt nothing. It was as if she were being held by a tailor's dummy.

Harriet had lost as much as Sasha. Not half a loaf, as he had said. Nothing so frugal. They had both lost an empire of the senses. Yet out of the blue – as if the sexual chemistry in her body, aware of this impending loss, had decided on its own to make a last fight for it – she felt herself stirring involuntarily in his arms. So that thinking this an intended response, Sasha doubled his efforts to revive their old sexual currency.

For half a minute, like a motor car running out of fuel, their bodies juddered and jarred together, went into brief and inconclusive spasms. Then, just as suddenly, as if a current had been switched off, everything died in both of them, and Sasha, pushing himself away, had hurried from the room.

Things had fared no better in the last few years between the twins' parents, Prince Pyotr and the Princess Sofia. Given their uncompromising views on each other's nature and the chaos of the time which forced them more together, their relationship went from bad to worse.

During the war and before the revolution the Princess, no longer able to travel abroad, to Paris or Nice or the German spas, on her adulterous commissions, increasingly fumed about the Palace. After the February revolution, with the collapse of the Tsar and his government, she feared the worst – what she had always feared – that the ravening horde of savage Russian workers and peasants would take over and put her and all like her to the sword. In this her views were correct, but premature, her worst fears being precisely realized some eight months later, in October.

After this, having made their escape from Petrograd to the castle, she was barely grateful. 'Out of the frying pan, into the fire,' she told her husband one evening in the ante-room in the south wing where the Prince slept alone.

'What would you prefer? That we swim across the lake?' Facing a mirror, the Prince, dressing for dinner, tried to subdue the two horns of his tufty hair with a brush.

'You should take more of a hand in things here for a start,' she told him scornfully. 'Rather than allowing Yelena to run everything.'

'It is her castle, her property,' he told her easily. 'She is mistress here. They are her decisions, and I feel she takes them well, by and –'

'She does not!' the Princess stormed, turning on him, with her proud but now frightened blue eyes. 'To think that she can defend this place against these marauding Red brutes when they come, as they will. Those Russian *scum*! – whom you and your Kadet party, by undermining the Tsar and his authority for so long, have allowed to take power. You and your spineless liberal friends. We have lost everything at the Palace – my hats and coats, furs, jewellery. Everything! It's intolerable! And added to that – that I have to consort now with Harriet and her bastard child.'

'Enough on that subject, Sofia.' He rounded on her sharply. 'We have talked of it before. You are the last person to take a moral stance on such matters. Holly is your grandchild and mine, and mother and child are our responsibility, whether she be married to Sasha or not. And as to our leaving here, I believe it right to stay put for the moment. We should not risk ourselves by leaving now.'

'Risk ourselves? That's not something you are ever likely to do. No, of course not! Like any decent man . . .'

He saw more fear than venom in her eyes when he looked at her, this woman who was arrogant yet afraid – and his wife. It was a combination which, even with his liberal ethic, he found difficult to bear.

So he said nothing, thus provoking her to continue her tirade. 'What would *you* do to save us if the Reds stormed into this room now? Wave your liberal principles at them?' He made no answer. 'Well? What would you actually *do* – to save yourself or any of us?'

He had considered this question before, and had not come to any sure answer. But now, taunted by her, he said, 'I would fight them, given arms.'

'And *kill* them?' She glared at him.

'Yes – if there was no alternative.'

She smiled at him pityingly. 'I don't believe you. You're a weak, shilly-shallying man, crammed full of vague, wishy-washy "principles". With a gun in your hand, you'd spend so long considering the issue you'd never manage to pull the trigger.'

'You are wrong,' he told her acidly. 'But think what you will. It makes no matter to me.' He hated her, not so much for scorning him as a man, but for putting her finger on one of the problems implicit in his liberal beliefs. The Reds were wrong, of course, theirs being a way of sheer violent coercion. But did this mean one should kill them if one had the opportunity? No, in theory. Yet after she'd left him with this last scornful sally, he kicked out viciously at the spindly leg of a small table by the doorway. It broke in splinters most satisfyingly. 'Yes, you are wrong,' he said out loud. 'I would certainly kill.'

Harriet, despite an outward show of calm and control, found her present situation at the castle very awkward, her memories bitter, and her future one which hardly bore thinking about.

She was in a bad fix. They all were. But unlike the Rumovskys, hers was almost entirely of her own making. She had quite lost control of her life. It was a position with which she could not come to terms. She was furious whenever she thought about it. Of course she had made a great fool of herself with Sasha. But now the implications of this were truly serious. If she had behaved more sensibly with him, from the very beginning – even if she had not taken up with him again, that day after his grandfather's funeral – she could surely have found a way of getting safely back to England before Holly's birth. Or failing this she might have found a future with Sandy that evening he had called on her, before he had gone up to the lake to rescue Yelena. Either way she would not now be at Ladoga herself, in such parlous circumstances. She had paid a great price for her romantic Russian yearnings.

She lived apart, in a suite of rooms in the north wing looking over the lake, including one made over as a nursery for Holly. This accommodation underlined her isolation, her uncertain status within the family. The twins remained distant towards her, while the Princess Sofia was icy. With Sasha himself, whom she nearly always saw in company with Holly, she tried to be congenial and familial, talking of their daughter. But in any conversation alone Sasha's demeanour was chill and inconsequential.

With Yelena she was rarely alone. And when she was, she felt a vacuum between them, as if they didn't exist in the same human world. So that when Yelena infrequently played with her niece, she did so as if Holly were just a visitor's child. It was worse than awkward, it was cruel, Harriet felt. Only with Prince Pyotr, with whom she had always got on well, did she have an open and, as the months dragged by at the castle, an increasingly confiding relationship.

It was largely due to Prince Pyotr's intervention and insistence that she was at the castle and alive at all. For it was he who, during the summer before, knowing how inept and indecisive Kerensky's provisional government had become, and how the Bolsheviks were thus likely to seize power in a violent *coup d'état*, he who, for their safety, had asked her and the child to come and live at the Palace, an invitation she had finally accepted just weeks before the October revolution.

So it was that she had escaped with the family to the castle, where, like the others in this isolated and enforced idleness, she had ample time to consider the mistakes and lost chances in her life during the last few years. And in all this unhappy recapitulation she perhaps came most to regret her losing touch with Sandy.

She had heard from the *dvornik* how Sandy had rushed into her house that misty afternoon. Almost certainly he'd been coming round to offer help, and possibly even to suggest a shared life together. And they had just missed each other.

Afterwards she had learnt how he'd left that same evening for Archangel. She had written to him several times, care of the Embassy, and then at the War Office in London, but without reply. Had he resumed active service in the army? Was he dead? She had made enquiries of him, with Sir George, the Ambassador. No Captain Woodrow was not on active service, he'd told her. His ear operation at the London hospital had been only partly successful, so that he'd taken up a staff job, in the Russian Section of the War Office. And taken up, in the intervening years, with another woman, Harriet supposed.

She'd had no rights with him, of course. She had treated him badly in those years before the war. She might well have married him then. Instead her infatuation with Sasha had lost her everything. Prince Pyotr had seen the true situation here – what affection she'd had for Sandy, and how very much more suited they would have been than she had been with Sasha.

The topic had cropped up between them earlier that year, in the short spring, when they'd been out walking alone together, with Holly, across the small meadow on Monastery Island – talking of the past, of life in St Petersburg before the war, when Sandy's name had come up, and the Prince had turned to her.

'You've hinted at it before, Harriet, so I hope you won't mind my saying it' – he'd looked at her diffidently – 'How much was lost, between you and Sandy.'

'Yes – who himself lost so much with Yelena. As Sasha and I did!' She made the best of this, smiling as he stopped to light a *papirosy*. 'What mismatchings,' she added, with unhappy irony.

She took his arm and walked with him to the clump of fir trees behind the deserted Monastery buildings, where a few of the remaining sheep and goats had gathered in the shade, Holly running towards them.

'I'm glad at least, Harriet, that you didn't go back to England. To have had the pleasure of these few years with Holly – I should have missed that sorely. Though I sometimes wonder why you didn't return, when you probably had the reasonably safe opportunity. I wonder why you've given the gift of Holly to Russia, as it were, to this mad country.'

'Well, the war, of course. U-boats. The danger of travel, especially with Holly.'

'You could probably have managed it, though. Through Sandy, the Embassy – if you'd really tried.'

'Possibly . . . But then!' She was suddenly enthusiastic. 'But then I really wanted to stay here in Russia in any case. Fifteen years now since I first came to live with you all. So Russia's my home, whatever happens to it. I could never so easily abandon the place. Or you people.' She'd stopped and turned to him, a fine light in her eyes, her freckled face alive with emotion. 'Dear Pyotr, I'm sure you knew it from the start, when I first arrived here – how naïvely attached I was to everything Russian, from Ivan the Terrible to Tchaikovsky and Chekhov!

Well, in my heart I'm still just as a fond of all that. Married to Russia really, for better or worse!'

She had felt suddenly resolute that spring day with the Prince, capable of anything, of overcoming any peril or difficulty in the future. She had established such a good rapport with him over the years – and she knew, at least, how he appreciated her. They walked on to the glade between the fir trees, where they helped Holly make a dandelion chain, the goats and sheep, curious or disdainful, looking on in a chewy, governessy manner. Yes, she so liked Prince Pyotr.

Indeed – the thought, unbidden and startling, flashed across her mind – she could so easily have loved him: this good man who, unlike the others in his family, had retained his decency; his warmth and fair-minded demeanour. A man who, in spite of all he had lost, in the way of his home, his career, his wife, had kept his head and his manners.

How bizarre love was, she reflected again, so often running quite against the grain of good sense, as it did for her in that instant, as it had done with Prince Pyotr's uncle Sergei, down at Orlov in the Ukraine years before, who had so fallen for her, writing her those difficult letters. And then, of course, there was just the same unsuitable, ungovernable force at work in the twins. Love could so suddenly and completely hold you up, like a bicycle puncture, delaying, even preventing you from ever reaching the right destination.

Reminded of Sergei then, she'd said, 'I wonder how things are with Tatyana and Sergei down at Orlov?'

'The Germans still control the Ukraine. So they should be all right. Though for how long . . .' The Prince had made a despairing gesture.

'What do you think will really happen here?'

'The Red Guards and their fledgling army – though there are fewer of them, are much more grouped together, disciplined and single-minded than the Whites – which is how they managed to seize power here, and why they are very likely to win this civil war. So I think it will end badly – for everyone like us.'

'Then should we not take the risk and try and leave the country now? Get to Finland or go south, to Orlov, and on to the Crimea, where we know the Whites are still in control?'

'Too great a risk at the moment. I've talked with Stephan. The lake, to the south and west, is totally controlled by the Reds. And that's the way we'd have to go, to reach either the Crimea or Finland. Better to wait a month or so, to see if the Whites can press home their various attacks, or if the British can get down from the north. Besides, Stephan has better ideas for our escape, if we have to, which he's working on. Yelena doesn't agree with his plans. She has this firm idea of doing battle with the Reds. She wants a stand-up fight with them. She's gone back to all that intense, irrational feeling. Frustration, anger . . .'

The Prince gazed out over the bay, lighting another *papirosy*. Harriet brushed her forehead, clearing away a straggly bit of dry hair. They had no soap now at the castle. Her skin was dry and flaky. 'Yes, those feelings she used to get rid of so well in her music. But in battle? She's no Joan of Arc.'

'I don't know. I remember so well her grandfather, when he told me he was leaving her the whole place here. He said she was just that, not St Joan but Catherine the Great! Well, we certainly know how she has these extraordinary powers – for good and ill.'

'All for ill really, when you think of it. Because she's lost her real gift in the process, her music. I hear them play together sometimes in the long gallery – nothing like she used to be. And quite lost herself as an ordinary, decent human being as well.' She paused. She didn't want to say how she really hated Yelena, and Sasha for that matter. So she compromised. 'Strange Linochka . . .' she said pensively, looking over the rippling blue waters of the bay. 'Cursed by the bad fairy at birth . . . I wish – I wish some ordinary magic of the world would come along and touch her.'

The Prince nodded. Harriet called the child. They turned and walked back across the meadow.

3

Sasha had not forgiven Harriet for her refusals, and in these resentful feelings, when they talked of Harriet, he found a ready ally in Yelena, whose book it suited to see him completely rid of Harriet at last.

The twins, bruised in their separate relationships, had been returned to each other, two sides of the same coin once more. But this regained closeness had led to a renewal of those old emotions between them which had never been resolved.

Neither could admit this, let alone act upon these inclinations, least of all Yelena whose feelings were so numb. They were no closer in that essential intimacy which Yelena had once wanted and which now tempted Sasha. The matter simmered between the two of them, until one afternoon during the hottest part of the summer, in late July.

They were in the estate office together, a few days after the Krupp cannon had been successfully fired. Sasha frowned unhappily. Yelena stood at one of the narrow windows looking out on the lake – Yelena who, unaware of the provocation, was flapping her thin muslin dress about by the skirts, raising currents of air about her legs against the heat.

'What a way we've all come,' Sasha said suddenly. 'Just to end cooped up here – me without Harriet, you without Sandy. And you and me . . .' He paused. 'Not really together.' Sitting at the vast, roughly carved Lapp table, fiddling with one of his grandfather's huge pencils, he couldn't see Yelena's face as it darkened.

'We have our music again,' she said sensibly, without thinking.

'For goodness sake, Linochka. Obtuse again! It's nothing like we used to play. Nothing resolved. Like our lives, which is why our music is so ragged.' He clenched the pencil savagely.

Yelena turned, annoyed herself now. 'How could our music be entirely resolved? Or us. Our lives are on a thread up here. Who knows where we all might be if the Reds attack, in a week or a month. On the run. Or more probably dead.'

'If you believe that then why don't we run now, before the Reds get to us, instead of playing toy soldiers up here with that old cannon? Get out and make for the Finnish border. Why stay here and wait to be massacred?'

'Because all the news is that the Reds are in trouble everywhere. The White armies will be in Petrograd before winter.'

'You can't be sure of that. So why take the risk of being caught here, in a place we could never defend against them indefinitely. If things turn in favour of the Reds they'll get us here, sooner or later.'

'There are no signs of things going in their favour. Just the opposite –'

'All right then!' Sasha stood up angrily, waving the big pencil like a baton. 'But you contradict yourself. You say the Reds may attack next week, which is why you and I can't resolve things. And then you say they won't attack, because they're losing everywhere. You can't have it both ways.'

Yelena, moving from the window, faced him now, feet apart, aggressive. Then she sighed, turned away, starting to flap her dress again. 'All right, I don't know what will happen. But I do know it's better to stay on a raft in a storm than try and swim for the shore. And how can we all *run*, with a small child, to the Finnish border? All that western shore from here to the border is held by the Reds.'

'We could bribe them. We have enough money and jewellery here –'

'They'd just take it all. Then kill us. They're a criminal mob. Better to wait here. Especially since we know the English troops have arrived at Archangel. They'll be coming south soon.'

Sasha, dropping this issue, turned back to the big table. 'Anyway,' he said, pausing before facing her again. 'All this talk about resolving out general situation. I was talking about *us* resolving things.'

'How do you mean?'

'You know what I mean.'

'Yes.' She swallowed. She could no longer avoid the issue.

'Of course you see! The terrible mistakes we've made – especially me – taking up with the others, simply to avoid doing that together.'

'But I can't do that now,' she told him quite simply. 'I've none of that feeling left in me now, for anyone. There's something in me – you know that. Once it was evil and now it's only a chilling ability to do good, that prevents me –'

He interrupted her, turning and simply taking her in his arms. 'Linochka, all that's nonsense – your strange powers for good or evil – when it's all just because we didn't make love together.'

She was so startled to find herself in his arms that it took her a few moments before she could even think of resisting. And when she tried to do so, she felt unable, all that sort of force draining out of her body – but replaced by another. It was as if some sealed well had broken deep inside her. The cistern smashed open. All the sensuous forces in her body, so long dormant, awoke and a stream of desire coursed through her. A furious hurry overwhelmed them, as they took to each other at last.

Looking over her shoulder through the window, Sasha saw a plume of dark smoke way out on the horizon of the lake. A ship was approaching the castle. Almost at once they heard the shouts from the look-out with field-glasses on top of the tower. And the voices on the ramparts beneath them immediately after. 'The Reds! A gunboat! They're coming!' Yelena, breaking from Sasha's embraces, stared out the window at the oncoming ship which had denied them each other. She was furious.

But, turning to him, she felt a quite different emotion, an equal love and desire, a certainty and courage. She had been touched by something human at last, in Sasha.

She said to him now, these new feelings of warmth and confidence flooding her face, 'The Reds don't matter, Sasha. Now we know we can be together like that any time.' She spoke quickly, anxious to encapsulate everything in the few minutes left to them. 'Yes! We don't have to run away from the idea any more, by running away from each other. Dear Sasha!'

She embraced him quickly. 'The Reds won't last. And then we'll be properly together.' She took his arm, shouting as they left the room in the tower. 'Come on! We have a future!'

Ten minutes later the first shell from the boat whined high over the tower and the next landed short, a hundred yards out in the water.

'A ham-fisted aim! And too far away. They surely can't be real navy sailors.' Yelena, still in her thin muslin dress and sandals, turned to Yevgeny, the head gamekeeper, and three other men who were with her on the ramparts, manning the Krup assault cannon. Stephan was far behind them, on the main island, behind the great arched gateway with its thick oak doors. Here he had mustered his dozen riflemen and two men at the machine-gun, hidden just beneath the granite boulder walls to either side of the gate, waiting for the expected attack from the mainland opposite.

Harriet, with Holly and Princess Sofia, was waiting inside the castle, their few things packed, ready to leave if necessary. Sasha and Prince Pyotr, with Leonti Filipov, captain of the *Prince Onegin*, together with his small crew, were down in the boathouse, the large cavern hollowed out beneath the ramparts behind the metal doors, all helping to get steam up on the *Onegin*. Everyone was in position, following the plan which Stephan had finally persuaded Yelena would meet every eventuality: if they could hold off the attackers, well and good. But if not, opening the metal doors, they would make a sudden escape in the steam yacht down to the end of the lake and put their other plans into operation.

Yelena, on the ramparts, watched the ship approaching. 'Come on!' she shouted. 'Closer! Closer!' It was swelteringly hot. Shading her eyes against the glare she picked up the field-glasses. 'It's no proper gunboat.' She turned to Yevgeny. She could see the boat clearly now, through the glasses, less than half a mile away. It was one of the old wooden-hulled, double-decked lake passenger steamers which in better times had plied up and down the western shore. Some steel plates had been set up haphazardly round the foredeck and about the bridge, enclosing a small siege gun. The gun and the men behind it were protected, but nothing else. There was no armour-plating round the bows or at the side. Yelena smiled in anticipation.

The steamer was making fast towards the little necklace of reef islands which ringed two-thirds of the mouth of the bay. Given the vessel's size, it would have to take a channel either to the left or right of these, veering close to land, but avoiding the two pincer-like promontories which jutted out into the water, leaving a clear passage of less than fifty yards.

'Come on!' Yelena shouted exultantly, seeing the steamer take the right-hand channel. The only thing that could save it now was if the crew spotted the makeshift mines, made from the Krupp top percussion cannon shells, set in clusters on a line anchored by ropes, across both channels a few feet beneath the water. The steamer, given the narrow straits, couldn't fail to hit one of these.

She turned, hearing the sudden sound of rifle fire behind her in the distance, a rattling fusillade, then the stammer of the machine-gun. The expected attack on the landward side had started. Turning back she heard another shell whistling over the water. This time they all ducked, taking shelter. A moment later the shell hit the tower immediately behind Yelena, exploding high above her so that fragments of chipped stone fell down about them.

Then, before she looked up again, she heard a series of deeper, muffled explosions, sullen-sounding detonations, out in the bay. Peering over the ramparts she saw the waves and small dying fountains of water round the steamer. The boat had passed through the channel and was still coming steadily towards them. But its bow was dipping, sinking gracefully in the water, as if the captain were putting it through some extraordinary manoeuvre. The funnel continued to belch smoke. The steamer had not slowed, keeping a straight course while all the time ploughing downwards, the water rising gently up the bows, over the foredeck, rippling up the steel plates to the bridge. Two men jumped overboard as swirling waves climbed the funnel, the steamer maintaining its gradual decline. In another few moments it had disappeared, sinking neatly beneath the placid blue water.

Yelena, watching through the field-glasses, had hardly dared breathe. But at the end, when there was nothing there, not even a broken spar or a lifebuoy, she shouted triumphantly. 'That's that, then!' She turned to the men at the cannon. 'And without our firing a shot.' She felt victory already, the vigour of battle coursing through her, a feeling that was almost sensual.

Then, looking up, the saw the other boat out on the lake, a dark plume of grey smoke a mile away on the calm water, coming fast towards them. She picked up the glasses again. It was a real gunboat this time, a narrow, grey, metal-hulled ship with white numbers on the bow and a long-barrelled gun mounted on the foredeck: a Soviet navy boat. The old lake steamer, with its tiny crew, had simply been a blockade runner, a mine-buster, she realized. The gunboat would now have free access into the bay, where it could fire at close range and at will.

She turned to Yevgeny. 'The cannon. Man the cannon.'

On the main island there was a lull in the firing. Stephan, behind the machine-gun just beneath the boulder walls, peered up gingerly. There was no movement among the jagged rocks on the shoreline or among the trees and scrub above. In the absolute silence the sun glittered fiercely on the water as he swung the field-glasses round over the whole arc of land. There was no sign of any small boats anywhere. The Reds might have rafts hidden in the woods, of course, to cross the straits at some point. But meanwhile, hidden in the trees, they seemed to have taken up a purely defensive position to stop them escaping onto the mainland.

The real attack – he could hear the shells exploding behind him on Castle Island – was going to come from the bay, so that more men would be needed to defend the ramparts at the castle. Leaving the two machine-gunners and four of the riflemen up on the walls, Stephan took the rest with him, crossing the courtyard, running over the drawbridge to Monastery Island, and over the second bridge onto Castle Island, soon arriving on the ramparts with Yelena.

The gunboat, at full steam and nearing the reef islands, was making for the right-hand channel. Stephan ran to the cannon. With Yevgeny at the breech, he started to calculate the range, adjusting the swivel and elevation of the gun. A few minutes later, with the gunboat just inside the bay now, Stephan pulled the detonator cord. The shell struck the water beyond the target. They reloaded, expecting the gunboat to slow and open fire, for it was within easy range of the castle then. Instead the grey hull veered away, started zigzagging, but clearly following a course which would take it to the left of the castle, going straight past its sheer, rocky flank, making for the mainland behind them.

'They're not going to attack us directly,' Stephan shouted, 'but from behind, on the main island, joining up with the other Reds on the shore.' They fired the cannon again, the gunboat passing to their left. But, in having to swivel the cannon round in the gunport, their aim went astray. And before they could reload, the gunboat had passed from their field of fire behind the castle.

'Back!' Stephan shouted. 'Leave the cannon and back to the main island. That's where they're going to make their proper attack.' The men at the cannon and the riflemen started back towards the main island. But Yelena didn't follow. She saw the problem. 'Stephan, without the cannon we've no hope of disabling the gunboat. So when the boat gets behind the main Island, with that heavy gun they have, they'll be able to smash open the great gates and let the other Reds cross over from the mainland.'

'Well, even if they do, there's still the straw – and the fire – in the courtyard there,' Stephan told her. 'We retreat behind that, with the machine-gun, and see how they do! They can't reach us inside the courtyard with their heavy gun. Then we can retreat further if we have to – across to Monastery Island, burning the drawbridge. Then back here again, burning the next bridge, then take the *Prince Onegin*.'

The men were undecided now, gathering round on the terrace. Filipov, the captain of *Onegin*, had come up from the boathouse to establish the position, with Sasha and his father behind him. They held a rapid council of war.

'No, we have to disable the gunboat in some way before we leave on the *Onegin*,' Yelena said firmly. 'Because it can easily outrun us. And we can't disable it without the cannon. Move the cannon!' Yelena said abruptly. 'They won't expect that. Wheel it back, through the great hall across onto Monastery Island, and up onto the high ground there by the church.

There'll be a clear field of fire from there to the mainland, and the water the gunboat's making for.'

They looked at her doubtfully. 'Through the great hall? The cannon won't fit.'

'Yes it will. We'll make it fit! Come on. Get the men and the ammunition boxes and we'll start moving it.'

Nobody had any other suggestion, and, taken by her enthusiasm, they did just this, manhandling the cannon up the terrace steps into the great hall, forcing it through the big doors at the far end, and across the drawbridge onto Monastery Island, where they pulled the gun up onto the high ground, past the church and the Abbott's abandoned house next to it, finding cover in the small gatelodge beyond where the Sexton had lived, breaking a window here and setting the cannon up, where it gave straight down over the mainland and the bay to the right where the gunboat had now taken up position. The boat had turned and was already firing in repeated fusillades at the main gates less than a quarter of a mile beneath them. Their own machine-gun was still in position there, but firing uselessly, making no impact on the gunboat's steel-clad hull and deck.

Stephan and Yevgeny laid the range with the cannon. The gunboat, facing almost head on to the gateway, presented no easy target. On the other hand, the ship was stationary now. And with the gun sited on top of Monastery Island they had the advantage of height, and the bright afternoon sun behind them.

The first two shells went wide. But the third scored a direct hit just below the bridge. There was a cracking explosion, a succession of splintering sounds like several huge trees falling, echoing across the water. Soon plumes of dark smoke emerged from beneath the wheelhouse. Two men ran from behind the gun on the foredeck. One of them stumbled. Flames were rising from where the lower bridge had been holed.

Stephan disengaged the breech. The shell case, ejecting in a spume of hot white smoke, clattered on the stone floor of the gatehouse. Another shell was loaded, the cannon maintained at exactly the same range.

The gunboat, its engine turning now, trying to retreat, had begun to swivel round in the water, presenting a larger broadside target. The fourth shell hit the boat amidships below the water line. There was a fountain of water and this time a muffled explosion. The boat started to list and soon, with the bridge on fire, it was sinking.

'Right!' Yelena clapped her hands exultantly, smelling the cordite fumes, relishing the taste of this first victory.

'We'll light the straw in any case. They may still get onto the island and it'll give us more time.' Stephan turned to Boris. 'Yes, fire the straw, then bring the men back from the gateway, and the machine-gun, and we can take to the *Onegin*.'

They ran back to Castle Island, to the great hall, where they waited for everyone to gather, the score of riflemen, gunners, the Prince and Princess, Sasha, Harriet and Holly, Yelena – before Stephan and Yevgeny led them down the winding stone staircases and passages to the cavernous boathouse. The rush flares on the walls glimmered through the fog of woodsmoke from the funnel of the *Onegin*, so that everyone, coughing and holding handkerchiefs over their faces, had to be led in a line, hand in hand, up the stern gangplank.

Once on board the Captain took the boat gently forward, the bows pushing open the great doors. Several minutes later they were out in the brilliant afternoon light, churning full steam ahead through the blue water, a white froth swirling behind them, making for the mouth of the bay, through the now mine-free passage, out into the vast lake.

After nine months trapped on the islands there was an air of euphoria among most, if not everyone, on board.

Harriet, disassociating herself from the celebratory mood, stood in the bow with Holly, where her Teddy could act as look-out. She held the little girl in her arms, the two of them gazing south over the empty, blue-glazed, hazy ocean, the wind ruffling Holly's dark curls and setting Harriet's dry red hair all askew. The child was excited. Harriet had the air of a woman abandoned, sentenced, and now going into a terrible exile.

She had seen Sasha and Yelena laughing with the others on the bridge: Prince Pyotr, Stephan, Yevgeny and the Captain – all congratulating each other, brimming over with that typical Russian enthusiasm, so volatile and irrational, she thought, which took them from the depths to the heights all in a moment. It was a quality she had loved in these people before but which now she looked on with appalled astonishment.

With the castle disappearing in the heat haze behind them, did they not realize how they had finally lost everything? Lost their last home in Russia, in a land where Russia itself was lost, a whole civilization, the works of a thousand years, destroyed in the last few months? How in the circumstances could they be so naïve, so jolly?

Standing on the bridge with Sasha, Yelena saw Harriet alone in the bows with Holly. She turned now to her brother. 'Such a woebegone figure, unable to celebrate the least advantage with us. And so generally depleted, these last months at the castle.'

Sasha had the grace to shift awkwardly on his feet. 'Yes . . . But what's anyone to do about it?'

'*I'll* do something about it,' Yelena replied sensibly.

Yelena wondered how she'd ever felt jealous of Harriet. She was a pathetic figure now. Yes, she pitied her. And in her new mood of loving confidence with Sasha, and their triumph over the Reds, she decided she would go and apologize to her, for her long coldness towards her, and give her some words of cheer. She owed this to Harriet, she felt. And even more she owed it to herself – to the new rational and fair-minded woman she had become.

Besides, this might be one of the last opportunities she had of apologizing, of making amends. Once they were out, or had escaped to the Ukraine, or if the Whites regained Petrograd before that, Harriet wouldn't stay in Russia. Though she had lost her British passport in the chaos of that last day in the Palace, she was still a British citizen. The Reds might let her out. But one thing was certain: they were approaching the end of things together – she and Harriet.

'I'm sorry.' Yelena, coming up behind her, spoke so suddenly that Harriet started, turning sharply. 'I'm sorry – for being so stand-offish these last months. It's been difficult – all of us cooped up together at the castle.' She gestured over her shoulder to the tower where the old Imperial flag still hung limply in the heat. 'But now – we're on our way!'

'Yes,' Harriet replied shortly. She was not to be friends with Yelena again so easily. 'Yes, I hope you're right.' She felt none of Yelena's confidence. 'For the moment, though,' she went on, 'I assume we're following the other plan –'

'Yes – abandon the *Onegin* in one of the little hidden bays near Saritza at the end of the lake. Then split up. Most of the men want to go back north, where they have relatives and can filter back into the villages. We'll make for Novgorod – disguised with this collection of old clothes and things we have with us on the boat – lie low there, with Stephan's friend, the station-master there. He can get us false papers, hide us, if needs be, until we see how the situation develops – whether the White armies get up here or not. If they don't, we'll take trains and go south – make for Orlov and Uncle Sergei. But I'm sure it won't come to that. We'll be back in Petrograd before winter.'

'Yes . . . I hope so,' Harriet said, Holly starting to struggle in her arms.

'Let me down! Down! I want to go and see Captain Filipov now.'

Yelena took the child from Harriet, setting her on the deck and grasping her hand. 'I'll take you, Holly. We'll go and see him. Teddy, as well. He'll want to see Teddy!' The two of them walked away happily.

Yelena was so rashly confident, Harriet thought. And after nine months of having more or less ignored her, her sudden apologies and amiability rang false, seemed an impertinence indeed. Victory had brought all this about, of course, with Sasha regained in the last months up at the castle, and now against the Reds.

But what real victory was either? They were heading south now into reality – and that, by all accounts, was grim. The country elsewhere was seething with violence and anarchy, filled with starving and feuding people, mobs of peasants and demobilized soldiers fighting for food and land, ransacking the great abandoned estates. And above them, their ruthless political masters, the Bolsheviks, now pursuing a policy of Red Terror, with their Guards, spies and collaborators, all on the look-out for dissenters, shooting people out of hand, at the least excuse or for no reason at all; and with them Trotsky's Red Army, newly organized and disciplined now, and likely to win power everywhere against the widely separated and ill-organized Whites, whose will-o'-the-wisp battalions seemed to have their being only in rumour.

The one certain reality was that Russia was being torn apart by every sort of horror, by individuals and armies of men, Red and White, helped as the mood took them by armed brigands, anarchists and other freebooters, in a civil war where there were a score of different fronts and as many separate contenders for advantage. What chance did they stand of survival in this maelstrom? A lone family with a small child thrown into the midst of this terror, trying to survive, to hide, to travel from one strange town to another, on trains or on roads where they would have no help, amongst a rabble of desperate people and police spies who would cut their throats or shoot them if they discovered who they really were.

It had been relatively easy, in the chaos immediately after the revolution, to escape north the few hundred miles to the castle. Now, with the Reds consolidated and firmly in control of the whole north-west, to a line running somewhere south between Petrograd and Moscow, they were supposed to pass through all this Red territory, then travel farther on, through the shifting civil-war zones, a thousand miles to Orlov in the Ukraine.

Harriet didn't give much for their chances. They would be stopped, unmasked and killed at some point in their journey. And all they had for protection in this so obviously perilous endeavour were a few revolvers – which, if they were caught with them, would result in their immediate execution – some Kerensky roubles, jewellery and gold coin sewn into the hems of their old clothes; and beyond that simply the wits and over-confident schemes of Yelena, this superior person who patronized her now.

Harriet knew, though, that she hated Yelena for her own lack of power, her inability to control her life, or Holly's, in what lay ahead. She should, of course, be cursing her own lack of spirit. What had happened to it? She felt rooted to the spot with inertia, indecision. She was miserable and afraid.

Some minutes later Prince Pyotr came up to her, still in his linen summer suit, open-necked shirt and spotted cravat. Very much the image of an English gent, but for the large service revolver strapped round his waist. This was belted so tightly that the hems of the white coat were flounced out like a minute tutu. Armed and dressed thus, with his awkward, tufty hair and spectacles, he was an incongruous figure, a character in some theatrical farce.

His appearance did nothing to allay her fears, but seemed rather to confirm the illusory nature of all their plans and expectations. They were already in the midst of a performance: the antics of a troupe of strolling players in some ridiculous melodrama.

She wanted to tell the Prince of her feelings in all this. She didn't have to. It was clear from his first words that he knew of them. 'Dear Harriet, I know what you must feel: an undue levity among us just now, when it's clear we're simply out of the frying pan and into the fire. So very Russian, to make light of that. I think though . . .' He paused, as if unwilling to voice the thought for fear of her thinking it nonsense. 'I think it's our nature . . . to laugh and delay things until we're actually scorched by the fire. Of course,' he went on with nice irony, 'it's impertinent of me – to tell you anything of the Slav soul. How we Russians tend to postpone things to the last minute, with irrelevant argument, laughter, all the idiotic prevarication we go in for – because you know all about that yourself!'

'Do I?'

'Yes. We've sometimes talked of it: how alike we two races are, the Slavs and the Irish. Wayward, given to fantasy, relying on wit and last-minute invention to stave off the worst. But with the nerve and courage to rise above the worst in the end. The qualities you've shown in dealing with Holly these last years – qualities I've enjoyed and admired in you, indeed, ever since we first met – what is it? – seventeen or more years ago.' He paused, nodding his head at her appreciatively, smiling carefully. 'If I may say so, dear Harriet – in case I don't have the opportunity again – I can't think of anybody I've been happier to know than you.'

BOOK THREE

1918–1919

1

They heard the sudden clatter of boots on the stairs beneath them, doors bursting open, startled voices, then the thumpings of poles and hammers, of people probing, searching the rooms, opening drawers and cupboards, climbing onto tables and up ladders, clouting the walls and ceiling.

Yelena, with Harriet and Holly, lay in the shadows of the roof space immediately above the commotion, by the warm chimney bricks which ran up the gable end wall, absolutely still, hardly breathing.

It was dawn. They had woken some minutes before, and lit the Chinese lanterns, so that two faint pools of orange light illuminated the space between the tea-chests where they had been sleeping. The noises were louder now, coming closer, as the Reds moved through the rooms below, searching for valuables or guns, banging on the walls and ceilings, testing for some hollowness, a fault, a hidden panel or trapdoor which would lead them to a secret cache, or upwards into this concealed space under the roof of the tea merchant's old house in Kharkov. The two Chinese paper lanterns, which had come as a free gift attached to one of the tea chests from Hankow, hung from a low rafter, vibrating slightly.

They should have extinguished the candles, Yelena thought. But it was too late. They dared not move an inch. Silence was the rule up here, from dusk to dawn, when there were people – the tenants back from work – downstairs. A tiptoeing life. A life in whispers.

There was, in fact, no access to the attic, secret or otherwise, from any of the rooms beneath. And the Reds, the brutish Soldier-Deputies or the far more dangerous men from the Cheka who were obviously conducting the search downstairs, the Reds wouldn't know there was any hidden space up here unless they heard a noise.

Entry to the attic, the way the tea merchant Arkady Matushkin and his son Fedor had brought them up here three days before, and hoisted black bread, hot water for tea and some candle stubs each morning, was through a door in the gable wall at the far end of the long attic. It gave out, high up, onto a small platform, with a pulley and tackle above and a sheer fifty-foot drop beneath to the floor of the main warehouse, a large empty space now from which the tea, in its chests and sacks, had long since been stolen or dispersed by the Bolsheviks when the Red Army had taken over Kharkov two months before.

The attic had been the original tea storeroom to the enterprise and where Matushkin had recently hidden his more precious stock before the Reds arrived. Its only access was by block and tackle, the thick rope splayed out, towards its end, to the four corners of a wooden pallet. They had sat on this and been pulled up, one by one, to the little platform on high, which itself was invisible from ground level, hidden by curtains of sacking.

They were safe here, Yelena knew, hidden in these dark spaces, warmed in the evening and during part of the night at least, when there were fires downstairs, by the chimney bricks. Safer here than they had been at any other time during the last three months, on a journey which had brought the three of them, and they alone now, through every sort of horror and disaster, from Lake Ladoga to the town of Kharkov a thousand miles south, on the borders of the Ukraine.

Half an hour later the Red search party left, and soon after that all the worker tenants had gone from the rooms beneath, so that in the dawn, the sounds of the town muffled by the thick snow that had fallen intermittently during the last week, there was complete silence.

Yelena moved to the end of the attic, to the tiny opening, a break in one of the roof tiles at eye level, which gave a view over part of the town. 'Can't even see the spire of the church this morning, snow's coming down so thick.' She rubbed her chapped hands, speaking to Harriet, then turned back, her sunken eyes peering over the snow-covered roofs of the old houses, towards the Church of the Dormition, barely visible a hundred yards away on the main street.

Arkady Matushkin's large wooden merchant's house lay halfway along the Moskovskaya, Kharkov's main thoroughfare, on high ground overlooking the river Lopan. And from this little opening, in better weather, most of the street was visible, together with the tall belfry of the Uspenski Cathedral and the clockface of the town hall, so that they could usually tell the time, though no bells rang from any of the churches, the sounds forbidden by the Bolsheviks, who now controlled the city and most of the surrounding steppe to the north and west.

Yelena continued to gaze out through the spyhole. In a shaft of snowy light from it, Holly played with piles of tea, scrapings from the floor, using it like sand, letting it fall through her fingers, laughing at the tickling sensation as it seeped from cupped thumb and index finger down over her palm. 'Mama,' she said. 'Just feel it. Feel it flow through your fingers. Tickly!'

'Not so loud, Holly,' her mother warned her. 'But all right, let me try it.' She bent down and the child put a handful of tea on top of Harriet's cupped fingers and she let it fall through her hand, like sand in an hourglass, feeling the tickly sensation herself, smiling conspiratorially at her daughter.

Then, without looking down at Harriet, Yelena said in a desperate whisper, 'When will they come with the new identity papers? When will Fedor get them? So that we can get *out* of here, and try to find Sasha. It's nearly a week now. Stuck up in this cramped dark.'

'One of them will come this morning,' Harriet replied calmly. 'As soon as they're sure the tenants downstairs have all gone out. With hot tea and bread, and to take the slops out. One of them comes every morning. We'll ask them then.'

'We ask every day.' Yelena was openly petulant in her tone now, glaring round at Harriet.

'It's no use being annoyed with me, Linochka.' Harriet's voice had an edge to it now. The two women, though they had gone through so much in the last months and had survived it all, were not, even now, at ease together, reconciled to each other. 'The papers take time. Fedor said so,' Harriet went on, then stopped, gesturing vaguely. 'I don't know . . .'

There was silence.

'The slops,' Harriet continued eventually, looking towards the far corner of the attic where they kept the bucket. 'Well, look on the bright side, at least with the smell of tea up here we can't smell the slops. Or ourselves. We must stink to high heaven. Haven't washed for weeks.'

'Yes,' Yelena said shortly. 'The good smells, stronger than the bad. Must be thankful for that, no doubt,' she added with heavy irony. Then, treading softly back down the attic, she sniffed the air and smiled in genuine pleasure: Her nostrils, her keen sense of smell, her love of every happy odour, all these were regaled now by wonderful smells: of jasmine tea, orange pekoe and delicate lemon, of tarred and smoked teas and others that smelt of burnt pepper.

They were surrounded by tea, large wooden chests of it, sacks, smaller bags and boxes, hard black bricks of it, a dozen varieties and as many faint or pungent odours. The Cyrillic letters – 'Matushkin's Imported Hankow Teas' – stencilled on the various containers, with the titles beneath. 'Gunpowder Green', 'Szechuan Black', 'Broadleaf Lapsang Jade', 'Jasmine Chung Feng' – the boxes and sacks piled up in a line along either side of the attic, where, down by the warm chimney bricks, by moving a chest of 'Hankow Black Tar', there was an entrance to a hidden space, hardly six feet square, their 'bedroom', with a roughly filled straw mattress and sacking blankets.

It was here that they all slept, eased into fitful sleep beneath the cold carpet of snow on the roof by the soporific smell of tea – the odours, the vague dreams of warmer climes in India and China. It was here, in this small, cramped space, in the orange light from one of the lanterns, that the two women took turns in telling or inventing stories for Holly, or reading to her as a special treat, since they had read it a score of times already and had to ration it, *The Tailor of Gloucester*, as she cuddled Teddy: these two objects, the tiny book and the small, almost furless bear, together with a blue tea-kettle and Sasha's violin in its case which alone, among everything else they had taken with them from the castle, had survived with them now.

It was here, in the warmth they created together, that the cat joined them sometimes in the day and most evenings. They had called the stray Tom, since he was just that, a young Siberian

Grey with thick shiny fur, calm yellow eyes and short whiskers. A businesslike cat, independent, yet well-mannered, obviously used to being among decent people, for it had welcomed them all at once to its kingdom among the rafters, coming out from a corner, eyes gleaming, tail erect, purring. A good mouser, Harriet had remarked, noting its gleaming fur and well-fed condition. The cat, had it spoken in response, might have said how it welcomed them all – dispossessed, like himself, by war and revolution – by way of companionship, and in practical terms, in a sharing of food, of problems and burdens. Tom was a happy diversion for the two women, but a godsend for Holly.

It was here, in this even more hidden enclosure, shut off from everywhere, that they slept huddled together, with Holly snuggled in between them. So that when the child turned restlessly or half woke in a nightmare, she reached out in the dark for reassurance, to either adult body beside her, her mother's or her aunt's, without always knowing which was which, for both gave her equal warmth, both loving the little girl without having much of the same feeling for each other.

It was here in this stark shift between dark and bright, of snowy light and orange Chinese lanterns, that the two women lived suspended, quite beyond reality, in a dream-time, a mix of awful nightmare and waking memories of terror, the hours passing slowly, able for the first time in three months to consider those months calmly, the brutal passage which had led them here, under the eaves, with all their losses, with nothing left to them but Beatrix Potter and a tea-kettle; a teddy bear, a cat and a fiddle.

In her dream – or was she half awake, a drugged spectator of the awful vision? – Harriet saw Prince Pyotr again, beneath the apple tree, hollow-cheeked from lack of food, sparse hair blowing in the wind, smoking a *papirosy*.

The bandit Petrov, in another of his unexpectedly considerate gestures, had given the Prince the cigarette before their duel – the quite senseless duel months before, after they had made their way south, over five hundred miles, walking, by train and by cart, from Novgorod to the town of Orel on the borders of the Ukraine.

The preposterous duel in the apple orchard, under a vast

autumn sky with racing clouds high up, at the edge of the forest, where Petrov and his gang of ex-convicts and army deserters had waylaid them three days before.

Both men standing together among the rotten apples lying in the ragged grass of the abandoned orchard. Then the dream, the vision, suddenly jumped forward.

The two men already in position, backs turned to each other, twenty paces apart, the Prince in a peasant's white belted smock, billowy serge trousers, floppy boots, Petrov, despite the warmth, still wearing his long black leather jacket, with an army forage cap, jodhpurs, high boots.

Then the command 'Fire!' from the sidelines, where they were standing, forced to watch, the Princess Sofia in her dark red shawl, Sasha, Yelena and she with Holly in her arms. And now the scene began to stretch out, was agonizingly prolonged.

The Prince turning, unnaturally slowly, arm rising with the big revolver, clumsily held, half raised, hesitating, all so slowly. Then Petrov, already facing him, lifting his revolver easily, firing, quite casually.

Harriet always thought she could see the bullet itself, a dark, slug-like object moving slowly through the air towards the Prince, his own revolver still only half raised, before the bullet struck him in the chest, so slowly, that she could identify the detail, the flurry of torn fabric, the open wound, spots of blood, red and white flecks, all of it flying about.

She was there again in the ruined orchard, the wind blowing, rustling the boughs, the sunlight making speckled patterns on the grass through the leaves, a few last red apples swaying on the branches above her.

She could feel the breezy moistness of the day, the smell of damp fallen leaves, holding Holly tightly in her arms, hiding the child's face. The others beside her, held by Petrov's men, wrists bound behind their backs, all of them forced to watch this duel which the Prince had so rashly agreed to. The pointless gallantry, the bargain which Petrov had proposed and struck with the Prince. This pistol duel which the Prince would fight on behalf of his for long unfaithful wife's honour and by which, if he won it, they would all go free.

But if he lost, Petrov would have what he wanted: not either of the younger women, but Princess Sofia, this middle-aged but still attractive woman. The Princess Sofia who, ever since they had run into the gang and had been held in their camp in the forest beyond Orel, Petrov had fancied for himself. Petrov, the polite brigand, with his airs and graces and ideas above his station. Harriet had never been able to decide whether Petrov, in this particular need of the Princess Sofia, had been motivated by dreams of aristocratic equality, through rape in that quarter, or just by a perverse and brutal desire for an older woman. In any case, it was his determination that he should have the Princess Sofia, for one reason or another.

Harriet heard the laughter all round her now, Petrov's men beside her, observing this end to the duel, eating the good red apples. Their jaws champing, crunching unnaturally loudly. She tried to run to the Prince but couldn't move. Then the scene jumped back in time and she saw the Prince falling again, bumping up and down in the springy grass, slowly rising and falling, twisting and turning, crimson spreading all over his shirt.

Then he was calling, his savagely pained face turned towards her, but the voice calm and friendly, like other times. 'If I may say so, dear Harriet, I can't think of anyone I've been happier to know than you.' But suddenly shouting out in desperation then – 'Been happier to know! . . . Happier to know . . .'

His voice stopped. He lay quite still among the apples. There was silence. Stillness. Everything froze. Events had come to a full stop. Holly was like stone in her arms.

But suddenly the child was screaming. Everything started again. The movement much faster now. Petrov, replacing his revolver in its holster. Coming towards them. Towards the Princess Sofia, smiling. Then taking out a knife, cutting the cords on her wrists behind her back, pulling both hands forward, holding them tightly, smiling. The Princess dumbfounded, trembling, then screaming, as they grappled with each other, until he overpowered her. 'Come, Princess. You are mine now. That was the bargain.'

The Princess breaking free and running towards her husband. But Petrov catching, tackling her, the two of them sprawling, skidding among the apples. Pinning her down, then forcing her round towards him. 'No, Princess. The Prince and I made an honourable bargain. Had I lost, all of you would have been free. As it is, he has lost. And therefore you will come with me. That was the agreement. The others, of course, they are free to go.'

Everything in her dream froze again then. It always did. Everything stopped. Everybody standing like statues in the orchard. Petrov on his feet now, holding the Princess in both arms, as if about to embark on a waltz with her. Petrov's men, motionless, around them, apples halfway to their mouths. Holly no longer shrieking. Sasha and Yelena standing awkwardly, caught like ballet dancers in mid-step, straining forward from their captors. The Prince quite still at last lying under the old apple tree. The breeze gone. The branches above them frozen in a cold sun.

Things moving again then, much faster. The horses tethered behind the apple trees neighing. The rattle of bit and bridle. Two men dragging the Princess away, screaming. The men mounting. The Princess set astride the big bay horse, pommel forced between her legs, held by Petrov behind her in the saddle. Hooves stamping, whips cracking, shouting, the Princess screaming, a cacophony as the troupe moved off.

Then silence. The men gone away into the forest, on their horses. The slanting sun stopped in its course. No wind. Nothing. All of them standing alone in the empty orchard. Frozen.

The images jumped ahead then – a few days later, after they had buried the Prince in a shallow grave under the apple tree in the orchard, the four of them making their way south towards the Ukraine and Uncle Sergei's house at Orlov. Towards an equal horror, brought on by their hunger.

The group of barbarous forest dwellers, cut-throats and ruffians: a score of armed men, a few women, the old crone with a butcher's knife by the horse-drawn cart. All of them standing at the edge of the forest clearing near the village. The starving villagers surrounding the cart, its load covered in sacking. The meat for sale here. The furious bargaining. The hunks and lengths of bluish, sour-smelling flesh sticking out over the end of the cart, a skinned thigh, half a buttock. Human flesh.

Then the dark red-patterned shawl on one of the women.

And the black leather jacket which the leader of the group was wearing. Princess Sofia's shawl. Petrov's jacket.

All of them turning from the cart, walking away casually, trying not to run, not to be sick, moving out of the clearing, back into the forest. Then running. Running . . .

Yelena woke with a start, sweating in the cold of the attic. This time in her nightmare it had been the feeling of scorching heat, the images of fire. So vivid. The wide wooden balcony of Uncle Sergei's great house at Orlov, where she and Sasha, long before, during those hot midsummer holidays, had played their music together. The balcony looking out over the English garden, flames engulfing it. The fierce crackling sparks in the cold night sky, the sound of splintering, the grand piano falling as the balcony collapsed, the piano landing with a great tinkling crash on the terrace beneath.

In her nightmares, the sequence of events at Orlov over those few days a month before varied each time. Sometimes the visions started with the rough mounds of earth under a cold autumn sky, out between Uncle Sergei's raspberry canes, the special Ruby Cascade bushes which he'd had from Sutton's in Reading.

Mounds of earth hidden between the canes concealed the shallow graves of the few loyal servants and estate workers who had resisted the mob of villagers, storming the big house a few days before they had arrived at Orlov, after they had made their way south in the month since they had left the forests outside Orel. These locals taking advantage of the sudden complete anarchy which had spread over the Ukraine just after they had crossed into the province.

Or Yelena first saw the haggard face of Uncle Sergei himself, nursing his wife Tatyana, who lay on a rough mattress under a blanket in the village church where the two of them had found sanctuary. Both withered, aged, numbed by cold, but Tatyana dying. The big, rosy-cheeked woman an emaciated shadow now. In the last stages of tuberculosis; not cholera or typhus – both of which had been rife for the last months in these southern provinces. But since the villagers thought she had been stricken by one of the two latter plagues and was therefore highly infectious, they had left them alone in the church.

Sergei and Tatyana had been able to live more or less unmolested in the big house ever since the revolution in Petrograd over a year before, a moment which had coincided with the onset of Tatyana's consumption, when they had gone south to Yalta for the winter, on the doctor's instructions, only to return in the spring, when her illness had taken a turn for the worse and she had wished to die in her own home.

Meanwhile, after the revolution and in their absence, the Ukraine had become an independent state, by terms of the Russian peace treaty with the Germans, under the nominal rule of General Skoropadsky, but in fact a puppet state, a German province occupied by Austrian troops.

However, late that October in 1918, the situation on the Western Front had deteriorated rapidly. The Front, and Germany, were both on the point of collapse, so that the Austrians had moved out of the Ukraine, General Skoropadsky had disappeared and, with the Red Army nowhere on the scene as yet, complete chaos had descended on the land, so that without any civil or military power, old scores and grudges were paid off everywhere.

Once more the great house, the model farm and the lands at Orlov had been stormed and taken over by the villagers, by landless peasants from the outlying districts, joined by thugs and hooligans and army deserters from the town of Varitsa fifteen miles away.

All these people had combined in a frenzy of looting, vandalism and expropriation of one sort or another. They had started first by ransacking the house, drinking the fine wines, feasting off the extensive larders, tearing cushions, bolsters, mattresses and sofas apart in their search for further valuables; then savaging the French wallpaper and the ancestral portraits in the dining- and ball-rooms, ripping the silk canopies in the bedrooms, destroying the library, the music room and the model dairy before drunkenly celebrating their destruction for several days.

Yelena, waking in the attic, saw it all again. The mayhem, the scenes, sounds, the hours of terror they had all lived through, watching events, as they had from time to time, from an upper window of the church.

The mob dancing down the wide village street in a drunken frenzy, stumbling, frolicking about, dressed in the contents of Sergei's and Tatyana's wardrobes. The women in bright silk ball dresses and fur coats, belted with strings of pearls, the men in English tweed suits and caps and top hats, flourishing shooting-sticks, other women waving light summer parasols over their heads as a thin snow drifted down, careering along the street on their way to the vodka distillery beyond the church.

And afterwards, when they had broken open the stores there, not touched since the Tsar's edict in 1914, the terrible violence which had followed on that. The sheer savagery.

She could hear again the mob approaching the church later that afternoon, the shouting and screaming, the jeering outside. Then the violent hammering on the door, when they'd thought it was all over for them, that the door would burst open in a moment, admitting the crazed swarm.

But no, the door had remained secure. They had not been trying to open it. They were crucifying someone against it – as they soon saw, when the several long metal spikes began to emerge, forming the corners of an inverted triangle as they were hammered through the wood, the tips thrusting into the church, with all the time the piercing screams of the victim outside, the shouts of derision from the crowd. 'That'll teach you, Yevgeny Ilyich!' 'And a suitable end for you and your schemings in the village over the years!' 'Let the sexton be killed against his own church door!' 'Yes! Let him be crucified against the door!'

Then, a few hours later when darkness had fallen, the flames in the clear night sky, the fire, rising up over the trees at the end of the street, coming from the great house, where most of the villagers had returned, for a further night's riotous drinking.

Sergei's fire, for he had started it, destroying the house and all that, in forty years, he and Tatyana had made of the place, the happiness they had had there – determined, not on revenge or murder, but that this should be his own last gift to the place, to preserve it, the inviolability of their own memories of it, by destroying it.

Seeing the village street quite deserted, Sergei had left by the back of the church half an hour before. He would return in a moment, he'd told them. But he had not come back. And later they had seen the flames. She and Sasha had run out into the lightly falling snow, down the street, into the parkland, and through the English garden towards the house, approaching it from the back.

The whole place was ablaze when they got there, with no sign of Sergei. Smoke and flame rising from the windows. Screams from inside. Some of the drunken revellers running from the house, clothes on fire. Others jumping from the windows. And then, as they watched, the wooden balcony disintegrating, the grand piano falling. Flames. Nothing but flame and fire.

The Red Army detachment, coming from Kharkov to the east, had arrived next day, at once imposing order on the village. The Bolshevik Commander came to the church that afternoon, two men following behind, bringing Sergei with them on a stretcher, half alive. They laid him down gently near the door, beneath a small icon with a candle still burning underneath it. His face was bruised and cut all along one side, and his body, on the same side, was soaked through, covered in icy mud.

The Commander took off his fur cap. 'We found him in a ditch, near the river, an hour ago. We have given him what medical attention we can. He is dying. Of cold, I'm sure. He's been in the ditch all night. With a leg broken, which we have put in a splint. But I think it best that you look after him now. We can take him to the priest's house, light a fire there . . .'

The middle-aged Commander was distinctly military – but in the old Russian manner: clipped Petersburg speech, an impatient air of authority, pedantic. It was clear he was a reasonable man. He must have known full well that they were all relations or friends of the owners of the big house, all of them connected with the same aristocratic and discredited family. But he asked no questions, made no demands, offered no threats. Clearly he was infuriated, horrified by the crazed behaviour of the villagers, the looting, murder, above all the crucifixion of the sexton against the church door.

He turned to them. 'Yes, you will have the old man to look

after you now. I will see that you have some food, and warmth, for the snow seems to be setting in.' He turned away. 'As for the others . . .' He gestured towards the door. 'Responsible for that atrocity. We found the ringleaders. They have been shot. We Bolsheviks will not tolerate anarchy and disorder. You will be left undisturbed in the priest's house. The old man does not look as if he has long to live. Nor his lady, it would seem.' He glanced at Tatyana, lying to the side of the church, being tended by Harriet at that point. 'You will want to bury them here, I imagine. We shall stay at Orlov for several days, regrouping, before pressing on to Kiev. But you should not stay on here after we leave. We cannot shoot all the villagers . . . And this is likely to be a major front in the war zone for some time to come. I will issue you others with temporary papers, safe-conduct passes, which will allow you to go back through our Red Army lines to Kharkov, which is entirely in our control now. You will be safe there. But your transit passes will no longer be valid after you arrive there. You will need proper identity papers then.'

The Commander walked away, putting on his fur cap, about to leave. Then he turned back. 'In Kharkov I have no control. You should remember that. There is a Political Commissar in charge at Kharkov, Comrade Leonti Drushov. He is not like me. You understand? He is much more searching in his investigations, as are his men. You will need proper identity papers in Kharkov. I suggest, when you arrive there, you go at once to Arkady Matushkin's house, on the main street, the Moskovskaya, near the cathedral. He is a tea merchant. You will see the sign. A big wooden house. He will be in a position to help you. Go to him at once . . .'

The Commander had brought his heels together, bowing briefly, in the fashion of an officer of the old Imperial army, before he left.

Or the dream, the memory, which Harriet and Yelena both shared – thoughts of the time, the day, the hour when Sasha had been taken from them.

Memories which nearly always started with images of the White Army Colonel's ambiguous face. Its nervy mobility, sudden changes of expression. Genial or abrupt, sensible or manic, amenable or murderously chilly – a face that went from one mode to another in an instant.

Colonel Leonid Skolimsky, Colonel in His Majesty's Imperial *Gardes Chevaliers*. The nearly white, short-cropped hair, the regal moustaches. The aristocratic bearing. The keen blue eyes, glaring, aggressive. A proud, honourable face. An old scar running down over his chin. The lineaments, the wounds of courage and conviction, of over forty years' service in the Tsar's cause, of duty and commitment to the Emperor, the Empire, the army, and now to the White cause, to the counter-revolutionary forces; part of Geneval Denikin's southern divisions, as they battled their way north, to Moscow and Petrograd, to regain these cities from the Bolshevik scum and set things aright for Holy Mother Russia.

A face of honour . . .

But behind all these first views lay a man corrupted, full of suppressed rage, cornered, out of control, nurturing wild schemes, a nature that had turned barbarous. A madman.

The Colonel had lost all proper sense and moral direction. The cumulative effects of six months fighting the Reds, in a series of ever more brutal battles and skirmishes, had unhinged him. His battalion of assorted cavalry and infantry – officers from his own and other disbanded Guards regiments, more soldiers from the old regular army – had been whittled away from some five hundred to one hundred and fifty men, as they had fought to and fro, sometimes with other White brigades, more often on their own, up and down the steppe from Orel to the Sea of Azov.

A constant war, on ever-shifting fronts against an enemy whose strength was equally varying and uncertain, so that tactics often had to be changed several times in the space of an hour, where triumphant sallies turned into immediate retreats. A war of ambushes and direct assaults, on horseback against armoured trains, with field-guns on high bluffs against Red Army river boats, or using siege tactics, for days on end, against a Bolshevik-held town.

A war in which, with this uncertainty of terrain and of enemy power and position, victory could turn into defeat overnight, where prisoners were never taken, simply executed, and which thus brought out the worst in the combatants, an equal brutality on both sides. A vicious civil strife, fuelled by real hatred with no quarter given.

Knowing all this, for himself and his men, the Colonel, in gradually losing his many engagements, had come to live on his nerves and begun to lose his mind instead. His judgement had become increasingly suspect, to the point when, on learning some months before how the Reds had murdered his patron and master, Tsar Nicholas II, along with his entire family at Ekaterinburg, the Colonel had lost almost all sensible control of himself.

At that point there had seemed no purpose in his war. For without the Tsar or his son, or any of the other Romanovs, for all the Grand Dukes and their male progeny had either been killed as well or had escaped the country, there could be no hope for Russia in the future. Russia *was* the Tsar. Everything stemmed from him, whoever he was: the Tsar was the Little Father of the Empire. Without him there could be no family of Russians. No Russia.

Now, in any case, the Colonel himself was beaten at last, the remnants of his small army trapped in the ruined town of Romny, between Kiev and Kharkov, encircled on three sides by the Reds, with no possible escape, except east, through the deepening winter snow, towards the Volga and, beyond that, Siberia. Even the Reds, he knew, would not think him foolish enough to set out that way at this time of year. So that, having demolished the town and killed many of his troops, but then having more urgent engagements south towards the Crimea and west into the Ukraine, the Reds had left him and his men alone, although no doubt they would return in a week or so to finish them off.

So when the twins with Harriet and Holly were brought to him that evening, Colonel Skolimsky was on the verge of a complete breakdown. But he soon recovered, for in their arrival and in his realizing who Sasha was, he thought he saw not only his own salvation and that of his men, but above all that of Holy Mother Russia.

They had met the Colonel in his faded green horseguard's tunic sitting at a table in the library behind the ruined town hall of Romny, his lieutenants around him, poring over maps, with the library books strewn all over the floor, blown across the room from shelves on a far wall holed by the Reds in their last assault on the town.

Outside in the square, by the church and along the main street, his men were camped in ruined buildings and behind barricades with their few field guns. A raggle-taggle, depleted, exhausted army, now finally and irretrievably cut off from the main White forces to the south when they had gone too far north, too fast, their supply lines overextended, stranded now in the small provincial town. And it was here that Yelena and the others, making for Kharkov along the broad, tree-lined *chaussé* from Kiev, had arrived late that afternoon.

Their safe-conduct passes from the Commander in Orlov had allowed them to pass through the Bolshevik rear lines. But after four days' moving across the ruined countryside, on farm carts, on barrows or on foot with hundreds of other refugees and stragglers, they had found the way to Kharkov barred to them. The bridge at Lubny over the fast-flowing river Sula had been dynamited by the Reds a week before. The only way to cross the river was to go twenty miles north to the next bridge at Romny.

Three days later, now with only half a score of other stragglers, they had arrived at the outskirts of the town on the river road, only to look up at Romny bridge and see its broken arches in the snowy twilight. There was no crossing here either. They would have to look for shelter in the town itself, which lay ahead of them, to the left. A ruined and deserted town it seemed as they made their way up the long main street with their bits and pieces – until they saw the barricades rearing up ahead of them, the piles of stones and smashed masonry, the sentries behind who challenged them.

Arms raised, they had come forward, stumbling up over the stones, to be met, not by Red soldiers, they saw to their astonishment and relief, but by Whites, by men of the old Imperial army dressed in every sort of uniform, field khaki, green guards' tunics, an officer in a gilt-braided cap.

Half-blinded by the snow which had come on in fierce little squalls with the night, they could hardly believe it. They must be mistaken. But no, it was true. These were men of the White army. After over four months travelling south, through every kind of terror and disaster, in search of sanctuary in White-held territory, at last they had found this. They were saved.

They had been taken at once to the town hall, to the small library at one end, where the Colonel sat morosely at the table. Sasha, discarding the snow-dusted blanket from his shoulders, had introduced himself. 'We are the Rumovskys,' he said. 'I am Prince Alexander Pyotrovich Rumovsky. My sister, the Princess Yelena, Miss Boulting, the child Holly . . .'

On hearing the name Rumovsky the Colonel's dulled expression changed. He stood up, smiling. 'Prince Alexander Pyotrovich . . . Princess Yelena . . . I am honoured indeed. The Petersburg Rumovskys? The Palace on Nabereznaya? The castle on Lake Ladoga? But of course, I know of you all – very well. And had some acquaintance with your father, indeed – Prince Pyotr Mikhailovich, at court and when he was a deputy minister. Is he with you?'

'No. He was killed over two months ago, south of Orel, in the forests there, a duel, on the long journey we've made from Ladoga.'

Sasha explained what had happened to them all, his voice weakening towards the end, for he was quite exhausted. Harriet and Yelena meanwhile had already taken chairs, with Holly on Yelena's lap, where her aunt was quietly showing her pictures from one of the library books which she had picked up from the floor: a collection of Afanasiev's fairy tales, the page open at *The Little Daughter of the Snow*. 'The snow girl,' Yelena whispered in Holly's ear. 'She comes alive and sings. Remember?'

> 'Yet I'll laugh and sing and play
> By frosty night and frosty day –
> Little daughter of the snow.'

Holly nodded vigorously. 'We'll take the book with us. Now we have *two* good books to read!'

'Please, Prince Alexander Pyotrovich,' the Colonel had interrupted Sasha, 'there is no need to explain further. You must all rest and have some sustenance. The officers' mess next door. There is something of a fire there. And there will be tea. I will arrange food and join you later. He turned to one of his aides. 'Captain, escort them to the mess. See that they are made as comfortable as possible.'

After they had left the library the Colonel turned to his second-in-command, Brigade Major Anatoly Suslov, speaking in tones of happy astonishment. 'Rumovsky, Prince Alexander Pyotrovich Rumovsky! You heard him say it, Major. And he is! I know of them well. And knew his father. The two of them there, they are twins, musicians previously, well known in Petersburg before the war. Child prodigies.'

'Yes, but why should they so particularly absorb you, sir?'

The Colonel had started to pace the room, eyes darting about, with an expression of almost manic excitement now. 'The Rumovskys of Lake Ladoga. You don't know the lineage there, Major, as I do. That youth, Prince Alexander Pyotrovich, his ancestor, a great-great-grandfather and more, was Prince Pyotr Alexievich Rumovsky, brother to the first Romanov Tsar, Tsar Mikhail in the early seventeenth century. So these Rumovskys are in the direct blood line of the original Romanovs. Prince Alexander Pyotrovich – that youth you met just now – he is a cousin of our last Tsar, Tsar Nicholas II . . .'

'Indeed. But what –'

'What luck, Major!' The Colonel rounded on him. 'This man is almost certainly the last Romanov, of the direct blood line, left alive in Russia now. The others, the Grand Dukes and their male heirs, we know they are all dead, or that some few have escaped abroad. This Prince Alexander Pyotrovich is the last Romanov on Russian soil!'

'So? What may we take from that?' The Major remained puzzled.

'Don't you see? We must save him. Save him for his role as the new Tsar, when we have regained Petersburg. Meanwhile we must take him east with us.' The Colonel had returned to the table and was prodding the map with a finger. 'Take him east, into Siberia, until we can join up with Admiral Kolchak's White armies beyond the Urals. We know the Admiral is already at Omsk and probably already on the move towards us, making for Ekaterinburg, to revenge the deaths of the Emperor and his family. We shall meet him at Ekaterinburg more than likely, then turn and fight together, back to Moscow and Petersburg. But with the prize, Major! A new Tsar. Tsar Alexander Pyotrovich Romanov! Yes, we must take him east.' The Colonel thrust his finger vaguely on the map of Siberia, where it touched nothing but wide open spaces, no town or river, no possible human habitation. 'Yes, east to the rising sun, Major, so that one day Prince Alexander Pyotrovich may be crowned Tsar.'

The Brigade-Major looked at his chief in covert alarm. He knew of the Colonel's monarchist obsessions, of course, and had noticed how he had taken the pressures of the last few months increasingly badly. There had been a number of incidents: sudden tantrums, broken glasses in the mess, shouting insults, a wilful misreading of maps, so that the Major had seen the worrying possibility that the Colonel might crack up altogether. But not in this way, that he should propose such an irrelevant, hare-brained scheme.

Now that the Reds, their troops called away on more urgent engagements, had left them alone temporarily, they should certainly try and break out from Romny at once in the only way open to them, north-east towards the Urals and then make for Omsk, where Admiral Kolchak, with a White army of some forty thousand men, was known to have set up a Provisional Government of Siberia. This was a feasible plan. They might make it, even in midwinter.

But to take these people, with a small child, simply in the vague hope that this Prince Alexander Rumovsky might one day be crowned Tsar back in Petrograd – the whole idea was preposterous. The civilians would be a severe encumbrance. Speed would be of the essence in any break-out. It was madness. The Colonel had finally gone off his head. Yet the Brigade-Major couldn't quite say so. Instead, to deter him, he made the obvious practical point. 'But, Colonel, we would have to take his sister and the other woman and her child with us as well. And we clearly couldn't do that – in midwinter.'

'No indeed,' the Colonel interrupted, agreeing with him at once. 'Of course not, Major. That would be a gross imposition, to subject the two women and the child to the rigours of such a journey. They will have to stay here. They will have to stay behind.'

2

Holly was still asleep at the other end of the attic. Harriet and Yelena stood in a shaft of morning sunlight beneath the little spyhole window. The snow had stopped overnight and an unexpected thaw had set in. They could hear the water dripping from the roof, running down the gutters. Sounds of spring, when it was not spring, when the real winter was still to come.

'What made it worse with that madman Skolimsky,' Yelena continued, her whispers increasingly harsh, 'was his lying to us. Pretending he was being considerate in not taking us with him. Suggesting how we should best get down to the Crimea . . .'

'Yes, a madman. And worse,' Harriet agreed. She felt disinclined to say any more. Yelena, on their journey through the great oak forests to Kharkov and ever since they had arrived in the attic, and sometimes even in Holly's hearing, had so harped on Skolimsky's treachery, his forcible abduction of Sasha, going through every detail of events in Romny over and again, that Harriet had little more to offer by way of sensible comment on it all. This annoyed Yelena now.

'You're unconcerned about it! How do you think Sasha must have felt? – being dragged away like that.'

'He must have hated it.'

'He wouldn't have gone willingly.'

'Of course not.'

'We have to follow him. Get him back. You think he wants to be dragged across Siberia and crowned Tsar, if they ever return to Petrograd? What nonsense!'

'Yes, absolute nonsense –'

'And that Sasha should be taken from me again when everything had been going so well between us – that's the worst thing of all.'

'Well, the worst thing except death.' Harriet was annoyed now, losing patience with Yelena. 'And he's not dead. And besides, what makes you think you're the only person who might miss Sasha? *I* do as well, as Holly's father and as a friend – and as someone I've loved. So it's just sheer egoism on your part when you talk of Sasha in that way, as if you were the only damn person who's been deprived of something there.'

Harriet had lost her temper by then. She had intended to. She felt better for it. But now Yelena retaliated in the same angry vein, so that a shouting match ensued, in whispers.

'You? You've lost nothing that you shouldn't have had in the first place – as governess, remember. That was your position with us, not mistress –'

'How dare you –'

'I do dare! Quite irresponsible of you, seducing him, having the child and then hanging on in Petrograd, when –'

'And *your* attentions towards him?'

'I've never made love with him!'

'Only because he was sensible enough to refuse it.'

Yelena paused. 'How do you know? Anyway, your goings-on with him have been much more unsuitable –'

'All right. So we've both been at fault, which doesn't give you any advantage over me, in loving or losing him. You're still such a smug, self-suiting little hypocrite. And so blind to your best interests.'

'He's my best interest. He's my twin brother –'

'Yes, but that never meant he had to live in your pocket – or your bed – as you wanted him to do, bullying him for years. Why can't you grow up, Yelena, once and for all. And get rid of your fixation about Sasha – and, yes, I had it, too, but it's long over. For you it goes on and on, and it's such a tiresome bore, doing nobody any good, least of all you.'

'How do you know? I know the good he's done me.' Yelena was openly aggressive now. 'And I'll be able to follow him and get him back, because soon I'll be able to "see" him, like I used to. See where he's going, where he is, with the powers I have. I still have those gifts, you know!'

'Do you indeed? I've seen no evidence of it over the past four months.'

'Of course not! You wouldn't, because Sasha was with us all the time. But now he's gone they'll come again.'

'I hope they don't. They've been the greatest curse of your life, those "gifts".'

'I still have those powers, you needn't worry.'

Yelena smiled in a dismissive, superior manner, so that Harriet nearly lost control completely, wanting to smack her. Instead she said, 'You know, in a way Skolimsky's done you a favour in taking Sasha off –'

It was Yelena now who tried to hit her. But even though both of them were weak and half starved, Harriet was the stronger. She grasped both of Yelena's wrists firmly, then twisted one arm. 'No you don't, you little wretch.' She turned the arm further. Yelena resisted for all she was worth, trying to force Harriet's arm upwards, but failing. 'Where's your power now?' Harriet gasped. She forced Yelena's arm further round. 'You could send me spinning couldn't you? – if you still had those powers. You could kill me, like you tried to kill Sasha. Where are they? Where *are* they?' Again she twisted her arm, Yelena's face creasing in pain.

Suddenly the anger, the violence, died in Harriet and she let Yelena go. 'No, don't try and hit me again. It's pointless.' Yelena didn't attempt it. 'I'm sorry . . .' There was silence.

Harriet was shocked. And yet, she saw some possible good in the event. In this sudden explosion of violence they had reached a climax in their long anger with each other. They could surely only go forward in some more reasonable manner.

'It's all so pointless.' Harriet turned away. 'Let's drop it all for goodness sake, Yelena.' She turned back to her, speaking in tones of meticulous reason. 'Drop our battles, drop everything except the future. And the point is that when we get out of here we can't hope to follow Skolimsky up to Omsk or anywhere else. We'd never manage it, even if we knew which way they'd gone.'

'There's only one real way from here to Omsk.' Yelena spoke in more reasonable tones herself now. 'The railway. To Voronezh, then Penza and on to Samara, and from there the link with the Trans-Siberian to Omsk, where Skolimsky expects to meet Admiral Kolchak.'

'There's no chance of our catching up with Skolimsky, by

train or any other way. No point in even trying to follow him. Two women and a small child. We'd never make it. We have to accept Sasha's loss. And hope he survives. We have to go south now, to the Crimea, which is only a few hundred miles away and which we know is still in White hands.'

'You think we can just abandon Sasha like that?' Yelena's aggression was rising again.

'We're *not* abandoning him. We're simply not in a position to follow him. And he wouldn't expect it.'

'I'd expect it of him if I was in his shoes and he'd been left behind with you.'

'Well, that would be very selfish of you, Linochka. Sasha would expect us to survive. It's our duty to survive, if we can, and that means not taking any unnecessary risks. Or at least it's mine. I'm not following Sasha across Siberia. I'm going south to the Crimea, if I can, with Holly. My first duty is to her.'

Yelena glared at her, trying to outface Harriet. But failing, she turned away crestfallen, so that Harriet felt a spasm of sympathy. 'Linochka, it's not the end of Sasha. I'm sure he'll survive. But it would certainly be the end of us if we tried to follow him. Yelena, if we don't pull together and be sensible at last, if we can't drop the past and all the mistakes we've both made, then we're finished. Just think of *us*, of you and me and Holly. And the *future* there.'

'The future?' Yelena asked miserably. 'What future? Just more days stuck up here in the dark, not able to do anything or get anywhere . . .'

Yelena was suddenly terribly afraid. She started to cry silently, gulping sobs in the corner of the attic, turning away, shaking with grief, self-pity. She had come to the lowest ebb in her life. Half-starving, marooned in this cold dark attic, with no more money or jewels in the hem of her clothes, no identity papers, no way out, all her family dead, Sasha lost – and all her old powers seemingly gone as well.

'Why?' she asked bitterly. 'Why . . .?' She tried to encapsulate these terrible despairing thoughts. 'What's happened in our lives? How has it all come to this?'

She started to snivel; then came the choked sobs again. Harriet had not seen her like this since she was a child. She was touched, wanting to comfort her, as she had when she was a child. But she held back. Perhaps only in this real pain, in reaching these depths, would Yelena come to see sense about her past behaviour or about what they should do in the future.

'I've wondered just the same thing, Linochka.' She took a gentler tone with her. 'How we've both come to this. It's the revolution, it's political things. But in another way, though . . . We've brought ourselves to this dead end'.

'How?' Yelena asked abruptly, again showing signs of aggressive recovery.

'It's obvious. By doing so much that was wilful, selfish, improper. I know that now. And you ought to know it too. Just not the way to behave. Or live. The whole thing with Sasha was totally wrong, with both of us. And that's one reason for everything going downhill, why we've got into this terrible fix.'

'How? What difference would it have made to us now – if we'd behaved differently towards Sasha in the past?'

'The wrong moral life can lead one into all sorts of material disaster. I should have gone back to England, before the revolution, if I'd not been so concerned with Sasha. Instead my impossibly romantic notions kept me here with him, and lost me Sandy. And you could long ago have done sensible things with Sasha, instead of trying to seduce him, then burn him alive at Ladoga, and so on, which led to all your troubles up there. The whole thing with Sasha, Linochka, is that *we* did it. Made the stupid choices. Did the stupid things. Our responsibility. And we have to get out of it all, *together* now'.

'But we can't, that's the whole point. No identity papers –'

'No! Get out of it in our *minds* first. Get rid of all the rubbish, what's selfish and stupid there. Get things on a proper footing at last. Now's our chance, when we're at rock bottom with absolutely nothing, to think and do the *right* things for a change. That's our only way out.'

Yelena, with a vague nod and a half-assenting expression, seemed to see something of all this at last, so that Harriet, suddenly moved, hugged her quickly. 'I'm not being governessy, Linochka. I want to find the right answers – between you and me, and you and Sasha, and me and Sasha. I want him back as well – because I want to make it proper at last, between all three of us. And come to decency and loving sense between us all. I want that more than anything in the world. So let's try and be real friends, you and I, for a start! You'll see, things will change now.'

Yelena nodded, seeming to agree again. Then Holly woke at the far end of the attic and Harriet turned away. She felt she'd embarked on perhaps the most important thing she'd ever attempted with Yelena; that with this moment's physical affection, which Yelena had accepted, she had made a first step towards helping her escape from her so disabling obsessions, her juvenile assumptions, to bringing some light and reason to her sullied heart.

Of course Yelena's vague assent was only a beginning. She knew her nature so well. Yelena might easily return to her old obsessive ways. She mustn't push things, assume too much by way of any final understanding in this mercurial, unhappy, unresolved woman.

But, having made this start, it was her task now to help Yelena unravel the tangles in her heart, to bring out the good, true spirit, the glorious person which she was sure was hidden there.

What at least was certain was that after so long struggling in a morass together – of enmity, rivalry, idiocy and mutual disgust – she and Yelena had found some solid ground together at last. They had come to a watershed. In this brief warmth between them just then they had surely found the beginnings of reason, of mutual affection and respect. The journey they had to make now wasn't across Siberia but a voyage, an adventure of hearts and minds between them both.

Later that afternoon the thaw ceased and the cold returned. The water stopped dripping from the roof and it began to freeze hard again. There was silence everywhere, until just before the light died when it was suddenly broken in the empty warehouse below them. The big doors opening, heavy footsteps, voices. Another raid, they thought. But this time for them. It could only be for them. Their hiding-place had been discovered. This was surely the end.

The two women, with Holly, stood quite still by the door in the gable wall of the attic. Now they heard the voices coming towards them more clearly. A coarse, dictatorial voice and a more cultured one, rising from the warehouse floor just beneath them.

The arrogant man was speaking. '. . . must understand, Comrade Commissar, that I have not only complete political but also military responsibility in Kharkov and the region. I've had no notice of your coming down here with this "cultural" train of yours. Certainly I've been expecting, I've put in most urgent orders for trains from Moscow – locomotives, wagons, carriages, anything to replace the rolling stock we found down here, most of it out of order or destroyed. I need trains to get our troops to the various fronts. I need hospital trains as well – any sort of trains. And I thought when you arrived that this was one of them. Instead it turns out to be a train filled with bloody singers and musicians, books and pamphlets! A "cultural" train when we're fighting for our lives down here. I can't believe it –'

'Comrade Commissar Drushov, not cultural. It's an "Agitation and Propaganda" train. Our purposes are political – to spread the Soviet message. To re-educate the proletariat, and the peasants, as we move through the countryside. Lectures, pamphlets, books, theatre and kinema shows, musical performances –'

'Yes, a whole train given over to such nonsense – balalaikas and poetry. A train *we* need for our troops or for the wounded. It's crazy . . .'

The footsteps moved away, then back again, this time stopping right beneath the door in the gable wall so that Yelena could hear the voices with total clarity. The more cultured voice, with a Moscow accent. A voice she remembered. The circus? The watchmaker's shop?

'. . . this train – I myself – you know I come here with the direct authority of the People's Commissar, Comrade Zhandov in Moscow, at the Commissariat for Culture . . .'

Yes, of course! – It was Miki's voice – Miki Ostrovsky, not seen in nearly three years, since she had kissed him goodbye between the snow banks outside the watchmaker's shop in Petrograd. The other man of course must be Commissar Leonti Drushov, the ruthless political chief in Kharkov, who the Red Army Commander had warned them about in Orlov.

'. . . I've no wish to put you out, Comrade Drushov. All I ask is that while we are here, for a week, we may use this empty warehouse before we move on to Voronezh and Penza and then back to Moscow – use the place for our work with the people of Kharkov. To give them kinema shows, lectures, concerts, distribute pamphlets. And to audition local people, since we've lost several of our performers. Illness. And two were murdered in a village outside Kursk. Moved away from the train into the forest and were set upon by bandits. We've suffered as well in this class war against the Whites.'

'A class – to judge by your smart Arbat street-accent – from which you come yourself, Comrade Commissar.'

'Yes, I do, as do quite a few others – commanders, soldiers in our Red Army and officials in our various political Commissariats. But we are all the same now. We may fight in different ways, with rifles or with typewriters and kinema projectors. But as Bolsheviks, first and last. The cause above the man, Comrade Commissar! We are all soldiers of destiny, whether we come from Arbat Street or the Petrograd slums.'

'Fine words. I'd expect no less from someone in your fancy line of business. But let me tell you something. Down here we have to deal in hard facts, not words. This warehouse is soon to be made over as a military hospital. So you can't have it for your cultural games. And let me tell you something else. I'm commandeering your train, right now. There's much more urgent use for it down here than your kinema and theatre shows. And I don't care what Commissar Zhandov says up in his "cultural" bureau in Moscow. I'll take the matter up with the Commissar of War, Comrade Trotsky himself. If there are any questions, he'll certainly support me.'

There was a pause. Then the more reasonable voice, relaxed to almost an impudent degree. 'Well, of course, I see your position, Commissar Drushov. On the other hand, we'd only need the warehouse for a week or less. And – and I do have a further authorization for this journey to Kharkov . . .' There was another delay. 'You see? Order Number 2329, from the General Secretary's bureau in the Kremlin. Signed by Comrade Lenin himself. We spoke several times before I left Moscow. Comrade Lenin is very keen on these "propaganda" trains, on re-educating the masses. He believes this second only in importance to our winning the war against the Whites. This train, you see, is the first of its kind. It was Comrade Lenin's idea in fact, which is why he has especially authorized it. I'm sure he would be annoyed – if you countermanded his orders and took the train yourself . . .'

A further pause, then the unwilling tones: 'Yes . . . I see. Well, a week then, and no longer.'

'No longer. We go north-east then, Voronezh and up to Penza, following in the wake of our Red Army successes there – to fight the other great battle, Comrade, for the future soul of Russia!'

'Fine words. You will learn that bullets are far more effective in the end . . .'

The two women recognized the tones of ironic disgust, the hatred even, in Drushov's voice before the men moved away and they heard no more. Yelena didn't need to hear any more. It was clear to her, at least, that if the Whites, in the shape of Colonel Skolimsky, had so completely betrayed them, here was a God-sent chance that the Reds might save them – and more than that, since this 'cultural' train was going north-east right up to Penza, this would put her, at least, well on her way to following Sasha.

'That was Miki Ostrovsky,' she whispered excitedly to Harriet when the men had left the warehouse. 'My great friend from Ciniselli's circus, three years ago. Clown and conjuror – or he was. You met him several times. He came to the Palace – before the war.'

'The voice was vaguely familiar –'

'Miki! Of all people. He was a secret Bolshevik before the revolution. But now he's Commissar in charge of this "cultural" train full of poets and people –'

'And going back to Moscow,' Harriet put in with enthusiasm.

'Yes.' Yelena was not so interested in this idea. 'We'll have to get in touch with him. But we can't involve Arkady or Fedor. Whether we get our new identity papers or not, we'll simply have to take our chances with Miki direct – and attend this audition.'

'Audition?'

'Of course. He said he's looking for replacements. Singers,

actors, musicians. Well, we'll do piano and violin. Sasha's violin. We have it here.'

'Yes – except I've not played the violin in years.'

'Nor me. But we *can* both play it. And the piano. We'll decide who plays which later.'

'What happens if Miki Ostrovsky's changed about you? He may betray us. It's three years since you last saw him. And he's a much more important Bolshevik now, talks to Lenin himself.'

Yelena smiled. 'No. I know him well. He won't have changed. Either as a Bolshevik – or about me. He wanted me as much as the cause, wanted both together in the old days.'

It was mid-morning, the warehouse pierced with bright frosty light from the rows of high windows. Yelena's introductory piano notes were so distinct in the chilly silence, so carefully spaced, with delicate echoes, that the music seemed to stop altogether at moments, to lie suspended over the heads of the audience, poised like a wave.

Then suddenly Harriet's violin came in at this apex of pendant sound, the essential key, the partner who would unlock the melody, so that the music took flight, rushed forward, flooding the warehouse with glittering notes. Piano and violin together now, one encouraging the other in vivid counterpoint, provoking yet controlled, neither instrument allowed to gain ascendency in this first movement of Cesar Franck's Sonata in A Major.

There were a dozen other applicants – local actors, poets, singers, musicians, with their friends and supporters – auditioning for places on the propaganda train. A widely assorted lot, running from an elderly schoolteacher with a bushy beard essaying youthful passion in an unconvincing rendering of Myakovsky's revolutionary poem 'Our March', to a tense young woman in a Cossack hat who sang, and played the balalaika badly. So that it was some time before they had had their turn in front of Commissar Ostrovsky and his aide, a serious-faced, intellectual-looking young man, in spectacles, with a notebook and a lot of pencils, who, in wearing greasy overalls and an oil-cloth cap, seemed to be trying to pass himself off as a locomotive engineer.

They had finally had their new identity papers from Fedor

Matushkin, so that they had been able to practise their pieces earlier that morning in the warehouse: two traditional ballads, 'Sing, Soldier, Sing!' and the evocative 'Land of my Sixteenth Summer'. Russian ballads which they both knew well and had sung together often before, with Sasha, and which Yelena sang then to Harriet's piano accompaniment, before finally playing the A Major Sonata together.

Harriet didn't find the violin part in the Sonata too difficult, though neither her playing nor Yelena's was entirely sure. But this didn't matter. It was appropriate, indeed. They should not appear too expert a duo in this provincial town. As it was their performance was better than that of any of the other applicants, and afterwards, when Miki and his aide had compared notes, and had come and spoken to them, they were taken on at once.

How soon had Miki recognized them, Yelena wondered? More or less at once, when they had come up to the front of the warehouse and had started to perform, or only later when they'd approached him? She couldn't tell. The mobile features she remembered were quite still. A mask, looking at them both as complete strangers. But not the chestnut-brown eyes. They were quite different, flickering with suprise, emotion. In his eyes she saw complete recognition.

'Comrades, you play – and you sing – well. Very well! Where did you study your music?'

'Kiev,' Yelena said at once, following the lines she had agreed on with Harriet. 'The Conservatoire there. With Mischa Khlebnikov. He was our teacher,' she added truthfully, speaking of the dandy with the silver-topped cane who had taught her and Sasha on the terrace years before at Orlov. 'We are refugees here,' she went on. 'After the mob took over in Kiev a month ago we managed to get here. Things have gone badly for us.'

'Yes, indeed. I'm sorry.' Miki turned to his aide, took a list of names from him, together with their new identity papers. He looked at them, comparing them. 'You are sisters, I see. Irina and Marina Kirilovna.' He turned to Harriet. 'Marina Kirilovna, your maiden name – now married to Dmitri Nikolaivich Bedayev, with your child Nastasya.' He glanced down at

Holly, who had come to stand with them, looking up with interest, sucking a thumb.

'Yes. Irina is my younger sister.'

Yelena, hearing this in public for the first time, thought the lie must be transparently obvious, and silently cursed this new predicament they had been forced into. Fedor Matushkin, organizing the forgery of their new identity papers, had returned with them in this form. The printer in Kharkov, who had done the work, had either misunderstood the instructions or had invented the relationship on his own account, as a more suitable, believable cover.

'Sisters. I see . . .' Miki nodded, a flicker of ironic surprise in his eyes.

'My husband was killed in the rioting in Kiev a month ago,' Harriet said, furthering her agreed role.

'I'm sorry.' Miki turned to Yelena, looking at her carefully. 'But you are not married, Comrade Irina?'

'No.'

She looked at Miki. In his long sheepskin coat, which still only came down to just below his knees, his bright red muffler and incongruous flannel trousers stuffed into English riding boots, Miki, Bolshevik Commissar though he was, was still the inspired daddy-long-legs. This gangly figure, his eyes touched with affection, humour, was still the man she remembered, but better, because power became him, not as dictatorial licence but as something which promoted his essential virtues.

No, he hadn't really changed. She sensed that much of what they had shared – during that first mad dance at the ball in Petersburg, the shipwreck of 'The Drunken Boat', his ventriloquism and talk of revolution, the theatrical disguises and their inept love-making – that some of all these memories were tumbling about in his mind as he looked at her.

She felt that he had forgotten nothing, and that now, in this meeting, they had come to another crossroads where, like the earlier ones, she would find difficulty in escaping, in taking a separate direction.

Miki looked over her shoulder then, his face clouding. She turned. Commissar Leonti Drushov was standing behind them. Remembering his voice, she expected to see a coarse and ugly man. But this was not so. He was handsome, fair-haired, firm-featured, clean-shaven, with a strong chin, in his forties. Then she looked at his eyes. They were not of the same agreeable cast at all. Pale blue, staring, malign.

'Yes, indeed!' He spoke brightly, looking at the two women. 'A fine performance – though I'm no judge of such things.' He put out his hand casually to Miki. 'Your identity papers . . .' Miki handed them to him. Drushov looked at them intently. Then he looked back at the women. 'You don't look like sisters,' he said curtly.

The women said nothing. Then, out of the blue, her little face tilted up fiercely, Holly said loudly, 'Yes, they are.' She pointed to Yelena. 'She's my aunt. Of course she is!'

Drushov said nothing more, handing back their papers. But it was clear that he remained unconvinced, suspicious of all three of them.

3

'You *have* changed though, Miki.' Yelena, in the train, looked across the table in the private compartment. 'There's nothing so nervous about you, like there used to be. Worried or wistful, I remember, when you were doing your turns at the circus.'

'No,' he said with some authority. 'Because I'm no longer just a performer. I'm producer as well! On the train here, I have control of everything. And I like that. Besides, it's been sink or swim for me since the revolution – and I've swum.'

'Yes.'

The train lumbered slowly through the night, the wood-fired engine, sparks rising from the tall-funnelled smoke-stack into a cold cloudy sky, pulling it slowly north-east across the steppe.

They had left Kharkov well after midnight, delayed until a Red Army troop transport had departed in the opposite direction, going south towards the Caucasus. This delay had allowed Yelena her first proper talk alone with Miki, in the privacy of his office compartment, since in the last few days they had met always in public and had spoken only formally, as if they were total strangers. Now, sitting across the table from her, with Harriet and Holly and Tom the cat down in the dormitory carriage with the other performers and technicians, they could talk freely for the first time.

'Yes, you've swum,' Yelena continued. 'A producer. A Commissar, in charge of your own train – and all for the greater glory of the revolution. All that you once said you'd be. You've got what you wanted.' She gazed at him. He was still in his sheepskin coat and fur hat, for it was cold in the compartment. His face was set now in the same calm expression of authority.

'Yes, all I wanted. Except you,' he added. 'If you remember when we last met? Strange to have you doing things for the revolution now, with me, that I suggested we do together three years ago.'

He might have smiled at this, she thought. But he didn't. 'Doing it perforce, though,' she said. 'And by chance.'

There was an electric fan on the table between them, a summer facility in this old first-class carriage from the Tsarist times. He toyed with it, switching it on so that there was a sudden icy breeze before he turned it off.

'Chances like this are meant in some way though,' he said. 'Don't you think?'

'In what way? You could have refused us the chance to come with you.'

'No, I meant your chance to work for the revolution, with your piano playing – as you will be now. And to come back to Moscow at the end of this tour, you and Miss Harriet and the child.' Yelena didn't comment on this. 'Or do you have other plans?'

'Well, I told you. Sasha, with that awful Colonel Skolimsky, they've gone east, to try and meet up with Admiral Kolchak in Omsk.'

'And you expect to follow them?'

'I had hoped to, yes. But now I don't see much chance of that,' she lied.

'None at all.' He was brisk. 'Coming on for real winter now. Two women and a child going east, beyond our lines. You wouldn't get far.' He looked at the curtained window, sniffing, as if smelling the grey cold outside, drumming his fingers, mimicking the regular beat of the wheels. 'Most of my own family got out to Finland just after the revolution. But you've lost everything.' His eyes suddenly turned back to her now, in their skittery mode, blinking in the electric light from the green-shaded table lamp. 'I'm sorry.'

'Yes, we've lost everything.' She started to shiver. Not so much at this thought, but at the idea of a whole future stretching ahead of her without Sasha. Now that she was moving at last, no longer trapped in the attic, and with the security of Miki and his train, she felt she should be looking for, following and finding Sasha. Of course he might be dead already, Skolimsky's men caught by the Reds or in an ambush by anarchist bandits or cannibal forest dwellers. He might be butcher's meat now, as her mother had become. Her mind went numb at this idea. She couldn't contemplate it. And in order not to – she had to think of Sasha as alive and therefore she had to follow him and find him. But Miki must not know this, nor Harriet, not anyone.

'Do you want to try and get out to the west when we return to Moscow?' Miki asked.

'No, not really –'

'Well, then – nothing to do but go forward with us, the Soviets, fill your life with that, and your music. I can arrange this when we get back to Moscow. I told you three years ago, the same thing. But now it's all happened – that new world I spoke of then. We're in it. It's all about to come to pass. And you can share it.'

He looked at her, with the same sensible gaze. But there was the glimmer of something else in his eyes: a hope, an invitation to share all this new life personally, with him. Of course . . . She was not surprised. He had loved her once, but had got nowhere with Sasha there, and afterwards, before she took the castle over, because she had felt quite useless to him or anyone else. Now, with Sasha, the castle and everything else gone, he felt again he might get somewhere with her. So that now, just as before, she was in a quandary with Miki.

She believed that Sasha was alive somewhere ahead of her. She had to believe in this. Yet she couldn't stay on the train indefinitely if she was to follow him – this train which would take her back to Moscow.

If only she could have had one clear message from her brother – a message, a vision, from him or of him, as she had had in the old days, to know that he was alive. But though, in the weeks since he had been taken from them, she had tried to invoke him, by thinking of him, concentrating, sending her thoughts out to him, there had been nothing in return. Her gifts in that way, for good or ill, as Harriet had confirmed in the attic – they had all quite vanished.

'Well?' Miki asked.

'Well what?'

'You're dreaming, aren't you? The past, not the future. Sasha. You really want to follow him, don't you?

'No.'

'Sasha's gone this time. Look at the map.' He put a finger on the map in front of him. 'You haven't a chance of following or finding Skolimsky. If he's making for Omsk – it's nearly a thousand miles away. He'd first have to go north-east through this Red-held territory. And even if he got through it and up to Samara –'

'Why shouldn't they get to Samara? Skolimsky fought for months successfully against you people –'

'Then he's got more than five hundred miles of Siberia to cross to get to Omsk –'

'Yes! But none of Siberia is in Red hands now. We know that. The Czech Legions – all those allied ex-prisoners of war who were being sent back home via Vladivostok – they've beaten off the Red garrisons in the railway towns. The Czechs control the railway now, so that once Skolimsky got onto the Trans-Siberian line at Samara he could easily reach Omsk to meet Kolchak. Or go on right across Siberia on the railway and out the far side, if he wanted, to Vladivostok. Or to Harbin in Manchuria, which is the real White army headquarters apparently. Well, we could do just the same, once we get onto the Trans-Siberian –'

'"We"? You'd take Harriet and the child with you? You think they'd come? When Harriet has the chance now of getting safely back to Moscow, and then back to England if she wanted to. I could help fix that.'

'Yes. Yes, I'm sure you could . . .'

The train rattled over some points, the table suddenly vibrating in the silence. She looked round suddenly. The compartment door had swung open, with a rush of cold air from the corridor. She expected to see Sasha standing there – a vision of Sasha perhaps. But there was no one. The door had swung open as the train had rounded a curve. Now it swung gently back again as the rails straightened. When she turned Miki was looking at her gravely.

'I suppose you expected to see Sasha there?'

'No –'

'Always Sasha . . . I can see it in the way you look, in your eyes. Look the other way, Yelena. The future, not the past. Think about it.'

She thought about it.

'The cause above the man – any man or woman – Yelena,' he went on. 'Your cause, music. Mine, the revolution. I said to you, when we first met at that awful ball in Petersburg before the war. The new – that was what was needed. Well, it's actually here now, all round us. And you're already part of it, on this train. Take it this time, Yelena.'

'Take it? Take your revolution which has taken everything from me: my parents, Sasha, my home, everything.'

'Yes, I can see that. But the revolution could have taken your life as well. And it hasn't. Or not yet. So you have another chance now – of surviving with it, not against it. There won't always be bloodshed and civil war. That will end. We will win. Then there will be better things, everywhere in Russia then – unimagined things, a new world.'

He was so sure, Yelena thought – as clown and conjurer in the past at Ciniselli's circus, and now as Commissar. He was so credible, just as he had been three years before in his talk of revolution. The difference was that what he had forecast then had come to pass and that where previously he had been an outlaw, now he held real power, which he was offering to share with her. She had only to attach herself to his star, to rise with him into this glorious new Soviet firmament.

He looked at her, waiting for some response. She had to say something. So she temporized, where she didn't actually lie, just as she had done with Harriet a week or so before. 'Yes,' she said, 'I'm sure you're right. There's really no chance of following Skolimsky, of getting Sasha back. A new world . . .'

She didn't believe in Miki's new world at all. But she would certainly give the impression of believing in it – for as long as she needed his protection, the security of the train, and for as long as the train was travelling north-east to Penza, with a connection from there to Samara, where the line linked up with the Trans-Siberian railway.

For the next few weeks, through the grey-skied days of a deepening winter, they trawled slowly through the snowy steppe making for Penza in a roundabout way, via Voronezh and Saratov, stopping at smaller towns in between – Biryuch, Bobrov, Korotoyak, Pavlovsk, Zemlyansk.

Lectures, kinema and theatre shows, concerts, recitals were

given, and Soviet propaganda books and pamphlets distributed, to a sullen, half-starved, war-torn populace who attended these events for every reason other than those Miki intended.

The train – 'The Vanguard', with the name emblazoned over the front of the locomotive – was not admired for its cultural and political messages. It was envied for its material comforts: the electricity generator, fuelled by precious oil, which gave light and power; the large supply of firewood in the double tender behind the locomotive, which served to heat the carriages as well; the stores of food, much of it tinned; the flatcar at the end of the train carrying a snub-nosed Peugeot motor, adapted as an armoured car with half-track wheels – and its even more precious supply of gasoline.

The people secretly scorned or ignored the train's other facilities: the printing press which produced a small newspaper at every stop, the kinema projector, the library with its stacks of revolutionary pamphlets, the coloured slogans and heroic pictures painted on the side of the carriages.

For the richer *kulaks* the train's real message was that, in its total irrelevancy, it could only be a harbinger of more settled times. If this meant peace under the new Soviet regime rather than under the Whites, it made little difference to them. One sort of peace in Russia had never been any better than another. But whatever, it would allow them to return to their usual way of life, to hoarding their grain, selling it dear and generally oppressing the peasants.

For the peasants, though, the purposes of the train were equally irrelevant: they saw in its material extravagance evidence of indubitable Soviet power which would soon, they hoped, come to their aid in a more palpable manner. So they thought it politic to show willing, to seem anxious for this cultural and political fodder, that they might, when better times came, be known as enthusiasts for this new order and thus be first in line for its more tangible benefits. So both factions, while rarely either enjoying or understanding these events, attended them with a show of enthusiasm.

An exception to this feigned interest was the music, the popular concerts. Both *kulaks* and peasants took to these with genuine appreciation, to Yelena and Harriet when they sang and played traditional Russian ballads, Harriet sometimes using a balalaika now, or Yelena a concertina, in station waiting-rooms or railway depots or concert halls in the larger towns.

And they took to Miki's conjuring tricks, if not to their implied Soviet messages: rabbits out of a hat, a red rabbit emerging where there had been a white one before; an endless stream of large silk handkerchiefs pulled from the same hat, one attached to the other like a line of washing, pure white before but now emblazoned with bright red letters, 'Forward the Red Guards!' 'Down with the Whites!'

So, too, just as Yelena had been years before on entering the watchmaker's shop in Petrograd, they were astonished by Miki's ventriloquist's act, in which, with one hand, he manipulated a small dummy figure dressed as a fat banker capitalist in a top hat and tails, while he carried on an ever more scathing and angry dialogue with it – a severe economic lesson to which the greedy banker succumbed in the end, falling forward, disgorging a lot of coins and jewellery from his mouth.

So far as these particular entertainments went, the train was a success. So that Yelena, in touch with an audience once more, responded, finding some vitality and hope again, at least while performing the music.

In larger towns, with concert halls where they gave piano and violin recitals to somewhat more sophisticated audiences, Yelena found herself playing with Harriet almost as well as she had with Sasha years before. Harriet had polished her old skills on the violin, as Yelena had on the piano. They made an attractive pair, both in themselves and in their playing, much admired by the few truly knowledgeable in these audiences.

Yet this success, and their subterfuge of appearing as sisters, troubled Yelena. She felt she was betraying Sasha. Harriet, sensing this, offhandedly suggested they try new pieces, sonatas which she knew that Yelena had rarely if ever done with her or with Sasha, from musical scores which the train carried or which they found *en route*: Rachmaninoff's 'Rhapsody on a Theme of Paganini', Liszt's *Erlkönig* – so that Yelena might see herself as embarking on new matters with her, in music, in life, untrammelled by the memory of Sasha.

This worked in performance. But at other times Yelena

brooded, conscious of having abandoned her brother and of living a lie as Harriet's sister. She looked at the big map in Miki's office surreptitiously, measuring the distances they still had to travel before they reached Penza or Samara, impatient at the train's snail-like progress zigzagging across the steppe. She would watch the flight of birds in the sky from some barren village or the window of a frozen waiting room, longing for flight herself, escaping the delays of this snowbound land, free of the earth, in search of her brother.

Meanwhile Yelena, with Harriet and Holly and the cat – now known as Tomcat, who had become the train's mascot – made a semblance of family life for themselves in the small compartment of the dormitory carriage which they had to themselves, sharing the two bunks, one above the other.

There were three other young women in the compartment next door, vigorous and alive with the joys of this cultural revolution. Katya, who ran the *Vanguard* news-sheet; Mousia, an artist, who was in charge of the stage set-ups, the stencilling and illustrating of slogans, and Elizaveta, the librarian, who organized the distribution of the books and pamphlets.

Beyond them in the five other compartments more than a dozen men had their quarters: the chef and a quartermaster, three actors, Miki's aide – the serious young man in the oil-cloth cap – the kinema projectionist, the two locomotive engineers and a fireman, a motor mechanic and driver and four Red Guards with rifles, who also manned the machine-gun, kept for emergencies, hidden under a tarpaulin on the flatcar with the Peugeot motor at the end of the train.

Handpicked by Miki, they were a dedicated lot, brimming with enthusiasm for the task in hand, this great propaganda and cultural mission which would result in the re-education of every *kulak* and peasant in sight. It was a task which left no time for petty or personal antagonisms. So that, recognizing Yelena's and Harriet's musical skills, the rest of the crew got on well with them and, when they had time, made a pet out of Holly.

Miki, without remotely favouring the two women, took a particular if covert interest in Yelena. Like Harriet, he knew well her chameleon nature. He didn't quite trust her. He noticed her one day taking an undue interest in the Peugeot motor, when it had been driven off the flatcar at a station. She was fingering the controls, the steering wheel, talking to the mechanic-driver.

Later, finding Harriet alone, sorting pamphlets in the library, Miki mentioned this interest of Yelena's. 'I get the feeling she's about to take flight. Or wants to. Has she really got Sasha out of her system?'

'I don't know. I hope – I think so.'

'She can't be so mad as to want to follow him –'

'She can! Her flirtatious Baltic mother was only one side to Yelena. She has others. And not just that Slav thing either, the soulful, compassionate feeling – but Tartar. I've often thought it – in her craftiness, cunning, cruelty.'

'Tartar?'

'Yes. Half you Russians are – Asiatic, the golden horde. Remember?'

Miki was put out. 'All the same, she'll surely come back to Moscow.' He spoke with sudden pleasure now. 'You all will. And as I've told you, if you want to get back to England – I could help you there.'

'Yes . . .'

'You seem uncertain?'

'It's just – what happens to Yelena?'

'You've probably guessed, if you didn't know already, my feelings about her. I hope she'll come back and work with me in the new Cultural Ministry in Moscow.'

'Yes, I know what you feel about her.' She looked at this tall, stringy creature, liking him, knowing him to be a good man, for all his Bolshevik enthusiasms. 'And, yes, you'd be a blessing for her. In practical ways, too. After all, she has no one left in Russia now. Sasha gone and all her relatives dead or disappeared.'

But still Miki felt, from her indeterminate expression, that Harriet wasn't certain of all this. 'Is it . . . Is it that you'd like to stay on in Russia yourself, with Holly? I could arrange something musical for you. Work in the Moscow Conservatoire, teaching, or a job in the Cultural Ministry.'

He saw the expression on her thin face, her freckled skin and cornflower-blue eyes, become even more uncertain, as if she were trying desperately to see into the future, so to make sensible decisions now, but quite failing. 'Yes,' she said suddenly, before realizing this was not the answer she meant. 'I mean, no. Of course I have to try and leave, for Holly's sake. And my parents; they've had no word from me since we left Ladoga. They must be worried stiff. Of course I have to try and get home as soon as I can.'

Harriet wondered why there had been any doubt in her mind about this. Holly's welfare was paramount. Yet aside from this all-important consideration for Holly's safety, Harriet sensed that one part of her didn't really want to go home at all – to her cold and critical parents in the wilds of West Cork, or even to her good friends in west London.

What she didn't want to admit was that she couldn't readily contemplate a future outside Russia, away from the twins or the Russian people. She needed them for all the wrong reasons, for their mad inconsistencies, their naïve innocence which provoked the governess in her, their forthright passions which tempted her to subjection there. They were a people who licensed the reprehensible and contradictory sides of her own domineering yet wayward nature, her need to be governess with these people, and yet their victim. Russia fed all that had been condemned and repressed in her own Victorian background and upbringing, all her – as she felt them to be – shameful needs and notions. Russia was her life blood in this way. Yet by her reason and her better nature she had to deny this. So she said then, 'No, of course I have to get home, as soon as I safely can.'

'I could help you then.'

'And look after Yelena?'

'I'd hope to, if she'll let me. The trouble of course is Sasha. They're really so bad for each other, when they're together.'

'Yes, I realize –'

'Always a rival there.'

Harriet thought it better to break off this line of conversation. She shrugged her shoulders, relaxing. 'Of course, it's all such nonsense, when the issue should be so simple.' She smiled at him. 'If I was in her shoes – with you – well, I'd jump at the chance!'

But she wondered about her motives here. Did she not rather mean, in this encouragement of Miki's suit, that he would be an admirable means of getting Yelena away from Sasha: a bait, a cure, as she herself had been for Sasha? Yet if Miki took up with Yelena it would surely be a repetition of this unfortunate pattern, result in another unhappy relationship, a recipe for a further disaster. So – in all honesty she thought – she could not encourage the match. Yet she couldn't say so now. She had to dissuade Miki in some other way.

'But since I'm not in Yelena's shoes,' she continued, 'well, I shouldn't try and put myself in them. You know,' she went on briskly, 'we really spend far too much time concerned with Yelena and Sasha. When we should be getting on with our own lives. On the other hand, in simply practical terms, since they are separated now, Yelena's going to need you. Or me.'

Miki wondered why she'd put it this way, as if they were somehow rivals for Yelena's affections. Then he thought – was she frightened of losing Yelena – to him – now that, with Sasha out of the way, she had Yelena all to herself?

Yelena, while Harriet was out of their compartment that evening doing some washing, read Holly a bedtime story, one of her favourites from Afanasiev's collection, *Alenoushka and her Brother*, which, given its theme of parental desertion, Harriet would not have chosen. Holly, her busy, often so pugnaciously involved, little face in repose at last, was tucked up in the lower bunk.

'"Once upon a time there were two orphan children, a little boy and a little girl, brother and sister. The little boy was called Ivanoushka and the little girl's name was Alenoushka. They set out to walk through the whole great wide world . . ." '

As she continued, Holly dropped off to sleep. But Yelena went on reading – the story of a brother and sister in which Ivanoushka, thirsty but ignoring his sister's advice by drinking water from a sheep's footprint, is transformed into a lamb; in which she herself is later drowned, with a stone round her neck, by an old witch; only to be rescued from the bottom of a river by a fine gentleman when she kisses the lamb, still waiting for her on the river bank, who returns to the original form of her brother so that they all live happily ever after.

She finished the story and gazed at Holly's sleeping face. She looked more like Sasha than Harriet. The toss of thick dark curls, the bowed lip above, the thin one below, the tiny pointed ear lobes, pointed chin. Sasha was there in this child's flesh and blood, she thought. She touched Holly's hand. She was touching part of Sasha. Sasha's hands, those long fingers of his which she had taken and looked at so carefully, that day on the terrace of Orlov years before – a moment she remembered so well, when she had first realized how she wanted him.

It was strange that Sasha should actually be here, half of him at least, in this other person, an essence, a miniature of him in this child, when he himself had so completely disappeared. She was suddenly angry, jealous that the child should be Harriet's and not her own, not a part of her that she could now remember Sasha by, a joint creation, a child who would then look like both of them, their twinship moulded into one person, incontrovertible evidence of their love for one another.

Miki and Yelena drove fast beneath a lowering grey sky, over the compacted snow on the road, between the tops of birch trees sticking up through the creamy folds on either side of them.

'It's wonderful!' Yelena shrieked, the keen air stinging her face. 'To be in a car again.'

Miki couldn't favour either of the women in front of the others on the train. But now, a few days later, when he had to drive to the town of Valuiki some miles away from the railway station, he'd been able to take Yelena along with him. He'd been told of a group of *Tziganes*, gypsy dancers, marooned in the town for the winter. He thought he might be able to use them for his propaganda and so had brought Yelena with him, in the Peugeot motor, with the excuse of her being his musical adviser.

Yelena drew the collar of her sheepskin coat closer about her neck. As a member of Miki's troupe, as an 'Artist of the People', she had been able to abandon her peasant disguises, her ragged shawls and filthy blouses. Now she had a sheepskin coat, a fur hat, high leather boots and a serge tunic beneath. After a month of such warmth and regular food the colour had come back into her cheeks, her face filled out, the deep dark eyes sparkling now, even in the sour grey light.

Miki turned to her. 'You've seen these gypsy dancers before, I'm sure.'

'Yes. We used to have them every winter at the castle on Lake Ladoga. My grandfather kept them, as part of his boyars' court, a whole troupe of strolling players, actors, dancers. Extraordinary.'

She told Miki something of all that had happened to her at Ladoga since they had last met: her madness, the violent fight with Sasha, the child she had had, stillborn, all the disasters which had befallen her there; the evil that had possessed her.

Miki was astonished. 'I didn't know about these powers. How did they come?'

'I hardly know myself now. They've gone so completely from my life. But I was born with them, according to an old Lapp woman, a soothsayer that my grandfather took me to see – born under the sign of the great wind god, Bieggolmai, who gave me the powers. But they were really nothing but a curse . . .'

'You're not even in your mid-twenties, yet it's as if you've lived through centuries of Russian history. That boyars' court, the last of the Tsarist years with all those awful balls in Petersburg, the revolution, the civil war, and now this new world that's coming. What next? That's the question.' She didn't reply, so that he had to continue. 'If you don't want to be part of this new Russia, then what? You can't go back to anything of your old Russia, that's certain. You could leave, like the other Whites, tens of thousands of them now, gone west, or east. Do you want that?'

'No, I don't know. Possibly –'

'What would you do? Among all those decayed aristocrats and generals and malicious, gossipy old women? In Nice or Paris. Drive a taxi, or play the piano in some bar or nightclub as many of them are forced to do, I gather.'

'Yes. Or rather no. I wouldn't much want to do either.'

'No?'

'I don't know. I'm not sure.' She didn't look at him, keeping her eyes firmly fixed on the road ahead.

She was so unforthcoming and uncertain, he thought, just as Harriet had been with him a few days before in the library. These two, whom he remembered as women of such decided opinions and intentions, seemed to have nothing in mind now for their futures. Of course the long and terrible journey they had made down here, the tragedies *en route*, must have numbed them. That was to be expected. He longed, as before, to help Yelena, to bring her back to faith, security, to love itself, through him and the whole new Soviet world which was opening up all over Russia now.

But he didn't have much hope. He had already offered her all this in the watchmaker's shop three years before, and most of the same in their first talk in his compartment a few weeks previously. She had remained impervious to all his suggestions. What use to make them again now? He lacked the key to her soul, the key that was still Sasha, and he would have to leave it at that.

Yet strangely, he reflected afterwards when they had reached Vuluiki, she had barely mentioned Sasha on their journey to the town, and hadn't used him as any excuse for not accepting his own offers. Had she finally accepted that Sasha was gone from her life, for good? Or had she just reached a complete emptiness of soul, with Sasha's departure and the earlier tribulations of her journey, all the wells of her spirit dried up, where there were no juices to propel her forward, one way or the other? A *tabula rasa* waiting for some new imprint? He had no idea what that might be. Nor, it seemed, did she.

The red-skirted women with their tight-fitting, gold-threaded bodices approached the men with gliding grace, advancing, retreating, promising, refusing, in steps of careful, stately ritual. Then a sudden change of pace. The men taking over, circling the women, stamping their feet viciously, right in front of the women, fired with frustrated passion. Their anger dying then, the delicate circling continuing, very close to the women now, but never brushing even the skirts of their partners, rising on their toes in soft leather boots like ballerinas, the women pretending acquiescence, before suddenly stamping their own feet, spurning the men, retreating – then all this was repeated, to the vivid music of the fiddles and concertina, this electric *contredanse* of passion.

'"The Dance of the Eagles". Georgian. They're Georgian

gypsies,' Miki said, turning to her as they watched the troupe in the main hall of the gymnasium at Vuluiki.

Yelena was spellbound. But in the end she said, 'What possible Soviet propaganda could you make out of that?'

'None. But it would get the people in. An audience – then the messages, afterwards.'

'Rather cheating, isn't it? Mixing art and politics?'

'Not at all. It's catching the fish. Christ was expert at it. The miracles first, then the message. "I shall make you fishers of men" – all that. We're just doing the same thing.'

'But you don't believe in Christ.'

'No. But if you cut out the going-to-heaven business Christ's message is just the same as ours – with the difference that we are in the business of heaven on earth. Christ was like Lenin. He had to overthrow the Roman yoke to bring in the new millennium. It's the same with us.'

'You have all the answers very neatly.'

'I don't. I'm not a politician. I'm on the miracle side of things. Art, the loaves and fishes, creating things out of nothing. And there aren't any "answers" in art. Only feelings of rightness, balance, perfection sometimes – all of which is pleasure. And that's my job, to give this to everyone now, not just the awful booboisie, the rich fools and stuffed shirts in Petersburg or Moscow . . .' His enthusiasm died in this excited interpretation of Soviet doctrine. He was suddenly bored by the whole theme, looking at her now with great candour and emotion. 'But enough of politics, revolution and the coming millennium! I don't really want you for that. But for you yourself. Come with me, Yelena. Come just for *me*, this time?'

It was a personal invitation now, and one which she had long expected. But after her talk with Harriet in the attic she knew better than to bring Sasha up as a reason for refusing him. She knew how to handle the topic of Sasha and her emotions – in silence, like the dancers, the women who, for all their suggestive provocation, remained inviolate. Well, she could do the same. So she had prepared a different answer and gave it now with confidence.

'Yes – yes, all right, Miki. I will come with you.'

It was like the dance they had just witnessed. Advancing, retreating, promising, refusing, promising again. A ritual of courtship without any final consummation. Part of a game. It had to be that way, she thought. She had no alternative. Miki looked at her in happy astonishment. She wished he hadn't believed her.

Miki, when next alone with Harriet, told her of this development. Harriet was astonished. And though, in her last talk with Miki, she had recommended such a suit, now she backtracked openly, putting into words what she had felt at the time.

'Don't be too certain, Miki,' she told him carefully. 'It could just be a ploy to stay with you, with us, on the train, before she gets off at Penza, where it links up with Samara and then the Trans-Siberian – and from there straight to Omsk where she thinks Sasha will be.'

'But she hasn't mentioned Sasha, not since we first spoke of him just after we'd left Kharkhov – when she simply agreed with me that it'd be crazy to try and follow him.'

'Even allowing her good sense there, it could still be the old story of Yelena. You know some of it, I'm sure, already. Yelena takes up with men – with you, with Sandy Woodrow – and there was that American, Quince, you remember him from the Petersburg days before the war? She takes up with them but just as a distraction from, or as revenge upon, Sasha. And quite likely that's what she's doing with you, now that Sasha's gone once more. A distraction.'

'But she was so sure! The way she said it.'

'The actress in her –'

'But you thought it a good idea the other day: she and I together.' He looked at Harriet, puzzled, fearing something in her now.

'Yes, I did.' Harriet paused, puzzled herself for an instant before continuing quickly. 'Until I thought about it. And anyway, I never imagined she would agree to being with you. Properly.'

'Well, she has. And I feel she's sensible about Sasha now, at last.'

'All of us – me, Sandy Woodrow, Sasha himself – have thought just that often enough. But it's never been true in the end.' She gazed at him, aware how she was exaggerating somewhat, even playing devil's advocate. But she thought it justified now.

The essence of what she had said she knew to be true. 'The plain fact, Miki, is that in living with any man Yelena would end up making his life a misery.'

Miki looked miserable then. Harriet hated hurting him. But better this now than for him to suffer far greater pain and disappointment later.

Yet perhaps she wasn't being quite fair to him. She turned back, speaking in a more hopeful tone. 'Of course, it's really none of my business – and you could be the one special person who worked for her. There are such people, people made for someone else. So you mustn't take my word on everything I've just said.'

'No.'

But it was clear that he had taken her words to heart, so that Harriet felt a dreadful stab of guilt after he'd left, for having, as she suspected, more or less killed off in his mind any idea of a happy relationship between them.

The following day, without Miki's having talked to Yelena alone again, or Harriet having an opportunity of talking to her about her conversation with Miki, the train was held up by a heavy snowdrift which had blown down off the surrounding forested hills into a cutting, completely blocking the line in an isolated section north of Saratov. They had spent all morning under a leaden sky with shovels clearing a passage forward.

Now, towards midday, they were nearing the end of the drift, for they had just unearthed a small railwayman's hut and beyond it could see the end of the cutting where the snow flattened out.

Then, with a sudden flurry of fresh snow sweeping down from the forest on the hill above them, they heard the sound of a train approaching, down line, a plume of dark smoke shooting into the sky, before it rounded a bend and stopped a hundred yards behind their own carriages. Hardly a train, they saw, just a locomotive, a single carriage and a flatcar behind with armour plating built up around a field gun with its barrel poking out.

Yelena, working some distance in front of their own engine,

with Harriet and the others, and Miki just ahead of them at the snow face, thought only that they would have some assistance now, relaxing on their shovels, watching the men in the distance disembark and walk towards them. But as they came nearer, skirting their own train, Yelena saw they were a group of a dozen Red Guards, with rifles, a man in front in a leather jacket and fur collar, a tall man with strong features and pale blue eyes under his astrakhan hat with a red star pinned on it. It was Commissar Drushov.

The guards fanned out around them, covering them with their rifles. Drushov took off his hat and shook some snow off it, smoothing his fair hair before replacing the hat. He seemed in no hurry. Finally, having surveyed the scene, the work they were doing, he addressed Miki.

'So, Comrade Commissar, we've finally caught up with you. You – and your friends.' He looked at the two women. 'Irina and Marina Kirilovna.'

'What's the matter? What do you want, coming all this way after us?' Miki was curt.

'Trains, Comrade. Trains. I told you. Yours. And we need traitors, too. Counter-revolutionaries, like you and your two friends here.' He looked over at Yelena and Harriet. 'The Princess there, Princess Yelena Rumovsky and her English friend!'

'Princess who? Rumovsky?' Miki leant on his shovel, quite relaxed. 'I've no idea –'

'Ah, yes, you do. You must have known, employing them so readily back in Kharkov. I was suspicious of them then, and of course I was right.'

'I've no idea what you're talking –'

'No? Well, it makes no difference. We're taking you all straight back to Kharkov. Your train of poets and musicians. And you and these two women, enemies of the people. The three of you will be tried in a People's Court.'

'Rumovsky? Who are these Rumovskys?'

'Leaders of the old regime, Comrade!' Drushov was almost genial now. 'The Princess's father was a Tsarist minister, related to the recently deceased Nicholas Romanov himself. White class traitors, counter-revolutionaries.'

'You know this?'

'Yes, I know it. The printer in Kharkov who forged their papers and his friend the tea merchant, Matushkin. We have them both. They were only too ready to tell us. In the end. So, back to the train, the three of you and the child, *my* train, not yours. Yours will be pulled along backwards until we get to Saratov.'

They could do nothing. A flock of crows rose suddenly, spiralling up like tea-leaves from the bare oak trees on the ridge above them, cawing stridently. The guards rounded up everyone, the whole troupe, leading them back down the line.

Yelena, coming to their dormitory carriage, started to climb up the steps at the end of it.

'*My* train,' Drushov reminded her. 'All of you, in *my* train.'

Harriet turned to him. 'My daughter. She needs things. And we have a cat. We have to take him.'

'A *cat*?' Drushov appeared to be astonished. Then, smiling, he was heavily ironic. 'A performing cat no doubt! Go and get your stuff.' He gestured to one of the guards. 'Go with them.'

The rest of the troupe, with Miki, were led on down the line to Drushov's train, while the two women, with Holly and the Red Guard behind them, stepped up into the dormitory carriage and moved down the corridor to their compartment. Once inside they closed the door, the Guard waiting for them just outside.

'What now?' Yelena whispered as they got their things together.

'God knows. Escape if we can –'

'How?'

As they spoke they heard the sudden sound of rifle fire, repeated volley after volley, coming from somewhere above them, on the corridor side of the carriage. Peering out of the door of their compartment they saw the Red Guard at the end of the corridor now, crouching at the open doorway of the carriage, rifle aimed at the line of trees on the hill above them, firing repeatedly.

From the big window in front of them they saw some distant figures, running from tree to tree on the hill, several hundred yards away, taking cover behind the trunks, firing again, the shots echoing through the cutting, the attackers moving forward once more. Then the window next to them shattered.

They ducked and lay flat out on the floor of the corridor. The firing increased as Drushov's Red Guards returned the fusillade from the hill.

Several minutes later Yelena peeked out of the window. A score of men, out of the trees and spread in a line, were running diagonally down the hill towards Drushov's train, taking cover in mounds of snow, then firing again as they gradually closed with their prey.

She could see some of them now, dressed in all sorts of clothes, in old military uniforms, with army forage caps, others in sheepskin coats with bandoliers round their chests, in Cossack hats. A mob of famished forest dwellers or anarchist bandits. The firing reaching a crescendo all around them, from Drushov's train and from the encircling raiders. There were shots and cries from somewhere down the line, before a final bout of rifle fire, then silence.

Harriet stood up gingerly and looked about her. The Red Guard at the end of the corridor was dead, slumped over the edge of the open doorway. Going to the next shattered window, she peered out quickly, craning her neck, looking down the cutting. There was no one there. But on the hill above her she saw the attackers, their backs towards her, still concerned with Drushov's train a hundred yards down the track.

'Come on!' Harriet said, taking the initiative. 'Now's our chance. We'll get out the other side of the carriage, then up the cutting to that railwayman's hut. Quick, before they turn their attention to us!'

'But we can't leave Tomcat – or my teddy and my books,' Holly said urgently.

'No, nor the violin for that matter,' Harriet added.

They gathered up their things, wrapping them in blankets, and put Tomcat in his covered basket, then went up the corridor and stepped out of the carriage by the door on the other side, and ran up past the engine and on along the cleared track, clutching the violin case, their blanket bags and the wicker basket.

Without the cover of the train now, they put on an extra spurt towards the hut ahead. None of the bandits turned to see them, as they leapt over mounds of snow and abandoned shovels, rushing forward to the door.

Then they were inside it, gasping, the door closed behind them. They waited. Five minutes, ten, before the firing suddenly broke out again. Yelena opened the door a fraction. She couldn't see Drushov's train. It was hidden on the bend behind their own. But she noticed the regularity of the shots, single rifle shots, one after the other, sharp cracks echoing up the snowy cutting as one after the other the bandits executed the surviving occupants of both trains.

4

They were still in the hut, shivering, distraught. From the slightly open door they had seen nothing of the executions, for their own train, on a bend in the cutting, had hidden this from them. But they had seen the bandits afterwards, coming with their pack-horses, pillaging both trains of all that they wanted by way of food, clothes, weapons, fuel – when they had disappeared up into the forested hills fifteen minutes before.

'We'll have to go back, one or other of us,' Harriet whispered 'But not with . . .' She nodded towards Holly, sitting wrapped in a blanket, holding Tomcat. 'We must. Some of them may still be alive – Miki even. We can't not.'

'I'll go.'

Yelena left the hut, hurrying back down the cutting, past their own train and round the bend, to be confronted by the carnage.

The bodies of their friends, along with Drushov's Red Guards, lay in a rough line by the side of the track in front of the armoured flatcar at the end of Drushov's train. They were spread out in various haphazard but sometimes comfortable-seeming positions; they might have been asleep, embracing the snow, on white sheets strangely patterned with red. There was no sound – no birds in the chill grey sky or in the trees on the hill above, no movement anywhere – only the slow hiss of steam from the two locomotives.

Yelena walked down the track. She could barely look at each corpse. But she had to. She found Miki's aide, the serious-faced young man, looking even younger now without his spectacles. The pencils he carried were all strewn about him. The bandits had robbed him of everything else, but not these precious objects of his, which they would have no use for. There were the three girls – Katya, Mousia and Elizaveta – who had shared the compartment next to them, grouped together in the red-stained snow, piled one on top of the other almost, as if, holding hands, they had been playing Ring-a-Ring-of-Roses and had all fallen down in a rush, together. But there was no sign of Miki or Drushov. She stepped up into Drushov's carriage. Apart from several of his Red Guards, killed in the attack, it was empty.

The whole carriage had been ransacked. But one of the Guards, lying on his side in the doorway, had a holster at his waist. She pushed him over with her foot and opened the leather pouch. The revolver was still there. The bandits had missed it. It was loaded. To be found with a gun by the Reds was to face instant execution. On the other hand, in their present circumstances, the gun might be the saving of their lives. Yelena kept it, stuffing it away inside the waistband of her tunic.

She went on up the line, getting into their own train, walking through the carriages. There was no sign of Miki here either. Another of his tricks? The conjurer, the illusionist. She remembered his mysterious disappearance, his escape from the police in the museum in Petrograd. Had he somehow managed the same thing here? Or had they taken him – and Drushov – as a hostage or for some other reason? She returned to the railwaymen's hut.

'Miki's not there,' she told Harriet. 'Or Drushov. The bandits must have taken them for some reason. Or they escaped somehow.'

'Thank God. Miki may have survived.' Harriet shivered. Holly shivered in her arms.

'The engine,' Yelena said. 'Our engine. They'd started to get steam up this morning. It'll be warm on the footplate.'

They took their things, walked back and climbed up onto the footplate of the huge locomotive. Yelena opened the firebox door. The embers of big logs glowed inside. She threw some more on from the tender behind her, leaving the firebox door open, so that soon the heat glowed out at them. They sat on logs, warming themselves, Tomcat sitting in front of them, Holly clutching her furless Teddy, sucking her thumb.

The engine started increasingly to hiss and sigh. Yelena looked up. The boiler pressure gauge was rising slowly. 'Of course!' She was suddenly excited. 'That's the answer. The bandits may come back – and since we have to get out of here anyway –'

'What?'

'We can't go back, with Drushov's train behind us. But we can go forward. The cutting's almost entirely cleared and the snow plough in front will push us through the rest of it. We'll take this train.'

'How? How to drive it, I mean? The drivers are all dead.'

'Oh, I can drive it all right. I've seen Johnny Quince do it – the American railway man in Petrograd. I was with him up on the footplate when he was driving it. He showed me.' She got to her feet. 'Look! It's easy enough. You check these two gauges – the water and the boiler pressure. When the finger goes into the green section of this dial – here – it means you have sufficient steam to drive it. Then you let the brakes off – spin that wheel over there. Then you move this long handle.' She took the end of the regulator handle. 'And push it gently forward. That lets the steam into the two cylinders in front – and you're off!'

'Where?'

'The next station, Balakovo. I've seen it on the map in Miki's office. We go straight on up north, with the Volga on our right, then there's a great lake, you'll see it, then across the river and there's the town of Balakovo, the next stop, about eighty miles away from here.'

'And if another train comes towards us? It's only a single line.'

'There'll be a signal up against us. We stop. Come on – we've no other way of getting out of here. Pile more logs on, get steam up. We can try it, at least.'

Fifteen minutes later, having stoked the firebox up to a great blaze so that the finger on the dial had moved into the green section, Yelena spun the brake wheel, then moved the regulator gently forward. There was a tremendous juddering, a vicious hissing escape of steam, the wheels spinning on the icy rails, before they gripped and the whole train lurched forward, gathering pace, the snow plough pushing through the last of the drift, smoke bellowing out in great throaty gasps, straight up from the cone-funnelled chimney stack.

In another ten minutes they had left the hilly area and were rushing along, at something a little above running pace, through the levelling wooded countryside. Soon, distantly beyond the trees, they saw the huge flat expanse of ice, ahead of them to their right, covered in blue tinted snow from the sunlight which had suddenly emerged from a gap in the clouds.

With the two women moving between tender and firebox stoking logs, Holly stayed out of the way, in a corner at the back of the footplate, holding Tomcat in his basket, a blanket over the top. Harriet kept an eye on her, noticing her fierce little face, the turned-up nose and piercing blue eyes, the determination there, in her sharp, all-encompassing gaze, as she seemed to be willing the train forward. Her eyes, as she got older, were an increasingly astonishing feature. Even in repose they tended to glitter with intensity. Now they blazed, as if fuelled by some strange power quite outside her consciousness . . . In all this – with the same nose and eyes – she was so like Yelena had been as a child, Harriet thought.

They arrived at the small railway town of Balakovo without mishap some three hours later, to be greeted as heroines by the few Bolshevik troops left in the place. They had rescued a valuable train. Balakovo had been taken and occupied by the Reds only a few weeks before. Their brigade had pushed on forward then, up the railway, north, pursuing the Whites, towards Penza and Samara, so that the town was controlled now by only a score of Red Guards with a Red Army officer in charge, a Captain Sverbeyev, a young cavalryman on crutches, wounded in the leg during the attack on Balakovo, who had thus been detailed to stay behind and take charge of things in the town.

The Captain was a countryman, from the steppes. Naïve and enthusiastic, with the glimmering of a moustache, to him this business of revolution and civil war was a vast excitement, opening up a whole new world, giving him power and promotion in the Red Army, so that he was bitterly disappointed that his wound had put him out of commission, temporarily denying him a part in the drama, the furtherance of his fantastic adventures.

He made up for this now by seizing his chances with the two

women, these attractive Amazons of the revolution, taking chivalrous charge of them and going out of his way to please them. He put them up in the town's only hotel, a dingy wooden building on the single main street, entertaining them there to supper late that afternoon.

In their honour he broached precious army stores, so that apart from *shchi*, the cabbage soup, which was still to be had, they ate salted pork, half a loaf of real rye bread and drank tea with which there was an even more precious spoonful or two of sugar. A feast, in the circumstances.

The hotel proprietor, an old and partly blind man, stumbled to and fro from the kitchen to the grimy dining-room. There was no one else there. The Captain, having demolished his soup at a rush, raised his glass of tea to them. 'Yes, you have done magnificently! I've sent some engineers and a platoon of Guards back to the cutting.' He belched a fraction, then gulped again at his glass of tea. 'They'll pick up the dead, bring back Commissar Drushov's train and repair the telegraph wires. So we'll be able to get through to Saratov and then to Kharkov first thing tomorrow morning. Tell them what's happened. Though they may have sent another train up already from Saratov, to see what's happened to Commissar Drushov. He's an important man, Regional Commissar.' The Captain attacked his pork then for half a minute. 'Of course,' he said with his mouth full. 'I don't understand . . . what Commissar Drushov was doing . . . following your train up from Kharkov.'

'I've no idea,' Harriet said easily. 'We weren't there when he spoke to Commissar Ostrovsky. We were in our carriage, just before the firing broke out.'

'Well, we'll know soon enough when the telegraph wires are repaired in the morning. And then we can get you all back to Kharkov.'

This, the two women saw, was exactly what they didn't want. In the morning, with the telegraph restored, Captain Sverbeyev would discover the reason Drushov had followed their train. In the morning, when the Captain had been in touch with Drushov's men in Saratov or Kharkov, they would be unmasked, known for who Drushov thought them to be: White counter-revolutionaries, traitors, enemies of the people. They had to get away from Balakovo before next morning.

Harriet looked out the window. It was snowing again, slanting flakes blown by a stiff wind.

'We'd really prefer to go north, back to Moscow, where we come from,' Harriet said, not pleading but in tones of some urgency.

'I wish you could.' The Captain picked his teeth. 'But from here, north to Moscow, you'd have to go via Samara where our brigade is fighting at the moment. And the line is blocked before Samara. You could only get to Moscow by going back to Voronezh and Kharkov.'

'I see –'

'But you'll get back to Kharkov easily enough. And after your brave efforts with the train up here they'll welcome you with open arms and arrange for you all to return to Moscow.'

'Yes. It's good of you . . .'

'I'm honoured. And now, I have something special, for the little girl particularly. A tin of fruit!' He beamed at them, picking his teeth again, before calling the proprietor.

They could not go north on the railway, the two women realized – and they must not go south. They had only a few hours to find a different form of transport and go somewhere else. Harriet saw only one possible answer. She must work on it at once. After they had all made a fuss of the fruit salad, devouring the small helpings with exaggerated relish, she broached the topic casually with the Captain.

'You must be keen on horses, as a cavalry man. You have some with you here, I imagine –'

'Oh, yes!' He interrupted, taking the bait immediately. 'Horses are my life. Before the revolution I worked at the famous horsebreeding centre at Hrenovoye outside Voronezh. Just as a groom then, of course. We bred them for the Tsar's army, some wonderful animals. The short-tailed Ardennes horse was good. But the best cavalry horses we bred were a cross between an Arab stallion and our own Russian palominos. Strong, wide-chested horses. But fast! We have several with us up here.'

'Do you? We'd love –'

'Oh yes,' he rushed on, quite taken up with the subject, 'after the revolution, you see – I was put in charge of Hrenovoye, and later helped organize a Red Army cavalry brigade, out of the horses there, and was made a Captain then. But now – my leg . . .' He tapped his thigh ruefully.

'I *am* sorry,' Harriet commiserated with him. 'But we're keen on horses, too. We both are.' She looked across at Yelena, who nodded. 'We used to ride a bit. Would you show them to us? These cross-bred Arab-Palominos especially. We'd be very interested.

'Yes, of course.' The Captain was more than pleased. 'They're in the livery stables behind the hotel. The place used to be a post-chaise inn before the railway came. Most of the horses are out of commission, one way or another, lame or cut about in our last attack. But come and see them, certainly.

The Captain held an oil-lamp, leading them down between two rows of loosely tethered horses. The stables contained everything they would want: a collection of high-pommelled, leather-pouched military saddles, bridles, martingales, nose-bags. Harriet smelt the familiar odour of leather, the warm dung, the acrid rumours in the straw. The horses stirred in the lamplight, the Captain patting their rumps.

'This is Misha. Pure-bred Ardennes – our Commandant's mount. Lame, fetlocks badly torn. He's taken my horse up the line, more's the pity! And this is Ivan, a cross-bred Arab-Palomino. And his half-brother, Sadko – by another sire – next to him.'

'Beautiful,' Yelena said. 'Are they lame?'

'No. Both were injured in the attack on the town here, over three weeks ago. Shrapnel. But they're fine now. They're quite recovered . . .'

They walked on down the stables, towards the big double doors at the end. They heard the snow blowing against them, the night coming on, in fierce squalls.

Later, in their bedroom, the two women discussed matters. 'It's the only way,' Harriet said. 'At first light or even before – those two horses, Ivan and Sadko. We can both ride, after all.'

'But Holly and Tomcat – and the violin?'

'The saddles are huge. Holly can sit before me. Tomcat will have to go cushioned with his blanket in one of the big saddlebags, and the violin in another.'

'And go where?'

'Across the Volga lake here, on the ice. You said you'd seen the whole area on Miki's big map.'

'Yes.'

'Well, draw it for me.'

'No pencil, or paper –'

'Here, on the dust of the dresser.'

Yelena, remembering the detailed, large-scale map of the area in Miki's office, drew a map of the immediate area with her finger, Harriet looking over her shoulder. 'We're here,' Yelena explained. 'On the left bank of the Volga, at Balakovo. The railway goes straight on up this left bank, for a hundred miles or so, then crosses the river again before going north for Penza and Samara.'

'So if we were to go west, straight across the bottom of the lake here –' Harriet moved her finger over the dust, 'and then turn and go north-west, along one side of the triangle, across country, we'd get to Penza just the same, while avoiding the Reds fighting up the railway line to the east.'

'Yes, I suppose we would.' Yelena looked at her in surprise. This was a new Harriet, taking the initiative now, in going north – pushing north in one way or another, towards Penza, Samara and the Trans-Siberian line, which led to Omsk and the chance of finding Sasha. Once they got to Samara, if they did, they would surely be beyond the Red Army lines, so that they could not then turn back into European Russia. No chance then of their getting out of Russia by way of the Crimea or Moscow. They would only be able to leave the country by going east, across the whole of Siberia. Yelena saw that Harriet, in proposing this hazardous ride north, was committing herself, and Holly, to the possibility of a subsequent and even more hazardous journey across Siberia.

'I can see what you're thinking.' Harriet wiped the dust off her finger. 'Why am I pushing for the idea of going north now – towards the Trans-Siberian and the possibility of finding Sasha? Well, I told you the other day, I want to find him as much as you do. Make things right and proper between us. Remember?'

'Yes.'

'So that's what we should do. Besides', she continued briskly, 'we *have* to go north – because we can't go back, unless we want to end up in the hands of Drushov's men.'

'No, I see that.'

'So . . .' Harriet shrugged. 'It's either the devil – or the deep blue sea.'

'Or out of the frying pan and into the fire.'

They thought about this for a moment, before they both smiled wanly at each other. It was Yelena this time who hugged Harriet impulsively. Confronted by this most practical evidence, it was clear that Harriet was with her now, collaborating with her, in going north.

'Yes,' Yelena continued. 'But we'll get out of the fire now as well. You were right – it's much easier to – well, you can really do *anything* with someone, if you're friends.'

Harriet nodded. 'Yes, it should work. After all, we both used to ride a lot, at Orlov and Ladoga. And, goodness me – I used to hunt all the time in Ireland. And the two horses couldn't be better. Ideally suited.'

'Will we really be riding on those big horses then?' Holly interrupted, looking up, gazing expectantly from one woman to the other.

'Yes. Yes, we will,' her mother told her.

'Good,' she said. 'That'll be even better than going on the engine of the train.'

The snoring innkeeper caused them no problems when they crept downstairs with an oil-lamp half an hour before dawn next morning and made their way out to the livery stables. Ivan and Sadko seemed pleased at the prospect of an outing. They saddled them up and stored away their things, with some food they'd saved from the previous evening in the big saddlebags. Tomcat didn't care for the smell of the horses or the idea of travelling in a pouch behind Harriet's stirrups. But by now he seemed to know the position, the whole situation, of this increasingly fraught journey: they were all in the same boat and he had better stay in it, with them, if he wanted to survive.

When dawn broke Yelena opened the big double doors. The snow had stopped. The light beyond was dazzling. The sun, for the first time in weeks, had made an appearance, just rising behind the stables, casting long shadows ahead of them on the crystal white waves which lay over the submerged fields, running away from the back of the town to the west. They mounted, spurred the horses gently forward, their hooves sinking deep into the snow as they followed a vague track between two rows of birch trees, making for the great lake which lay ahead of them down the long slopes.

They crossed the three miles of ice over the lower part of the lake in less than half an hour; then, reaching the shore line, they rode due north, finding cover below a high bluff of wooded land which bordered the western side of the lake, too steep to allow for any landing-places or habitation.

After another three hours, with the sun glaring off the snowy lake and the horses beginning to sweat, they came to a gap in the cliffs, to the mouth of another smaller frozen river, a tributary which led into the lake, and which seemed to flow from the north-west, from forested hills running into the distance, away above them to their left.

It was after midday. They had only another four hours light in which to find shelter from the freezing night. The tributary seemed to offer the best hope of this. There would be a settlement, some houses or even just a logger's cabin on its banks farther upstream. They left the lake, riding between steep wooded hills to either side, without sign of any life.

An hour later, with the sun sinking in the sky, the river began to narrow and the banks became less sheer, replaced now by thickly forested hills sloping up to either side, timber country of pine and birch, but still empty of any sign of human settlement.

Pressing on, the river became increasingly narrow and split by small islands, leaving widths to either side of only half a dozen yards or so, which finally explained the lack of any settlements here. The river wasn't navigable.

The sun had disappeared, hidden by the hills, as the stream narrowed still further, so that they rode beneath a canopy of icy pine branches, some so low that their faces brushed against clusters of pine needles, which dusted their cheeks with falls of powdery snow and left a faint resinous smell in their nostrils.

Now, with the sun gone, in the snowy green gloom beneath the trees, it was suddenly very cold. They had eaten most of the bread they had brought. Holly, despite the wrappings of a double sheepskin coat and her squirrel-fur hat, began to shiver. Her cheeks were blue with cold. The horses' sweat had started to freeze, leaving a white sheen of crystals along their flanks, their tired breath rising in languid white spumes, hooves echoing ever more slowly on the lightly powdered ice.

They had ridden a good fifteen miles up the twisting, narrowing stream. And there was nothing – no settlement or shelter – nothing but a frozen forested wilderness ahead of them, when in another hour it would be dark and they would certainly freeze to death overnight.

Neither of the two women said anything, clenching their teeth against the cold, the chill breeze that had come to sweep down the narrow, thickly forested valley, rustling the pine branches, throwing grits of ice in their eyes. Then, rounding a bend in the stream, they saw a windmill, its sails catching the last of the slanting light, sticking out above the pine trees on a rise above them to their left: four dark triangular sails, turning quickly in the stiff breeze.

'It's – a windmill!'

'Yes.'

'But it can't be. There are no fields here, no grain to mill.'

'No. But it is a windmill . . .'

The elderly man was suspicious. He had introduced himself in an equally wary manner, with careful formality. 'I am Mikhail Ivanovich Karasakoff, *barin* of this settlement.' Dressed in the old Russian fashion, in a simple linen kaftan, peaked cap and pantaloons thrust into high boots, he moved to the table where the map was. Harriet followed him, anxious to hear what he said, for he spoke Russian in an equally archaic manner, and his voice in any case was difficult to hear against the rattle of cogged wheels and other machinery worked by the wind sails in the long room next door.

'Yes,' he said, 'from what our agent last told us, the territory ahead is all held now by these accursed Reds. And you would have to get to Samara before you reached that railway that crosses Siberia now. And by train from here to Samara – well, our agent told us: the line is down in that direction, somewhere before Penza.'

He looked at Harriet, then at Yelena, who was sitting on a

stool, exhausted, holding Holly on her lap, with Tomcat at her feet, by a small fire.

Harriet saw the icicles melting on Karasakoff's bushy beard. Though still light outside, it was well below zero and he had just walked up the hill to what seemed to be the estate office, next to the workshop, of this settlement by the frozen river. He turned to her again, strongly built and burly, though he must have been well into his seventies. 'You say you want to get to the territory held by the Tsar's people, these "Whites". You will not get there by train, not now. By sledge perhaps, with horses. You have money?'

He looked at her hopefully, taking off his spectacles. They were old and gold-rimmed with small, perfectly round lenses. They might have come from a museum. He wiped the glass with a lace-bordered handkerchief drawn from inside his kaftan.

'No, we have no money.'

Harriet went over to the window, looking down over the settlement of these Old Believers. There was a small church, the centrepiece of a dozen or more well-built log houses nestling in a semicircle, backs to the wilderness, forming a sort of stockade on one side, facing the frozen river on the other. Behind the houses were small cultivated fields, running up the side of the hills, and beyond them the higher ground, covered in snow-laden birch, pine and oak trees.

A woman crossed the path below her, carrying two wooden pails on a yoke across her shoulders, with a bundle of straw, and went into the barn-like entrance of one of the log houses, where at once some pigs and small brown cows came to the doorway for their feed. Harriet was surprised – the animals living in the houses like this. Then she noticed the wooden steps leading up to the first floor of each house. Of course, they kept their stock on the ground floor, so that their heat in winter would seep upwards, warming the humans above. The Old Believers – a clever, frugal people.

She turned back from the window. 'No, we have no money, or anything else. But you have seen our identity papers. We are not criminals. And we are not Reds either. You can surely see that as well. The train we were on, I told you, it was ambushed by bandits. We were going north, trying to get to the territory of the Whites.'

'Indeed.' The old man stroked his beard and chewed his lips. 'I can see that. You are from another class altogether. As we are here, and have been for hundreds of years. We, of course, are not "Reds" either – those antiChrists. But we have no wish to provoke them, or to advertise ourselves to them. Or to anyone else.' He looked at her doubtfully. 'We have lived and worked alone here, in this valley, for many generations, cutting and shaping wood, at the water wheel by the river in summer, up here with our wind sails in winter. Furniture, spoons, dolls, toys, exchanging them for things we need with our agent. We mind our own business. Some of these Reds have been here already, uncouth men, making enquiries. They left – winter was setting in. But they said they would return in the spring. You would be a difficulty.'

'But you can see,' Harriet appealed to him, 'with the child – we can hardly move on now. The Reds will not be back in midwinter. The hill passes must be blocked.'

'Yes, indeed.'

'We only found the settlement by chance, taking our horses up the river on the ice.'

'Indeed, you were lucky. The ice on this river is not normally so thick as to allow such weight.'

'We could work for you, earn our keep, until the spring.'

'There is work here. But it is not of your sort. Furniture making, the cutting and shaping of logs, the men do that at the lathes and benches next door –'

'And the women? That lace-bordered handkerchief I notice you have. And your fine linen kaftan? You make all your own clothes here, I am sure. And that woven carpet by the table over there. Could we not work at these things, with the women, on your looms? Forgive me, but I know something of you Old Believers, your self-sufficient way of life, of how you disagreed with the Patriarch Nikon's reforms in the seventeenth century, and retained all the old styles of the Orthodox faith. I have much respect for your old beliefs,' she added, which was true. She knew how these people, by refusing these reforms, had suffered terribly – thousands of them burnt alive, often in their churches, the rest forced into exile, where most of them, by their co-operative skills and hard work, had formed thriving colonies, way beyond the new Orthodox pale, as woodcutters and carvers, in isolated hills and valleys, or as farmers in the middle of nowhere.

The old man, though he did his best not to show it, was pleased with her knowledge and comments. 'Indeed,' he said cautiously, shifting uneasily on his feet. 'Well, I would have to talk to the Elders of the Congregation.'

They were taken in by a particularly devout and taciturn middle-aged couple, the Timashevs, Natalya and Nikolai, whose two daughters had both left home, marrying with other Old Believers who lived in a further settlement up river. Their house was one of the smaller wooden *izbas*, by the river bank. They slept, all three of them, in a loft which jutted halfway out over the kitchen, used for storing grain and hay, reached by a wide ladder. Here – under the eaves again, but far warmer, for the kitchen stove was just beneath them and kept permanently alight – they slept on a wide straw mattress between old patched linen sheets with homespun blankets.

Having blessed themselves repeatedly first thing each morning, all standing in front of a collection of small icons to Saint Vladimir and others in the 'Beautiful Corner' of the *izba*, they ate *kasha* for breakfast with black bread and brick tea, sweetened with wild strawberry compote – the bread and tea again at midday and a supper from a large store of preserved fruits, pickled vegetables, dried mushrooms and salted pork or river fish. There was *kvass* to drink, or buttermilk from the several cows in the barn beneath them. They lacked for nothing in the way of these simple provisions and domestic comforts, while Tomcat, too, found a settled ease at last, by the stove or roaming the hayloft in search of large mice.

Throughout the frozen winter days Harriet and Yelena, with Holly sometimes in attendance helping with bobbins of thread and skeins of wool, worked at looms or with needles and coloured threads, with a dozen other women in a large wooden hut by the river.

There were two tall American stoves at either end, always bright with small logs, so that their fingers were kept warm as they pushed shuttles to and fro, creating carpets in variously coloured wools, or did embroidery on cotton or homespun linens, saturating the fabric in floral designs, or worked on church vestments in gold or silver thread; or created clothes for a bride's trousseau, a girl of the settlement who was to be married in the spring: embroidering elegant festival *sarafans* for her, long flowing pyramid-shaped tunics with billowy sleeved blouses made of silk or brocade; or created marigold and daisy-chain designs on the apron of a *ponyova*, the traditional homespun dress of these Volga Slavs; or worked on little red felt over-jackets, threading sequins and gilt braid, lining them with russet silk, trimmed with sable or fox.

On other days, with bright paints – red, purple, yellow and green – they decorated birchwood spoons and platters and delicately carved wooden toys made by the men up on the hill: farm animals, dolls and mechanical toys, of dancing bears and bears that sawed wood or carried water. And later on, when they were more adept, they worked with lace, the finest *guipure russe*, edging blouses, collars, handkerchiefs and silk shawls.

With this work, in these designs, for *sarafans* and *ponyovas*, toys and platters, the two women found a creative absorption, a release from the nightmare of their recent lives, and kept their fingers nimble.

The ancient Slav motifs which they used in their designs: the lozenge as a symbol of the bride's new house, the sun as earth-mother worked in red and black, the brilliant birds and flowers and mythical animals which they set on cloth or bowls – these were magic symbols, to promote fertility or to ward off evil spirits. And working on them had the same calming effect on both women. The dark of their lives was rolled back by these happy emblems and bright colours.

For the first time since they had been at Ladoga over six months before the two women now had a secure base together, with food and warmth and useful work to do. No longer on the run and with no possibility of their leaving, in pursuit of Sasha, for Moscow, the Crimea or anywhere else, everything eased between all three of them as the days went by.

Holly, nearly four years old now, went to the small village school, and all of them observed the formal customs, the archaic rituals of the community. They attended the small plain church, singing the original chants and responses of the faith, making the blessing with two fingers, not three. Seen thus to be in agreement with the old faith, posing no threat to the community, mixing and working with these Old Believers, they were accepted by them, if in a somewhat dour and distant manner.

It was clear of course to everyone that they would not be there indefinitely. But for the time being, with the passes blocked and until spring came, they were sealed into the snow-filled, ice-bound river valley, secured in this Arcadian world of seventeenth-century Russia.

No one came and no one left. They lived suspended in a time out of war. Not even the vaguest news of the civil war filtered through to them in this lost domain, so that it seemed at times as if they might indeed stay here indefinitely, and would enjoy doing so, involving themselves increasingly with the serene life of the community, celebrating their saints' days and winter festivals, their births, deaths and impending marriages, riding out for short forays with Ivan and Sadko on tracks through the pine woods up into the hills, building ice slides for the children, teaching them to skate on the frozen river.

Now, for the first time in many years, Harriet and Yelena were friends together, able to talk without argument, spite, anger, free of all the lies and exaggerations which enmity or fear had brought to their conversations before. They were able to begin at last sensibly to consider their lives, past, present and future, with calmness and truth.

Where there had been coldness or recrimination, now there were the beginnings of honest words, exchanges and queries conducted in gentler tones. For Harriet it was the start of that journey – a voyage into Yelena's unhappy soul, to try and bring some ease there, and to her own equally bruised spirit – the largely self-inflicted injuries of the heart in their relationship with Sasha which had come about, for both of them, for much the same obsessive reasons.

They spoke again of their need to find Sasha. But they talked of this now as a distant, idealized conception, without discussion of the practicalities, of how they might achieve it.

Sasha, since he appeared now so necessary for their future

peace of mind, assumed a solidity for them in advance, without mention of how, or even if, they might meet him again. In this way he took on the form of an answer to an equation to which there was no prior formula.

So set were they on a sensible reconciliation, so sure that it would come about, that they omitted the hero's part in the drama. The two heroines took over his role, giving him lines, attitudes, moves, which, if he ever came on stage, he might never make or speak at all. A play where the dialogue was entirely one-sided – two voices making overtures, plans, inviting responses which, going unanswered, they gave themselves.

'Yes, he's bound to see a real change in us, when we meet.'

'We'll find him – once we get to Omsk on the Trans-Siberian. And even if he's not in Omsk then we'll find him somewhere else farther down the line. He'll be with Skolimsky's men after all, and we'll hardly miss them.'

'Yes. And then we can get out the far side, at Vladivostock, and make a life for ourselves – abroad, in America or England.'

This was their happy fantasy, that even in all the lengths and breadths of Siberia, they would readily find Sasha, and would at once form a perfect understanding with him – and a sensible life all together, somewhere else, ever after.

5

Yet their idyll in the colony, they knew, could not last. The *barin* had told them, and had since reminded them, that when spring came and the passes were open the Bolsheviks would certainly return to the settlement, where they would be seen as strangers, with consequent enquiries and trouble all round.

But the two women knew more than this to their disadvantage. Their identity papers named them as two sisters, Irina and Marina Kirilovna: the counter-revolutionary couple who Drushov and his men had set out to find, along with the traitor Commissar, Mikhail Ostrovsky.

The Bolsheviks in the immediate area would certainly know all this by now as well. So, too, would Captain Sverbeyev at Balakovo, whose men might well be the first to arrive at the settlement when the passes opened. They would have to leave the colony before any Reds arrived, before spring came, and get right away from the area as quickly as possible.

Their departure was precipitated a few days later, in early March, when winter still had a fierce grip on everything, with the sudden arrival of a tall man, wrapped in elkskin furs, with a rifle slung over his shoulder, who appeared on the river ice one morning with a pair of horses and a large empty sledge.

Yelena and Harriet, in the workroom with the other women, saw him come, dragging the big sledge off the ice, being met by Karasakoff. It was the trader, the women told them, the colony's agent for the sale of their furniture, carpets, clothes, toys, spoons and platters. The colony were somewhat surprised to see him. He had arrived earlier than usual, and by a way he never came – risking the river ice, and not by the hill passes, which were not open yet.

Some time later Yelena and Harriet were called from the workroom by the *barin*; they went with him to his *izba*, where they met the agent, a thin figure, a man with eyes too close together, with tightly curled dark hair, still in his elkskin coat.

Karasakoff put on his gold-rimmed spectacles. 'This is our agent Nikita Sergeivich Rogovsky.' The women looked at Rogovsky, his chilled, cadaverous features, suspicious eyes. He returned their gaze in a somewhat alarmed manner, then spoke to the *barin*.

'Yes. It must be them – two women, and a child. But is there no man with them? There was another on the train, a Commissar himself.'

'No.' Karasakoff shook his head. Rogovsky seemed relieved to hear this. Then the headman turned to Yelena. 'He says the Reds are looking for you everywhere. He has come upriver to take his trade with us, earlier than usual, and to warn our settlements, in case you had sought sanctuary with us. He says the Reds will be up here as soon as the passes are open. Or risk the river, even before that, as he has done.'

'Looking for us? Why?' Yelena asked innocently. 'We've done nothing. We were ambushed on that train by bandits, trying to get north to the White territory, as I told you.'

'None the less it is you, and this other man, who was with you on your train, who the Reds are looking for – particularly a man called Drushov, who is regional Commissar here.'

'But it can't be!' Yelena burst out. 'Drushov must be dead. Or the bandits took him.'

'No, Commissar Drushov was not killed. Nor was he taken by the bandits,' Rogovsky said. 'I have heard all about it along the river. Drushov escaped with some of his men, down line, before the final assault on his train. He was badly wounded, in the face, for I have seen him – so that he lost his post as Regional Commissar in Kharkov. But now he's Commander of a special Red Army group, up here, charged with finding and destroying these anarchist bandits in the hills around. Since his face was ruined, and he lost his important position in Kharkov, he has taken it as a personal mission apparently, to find and kill these marauders. And as well – he's given particular directions everywhere – that both of you, and a child with you, and the man you were with who was in charge of your train, a Commissar Ostrovsky, that all of you should be found, with a large price on your heads . . .'

'But why? Why us?'

'It's obvious, isn't it?' The agent smiled. His tone was amicable. He was simply giving them a friendly warning in all this. But his small eyes betrayed him. They were greedy.

'What?'

'Well, it's obvious to the Reds at least that since both of you, and this Ostrovsky, were the only people who escaped the massacre – you weren't to be found among the dead bodies – well, they think you were in league with the bandits, and therefore responsible for the deaths of all those Bolsheviks, on both trains.'

'But it's not true,' Yelena said. 'None of it. We had nothing to do with the bandits. And nothing particular to do with Commissar Ostrovsky either. We only worked as musicians on his train.'

'Yes, of course. I believe you . . .' But Yelena could see that neither of the men believed her. They clearly now thought them to be not loyal Whites but wicked anarchists, worse than the Red antichrists. They looked at both women with misgivings – as well they might, Yelena thought. If their presence was discovered here, in the light of this news they and everyone in the colony would be put to the sword by the Reds.

The old man spoke then. 'Whatever the truth of things,' he said gravely, 'it makes no difference to us. The fact is that the Reds are looking for you, with a price on your heads. All of us here of course are against the Reds. But we must not provoke them. You will have to leave, as soon as possible. And make it out afterwards, if you are called upon to do so, that you have never been here.'

'Leave? How?'

'On the river. With your horses, before it starts to thaw, the way you came.'

'Yes, we will leave then,' Yelena said as brightly as she could. 'And yes, of course,' she added, 'we won't mention that we've ever been here.'

The two men gazed at them, Rogovsky even more distrustfully now. He shifted on his feet, gazing momentarily at his rifle in the corner. Of course, Yelena saw, his own trade here, his very life, was at risk now as well. She could see what was in his mind. He didn't believe they would keep their mouths shut.

These two women – they had only to be caught by the Reds and tortured to give away not only the fact that they had been sheltered by the colony all winter but that he had warned them of their danger.

So both women were surprised when he said, with apparent concern, 'No, I can take you down the river here, on my sledge, first thing tomorrow morning, with your own horses running behind. I'll let you off at the mouth, where it joins the lake and the big river. You can ride north then, get well out of this whole area.'

Yelena was immediately suspicious. But she agreed. She had to. Neither of the men must think she was in the least anxious about this means of departure.

'But what of the war?' Yelena took the opportunity of asking Rogovsky. 'We were making for Samara when the train was ambushed in December. How far north must we go now to reach White territory?'

'Samara, which was in the hands of the Czech Legions, is now controlled by the Social Revolutionaries, not the Bolsheviks.' Rogovsky, encouraging their departure north, embarked on a résumé of the situation with great good will. 'But the Social Revolutionaries have no real power. The Red Army are in the area all about the city and use it as they will. However, the Reds are doing no more than hold the line up there, between Samara and Kazan, where they are not now actually in retreat.'

'Admiral Kolchak's forces are winning then?' Yelena was encouraged.

'Yes, it would seem so. "The Supreme Ruler" has gathered a large army together, nearly half a million men, from the east and has the help of British and French troops now. In the north they've been successful for some time, advancing right up to Perm, west of the Urals, which they took two months ago. So the Whites are ready there to make a dash straight through to Moscow. And in the south to counter-attack all along the Volga front, down to Kazan and Samara. If you got to Samara, laid low, and just waited, the Whites might be there in a month. I pray they are. So, if I leave you – I'm going south towards Saratov – at the mouth of the smaller river here, you should make Samara, up river on the ice, with your horses in about a week. Keeping clear of of the Reds, of course,' he added with a smile, as if this would be an easy matter.

Yelena was certain then that Rogovsky could not wish them well. She knew the vicious reputation of the Reds when they caught bandits or White counter-revolutionaries behind the lines – as he would know himself. Had Rogovsky genuinely meant to help them he would have advised them of the real dangers of such a journey. All this was a charade on both their parts. Rogovsky was going to turn them in – or worse.

Back in the Timashevs' *izba*, as they began their packing, she confirmed her fears to Harriet. 'It's obvious – Rogovsky's whole attitude. He's offered to take us downriver just to save his own skin and his trade with the colonies up here. As soon as we're out on the lake he'll take us straight over to Balakovo, turn us in to the Reds and claim the bounty.'

'Yes.'

'Only one thing to do. We'll turn the tables on him, take his offer, then take his sledge and horses and make up the Volga ourselves.'

'How?'

'Overpower him, going downstream, before we get to the lake. Use the gun – the revolver I took from that dead Guard in the carriage. Shouldn't be too difficult. Rogovsky won't be expecting it. It's the only way – unless you want to stay here and wait for Drushov's or Sverbeyev's men, and have us and probably the whole colony slaughtered.'

'Yes.' Harriet was doubtful. 'I'm not sure about the gun and overpowering him –'

'Shoot him, if need be!' Yelena was adamant. 'Because that's quite likely what he has in mind for us. He'd be sure to clear his name, and keep his trade with the colony, by killing us all first and *then* taking us in. Because then there'd be no chance of our telling the Reds we'd been sheltered by the colony or been warned by him – and he'd get the bounty.'

'*Shoot* him?'

'Yes! It's kill or be killed in this civil war.' Suddenly, as before when she was in charge of the military plans at Ladoga, preparing to do battle with the Reds, Yelena felt a burning need to retaliate. A will to win, at any cost and against whatever odds, invaded her mind, coursed through her veins.

Her eyes blazed. 'We've known this long enough, all the way down from Ladoga. It's just that we've been lucky, never having to kill someone ourselves. Now we may have to. No fine feelings, not now, if we're to survive.' She glared at Harriet. 'Look at the Reds! – and all we've suffered as a result of their damn revolution and killings – losing Papa and Mama, Uncle Sergei, Arkady and Feodor Matushkin, probably Miki, possibly Sasha. So if we're thought to be anarchist bandits now – then we *will* be, if necessary.'

Harriet was not persuaded by these arguments. Yet, if it came to the point, she supposed there was no alternative. 'Yes, all right . . . But what afterwards, if we survive, going up the Volga?'

'Simple enough. Do as Rogovsky says. The Volga goes straight up from here to Samara. Get to Samara and lie low. Wait to see if the Whites get there – and if they don't, then we try and take the Trans-Siberian line east.'

'We'll be going straight into where the Reds are fighting, though. Rogovsky said so, all round Samara and beyond.'

'Have to risk that. But better up there – because they won't notice us in the chaos of the war. Better that than to stay down here where everyone is looking for us. And then another thing – once we're rid of Rogovsky, we can take over as traders, with all his wooden plates and toys and clothes and things. Sell them – we've no money – or barter them. And that'll give us a genuine reason for travelling, a perfect excuse if we're stopped.'

'Two women traders? Hardly likely.'

'I'd thought of that!' Yelena was joyous with her inventions now. 'Rogovsky's a thin, tallish man. Your size almost. You take over his clothes. Go as a man.'

'What? How could I –'

'Of course you can! But much more – you *have* to, because Drushov and his men will be on the lookout for two *women*. So one of us will have to change. And I'm too short. Besides, it would be far more believable to go as husband and wife, with a child, than as sisters, since we don't look alike. And safer, too, than travelling as two women.'

'As a man? How?'

'Crop your hair of course, now, and you put on your

astrakhan hat first thing in the morning before we leave. And we can make a moustache for you here as well. Bits of your hair, with some glue from the workroom – stick it onto a strip of silk, then stick the whole thing on later after we've got rid of Rogovsky. And bring some burnt cork with us, to darken and coarsen up your face and hands. And then there's your identity card, if we're stopped. We'll scratch out your dead husband's name, Bedayev, altogether. And do the same with the last two letters of your maiden name there, make you the masculine "Kirilov", not "Kirilovna". Then change your first name from "Marina" to "Mikhail". Half these Red Guards and Soldier Deputies are illiterate anyhow. They won't notice. So you see, it all fits!'

They stopped talking. Holly, who had been at the far end of the loft, came up to them clutching Tomcat in her arms and talking to him. 'Yes, Tomcat, we're going on a sleigh ride tomorrow, so you'll have to get into your basket again. A sleigh ride – like Father Christmas with all his presents! Aren't we, Mama?'

Her mother nodded.

Later that evening, up in the loft, Yelena, with some glue and a pair of scissors taken from the workroom, first cropped Harriet's bushy reddish hair, right round, quite high up on the neck. There were no mirrors anywhere in the colony, so Harriet couldn't see the effect.

'Ghastly?' She looked up at Yelena.

'No. Looks quite good really. At any distance you look like a man!' She trimmed some straggly bits of hair to make the moustache, then took the hardened chips of glue and melted them on the end of a broad knife over the tallow candle flame. She smeared the sticky result over a strip of skin-coloured silk and arranged the tufts of hair along it, trimming these before attaching it on Harriet's upper lip with a spot of glue to either end. 'Looks even better! Just like the charades we used to have in the Palace. Now we'll try the burnt cork – we can wash it off afterwards.'

Holly, beside them, had been watching all this with fascination. 'Mama, why do you have to look like a man now?'

'It'll be safer on the sleigh that way.'

'But you must have a big white beard and a red coat to look

like Father Christmas.' Holly was puzzled, about to be disappointed, but equally determined not to be.

'Yes, I know. But sometimes Father Christmas has to make do with less.' She looked at the bright pugnacious little face staring up at her in the candlelight. And it struck her then – yes, she would kill, without hesitation, if this were the only means of preventing harm to her daughter. Thinking this, she turned to Yelena. 'What of Rogovsky's rifle? After we've ditched him. I'm surprised he has one, openly. The Reds would kill him at once –'

'He must have a special permit for it.'

'I can use a rifle. All that target-shooting I used to do with Sandy in Petersburg.'

'Yes, if we find he has a permit, we might risk taking it with us, or hiding it beneath the sledge.'

Yelena leant forward, putting some finishing touches with the burnt cork beneath Harriet's chin. She looked at her appraisingly. The cropped hair emphasized the feminine length of her neck. 'You'll have to keep the collar of your coat up and wear your scarf all the time. Neck's too like a woman's.'

'I am a woman. It's all very well for you – with your short hair you should have been the man. Always were something of a tomboy anyway.'

'Well, I can't be. Told you, I'm too short. Though tall women quite often marry smallish men. Remember short Uncle Sergei and tall Tatyana. And how keen Sergei was on you . . .'

'Yes. Yes,' Harriet said, admitting this in a matter-of-fact tone. 'Sergei – he so wanted – well, yes, me.'

Yelena nodded. 'I knew that years ago.'

'So difficult all that was. So difficult to find the right person.'

'You don't have to tell me.

'Perhaps there never is any other "right" person – just the possibility of being that in oneself.'

'Yes.'

Yelena crumbled the end of the burnt cork in her fingers, the soot falling on Harriet's coarse linen skirt, which she had made herself in the colony. Yelena brushed it off absentmindedly. Neither of them looked at the other. They were thinking of themselves alone now; not of Sasha or Sandy or Sergei, or Miki or Johnny Quince. Without their realizing it until that moment, in all these plans and subterfuges, the bias of their lives had entirely changed.

Instead of pursuing Sasha or indeed anything, the three of them were now being pursued themselves – so that they had only their own lives to consider, and a care for one another, in which it was now tacitly agreed by both of them then that they would fight to the death, to survive together.

In the event, moving off at first light through the mist-shrouded valley, they didn't have to shoot Rogovsky. Halfway down the smaller river, in the gloom of the overhanging pine branches by the islands, Yelena, sitting with the others under a wolfskin rug among the boxes of carpets, toys and clothes, asked Rogovsky to stop, that she might relieve herself.

She went into the shadows of the pine trees, waiting until she saw his back turned. Then she took out the revolver from beneath her sheepskin coat. Emerging from the trees she returned silently across the ice, towards where he was sitting on the raised seat, levelling the gun.

She got to within a few yards of him before he turned.

'Get down,' she told him calmly. 'Throw over the rifle – to her. Then keep your hands raised. And remember, just as we killed all of those Reds on the train – I'll kill you, if you do anything suddenly – or stupidly.'

She meant every word, filled with sudden venom and energy. And it was clear that Rogovsky recognized this firm intent in her voice. He did as he was told. He got down from the seat, threw his rifle over to Harriet, who was standing on the ice now. She kept him covered with it.

'Take your clothes off,' Yelena told him sharply.

'What?' Rogovsky was appalled at this idea.

'All of them, coat, hat, boots, trousers, the lot!

'But I'll die of cold.'

'You'll die sooner if you don't.' She raised the revolver at his heart. He started to get undressed. Harriet picked up his clothes from the ice, while Yelena kept him covered now. Soon he was shivering and almost naked, except for a pair of dirty longjohns.

Harriet meanwhile had hurriedly undressed down to her under-clothes. Her naked legs and arms, exposed to the icy chill, began to shake before she put on Rogovsky's clothes: his thick serge shirt, pantaloons, elkskin coat and fur-topped leather boots. Yelena looked at her. They fitted well enough.

Yelena threw Harriet's clothes to Rogovsky, her skirts and blouse and boots. 'There,' she told him. 'If you hurry, that'll get you back to the colony, before you freeze.'

'But these are women's clothes,' he expostulated. 'I can't wear –'

'Oh yes you can. And be thankful you got off with your life.' She moved away. But then she turned back and walked up to him, raising the revolver again. 'Or shall I shoot you?' she asked thoughtfully. 'Just to make sure you keep your mouth shut – about our meeting'. She tightened her grip on the revolver, easing a finger on the trigger. Rogovsky yelped in fear.

'No! No, I'll say nothing. I promise. Nothing.'

She lowered the gun. 'No, you won't, will you?' She raised it again. 'Because if you do, we'll get to hear of it, me and my friends up in the hills. And we'll come back – be sure of that – and kill you some other time.'

A minute later Yelena, up on the front seat, flicked the horses' rumps and they set off at a smart pace down the river ice. Their sharp-shod hooves kicked up gobbets of snow as she urged the two horses on, Harriet, Holly and Tomcat in his basket, under the big wolfskin rug, Ivan and Sadko on their long tethers following on behind – with Rogovsky soon in the distance, dancing about, bootless, over the ice, forced as he was by the freezing cold to get into Harriet's clothes.

Farther downriver they stopped again. To their dismay, in going through Rogovsky's pockets they found nothing of any use or value – no money, not a kopek, only the rifle permit.

'He must have had some money and other papers and things. Hidden them somewhere in the sledge.'

'Or in a pouch under his long-johns. He's a travelling man.'

'Well, with the permit – we can probably change the name – let's keep the rifle. Strap it under the sledge.'

'Even better – take it to bits.' Harriet had been looking at the gun. 'See, the bottom, it screws off.'

Harriet unscrewed the rifle butt and they hid the pieces carefully, the barrel and stock between two of the slatted boards at the bottom of the sledge, where it fitted snugly and invisibly when they had covered it with moss from the river bank, the butt in the bottom of one of the horses' nosebags.

'We'd better hurry, with the disguise.'

They'd brought matches, candles and the hardened glue with them. Yelena heated the chips in the flame, smearing the back of the silk before sticking the moustache on. Then, with the burnt cork, she lined and darkened Harriet's face – eyebrows, cheeks, chin and hands – rubbing the soot, thinning it out over her pale freckled face. 'There, with the scarf kept well up, a suitably gruff expression and a lower tone of voice, you'll pass as a man. As long as you don't get *too* close to anyone.'

'I won't.'

'Rather distinguished-looking to be a trader, that's all.'

'Same goes for you. You're not much like a trader's wife.'

They looked at each other, worried by this, before Yelena said rather glumly, 'Nothing to be done about it. We'll just have to have rows and treat each other badly in public. We're married now after all.'

Holly, who had been watching all this, wasn't happy with the final transformation. 'You're not a bit like Father Christmas,' she said crossly. 'Or Papa.'

They had forgotten Sasha. Harriet felt a stab of guilt. 'No, I don't look like Papa. I'm dressed like this now so as we can find him more easily. So you must remember, as I told you – if anyone asks you, or if you're talking about us with other people, that I'm your *father* now, and Linochka is your mother. Understand?'

'No. It's not true. And Linochka's my aunt, not my Mama.'

'No, but we have to *pretend* it's true, do you see?'

'All right. But I have a real father still, don't I?'

'Yes. And we'll find him.' Harriet picked the child up, holding her tightly, looking over Holly's shoulder at Yelena dumbly. 'Here, Linochka will take you. I'll have to drive the horses now.'

Yelena took Holly in her arms, snuggling her tightly herself for a moment, looking in turn at Harriet. They'd had to invent a family – father, mother, child. But now she suddenly felt as if all these relationships were true – that they *were* this family.

A few hours later, the mists cleared under a hazy blue

morning sky. They were out on the lake, travelling north towards where it narrowed into the river proper. The Volga lay ahead of them, frozen hard as steel, coursing through a great white lopsided valley. To their left rose glacier-like cliffs; on the other side, a mile away, nothing but a vast expanse of flat land with a few trees half buried in the snow. On this eastern bank, which they made for, poles marked the course of cleared snow which the sledges were to follow.

Further inshore river steamers, barges and great rafts soon came into sight, tied up along the bank, locked in by extra pilings to stop them being crushed by the ice. There were a few settlements and small ports here, so that soon, as they raced along, they found themselves part of other intermittent river traffic, behind and ahead of them. Small sleighs and larger sledges and sometimes a *troika* galloping fast, and once they passed a whole convoy, a score of slow-moving sledges, hauling goods down to the Black Sea ports.

They were exhilarated, gazing with slit eyes at the sparkling panorama unfolding in front of them. The cold was penetrating. The icy air stung their faces. The sledge seemed weightless as it skimmed over the blue-glazed ice. In this liberation after the long winter locked in the colony, they were too excited to be fearful of the future. They had forgotten happiness like this, times when they had skimmed over the Petersburg streets years before, in Pushkin's wonderful winter weather. '"The glories of those frosty days"!' Yelena shouted up at Harriet. '"Our secret promenades on sleighs".'

They must win, Yelena thought. In the daring of such escapes they surely could not lose.

6

They made fast progress upriver. By alternating the pairs of horses, Ivan and Sadko taking over from the other two every so often, they were able to keep going for most of the daylight hours in the four days that followed, stopping only for half an hour now and then, to rest, feed themselves from the dozen loaves of black bread and pickled vegetables they had brought with them, and give the horses their nosebags.

The weather stayed bright, but cold so that they nearly froze at night, sleeping rough in the sledge as they had to, so as not to attract attention by calling at any of the small settlements along the river. They survived by making a tent with the wolfskin rugs and elkskin coats, sleeping beneath this, huddled close together, with Tomcat, finding warmth under the colony's homespun blankets, between the cargo of trunks and boxes, with the horses managing as best they could, covered in other rugs and carpets, tethered in whatever shelter they could find among trees on the river bank.

Yelena was right about the need to disguise themselves as man and wife. Her scheme saved their lives. They were stopped twice on their first two days travelling by Red Guard patrols, who indeed were looking for two women with a child, asking if they had seen such. Luckily, both patrols were in a hurry and, with Yelena doing most of the talking, their disguises held. They had been practising their rough Ukrainian accents, becoming adept at this, as Harriet did in developing a much lower masculine tone of voice.

But worse was to come. On their third day out, an hour after sunrise, round a curve in the bank so that they had no warning of them, they ran straight into a larger group of Red Guards at a small jetty, waving them down with their rifles.

The Guards had time on their hands, and were an illiterate

and venal lot, pretending bureaucratic knowledge, gazing at their identity cards, one of them inspecting them upside down, before handing them back. They were much more interested in the boxes and trunks on the sledge, opening each of them, disappointed in finding they only contained carpets, wooden toys and spoons, brightly coloured plates and bowls. The Red Guards had hoped for food, money or other real valuables as a bribe at least. They became frustrated, annoyed and vindictive, picking roughly through the boxes, strewing the contents over the ice and on the jetty. One of them was poking about along the bottom of the sledge, near where the rifle barrel was hidden. He came across Sasha's violin case and opened it.

'You trade in this, too?' He held up the violin to Harriet.

'Yes, at Samara.'

'I'll have it.'

Harriet was aghast. 'It's worth nothing.' Her voice rose several tones, becoming almost feminine. 'It's only a cheap fiddle. Just a few rubles –'

'Give me the rubles then –'

The Guard paused, looking at Harriet carefully. 'What's wrong with your voice? It's gone like a woman's . . .' He peered at her closely now. 'And that moustache. Something funny about you, for a man. Let me see your identity card again.' Harriet felt herself shaking inside her fur coat as she reached for her pocket.

Suddenly the Guard, spotting something over Harriet's shoulder, shouted at her: 'All right, get this stuff and the sledge out of the way. Quickly!' At this the half-dozen Guards started scurrying about in a panic, some of them taking hold of the sledge, pulling it off the cleared course in the snow. The two women, leading Ivan and Sadko to one side, turned round, looking downriver, where they saw the reason for this commotion.

A score of sledges were racing towards them, the first with a Red Army flag flying beside the driver, the other big sledges following, filled with white-uniformed soldiers.

The Guards, in a rough line at the edge of the cleared path, had come to attention, saluting, while the two women, next to their own sledge, were tucked in behind the jetty a dozen yards away.

They were close enough, however, as the column slowed on the bend, to get a glimpse of the man next to the driver in the leading sledge – a man with half his face chopped away, a hollow of livid flesh where his cheek ought to have been. It was Commissar Drushov.

The guards confirmed this after the convoy had passed, speaking among themselves, mentioning the Commissar's name, before one of them approached Harriet. 'Right, get out of here,' he told her. 'And count yourself lucky that you weren't stopped by them. Or that they didn't stop themselves, for that matter . . .' He looked after the disappearing cavalcade with relief, the horses kicking up a storm of ice and snow as they galloped away upriver.

'Who?' Yelena asked.

'Who?' The man grunted, blowing his nose through his fingers. 'That was Commander Drushov and his special Brigade, out looking for the bandits.'

'We've nothing to hide. I'm a good Bolshevik.'

The Guard laughed now. 'As if that mattered. Nothing matters with Drushov. He kills good Bolsheviks, too.'

'Where's he off to?'

'Samara, it must be. Same as you. But I'd keep well clear of him.'

'We will. Thanks.'

Later, stopping farther upriver, the women discussed the matter. They remembered the fear on the Guards' faces, and their own horror at this half-visaged man, this apocalyptic figure and his fierce troop as they had rushed past. Drushov, they reminded themselves, had been looking for them as much as anybody. Had he stopped he would surely have recognized them and that would have been the end of things.

'We can't go back.' Yelena looked downriver. 'And we can't lurk about in this cold. We'll have to risk it. Delay our arrival at Samara – and hope they've left by the time we get there. Besides, they probably won't be there at all. They must be hunting the bandits in the hills, after all, not the towns. In any case, Samara's a big place. We're not likely to bump into him.'

'Worth the risk?'

'To freeze – or not to freeze?' They looked at each other. They said nothing more.

They delayed their passage as much as they could. But by the end of the afternoon on the following day, making due east now towards a great bend north on the river, they saw the blue dome of the big cathedral on a spit of land, gleaming in the slanting light in the distance ahead of them to their right. And soon a succession of square, white stuccoed villas came in view along the river front, glittering cubes across the ice – the snow turning carmine, dusky scarlet, blood-red in the setting beams of the sun. They could delay things no longer. They were arriving at Samara.

Coming closer to the town they saw the elegant riverside villas and their gardens had been taken over by Red Army troops, in tents and makeshift huts all along the river bank. So that they had to moor the sledge and tie up the horses on the frozen mudflats half a mile away upriver. Here, living in some ramshackle wooden huts on the bank they found a group of fishermen, their small boats pulled up on the banks and lying under cover in rough A-shaped boathouses. Some of the men were out on the river at their winter work, sitting motionless on stools, like heavily wrapped statues in the slanting red light, over holes they had bored in the ice, lines sunk in the water, scatterings of small silver fish by their thick felt boots.

Yelena spoke to one of the older men while Harriet was tethering the horses. Her husband was a trader, she told him. They had goods on the sledge. No food or valuables, just rugs and wooden spoons and so on. She offered him two homespun blankets, with the promise of more to come, if they would guard the sledge and look after the horses. The man agreed. Of course they might rob them of everything by the time they returned. But there was no alternative. They left Tomcat in his basket with them, arranging as part of the bargain that he should have some fish for his supper, and set out for the town.

The first thing they saw were some camels, tethered outside a yard doorway in the suburbs – flabby humped beasts with large moist eyes and long lashes, first signs of the Orient here, which excited Holly, until they realized, from anguished groans and neighing shrieks, that the animals were being slaughtered behind the doorway. They hurried on.

There was no sign of Drushov or his white-coated Special Brigade when they got to the town. But it was equally obvious there would be no place for them to sleep or stay there either. The town, with its grid pattern of small streets bisected by half a dozen long main thoroughfares, its old dark wooden merchants' houses and newer white stuccoed buildings, its shuttered banks and shops and abandoned tramcars, was in a state of continuous flux, filled to overflowing with contrary movement: waves of soldiers, refugees, beggars and harassed citizenry washing to and fro up and down the main paved boulevards and across the narrow slushy, unpaved side streets.

The Red Army was everywhere. Despite the supposed control of the Social Revolutionaries and their Constituent Government of Siberia, it was clear that the Bolsheviks ran things here now – that they had commandeered all the hotels and many of the houses. Armoured cars and gun carriages rattled up and down over the cobbles and tramlines, interspersed with groups of infantry and cavalry. Bedraggled, hungry-looking soldiers, some bandaged or on makeshift crutches, loitered at street corners, chewing sunflower seeds or gazing into the largely empty shop windows: grocers', bakers' and butchers' shops which, when they were open at all, contained nothing but scraggy bits of camel or horsemeat and slices of crumbling turnip cake.

Fresher-faced young men, new Red Army recruits with bandoliers and assorted rifles, caps at jaunty angles, marched with vigorous if irregular step to the strains of several discordant harmonicas, towards the railway station, where engines whistled and steamed in the distance. They were obviously embarking for some Front. So that when the two women – after a long walk up the main Dvoryanskaya street and through a big square with a vast ruined statue of Tsar Alexander II – reached the station themselves, it was clear that, as civilians, they would stand no chance of getting on any train going east on the Trans-Siberian line.

They felt safe enough among the milling crowds. But it would soon be dark. The sky had turned to deep crimson, with a freezing mist creeping up from the river. It would soon be bitterly cold. They dreaded another night under the wolfskins on the sledge. They were famished. They couldn't get on any train. Yet they couldn't stay in the town without food and shelter – and how could they pay for these things in any case without a kopek? They could sell or barter the goods they had brought with them on the sledge next morning, no doubt. But meanwhile, right then, what were they to do? And in the longer term – what was happening at the Front? Where was it? With all the comings and goings in the town, were the Reds advancing or retreating? Would the White Army arrive – in a week or a month – if they stayed where they were, lying low?

They needed answers to all these questions and problems. But first they had to eat, to find some warmth and somewhere to sleep. They couldn't even line up at the stall outside the station selling foul-smelling *piroshkis*. Holly, grasped by either hand between them, was shivering. She wouldn't cry. She never did. But it was clear she was at the end of her tether. They all were.

Yelena was forcibly pushed into the woman as they were coming out of the station, all four of them caught between two opposing waves of milling soldiers.

'I'm sorry . . .'

They separated. Yelena had time to observe her before they were forced together again in another mêlée farther on. The woman was on her own, in her late twenties perhaps, dressed in worn, very ordinary clothes, with rather an ordinary face. Yet she was attractive, Yelena saw, in an unexpected way. The small restrained face, unexceptional at first glance, was original, even provocative at a second: the decided nose and chin and piquant lips betraying the other less adventurous facets – the pale-coloured skin, the blameless cheeks, the severely tended short-cropped dark hair – and the deep brown eyes which, unfathomed, took no sides in the battle, yet clearly waited their occasion, to cast a deciding vote, in favour of brio and valour.

Yelena, noticing these conflicting elements, saw them repeated in the woman's nondescript clothes, which belied a clearly determined personality, a woman of character and quality, in her face and bearing, in the way she battled her way forward through the unheeding mass of people – so that Yelena decided to risk speaking to her, in her own Petersburg accent. 'Trying to get any train here, it's impossible, isn't it?'

The woman, having glanced back at Yelena while still struggling forward, said automatically. 'Yes. Nothing to be done. Except get out of here. In one piece.' She spoke in a cultured manner as well, which was at odds with her meek appearance, in short, staccato sentences, severely, like an impatient army officer. Then she turned, looking at Yelena in alarm, as if she'd said quite the wrong thing. She hadn't. It was the accent she had spoken with, the same upper-class Petersburg tones as Yelena, that had alarmed her, that in doing so she might have given herself away.

'It's all right,' Yelena reassured her. 'I'm from Petersburg myself. We all are.' She gestured to Harriet and Holly behind her.

Outside in the forecourt of the station where there was more space the woman strode off hurriedly. But Yelena again took the risk of following her, of saying, when she came up to her, 'It's perfectly all right. Don't worry. We *are* from Petersburg. An old family. The quays. Nabereznaya Quay.'

The woman had turned again, this time unwillingly. 'Yes?' she asked coldly. 'Should I know you?'

'You might have done. Might know of us, at least.' In her desperation Yelena took a further risk. 'I'm Yelena, Princess Yelena Rumovsky. You may have known my family, the name. My father was a minister in the Duma. My brother and I played the piano and violin there, gave concerts, at the Conservatoire and the Maly Theatre, before the Revolution. Alexander, the violin. I played the piano.'

At this news the woman paid her proper attention at last, looking at her carefully and then at Harriet, who had come up behind them, with Holly. Finally she spoke again, clearly deciding to risk things herself.

'Yes. Yes I do know of you both. I went to quite a few of your concerts then. You and your brother.' She glanced at Harriet again. 'I remember particularly your both doing Franck's Sonata in A Major. At the Conservatoire.'

'We need help,' Yelena interrupted her. 'We've just come here, on the run, from the south. We've no money, food, shelter, nothing. And a young child.' She gestured to Holly. 'We're trying to get to White Territory, on the Trans-Siberian, to Omsk and General Kolchak's forces. Can you help, if you're living here?'

The woman looked at Yelena carefully again, then said

quickly, 'Yes, I think I can. I'm marooned here myself. But I have work.' Peering closely at Yelena, then at Harriet and Holly, she weighed the matter further. 'Yes. I think I can get you both some work here.'

'Work? Some food and shelter would do us.'

'You'd get that as well.'

'Where?'

'I'm working at a *kumys* house, right on top of the hill here. The Villa Annayevo. Come up there in an hour. Can't miss it. Big ornate white building. Come to the side entrance. An arched doorway. There'll be guards. But I'll have left instructions.'

'The Villa Annayevo, a *kumys* house –'

'Yes. You know. The camel and mare's milk cure here. It's the only *kumys* house left in the city. The Reds opened it again when they got here last October. To treat senior Bolsheviks, Red Army officers, and so on. So be careful what you say. Have you got identity cards, food coupons?'

'Identity papers, though they're forged. But no coupons.'

'You'll probably be all right. You'll only be questioned by the head doctor there, Dr Bibikoff. And we need help, dairy hands, servers, and he only takes women of "good family". Be there in an hour. Shouldn't be heard talking like this together.'

The woman was about to turn away. 'Who . . . who should we ask for?' Yelena said.

For the first time, if only for a second, the woman hesitated. 'Rayevsky. Nurse Anna Rayevsky.' She made to move away again, before turning back. 'There's only one thing . . .' She gazed at Harriet's dark features, the limp moustache, the thin, fine fingers clutching the collar about her neck. 'You'll have to get rid of your disguise. May have worked on your journey here. But close to – it's pretty clear you're a woman. Not a man.' Harriet was dumbfounded, fingering the moustache suddenly. The woman shook her head, the slightest smile on her lips. 'It's no good. Take it off. Clean your face. Besides, Dr Bibikoff only takes women. I know about your friend here.' She glanced at Yelena. 'You can tell me who you are later.' Then she was gone.

Harriet, unmasked, was outraged. 'Nurse Anna Rayevsky indeed! Well, if I'm not a man that's certainly not her name either.' Harriet looked distrustfully after the figure dissapearing among the crowds. 'And what's she doing, obviously a White, working with a lot of Bolshevik bigwigs? It's a trap. It must be.'

'How? She couldn't have expected to bump into us. Anyway, she said she was marooned here. She's probably on the run herself, making for White territory, and has got a job nursing here meanwhile –'

'Because she's a woman of "good family" – as she knows we are now. But what does that mean? Why should a lot of important Bolsheviks only employ people of the old regime, which is what it amounts to?'

'I don't know. We'll find out.'

'I don't think we should risk it. There's something not quite right about her, about the whole thing. It's likely to be a trap of some sort. And even if it isn't – there's a risk, in our running into these Bolsheviks, not to mention the fact that some of the patients in these *kumys* houses are tubercular, infectious.'

'I know. But this whole journey is a risk!' Yelena, in her tiredness and hunger, and close to breaking, was suddenly angry. 'What do you want to die of? Cold? Starvation? A bullet? A murderous Commissar? Tuberculosis? Take your choice, it amounts to the same thing in the end.' She glared at Harriet. 'This whole business is one long risk. And if we stop taking them – we'll lose. All the other ways of dying will catch up with us. Anyway, have you any better ideas?'

'No, I suppose not. Not for tonight anyway. But we shouldn't tell this woman, or anyone else, about the sledge and the horses upriver, in case we need them again, to get away.'

'All right,' Yelena said, in a much brighter mood now, though Harriet was still annoyed. 'So let's go back to the sledge, for Tomcat and Teddy and the violin. And for you to get rid of that moustache and be a woman again.'

'Thanks . . .' Harriet was petulant.

'She was right. Pretty hard to turn you into a man.' Yelena, head to one side, gazed at her happily. 'Besides, I didn't much care for you as a husband.'

'No. Nor I you – as my wife . . .'

Harriet smiled at last. They were both anxious to be themselves again. Yelena touched Harriet's arm. 'I'll go back for the things. You two stay here – you look exhausted – by the wall here. Don't move. We have to have Tomcat and Teddy. And the violin. I won't be long.'

Harriet was immediately uneasy. 'No,' she said. 'Let's not separate, anything could happen.' She looked at Yelena anxiously. 'Let's stay together. I'm not that tired. We can all go back.'

'Yes, we'll all go back,' Holly agreed. 'I'm not that tired either.'

They walked up the river bank. The sledge was still there, covered up, untouched. And the four horses were there, a pair of them inside each of two boathouses, at their nosebags. Tomcat had had his fish supper and was in one of the wooden huts, next the small stove, washing his whiskers amongst a group of old men. Harriet explained the position to them. They would be spending several nights in the town and would return in a few days' time. There would be more blankets for them then. The old men nodded. Two of them were already wrapped up in the blankets they had been given before. They took Tomcat with them in his blanket and basket, and the furless Teddy and Sasha's violin, and on the way back to the city Harriet got rid of the moustache, cleaned her face and let the remnants of her hair fall down from beneath her astrakhan hat.

By the time they returned the light had faded and a few oil-lamps and candles showed in the windows. There was no electricity in the town now. Soldiers clustered round flare-lit stalls with their tea-kettles looking for hot water. At another stall two swarthy Georgians were selling tobacco and tea, in minute quantities, in furled cones of newspaper.

When they got to the hilltop twenty minutes later it was dark, pale-blue dark with a bright half-moon and a shimmer of stars, the mists dissolved, crystal clear and icy cold. From the ridge looking north over the town, they saw the great bend in the Volga; to the west, on their left, the vast snow-covered land bisected by another wide coil of ice glimmering with a faint blue iridescence, twisting away into the last of the sunset, a vague pink flush on the horizon.

Immediately above them the white Villa Annayevo gleamed in the moonlight. It was a long two-storeyed building, set on its own, surrounded by decorative iron railings, with a wide view over the town and the river – its ornate stucco balconies, cornices and pediments giving it the air of a confectioner's elaborate creation, over-iced and sugared.

A gramophone played from somewhere beyond one of the brightly lit central windows, with a chandelier just visible. Electric light. A generator thumped faintly in the background.

Walking round to the side the two women approached a big arched doorway with a high wall running away beyond it. Two armed Red Guards stepped from the shadows, challenging them. They gave Anna Rayevsky's name. One of the Guards pulled a bell and a minute later the big doors opened, and they saw Anna standing there, in a white smock now and a nurse's cap. They went in. The doors slammed behind them.

They had entered a small ornamental park with trees and chalets, running down the other side of the hill in a series of stone terraces, with columns and arbours, draped in meringue folds of snow, sparkling in the moonlight. On the far side was another lower building, an annexe to the villa, which Anna led them towards, explaining as they went.

'We're coming to the staff quarters. And the offices and laboratories. The stables, with the mares and camels, are down the hill at the end of the park there. You'll meet the doctor. Doctor Anton Bibikoff. Runs the *kumys* house. You've brought your identity papers?'

'Yes. But no food coupons.'

'That won't matter. Nor will your Petersburg accents. Not with Dr Bibikoff. I've told him you are both Rumovskys, for the time being. From the Palace on the quays. He knows the place. And about the Rumovsky family. So that's all right. But you've obviously been travelling under assumed names. And for the sake of form here you should go on using them. What are they?'

'Well, I'm Irina Kirilovna. And I am . . .' Yelena hesitated. 'Or I was – married to my husband here: Mikhail Nicolaivich Kirilov.' She looked at Harriet. 'And that's a problem, because my husband's a woman now. And the identity papers show him to be a man and –'

'That won't matter,' Anna broke in, impatient with these subterfuges. 'We have facilities at the Villa for changing identity papers. And the child?' She looked down at Holly. 'Who does she belong to?'

'She's mine. She's Holly,' Harriet broke in. 'Though we've been calling her Nastasya. On the identity cards –'

'Your husband? He died on the journey here?'

'No. At least we hope not. And he wasn't actually my husband –'

'It doesn't matter. You can tell me all about it later. And Dr Bibikoff won't be interested. There is one problem, though, which he will be interested in. I know Princess Yelena here plays the piano. But you?' She looked at Harriet. 'Do you play any instrument? The piano? Or even better the violin? I see you have a violin with you.'

'Yes, I do, as it happens. I can play both. But why?'

'Good! Because I said you did. Took a risk. But come on. He's expecting us.'

The doctor's room, the first off a long corridor running down the centre of the annexe, was well ordered and lit. A small, brisk, late middle-aged man with a pince-nez and white hair cut *en brosse* sat at a heavy mahogany table. Medical charts and graphs hung behind him on the wall. The doctor sat at one end of the table, facing an ornate brass inkstand, quill pens, neatly stacked papers and files – all seemingly untouched. There for show, Yelena thought. The rest of the long table was taken up by a number of labelled test tubes, in racks, filled with milky fluids, in various stages of gassy fermentation. There was a faintly cheesy smell in the air.

Anna spoke. 'These are the Kirilovs. And their child Nastasya.'

The doctor stood up, but offered no hand, made no attempt at any formal introduction. Taking off his pince-nez, he gazed at the two women intently. 'You have your identity papers?' His voice was confident, upper class, St Petersburg. It was clear he had nothing to hide here. Harriet handed the two cards to him. He gazed at them briefly. He made no comment on the fact that he was now confronted by two women. 'Your food coupons?'

'We lost them.'

'They can be replaced,' he said at once, as if this was a matter of no importance. 'And your identity cards as well.' He resumed his seat now, leaning back in a very modern office chair – Harriet had seen them in Petersburg, they had come from America – which tilted to allow for more relaxed positions. 'Of course, you have no experience of this sort of work, in a *kumys* house, or a clinic of any sort?'

'No. We –'

'It doesn't matter. We don't need you for that.' He dangled his pince-nez by the string, letting it swing in front of his eyes like a metronome. 'I understand you are both very musical. Two pianos, or piano and violin? I see you have your violin. We would like someone here for that, to divert the patients, in the evenings.' He looked at Harriet. 'Which of you plays which?'

'I play the violin,' Harriet said, trying to hide her surprise at this turn in the interview, holding up the violin case. 'My friend the piano.'

'Good! And you can both play well – that is what Nurse Rayevsky has told me – and that is what counts. Not that we have a very discerning audience here. But they are important people. Senior figures of the revolution among our patients who have come for the "cure", some from Moscow, indeed, important Bolsheviks, political Commissars, Commanders of our Red Army suffering from anaemia, pleurisy, battle fatigue, nervous complaints of one sort or another. They deserve the best.'

'I'm sure we can provide that,' Yelena said, going along with this surprising form of work in the *kumys* house with more confidence. 'We have some considerable experience already – playing for Red Army troops on the southern Front: revolutionary music, songs, ballads, Mayakovsky's poems –'

'Oh, no!' The doctor was aghast. 'Not that sort of music at all. It would upset the patients. Memories, anxieties – it would disturb them. We require lighter music, the popular classics, operetta, *The Merry Widow* – that sort of thing.'

'I see. We could provide that equally well.'

'Good!' The doctor stood up now, briskly happy. 'You will start tomorrow evening then, after dinner, in the *kurhalle*. You will receive bed and board here, and a small wage. Nurse Rayevsky will show you to your accommodation. A room to yourselves – and your daughter – since you will count as senior staff here, with the responsibilities that go with such positions. I must emphasize the importance of your duties here. Entertainment, taking the patients' minds off things. Boredom is as much of a problem with these men as their illnesses. We aim to treat the whole man here, not just the physical symptoms. You see?'

'Yes, Doctor.'

'Our patients here deserve only the very best.' He repeated this concern with emphasis. 'These Commanders of our glorious revolution.'

There wasn't a hint of irony in his voice. Yet there was clearly something quite insincere in his attitude, Yelena thought. This fusspot, with his old-fashioned hauteur, was obviously a man dyed in the wool of the old regime. What was he doing running this privileged *kumys* house for these leaders of the revolution? The whole situation was bizarre. She looked at Anna Rayevsky. Her face, without expression, gave nothing away.

'Come with me then,' Anna said. 'You will need to meet the housekeeper for your bedding. And more suitable clothes . . .'

The housekeeper was a dumpy, middle-aged woman with a dimple on her cheek and white hair tied up in a bun beneath a white bonnet, a woman of a now quite vanished class. Yelena had known such women before the revolution, senior household servants, part of the family, who had run all domestic affairs in grand houses in Moscow and Petersburg: competent women like this one, knowing exactly her place in the scheme of things here, who took them upstairs then, handing them out bedding, blankets, towels and even a bar of tallow soap from a huge linen cupboard, before taking them to another even bigger cupboard, filled with a collection of well-cut men's and women's clothes, all of them obviously made before the revolution.

Again, as with Dr Bibikoff, she asked no questions, made no remarks – on the state of their clothes or anything else about them, simply saying that they would need suitable evening wear, to appear in front of the patients. 'Some of our earlier patients here,' she told them, 'in former times, they left these behind.' She fingered a long black silk chiffon evening dress with a plunging neckline. 'And this might suit you,' she said, handing another smaller evening dress, in dark crepe, to Yelena. 'Choose what you will. And you need not fear contagion here. The men are convalescent, not infectious. And these clothes have all been thoroughly fumigated. But come, there is some food for you. You must be hungry, after your journey.'

The housekeeper made no enquiries about how or why they had arrived in Samara in this considerably dishevelled state, remarking only that their cat would have to be kept under control. It could not be allowed into the main villa, since fur of any sort would be an irritant to some of the patients with their breathing problems.

She took them downstairs to a small staff dining-room off the kitchens where, though supper was over, places had been neatly laid for them at a long table.

The food, though it was largely remnants from the supper served earlier to the patients, was, by the standards of the time, tasty and lavish. There were thick pork cutlets, with potatoes, preserved pimentoes, sugar, tea and, most surprising of all, white bread, a thing the two women had not seen since before the revolution.

Anna, released from her duties, came into the dining-room later, with some of the other nurses, who wandered round, filling their tea glasses from a large silver-plated samovar in the corner. 'Eat as much as you want. Nothing is thrown away here,' she told them. 'Except to our pigs beyond the stables. There'd be riots in the town if they knew what we ate here.'

The two women were introduced to the other staff afterwards. In their neat white tunics and caps it was very clear by their voices and general demeanour that none were from the old peasant or new proletarian class. They might all, indeed, be described as coming from 'good family'.

Anna took them upstairs to their bedroom afterwards. It gave out over the garden, with two metal dormitory beds and a mattress between them for Holly.

'It's all quite simple. Or relatively simple,' Anna explained in answer to their questions. 'Dr Bibikoff ran the place before the revolution. The best *kumys* house in Samara. Apart from Dr Postnikov's establishment, but that was closed down. He wouldn't collaborate. But Dr Bibikoff collaborated, and was allowed to hold on to the Villa Annayevo by the Reds when they got up here last October. They took it over. And most of the old staff with it. They wanted somewhere for their Commanders and Commissars to recuperate – and were prepared to go along with the old regime here. So long as the whole thing was kept quiet. As it is. Which is why it's guarded all the time. And why they won't employ anyone from the town. They'd give the game away. The very idea! These important Reds up here living like lords. So Dr Bibikoff only takes on people like you. Or me. People who can be relied upon to keep their mouths shut. For one reason or another.'

'Because they're really Whites, on the run?'

'Many of them. Yes.'

'So Dr Bibikoff knows all about us? And you?'

'Yes.'

'You're on the run as well?'

'Yes. I'm trying to get to Omsk . . .' She hesitated.

'You needn't tell us, if you don't want to. We had to tell you who we were. Or who I was. This is Harriet, by the way. Not my husband, of course. She used to be our governess, me and Sasha, my twin brother, when we were little, in Petersburg.'

'Yes, I'm Harriet Boulting, from Ireland. Their governess in Petersburg.'

'And our friend now,' Yelena put in. 'Though Sasha has disappeared, on our way here, abducted by a madman, a White Army Colonel . . .'

'Yes, I see,' Anna said, before looking over at Holly, playing on the bed with her almost furless Teddy. 'And your husband, Holly's father?'

'No,' Harriet said at once. 'Holly's father is Alexander, Sasha – Yelena's brother. Though he's not my husband. We're not married,' she added, intent now on telling the whole truth at last.

'I see,' Anna said. But she didn't quite. She tried again, looking from one woman to the other. 'First you were their governess. Then you married – no, you didn't – Sasha was simply the father of your child. Then you became Yelena's sister, Marina and Irina Kirilovna you both were. Then you became Yelena's husband, in disguise. And now you're back to being your own self again – Harriet Boulting, from Ireland?'

'Yes. Yes, that's about it,' Harriet said.

There was silence as the three women contemplated this summing-up of the situation. Harriet and Yelena, hearing this objective précis, were aware, perhaps for the first time, of the bizarre shapes and passages of their lives. They looked puzzled. Yelena realized she could make no immediate explanation of these peculiar connections and subterfuges.

Instead she laughed.

A moment later the other two women joined in. They all laughed, Holly joining in without understanding why – all of them soon embroiled in bouts of uncontrollable laughter. None of them had laughed like this for months, years. It was a wonderful release, from every sort of pent-up fear and emotion, the horrors of their journey – when Harriet and Yelena could now share these strange connections with another woman, a stranger. Suddenly they were all three of them, with Holly, firm friends.

'What a situation!' Anna said at last, holding her aching sides.

'Yes.' Yelena wiped her eyes.

'Yes,' Harriet added, recovering herself.

All of them relaxed then and Harriet and Yelena told Anna most of what had happened to them, in their lives, and with Sasha in Petersburg and Ladoga, and in the nine months since they had left the lake – omitting only any mention of the fact that Commander Drushov and his special Brigade were pursuing them, since clearly this would jeopardize their position at the Villa.

Anna listened attentively. She was a good listener. At the end of their account she surprised them by her complete acceptance and understanding of the difficulties of their relationship with Sasha when she said, 'How unsuitably close one can get to people. Whether they be a brother and sister, a governess, or someone else's husband or wife – it makes no matter. When that closeness occurs one has to run away at once. Or stay and accept the consequences. As you both have. And as for your journey – what a truly awful time. I, by comparison, had things easier . . .' Anna considered how best she might embark on her own tale, since this, though not asked for, was now vaguely expected by the two women.

'We are from Petersburg. I and my husband, Ivan Pavlovich Rayevsky. We lived on Furshtatskaya. He is in the Imperial Navy. Just before the revolution he was posted to Odessa. The Black Sea Command, under Admiral Kolchak. To the battle cruiser *Kiev*, as second officer. I stayed on in Petersburg. I was to have joined him in Odessa. But the revolution stopped that. And Ivan went east to Vladivostock. We have been separated ever since.' She paused, looking vacant for a moment, then dutiful – concentrating, as if she wanted to remember the man, more truly, exactly, but couldn't. 'As far as I know – there were messages earlier – he got to Vladivostock with Admiral Kolchak. So he should be alive. The Whites – with the Allies now – have always held Vladivostock. I've been trying to reach him ever since. But by going east, since that's where he is. And because my family had a secondary property near Nizhny-Novgorod I first went there. But the house and estate had been destroyed. My cousins were dead or had disappeared. I managed to get a riverboat then, last autumn, right down the Volga, here to Samara. Because I knew Dr Bibikoff already. I'd come here with my father several times before the revolution. He'd been taking the cure. The doctor gave me work as a nurse. I am a nurse. I qualified in the Pokrovsky Hospital, in Petersburg, and I've been here ever since. Waiting to get to Omsk. Or for the White armies to take Samara. Like you. So there you are. And the news is good. We overhear it from some of the recently arrived Red Army officers. Since December, when they took Perm, the Whites have been attacking all along the Volga front – Admiral Kolchak's great army from the east. So, if we simply stay put here in Samara, the town is likely to be taken by the Whites, in a week, a month. Meanwhile, lie low!' She smiled at the two women. Apart from the laughter, it was the first time she had done so. She was not given to easy smiles. 'Yes,' she added, with an equally unusual emotion in her voice, 'Admiral Kolchak. Now that he is in charge of everything, we shall certainly win.'

7

The Whites did not take Samara in a week or a month. Instead Harriet and Yelena, with Holly and Tomcat, settled into the life of the Villa, a completely sealed existence, like that they had shared with the Old Believers, quite cut off from reality.

But this time, instead of the saintly austerity by the frozen river, they lived in circumstances close to luxury, amongst an enclosed order, as it were, of Bolshevik and bourgeoisie in unholy alliance.

Here the old bourgeois ministered to these Red leaders, tending their various maladies, cosseting men most of whom knew well how they were members of a discredited and traitorous class, men who, in any other circumstances, would have given immediate orders to imprison or execute them.

But here the situation was quite different. Both these normally utterly opposed factions needed each other now – the important Bolsheviks to be cured by competent hands, through services they would not get in any Red Army hospital, while the competent bourgeois hands relied upon the Bolsheviks' protection for their lives. The Villa Annayevo, with its decayed Second Empire décor, its Corinthian pillars and marble fittings, its huge gilded mirrors, was, in another way, a hall of mirrors, where everything was reversed and distorted, where the bourgeoisie held real power, dictating to these standard bearers of the new regime – so that everybody in this sealed orbit lived as though in a spellbound kingdom where everything had been frozen in a quite bizarre and contradictory way.

The Bolsheviks acquiesced in the manners and mores of a pre-revolutionary world, while the staff could pretend that the revolution had never really happened. The Reds, lulled in this time-warp, soon ceased to think of the levelled and levelling world which they had created and which lay outside the Villa, while the others were encouraged in their belief that their own old Tsarist world would soon be re-established everywhere in Russia.

There were over a score of patients at the Villa. In the daytime they wore grey cotton tunics, while undergoing the various aspects of their 'cure' – taking up to five bottles a day, at carefully prescribed intervals, of fermented, gassy mare's or camel's milk, or lying immersed in heated Volga mud baths which they took in deep tubs in the marble basement, or undergoing vague exercises in the small gymnasium. At other times they re-read or discovered Russian classics in the library, or played ping-pong or billiards in the games room, where some few – surreptitiously or until they were reprimanded – re-fought earlier Red Army campaigns with the various coloured balls. They strolled and chattered, or sat about in the *kurhalle*, a large oval room in the centre of the Villa, with pillars and a silent marble fountain in the middle, surrounded by little tables and reclining chairs, warmed by two huge tiled stoves at either end.

In the evenings the men dressed more formally, in uniforms or decent suits and, having taken supper in an adjoining room, adjourned to the *kurhalle* where a more informal mood prevailed, especially towards seven o'clock, an hour the men came increasingly to look forward to, when the two women ascended the small dais by the bay window.

Yelena, in the dark crepe dress, took her seat at a grand piano, while Harriet, wearing the black silk chiffon, went to the music stand with Sasha's violin – the two women first tuning their instruments enticingly, before embarking on spirited renditions of Lehar's *Merry Widow* and Offenbach's *Gaité Parisienne*: evenings of seemly, pre-revolutionary pleasure where, under the watchful gaze of Dr Bibikoff, himself now in evening dress, some of the patients, those men who cared, or who knew how, were allowed to dance under the bright chandelier, waltzes or polkas, either with each other or, at a suitable distance, with women of the staff, appointed to the task by the good doctor.

The White armies never reached Samara. Instead, as news from the *kurhalle* confirmed in the succeeding weeks, Kolchak's forces – his huge Siberian army – though successful earlier in the year on the Northern Front in the Urals, had run out of steam on their southern flank in their push for the lower Volga. Here there was a stalemate, with the 5th Red Army and Kolchak's Western Army temporarily poised, some hundred miles north-east of Samara, on a line between Ufa and Kazan.

However, apart from their hopes postponed here and consequent feelings of impatience and indecision, all went well for the two women and Holly at the Villa. They were well fed and cared for – as were the horses, by the fishermen upriver. Either Harriet or Yelena sneaked out to the settlement every few days, bringing the horses fodder which they stole from the mare's stables at the end of the park, while paying the fishermen out of the small wage they received or with blankets from the sledge, not so welcome now, for the weather had turned milder and there were hints of spring in the air.

Harriet's and Yelena's impatience to be out of the Villa was due not only to their ambiguous position among the Bolsheviks there, to their need to be either rescued by the Whites or to get to Omsk, but to another factor which they had recognized from the start but which, among every other plan and contingency discussed, they had not spoken of: the fact that, since the Villa was specially for the use of these Red Army Commanders and Commissars, there was, among the latter, a remote chance, as a result of some relapse or illness, that Commissar Drushov himself might at some point turn up at the Villa, to take the 'cure'.

He did.

The women had no warning. And but for the fact that Drushov had stayed in his room on his first evening, he might have been part of their audience and would have seen and certainly recognized them in the *kurhalle* that same night.

As it was, Yelena, visiting the kitchens next morning, had seen Drushov's name added to the list of patients which was kept there. At the same time she became aware of unease among the staff, a fluster in the corridors, frowning faces and a more than usually preoccupied Dr Bibikoff.

Under the excuse of renewing their bedding, Yelena went at once to see the dumpy housekeeper Maria, soon getting her into conversation in the matter, whereupon the woman confirmed her worst fears. Yes, there was indeed a new patient, she told Yelena.

'A Commander Drushov, head of some special troops looking for bandits. And now he's come here, more's the pity, because he's a brute. Suffers from neuralgia – half his face was shot away in some ambush last year – and from gout. So he's to take mud-bath cure. A man with a most unsavoury reputation apparently,' she added.

'Oh?'

'Yes, as a result of his earlier wounds, the doctor said. Revengeful. And with an evil nature anyway. We've already had problems with him. Insists on all sorts of special consideration – to eat in his room, and that he should have alcohol, which is forbidden – and, worse, drugs, which we don't have here – cocaine and the like. Apparently he has a small supply. And worse still,' the housekeeper lowered her voice, 'he's a killer. Kills for the sake of it. And not just bandits. Anyone who crosses him: Bolsheviks, women as well. So keep out of his way. Though for the time being he's staying up in his room, except for his mud bath at noon. Nurse Rayevsky has had the bad luck to be delegated for that. The doctor thinks he'll be here for some time.' The housekeeper turned back into the linen cupboard. 'The brute has already fouled his bedding,' she said over her shoulder. 'I wish we were rid of him.'

Almost at once, inspired by this last comment, Yelena knew what she must do. She must get rid of Drushov herself, at once, before he had time to discover their presence in the Villa. She would kill him by some means, and without telling Harriet in advance. Harriet would only argue the toss, attempt to dissuade her. She must kill Drushov herself, now, and have done with it, before she had any second thoughts or before he killed them. It was kill or be killed, she reminded herself.

But how to kill him?

The mud bath, of course. She would drown him in it, make it seem like an accident. She had seen the two deep tubs in their cubicles in the marble basement, where the patients, having been covered with buckets of hot mud taken from a heated cauldron, were left to lie alone, immersed in the stuff up to their necks for an hour or more.

She would dress in a nurse's smock and cap, go down to the

basement, and wait her opportunity, hidden somewhere – she remembered a curtain between the anteroom, where the patients took a shower after their treatment, and the room beyond with the tubs. She would wait until Anna had covered Drushov in mud, and left, and then drown him.

An hour later, just after midday, having provided herself with a white smock and cap from the laundry room, Yelena stole down to the basement. Even before she reached the bathroom, moving through the anteroom, she was enveloped in wispy white fumes. And when she stopped, hiding in the folds of the curtain by the entrance, and peered inside the bathroom, she saw a fog of sulphurous steam swirling round the place.

She heard the mud sloshing about, being tipped into the tub in the left-hand cubicle. A moment later Anna emerged, with an empty bucket, refilling it from the large cauldron of heated mud at the end of the room before she disappeared back into the cubicle again.

No one went to or from the cubicle to her right. It must be empty. Yelena considered matters. She saw the large wooden paddle, set on the lip of the cauldron, used for stirring the mud. When Anna left she would use it, to knock Drushov unconscious before she pushed him under.

She had no immediate opportunity. In the next instant there was a shout, a man's voice, and a piercing scream – Anna's. The sounds of a struggle, of mud slurping about, in the cubicle to her left. Yelena rushed forward, tearing the curtains open.

At first, in the steam, she couldn't see exactly what was happening: just two muddy bodies intermingling, swaying, struggling, shouting, screaming. Then she saw the man. It was Drushov all right. The fair hair, the purple scarred face like a big half-eaten beetroot. He was standing up in the full tub, naked, covered in slimy grey mud, struggling with Anna. He had his arms to either side of her, by her waist, pulling her tunic off, so that she was half naked.

In another moment, as Yelena watched, and without Drushov's even noticing her arrival, he had stripped the flimsy cotton, her slip and knickers off completely, before he lifted her up into the tub with him. They struggled viciously now, caught in a furious embrace, so that Anna was immediately daubed in the smooth grey paste. Drushov's hands were pressed on her back, her buttocks, pummelling, pulling her to him, subduing her with his powerful arms, his thighs, gobbets of mud flying about through the steam, in the fury of their battle, before he finally got the better of her.

Now he turned her round suddenly and, still gripping her by the waist, but from behind now, he pushed her down into the tub, where she crouched on all fours like a dog, her head sinking into the mud, before he set upon her from behind, to rape and drown her at the same time.

Yelena rushed out and got the big wooden paddle, then returned with it. She brought the broad blade down on the back of Drushov's head with all her strength. Striking him again and again, furiously, about the head, the neck and shoulderblades. Twisting half round, he sank down, facing her, lying on Anna's back, the whole weight of his body pressing Anna deeper beneath the squelching paste.

Yelena dug both arms into the seething morass of mud and flesh, trying to pull Drushov's body away, to the side of the tub, so that Anna, now entirely submerged, but struggling and still alive, could rise up and get clear of him.

Anna managed this, getting to her knees, blinded, choking with mud, great vomits of it coming from her mouth, before she stepped out of the bath, when Yelena had Drushov, now almost entirely beneath the mud, all to herself.

She jumped into the tub, straddling him, putting all her weight on him, pushing him down under the smooth grey swirl. Down, pressing him down with every ounce of her strength and weight. He was half conscious. But still he struggled. He wouldn't stay down.

Both her arms on his shoulders, her thighs pressing at his waist, pushing on his midriff, she hammered away at him, until his ravaged face finally sank beneath the mud. She kept it there for a minute, until there was no movement, just a few bubbles, rising up, breaking on the surface. Yelena took her arms away, relaxing. He was gone. He was dead.

Suddenly the mud erupted straight in front of her. The hideous face, two arms, the whole slimy torso rushing up at her like some nightmare sea monster from the depths. The arms gripping her round her neck, the face a horrifying mask, even the eyes mud coloured, staring at her. Then his grip tightened round her throat, the arms pulling her down, down, as they struggled furiously again. If he was to drown, his eyes seemed to say, then she would drown with him, in a last fatal, violent, sexual embrace.

They swayed to and fro for moments on end, one with the advantage, then the other. Yelena felt she was losing the battle. She prayed for the return of all her old powers. And the prayer seemed to be answered. She felt a new strength, an electric surge in her arms. She forced him back now, forcing, farther and farther, seeing him sink again, both their bodies shivering with the exertion until, with a final thrust, Drushov disappeared beneath the mud once more.

This time she kept her hands round his neck, tightening the grip about his throat, pressing down on him with her whole body, feeling the last spasms of squirming flesh beneath her, lunging down on it repeatedly, killing it.

Suddenly the body went limp, unmoving. The surface of the mud became calm, without bubbles, the grey sulphurous slime enveloping Drushov, entombing him.

Yelena got out of the tub. Her own smock had come adrift in the struggle. Panting, gasping for breath, she stood there, almost naked, her whole body covered in a glistening grey skin, like a savage – dripping, steaming from top to toe, victorious.

Anna crouched on the wooden duckboards by the tub still recovering, coughing, clearing her mouth, eyes, her nostrils. But when she stood up and saw what had happened she said simply, 'We must get out of here, quickly.'

'We? There's no need for you. You can say it was an accident.'

'No. They won't believe that. And in any case, even if they did, they'd say it was my fault, my responsibility. Or his cronies would – his Special Brigade are in town apparently. I certainly have to leave as well. And get well away from here, if I can.'

'Yes . . .' Yelena was bemused for a moment. Then, starting to think, her mind worked fast and she spoke quickly. 'All right, then we'll all get out. And you can come with us. I haven't told you. We have a sledge and horses – half a mile upriver on the frozen mudflats, a fisherman's settlement there.

We'll take the sledge north. They'll be looking for us on the river probably. But they won't expect us to go north, towards the Front. Meanwhile, we'll lock the basement door. When's the next patient due?'

'Not till this afternoon. Two o'clock.'

'That'll give us an hour's start on them, at least. So let's get this mud off next door, quickly.'

Anna ran a finger down her flank, scraping the glutinous mess away. 'Thank you,' she said, getting some of her composure back. 'He was going to kill me.'

'Yes, I saw that.'

'Thank you for saving my life. You did.'

'You did the same for us, when we came here.'

'The only thing – how on earth did you know? To turn up here? At just that moment.'

'I didn't know. I came here to kill Drushov myself, in any case. I'll explain later. Come on.'

Having showered in the anteroom, they locked the basement and went in bathrobes back to their rooms, Yelena having arranged to meet Anna at the fishermen's settlement. 'As soon as possible,' she'd told her. 'We have to hurry.'

When she met Harriet and Holly in their own bedroom, she was in even more of a hurry. 'Can't go into it all now,' she whispered to Harriet. 'Except that Drushov was here. He's dead. I killed him. Anna was there, too, so she's coming with us. In the sledge. But we have to go now. Just with Tomcat, Teddy, the violin and as many warm clothes as we can wear. *Now*!'

'But –' Harriet was aghast.

'*Later*, I'll tell you. We have to go at once, separately, no calling attention to ourselves until we get well away from the Villa – then run!' Harriet asked no more questions. They gathered their things together.

Less than an hour later they were with the fishermen on the frozen mudflats. It was still cold, with a chill coming off the river. But the sky had changed. The grey skies or the hard blue domes of winter had gone. There were fluffy white clouds racing along from the south. They got the horses out, harnessing them in line abreast this time, for added speed, Ivan and Sadko in the centre, the other two as outriders, loosely attached, *troika* style.

'The rifle,' Yelena whispered to Harriet. 'We must get the barrel out, and the bullets from the floorboards, and the butt from the haybox, and put it all together when we get away from the fishermen. I've got the revolver. But I'll give it to Anna, because I'll have to drive and you're good at rifle shooting – the two of you at the back –'

'Why? What do you expect?'

'That we'll be followed on the river very possibly, by Drushov's men, his Special Brigade. Anna says they're in town, and when they find Drushov dead –'

'But we can't fight them all off!'

'We may have to, have to try. Come on, let's see if we can lighten the sledge – as much speed as possible.'

They unloaded some of the heavier boxes with carpets in them, giving them to the fishermen as a final payment. They kept all the blanket boxes, against the cold, and the ones filled with wooden bowls and spoons which they could barter in the future.

One of the old fishermen, seeing they were off on the river, came up to them. 'You are not travelling far on the ice?'

'No, southwards, a few miles. Back to Saratov eventually,' Yelena lied.

'You will know yourself, and your friends . . .' The old man looked up at the puffy white clouds, then raised a finger, licking it. 'The wind has changed, these last days. From the south now. The thaw is here. And the ice will crack, without warning, as it always does at first. You will need to take care. The signs are in the wind, and in the groaning of the ice, waking from its long sleep. Spring is almost here, God be praised. I wish you well . . .'

Five minutes later, having bought some small fish, adding to the food which they had managed to bring with them from the Villa, they were out on the river, heading south while still in sight of the fishermen, but then, beyond the lip of land, swinging round and going north: sixteen sharp-shod hooves in line, thundering on the ice, the horses' galloping fast, happy in their release, north towards the great bend in the river.

They kept to the cleared track on the ice at first, racing

between the wooden marking poles, close to the left bank. But soon, approaching a number of wooded islands, the track divided, the wider one crossing diagonally towards the right bank a mile away.

They took the less frequented track, a narrow passage between the islands and the near bank. But the going was rougher here, with lumpy ice under the sledge so that they bumped about and were forced to slow. The heavy going loosened one of the horses' shoes, so that they had to stop, to take it off completely.

But this gave them the opportunity to organize themselves on the sledge: to put the rifle together and check the ammunition. There were five shells already in the rifle magazine and twenty more in a small cardboard box. Harriet took up a position with the rifle at the rear of the sledge, where she had some cover beneath the tailboard. Anna, with the revolver, crouched beside her. Holly with Tomcat hid between the boxes in the middle, with Yelena driving the four horses from the raised bench in front, but ready, at the first sign of pursuit, to climb down and use the reins from a crouching position, covered by the boxes behind her.

Before they set off again, in the silence of what was now an almost balmy early spring afternoon, they heard a series of long-drawn-out groans and cracks from somewhere beyond the islands ahead of them, followed by pistol-shot cracks echoing towards them in the mild air. But in the shadowy lee of the wooded island, the ice beneath them was hard as steel.

Five minutes later, reaching the top of the island, they came out onto a wide expanse of lake ice, pearly-sheened in the cloudy sunshine, with the far bank almost invisible now. But a mile ahead was a clear view of the narrowing river, with steep banks to either side, the entrance to the gorge and the great bend in the Volga.

At this point their smaller cleared track on the ice joined again with the wider track coming from the far bank which they had left half an hour before. And there, less than a mile behind them, making great pace towards them in a flurry of snow, they saw the dark horses pulling the leading sledge and behind this three or four other sledges with white-coated figures: Drushov's men, his Special Brigade, pursuing them.

Yelena flicked the horses' rumps with the long snaking whip, and the animals surged forward, so that it seemed at first that they would easily outrun the slower and more heavily laden cavalcade behind them.

They might have done had not another shoe come loose, on the second of the outriding horses, so that he broke pace with the other three, slowing them. Yelena could only cut him loose. She struggled to release the makeshift traces, leaning out dangerously over the edge of the sledge as they raced along, icy splinters cutting her face, her eyes closed so that she fumbled things. By the time she'd done this, with the horse free, dropping behind them, they had slowed right down and the Brigade had gained several hundred yards on them.

The women heard the echo of thundering hooves over the ice behind them. They saw the leading driver, leaning forward, whipping his horses on. Then they heard the first rifle crack as the soldier next him opened fire, the shot ringing over the ice, passing over their heads. Then a second bullet hit the tailboard right beside Harriet, where she was crouching with the rifle, leaving a huge splinter six inches from her arm.

Harriet returned the fire. The first kick of the rifle surprised her, the barrel leaping upwards. The second shot kicked high as well. She gripped the rifle more securely, finding the balance of it with the third shot which, to her dismay, hit one of the two leading horses. It stumbled and fell. The sledge crashed into it, tipping over, the soldiers tumbling out onto the ice, with the other sledges behind swerving off the cleared track, narrowly missing the tangle of men and animals – so that their pursuers had to slow, spreading out now, in line abreast, delayed by having to travel on the snow, a manoeuvre which lost them a hundred yards or more.

But in this regrouping, one of the following sledges, allowed free passage on the cleared track, proved faster than the others had been. It gained on them steadily, the driver hidden from them, crouching below the raised seat, a white-coated soldier next to him using the seat as a rifle rest, firing repeatedly at them between the horses' flowing manes. Harriet fired twice more, emptying the magazine without luck, before she had to stop to reload. Anna took up the barrage with the revolver, but to no better effect.

It was a race between them and this leading sledge as they approached the narrowing banks of the river ahead – a race they would lose, Yelena saw, for their three horses, lacking condition unlike those of their pursuers, were tiring now, slowing, faltering. They had given their best.

Rising up in the seat for an instant, Yelena saw, a quarter of a mile ahead of her, the dark lines on the ice: jagged patterns crossing the lake at right angles to them. Another quick view confirmed her suspicions, her worst fears. The dark line – the one long, gradually widening dark line which lay straight in front of her, was black river water. The ice ahead of them was breaking up, great floes being cracked apart by the torrent issuing from the narrowing banks at the great bend in the river. They were no longer, any of them on the sledges, part of the main. They were galloping, all of them, on one vast ice floe, an island, separated from the rest by an ever-widening gulf of water.

Yelena saw they only had one chance. She must drive the horses towards the widening space in front of them as fast as she could and hope they could jump the gap, taking the sledge over with them – the others behind, when they reached it, would find the break too wide, and they would have either to pull up or flounder in the water.

She stood up again in the racing sledge. A bullet whined over her head. The gap ahead of them was already too wide, she saw. But to her right, a hundred yards away, it was narrower. She would try there. She reined the horses round, swerving off the cleared path, racing across the snow now, getting a last furious effort out of the horses, flicking them with the whip. They managed a full gallop again, their hooves and the rifle shots all round them muffled in the cover of snow, so that it was strangely silent now.

Yelena could see the dark swirling water fifty yards ahead. The gap between the two ice floes was widening every moment. Two yards, three, four? She didn't know. And didn't care. There was no stopping now. She gave a last flick of the whip to Ivan, the Arab-Palomino straining forward valiantly, taking the other two horses with him.

There was almost complete silence then. Yelena heard

nothing. No rifle fire, no sound of hoofbeats, no singing of the sledge runners. Silence.

The horses took the jump together, all three animals soaring upwards, the sledge rising after them, everything free of the ice for a long second, the heavy sledge twisting in the air as they all hung on to the sides for their lives, before one of the runners hit the other side with a great tilting crunch – then righted itself, the hoofbeats continuing, the runners singing, Yelena's hearing coming back.

She looked behind her. The leading sledge was approaching the water at full gallop. The pair of horses jumped – and just made it. But the sledge never crossed the gap. The bottom of it hit the side of the ice wall amidships, snapping the horses' traces, so that a moment afterwards the sledge and the men were all sinking in the icy water. The other three sledges, seeing no chance now of jumping over, managed to pull up just in time, the soldiers scrambling out, firing wildly.

But already Yelena and the others were well ahead of them, the rifle shots dying in the air. Soon they were out of sight of their pursuers, hidden by the high banks on the great circling bend in the river, in shadow now, galloping upriver, on ice that was hard, unbroken.

BOOK FOUR

1919–1920

1

Robert Hodgson, British Consul at Omsk, sipped his boiled water and thought to keep his distance from the scruffily dressed woman sitting opposite him. The water supply was polluted. Dysentry was rife. Worse still, typhus was everywhere, among the tens of thousands of retreating, panic-stricken refugees and White Army troops. A death which would take you in a week, he knew, with the 'mulberry blush' and an agonizing delirium, the result of someone else's body lice, malignant ticks which, he'd heard, could jump across sheer space before attaching their death warrant to you.

It was his duty, as a Britisher, to survive. Much would depend on him in the coming weeks. He was a strong and decisive man and he intended to remain so, among these demented Russians – the ill, the spineless, the unhinged, whose numbers increased daily in a city where almost everyone not losing their life was losing their head.

Meanwhile he cursed the unusual late summer heat. It was mid-September. There should already have been a coolness in the air, clear hints of the harsh Siberian winter. He sweated in his office above the Commercial Bank of Siberia in the tall new building on Nikolaiskaya square. The ceiling fan no longer worked. The windows were closed against the foul smells carried all over the city in sharp dust squalls from the steppe.

The woman continued her story, a lengthy and surely exaggerated, if not largely imagined tale, he thought. He must be careful of her. She might well be a Red agent. His gaze wandered across the square, to the dun-coloured domes of St Nicholas' church, the pillared façade of the Cadet School next to it, other pompous stone-built modern buildings, banks, offices, hotels. But just beyond these lay endless fetid alleyways of crumbling wooden houses, shacks, the tower of the mosque rearing in the distance of the old city, and beyond that nothing but empty flat lands, the tawny endless steppe.

This capital of White Government in Siberia was really no more than a squalid provincial outpost, still a caravanserai belonging to Mohammedans and Khirghiz tribesmen with their camels and tents, masquerading as an important capital city now, with a few trams and motor cars. He hated the place. It was worse than Khartoum, where he'd once had a posting.

'We stayed the winter, across the lake on the Volga from Balakovo, at a colony of Old Believers . . .' The woman's voice, well modulated, penetrating, had a slight Irish intonation. He mistrusted her for that as well as for her strange story.

It was late afternoon. He longed to be rid of this awkward customer, longed to be back in his cool room across the square in the Rossiya Hotel. He could see the hotel, on the corner of one of the broad, dusty boulevards that ran towards the Irtush river, see the other avenues that led to the railway station two miles away, and to the huge *Stavka* building a mile distant to his right, where General Kolchak had his Siberian Army Headquarters.

Engines whistled and shunted endlessly in the distance. Immediately beneath him a loud, continuous uproar rose from the square, shouts, arguments, pleas, imprecations from just a fraction of the thousands of refugees who had come to overflow the city in the last few months: a horde of filthy, distressed humanity desperately seeking money, food, shelter, above all an exit by train from the city, camped everywhere meanwhile on the outskirts under sackcloth or cardboard tents, with many more just living in holes burrowed in the earth, like animals.

Yet behind all this desperate commotion he could just hear the faint lilt of a waltz from the Romanian orchestra which played every day in the late afternoon and evening on the covered terrace of the Officers' Club at the Casino nearby. Here, at that very moment, the corrupt White Army officers with their wives or mistresses would be sipping tea and drinking iced beer sent up from Harbin nearly three thousand miles away: gorging on luxuries which had taken the place of essential allied military supplies from Vladivostok – wagon-loads of comestibles, tobacco, fine wines attached to army trains by means of bribes all down the line, and sold in Omsk, when the officers had taken their fill, for twenty times their worth.

How he hated the place – and the people. And worst of all what emanated from the latter: the foul air, which he hardly dared breathe, reeking of sickly excretions, the acrid smoke of camel-dung fires, a smell of general human decomposition, of fear and death.

The situation in Omsk was already quite out of hand, though no one in power would admit it. Things were coming to an end in Omsk, he knew. Soon the troops of the Allied Intervention – the British, French, Americans, along with Kolchak's demoralized armies and the unhelpful Czech Legions who still controlled most of the Trans-Siberian railway – soon the whole ramshackle caboodle of antagonistic military alliances in Siberia would disintegrate. There would be nothing to hold the suppurating body of the city together then. The Red Army had moved well beyond Chelyabinsk, less than four hundred miles away to the west, and were coming on down the line at the rate of twenty miles a day. Very soon the bloated Russian Military Command in Omsk – there were over four thousand staff officers attached to the *Stavka* alone – would be packing up. Then they would turn and run. For the infantry and civilian refugees, with little or no chance of getting on any train, it would be murderous rout. *Sauve qui peut* and let the devil take the hindmost.

The few remaining British troops, the staff officers of the British Military and Railway Missions, would no doubt get out in good order. Nearly all the British civilians in the city had already left for Vladivostok. But not quite all. His gaze returned to the woman as she continued her story. This Miss Harriet Emily Boulting, a tall, bizarre, red-headed figure spinning a fantastic yarn . . . He must be careful here. Yes, indeed. The Reds had infiltrated spies and propagandists of all sorts into the city.

'You say,' he interrupted her then, 'that you travelled by sledge, in mid-March, along the river ice, from Samara up to Simbirsk and on to Kazan, arriving there in mid-April?'

'Yes.'

'But the ice on the Volga would have broken up by then.'

'It hadn't. It had only started, down stream. Else we would have been drowned, wouldn't we?' Harriet smiled a fraction, toying for a moment with this over-confident man, somewhat florid of feature, brilliantined hair parted in the middle. He had rather the air of a stage-door-johnny, she thought, sitting beneath a long outdated portrait-photograph of Edward VII and, more incongruously, a large map of the London Metropolitan and District Railways.

'Yes,' he said, not the least taken aback. 'But by then you would have arrived in the middle of the battle zone, on the Volga front. The Red Fifth Army and Kolchak's Western Army were fighting then on a line between Kazan and Samara. Yet you survived, three women and your child, in the middle of all that fighting. And further, you all passed through the lines, eastwards, to Omsk. May one ask how?'

'I was coming to that.' She glared at him. 'We became camp followers at first, attaching ourselves to the rear of General Frunze's Red army, on its central front. We were stationed at Koschtschakovo, just east of Kazan, which was a Red Brigade headquarters – the leading 27th Assault Brigade – under a Commander Matakov. We did washing, cooking, general duties. And Anna Rayevsky, a qualified nurse, worked with Dr Chicherin at the field hospital.'

'"General duties"?' He looked at her with the faintest hint of salaciousness, which infuriated Harriet, so that she responded with information she had not intended to divulge.

'No, not prostitutes. We did guard duties, went on patrols.'

'Do I take it that you were armed?' Mr Hodgson spoke innocuously, sipping his glass of water.

'Yes.'

'Ah!' He leant forward, suddenly accusatory. 'So you actually fought for the Reds?'

'Yes.'

'That could well be construed as treason, Miss Boulting –'

'What nonsense! The Red Army is filled with officers and men who fought with the Whites. Besides, we had no alternative if we were to survive. We were asked, when the front just beyond the town was being pressed by Cossack cavalry. There were a score of other women. They volunteered.

We went along with them, were involved in several engagements against the Whites.'

Hodgson was appalled. 'I can hardly believe it, that you, a British woman, should have –'

'Do you mean I shouldn't have done this? Or that you don't believe I did it?'

'Both,' Hodgson said, before he saw the trap he had fallen into. 'I mean –'

'You mean, Mr Hodgson, that, if you don't believe me, then I couldn't have fought for the Reds at all, could I?' Hodgson said nothing. 'In fact, it's perfectly true. See, I can prove it, below my shoulder, the bullet mark.' She pulled up the sleeve of her blouse, displaying a heat scar running across her upper arm.

'You might have come by that in other ways. You must allow my suspicions. We've had many instances of Red infiltrators in Omsk.'

'No, Mr Hodgson, I am no Mata Hari.'

'How did you get across the lines then, ahead of the Red Army?

'The Reds, as you know, by late May had taken the offensive, successfully counter-attacking in the Urals, then all along the Volga Front. We were first in the advance, as part of Commander Matakov's 27th brigade, on the central front, making for Ufa. It was like a knife through butter against the White troops – except with General Kappel's, who showed a fight. But the other White troops either deserted and ran or came over to the Reds. The whole White front around Ufa when we got there had collapsed. It was wide open. Chaos. There was no one to stop the advance. But General Frunze, who by then was in the vanguard with the 4th Red Army, decided to consolidate his position at Ufa. We were quartered there for nearly a fortnight. Then an opportunity arose for us to get out, east, on our own. The field hospital had been set up in a forward position, with tents, beyond Ufa, out in the steppe. The three of us by then were attached to the hospital. All round us, out in the sandhills, there were Khirghiz tribes with their camels and goats, nomadic people –'

'I know of them. We have many of them here.'

'Which is exactly how we got out. Anna Rayevsky had

travelled in these parts before the revolution, with her father. Spoke some of the Khirghiz language. She became friendly with a group of them. With the onset of summer they were moving their herds east, towards the Irtush river, here, to Omsk. Anna persuaded the headman to take us with them.'

'The Khirghiz tribesmen are not given to easy association with strangers. Quite aside from the fact that, had the Reds caught you with them, crossing into White territory, they would have massacred the lot of you. So I'm bound to ask how you persuaded them.'

'They hardly needed persuading. They needed us, in the event. Typhus had broken out in Ufa. Some of the Red Army troops caught it. Dr Chicherin had drugs for it. Anna administered them, inoculating the men. Then some of the Khirghiz, visiting the town, caught typhus. The Reds wouldn't spare any drugs for them. The tribesmen died. But Anna explained to the headman she'd met that none of his tribe would die if she inoculated them, in advance. They took us on that understanding. We left with a supply of the drug, syringes and so on. She inoculated them. None of them caught the disease. That's how we got here. It took us over two months.'

'I see.' Hodgson mopped his brow. 'But again, you can show no proof of this. All I have to go on are these Soviet identity cards of yours, and the other women.' He picked up the soiled cards from his desk, then let them drop hurriedly, as if they might be infected. 'And your card, Miss Boulting, shows you to be a Soviet citizen, of quite a different name. A Russian . . . We are fighting the Soviets. Have you no British passport, or at least a Tsarist *laissez-passer*, either of which you would have required for entry into Russia before the revolution?'

'I lost my British passport over two years ago, in the chaos after we had to leave the Rumovsky Palace in Petrograd.'

'I see. Though again, even this Soviet identity card – it cannot be yours. It shows you to be a man, one "Mikhail Kirilov". You can hardly expect me –'

'I told you, that was an identity I assumed after we left the colony of the Old Believers. I disguised myself as a man, with the Princess Yelena as my wife, because Commissar Drushov was looking for two *women* after the train was ambushed.'

'Ah, yes – the Bluebeard Commissar Drushov, that your

friend the Princess – your "wife"? – disposed of in a mud bath in Samara.' Mr Hodgson sighed. 'Before, that is, you all set off on that extraordinary journey up the ice on the Volga in the sledge, pursued by Red shock troops, when you jumped the gap in the ice floe . . .' He looked at her, almost smiling himself now.

Harriet leant back in her chair. 'Mr Hodgson,' she said easily, 'I care not one whit whether you believe me or not. The simple facts are that I'm British – or rather Irish, and more than ever glad of that in the light of your attitude – and that I am in need of your assistance, I and my child and my friends.' She leant forward then. 'And what I should further emphasize, as I've mentioned already, is that General Knox, Commander of the British Military Mission here, is a close friend of mine and of the Princess. Where we lived – the Rumovsky Palace – it was next the British Embassy on the quay in Petersburg. General Knox would immediately recognize us, vouch for us, and would certainly do everything he could to help us.' She looked at Hodgson carefully. 'I'm sure the General would find your present attitude . . . unhelpful, to say the least.'

Mr Hodgson was not to be put out. 'He might. But unfortunately General Knox is away at the Front for the moment. And therefore cannot help you – or me – in this essential matter of identification.'

'Yes, I know that. I have been down to his personal railway carriage near the *Stavka* building. He is away for several weeks, at what remains of the White front.'

'Indeed . . .' Hodgson was put out this time. 'You have been making military enquiries.'

'I'm not a spy. They trusted me down there. But as a civilian I have to come to you for identity papers, a *laissez-passer*, to get a train out of here'.

'Your friends, of course, as Russian citizens, would have to apply to General Kolchak's HQ here, at the *Stavka* building.'

'They've already been there. But found the whole place in hopeless confusion, with this retreat. Impossible to see anyone senior enough to help them. So that naturally I would hope, given these circumstances, for some assistance from you.'

'One might hope for that, yes. Unfortunately, as you may have gathered, it's no easy matter for civilians to get a train east at the moment. Tens of thousands of refugees attempting the same thing, when the few trains are needed for the troops, the wounded very largely –'

'More to get the White Army brass hats and their wives and mistresses out before the Reds arrive.'

'I think that too severe, Miss Boulting. There is no general retreat here. They are simply moving the wounded back from the Front –'

'That was not the impression the Princess Yelena got at the *Stavka*. They were burning files, panicking like rats on a sinking ship.'

'I couldn't comment on that –'

'You could, on the other hand, advance me some funds, pending General Knox's return, when he will at once identify me and reimburse you. Or I will myself when I get home.'

'I repeat that I cannot advance funds without proper identification. And you should know how in any case Omsk rubles are practically valueless now. However . . .' Hodgson considered things. 'In the light of what you say of your friendship with General Knox I will allow you some British Military Mission chits – coupons which you may use as payment for food and services at the Commercial Hotel, but only there.'

'And a room?'

'Yes, a room. If you can get one.'

'Perhaps you might use your influence? I understand that hotel is occupied almost exclusively by officers of the two British Missions.'

He looked at her circumspectly. 'Yes. Yes, I will see what I can do.'

'Perhaps you might telephone them now, so that I can go round at once?'

'Yes.'

'Thank you, Mr Hodgson. I'm sure the General will be very grateful to you. It will be such a relief to have a room. We have not bathed or washed properly – for months . . .'

Mr Hodgson had stood up, taking a booklet of coupons from a drawer. But now, on hearing this news, he left them for her to pick up on the desk.

'Oh, you need not fear typhus infection, Mr Hodgson. We –

all of us – have been inoculated. Can it be that you yourself – have not been?' Mr Hodgson, taken aback, said nothing. 'I should strongly advise it. A most painful death . . .' She turned and strode out of the room.

Having pushed her way across the teeming square, she went into the equally crowded lobby of the Commercial Hotel. British officers, languid in the heat, were sipping tea under the faded potted palms. She spoke to the desk clerk, showing him the coupons, asking for a room. He shook his head, smiling inanely. 'You should have had a phone call from the British Consul. May I see the manager?'

Both clerk and manager made a tremendous fuss: the hotel was full. But Hodgson had indeed made the call and a poky room on the top floor was eventually found for her, looking out the back, across a dusty, unkempt beer garden, with a view of the crumbling walls of the old city fortress and the mosque in the distance: a long, narrow carpetless room, two iron bedsteads, thin mattresses, peeling wallpaper, washstand and bowl, nothing else. It was hot and hideous. But there was a shower bathroom on the floor below, with water available for half an hour each day. She longed for a shower, the flow of water over her grimy body . . .

But first there was Holly, Yelena, Anna and Tomcat to see. They were camped at the back of the White Officers' Club – they had taken over the casino – in the park half a mile away. She locked the bedroom door and walked over there.

It was nearly seven o'clock. The sun still burnt from a cloudless, ashen-blue sky. But it was cooler, the streets more crowded than before, the time of the evening promenade, with the cry of the muezzin from the mosque tower as she passed near the old fortress gates. She walked through the arid park to the Casino Club and went to the kitchen yard at the back of the long, white stucco building. Yelena and the others were resting in the small storeroom beyond the kitchens. It was filled with empty crates and bottles and smelt of sour beer. But it was the best that Eugene Popesco could arrange for them when he had taken on the two of them as reserve players in his Romanian orchestra.

It was the interval between the late afternoon and evening performances. The two women, with Holly between them trying to tempt Tomcat to some scraps, were sitting in the shadows on cushions which they had taken from the terrace chairs in front. Harriet flourished the coupons at them.

'Success! Hodgson finally gave in. Coupons – for the Commercial Hotel. Food – and a room! And a bathroom on the floor below. Water – a tiny trickle from the shower!'

Suddenly she stopped her rejoicings. Anna, sitting against the wall, was staring vacantly ahead of her, unsmiling, making no response to this good news. Yelena, putting a finger to her lips, got up quickly and went outside, walking with Harriet to the end of the kitchen yard.

'It's awful for her,' Yelena said. 'She found out today – at last at the *Stavka* – her husband, she's just missed him. He'd come up here with General Kolchak last October, as part of his staff. He was put in charge of naval operations on the Upper Volga. When the Whites made their big push towards Kazan in the early summer, his gunboat was more or less blown out of the water from high ground, by several Red batteries just above Kazan. He knocked one of them out, fought like fury. But was badly wounded – in the shoulder and chest. He survived. Rescued half his crew apparently, and they got back, first to the White Army command at Chelyabinsk and eventually here, where they sent him out on a hospital train to Harbin just two weeks ago.'

'How terrible.'

'And all the worse –' Yelena turned to Harriet urgently, 'because I had such good news today at the *Stavka* – we both went there together. I finally got hold of someone who talked sense – a staff Major called Petkov, in the Army Transport section.' She put her hand on Harriet's wrist, gripping it. 'He wouldn't tell me much at first, until he was sure I was Sasha's sister – and I could prove that with Sasha's violin I'd taken with me, with his name on it, and told him things about the family and the Palace in Petrograd, which he knew about. And then he told me – yes! He'd seen Colonel Skolimsky! Skolimsky and a straggle of his troops arrived here a month ago. But he went straight on down the line to Harbin, in a sealed carriage.' Yelena beamed. She was breathing quickly, the sweat forming beads on her brow.

'But Sasha? What about Sasha?' Harriet was equally on edge.

'Yes! Sasha was with him. Major Petkov knew that, but it was all very hush-hush and he swore me to secrecy. He knew that Skolimsky had a young man with him, a Romanov prince, he'd been told, a cousin of the Tsar. And that they were taking him down the line, out of harm's way into Manchuria. So that when the Whites won the war this Romanov could be crowned as the new Tsar. So Sasha's alive! He's gone east, in a special train, to Harbin, and all we need do is follow him there.'

'But didn't you tell this Major Petkov that Sasha had been abducted by Skolimsky?'

'Oh yes, I told him all that – the whole story. But there was nothing he could do about it.'

'And didn't Sasha kick up a fuss when he got here? Didn't Admiral Kolchak know about it? Didn't he see Sasha?'

'Exactly what I said to Petkov. But Kolchak didn't know anything about it, not until afterwards, because he'd been away at the Front. Sasha was gone by the time he got back. And Kolchak's away again now, and the whole *Stavka* in chaos what with this retreat. So Petkov says there's nothing to be done. That we'll simply have to follow him down the line, get to Harbin – if we can – and take the matter up with General Horvath, the Governor there.'

'But will Petkov help you – us – get on a train, as civilians?'

'He'll try. But first we have to get White Army transit papers. And that's another department at the *Stavka*. It'll take time, a week or more, with the chaos there.'

'Same thing with Hodgson. He won't give me any transit papers until Knox gets back.' Harriet told her of her meeting with the Consul. 'Still, it's a start,' she said at the end, as they walked back to the storeroom. 'Sasha's alive. And so is Ivan. And we have a hotel room. How is Anna taking it?'

'Stoically. She was due back at the hospital tonight. And she's going. Holly's being a help, playing, talking to Tomcat with her. But it'll all be much better in the hotel room. Is it nice?'

'No. It's ghastly. But it's ten times better than this.'

'Good . . . But come on, it's nearly half past. We're on in ten minutes. Lehar and Strauss. Oh, Harriet!' Yelena turned suddenly to her again. 'I'm so happy about Sasha. But sad for Anna.'

'Yes.'

'She's come to mean as much to us as anyone.'

The three women, after months crammed together in Red Army bivouacs and Khirghiz tents, had refined the art of living at close quarters. In their narrow room at the hotel, with its two small beds, they still had to maintain this. And yet it was different. There was safe space beyond the small room, sitting out in the shade, on the guttering between the two sloping roofs, walking the long corridors, sitting in the lobby or the dining-room, best of all in the bathroom, the sheer luxury of flowing water, if only for a minute or two each day. In these places they could be alone. As well, for the first time in nearly two years, since leaving Petrograd after the revolution, they were safe, without immediate fear of the Reds, without the need now for any kind of subterfuge.

For Harriet and Yelena all their earlier disguises and confusions were no longer necessary. Though greatly changed, in themselves and with each other, they were two women again, with all that entailed by way of hopes and needs. And the same was true of Anna. She no longer had to maintain the various fictions of her life.

Once installed in the hotel room, she had the time and the need now to unburden herself, to tell them the truth of things with her, late the following Sunday evening as they sat on in the dining-room, after the second dinner service, with Holly in bed upstairs.

Her name, as Harriet had suspected when they'd first met in Samara, was not Rayevsky, nor was Ivan Pavlovich Rayevsky her husband. Ivan was her lover, she told them then, and she had taken his name, as wife, in forged Soviet identity papers arranged for her in Samara by Dr Bibikoff.

She had been married though, to a man called Anton Vasilievich Suvorov. It had been an early marriage, when she was twenty-two – seemingly a most suitable union between two old St Petersburg naval families, the Suvorovs and the Denisovs, her own family.

Anton had long courted her. An older man, worthy and reliable. He shared some of her interest in music, encouraged her in her nursing studies (which were thought very daring) and had taken her on short trips out to sea whenever he could. He was kind, painstaking, loving. There was much good in the relationship. Yet it did not work. There was no spark to it. The marriage began to go astray within a year or two.

Then she had met Ivan Rayevsky, a chubby, bearded, curly-haired colleague of her husband at the Admiralty, where they both worked on the Home Fleet Staff.

Ivan was quite different. He was unreliable. He was thought to resemble Gogol somewhat – in looks and in his witty attitudes to bumbling Admiralty officialdom. He was scoffing, untidy and preoccupied – always thinking of something else whenever they had met – of battle plans, squadron orders, dreadnought cruisers. He was quick and unconventional. Admiral Lord Nelson was his hero and he seemed not to have the slightest interest in women; nor she in that sort of man. Yet they had taken to each other, a *coup de foudre*, one afternoon walking the Admiralty Quays, while he had been describing to her Nelson's wonderfully original strategies at the Battle of the Nile.

They had fallen in love, resisted, succumbed. Her husband had found out. There had been arguments, tantrums, fights, desertions, returns – the whole gamut of usual, shaming things. Halfway through the war her husband had finally left her. Divorce proceedings were put in train. After several months of intense happiness with Ivan in Petrograd, he had been posted to the Black Sea Fleet under Admiral Kolchak's command, finally going with him, after the revolution, to the Pacific Fleet at Vladivostok, when she herself had then set out to cross Russia to find him, only to discover now that she had missed him by a few weeks, that he'd been taken down the line to the hospital in Harbin badly wounded.

'So you see,' she told them, as she sipped her tea, 'my situation – it's been somewhat like yours. Barking up the wrong tree first with Anton. Then very possibly barking up another now – with Ivan.'

'But why?' Yelena was surprised. 'When you say things were so good between you and Ivan?'

'Never lived properly together, though. All the drama of the mistress thing. That inspired but unreal level. I'd hoped it would be real one day, when we married, which was our intention –'

'Was? But isn't it still? When you meet, in Harbin. He's only wounded –'

'I'm not so sure now. We were wonderful as lovers. But in living a life with him – well, that would mean so little time with him. Unlike my husband, Ivan was always a seagoing naval man. And if he recovers, he'll mostly be at sea again and I'd be a wife to him every three months at best. That would be awful. I have a strong feeling for day-to-day events. I'd want to share that with him.' She smiled. 'Though God knows it mightn't work with him. We're not very alike in feelings apart from those we have for each other, nor in outside interests. I love music – concert going, musical soirées, musical people, that whole world. He's not so keen. The few concerts we went to together – including that one of yours, Yelena – well, I know he found it all pretty boring. He tapped his foot, poor man, in what he thought to be the rhythm of the music. What he really likes is looking through a telescope at mysterious coloured flags which spell out messages like "Attack!" or "Engage the enemy more closely!" Of course, I love him for it. That enthusiastic boyish nonsense. But it mightn't have made for a life together, these differences.'

'But like it or not, isn't everyone really utterly different?' Yelena asked. 'So that if you're close to them, and want to get on with them you *have* to compromise, in any case, with whoever they are.'

'Yes. But in practice compromising doesn't solve problems. It patches them up, delays facing them, makes them worse. Compromising usually means that one person doesn't know there are sizeable holes in the ship, that it's sinking.'

Harriet nodded very slightly, knowing how true this had been for her with Sasha.

'Or look at it from the opposite angle,' Anna continued. 'Is it possible to be absolutely in tune with another person? To find a real soulmate?'

'Yes. Yes, it is!' Yelena said at once. 'What I had with Sasha. Exactly!'

There was a pause. Some British officers rose noisily from a table nearby. They would have whisky from Army Rations upstairs in their rooms. It was considered bad form to drink this imported liquor in public, in front of the Russians.

Harriet filled the silence after the men had left. 'I'm sure, in the end with someone, it's all about finding – and doing – what sensibly *works*, about decency and loving reason, that these should prevail.' She knew at once that this was rather too obvious and facile a point – one simply which she desperately wanted to believe and put into action herself.

Anna sensed this, too. So she said, 'In the *end*, yes. But by then the boat is sinking, isn't it? The goodwill and decency come too late. Loving doesn't start by reason, or live by it. Or end by it.'

'Yes, but one has to try for reason, all the same.'

'I think that's sighing for the moon, Harriet. Once you start having to try in love, you're at the beginning of the end. Road to hell – paved with good intentions.'

Though General Knox, on his return from the Front a week later, had at once identified Harriet and Yelena, and Mr Hodgson had given Harriet funds and a British Consular *laissez-passer*, it took Yelena and Anna, since they were apparently Soviet citizens, nearly a month before they were able to persuade the *Stavka* authorities to give them first of the new White Government identity papers and then the rail transit passes which were needed for all three women.

So it wasn't until the end of October, some weeks after the first snows had come and winter had suddenly pounced on the city with its freezing claws, the thermometer dropping to twenty degrees below zero, that all of them finally managed to get away from Omsk.

They sat now – with Holly, the now quite furless Teddy, Tomcat in his basket and Sasha's violin – in a staff compartment of a White Army hospital train, going east, to Irkutsk, and then to Harbin 2,500 miles away, with a trainload of wounded men. Anna was formally attached to the train, as one of the nurses. Major Petkov had managed to secure places for Yelena and Harriet, assisting her. They were just in time. This train would be one of the last to leave Omsk. The Reds were less than a week away from the city. Omsk, as the women left, was in a state of complete collapse and panic.

General Knox himself had come to see them off, and now, with the ringing of the third bell, they could see him, a tall figure, head and shoulders above the throng of people, with his Sergeant, waving at them, as the long train pulled out. Yelena waved at him until the last moment, when his braided cap had disappeared, tears in her eyes for this man, his kindnesses, and for the fact that, in seeing and talking to him over the last few weeks, he had been a reminder of her past life, of her family, her home, the pre-war years in St Petersburg. In the trials of mere survival for so long, Yelena had forgotten this life. It had happened to another person, in another country, in an earlier century.

General Knox had been astonished to see the two women again. He had entertained them to supper, with Anna and Holly, some weeks before, in his private railway carriage by the *Stavka* building, listening to their tales.

'Your parents, Yelena – I am so very sorry. I much admired your father. A tragedy . . .' He'd looked across the green baize table on which they'd eaten, in his map room, drumming his fingers lightly on the cloth, thinking. 'But then, that you both – that all three of you – should have survived is more than something. And the little girl.' He'd looked across at Holly. 'And the cat!' His eyes had rested a moment on the wicker picnic basket with its half lid open, Tomcat inside, having eaten some scraps supplied by the General's batman-cook from the tiny kitchen next door. 'A cat across all those distances. How did you manage it? That he did not run away at some point?'

'Oh, Tomcat knows which side his bread is buttered on,' Holly piped up. 'So Mama says.'

'I see. Yes, he would, wouldn't he?' Knox had smoothed his luxuriant moustaches, offering the women tea. 'No coffee, I'm afraid. But always tea in Russia, whatever the chaos.' He'd stood up then, gone to a cabinet. 'Will you permit me to smoke?' He'd lit a small cigar, standing at the end of the compartment. 'As for Sasha, I'd heard nothing of what Major Petkov told you, Yelena. All this terrible nonsense of Colonel Skolimsky, abducting him. Simply criminal. And while it's true he must be the last Romanov alive on Russian soil, it's most unlikely now that the Whites will ever be back in Petrograd to crown him. A fairy story. When you get to Harbin you must see General Horvath, the Governor there, at once. I'll have a letter for you to give him, vouching for you. And one to the British Consul there, a Mr Sly – strange name. So you should be able to get Sasha out of whatever fix he's in, if he's not done that for himself by the time you reach Harbin.'

'Thank you – thank you very much.'

'What will you do then?' he'd asked more briskly.

'England, I hope,' Harriet had said. 'I have good friends in London, in Chiswick. We can all stay there initially, I'm sure. Though for Anna –' She'd looked over at her in the shadows of the compartment. 'It rather depends on how her friend is, when we reach Harbin. She, he, may want to come with us, if they can.' Anna nodded.

'Good. I'll give you another letter, which should allow you passage on any British ship out of Vladivostok. Funds? – apart from what Mr Hodgson has arranged, in these almost worthless Omsk rubles.'

'I have ample funds, in London, General. Meanwhile we will get by with Omsk rubles. And we can work in Harbin, if needs be. We've managed that way before.'

'Indeed you have. I should warn you confidentially of one thing, though. General Horvath is a wily customer. Corrupt, as are most of the military and civilian authorities there. If they see any advantage in holding Sasha as a potential Tsar, or for any other reason, they'll take it. Most of them believe, in the cloud-cuckoo land they all live in down there, that the White Russian cause will prevail, that they'll all be back in Petrograd and Moscow in no time. Hopeless optimists, in the Russian manner . . .'

'Yes, but then we are, too, General.' Harriet had smiled at him.

'*Not* hopeless, though, Miss Boulting! There's the difference. I have only some whisky with me. But would you join me in a toast? To your future success and prosperity? I'm sure you all, at least, will be out of here very soon.'

It wasn't until they had left the carriage, with Yelena and the others walking ahead of them, that Harriet, encouraged by the alcohol, had asked the General if he'd had any news of Sandy Woodrow, his assistant military attaché in Petrograd.

'Yes, I have. Or I had, months ago now. He was with the War Office, at their Russian desk, in London. I saw him there briefly in October last year, just before I came out here.'

'He was well?' she'd asked easily.

'He was well.' The General had looked at her with equal ease, though he was perfectly aware of the emotional element behind her innocent query. He well remembered the close relationship between his junior military attaché and Miss Harriet in the days before the war in St Petersburg. 'He remains slightly deaf, unfortunately. They were able to do little about his hearing at the London Hospital.'

'I'm sorry. Is he married?' she had continued in the same tone of mere social enquiry.

'No – he wasn't then at any rate. He was rather champing at the bit, though, wanting some active work, since the war with Germany was soon going to be over. An active man, as you will remember.'

'Yes.'

'You may see him, I imagine, when you get back to London. If he is not still there the War Office will know where to find him.'

'Yes.'

She had smiled at the General then, but faintly, rather looking through him, thinking of Sandy. The years had run back for Harriet then, to life in a vanished world, and time: to a man she had loved and lost, in the mists of Petrograd, over three years before.

And now, as the train pulled out of the station, she realized she was taking the first real steps back into the renewed possibilities of all that kind of life, a life which she hoped again now might offer her an appropriate love, a future with – well, just possibly with Sandy.

Yelena, too, as she waved goodbye to the General, thought of similar things: of Sandy, since Harriet had told her briefly of her talk with the General, but more of Sasha. It had been easy enough, in Sasha's absence, to agree with Harriet that she must form a more balanced relationship with him. But in the event – if and when they met, in his renewed presence – would this be so easy? Would it be possible even?

She had not seen him for a year, had been without any 'sight' of him, had lost that clear sense of him – the shapes of face, feel of skin, the honey-and-oatmeal smell – so that desire for him had gone as well. But, just as desire could first come in a flash, against every good intention, so it could return, couldn't it?

For all three women, as they started out on the long train journey home – to some kind of home, at least – there were these questions, the hopes and doubts of the heart. Would there be, in this return to something like ordinary life which lay ahead of them, down the line in Harbin, and across the oceans in London, any happy end? The loves they had had with Sasha and Sandy and Ivan would soon almost certainly have to be confronted again, as dead ashes or as still living hopes in the shape of the men themselves.

Or had they left all that agonizing emotion behind them now? The high drama, the intense but quite possibly ill-founded happiness of Anna, the foolish and obsessive regard for Sasha which, for the other two women, had brought them both to such degradation? Had they, in the meantime, found something better and safer which would sustain them, their own undemanding affection for each other, born of trust and triumph in their journey. In these last months together, surviving every hazard, the three women had reached a sure understanding. They were happy together. They were mother and aunts to Holly. All four lives were interdependent. So they feared any resumed emotional ties with these men.

And yet another part of them wanted this – wanted the love that came with men. This had not died in them. The feeling had slept. But now it stirred again. They could not deny it. They wanted to give it flesh, but were wary of just this – how the flesh might run away with them, lead them to disaster once more. The problem lurked vaguely ahead of them, across the endless steppe, over the horizon.

It was not one which could long absorb them, though, as the train rumbled slowly through the frozen suburbs of the town, the vast expanse of shimmering snow on the steppe beyond blue tinted in the slanting afternoon sun.

Their own problems paled into insignificance as they saw on the road beside them the thousands of diseased, infirm or starving refugees, some lucky ones with horses. Trudging, stumbling, many falling as they walked, carrying sacks and bundles, many dressed just in rags against the oncoming freezing night.

As the train pressed forward down the branch line from the city to Omsk junction where it joined the main Siberian line they saw a world sometimes more filled with dead than living; the cadavers of horses, hacked about for meat, lying to the side of the road, the human corpses spreadeagled, scattered with them on the snow.

Half an hour later, stopping at Omsk junction, there was a different view of the dead. The naked typhus-ridden bodies, ejected from earlier trains, frozen solid now, were piled up in scores, like logs, beyond the equally frozen water tower, where icicles hung from the top, long and thick as the frozen legs of the dead.

The dead were lucky here, the living simply piteous. Before the train had come to a halt at the junction, desperate crowds had stormed it, trying to force themselves on board, stopped only by the armed guards, brutally repulsing them at each entrance.

The three women forgot their problems then, as the train, barely stopping, moved on and was shunted into a siding some way beyond the station.

A siding? Why were they being taken into this distant part of the junction filled with nothing but old depots, warehouses, lines of broken-down wagons and engines?

Their train came to a stop. After a few minutes Yelena leant out of the window. Rounding a curve in the siding, she saw another train shunting back towards them. A hospital train, four long carriages, with the same title and Red Cross markings on the carriages as their own.

She was surprised. There had been no word of this. There was no hospital at the junction. There was a lack of activity and an air of silence in and around the four carriages, no lights, all the window blinds pulled down – as the train approached them, the buffers clashed against their own, and they were joined to it.

Yelena turned back to Harriet. 'I don't know what's happening. Another hospital train. But there doesn't seem to be anyone on it.'

Yelena looked out again. 'Oh, there are people out there

now. A lot of them coming. Why, there's Major Petkov, my Army Transport friend from the *Stavka*.' She gazed down the tracks to where a group of White officers had stopped under a pylon light next to the new carriages. 'And there! That's Admiral Kolchak! I'm sure it is. Talking to Petkov. What on earth is the Admiral doing here?'

Harriet took her place at the window. The Admiral was shaking hands with Major Petkov and half a dozen other officers and some civilians who were about to board, along with several platoons of soldiers, climbing up into the last of the new hospital carriages, with rifles and machine-guns.

'A hospital train filled with soldiers? Where are the patients?'

The snow had started to drift down with the onset of night, big white flakes floating through the faint lamplight as the whole train pulled out of the siding, with Admiral Kolchak standing to attention, saluting.

A few minutes later Major Petkov, in a bearskin greatcoat and hat, came into the staff compartment, calling all the dozen nurses together. 'You'll be wondering,' he told them, 'about these new hospital carriages attached to the train. Empty for the time being. We're to pick up some more wounded farther down the line, at Novonikolayevsk and Irkutsk. Senior officers and some important White political figures, wounded in local skirmishes. So I shall be accompanying you, with troops, the better to protect the train . . .'

He looked round at the women, smiling. Yelena sensed, from his forced smile and somehow unconvincing tone, that Major Petkov was lying. There was some other reason for his presence, and that of several score soldiers on the train. The new hospital carriages could surely not be empty, Admiral Kolchak would not have come down to the remote siding to see off and salute a lot of empty carriages.

She didn't speak of her suspicions to Harriet or Anna. She bided her time. Several hours later, when they had seen to the wounded and things has settled down for the night, Yelena, treading silently down the corridor, tried the interconnecting door between their staff carriage and the next, the first of the new hospital carriages. It was locked, as she had expected. But all the interconnecting doors on these trains used the same bolt key. She had one with her now, and she opened the end door.

It gave out onto a platform, above the rattling buffers and couplings, the train jumping about on the ice-encrusted tracks, the air freezing her cheeks at once in a night that had become moonlit now, the falling snow gone. She moved across the buffers. There were two locks on the door ahead of her, top and bottom. She turned the key in each, then pushed. The heavy door opened a foot or so so that she could peer in.

The carriage was almost in darkness, illuminated by two small swinging oil-lamps. There were none of the triple-decked hospital bunks to be seen. They had all been cleared out and replaced by dozens of heavy wooden boxes, right down the carriage, piled to the roof. She could make out the black stencilling on the nearest. The two-headed Imperial Eagle and, beneath that, the legend: 'Imperial State Bank, St Petersburg'.

Of course, she thought, she'd heard about this. It had been a great coup for the Whites when they had captured the old Imperial State Gold Reserves from the Reds at Kazan earlier that year and taken it back to Omsk. But it was rather a different and much more dangerous matter for them to be taking the gold on to Irkutsk now, in a practically unprotected hospital train. If their lives had been at risk before on this journey, they were doubly in danger now.

2

Yelena spoke to Major Petkov next morning, at the end of their carriage, with its interconnecting doors into the first of the bullion carriages. She was blunt with him. 'Major, I know what's beyond these doors, in those four extra hospital carriages.'

'I don't quite follow?' He appeared genuinely puzzled. 'Nothing but empty bunks. I told you all yesterday.'

'A pointless exercise, Major. I've seen what's in there, the Imperial Gold Reserves – the bullion the Whites captured at Kazan earlier this year.'

'I see.' The Major, confronted with this truth, seemed equally perplexed. He shivered momentarily in his white bearskin greatcoat. 'How did you find out?'

'It hardly matters.'

The Major suddenly touched his nose anxiously. Frostbite was a permanent danger now. It went for one's exposed extremities. One never felt it strike, and he had been moving between the carriages, in the open, in close to thirty degrees below.

'It's all right, Major. Your nose is still pink. But had you expected to keep the whole thing hidden for the duration of the journey?' she continued.

'Yes, I do expect that.' He was suddenly formal, severe. 'No one must know. That's the whole point of the exercise – in attaching the bullion, in hospital carriages, to the back of a genuine hospital train.'

'Against the rules of war, surely?'

'"Rules of war".' He smiled faintly. 'As if there were ever any such in this war. The bullion has to be safeguarded at all costs. This is half of it. General Kolchak will bring the rest with him when, if, he leaves Omsk. He still thinks he can defend it.

But if he can't, or if the Reds get the other half, he'll use this part of it to set up another White capital at Irkutsk. Hence the subterfuge.'

'But you put all of us – us and the wounded men here – at an even greater risk.'

'Only if you, or anyone else on the train, allow word to get out of what we're carrying. That's why we're doing it this way. Had we loaded the bullion on freight wagons in Omsk someone and soon everyone would have known of it. And word would have travelled down the railway. There are guerilla groups to either side of us all down the line, you know, who'd do anything to get their hands on the bullion. Red partisans, convict and anarchist gangs to the north in the *taiga*; bandits with their private armies to the south of the line around Irkutsk; the Cossack Ataman Semenov or some of the Manchuria "Red Beards", the warlords in the same area –'

'Exactly, we've heard of them already.'

'All the more reason, Princess Yelena, why no word of what you know should leak out, not even to your two friends. If it does get about that we're carrying bullion to the value of about fifty million pounds sterling, none of you are likely to get to Harbin alive. And you have your brother Alexander in Harbin. Do you not?' he added pointedly.

Yelena told Harriet and Anna at once.

'Fifty million sterling?' Harriet remarked afterwards. 'The straw that breaks the camel's back . . .'

'On the other hand,' Anna said, 'we'll get to Irkutsk and then on to Harbin a lot quicker because of the bullion. I've noticed, we have two engines on the train, and an extra tender. And something else. After we left Omsk Junction, we were switched to the westbound line, where there are almost no trains coming up from Irkutsk, whereas the eastbound line, which we'd normally be on, is clogged full of trains. We'll get to Harbin quicker.'

'If we get there at all.'

Anna, in her Red Cross uniform, with a heavy serge coat over that, left them to tend the wounded farther up the train, leaving Yelena and Harriet alone, with Holly, to finish off some black bread and a glass of tea which had been their breakfast.

Holly was feeding Tomcat some crumbs. 'Why is the train being full of gold a bad thing, Mama?' She didn't look up. 'We could spend it. We'd be very rich.'

'Well, we can't, because it's not ours. And you can't spend gold anyway. It has to be turned into money first. Into coins. And you're not to tell *anyone* about it, what we've been talking about. All right?'

Holly looked up doubtfully now. 'All right. It's a pity, though. With all that gold, we could buy nice things, something nice for Papa when we see him, in Harbin.'

Holly returned to feeding Tomcat. The two women said nothing. Instead Harriet started to rub some of the ice off the inside of the window. The view outside, with a pale sun up now, was almost invisible. Overnight the carriage window had become thickly encrusted with ice, inside and out. They shivered in their great coats. There was some heating in all the carriages, supplied by two stoves at either end, which depended on their stocks of birch wood, kept in bunkers beside each stove.

The women knew it was essential to keep these stoves going. With the temperature falling outside all the time, and with a constant freezing wind from the *taiga*, if they were delayed, if the wood gave out, they would very likely all die of frostbite and cold within twenty-four hours.

With Anna in charge and the other two helping her, the three women ministered to some fifty wounded men who lay in their carriage in tiered bunks. They fed them – often spoon-fed them – with cabbage soup and rye bread and glasses of tea. They washed their cut and battered bodies in what little water they could warm up on the stoves, swabbing and bandaging their shrapnel gashes, their broken and sometimes amputated limbs.

There were not, as yet, any typhus cases among the patients. But four of them died before they reached the next main station at Novonikolayevsk a week later; their bodies were bundled out in sheets and left among piles of other frozen corpses in one of the station warehouses.

It was hard, messy, sometimes ghastly work. But all three women knew their luck. They had only to glance out of the carriage windows to confirm this – seeing the never-ending, straggling lines of wretched people moving sluggishly eastwards along the great Siberian *Trakt* which the railway followed: men, women and children on sledges and horseback but mostly on foot, heads bent into the bitter wind, for the weather had changed into squally, grey, drear freezing skies; troops, bedraggled infantry and skeleton artillery brigades dragging battered guns; officerless platoons and groups of officers without men, the debris of the White armies intermixed with convoys of haggard civilians, dressed usually in nothing but sackcloth and bast shoes.

All of them looked up at the train with hopeless rage or envy, like people shipwrecked far out to sea watching a ship pass close by them, knowing it will never stop, looking fearfully over their shoulders as if towards approaching sharks, expecting the next train to be the murderous vanguard of the Red Army.

It was a continuing nightmare vision, only erased with darkness when, with the blinds drawn and the swinging oil-lamps lit, there was a period of calm among the wounded after supper. Then the three women helped the men in other ways, taking dictated letters from them, playing chess, reading aloud, from Afanasiev's book of Russian fairy tales which Yelena still had with her, or with Yelena and Harriet taking turns with Sasha's violin, playing short classical pieces or more often traditional Russian airs, which the men loved more than anything, taking up the Russian ballads in chorus, humming then breaking out in deep, sad, throaty voices.

Later still, with Holly asleep in the top bunk of their tiny compartment, when things finally settled down for the night, the women took turns to stay on duty. It was Yelena's turn that evening, so that Anna and Harriet were alone in the compartment.

'That Major Serizov,' Harriet said. 'I was taking a letter from him, to his wife. He has six children, can you imagine! He can't be more than thirty-five.'

Anna was getting ready for bed, keeping her coat on, wrapping herself in two blankets as well, from head to toe, and cleaning her face with the inside of a stale heel of rye bread, which all the women used for this purpose. 'I'd like six children, growing up all round me like flowers,' Anna said with a sudden urgency which surprised Harriet. 'Yes, I know,' she went on. 'I don't seem the sort for it. Hard-headed. Practical. You might even say cynical. Not the motherly type. But I am. Just don't admit it. Least of all to Ivan. Because he's not really interested in children.'

'No.'

'Was Sasha?'

'Yes. But more as a lever. To get me to marry him. To be fair – it was my fault to begin with. I was obsessive then, taken by the wayward part of him, and wanting the physical thing, which kept us together – falsely, of course – but which neither of us could quite let go of, when what I wanted was a bit of ease and sanity with him then – which I might well have had with the rational Sandy, the Englishman. Sandy Woodrow. The man I should have married.'

'One needs both. The raffish and the rational. And it's the same for men, with us, I'm sure. It's the way to make things work. It's a sort of controlled tension that's needed between two people. To keep an interest going. The secret is never being too certain of the other.'

'Yes,' Harriet agreed. 'Yes.'

They climbed up into their bunks then, as the train rumbled slowly through the snowy night. There was silence, before Harriet suddenly spoke again. 'Do you know something? What I'd really like with someone are the small things – to share those. Books or whatever, letters, old photographs – all the bits and pieces I had with me in Petersburg. I'd like to go through those with someone I was really fond of. And I'd like to write them letters, and silly picture postcards, and to receive them. And make cups of tea for each other and messy jam sandwiches. To *collaborate* with them, in small things. That's what I'd really like most. I feel – these last years, longer – that I've been living with only one leg. That I'm only half of myself.'

'Yes,' Anna agreed finally in the darkness. Then, after a long pause, when Harriet thought she had dropped off to sleep, she suddenly continued in a wide awake voice. 'With me the small thing would be the chatter I had with Ivan, in those few months together in Petersburg. Small things. I hardly thought about it then. Not talk about important things. Just gossip from his day when he got back from the Admiralty. Naval matters, rather boring. But soon he took off on ridiculous tangents and was telling me about the Battle of Trafalgar and Lady Hamilton and "Kiss me, Hardy". And suddenly we were roaring with laughter. Going from one nonsensical thing to another. Each topping the other. All very fast. When at the end of it, or halfway through more often, we just wanted to jump into bed together.'

'Yes . . .'

Then they both slept.

Yelena sponged the young Captain's legs and thighs, with a little warm water. The fair-haired man could do almost nothing for himself. Shrapnel had pierced his chest, arms, his throat and head. He was bandaged most of the way up from his waist. Only his eyes and mouth were properly visible, though with his larynx cut about he could do no more than utter vague grunts.

Yet from his waist down he was entirely unharmed. He was fit and powerful here, virile. It seemed very strange to Yelena that the top half of his body – arms, speech and therefore thought – should be without expression, while the lower part was more than normally active. He moved his legs about. They itched. He had bed sores. He exercised his legs. He arched his knees, up and down, offering his thighs to her, turning them, so that she could tend and cleanse them.

The Captain was perfectly conscious, but could do nothing, express nothing, except with the lower parts of his body, which performed and moved about just as any man's body would, especially under the touch of a woman's hands. The whole situation stirred Yelena. She told Anna of the young man's reactions.

'It's usual enough. Seen it before, in men wounded like that. Almost automatic so far as I can see. Lying in bed immobile. The whole business down there – just sets itself up of its own accord almost. To make love.'

'Yes.'

They were walking down the corridor, the train suddenly lurching over the ice-encrusted rails. 'I've felt just the same – well, long ago,' Yelena said. 'Just the same. The whole feeling coming over me, beyond my control, for no good reason, wanting that very much.'

'It's good. It's a good feeling.'

'Which we aren't supposed to have. Sandy – I told you – he was very put out by that in me.'

The carriage lurched again and Anna steadied herself against their compartment door. 'You were unlucky then. It's the most extraordinary feeling. With the person you're lucky with. Like going through endless smaller and smaller doors. Then rocketing out – a sort of agony – into a quite new world. Colours and feelings you've never dreamed of before. A world that's greater and wider and newer and quite different each time. What an adventure. And *learning*! When you're lucky.'

'Yes. But it's not supposed to be seen that way –'

'But it is. It *is*.'

They went into their empty compartment. Anna rubbed at the window, trying to clear a patch in the ice. 'And yet in another way that part of loving is such a down-to-earth, simple, giving thing, really.' Anna gazed out through the still opaque space at the passing steppe. 'If that captain wanted to – and I'm sure he does – and if he wasn't in there among all the others – I'd make love to him myself. As a simple gift.'

'Yes.'

'It must be about whole-hearted, lifelong commitment,' Harriet said. 'Whatever else it's about.'

They had stopped at the big station of Mariinsk another week later, talking of their hopes again, as a relaxation, as a way of breaking the monotony of the horror, the harsh reality all about them. Another three of the wounded had died and been bundled out of the train half an hour before, including the young officer whose legs Yelena had tended, and without Anna's having had the chance to ease his pain by making love to him.

They were playing chess, as they sometimes did, one with another, or with the men – Yelena playing with Anna on this occasion in their compartment, with Harriet leaning over Yelena's shoulder, the door half open, so that they could keep an eye on Holly standing at the carriage entrance between two armed soldiers looking out at the hordes of people.

'It's about what's possible, more often,' Anna said. 'You're never going to get it all. The loving companionship, the jokes, the happy collaboration, jam sandwiches and sharing old photographs. And the physical thing.' Anna moved a pawn.

Yelena studied the board for half a minute. Then she suddenly looked up. 'Why not?' she said abruptly. 'Why not get it all?' She moved her second bishop out. Her first bishop was already facing Anna's queen on a long diagonal, with her King immediately behind the Queen. 'Why not?' Yelena said again, more urgently now. 'Everything – it's not too much to hope for, especially after what we've all been through. You two – you're either cynical or sentimental about our chances with – with whatever man we might meet in the future. Why shouldn't we hope for everything? Soulmate and old photographs and bed! Why do we have to think of settling for less? Why not *more*?' The other two were startled at this outburst, Anna taking her mind off the game, looking at Yelena. 'Yes, we *can*,' Yelena went on, almost willing the idea across to them with her fierce blackberry eyes. 'We can hope for everything now. And get it. We must. I do. We can. We *will*!'

When they returned to the game Anna saw she was in a quandary. To move her Queen, as she had to, would be to put herself in check from one of Yelena's bishops, while Yelena's other bishop was poised to take her King's pawn, which in turn was covered down the centre by Yelena's Queen. Yelena would have checkmated Anna in a few more moves. But they stopped the game suddenly. Holly, Harriet saw, who had been standing out in the corridor, at the carriage entrance, a few moments before was no longer there.

Holly had been watching the hapless, bewildered crowd of refugees streaming up and down beside the train in the thin snow, some of them trying to get into the train, or even get a foothold on the carriage steps, only to be repulsed by the guards.

There was pandemonium. An old woman, with three vast bundles over her shoulders, shrieked as she fell back, pushed off the steps, landing in a heap on the crushed snow. A young man, berating the two guards, was struck with a rifle butt as he approached them. On the wooden station wall opposite – where hundred of messages had been pinned by earlier travellers trying to regain contact with relations following after them – a whole family, reading some unfavourable message, broke into loud wails.

Holly, sucking her thumb, clutching her furless Teddy, peering between the legs of the two guards, was fascinated by the turmoil, the uproar, the spurts of sudden steam, the station bells, the whistles of the departing trains.

Then, as one of the guards moved backwards suddenly, the teddy fell from her arm, down the steps, and into the crushed snow, where almost at once it was swept away by running feet. Slipping between the guards' legs so that they'd hardly noticed her, she had climbed down onto the shallow platform, had seen the teddy, kicked some way ahead of her, and was pursuing it now, helter-skelter, down the platform, as the animal, caught up by other feet, was taken farther ahead, eluding her, as she followed it hither and thither, approaching other platforms and trains, when suddenly she was quite lost.

She gazed about her, caught in the crush of people. Haggard, frightening faces, bearded figures, an old crone in torn shawls glowering at her.

'My Teddy,' she shouted despairingly, running forward, looking everywhere, between people's boots. 'My Teddy! Have you seen my Teddy?' No one took the least notice of her. They had all lost, and were searching for, more than a teddy bear.

Gazing wildly about her, Holly was desperate. Teddy was lost. But so was she. There were so many trains and platforms about her now, and carriages and people, swarms of them, pushing her about, off balance, so that she crouched down on all fours, looking for Teddy at ground level, only to get splinters of icy snow kicked in her eyes, tears streaming down her cheeks. Though not crying tears, she knew. She wouldn't cry.

Then, standing up, she suddenly saw the animal. A big man just ahead of her had picked up Teddy and was looking at him. She rushed up to him. 'My Teddy! That's my Teddy.'

The man turned. She was surprised at his face, his dress. He didn't look like the Russians did. He had a flat fur hat and a pigtail, slanting eyes, a wispy beard and a huge fur jacket over a sort of skirt and baggy trousers. But he understood her Russian perfectly well.

She looked up at him. 'That's my Teddy. Thank you – for finding him.' She held her hand out. The man started to hand it to her, then stopped.

'You speak Russian in a strange way, little girl. And your clothes are very fine. Who are you?'

'I'm Holly Boulting,' she said at once. She was desperate to get Teddy back, and get back to her train, which might be leaving at any moment, so that she rushed on saying the first things that came into her head. 'Yes, I lost my Teddy. And now I've lost my train. Could you help me find it as well?'

'Yes, but what *echelon* is it, little one?'

'What?'

'What train are you on?'

'Oh, it's up there. The gold train –'

These last words escaped her before she knew what she was saying. Ever since she'd heard the talk between the three women about the last carriages being filled with gold she'd seen the train as a magic train, filled with nothing but gold, piles of it, glittering heaps, just like in the picture of the King, in his 'counting house, counting out his money', in the book of nursery rhymes.

'The gold train?' The strange man bent down to hear her better, peering closely at her with his slanty eyes.

She shook her head from side to side. 'No, the hospital train. Lots of wounded soldiers. Up there.' She pointed through the drifting snow.

'Come, I will take you back to it.' He took her hand, and then pushing – even kicking – people out of the way, he forced a passage right up the platform, and then across to the next, where Holly saw the red crosses on the carriages of her train. The man led her up past the four sealed carriages, the blinds down and doors locked, with a few soldiers moving up and down beside them.

'Not here, farther up,' Holly told him. 'These carriages are empty, for the very ill at the next station,' she went on, trying to cover up her earlier mistake.

'I see,' said the man. He looked at the carriages carefully as he passed. A moment later Harriet, followed by the two women, rushed down the platform towards them.

'Holly! Thank God!' Harriet picked her up, clutching her,

thanking the man profusely, anxious to offer him some reward, which he declined politely, bowing slightly, his sharp dark eyes appraising everything he saw – of this foreign mother and child, these privileged people and the rest of the hospital train ahead of him, where the carriages, as he saw from the lights behind the blinds, the movement of nurses by the doorways, were clearly occupied with wounded soldiers – as the last four carriages, equally clearly, were not.

He watched the train pull out into the night. '"The Gold Train"?' he asked himself. 'But of course, of *course*! The Kazan Gold reserves . . .' He turned immediately and left the station.

Holly told her mother everything that had happened, omitting only the fact that she had referred to the train as the 'gold train'. She didn't dare tell her that. Besides, the man wouldn't have understood what she was talking about.

They reached Irkutsk, by Lake Baikal, ten days later. Yelena, who had been told by Major Petkov that the bullion carriages were to be uncoupled here, was surprised when they pulled out of Irkutsk to see them still attached.

She managed to speak to him about this the following morning, as they traversed the southern shore of the great lake, negotiating scores of tunnels cut into the rock, so that as they spoke in the corridor their faces were alternately set in brilliant light, then cast in dark shadow.

The Major was guarded and anxious in his replies. 'It's been decided to take this part of the bullion reserve over the Manchurian border and on to Harbin. In case there is to be a final retreat there. Irkutsk is no longer to be relied on as a future White Siberian capital. Political control there is now in the hands of a mixed group of Social Revolutionaries and Menshiviks. The bullion would have been at risk there, even if the Reds didn't get it. So we're taking it on.'

'How will you explain this to the other nurses? They're already surprised that we picked up no wounded soldiers for those four carriages in Irkutsk. Some of them are suspicious anyway – suspect what you're carrying in there.'

'Let them suspect,' he said shortly.

'They may gossip.'

'No. There will be no gossip. Because from now on none of

you, unless accompanied by me or some of my men, will leave the train. There will be no gossip. The matter is far too important,' he added, anxious again now, looking through the window at the quite different landscape they had entered, having finally left the tunnels.

The flat steppe had gone. There were snowy views ahead of them: bleak hills and cloud-covered mountains beyond, sullen crags, small frozen lakes and ice-bound rivers twisting between steep ravines.

'Yes,' the Major continued. 'No one will leave the train now. And further I shall be taking Nurse Rayevsky from your carriage. We have an officer in our staff car at the end. He is sick.' He didn't elaborate.

'Typhus?' Yelena asked.

'I don't know.' The Major waved his hand impotently.

'You can rely on my discretion.'

'It may well be typhus. And if it is, and if it spreads to the other men, our guard on the train will be much depleted. Which is exactly what I don't want. Obviously.'

'Obviously?'

'Yes, Princess. I had never expected to take the bullion beyond Irkutsk. It was to be left here, pending Admiral Kolchak's arrival. Now I must take it along the Manchurian borderlands. Soon we'll be in territory where neither the Czechs nor the Whites have any real control.'

'Of course – Semenov, the Cossack Ataman, rules these parts.'

'Not only him. There is his even more evil friend, Ungern-Sternberg, with his own private army. And the *Hun-huzes*.'

'The Red Beards?'

'Yes. Manchurian robber warlords, of one sort or another. Several trains have been ambushed and plundered – we heard in Irkutsk – in the last month and more before.'

'But surely they wouldn't attack a hospital train? No plunder there.'

'Yes. That's what I hope.' He looked at her confidently. But his eyes betrayed his anxiety. 'Will you ask Nurse Rayevsky to come and see me? And to bring all her things.'

Four days later, at the little town of Manchuli, the frontier station, they crossed into Manchuria, taking the spur line of the Chinese Eastern Railway which would lead them south-east, over the snowy plateau near the mountains, then across the desert steppe, for four hundred miles, to the town of Harbin.

Yelena, up early that morning, was sitting by the compartment window, gazing out through the small circle of glass which they managed to keep clear of ice. Suddenly, the train crawling along very slowly, above a frozen river to their right, she caught sight of something. She leant forward, nose to the glass, riveted.

She could never have imagined such a thing; an illustration from some Chinese legend: the half-dozen dragon-prowed, black-hulled, black-sailed Chinese junks, emerging mysteriously out of the misty pearl-pink sunrise, sailing along the frozen river beneath them.

There was sufficient wind to drive the boats at a fair pace, men fore and aft with long sticks steering the craft as they moved over the icebound river just below them, the river running parallel to the railway, the track cut into the side of a steep ravine towering above.

Junks sailing on a frozen river? It was impossible. But then she saw it. Of course! The boats had sledge runners attached to either side, right down the length of their hulls. She was entranced. Since Anna was quarantined now in the last carriage with the troops she had only Harriet and Holly to share the sight with. She called them to the window.

'Look! Chinese junks, skating along the ice.'

But before they could get a proper look at them, the train ground to a halt. Almost immediately afterwards the firing started. Rifle and machine-gun fire from somewhere above them, coming from the top of the ravine. Bullets raked through the carriage roof. All three ducked to the floor, pushing themselves under the bunks. 'Oh, God,' Yelena said. 'How did they get to know about the gold?' Holly, across under the other bunks, huddling with her mother, clutching Teddy, said nothing.

In the last carriage Major Petkov, who had just finished breakfast with three of his officers, saw the bullets splintering through the roof, in a line, spattering down the central aisle.

They threw themselves aside just in time. Several of his men in the top bunks were hit. But he had the others – half his complement of troops already dressed and on duty – out of the carriage, by the doorways facing the river, in a trice, manhandling the two Vickers machine-guns down to them, onto the track overlooking the river, using the cover of the train to set them up.

Sending the Telegraph Sergeant back to tap into the wires and another officer to help the machine-gun platoon on the second tender behind the engines, the Major took stock. The train, he saw, had been stopped by a rockfall, some hundred yards ahead at the mouth of a tunnel. The bandits were firing down at them at an angle of about 45 degrees, from positions all along the top of the ravine.

So long as his men stayed in cover behind the carriages, on the river side, they were safe enough. The ravine above was too steep and jagged for the bandits to get down to them. It wasn't the best place to ambush a train, the Major saw. They could hold them off indefinitely until help arrived via the telegraph. Or the bandits would retreat or run out of ammunition.

His men were crouched now, some fifty of them, with rifles and four machine-guns, all along the length of the train, their backs to the wide frozen river a hundred feet below down the cliff face.

The Major turned, looking over the crystal glitter on the snowy river ice, shading his eyes against the bright sun, risen now above the mountains to the south. He saw the half-dozen cargo junks, their ribbed black sails like larvae skins, approaching them. He had been in these borderlands before. Such craft were quite common in winter on the canals and rivers here. He was surprised only that, with the gunfire, the obvious signs of battle, they came on downstream towards the stalled train. Then he saw why.

Coming abreast of the train now, ranged in a line, all six junks furled their sails, the men with sticks fore and aft using them to brake their progress, so that the boats came to a halt broadside on to the train, less than a hundred yards away.

A moment later the cargo tarpaulins amidships in each junk erupted with a withering fire, bullets raking the train, hitting many of the men before they dived for cover beneath the carriages.

There was no cover for the troops then. On the far side of the train they would be exposed to the bandits on the ravine top. Their machine-guns pointing the wrong way, the men were trapped on two sides now, from above and below.

The bandits continued firing, in bursts, for some minutes. Major Petkov's men did their best to return the fire from beneath the carriages. But their sightlines were awkward and it was an unequal business. The Major, from his vantage-point crouched halfway along beneath the train, looked up and down the line. There was no sign of the Telegraph Sergeant he had sent back to tap the wires. He saw what would happen. The bandits had only to approach them along the tracks now, from either end, and they would be surrounded on all four sides.

Five minutes later he saw the first of them, downline, running fast towards them, hugging the cliffside, firing as they came. Turning upline he had a view of the same sort of people, approaching in the same fashion: small men, in heavy furskin jackets and rough pantaloons, with short carbines, running towards them from the mouth of the tunnel.

They were surrounded. Major Petkov had drawn his revolver already. He drew the sabre now from its scabbard at his waist. The bright silver blade glittered in the sunlight, as he prepared to break cover and do battle at close quarters.

Twenty minutes later it was over. The Major and most of his men were dead. In the hospital train proper, Harriet and Yelena, with the other nurses, saw little of the carnage, when the Manchu brigands, out-gunning the Major's men from all sides, had overrun the train, uncoupled the last four carriages, and pushed them backwards down the line to where the track lay immediately above the frozen river.

Now the bandits were feverishly unloading the heavy wooden bullion cases, roping them, then lowering them one by one down the sides of the sloping cliff straight onto the decks of the junks on the ice below, each junk pulled up in turn to receive the precious cargo.

Harriet and Yelena, peering round the side of their carriage door, saw something of all these latter manoeuvres, and feared for the worst, believing that when the brigands had taken the bullion they would turn their attentions to the women, at least the nurses in the other eight carriages.

But they were lucky. The bandits, knowing there would soon be other trains coming along the line, and seeing how heavy the work was, and delayed in this, had no time to waste in taking any women. They only took Anna.

Harriet and Yelena saw her go, led away hurriedly from the last of the bullion carriages, between two small, fur-hatted men. She stumbled, crossing the tracks, moving to the river bank giving down to where the last junk was moored beneath. The men picked her up roughly and put a rope round her neck. The two women thought they were going to hang her. But they slipped the rope round her shoulders, under her arms, tightened it and lowered her down the rock face onto the deck of the junk.

Five minutes later all the junks, sails unfurled, had moved away from the bank, the men pushing them out into midstream with their long metal-spiked sticks, catching the wind then and sailing away downriver. The huge sun had risen well up over the glittering valley. There was a breezy, sunny, frozen silence all round the train. Anna was gone.

3

A week later the hospital train crossed the delicate, latticework bridge spanning the half-mile-wide Sungari river at Harbin. On the far side, immediately below them, set along the steep bank, Harriet and Yelena saw the Chinese Town, a warren of narrow streets, small shops, hovels, a few pagoda roofs, everything covered in meringue folds of thick snow – the big flakes slanting out of the north. Turning, they saw the outlines, the church domes and tall buildings, of a large modern city coming in sight a mile away.

When the train finally pulled into Harbin's art-nouveau station they voiced their emotion mildly.

'Yippee!' Harriet said, lifting Holly in her arms. 'We're here.'

'Hurrah,' Yelena added quietly, holding Tomcat up to the window as the train drew into the platform, where the stretcher bearers and ambulance wagons were already waiting for the wounded.

'Papa?' Holly enquired much more boisterously. 'Will he be here to meet us?'

'No. Because he doesn't know we're coming. But we'll find him in the town somewhere. That's what we've come all this way for.'

'Yes.' Holly sucked her thumb.

Apart from this small disappointment, the two women saw their future in Harbin in relatively simple terms. They had letters of introduction from General Knox to the city Governor, General Horvath, and to Mr Sly, the British Consul. They had but to meet these two officials to set in motion their every plan: to find out where Sasha and the renegade Colonel Skolimsky were in Harbin, and to tell the Governor how the Colonel had abducted Sasha and abandoned them over a year before.

They would then tell the Governor how Anna, as well as the bullion, had been taken by some Chinese warlord in the ambush – and look forward to Anna's rescue when the authorities in Harbin mounted an attack on the bandits to retrieve the bullion, as they certainly would.

Harriet meanwhile would see the British Consul as soon as possible – who no doubt, and despite his name, would be more helpful than Mr Hodgson had been at Omsk. He would likely advise them about accommodation, advance Harriet funds, and eventually, when Sasha had been discovered and Anna had been rescued, facilitate their departure from Harbin. All of them, including Ivan Rayevsky, reunited with Anna by then, would take ship from Vladivostok back to England.

But things were not to work out as readily as they had imagined.

Immediately after the wounded had been transferred to the ambulances a senior White Army officer, a Colonel Maximov, with a lieutenant, called all the nurses up, together with Harriet, Yelena and Holly, and took them to a waiting-room where he addressed them.

'You have come through a great ordeal, all you ladies. I congratulate you.' He smiled wearily. A big man with a bushy moustache, he had the air of someone physically depleted, his uniform a little too large for him, harassed. 'As I'm sure you all know by now,' the Colonel went on, 'this bandit got away with half the Imperial State Gold Reserves. Well, I would ask you – require you indeed – not to speak of what happened in the ambush, or of the missing gold. It would erode morale here. We shall have the bullion back, no doubt of that, when spring comes and the passes open, and we can mount an attack on this warlord in the north. In the meantime, your absolute discretion in this matter, please. Sledges have been arranged to take you all to the army hospital.'

After the Colonel had finished speaking Yelena approached him. 'Colonel, I and my English friend here, we have several problems. We are not nurses, but came on the hospital train through the good offices of Major Petkov and General Knox, at Omsk –'

The Colonel was almost jovial. 'Oh, that's perfectly all right.

I'll arrange for you both to be billeted with a family. We have a list.' He was about to turn away to his aide.

'Colonel – there was a woman who this warlord took, our great friend Nurse Anna Rayevsky. She was in the last troop carriage at the time of the ambush.'

'Was she indeed? I'm sorry to hear it.' The Colonel showed avuncular concern. 'Well, we shall do our best, of course, to rescue her, and ensure her safety, when the time comes to mount an attack. I'll have her name and details.' He called to his aide. 'Lieutenant, please, a moment . . .' The Colonel turned back, about to present his compliments and say goodbye.

'Colonel, forgive me, but there is a further matter which is even more important. I am from St Petersburg, the Princess Yelena Rumovsky –' On hearing her name the Colonel's demeanour changed. No longer the competent army bureaucrat, and if only for an instant, he had a startled expression. 'Before we took the hospital train from Omsk we had crossed half Russia last year. But over a year ago, at the town of Romny in the Ukraine, we ran into the remnants of a White Army brigade commanded by a Colonel Skolimsky. This man abducted my brother, Prince Alexander Rumovsky, and took him across Siberia, to meet with Admiral Kolchak's forces, with the idea – since we are of the Romanov line – of making my brother the new Tsar when the Whites got back to Petersburg. When we got to Omsk last September I learnt from Major Petkov that this criminal Skolimsky had arrived in Omsk a few weeks before, with my brother, and had then been sent on to Harbin in a sealed train.' The Colonel, motionless, his jaw set in a firm line, listened to her rather coldly now. 'I have a letter here,' Yelena went on, 'from General Knox, confirming these facts. Well, my brother must have arrived in Harbin with Skolimsky some time ago. I'd obviously like to see him as soon as possible – and to expose this madman Skolimsky. I'm sure you will have heard of all this. Do you know where my brother is?'

The Colonel was suddenly abstracted. He took the letter, read it quickly, then returned it to her. 'This indeed is news to me, Princess. I have to say that to my knowledge at least . . .' He paused. 'No such Colonel Skolimsky, or your brother, have arrived in Harbin, in any sealed train. I should have known. Are you sure of your facts?'

'Absolutely. Major Petkov told me, at Omsk, in confidence – since the whole thing was supposed to be top secret.'

'Yes. Yes, it would be.' The Colonel was vague again. 'A new Tsar like that, in a sealed train . . . All I can suggest is that you speak to the Governor here, General Horvath. He would certainly have been informed of such a very confidential and serious matter. I would not have been told. If you'll forgive me now, Princess, I will see that the Lieutenant here arranges the best possible billet for you all in Harbin. Not easy, you know, so many thousands of refugees . . .'

Yelena couldn't quite decide about the Colonel. She felt he'd been speaking the truth about Colonel Skolimsky and Sasha not having arrived in Harbin – but that he was hiding something else. She wanted to speak to him again, to help her arrange to see the Governor. But, having spoken to the Lieutenant, the Colonel had disappeared almost at once out into the snowstorm.

Harriet, later that same day, visiting the Consul's office in a large, white pillared house down in the wharf district by the river, had no better luck. Mr Sly, the Consul, had left on sick leave for Vladivostok a week before and his replacement had been delayed by the bad weather downline, she was told by one of the two Russian secretaries who were running the office, both equally vague, who had spent most of the time chattering on the telephone.

Meanwhile Yelena had gone at once to the army hospital in the Gondatevka district to seek out Ivan Rayevsky and tell him about Anna. It took her some hours, in the chaos of the place, asking questions, walking endless corridors smelling of cabbage soup and disinfectant, before she found a nursing sister who knew about him, leading Yelena to the records room. 'Commander Ivan Pavlovich Rayevsky? Imperial Navy?'

'Yes.'

'He left here, his treatment finished – he'd a broken ribcage, fractures to the shoulder and arm – some months ago.'

'Where? Where would he have gone? You must have some address for him, in town.'

'No. You'd have to go to Army Records Section for that. At the *Stavka* building in New Town, end of the avenue.'

Yelena knew enough about the chaos in *Stavka* buildings to know she'd have a hard job there. Yet she had to find him. He and Anna had been so close and happy, had seen such a future together. He would want to know what had happened to her – at least that she'd been abducted by some bandit warlord, though God alone knew what had happened to her since.

Ten days before, Anna had been taken, on the last of the bandit junks, for three days downriver, sped by the wind, travelling day and night by the light of six huge paper lanterns attached in line abreast to the prow of each junk. Imprisoned between cases of bullion, bound by one foot with a rope attached to a bulwark, she was fed irregularly with bowls of sour rice. She could only assume the worst in this bandit's having taken her. Bandit? He was obviously more than that – a powerful Chinese warlord.

She met him only once during the bitterly cold journey. He had visited her on the first evening – a short, almost tubby man, built like a wrestler, fierce-faced, with very round, almost childish blue eyes. He was not red-bearded. He had no pigtail. He was almost clean-shaven and was dressed, unlike his men, entirely in European fashion: a heavy khaki army jacket, jodhpurs, riding boots and a flat cap. The only concession he made towards native dress was the short Manchurian rope-handled sword he carried in a scabbard at his waist. She noticed a gold chain round his neck, attached to some object beneath his jacket, glinting in the lantern light.

She had asked him for a blanket, in pidgin Russian. 'I understand you,' he had replied quickly, in almost perfect Russian. He gestured to one of his lieutenants, speaking in Manchu. A blanket was brought. She had asked, and he had said, nothing more – looking down at her expressionlessly as she lay on the dirty sacking before he departed. If his hopes were for rape or concubinage he seemed very uninterested in her, Anna thought.

Leaving the tributary, the convoy joined the larger Hulan river, travelling upstream now. Two days later the junks drew to a halt, next to a rough landing stage, at the bottom of a steep ravine. Here the bullion was unloaded by an army of coolies, taking a whole day, the gold bars unpacked from their wooden crates and laboriously packed again, stowed away in saddlebags set to either side on the backs of some seventy yaks and as many small mountain ponies, one of which Anna was given to ride, its bridle linked to the pony ahead, ridden by one of the warlord's lieutenants.

At daybreak next morning, they left the ravine, heading east, along the side of a long snow-filled valley, gradually climbing the slopes towards the glittering peaks of the Khinghan mountains in the distance. After a morning's relatively quick progress along a beaten track, they turned sharp north, before the two sides of the valley joined in an almost sheer rock face. They trekked upwards then, on a much steeper mountain path, which twisted higher and higher, between overhanging crags, across rope bridges, over ravines, through ever narrowing passes.

The weather remained clear and sunny. But the wind in the high passes was increasingly bitter, so that Anna, despite the blankets wrapped about her, nearly froze on the small pony.

They made camp overnight at a way station, a group of makeshift wooden huts, sheltered under a crag, alongside a rocky track, which gave over a vast ravine, dipping sheer for thousands of feet below them, and beyond that a valley where they could just see the frozen Hulan river, snaking about in the snow-filled wilderness far beneath them, the sun a huge ball of fire falling behind the shadowy peaks to the west.

Next morning, at first light, they travelled on along the track cut into the side of the cliff, in deep shadow for several hours as the sun rose on the other side of the mountain. So that it wasn't until nearly midday, when they emerged into the bright light at the end of the long ravine, that Anna saw an astonishing sight on the mountain top straight ahead of them – a heavenly city, it seemed, hovering in the puffy white clouds: a fortress with battlemented walls, a bell tower, a cluster of buildings, pagoda roofs.

At first she was barely able to distinguish the fortress walls from the snow-topped mountain. They were the same dazzling white in the midday sun, both towering up into a pure blue arc of sky. Then, as they came closer, she noticed another colour:

gold – a myriad sparkling gold flashes, dancing in the keen light, from the centre of the fortress walls.

It wasn't until they had ridden across a snowy plateau in front of the fortress, and crossed a drawbridge over a snow-filled moat, that Anna saw where the flashes had come from. Set into the great wooden double doors, opening now into a small courtyard, were hundreds of gold-topped nails making the shape of a vast sun.

Behind the thick, dilapidated walls, as the long cavalcade of yaks and ponies passed through the great gold-studded doors into the courtyard, Anna saw another wall in front of her, a concealing wall with a smaller gateway to one side. Riding through this second gate she found herself in a much larger courtyard, a big square, with all about her the remains of an ancient Manchu hill town, a Shangri-La set up here in the heavens centuries before and now quite gone to seed.

Around the great cobbled square there were lines of closely packed, mostly derelict one-storeyed houses, divided by small alleys and intersected by a long main avenue which led to a large pagoda-roofed building, a temple, at the end.

The yaks and ponies remained in the square, surrounded by swarms of dark-skinned mountain men, who at once started to unload the bullion onto high-wheeled carts, uttering small grunts of triumph, like pigs relishing a particularly good feed, as they proceeded with the heavy work. The bullion was moved across the courtyard to a larger, newer building, made of stone, guarded by riflemen, with a chimney on top, belching smoke. She could hear the sound of hammering from one side of the building, the vague roar of a bellowed furnace from the other.

Anna, between two guards and with the warlord himself strutting ahead, carrying a single gold bar, was led down the main street, towards the temple-like building at the end.

On her way, to either side, she saw ruined shopfronts, with the remains of vivid pictures above them – just as in the old Russian fashion – signifying their wares: huge blue and red boots against a star-spangled background over an ancient bootmakers; a pestle and mortar above what had once been an apothecary's shop, and farther on, against the wooden awning of what must have once been a theatre, a series of brutally depicted, terrifying masks, with a great brass gong in front, its ropes frayed away, the gong about to drop.

Nearing the temple steps Anna was astonished to see a small black motor car, brand-new but with all its tyres flat, parked in splendour, in front of the decaying building. The warlord patted the bonnet affectionately as he passed. They climbed the steps towards a series of sliding wooden filigree doors, each manned by a sentry, dressed in the old Manchu warrior fashion: heavily padded and ribbed smocks covered in chain mail, with long-backed and -sided helmets, holding tall penanted halberds.

Inside she entered a shadowy pillared hall, lit by a few lanterns, once a temple, but now made over, it seemed, as a tribute to King Midas. Outside, the wooden roof and walls had been eaten away by the weather. But inside, things had been renewed. The pillars, walls, the sloping ceiling had all been covered in hammered gold leaf, so that the whole space glimmered faintly. She had come into an Aladdin's cave, for around her now, in mouldering lacquer cabinets and on rackety shelves, she saw astonishing treasures, old and new: small terracotta statues of Manchu warriors, Buddha figurines, tall blue-patterned vases, embroidered silks and illuminated manuscripts; then cabinets full of golden birds and animals, gilded globes and daggers, gold knick-knacks of all sorts, a treasure trove of golden ornaments.

Ascending some further steps at the end of the hall, the warlord led her towards a series of tall white silk screens, each screen wonderfully embroidered and coloured with differently hued birds – parrots, pheasants, golden orioles. Then Anna heard the jazz music, soft but quite clear from behind the screens: 'Alexander's Ragtime Band'.

Drawing one of the screens aside, and dismissing the guards, the warlord led her into quite a different space: a separate room, contained within the screens, softly lit by yellow lanterns. It was furnished in a modern European style: a luxurious, heavily cushioned sofa, easy armchairs, a card table, an art-nouveau bureau with a scalloped horned gramophone on top, a cocktail cabinet.

A woman sat at the card table playing patience, smoking, with a glass beside her and a bottle of port. A slumberous-faced, almost middle-aged, dark-haired woman. A fine aquiline nose, deep-pooled eyes. A strikingly handsome woman, sensuously olive-skinned, dressed in dark silks, spattered everywhere with gold. Gold bracelets, necklaces, brooches, rings. Gold against black. She glittered everywhere. The warlord's mistress, Anna supposed. The woman looked up at Anna for a long moment, appraisingly, then smiled.

The warlord spoke in Russian. 'I have brought you the gold.' He put the heavy gold bar down on the card table. 'This – and thousands of others. More gold than any one man has ever possessed.' He paused, hoping for favour here. The woman gave none. 'And – and another present,' he went on, with less enthusiasm. 'A "modern" present.' He glanced at Anna. The woman busied herself, rounding up the cards, stacking them in a pile. Then she looked up at him.

'I have enough gold,' she said shortly. 'But your other present –' The woman turned to Anna. 'She looks of more value. Certainly more so than the last "modern" present you brought me. He was so surly. No interesting talk at all.' She gestured to Anna, her innumerable gold bracelets jangling in the silence. 'Sit down, my dear. My name is Masha. And this is my friend –' she made a vague gesture towards the warlord. 'My friend FuLang-Kin. Switch the gramophone off, will you, Fu?' She turned back to Anna. 'Much better, now you're here, to talk. I so miss good talk up here. Women's talk, you know. Nothing but men everywhere . . .' She glanced at Fu, allowing him a brief smile. He returned her look with one of unbounded adoration.

Anna sat down and the woman smiled at her much more warmly. 'A little port-wine? It will revive you before we eat. You must be tired, and hungry, after the long journey.

Yelena, in the subsequent days, could obtain no interview with General Horvath. Each time she went to the City Hall on the broad main street in New Town two miles down from the river, and even though she stood in line for hours, she had been unable to get near either of the two appointment clerks. The whole building was in a state of pandemonium, filled with refugees, petitioners, hundreds of people, among the tens of thousands who had flocked into Harbin in the last months, after their frantic retreat across Siberia, with the demoralized remains of the White Army.

Harbin was bursting at the seams now, the refugees desperately seeking help, accommodation, work. No one was in the least interested in Yelena's problem – a lost brother, abducted over a year before by a renegade White Colonel.

Meanwhile, seeing that they would need some sort of work themselves, pending the arrival of the new British Consul and obtaining an interview with the Governor, Yelena had made enquiries at Harbin's Higher Musical School, suggesting she might teach the piano there, or join the Harbin Symphony Orchestra which, as she had discovered, was playing with the Opera Company at the Railway Assembly Rooms in the New Town, where the season had recently opened with *Aida*.

She could not get to see the school's director, but she was snubbed by his deputy, a cocky man with a shock of 'poetic' long hair, who had never heard of her, or of her brother, even though she told him how they had both won the gold medal for piano and violin, at the St Petersburg Conservatoire in 1914. 'Madame,' he had said sniffily, 'we have here, at the school and in Harbin, many of the greatest teachers, musicians and singers in all Russia: the pianists Kolchina and Aptekareva, the tenor Muzzhukhin. And Lipovsky, the great bass. I am afraid there are no openings here. Though you might try with the Operetta Company, down at The Wharf in the Commercial Building. I believe they are playing *Sylvia* there at the moment,' he had ended even more sniffily.

The authorities had at least found them some accommodation – a room in the suburb of Modiago, in the house of a taciturn refugee dentist and his family, in one of the hundreds of new *dacha*-like houses which were being built everywhere round the city then. 'Wood and Lining' houses, the latter being simply sawdust poured between two walls of thin boards hurriedly knocked together, so that the rooms were freezing, only a few degrees warmer than the bitter December weather outside.

Yelena, unable to stand the cold, and leaving the other two with Tomcat and the dentist's wife and children round the single small stove in the kitchen, left early that morning to try once more at the Town Hall. And to look for work, and try and find better and warmer accommodation. She found herself paralysed in the suburban house, from cold – and in thought, action. She must get out and *do* something, anything. They had finally, after every sort of trial, setback and deprivation, escaped from Russia. Yet here they were now, in freedom, almost as badly off as they'd ever been.

She walked the several miles to the Town Hall in the city centre on New Trade Street. Though it was not yet eight o'clock, and the offices were closed, there was already a line of people issuing from the entrance right round the corner. It was hopeless. She didn't even bother waiting. Some more drastic means of contacting General Horvath was required.

She walked on down the avenue, passing from the administrative to the commercial district, where she stopped at the window of Filipov's *piroshki* shop. It was just opening. She could smell the baking pastries, the hot mincemeat, coming from the doorway and she was suddenly hungry. She gazed longingly into the window where they were setting out the various pasties. But she had very little money. The Omsk rubles which they had brought with them were quite valueless in Harbin. They had been living on a small initial allowance of Harbin rubles with which they had been issued at the station. She had not a kopek to spare.

FILIPOV'S PIROSHKIS. She looked up at the sign. They had been famous throughout Russia before the revolution. She and Sasha had eaten them almost every day in winter from street stalls or at Elysieff's café on the Nevsky Prospekt. Now she saw the pies again, available everywhere in Harbin, as almost everything was that she remembered from the old days, her old life, in Petersburg.

She walked on down the avenue, clutching her fur collar close against the freezing chill, pushing her way through the great bustle of people, along the wooden pavements, gritted and cleared of snow, everything tended to in the streets, as they'd been in every Russian city before the revolution.

She gazed at other shop windows, selling groceries, confectionery and cigars, furs and galoshes, skirts, corsets and silk stockings, all the latest fashions. She was astonished by the rich supply of goods on sale, seeing the hoardings on the street corners advertising things she no longer thought existed:

BORMAN'S CHOCOLATE, LOPATO CIGARETTES, GERASIM'S VODKA.

She still could not quite believe it all: this vast, throbbing city, with its tramcars and motors and throngs of well-dressed people; its blue- and gilt-domed churches, and the Cathedral of St Nikolayev just ahead of her now, built in the Old Volga style. A city which was part of a lost time, she saw, as well as being an eldorado now, set in the middle of Manchuria.

This city, which she'd known about before as simply a small railway town, headquarters of the Chinese Eastern Railway, which the Russians had built twenty years before to house the workshops and administrative buildings for this spur line so that they could take a short cut to Vladivostok, this railway town, which the Russians still controlled on a long lease from China, had now become a teeming metropolis, a city where everything from Filipov's *piroshkis* to the solemn tones of the cathedral bells still went on as if there had been no revolution, as if nothing had changed anywhere in the old Russian Empire, which in fact lay in ruins only a few hundred miles to the north.

Yelena went into the cathedral, the great bell tolling for the morning service, crowds of people crossing themselves repeatedly as she entered the huge circular nave, looking towards the gold-doored, jewel-studded iconostasis with its hundreds of glimmering candles in front, and hundreds more above her, set in circles on the vast chandelier that hung from the dome. And icons everywhere, against the pillars, the walls, lit by further candles set on spikes. Candles sold from boxes by old women in shawls right beside her.

She crossed herself, and taking out two kopeks bought a candle. She moved away from the throng of people by the door, towards the shadowy walls, where she would look for a suitable saint to make an offering to, of a candle and a prayer.

Work, she thought. She and Harriet needed proper work. Money for decent food and a place to live. And she needed to find Sasha. And Anna and Ivan Rayevsky. And needed to talk to General Horvath, and Harriet had to get in touch with the British Consul. She had a lot to pray for, she thought, as she found an icon to St Vladimir in one of the darkest corners of the cathedral, and stuck the candle on the spike. To pray for these things, yes, for she had long since abandoned the idea that she still possessed any strange gifts or powers.

It was hot in the cathedral as she stood before the icon. She started to loosen her fur collar, hearing the soaring chants of the priests and the choir behind her. It was hot and she had walked a long way, and had eaten nothing. The icon and the flickering candles beneath it started to blur before her eyes. The voices of the choir seemed to ring strangely in her ears. She fainted.

When she came to she was lying back, with her fur coat and collar open, on a chair in the concierge's hut, a kiosk where they sold candles and picture postcards of the saints by the entrance. One of the old women candle-sellers was leaning over her, fanning her with a newspaper, a glass of water in the other hand. Behind her stood a middle-aged couple, both in furs, with fox-fur hats.

'There – she's coming round.' The *babushka* turned to the couple. 'Lucky you found her, in that dark part of the cathedral. Only a month ago, in this cold,' she continued with relish, 'they found an old woman dead in front of St Vladimir.' She turned back to Yelena, glowering at her now. 'Yes, you were lucky, young Missy, that these kind people found you.'

The woman in the fox-fur hat came forward now. She had trails of fair hair, dipping down beneath the hat. 'Are you all right?' she asked. Yelena focused better on her now. She had a gentle face, plump, yet with an unexpectedly long and thin nose.

'Yes,' Yelena said, unconsciously touching her own turned-up nose, wiping it. She took a sip of water from the *babushka*. 'It's just – the sudden heat. And I'd walked a lot . . . and not eaten for quite a while.'

The woman came closer, putting her hand on Yelena's arm, looking at her, the large blue eyes filled with concern. 'Well, that's easily fixed. We were just going home for breakfast, to our restaurant. Come with us and have some breakfast.'

Yelena looked up at the woman, then at the portly man behind her who had taken his newspaper back from the *babushka* and was fiddling with it. 'But –'

'No, I insist. We have a sledge outside. We're down by the wharf. The sleigh ride and the food will revive you.'

Twenty minutes later Yelena hung her coat on a tall bentwood stand and sat down near the warm stove in the back room of the restaurant, by the kitchen, the couple opposite her. Their table was simply laid with a red check cloth. So much was red or orange in this old-style Russian restaurant, she noticed: the traditional red peasant plates set on shelves along the walls, with a score of red teapots, scarlet china hens to keep eggs warm in, orangey bowls, crimson mugs, platters, a large bronze-gold samovar bubbling away in a corner. And above the small central dais, which divided the front room from the back, the *pièce de résistance* in the décor: a fine papier-maché model of the Firebird, its tail feathers painted in every colour of the rainbow. The restaurant was called 'The Firebird'.

A woman, dark-featured in a white apron and cap, came in from the kitchen carrying a large tray. She set the dishes down: a huge selection of *zakuski*, *piroshki*, semolina *kasha*, hot *bliny*, pickled mushrooms, cucumber, a whole fresh-baked loaf of rye bread and a bottle of Gerasim's chilled vodka.

The man filled three small glasses. 'This, too, will revive you,' he said to Yelena, smiling.

They were called Yukhotsky, Misha and Nadya Yukhotsky, in their mid-fifties, Yelena thought. She heard their story, and they hers, over the long breakfast. He had been a successful businessman in St Petersburg before the war, as an export agent for meat and butter from Siberia, transported in special cold wagons and sent overseas, largely to England, where they made regular shipments to Hull and Norwich.

They had lost everything in the war and revolution, including their two sons. The first had died at the battle of Tannenberg in 1914, and the second had disappeared in the chaos after the October revolution. He had been on his way out of the country, on one of the last trains leaving Petrograd for Finland. They had later heard that the Reds had stopped the train just before the border, searched everyone, looted what they could, and then massacred most of the passengers, their son included, they assumed, for they had never heard from him since.

Afterwards, early in 1918, with business contacts in Siberia, they had managed to get to Omsk, where he had worked supplying food to the White Army, an enterprise he had maintained until a year before when, realizing that things would soon come to an end in Omsk, they had gone on to Harbin.

With the money they had saved, in Omsk rubles which still had value in Harbin then, they had bought what had been a run-down *bliny* and *piroshki* snack restaurant and transformed it into 'The Firebird' – in this two-storey building overlooking the river, with an apartment on top and a terrace outside for use in the summer. They had met a young Georgian couple in Harbin, Gregori Arkhip and his wife Sofia. Gregori had been an under-chef at the Metropole Hotel in Yalta. The two of them had taken over the cooking in the restaurant, making wonderful *shasliks*, fish *pilafs* and *kotleti* on the wood-fired grill. The place had become something of a success, Misha told Yelena gently.

'But now,' he went on, his round face, which was as plump as his wife's, reddening in the heat from the big porcelain stove, 'we have had the best possible success of all!' He turned to his wife, smiling at her beatifically. 'Yesterday, just yesterday evening when we were called to the Telegraph Office, we received a telegram from our son Ivan. He's *alive*! In America, in San Francisco. He survived the massacre on the train, and found out where we were eventually. A good customer of ours here – when he went to San Francisco, Ivan met him, quite by chance, and the man told him about us, where we were. Can you imagine?' He turned back to Yelena, shaking his head. 'We went to the cathedral this morning to offer thanks. To St Vladimir. Which is how we found you. You who needed help, in need of some divine intervention such as we'd just had. So that of course you had to come back with us, so that we all might celebrate this great good fortune.' He raised his vodka glass, but was unable to drink it. He broke down in tears.

'Misha, little dove.' His wife put her arm on his. 'Misha, we have both cried enough already,' she said with calm concern. 'We must ration our tears now, otherwise there will be none left for when we see Ivan again!' She patted his arm, then turned to Yelena. 'Yes, we shall soon be leaving, for America, with Gregori and Sofia. We shall start another restaurant, in San Francisco. There are many Russians there already.'

Yelena looked at the couple, moved to tears herself now, by

their warmth and generosity, the way they had shared their food and their feelings with her, all the best of the old Russian virtues which she remembered from her own life, long before, in Petersburg, and which she had not witnessed since. Suddenly Yelena was pleased to be Russian.

She told them her own story then, without restraint, warmed by the food and vodka. Earlier she had simply told them her name and something of the trip to Harbin. Now she elaborated, told them all, from the beginning, with Misha and Nadya interjecting from time to time.

'But of course, you are *those* Rumovskys – Prince Pyotr, who was a minister in the Duma, the big palace on Nabereznaya Quay . . .' Misha had lit a *papirosy*, and the smoke was curling up towards the ceiling where the Firebird was suspended.

'We are not musical, in that classical way,' Nadya had said. 'More the operetta, at the Arcade Theatre. We liked that, didn't we, little dove?'

'Oh, I liked the Arcade Theatre as well. Russian musical comedies!' Yelena said. 'I can play that sort of music too! *Bayaderki* or *Sylvia*.' She looked over at the dais between the two rooms where there was a piano. 'Look – I'll play some now.'

She leapt up, played a highly spirited medley from *Sylvia* and *Bayaderki*. Gregori and Sofia, hearing the music, came out of the kitchen to listen.

Seeing them, Yelena shouted out, 'Or Georgian music – I can play "The Sword Dance"!' which she did, so that soon Gregori had taken to the floor and, arms raised, feet flying, was dancing like fury. Soon, in one way or another, they were all dancing, singing, across the floor and between the tables, as Yelena played on, till they were exhausted. Then they sat down, at the table beneath the Firebird, breathless, happy. Misha poured more vodka, raised his glass.

'To you, Princess Yelena, who have made our day so joyous!' Then he looked up at the Firebird. 'And to you, great bird of Russia – and to this dear place, which we shall so miss.'

Almost before Misha had finished speaking Yelena knew what she was going to say. 'Misha Alexeivich, you need not lose this place. Or if you do, it could be to me, to me and my friend Harriet. Let us run it for you, after you leave. Or buy it from you. We could well have the money before you leave.'

'You?' Misha looked at her seriously. 'But you have no experience, a princess –'

'Yes! I have. As a child I practically lived in the kitchen of our palace. Especially at Easter, watching them make the *pashka* and the *kulich*. And all the Easter roasts and stuffings. All the smells – I loved it. I could run it, with my friend Harriet. Gregori and Sofia –' She looked at the Georgian couple. 'They could show us – the cooking – before you all go.'

Misha thought a moment, frowning, somewhat embarrassed. 'Yes, Princess Yelena, perhaps you could. The trouble is – we would need the money, before we go. This is our only capital.'

'I will find the money then,' Yelena said triumphantly. 'When the British Consul arrives. My friend Harriet, she has money in London – and he will advance her some, in English money which would have real value for you in America. You see, we must wait here in Harbin, until I find my brother. And our friend Anna Denisovna, wherever she is, with some warlord up in the mountains. We must wait here.'

Nadya spoke then, to her husband, who was still downcast. 'She is right, little dove. We have to sell to someone. Why not to the Princess here? Especially if we can sell for English money. Harbin rubles will be useless in America.'

Misha stood up. 'Yes, yes, of course. I was only thinking – how much luck can one expect in the course of twelve hours? I am frightened now only of running out of it.' He raised his glass. 'Indeed, The Firebird will be yours, Princess. Meanwhile, we have a small room upstairs, for you and your friend and her child. Come here, stay with us, and we will teach you the trade. Gregori here, there is no one better at grilling *shaslik* and *kotleti* in all Harbin, in all Russia!'

4

When Harriet saw the cosy and colourful restaurant, and being equally dispirited with their cold and cheerless accommodation in the suburbs, she took to the idea of buying it almost at once. She liked the Yukhotskys. She liked the small, yellow-painted room upstairs at the back, with an American stove, where they could live while they learned the trade. She wasn't so certain of this last idea – of being chef, waitress, cashier and whatever else, alone with Yelena. But it was clear they would have to wait in Harbin for some time, perhaps months, while Sasha was found and Anna rescued.

Yes, she would buy the place. The Yukhotskys wanted the equivalent of £250 sterling for it. She had herself nearly £1500 banked in London, as she had learnt by telegraph soon after her arrival in Harbin. Given this evidence from the bank, with General Knox's letter, and pending the arrival of a banker's draft from London, the new British Consul – who had now arrived, she'd heard – would surely advance the money. She now had all the more reason for wanting to see him.

The Consul's house and offices were just down the river road from the restaurant, in the commercial quarter of the wharf district. Harriet, wrapping up well in the piercing cold which had come on again, walked down there two days later, after they had moved into the little room above the restaurant.

The Consul's offices were to the side of the large house, up some steps which led into a waiting-room with a desk. The desk was unoccupied. There was an open doorway ahead which gave onto the hall of the main house. Looking through it she saw the hall littered with cabin trunks and packing cases. Two Chinese porters were manhandling the luggage, under the petulantly shouted direction of a smallish woman – an Englishwoman, overdressed in a lace-collared blouse, navy-blue velvet skirt and jacket. She bounced about, the curls in her fashionably cut fair hair flouncing in the same measure, as the porters stuggled up the stairs, hitting the banisters. 'Idiots!' she shouted.

This must be the new Consul's wife.

Harriet, unwilling to call attention to herself, moved about the waiting-room, glancing now and then at the charades in the hall beyond. The woman saw her at last.

'Yes?' She came through the doorway.

'I would like to see the Consul. It seems, the secretary isn't –'

'Oh, that Natasha,' the woman observed dismissively. 'She should be here. So unreliable.'

The woman spoke in an over-refined Home Counties manner, an accent more developed than real, Harriet thought. She was short and rather buxom – attractive if one liked that sort of *embonpoint* form. Competent, pleased with herself, yet somehow common.

'I have an important letter for the Consul,' Harriet said. 'From General Knox, head of the British Military Mission in Siberia. May I see him? I know it may be awkward. I see you are just moving in.' The woman, eyebrows raised, held out her hand for the envelope, as if it contained a tribute to her. 'I'm afraid the matter is confidential,' Harriet said. 'I would have to give it to the Consul personally.'

'Oh?'

'Yes.'

The woman, put out by this, retaliated brusquely. 'My husband – the Consul, Captain Woodrow – is presently with the City Governor, General Horvath. He will be some time. I suggest you telephone in future, to the secretary, for an appointment.'

'Captain Woodrow?' Harriet enquired. 'Captain Sandy Woodrow, by any chance?'

'Yes. But on the Foreign Office list now. Do you know him?' The woman looked at Harriet, *de haut en bas*, even though she had to look up at her.

'Yes,' Harriet said, with just a touch of venom. 'Yes, I knew him well. Some years ago now, in St Petersburg.'

'Oh, may I ask –'

'I shall call again, Mrs Woodrow,' Harriet interrupted her. 'The matter, as I say, is of a confidential nature.' With that she turned and strode out again into the blizzard. She was shaking all over. But not from the cold.

When she got back to the restaurant and had told Yelena of the meeting, Yelena was silent at first. Then she said, 'How surprising that Sandy should marry such a common woman.'

'Yes.'

'Except I don't suppose we know it all.'

'No.'

When Harriet phoned that afternoon she spoke to the secretary. 'The Consul is engaged,' she was told. 'No, I cannot interrupt him. An appointment? Perhaps some time next week. He is very busy.'

Harriet nearly lost her temper. 'Will you please tell the Consul that I have an important letter for him, from General Knox, head of the British Military Mission, and that I am coming round to see him at once, and that I shall wait for him as long as needs be. And my name, give him my name – Miss Harriet Boulting.'

She enjoyed slamming the mouthpiece back on its hook.

'I *am* sorry.' Sandy stood up from his desk. Behind him was a rather better portrait-photograph of Edward VII than the one at the Consul's office in Omsk, but the same map of the London Metropolitan and District Railway. He came forward, taking Harriet's hand diffidently. 'These secretaries. I'm afraid they are rather taking advantage, a new man here.' He looked at her quickly, dropping her hand almost at once, looking away, busy now. 'My dear Harriet . . .' He spoke to empty space. Then he looked back at her for another instant. 'Do – do please take a seat . . .' After further fiddlings around he resumed his seat behind the desk, as if grateful for the barrier it now formed between them. 'My dear Harriet,' he said again, 'I can hardly believe it.'

'Nor I.' She was more direct in her tone, approach.

He cocked an ear to her. 'I'm afraid – you must speak up. My left ear, it's never quite recovered.'

'*Nor I*,' she said again, more distinctly, though the words seemed forced and unreal now. 'It *is* unbelievable.' She tried to smile at him, but that seemed false as well. Though there was a stove roaring nearby, and it was warm, she felt herself beginning to shake again. He noticed her discomfort. 'But your coat, of course, I should have –' He jumped up, helping her off with it, so that standing in front of him she felt somehow naked.

'Yes,' he said. 'We'll have some tea.' He thumped a bell pinger on the desk and one of the secretaries, Natasha, put her head round the door.

'May we have some tea, please?'

'With sugar – we have some. Or the raspberry jam?' Natasha asked engagingly of Sandy, before glancing sourly at Harriet.

'Sugar, please,' she told her firmly.

As Sandy conducted some further business with the secretary, Harriet had time to observe him. Dressed in a Norfolk jacket, plus-fours and stout boots, he had the air of an English squire, somewhat at sea in China. His sparse reddish hair had thinned more since she had last seen him over three years ago. Now he was almost bald on the crown of his head. But the rest was the same: the fidgety alertness, the hesitant fire behind the calm grey eyes, above all the constant air of care and concern. How on earth could he have come to marry such a vulgar woman, Harriet wondered.

'So there we are!' he said airily, when the tea arrived on a tray. He looked out of the double-glazed windows. 'What weather!' he remarked. 'Worse than anything I remember in Petersburg.'

'Yes,' Harriet said brightly. 'Of course one doesn't suffer the same sort of miserable canal mists here – I imagine.'

His eyes blinked quickly. He turned away, clearly taking the allusion she had made to their failure to meet in the all-embracing vapours of Petersburg three years before. 'No, I imagine not. Though I've only just arrived.' He looked at her again directly. But he couldn't keep it up.

'Yes, like us. We've only been here – less than a week.'

'"Us"?'

'Me. And Holly. And Yelena,' she said evenly.

He nodded at each name with a faint smile, as if the three of them were distant, importunate relatives who had arrived without warning in Harbin for the weekend.

'Indeed.' He pulled himself together. 'You and Holly and Yelena! And Sasha?' he asked.

'No, not Sasha.' He was looking at her directly now, the gaze maintained, his face twitchy, perplexed. And she saw what a great burden of emotion he was carrying – of surprise, anger, regret, longing – none of which he could express. And she felt exactly the same. All they could safely talk about was the weather and the crops. Harriet, as she passed onto more formal matters, had to make a conscious effort to stay seated, to stop herself from running out of the office, as she told him her story, and Yelena's – the whole story of the last few years.

'Well, of course,' he said, 'as regards Sasha – I can certainly use whatever influence I have to get Yelena an interview with the Governor. And as for funds, for the restaurant, I can arrange for that at once. No need to wait for your banker's draft from London.'

The interview, formal and frustrating, was coming to an end. But neither knew quite how to end it. Harriet decided to take the plunge. She stood up. 'Sandy . . .' She spoke in as casual and friendly a manner as she could. 'Your wife – when I met her – she's so pretty – I'm pleased –'

'Yes! Yes,' he interrupted at once, as if to forestall any more half-truths. 'Mary. We met at the War Office. She was in the cypher department. From Bagshot. Married just a few months ago. Before I got the posting here. Not quite what I expected, nor she. But then with my knowledge of Russia, Russian military affairs – and with Mr Sly falling ill – I suppose I was possibly – a fairly obvious choice for the position.' He rattled on, striding to and fro about the office, flapping his hands about in a way she remembered, like a man pursued by bees.

'Sandy,' Harriet brought him to a halt, with a darker and finally genuine tone. 'Sandy, if it's a strain – and it is – we don't need to meet again.'

'No,' he said at once, before he rushed on. 'No – I mean that would be a pity. I do after all represent you, as a British citizen, all your interests, here in Harbin.'

'Mine. But not Yelena's. And quite apart from me – it might not be easy, between you and Yelena.'

'Have I told my wife, you mean?'

'Well, I wondered –'

'No. No, I've told her nothing of Yelena and me. Or of you.' He looked at her now, for an instant and for the first time, with an unconcealed longing. Then he scratched his ear, putting his head to one side quizzically, gazing at his boots, like a perturbed cockerel surprised by a worm, in a manner she remembered just as well as she did his flapping hands. 'You – and me. That was the last thing I could have spoken to Mary about.'

Sandy was able to arrange an appointment for Yelena with the Governor, General Horvath, very soon after this. She went to see him in the palatial Town Hall, being shown up the broad staircase by a flunkey into a suite of even more palatial rooms which the General occupied on the first floor. Cohorts of officials with no substance but much pomp and ceremony buzzed about guarding the approaches to his office.

Inside, finally, Yelena was overwhelmed by the violet-scented 'Court Water' – such as had been used at the Tsar's Winter Palace and the Rumovsky Palace years before – by the monstrous gilded furnishings, false Second Empire, and the heavy velvet curtains at the windows which obscured most of the snowy light. The General sat in a huge, throne-like chair behind a large marquetry desk, almost bare except for many photographs of himself, in grandiose poses at public functions, although there was only one such representation of the lately deceased Tsar, a grimy portrait hidden in the shadows behind him. The message was clear. Here, in the shape of the General, was a possible new Tsar.

He rose as Yelena was shown in. He was in full dress uniform, bemedalled and gold braided, with a paunch and a long white forked beard. He was a smallish man and he looked like a toy soldier. He took her hand. His was white and clammy.

'Princess Yelena . . .' He bowed a fraction and showed her to a high-backed, damask-cushioned chair. 'I am honoured. Had I heard earlier – your name – I should have seen you before.' He fussed over her unnecessarily: affable, patriarchal but sly, Yelena thought. Tricky. Just as General Knox had said.

She recounted her story, first of Sasha's abduction by Colonel Skolimsky, then that of Anna, and the taking of the bullion from the hospital train, at the hands of some unknown Chinese warlord. 'Though of course it's my brother, Prince Alexander, who I am most concerned about.'

'Naturally.' The Governor fidgeted in his huge chair.

'And this criminal madman Skolimsky. He and my brother must have arrived here some time ago, in that sealed train from Omsk. With the secrecy of this nonsense of his being the next Tsar, I can see that few would have known of their arrival here. But you at least, General, must know where they are in Harbin.'

General Horvath blinked several times and sighed. 'Yes, Princess. The business of your brother, as a Romanov prince in line for the Imperial throne, was certainly a matter of the greatest secrecy – as was the transport of the bullion on your hospital train. And yes, as Governor, I was aware of your brother's impending arrival here with Colonel Skolimsky, just as I expected the bullion. However . . .' He cleared his throat. 'The position is this, Princess: your brother and, a few months after that, the bullion, were both taken by a *Hun-huze*, a Manchu warlord well known to us, Fu Lang-Kin –'

'You mean –' Yelena was astonished at the implications. 'You mean that my brother, and then the bullion and my friend Anna Denisovna, were all taken by this same man?'

'Yes, Princess. Fu is the most powerful of the warlords in the north. A year ago he took over an old Manchu fortress, Shanyang, as his headquarters, on a mountain top above the Hulan river. A clever man, with a formidable intelligence network, all along the Trans-Siberian line, he obviously got word that a special train, carrying a particularly important passenger, a Romanov prince, was going to pass through his "territory". Well, Fu ambushed that train, some two months before he ambushed yours –'.

'And was my brother killed?' Yelena leant forward.

'No.' The General stroked one prong of his beard. 'But abducted again, if you will, though I had heard nothing of Colonel Skolimsky's having done this originally. Fu killed most of the others on the train, including Colonel Skolimsky. But he took your brother back with him, to his fortress in the Khinghan mountains. We had word of this from Fu some weeks later – that he knew your brother was a Romanov, a possible future Tsar, and was holding him hostage, against a large ransom.'

'A ransom? How much? When has it to be paid?'

The General fidgeted again. 'Yes, the ransom – that's just one problem – a hundred thousand rubles by the end of this month.'

'So soon?'

'Indeed. But there is a more serious problem now. The whole matter is changed since Fu took the bullion. Of course we will mount an attack on his fortress, to regain it –'

'Of course – and to get my brother back. And my friend Anna.'

'There are difficulties there, Princess. Firstly we cannot mount a successful attack on Shanyang until the passes open, in the spring. And secondly . . .' He played with the other prong of his beard. 'Secondly we have since had further word from Fu that if we do attack the fortress your brother's life will be forfeit, together with that of your friend Anna Denisovna. So you see Fu is holding your brother hostage, not against any ransom money, but against our attack. He needs your brother now as a hostage against billions of rubles rather than a hundred thousand.

'I see. Except – I don't quite see. Fu could spend the rubles, but not the bullion. It's all in gold bars, isn't it?'

'Fu particularly wants the gold, though. He's obsessed by gold. His last name, "Kin", means gold in Manchu. Fu Lang-Kin: he's known as "The Sun King". His fortress up in Shanyang is like Montezuma's, practically made of gold.'

'Oh . . .'

'But you mustn's despair, Princess,' he went on unctuously. 'I've had it on the best advice from our own intelligence people in these borderlands, your brother will come to no harm, so long as the bullion is secure with Fu. So we can play for time, think out the best course of action, until spring. Besides, Fu may be open to quite other lines of approach. A political bargain. He has ambitions to re-establish the Manchu dynasty in China, to become Emperor in Pekin, to westernize the country. He has pretensions to European civilization, and a Russian mistress, a Jewess from Harbin. We shall see. I will keep you informed. Though I ask you meanwhile to keep all these matters strictly to yourself.' He stood up. 'And now, your friend Anna Denisovna – you needed to know where her friend was in Harbin. I will see to that. I'll ask one of my aides. You say his name is Commander Ivan Pavlovich Rayevsky . . .' He made a note of the name. 'We will let you know where he is.'

After she had left the General, Yelena suddenly realized that Anna, if she was still alive, might be with Sasha at that very moment, both of them held captive in Fu's mountain fortress. They would have met and discovered who the other was, learning of all their mutual connections. They would have talked of everything. And Yelena felt a spasm of hurt. She wished she had been abducted: then it might have been she who was with her brother.

'We'll have to tell Holly something of Sasha's situation, at least,' Harriet said.

'Yes.'

Gregori was having a palaver with a Russian butcher woman at a stall ahead of them in the covered market at the end of the wharf. There were Chinese and Russian stalls. A vast display of winter produce. Frozen carcasses, fowl and fish of all sorts. Bear and venison haunches, whole sides of mutton, buffalo from the south, arctic hares, ducks, ptarmigan, pheasants, powan fish, huge salmon, everything icy and frozen.

Gregori turned to them. 'This is Polenka.' He introduced them to a small, bright-eyed woman in a red kerchief with blue-frosted, calloused hands. 'The best mutton here, for the *shaslik*. And for the special Caucasian pilaff we do. You need four whole shoulders for that. And rice – I'll show you where to get it. Chung-lu's stall at the end, by the clock. And his friend Ming next to him has the best herbs and spices. All you'll ever need. Almost as good as you'd find in Tiflis.'

They walked on, up and down the aisles, pushing through mobs of early-morning traders and shoppers. The two women were greatly taken by it all. They had not seen produce like this since before the war in Petersburg. The idea of getting their hands on it, of preparing and cooking this food, appealed to them.

They found the whole idea of running the restaurant together increasingly tempting, intriguing. Creating with their hands, since they no longer played music together. And the smells . . . The red wine gravy Gregori made to go with the duck, the tart arctic bilberry sauce he made for the pheasants, the burnt sizzle of mutton on the *shaslik* grill, the grated almond he used, with candied peel and raisins, in his special Russian rice pudding. They were entering a whole new world of the senses, at the restaurant and here in the market – coursing through this sea of exotic produce.

It was all wonderful, until Yelena's heart seemed to stop for a moment. The shape she saw then, just for an instant, at the end of the aisle, running round the corner. A black shape, a small black dog. A pug dog, she thought, like Samson, and like that other, his twin, which had later come to plague her.

She swung round to Harriet. 'Did you see it?'

She spoke so urgently, her face a mask of terror, that Harriet was alarmed. 'See what? What, Linochka?'

'That black dog – over there – running round the corner.'

'No, I didn't. Why? There are lots of dogs –'

'Yes, but that one was different. It was like Samson – and the other dog, the terrible one, that came later.'

'Linochka . . . No.' Harriet put her arm on her shoulder. 'It was just a black dog.' Harriet took her hand. 'Come on back to the restaurant. We had such an early start this morning, you're tired.'

'Yes. It was just a dog, I suppose.' Yelena forced a smile now.

'Come on back – and we'll try on our new clothes.'

In their yellow-painted room, after they'd returned laden with food, with Holly downstairs helping Sofia in the kitchen, they changed their clothes. Sandy had already advanced Harriet a sum of Harbin rubles and they had been to the dress shops in New Town. They had bought skirts, blouses, jackets, stockings, underclothes, shoes, all in the post-war fashions they had never seen before, which they thought too daring or imagined they would look foolish in, but had bought all the same. They tried the clothes on properly now.

'That navy serge is lovely. And warm-looking. But the hem, it's almost up to your knees!' Yelena remarked.

'Well, they're all wearing skirts that length.' Harriet looked uncertain. 'Aren't they?'

'Yes.' Yelena looked down at her own green cord skirt, short in the same measure. 'Just – it feels a bit naked.'

'I felt the same the other day, when Sandy helped me off with my horrid old fur coat in his office. Wanting to hide myself from him.'

'The feeling of not wanting to be seen, or touched, by someone you've been close to. I know it.'

'Yes. So much for my happy ideas about me and Sandy. Ridiculously romantic . . . Why shouldn't he have married? Quite expected. He never thought to see me again. I was dead, he was sure.'

'But why marry someone like her? Or what you say of her,' Yelena added, since she hadn't seen either of them.

'Why does one marry anyone? Never really tell, what sets a person off with another. He's not a fool. He must have seen something special in her.'

'Yes. Perhaps they found out they're very good, you know – in that way.'

Harriet sighed. 'Yes, perhaps.'

'I'm sorry.'

'What about Sasha?' Harriet passed quickly on.

'What is there? I don't know. Even if we had a hundred thousand rubles. Perhaps we should both talk to Sandy about it. Would that be difficult – his seeing me again? – even though he said nothing to his wife.'

'You, we, can see him without her. It's all reasonably official, after all.'

'Ivan,' Yelena suddenly said, changing the subject. 'We'll have to try and find him this morning. This house – he may have just a flat in it – it's somewhere down here, behind the wharf.' She looked at the note which one of General Horvath's aides had delivered the previous evening. 'It's off Kitaiskaya – "Commander Ivan Rayevsky, 17 Harbour Street". Would you go? Gregori said he'd show me how to do his lake bream this morning with lemon and herbs, butter and wine and a hundred and one other things.'

'Yes, I'll go,' Harriet said.

She turned away, frowning again, settling her new clothes in the cupboard. Clothes she might well have sported with an unmarried Sandy, Yelena thought, that very evening over baked lake bream in the restaurant. She went up to Harriet and hugged her. They said nothing, until Yelena suddenly burst out 'Your clothes are lovely. And the navy skirt shows your nice long legs and I wish I had legs like that and any man would be the luckiest in the world to have you. And we can't do anything about Sandy. Or about Sasha or Anna for the time being, but we'll stuff ourselves with the baked lake-bream tonight.'

Breaking apart, Harriet smiled. Her eyes were lightly glazed with tears. 'Yes, we will,' she said.

Harriet was surprised to find how Harbour Street, beginning with Russian shops and business houses, them crossing a small canal, immediately changed its character, becoming part of the *Fudzyadyan*, the Chinese settlement by the wharf which they had seen from the railway bridge on their arrival.

The road quite changed, deteriorating into a warren of haphazard, pot-holed streets, then alleyways, with small shops, with wooden balconies overhead and wide eaves over these that nearly met across the lanes, so that it was dark and almost dry underfoot, as she pushed among the pigtailed crowds.

The air smelt of coriander and garlic from the frying pots set above little fires in front of snack restaurants. Soon she was quite lost. The Chinese man she asked directions from looked at her, in her smart new clothes, as if she came from Mars. But at last, asking directions in a larger shop that sold iron-mongery, strange hoes and spades, she found an elderly man in spectacles with yellow, emaciated skin, sitting cross-legged on top of a brick stove, smoking a long ivory pipe, with its bowl two-thirds the way down. There was a sweetish smell in the air. He looked up at her. His eyes were bright. He knew nothing of what she wanted until she mentioned the Commander's name.

'Ah,' he said slowly, speaking in pidgin Russian. 'The Navy man, Commander Ivan. He not far.' He called to a boy at the other end of the gloomy shop. 'He take you.'

It was quite far. The boy led her some distance, almost down to the river bank again, stopping at the end of a squalid lane where they faced a single, ramshackle wooden house, with a balcony and clapboard walls, in the Russian fashion. The windows were shattered, the small porch almost derelict, the hall door boarded across. It looked deserted. 'Here, Missy,' the boy said, pointing to the back of the house. She went round to the back. The boy pointed again, up some steps to a back door. 'There Navy man Captain Ivan!' he said, giggling, before running away.

She climbed the rackety steps and knocked on the door. There was no answer. But she heard voices, a baby crying, and then a man's voice, in Russian. 'Do be quiet!'

She knocked again. An attractive, clearly pregnant Chinese woman, dark hair plaited in a single thick pigtail, in a faded padded jacket and with a baby held in the crook of one arm, opened the door. She gestured Harriet inside.

Harriet entered a room which was kitchen, living-room and nursery all in one. The place smelt of old cooking, of urine – and a sweetish smell, the same as in the ironmonger's shop. Opium. Her eyes becoming accustomed to the gloom, she saw the man. He was lying on some padded quilts in the corner, leaning forward, igniting the bowl of an ivory pipe from a small brazier of charcoal beside him. He looked up at her. She came a little closer. He was wearing a flower-patterned Chinese jacket, with a beard and a shock of dark curly hair, both unkempt. He had a fine aquiline nose and prominent ears. He did look a little like Gogol.

'Yes?' he asked her.

'Commander Rayevsky?'

'Yes,' he said. His eyes had an unnatural sparkle to them.

Harriet knew she couldn't go on with it. 'I'm sorry to bother you. I got lost, quite lost. The little boy, from the ironmonger's shop – he said there was a Russian nearby, who could show me the way – back to the wharf district.'

'You're not far.' He waved a hand vaguely behind him. 'The river is just down there, behind the house. Then follow the river road down, towards the railway bridge. You can't miss that.'

'Thank you.'

He smiled vaguely. The attractive Manchu woman smiled at her, bowing her out. The baby gurgled. They all looked happy. Ivan Rayevsky had gone native.

But Anna would hardly be so happy, Harriet thought, having crossed Russia, risking her life a dozen times, only to find her lover was living with a native woman, with a child and another on the way. This betrayal would certainly justify Anna's cynicism about men. Did Ivan, Harriet wondered as she walked away, tell his beautiful concubine merry stories about Lord Nelson and Lady Hamilton? She doubted it. She thought at once that, if and when she saw Anna again, she, at least, would not tell her of what she had just seen. Anna was not entirely cynical.

Yelena was puzzled when Harriet told her of the meeting later. 'The baby was four or five months old? And she's expecting another?'

'Yes.'

'So Ivan must have taken up with her at least a year and more ago, when he came through Harbin with General Kolchak from Vladivostok on their way up to the Front.'

'Yes. He'd dropped any idea of Anna a long time ago.' Harriet looked out the back window of their little room to the yard, where some black pigs were snuffling about in the snow.

'Or else he assumed Anna was dead. The way everyone – your parents, General Knox, Sandy – assumed we were all dead.'

'All the same, Anna kept her faith in him, through thick and thin. He might have done the same.'

'Sandy didn't – to be honest about it – with you.'

'No, but it wasn't the same. I – he and I – were never lovers.'

'No, nor me and Sasha. But I've kept faith.'

'Well, you'd no need to keep it – in that way.' Harriet turned to her.

'But I've not met anyone yet, have I?' Yelena said rather petulantly.

'You met Miki.'

Yelena said nothing. Harriet looked back at the black, pot-bellied pigs. They were rooting among the restaurant scraps, she saw now. 'The point,' Harriet said more forcibly, 'is that you and I weren't in the same committed position with Sasha or Sandy. Ivan and Anna were completely attached, from what she said. Talk, jokes, bed, the lot. And he threw her over, a year and more ago, when he couldn't have been sure she'd died in the civil war.'

'Well,' Yelena said, 'Anna knew he was unreliable. That was his great charm for her, the raffishness.' She laughed drily.

'But *that* unreliable?' Harriet asked. 'The man's a scoundrel. And gone to the dogs now, like so many other White Russians here – like the ones we saw when we had tea last week in the Hotel Moderne, those drunken officers with fur-coated adventuresses. Knaves and speculators, rogues and vagabonds, the lot of them. The wonder is that Anna, with all her hard-headedness, didn't see this in Ivan long before.'

'She's practical, but romantic, too,' Yelena said. 'Remember she told you she wanted a lot of children, growing up round her like flowers.'

'Yes. She's both. And she wants both. The raffish and the rational. All the same, to misjudge someone as much as she has . . . But then I suppose one just simply doesn't know, does one?'

Harriet gazed out the window again. The pigs were fighting now over something delicious in the scraps. She turned back.

'I tell you one thing,' she said decisively. 'We won't kill those pigs like Gregori's been doing here for the pork cutlets – Holly would be heartbroken.'

'No, we won't.'

5

Gregori had been anxious to kill one of the pigs, at least, for the final celebratory dinner at The Firebird two weeks later, in early February, just before the Yukhotskys and the other two left for America. But Harriet, who had now received her money from London and had paid the Yukhotskys, managed to prevail over the excitable Georgian chef. The pigs survived. Instead the guests were served quantities of *Zakuski*, caviare, fish pilaff, salmon *shaslik* and Pekin duck. They drank vodka in many flavours and a great deal of heady Manchurian red wine, made from the grapes of the wild vines which grew in profusion on the slopes of the volcanic hills to the north of the city.

All the regular customers and friends came, some scores of them, throughout the evening. Civilian couples, groups of White Army officers and their wives, men from the business community in The Wharf, some journalists from the *Manchurian Herald*, and Kaufman, the ebullient editor of the popular *Mouthpiece* newspaper, who was life and soul of the party for most of the evening. As well there were several Orthodox priests, patrons of the establishment, most notably the missionary Archpriest Demidov, histrionic and silver-tongued, who said grace, blessed the company to begin with and then delivered a rousing homily on how only Our Lord had a last supper but that everyone in the restaurant would meet and eat together again, at some point in the future, back in Holy Mother Russia.

Afterwards there was entertainment: singing, music, dancing. Two clowns from Iazko's circus arrived, in baggy silks and false noses, pulling rabbits and American flags from their sleeves. The small balalaika orchestra played ever more furiously. Gregori did his Georgian Sword Dance – and as final surprise Lipovsky, the great Russian bass, arrived and regaled the company with soulful ballads: 'Sing, Soldier, Sing' and 'Lost in the Tall Stand of Grain', Yelena accompanying him on the piano. After that Harriet, when Misha Yukhotsky introduced and commended her and Yelena as the new owners, was persuaded to join Yelena and play a duet with her on Sasha's violin, Tchaikovsky's '*Souvenir d'un lieu cher*'.

Yet it was not the full-hearted celebration it might have been. By early January, a month before, the White Army retreat along the Trans-Siberian *trakt* and railway from Omsk had become a complete rout, one town after another falling to the 5th Red Army. Admiral Kolchak, abandoning Omsk only at the very last moment in mid-November, had been held up repeatedly on the line by the Czech Legions on his way to Irkutsk. So that by the time he eventually arrived there, in mid-January, the city had changed its political colouring. The milder Social Revolutionaries and Mensheviks had been largely supplanted by a new hard-line Bolshevik Revolutionary Committee, under Lenin's command in Moscow, who were anxious now to get their hands on Kolchak.

When the Admiral and his entourage came at last to Irkutsk station, the Czechs, who had long since fallen out with Kolchak and the Whites generally, had handed him over to the Bolshevik Committee. He and his senior officers were at once imprisoned in Irkutsk jail, across the Angara river. The White cause in Siberia was finished. There was nothing but shipwreck now for all the White ideals, and Harbin in the last month had been increasingly flooded with tens of thousands of survivors from the north, crowding out the city, defeated, desolate.

But there was a further blow to come. It came that evening, towards midnight, when a messenger arrived, spoke to the editor Kaufman and handed him a telegram. Kaufman stood up. The music stopped. 'Your Excellencies, ladies and gentlemen, I have grave news from our agent in Irkutsk. The Supreme Commander, Admiral Kolchak, together with Prime Minister Pepeliaev, were both executed at dawn this morning, by a Bolshevik firing squad near Irkutsk Gaol. Their bodies were dumped into the Angara river, through a hole in the ice.'

There were gasps of horror, cries of 'Shame!', sobs, before the Archpriest Demidov stood up, blessing the air, intoning in a high voice the prayers for the dead, 'Eternal Memory . . .' After that everyone stood up and sang the old Imperial anthem, 'Bozhe Tsarya Khrani', voices gradually louder, until they raised the roof; every sort of voice, strong, cracked, dry, throaty, underlined throughout by the great booming bass of Lipovsky. The glasses on the tables and the decorative red Volga platters on the shelves trembled. Finally Misha proposed a toast. 'Long live Mother Russia, and we true Russians, now and until we return to our true home in the future.' Glasses were raised silently. There were more tears.

It was then that Yelena saw the two men who had just come into the restaurant, standing over by the doorway. Late guests, or perhaps gatecrashers. She went over to them. Before she was halfway across the outer room she recognized one of them. He was wearing an opera cloak with red lining, over a dress suit, with starched shirt and high collar, silver-topped stick in one hand, top hat in the other. She had seen the man dressed in just the same way, soon after she'd first met him nearly six years before, when he'd come to the concert she'd given with Sasha at the Petersburg Conservatoire. It was Johnny Quince, Roly-Poly Johnny Quince. And the man with him was the mournful, cadaverous Matty, his 'quantity surveyor.'

She went up to him and it was only then that he recognized her. 'Well, I never . . . I bet you don't remember me? I'm John William Michael Quince, from Charlottesville, Virginia. And this is my good friend Matty. We've just come from *Aida* uptown. I suppose we're too late for a table?' he added off-handedly.

Johnny, she thought, out of the blue, casual, cheeky as usual. Yet harbinger, as so often before, of renewed hope. He'd hardly changed at all in the five years since she'd last seen him on the train back from Dvinsk. The same cherubic face, bright blue eyes, crinkly straw-coloured hair – that air of mischief and power. Schoolboy and dictator.

'What on earth are you doing here?' she asked coolly, her heart beating faster.

'We often eat here. The *shaslik* – best in Harbin. And you?' He looked at her more seriously now.

'God, that's a long story.'

'Mine's quite short. Been over from the States and in and out of Harbin for most of the civil war. With the US Railway Advisory Board to Russia – Colonel Stevens's crowd. Advising on the Trans-Siberian. But now we're down here, dealing with the Chinese Eastern, up and down the line between here and Manchuli on the frontier. Nothing more for us in Russia. And the war there is really all over now. Just heard the news, about the Admiral.'

'Yes. New beginnings. We've just bought the restaurant here.' She glanced behind her where the guests were still proposing last toasts, embracing each other, tearfully.

'You have? Great. The entrepreneurial spirit. I was always telling you about that.'

'Yes. That lunch at the Astoria. Your capitalist schemes, which would share the Russian wealth about better than Lenin. Didn't quite come to pass.'

'No. Poor old Mother Russia.' He fiddled with his hat for a moment, thinking. Then he looked up at her, questioningly. 'Lot of water under the bridge . . .'

'"Poor old Mother Russia", "Lot of water . . ." You and your clichés, Johnny.' She teased him without thinking, falling at once into their previous routines, that centre of their friendship which was a quality of pure fun: the jokes, the clichés, the happy mutual provocation.

'Yes, Princess.' He nodded a little wearily. 'Beloved Mother Russia. And now it's all over. The onion domes and the colour.' He looked beyond Yelena into the restaurant, where the guests were still chattering furiously, saying endless goodbyes, to each other, to the Yukhotskys, to Gregori and Sofia. 'New beginnings, yes,' he said suddenly, looking back at Yelena in a manner both tender and personal, so that she felt a burning sensation, moth to flame, brushing close to this dangerously free spirit once more.

But Matty was anxious. He had noticed this moment between them. 'Come on, Johnny, it's time we went back. We can get a snack at the Hotel. Goodnight, Princess –' He paused. 'Still – Princess Yelena Rumovsky?'

'Yes. Still the same.'

Matty looked at her with a hint of disappointment. But Johnny's face remained blithely untroubled, as if he'd known from the start she'd not married.

'Out of the blue!' Johnny said when they got back to the Orient Hotel in New Town, throwing his hat and stick down on the bed of the suite he and Matty shared on the top floor. He took off his cape, reversing it, showing the red lining, and did a bullfighter's dance with it about the room, prancing, making little feints and retreats at Matty. 'Out of the blue!'

'Yes. And bad luck to it.' Matty poured himself a glass of water from the bedside carafe.

'I told you, one day – "True to the vision, true to the end" – I'd find her again, or that we'd bump into each other, one way or another.'

'Yes, so you did.'

Johnny put down the cape. 'A real bread-and-water man, aren't you, Matty? And no jam tomorrow.'

'No. Just life isn't like that. Like a dime novel.'

'You can't deny it, it's one hell of a coincidence. How would you account for it otherwise? If we're not meant for each other?'

'That's a five-cent novel.'

'Okay.' Johnny fingered the red lining of the cape, downcast for a moment. Then he looked up brightly. 'We'll see if we can't make it a real classic, bound in red leather.' He turned away, then back, looking at Matty with a mixture of frustration and affection. 'What *would* I do without you?' He set off then, strutting about the room, putting his opera clothes away, humming the slaves' chorus from *Aida* – loudly.

'Right, Holly, up you get, behind me, between us.' Johnny, with Yelena, lifted Holly onto the toboggan a few days later. And almost immediately, red scarves flying, cheeks stinging, they were off down the icy slopes of the Sungari riverbank. It was a Sunday. There were hundreds of others out, sliding on trays and toboggans in the bright sun. Their toboggan gathered pace, slewing and bumping about, Johnny gripping the lead rope fiercely, riding the sledge like a bucking bronco, grappling with it, keeping it on an even keel, amidst shouts and roars from all of them, until they turned over in a heap at the bottom of the slope, skidding out on the ice of the river.

Afterwards they had *bliny* at one of the many stalls on the ice, the pancakes smothered in butter, which Johnny got all over his chin, taking out a huge white handkerchief before turning to the stallholder and asking for more, in Russian this time, which he spoke well now.

Apart from his proficiency with the language, everything was almost the same as before, Yelena thought, when they'd first met each other, with Sasha, on the great ice slide in the Mikhailovsky Gardens in Petrograd, so many years, it seemed, before.

They walked along the river ice, between the throngs of people, in the keen blue air, towards the latticed railway bridge, Holly running ahead of them, as Yelena continued her story, which she'd started earlier.

'Jesus, I'm sorry. Your parents and all. Going like that. And then Sasha.'

'We were luckier than most.'

'You still have that "thing" you had for your brother?' he asked easily, turning to her.

She was shocked for a moment, hearing it put this way. A year before she would have been angry. 'No,' she said. 'No, that's all changed. I just want to see him back, alive, obviously. And Anna, of course, who's up there with him.'

'Well, that mightn't be too difficult. I know the area up there, from railroad surveys. Shanyang – it's not impregnable, even in winter. A brigade of decent troops, with artillery –'

'Yes, but the whole point is that this warlord Fu doesn't want to ransom Sasha now – just to hold him hostage against any attack General Horvath makes when they go for the bullion. Fu will kill Sasha – that's the message – as soon as they see any troops or artillery.'

'Yes . . .' Then, in a sudden burst of enthusiasm, Johnny changed tack. 'But, Princess, it could work out another way. We could parley with Fu on our own, now, before there's any attack. Do a deal with him. Offer him double the money. Or something else he wanted, some European toy. I know he's crazy about things from the West.'

'Why should he bother? He's got enough gold to buy anything he wants – buy up half China. And America.'

'Every man has his price.'

'Well, even if he did, how would we get up there?'

'I have a little plane here, with the Railroad Commission, a

Curtis Jenny with a ski undercarriage for the winter. I use it for surveys and getting up and down the line quicker. It's mine – and I fly it. We could take it up there, land on the ice of the Hulan river, then get up the hills. Or even better, land on the plateau. There's a big flat tableland right in front of the fortress. I was up there at Shanyang a year ago, just before Fu took it over, to take a look at the place. I know the area pretty good.' He looked at her, smiling.

Was he tempting, bargaining with her again? Like the battle of wits and wills they'd had on his train down to Dvinsk years before, when they'd played chess? He'd lost and afterwards they'd tumbled into bed. Then, too, they'd been looking for Sasha. Ostensibly looking for him. Was this the same? – for Johnny, at least. A play, a game, to get her again. Was it disinterested help? Or was there a payment expected from her in return?

They walked up the wooden steps by the railway bridge, to the top of the riverbank, as he played with Holly, swinging her up by the arms from one step to the next, then three at a time.

'I didn't ask you, Johnny,' she called up to him. 'Why didn't you marry?'

'How do you know I'm not married?' He paused in his swinging, looking down at her.

'I know you're not. The way you talk – and look – at me.'

'Matty says I talk – and look – at every girl that way.'

Then suddenly, at the top of the steps, disappearing behind the embankment wall, she saw the black shape again, the dog, the black pug dog. But almost immediately afterwards, when they got to the top of the steps and she looked both ways, she saw nothing.

'What's the matter?' Johnny was puzzled, seeing the fear in her face.

'Nothing. I don't know. I thought I saw something.'

'Not those strange powers of yours again?'

'No. No, I hope not.'

Anna remembered Masha's talk of an earlier 'modern' present which she had received from Fu – in the shape of an unsatisfactory man, a Russian, she assumed, surly and uncommunicative. Was he still in the fortress? Or had he been dispensed with – executed even? – being unable to fulfil Masha's social and conversational needs? He would not have been brought in as a sexual stimulant for Masha, that was surely Fu's prerogative alone. Or had the man been brought to the fortress for some other, quite different reason? Anna had no idea. Anything was possible in this bizarre mountain-top court, a mix of the fiercely medieval and the very modern, a world of terracotta Manchu warriors and Ming vases, set next to cocktail cabinets and a little motor car from Shanghai.

Anna was certain only of one thing. If she was to have any chance of getting out of the fortress alive she had to collaborate with Masha, play for time, find out how the land lay, perhaps meet this other prisoner in the fortress, when they might both be rescued, since obviously the Russian authorities in Harbin would find out which of the warlords had taken the bullion and would soon mount an attack to reclaim it. Meanwhile she would talk to Masha of 'women's things'.

She found Masha easy to talk to and appreciative of her modern attitudes – how a woman should not be dependent, should support herself, what she should hope for in, how she should deal with, men. Anna's and Masha's feelings here in many ways coincided – albeit that in Masha's case they were beliefs she had come to in a much harder school. Masha told her something of her life in the days that followed.

Her parents had been poor Jews, exiled from the Ukraine in one of the Tsarist pogroms forty years before. They had made their way across Siberia to Shanghai, when her mother had died and her father had married again, to a woman who hadn't cared for her stepdaughter. She'd been packed off to what was, in effect for Masha, an orphanage in Shanghai, a Catholic convent school, where at least she'd been well educated, anxious as she had been to better herself and put her unhappy past behind her.

Later, ousted from the convent and before she was twenty, she'd taken up with Sergei, a charmingly believable Russian, a man much older than she was, before discovering he was a pimp, running a high-class brothel, where she was forced to become one of the girls of the establishment.

'It was that or being chucked out on the streets and starving,' she said to Anna, playing cards with her one afternoon. 'But I did well in the profession. My clients were among the most important men in the city. They liked me. They tipped me well. I was able to hide and save a lot of money. I knew I could run the place better than Sergei. But first I had to get rid of the brute, the pimp who'd double-crossed me from the start. It was quite simple. I paid a couple of Chinese thugs to murder him. Afterwards I took over the bordello myself. And made a *real* success of it!

'Then I met Fu. Oh, before all the wars, six years ago. He came in one evening. He was an up-and-coming *Hun-huze* then, a budding Manchu warlord. I liked him. He was different. He wanted to learn about Western things, to educate, to better himself, as I had wanted. And he wanted to do things for China, when he had real power. To re-establish the Manchu dynasty, which had died out with the child Emperor Pu-yi in 1911. But Fu would be a modern Emperor: Western ideas, industries, an end to the old ways of China, the chaos that's brought. And you know,' Masha said, leaning forward, eyes glittering, tapping the table, gold bracelets jangling, 'that's what he's close to doing now. It won't be difficult, with this bullion. He'll be able to buy new weapons, recruit more troops. He has only one rival among the warlords here – the Old Marshal, Chang Tso-Lin, on the far side of the Hulan river. When Fu wins, the whole of Manchuria will be his! Then to Pekin!

'So you see, as well as liking, loving, Fu, I came to respect him, for his ambition, his will to succeed, in his world, just as he likes me for what I've done on my own, and the fact that I won't kowtow to him. That's what keeps us together. We know how far we can go with the other. With people, if they're to get on together – it's all about knowing where the boundaries are. Isn't it, Anna?'

'Yes,' Anna said, noticing how Masha looked at her then, as if to say how these precepts applied to their relationship as much as they did between herself and Fu.

Yes, for all this apparent equality between them, it was clear to Anna that Masha had to remain in control, have the last word with her: that she was in the position of Scheherazade and must keep her patron amused – and generally informed, too, of recent events in the wider world, a place where, it was clear, Masha had not been for some time.

The routine of Anna's day was largely dictated by Masha's nights with Fu – success or failure between them in the boudoir. Success meant that Masha did not appear in the silk-screened space in the great temple hall until the afternoon. Failure meant that Anna's company was required at midday, when they took tea together and Masha, for her breakfast, ate a quantity of sugared almonds and crystallized fruits from a supplier in Harbin.

Masha's quarters with Fu were in a series of lanes and small courtyards leading off the back of the old temple – a number of low, single-storyed houses, interconnected, with overhanging eaves and a long terrace beneath. Anna had a paper-windowed room in one of these lanes, furnished with lacquered tables, inlaid bureaux, a few awkward high-back chairs, and a *kang*, a big, hard-mattressed, gold-damask canopied bed set some four feet off the ground, with a brick stove underneath. Most of the furniture was in a state of near collapse, mildewed, eaten away by termites, damp-stained, secured in places with decayed yellow tasselled ropes. Above the other stove at one end of the room, set on a shelf, were some dead-looking dwarf trees in pots – prunus, cherry and quince. An old Manchu woman ministered to her needs and kept the stoves fed with small birch logs, while a pair of Manchu guards, in their padded chainmail smocks, patrolled the lane outside all the time.

Beyond the lane lay a walled garden, lying under snow now, but with a tracing of elaborately patterned paths, box hedges, frozen rivulets and a willow-pattern bridge. The paths at least were kept clear of snow, so that Masha and Anna could take walks in the garden, both dressed in heavy fur coats, Masha leading a pair of Pekinese dogs, Anna holding her box of strong Balkan cigarettes, which Masha smoked incessantly, and a gold cigarette lighter made by Morozov in St Petersburg.

Stopping by the little bridge Anna put her hand briefly on the snowy balustrade, only to jump back in alarm. Just beneath the dusting of snow she had touched a scaly body, a narrow head and a long tail. She looked down. She had partly uncovered a lizard. It wasn't real. It was made of gold.

'Yes,' Masha explained. 'This is the "Golden Garden". Fu

made it for me. In the summer you'd see all the ornaments his goldsmiths made.'

Masha led her farther round the paths, dusting the snow off other exquisite golden garden decorations: a tiny apple tree with golden fruit, a weeping willow with a gold nightingale perched in the upper branches, a plum tree with a gold spider's web spun between the twigs, a gold wasp eating a hole in one of the gold plums. Decorating the edge of the ornamental pond were snails, snakes, frogs and butterflies on golden lily pads, all perfectly sculpted, uncovered, as if in a fairytale, from the crystal snow, glittering in the bright noonday sun.

Anna was astonished.

'Gold, you see – it doesn't rust,' Masha remarked casually before they walked on, the two Pekes yapping.

'What presents he gives you,' Anna remarked equally casually.

'Yes. Anything that occurs to him, or his goldsmiths, or anything I fancy – all in gold. So that I'm tired of it. Until quite recently Fu and I travelled – to Shanghai and Harbin. I had "modern" presents then, as he calls them. But not for a year or more now – cooped up here. I long for "modern" presents.'

This gave Anna the opportunity she had been seeking. 'Yes, I heard you both speak – of a "modern" present, when I came. A man, who was unsuitable –'

Masha turned to her quickly. 'You should not have heard that.' She was suddenly annoyed. Then she relented. 'Though, yes, you are right. He was a sort of a present. In fact Fu had other reasons . . .' She dropped this line of comment, another factor in the matter suddenly occurring to her, a more pleasing aspect of it. She looked at Anna, her heavy lidded eyes flickering, smiling. 'On the other hand, now I come to think of it, the man concerned might well have uses, from your point of view. Might appeal to you, as he didn't to me.' Anna, at first, could not quite believe what Masha was clearly getting at. 'Why so surprised?' Masha continued, seeing her puzzled look. 'I'd like you to be happy here. You may be up here some time before Fu mounts an attack on Chang Tso-lin and finally reaches Pekin. You'd be free to go then, of course. Or not, as you chose. I'd like you as a companion then, too, in Pekin. But in the meantime, if the youth pleases you, I wouldn't mind at all, so long as he didn't get in the way of our walks and talks and card games in the daytime. You could meet him and see if you like him. I'll ask Fu when he returns.'

Masha in the role of procuress now, Anna thought, proposing this casual sexual scheme. Normally she would have laughed at the idea, and refused. But she didn't now. The surly youth might have possible ideas about escape. In any case she'd like to meet him. So she thanked Masha, accepting her suggestion.

'Who is he?' she asked off-handedly.

'A Russian. Of good family, I could see.' She didn't elaborate. They walked on round the garden, talking – from Masha's point of view at least – of more interesting things: the latest women's fashions, some domestic trouble she was having with Fu.

So it was in the guise of procured and anonymous lover that Anna met Sasha the following day. He was brought to Masha's silk-screened room late in the evening, while the two women, sitting on the easy chairs, were sipping port and eating bonbons. He was surly-looking indeed, Anna saw, and unkempt. A mop of uncut, dank dark hair, black darting eyes, jaws moving, grinding his teeth, saying nothing as the two women inspected him.

'So, I have a friend for you,' Masha told him. 'If you please her.' She popped a crystallized fruit into her mouth. 'Turn about, will you.' He didn't move. She repeated her command. The guard had to force him. 'What do you think, Anna?'

Anna thought the whole situation degrading. But she looked at the youth carefully none the less, appraising him in the manner Masha expected of her. 'Yes,' she said at last, in a low voice. 'Very nice.'

'You may have him then,' Masha said, in a most audible voice. She spoke to the guard in Manchu, then to Anna. 'He'll bring him to your room later. I'll see he's properly fed. They are not well fed down in the town. You can go to him later, when we've finished our game. But be sure and be back with me at midday tomorrow. Fu is away tonight.'

When Anna went to her room half an hour later, entering past the two guards – and a red lantern which had unaccountably been posted above the doorway – she found the youth sitting at the lacquered table, over a selection of dishes, supplied by the old woman: noodles, rice, bamboo shoots, pork fritters and much else, together with a bowl of *sake*, everything untouched.

He looked up at her as she came in, discarding her fur coat and galoshes which were among the few things she had taken from the train. Underneath she wore clothes which Masha had supplied, in the Chinese manner – a pale sky-blue jacket edged in gold thread with butterfly buttons up one side and a pink silk cheongsam, embroidered with peonies, cut up to her knee.

The man said, 'If you touch me I'll kill you. I'm not some animal to be pawed over by you or your evil mistress.'

It was an interesting way to meet a man, Anna thought. She couldn't help smiling. Seeing this apparent levity, the man added, 'You little tart, if you think you're going to get me into that damn great bed –'

Anna shook her head. 'No – you've got it all wrong. I'm a prisoner here as well. They kidnapped me – Fu and his men – over two weeks ago from a hospital train, up near Manchuli. How did you get here? Who are you?' She made a few paces towards him, cautiously.

'Fu kidnapped you? And yet you're obviously a bosom friend of his mistress,' the man added ironically. 'That doesn't make sense.'

'I can explain it all . . .' Anna came a step nearer, seeing him better now in the light from the lantern over the table. She could tell from his accent that he was certainly of 'good family'. Though one couldn't have told this from much else about him. He was haggard – this lanky, hollow-cheeked man with a dark tow of wild hair, in a dirty padded Manchu jacket and coarse pantaloons. There was a look of great tiredness, yet bitter anger in his deep-set eyes; the face of a man who for a long time had lived at the end of his tether: She felt a sympathy and liking for him. She was suddenly attracted to him. 'But who are you?' she asked again, since he had remained silent. 'It's all right,' she went on. 'I'm not a tart. I promise I'm not going to touch you.' He relaxed a fraction. 'Tell me – and I'll tell you about me. And eat. Have to keep alive. And Masha says the food is terrible down in the town. Let's eat. And talk . . .'

Since he was famished Sasha grudgingly agreed. Yet he remained on his guard. He'd learnt to be suspicious of everything in the past year. This woman was a possible danger. There was something not quite right about her – being abducted by Fu and yet being such a close friend of Fu's mistress. So he would hear her out first, to see if she rang true, and lie about his own identity meanwhile, give her a false name.

Certainly she seemed straight enough and he liked the look of her. Her face, which he had thought plain in the shadowy light, he now saw, after she had approached him, to be beautiful. A contained beauty, nothing left to chance in the design: the brown eyes humorous and honest, brown hair exactly following the shape of her head – small ears, nose, lips: a model face, which appealed to him, as did the similar neatness everywhere about her body: an equally well-organized body, narrow shoulders, small breasts, all set to advantage in her neat Chinese clothes. In fact – he was attracted by her. All the more reason to be careful, he thought. Still, there was no reason not to eat with her. He was starving.

So they sat down together, Anna and Sasha. They picked up the chopsticks, began their feast of a supper, and started to tell their stories to each other, in the shadow of the great damask-covered, gold-canopied bed, with the stove sighing beneath it.

'I'm Anna Denisovna,' she said. 'From Petersburg. Though a long time ago.'

'Andrei Dmitrievich Shilovsky.' He introduced himself with an invented name. 'From Moscow – an equally long time ago.'

They smiled at each other.

'How did you get up here? Why did Fu take you?'

Sasha had started to gobble up his food, going from dish to dish, setting into the rice, the slivers of duck, the spicy sauces, bean sprouts, bamboo shoots, noodles and pork fritters – so that his mouth was still half full when he finally replied. 'I don't know. I think I was a present for his mistress.'

Anna was startled. 'In what way? Surely not *that* way?'

'No. As company, to talk to, as a European, about the big world.'

'But that's why he took me!'

'Yes, since I signally failed his mistress there.'

'I've made quite a success of it.'

'So I saw.' He looked up at her sourly, then took a gulp of *sake*, washing down his last mouthful.

'Well, what else was I to do? The alternative, I thought – well, they'll execute me. Or put me in a dungeon.'

'Yes. Like me. That's where I am. Pretty foul place. Just next to where the executioner does his work. And you're right – it's quite a regular occurrence here. Chief Executioner, a big fellow, with an even bigger scimitar. Just one flash of the blade. I saw his technique with two coolies the other day. They'd been caught secreting some gold down at the smelter.'

'How awful!'

'Thought I'd be next . . .' He tucked into some more of the Pekin duck.

'That's terrible. But how did Fu get you?'

'I was on a refugee train, from Omsk, making for Harbin, two months ago now, which he ambushed just south of Manchuli.'

'But why ambush a lot of refugees? And why take just you?'

'I don't know.' Sasha moved on to the pork fritters, drank more *sake*, giving himself time to think. 'Fu's men, they searched all through the train. They were looking for someone, who they didn't find. Then all of us, the younger men, were lined up, and Fu came down the line, looking at each of us, talking to us. And he just picked me out.' Sasha shrugged his shoulders. 'Don't know why.' He was surprised at the facility of his invention here. He started to eat again. He'd not eaten like this in years. Then he drank more *sake*. He felt in a much better humour.

'I see,' Anna said, looking at him intently. 'Yes, I suppose he liked the look of you . . . As a social "present", I mean, for his mistress. All seems a bit strange, though.'

'Yes, it is.'

'Does Fu have any more "modern presents" like you, like us, shut up in the dungeons?'

'None that I've seen. Unless the Lord High Executioner got them before I arrived.'

He smiled. Anna smiled. She liked his dry humour. She found herself staring at him, held by his gaze. 'And what about you?' he asked. 'What's your story?'

'Mine? I've been traipsing across Russia for a year or more – all sorts of adventures – from Samara to Omsk, making for Harbin like you, with two women I met in Samara. We became great friends. Until I was taken from a hospital train we were on. I'm a nurse. In fact the last four carriages were carrying half the State Gold Reserve, gold bullion. That's why Fu went for it. And I was the only woman in the last troop carriage, where I was looking after one of the officers. Fu took me – yes, as a "present" for his mistress, as it turned out – leaving all the wounded in the real hospital train, along with my two friends. They must have all got away, thank God.'

'I see . . .' They gazed at each other. Sasha's head drooped. He was dog tired. Then he pulled himself together, taking more food, more *sake*. Then he slumped again in the high-backed chair. 'Sorry, I'm exhausted.'

'Yes . . . Yes, you must be.' Anna, pulling herself together as well, became more her businesslike self. 'You look pretty tired. What a time you've had.' She stood up. 'You must stay here. Of course. That won't be a problem. I'll make it clear to Masha that you're perfectly "satisfactory" – in that way . . .'

She smiled a fraction, as he did. 'That's good of you,' he said. 'I wouldn't want to disappoint you – in that department.'

'No . . .' She looked over at the great bed. 'You can have that ghastly bed behind you. I'll sleep on the floor, these cushions.'

'In my present state you'd be quite safe to share the bed, I assure you.'

'Yes, and you with me. I'm exhausted, too. I wouldn't be much good as a tart, I'm afraid.' They nodded, believing themselves secure, in their exhaustion, from any such temptation.

In the event they were not safe at all in the large bed together. Half undressing in the shadows they lay down wide apart, and soon fell asleep, sated with food and *sake*. But in the bitter cold that came on when the stove died beneath them in the early hours of the morning, they found themselves, in their twisting sleep, nearing each other for warmth, despite the heavy damask covers.

They half woke in the darkness, only the soft light from the red lantern outside faintly illuminating their faces. They touched each other more consciously then, before suddenly clinging together, as anonymous lovers, in the sensuous, irresponsible manner of drugged half sleep. They took to each other with the keenest sort of appetite then – the lovemaking that can come with simple liking between two strangers.

When they woke she saw the dwarf cherry tree, above the other stove, had put on buds, a shower of tiny raspberry-coloured petals. The old woman brought them breakfast. Halfway through, lifting a bowl of tea, Sasha looked across at her.

'I'm sorry,' he said quietly. 'I quite misjudged you – thinking you were a great pal of Masha's, in league with her.'

'I can explain all that.'

'Yes. I simply thought, being a close friend of hers, you might be up to some trick with me. So I didn't tell you my real name. I'm not Shilovsky from Moscow. I'm Rumovsky – Alexander Rumovsky, from Petersburg – still a long time ago!' He smiled at her. 'I'm Sasha Rumovsky. I'm sorry –'

He paused, astonished at her expression. There was such surprise in it at first that this hid all the other emotions, which began to emerge immediately afterwards – disbelief, horror, embarrassment, when she closed her eyes as if she simply couldn't face the issue.

'What's the matter?' He half rose in the chair.

She opened her eyes at last. 'Everything. And nothing.' Then she smiled at him, her face showing only pleasure. 'Well, what does it matter? I have to be honest – I'd have wanted to do what we did last night anyway – even if I'd known you were Yelena's brother, and Harriet's old lover . . .'

It was Sasha's turn to look astonished.

6

'You see, Suchitsky,' General Horvath dabbed at his forked white beard, 'we can no longer have as our major concern this Prince Rumovsky up at Fu's redoubt. We must concern ourselves now, as a priority, with the bullion.'

'Yes, Governor.' General Suchitsky, Commander of the Harbin Garrison, was not so certain of the Governor's change in priorities here. The two men, in General Horvath's office, were looking at a large-scale map of northern Manchuria. Both had swagger sticks, which they had been manipulating over the map, almost fencing together with them at times, as they prodded about the mountains and rivers of this vast wilderness.

'It's perfectly clear. We have to have the bullion back, down here. Because the rest of it is gone for good, taken by the Reds at Irkutsk, from the Admiral's train before they executed him. And we need the gold in Harbin to consolidate the army, regroup, buy new weapons, so that we may counter-attack against the Reds.'

'Yes, absolutely, Governor.'

'And we need the bullion before Fu melts it all down, for those knick-knacks he has all over that Sun Palace at Shanyang. You know his habits.'

'I do.'

'So we must attack at once, now, before the passes open. What are our chances?'

They pondered the map again. 'Not good, sir. Easy enough to get a brigade or more, by train, up to here, the station at Hulan Ergi.' He pointed to a railway town some two hundred miles north-west of Harbin. 'Which gives us ready access to the Hulan river. We can sledge up the river, sixty, seventy miles or so, as far as here, this bend, before the ravine. There's a landing-stage here which Fu uses. Beyond that the river's too narrow for any sort of navigation From the pier – well, with a brigade it would be about two or three days' march up to Shanyang. Mountain track at first. But then much steeper, a path cut into the cliffs, which is the only way up in winter. Not easy . . .' General Suchitsky looked doubtful about it all. But General Horvath was not to be deterred.

'Yes, yes, General. But our troops have fought such engagements before, in the high passes, in winter. Against . . . well, these men are just bandits!'

'Our troops are somewhat demoralized at the moment, sir. And Fu and his men are something more than mere bandits. I have to say it would be difficult indeed. Fu's men would have word of our coming as soon as we went on the Hulan river. So we'd be open to attack, from the high ground, all the way along it. And an even easier target up the mountain track and the higher path. As a fighting force we would be very much depleted by the time we reached the fortress.'

'What would you do then, General?' The Governor eyed his friend carefully, smiling slightly, seeing that he would have to make a different approach now. 'By all accounts Fu has the equivalent of some fifty million sterling up at the castle. Equip a whole new army down here? You would be responsible for that – and the budget, of course . . .' The Governor licked his lips for a moment, eyeing his old comrade-in-arms.

'Yes. Yes, I see that –'

'Surely a brigade of really fine troops could be mustered? The pick of the bunch. It's worth it. And besides, we have to! You and I, after all, are now the military and civilian leaders of the White cause. The Whites – here in Manchuria, in Russia and overseas – they rely on us: to create a new army, regroup, counter-attack against the Reds. With the bullion we could do that. What do you say? We could split the bullion fifty-fifty. Half for you to equip a new army. And half for me for – for government use here in Harbin.'

'Yes. Yes, I agree.' General Suchitsky was suddenly more helpful now. 'I mean, I agree it's possible to succeed in an attack at this time of year. There's only one point, Governor – to return to this Prince Rumovsky – I understood from you that in the event of our attacking the castle Fu would execute him, this possible new Tsar.'

'Oh, we need not detain ourselves with that overmuch. It's the bullion we must have. Besides, the youth is only a distant cousin of the last Tsar. And there are some other Romanovs, overseas, to crown when we return to St Petersburg.'

'I see, yes.' General Suchitsky looked doubtful again. 'You mentioned as well, sir, last time we spoke, that his sister, the Princess Yelena Rumovsky, had recently arrived here, that you had met her. Since the Prince's life would be very much at risk, she would be disturbed to know we were about to attack Fu's fortress –'

'She need not know, General.' He turned to him, imperiously formal now. 'She must not know. Obviously the whole attack must be kept most secret.'

'Yes, Governor.' Suchitsky paused. Then he continued more enthusiastically. 'Of course, it suddenly strikes me – before, or to coincide with our sending the troops up to Shanyang, we might make another form of attack, to soften up Fu's defences at the fortress.'

'Yes, Suchitsky?' The Governor was happily alert now. 'What had you in mind?'

'Let me explain . . .'

Sandy, shocked in his meeting with Harriet, was not anxious to meet Yelena. He had indeed kept hidden from his wife all that had happened between him and the other two women in the years he had lived in St Petersburg. Latterly, he had told Mary that Harriet had been simply a distant friend, a neighbour, in the Palace next door to the British Embassy, who, in the chaos of the revolution and the civil war, he had thought dead, never expecting to see her again – this last, at least, being perfectly true.

But Mary felt he was hiding something here. She had been made suspicious from the start by Harriet's high-handed behaviour with her in their first meeting – the woman's insistence on seeing Sandy alone, on a 'confidential matter'. The woman's whole attitude suggested a closer connection with her husband than he had admitted.

So, in the light of chance sightings of the woman and having made some enquiries, she carefully prodded Sandy over dinner a week later.

'That woman who came to see you the other day in the office – Miss Boulting. I've since seen her out walking on The Wharf – with her daughter, and a friend, the Princess Yelena Rumovsky, who also lived next door to you in Petersburg, at the Rumovsky Palace.'

'Oh? Have you . . .' Sandy continued picking at his food, at the attempt which Mary had made with Hu the cook, to prepare a typically English meal.

'Yes, and I've seen them both in the covered market, out shopping for food. Did you know they've bought The Firebird restaurant down the road?'

'Yes. Yes, I did know. I advanced Miss Boulting the money for it, in fact. £250.'

'You did?' Mary feigned surprise. She knew this already. She had seen the Consular accounts, after she had made earlier enquiries. 'You must have known her very well before – to do that.'

'No, she had proven funds in London. There was no risk.'

'All the same, £250 –'

'She's a British citizen, Mary. I'm here to do exactly that sort of thing for many of them.' Sandy pondered the undercooked stew.

Mary changed tack, leaning forward, relaxing, smiling. 'Do tell me, Sandy – you're so reticent about your Petersburg days. The things you did, the people you met!' She twinkled at him.

'You must speak up, my dear. My bad ear.' He turned the other ear to her. But she knew he had heard her.

'It doesn't matter.' She retained her smile. 'I'd like to eat at The Firebird, Sandy. Can we? They say it's an excellent restaurant – and we so liked going out in London.' She spoke quite loudly, ensuring that he could not make the excuse of her being inaudible.

'Yes, we will. But for the moment, settling in, I've so much on. Later . . .' He tidied his plate, leaving much of the glutinous meat and vegetables. In other circumstances he would, indeed, have liked to eat at the restaurant.

'Dessert?' Mary said brightly. 'I've managed to show Hu how to make a good English rice pudding.' She smiled again. She knew well how Sandy liked to eat out in London, to try new restaurants. So she had further confirmation now that he was hiding something about this woman. There had been some emotional tie between them, or more – and worse. Oh yes, she knew of her husband's appetites here. They shared them. It had been such a factor in their wanting to marry, she remembered. But that he had shared these things with another woman before her, who had now come back into his life – well, that was another matter altogether. It shocked, it threatened her. He must have had a full-blown affair with this Miss Boulting, she decided. Why, it was even possible that the child, the little girl that Miss Boulting walked about with, was Sandy's child. She would keep an eye open, make further enquiries.

General Knox, in the final rout and retreat of the White armies from Omsk, and then Irkutsk, had arrived back in Harbin some days previously, at the headquarters of the British Military Mission in New Town. He had already met Sandy, who had told him everything of Harriet and Yelena's safe arrival, though General Knox had not yet met either of the women himself.

But the following day he had come down to see Sandy in his office on a matter of urgency. 'I've had word, last night, from one of my more reliable contacts at the *Stavka* here, that Horvath and Suchitsky are going to attack Fu's stronghold, to get the bullion back – now, before the passes open.'

'But the Prince – Sasha's up there, as you know.'

'Exactly, which is the problem. Fu is likely to kill him as soon as he sees any troops approaching. Fu still believes that Sasha, as a Romanov prince, is a very important figure with Horvath, as a future Tsar – although he's not. Horvath knows very well the Whites are never going to return to Petersburg now. Doesn't care a damn about Sasha. He just wants to get his hands on the bullion.'

'Sly as ever.'

'Yes. The point is, I feel responsible for Yelena and Miss Harriet. I arranged for their passage on that hospital train, gave them letters to Horvath and so on. I'm going to have to do something.'

'What?'

'I'm not sure. I've no power now to stop any such attack, and it's all top-secret. But we'll have to tell the Princess.'

'Will you tell her?' Sandy was keen not to have to.

'Can't really. Too obvious – my military connections. You must do it. And give no hint of your source. Just say you know it's true – that they'll attack in a week's time. And for her to keep mum that she heard this from you. Then she can take it up with Horvath herself. She might be able to stop him. She should know about it in any case.'

'Yes. I suppose so . . .'

Sandy wondered how to approach the matter, whether he could avoid Yelena and simply tell Harriet, asking her round to his office. But this might not be a good idea. He was well aware that Mary was now generally suspicious of his relationship with Miss Boulting. Besides, Mary helped him now in his office, with his appointments, typing, coding and deciphering messages to and from London. She would know if either Harriet or Yelena visited the office. And he would not be able to tell Mary anything of the conversation afterwards. It was top-secret. This would make her additionally suspicious. There was nothing for it. He would have to see one or other of the women himself, at the restaurant.

He went out that afternoon, putting on his fur hat and *shuba*, for it was snowing, setting off down The Wharf in the heavy slanting flakes, having told Mary he was quite out of tobacco. This was a mistake. She checked the drawer in his bureau, saw the unopened tin of St Bruno Coarse Cut, and at once set out to follow him, seeing him enter The Firebird fifteen minutes later.

Yelena was laying places for supper on the red check tablecloths when Sandy opened the first of the two glass doors, walking in out of the snow. They were having Gregori's Caucasian pilaff as the main dish that evening, Harriet cooking it in the kitchen behind, so that the outer rooms smelt delicious already, wafts of sizzling mutton and red-wine gravy redolent on the air.

They looked at each other, startled, saying nothing. Sandy blinked – his head awkwardly to one side, snow all over his coat and in his eyes. He looked like a drowned rat, Yelena thought, just as he had all those years ago when he had come in out of the rain, into Watkins's English Bookshop in Petersburg.

And now he was married. This good man who had so

wanted to marry her, whose child she had miscarried up in Lake Ladoga, when he had afterwards rescued her, but whom she'd refused a second time, unable to touch him. Looking at him now, all this flashed through her mind, so that she felt a stab of vast guilt and loss, of all that she had done and failed to do with him.

'Sandy,' she said at last, quite evenly. 'Come in, take your wet things off . . .' And again the memory, of how she had done just this, taken everything off, that first time in his Petersburg flat.

'Yelena . . .'

He looked at her, practically speechless, thinking, just as she had, of everything he had done with this woman, the love he'd had for her. A whole future life gone missing there, with Yelena, as with Harriet, who came out from the kitchen just then, wiping her hands. Two women who had meant so much to him, whom he'd thought dead in the civil war, had now come into his life again, standing in front of him, so that he was tempted by both of them once more, just as he had been in Petersburg. In all his emotional confusion then, hating one, loving the other, then *vice versa*, running between them like a madman, only finally to lose them both. What a disaster, he thought now – a disaster that he had married Mary.

Yelena came up to him, smiling warmly. 'Do take your coat off –'

'I've something important to tell you,' he interrupted her.

'You're mad,' Harriet said forcibly. 'You shouldn't even *think* of going up to the fortress in that aeroplane with Johnny.' They talked nervously later that night after the restaurant was closed. 'Landing on some mountain top, on skis! And even if you manage that, this warlord Fu, or whatever his name is, will simply keep you two as hostages as well – and kill you when the troops attack.'

'But Johnny says he has a scheme, some way he can persuade Fu to release Sasha. Not with money, a "toy" he said.'

'A toy? He really is mad. One of his mad American schemes–'

'He's not mad! He's run railways all over the place. In America. And in Russia! I've seen him – at the big junction at Gatchina in the old days – succeeding in things that no one else could have done. He has tremendous ideas, and energy, and they work. I wouldn't think of doing this with him otherwise.'

'But this isn't railways, Linochka, something he knows about. This is *Boys' Own Paper* stuff. Amateur heroics, while Fu is a warlord, quite ruthless. You saw what he did – killing so many in the ambush.'

'All right then!' Yelena looked at her fiercely. 'What else do you suggest? They're going to attack the fortress in less than a week's time. And Sasha and Anna could be dead by then. And if I had done nothing to save them – given this opportunity – how do you think I – *we* – could live with that for the rest of our lives? So I'm going to do it. I trust Johnny.'

They glared at each other, but said no more.

Yelena met Johnny in the busy lobby of the Orient Hotel next morning, telling him of Sandy's bad news. She thought he might have had second thoughts about the whole plan. He hadn't. Just the opposite. 'Good,' he said, sipping his coffee. 'That means we really have to move at once.' He glanced out of the window, where the snow, which had been falling steadily all week, was lighter now. 'And the weather's clearing. All this snow's been coming from the north. If it's easing here it should have cleared altogether up on the Hulan river. I'll get a proper forecast on the railway telegraph, what it's like up in the mountains. The US railroad Commission – we have a man at the railway town of Hulan Ergi, near the Hulan river. He knows the area and the weather up there. Could leave in a day or two.' He wiped his mouth with his big white handkerchief, turning, looking for a waiter. 'More coffee?'

'Johnny,' she said urgently. 'Is this going to work? What exactly is your plan? Fu is not someone to play games with. Even if we get up to the fortress he may just hold us as hostages as well, and kill us as soon as he sees Suchitsky's troops coming.'

'We have nearly a week before they're going to attack. That'll give me plenty of time to bargain with Fu, after I've landed the plane on the plateau next to the fortress.'

'Bargain with *what*, though?'

'Something Fu will want very much, a new "toy". I told you, he's crazy about the latest western developments.'

'What new "toy"?'

'It'll be there right in front of the fortress gates for him when we land. A golden bird, for the Sun King. He won't be able to resist it.'

'A golden bird –?'

'Yes, Princess!' He leant forward, touching her arm, his face alight. 'I mean the aeroplane, the Curtis Jenny, and I'll have it painted all gold before I leave. He'll probably never have seen an aeroplane before, let alone think he'd ever have the chance to fly one. He won't be able to resist it, I tell you!' He turned to the waiter who had just arrived. 'Some more coffee and pastries, please.'

'But Fu won't be able to fly it. It'd be no use to him.'

'Ah, but I'll fly it for him, with him in it first. Then I'll teach him.' He smiled. 'At least, I'll start to teach him. Then at some point I'll get Sasha and Anna into the plane, and we'll take off from the plateau.'

'You keep saying "I", Johnny. I'm coming too, you know.'

He looked at her, startled. 'But you were never coming, Princess. It was just me –'

'Oh, no. If you risk it, I risk it.'

'If you came there wouldn't be room for the other two. It's only a two-seater. And besides, taking off from that plateau, it's five or six thousand feet above sea level. Thin air. The engine doesn't work as efficiently at that height. And I'd need all the power I could get, taking off with Sasha and Anna. You'd endanger the whole scheme.'

'I'm coming, even if I have to walk back down the mountain. We do it together. Otherwise you needn't bother helping me at all. Besides . . .' She looked at him, wide-eyed, eyes flashing. 'I'm not heavy, nor Sasha – thin as a rake, he used to be. And Anna is a small woman. We'd all be about equal to one big man.'

Johnny nodded as she spoke. 'All be about equal to one big man?'

'Yes. We'd all about equal your weight, Johnny. You great roly-poly. So you'd better stop eating those pastries. Starve yourself a bit.'

'Yes, Princess. Yes, I'll do just that . . .'

'I'll come back,' Yelena said to Harriet, two days later, the night before they were due to leave. 'We'll all be back – me and Sasha and Anna and Johnny. Don't worry. I feel it in my bones.' Yelena did feel this. And Harriet sensed this as well. Harriet was worried none the less. 'We're not going to lose now, at the last fence,' Yelena went on. 'Besides – you remember that old fortune-teller woman up at Ladoga, she told me: I'm under the sign, I have the protection of the great wind god, Bieggolmai. Who better to see us all safe in the aeroplane – there and back?'

'Yes,' Harriet said, feeling more confident now, remembering all the old good magic in Yelena, how she had dispersed the wolves on the great lake when she was a child and had cured the local people there later. There were these extraordinary powers in Yelena, seeking the good. Harriet could not deny it. She must not deny it now. This, she thought, was the last hurdle for Yelena in her long journey to becoming a full and glorious person. And perhaps her own last obstacle as well, in making good all her flaws and failures with the twins. If she couldn't actually share the risk with Yelena, she must, at least, believe in her. 'Yes, Linochka,' she spoke more confidently still now. 'You're right. You'll be back, with Johnny and Anna. And Sasha –'

'Yes, with Sasha! And then – then we can make everything right and proper.'

By next morning the weather had cleared completely. The day was bright and sunny. But the air was still freezing, so that the snow made a crunchy sound under the car wheels as a grim-faced Matty drove them off the road and along a track towards the aerodrome. It had been built by the White Army Air Corps, a large hangar, control tower, fuel stores and buildings on the flat land on the other side of the Sungari river, beyond the railway bridge.

A Russian mechanic met them as they drew up by the hangar doors. A dashing fellow, his pidgin English was highly Americanized.

'How is she, Alexei?'

'She okay, boss. The paint – it all dry swell. She fine and all ready to go.'

Yelena looked beyond the mechanic, into the shadows of the hangar. There were some other larger aeroplanes there, and several smaller ones.

'Those big ones are Airco's – De Havilland Nines. British bombing planes the White Russian Air Corps uses,' Johnny told her. 'And the smaller ones are Sopwith Camels – fighter planes. Regular little Armada they have here.'

They stood aside as the Curtis Jenny was pushed through the doorway. When the plane came out into the bright sun Yelena had to shade her eyes. Almost every inch of it was covered in a glimmering sheen of dazzling gold.

'My God, Johnny! It's wonderful!'

Johnny smiled, then turned to Alexei. 'Gasoline strained and tank full up, okay?'

'Yes, sir, seventy gallons, through muslin, boss. And six more barrels of it waiting when you land at Hulan Ergi. And the engine – well, you saw yesterday, boss. Strong, like an eagle. Sweet.' He patted the engine cowling.

Johnny turned, looking at the wind-sock on the far side of the snowy expanse in front of them. 'Wind's steady from the south-east. Be on our tail most of the way.' He walked round the plane then, checking everything, pulling at struts, tweaking the ailerons and tail rudder, peering at the ski undercarriage, putting his fingers into odd places, inspecting the tips afterwards, smelling them. 'Good. You did all the wires and pulleys – that mix of grease with a little pure alcohol I showed you?'

'Yes, boss. She no freeze up.'

Johnny turned to Yelena. 'Inside the hangar. The flying gear. We can get togged up. There's a big fur coat, flying cap and goggles. They should fit you. Go ahead and try them on.' After she'd gone he turned to Matty, sighing – Matty, sour-faced, who had said almost nothing on the journey out to the landing field. 'Matty, we went through it all before.' He blew his nose with a big handkerchief, ruffling his straw hair. 'So there's no point in hell in looking glum about it. I've landed on snow plateaux oftentimes before. I've been flying this machine for two years without any real trouble. And in most kinds of weather. I know the machine – and the terrain – like the back of my hand. I fly it as well as I drive a locomotive –'

'Yes, Johnny, but –'

'And no, I'm never overconfident, never go beyond what I or the plane can do. That's why I'm still here. That's why I'll be back.'

'Sure, I know all that. The point is – why risk things, in this case? To put it bluntly, this isn't railroad business. You have a lot of shareholders back home, with the Philly–Reading railroad. Your father and mother . . . And Johnny,' he rushed on, 'you have a wife! Whether you like it or not, she's still your wife.'

'Just keep your voice down. We went through all that too. She ran out on me more than a year ago –'

'No matter –'

'Just shut up, Matty. Okay?' He smiled then, patting his arm. 'Let me handle it – the way I'm handling it.'

'You should have told the Princess.' Matty was stony-faced.

'I'll tell her when I get back. Besides, what are you talking about? I've not asked the Princess to marry me. Just doing her a favour in the meanwhile – before I ask her. See?' He took him by the shoulders, shook him gently. 'Nothing ventured . . . You know me.' Then he smiled, a huge smile. 'So long, partner!'

Ski-ing, skimming, straining, roaring along the crunchy snow. Yelena in the front observer's cockpit, cold tears searing across her cheeks, until she adjusted the goggles, the plane making straight for the latticework railway bridge. They surely couldn't avoid it. She crouched down in the cockpit waiting for the crash, the burst of canvas and metal all about her.

But when she looked up again, her stomach suddenly heaving, they were soaring, floating, the engine with a different tune, tiny spats of oil hitting the small windscreen in front of her, Johnny shouting something in the cockpit behind her, the horizon shifting dramatically now, tilting, sinking, disappearing, the plane rising, shaking, then suddenly veering, so that she leant away from the sheer fall beneath her, seeing the railway bridge swinging round right below as they heeled over it, turning north, the plane righting itself, surging upwards then into the wide blue sky.

Three hours later, having stopped to refuel at Hulan Ergi, they were flying north-east along the valley of the Hulan river, with the snowy peaks of the Khinghan mountains coming up ahead of them, to their left.

In the thin air the view was incredible. A long line of hazy, pearl-blue mist on the far horizon, cut by the shimmering peaks towering up into a sky that seemed an unnatural colour, a deep, then deeper violet. Beneath her the sun slanted across ravines, in a stark contrast of brilliant light and deep shadow. For Yelena it was stories from her childhood come true. A magic carpet over Baghdad. *The Phoenix and the Carpet.* Cook and the children gliding over towers and tropical isles. Yet something better than all that. A reality of feeling here, looking down, for the first time, as if at the whole masterplan of the world. And thinking 'Here I am – where I ought to be.' The world at last understood, without end, without thought of past or future. She was freer than she had ever been before.

At fifteen hundred feet they followed the course of the frozen river, broad and straight at first before it entered the foothills of the mountains and then began to twist through ever narrower ravines, the lower, snow-covered peaks of the Khinghan mountains soon coming into view.

Fifteen minutes later, having gradually risen to three thousand, then four thousand feet above the valley, Johnny banked the plane away from the river, the plane heading due north then, and still rising, levelling out at five thousand feet, heading for the first of the peaks in the distance. Flying for another ten minutes, they crossed the peak and flew over a valley, rising almost sheer on the far side to a plateau with a craggy, snowy hump set above it.

The sun was behind them now – when Yelena suddenly saw a yellow sparkle, just below the crag, and then a brilliant sunburst of light, a glitter of gold, coming up straight ahead of her on her left. A few minutes later she could distinguish the wide fortress walls from the snowy background, and a great doorway studded with points of gold. They were making straight towards the golden fortress city of Shanyang.

And then it was there, clearly in focus, when they were banking right over it, a few hundred feet above the scurrying people, alarmed, looking up at them, from the courtyards and alleyways, a plume of grey smoke, a great pagoda-roofed building, a bell-tower, a snowy garden, as they kept on banking to the left, circling round steeply, so that her stomach lurched about again, before they were dropping sharply, still turning, facing south, and then south-east, making for the plateau, heading into the wind now, straightening, dropping, the engine cutting, spluttering, falling, gliding fast just above the long flat glittering blanket of snow. Then touching, the skis skimming the surface, gently, a sudden jolting, a series of twisting bumps and punches as the skis hit into the crisply frozen snow and the plane landed, coming to a halt halfway along the plateau, the golden bird at rest on the shimmering surface, a few hundred yards from the fortress's golden gates.

Johnny helped Yelena down from the front cockpit. The great fortress doors had opened and armed men came towards them, but gingerly, afraid. 'See, we made it!' Johnny shouted. Yelena embraced him quickly. 'You did, you did . . .' Then he took out his huge white handkerchief and waved at the approaching men. 'Peace,' he shouted out in Russian. 'Peace!'

And now there was one man, they saw, emerging from all the others, striding forward eagerly, with a rolling gait, in jodhpurs and a heavy khaki jacket – Fu himself. He made straight for the golden plane – not fearfully, as his guards did, standing back with their rifles levelled, but with an admiring and proprietorial air, as if he already possessed the machine.

Close to it now, he patted the engine cowling, and got his fingertips burnt. He blew on them. Johnny looked at Yelena knowingly. Fu turned his huge head to them, smoothing the curly black ends of his moustache, his clever face touched with a half smile. 'I have heard much of these birds,' he said slowly. 'And seen them from a distance. But not like this. A marvel.' He walked up and down the fuselage, touching things more carefully now: the wing, the tail rudder, craning up and gazing into the rear cockpit, enchanted by all he saw. 'And all in gold,' he said, returning to them, looking at Johnny steadily, wary now.

'Yes, Fu Lang-Kin, all gold. A golden bird . . . And I'll give it to you,' Johnny went on in Russian, 'and I'll show you how to fly it, if we can strike a bargain. If we can talk?'

Fu, his face a mask now, nodded slowly, saying nothing. Then he held an arm out. 'Come,' he said.

Yelena and Johnny, with Fu striding ahead of them, were led

towards the fortress walls. They crossed the drawbridge over the moat. Yelena looked up at the great gold-studded doors, opening now in front of them. An enchanted castle, she thought.

Inside the walls Fu, with one of his lieutenants, led them into a small courtyard, then through a gateway set at the end of a second concealing wall, then into a large square and down the avenue towards the temple at the end. They passed the little motor car and climbed the steps, with the guards in their Manchu warrior dress, then went into the great gold hall and up the further steps at the end and into the white silk-screened 'modern' room with its gramophone and cocktail cabinet.

It was empty, the stove roaring at the far side. The room had been tidied up. Fu took a seat on one of the few Chinese pieces of furniture, a high-backed lacquered chair, then graciously gestured the other two towards the chintz armchairs.

'You spoke of a bargain?' he said when they were all seated.

'Yes,' Johnny spoke slowly. 'The gift of the gold bird, and my showing you how to fly her, in exchange for the two Russians you have here, the man and the woman.'

Fu drummed his fingers on his knee, sitting bolt upright. 'Is that all?' Johnny nodded. Fu sniffed. 'How long will it take? That I may fly the bird myself?'

'Depends on how she likes you. A few days. Or more . . .'

'You will not have the man or the woman until I can fly her.'

'All right. But can we see the two people meanwhile?'

Fu smiled. 'I am not such a fool, my friend, but to see that you might fly away with them, on the bird, before you showed me the use of it. You will be kept apart, you two, in quarters together, at the Inn of the Dragon by the gates.' He stood up. 'When will we start the teaching? Now?'

Johnny had to play for time. 'No, tomorrow, Fu. The bird must rest after her long journey.'

They were led away by an aide.

7

Anna and Sasha, in Anna's room that morning, had heard the aeroplane – then seen it from the garden, flying over the fortress. 'Who can it be?' Anna had asked, looking up at the golden machine banking steeply overhead. Then they had lost sight of it beneath the walls, hearing the engine splutter before finally cutting out as the plane landed.

'Who knows? Some madman – to bring an aeroplane up here.'

'Yes. But not Chinese. They must be European, Russian.'

'They've come from Harbin, about the bullion, no doubt,' he said. 'Perhaps to do some deal with Fu about it.'

They walked on across the snowy garden towards the little bridge and the frozen ornamental pond. 'Or could they have come about us?' Anna wondered. 'To get us out, in some way?'

'God knows. I wish we were out of here. Get to grips with real life again,' he added, without much conviction.

They had come to the pond with its gold animals crowded round the edge; the snake, the hedgehog, the snails, the big bullfrog. Anna knelt down, brushing the snow off them, displaying the splendid frog last, so that it gleamed in the sun. 'These gold animals,' she said. 'We won't believe it all afterwards, if we do get out of here.' She stroked the frog. 'I'd like to take this with me.'

'You will – I hope. Me. The Frog prince!' Then he went on equally casually, 'I'm glad I met you.'

'Me too.'

What had started as a need for warmth, an animal hunger, a simple attraction between them, had become something more. Nearly a month had gone by since their first night together. They had since talked of everything – their separate lives in St Petersburg before the revolution, the separate journeys they had made across Russia. They had talked of their relationships, their stupidities and losses there; Sasha with his sister and Harriet, Anna with her husband and Ivan. They had spoken of everything eventually.

They had squared their consciences and had come up with logical, reasonable answers for those people with whom they had commitments – Yelena and Ivan, Harriet and Holly – if and when they found themselves in the real world again. As indeed they might not. They knew well the dangers they still faced. Despite Masha's accommodating attitude towards them they were hostages. Fu would have the last word as to their lives. Theirs was a love, they thought, born and nurtured in peril, yet none the less real for that; so that they were determined to hold onto it – later, in safety, if they found that. With the arrival of the aeroplane, and some possibility of release, they talked of these things again.

'We have to remember, Sasha, we've done nothing wrong. That's the point. Neither of us is married. Yelena's your sister, and we've talked of all that – there's no future that way with her. And your relationship with Harriet is long over, which shouldn't prevent your being a good father to Holly. If and when we get out of here, we should all of us be able to look at these things like decent civilized people. And for all the mistakes we've both made in the past, this is *our* chance now.'

'Yes . . .' Sasha looked at her, silent now, thinking. 'Yes, of course,' he went on more briskly. 'Our chance. Nothing wrong. Decent, civilized people.'

The two couples were set quite apart in Shanyang. Sasha and Anna did not know who had come in the aeroplane, while Yelena and Johnny had no idea where Anna and Sasha were hidden in the maze-like fortress town. Johnny couldn't risk many take-offs and landings with Fu on the high plateau, one or two at the most. He had to play for time, knowing that they had less than a week before General Suchitsky mounted his attack, when all their lives would be at risk.

Meanwhile he and Yelena were put in a dingy, extremely primitive room in the Inn of the Dragon. Guards were posted outside the door, so they were forced together in the dusty room, with its single paper-glazed window and narrow bed covered in moulting yak hides; a room – and a bed – they realized they would have to share, unless one of them slept on the hard board floor, without any coverings.

'Now what?' Yelena asked, trying to cheer up the ancient, flat-topped brick stove which had been lit for them.

Johnny moved about the room uncertainly. 'Well, Fu's men didn't find the automatic I'm carrying strapped on the inside of my leg.'

'A gun? So what? We were never going to shoot our way out of here. What are we really going to do?'

'Play for time. I'll show Fu the workings of the plane first, cockpit controls and so on, them taxi up and down the plateau. That'll take two days. Then maybe a flight around the fortress. Another day. I have enough fuel. We filled her right up at Hulan Ergi.'

'Yes, but *then* what? – since Fu's never going to be able really to fly the plane, not in a month of Sundays.'

'No. We've got to somehow find Sasha and Anna. Then get them out of the fortress. And out into the plane –'

'Simple!'

'I'll think about it. I have to go out now, with one of the guards, to rope the plane down and cover the engine in furs against the frost. I'll have a good look round while I'm out. Maybe I'll get a lead on where they are. Then supper. Fu said at least there'd be supper here. Supper and bed. Nothing much else we can do.' Johnny left her.

Yelena crouched over the brick stove afterwards. Yes – supper and bed, there wasn't anything else for them to do. It would be dark in a few hours. Supper, yes. But bed together? No. At least not in that way.

In the event, when Johnny came back and after they'd been brought a meagre supper of rice and some thick cutlets, which might have been either yak or horsemeat, and they were preparing for bed, he saw the position the same way. 'It's okay, Princess – don't worry. I didn't come up here just to find a good excuse to make love with you. But I'll tell you one thing – I'm sure as hell not going to sleep on the floor. We're going to be in that bed together, with every bit of covering we can get, and any warmth we can make together. Otherwise we'll *freeze*.'

They slept together under the grimy yak blankets in all their clothes and furs, even their leather flying helmets with the ear-flaps, it was so cold. They passed a completely chaste night, lying crushed together in the narrow bed like two mummified aviators.

The next morning, gazing through a tear in the paper-glazed window, Johnny looked at the stone building nearby, its chimney belching smoke to one side of the large courtyard. 'Christ, a regular factory! You know what they're doing there? – melting down the Tsar's gold.' Then, taking up the fieldglasses he had brought, he swung them right round the square, to the other side, before focusing on another stone building. Men were carrying tar-paper packages out of it, he saw, and coils of thin black rope, it seemed, and what looked like a huge collection of irregular-shaped wooden garden trellises, taking them across the great square over to the high wall, the concealing wall which faced the big gates on the far side. 'I can't make out what they're doing here.' He handed the glasses to Yelena.

She watched the movements for a while, as the men set up the trellises on the wall – in all sorts of patterns, she saw now, making the outlines of pictures: a dragon, a junk, a bear, and at the centre, two ducks. It was only when the men, with ladders, began to attach the little tar-paper packages all along the outlines of these images, linking them together with the black cord, that Yelena realized what they were doing.

'I know! They're preparing a huge firework display. The black cord – it's fuse string, like they used to light all the chandelier candles at the Easter Mass in Russia. The Chinese invented fireworks. Of course! Fu's going to have a gigantic firework display!'

It didn't take Johnny long, when he had looked at the trellises with the glasses, to guess what the impending display was all about. 'It's two mandarin ducks, as the centre-piece,' He turned to Yelena. 'The symbol of eternal love out here. I bet it's Fu's birthday. Or more likely his mistress's.'

Johnny was right. It was Masha's birthday and Fu had arranged an evening of festivities for her. Fu confirmed this with Johnny when they had all gone out together later that morning, through the gates and onto the plateau, when Johnny gave Fu his first flying lesson.

He'd shown him how the ailerons and the tailplane worked, then sat him in the pilot's seat, in the rear cockpit, explaining the controls. 'Now that's the altimeter, shows you how high you are above ground. And the other big clock next to it – tells you how fast the engine is going round, revolutions per minute . . .' Fu had nodded, smiling beatifically, fingering the controls, the switches, peering at the dials – though barely understanding anything about it at all.

Later, to keep the engine in good shape, Johnny, with Fu on the throttle, had swung the propeller and started her up. Then he'd taxied, with Fu in the observer's seat, up and down the plateau. Fu was enchanted. But he didn't invite either of them to the birthday celebrations.

Back at the Inn Johnny said to Yelena, 'Well, maybe this party will give us a chance of getting to Sasha and Anna. I've been at some of these Manchu parties. They eat – and drink – till they collapse.'

'How will that help us – to get to them?'

'Several ways. Sasha and Anna – they must be somewhere up beyond the temple, that silk-screened room with all the modern furniture we were in. I know the layout of these old Manchu fortress towns. Fu's private quarters will be beyond the temple – a lot of low houses, in a series of small streets, courtyards, with a private garden beyond. They'll be somewhere up there. And if we can get up there tonight, when everyone's drinking and feasting and watching the fireworks –'

'They'll still have the guards on the door here. And we'd be seen – walking about outside, up that main street.'

'I've thought of all that. First, we can jump out of this paper window – not far from the ground. And the guards'll never hear us with the racket from the fireworks. Secondly, it'll be dark this side of the inn, away from the square. And we'll have something of a disguise. Look!' He turned to the bed, on which lay the collection of yak coverings, picking one up and draping himself with it. 'See? Most of the people here wear these crummy things, with hats of the same stuff. We can cut out hats from them as well. And then – our faces. We can shadow them, put on slanty eyebrows, the lot – from the charcoal of the candlewicks in the lanterns here. Anyway, no one will bother with us. Most of the people will be drunk by then. We can slip by them.'

'But then what? Even if we find them? How do you expect to get them out, through the locked main gate, and onto the plane – in the middle of the night?'

'I don't. Not at night. But once we find them – we'll get them out at first light.'

'How, for goodness sake?'

'You'll see. You see, there's one thing Fu values above all others – more than the aeroplane, more than all the gold in the world. His woman! His Jewish mistress.'

Fu, after his flying lesson, had gone to see Masha in the silk-screened room. As a treat, she allowed him several embraces.

'So,' she asked. 'How was your flying lesson?'

'He has showed me well. It will not be long. I shall fly the bird very soon!'

'Indeed,' she said encouragingly. 'And you will then let the man, the Russian they want in Harbin, go?'

'Of course not. I shall keep them all here, the American and his girlfriend, the Romanov prince and the woman I took for you with the bullion. All of them, as hostages against the attack they will surely make from Harbin for the bullion, when the passes open in the spring.'

'I see. Though Anna is my friend now. She, of course, will not be included in any of this hostage business.' She looked at him steadily.

'No,' he said at last. 'Not if you say so.' Then he brightened. 'The other three would be sufficient. And now, your birthday gifts?' She nodded, and Fu clicked his fingers. There were footsteps at the end of the temple. Fu pulled one of the silk screens aside, leaving a view right down the pillared hall. A procession of Manchu warriors, dressed in the old style, approached, each bearing a gift on a lacquered tray. They came forward, in slow procession, the warriors climbing the last steps before laying down Fu's gifts, an Emperor's tribute to his mistress-Queen.

Masha glanced at the trays. All together they made up a

Noah's Ark of golden animals: elephants, tigers, bears, monkeys, whole families of them, in all sizes. But the centrepiece, which even Masha stood up to inspect, was something special – two solid gold mandarin ducks, with jewels for eyes and coloured jade, emeralds and rubies for feathers, set on a mirror of water on a tray shaped as a pond, with a golden bridge and tiny gold trees all round. Jewels and mirrored gold – it sparkled magnificently as Masha picked the tray up and moved it about in the light from the paper lanterns. 'It's wonderful, Fu. Thank you.' She went over and kissed him, in genuine thanks, though she had another motive. 'Fu, there's a special favour for my birthday I'd like to ask of you – that after the public celebrations, in the square this evening, we might have a little "modern" party, up here, with Anna and her friend, the Romanov prince, and the other two who came up in the aeroplane. I'd like to meet them.' She looked at him openly, without a hint of pleading.

'But Masha, it would be unwise – their meeting.'

'Why?'

'They are all hostages. They might make plans for escape.'

'The two in the aeroplane have no idea they are hostages!'

'No. But they are. And they came for the other two.'

'Well, let them meet them, as evidence of your good intent. Besides, none of them can expect to improve their chances of escape because they are all together, here, under your eye and mine. It would give me such pleasure, a party! Like we used to have in Shanghai and Harbin, in the Orient Hotel. You remember? You enjoyed them then, and the fun you and I always had afterwards . . .' She went up to him, touched his moustache and brushed her lips against his.

'All right. I will ask this American and his girlfriend, and we will have a little "modern" party, after the festivities.' She kissed him again.

Later Anna took tea with Masha. Anna wished her a happy birthday, apologizing that she had no present.

'Your company is a sufficient present.' Masha lit a cigarette. She was in good spirits. Anna looked at the gifts all round the sofa. Then, more closely, at the mandarin ducks on the pond.

'They're beautiful – incredible!'

'Yes. Fu overdoes it, though. With these gold knick-knacks. I'd give them all away for a trip round the shops in Harbin or Shanghai.' She drew on the cigarette. 'But we don't go shopping any more.' She stood up and paced about. 'I do wish Fu would get on with his wars, so that we can get to Pekin. He only has to beat the Old Marshal up here, Chang Tso-Lin, to control most of Manchuria. But he dallies, with these gold presents for me. A glass of port-wine? To celebrate?' She poured two glasses.

Anna toasted her. 'Happy birthday!'

'How is your friend, the young gentleman? You are still finding him – satisfactory?'

'Oh, yes . . .'

The two women had an unspoken arrangement, that the 'young gentleman' should not be part of their own social life together. He was for night-time pleasure, that was all.

'Forgive me for asking,' Anna said later when, warmed by the port and encouraged by the generally festive air, she risked the question. 'I saw that little aeroplane flying over the fortress yesterday, and heard it land. I wondered who it might have been.'

Masha sipped her drink. 'Two people from Harbin. Anxious for their gold, offering some deal with Fu,' she said easily, continuing the lie since, liking Anna so well, she was not going to tell her anything of Fu's bargain with the American, or that, in the longer term, if Fu failed to fly the aeroplane and the Whites attacked the fortress, her lover's life would be forfeited.

'Nothing to do with me?' Anna enquired equally casually. 'Or the young gentleman?'

'No. They want the gold back, that's all. Besides, Anna, you will soon be out of here in any case, with me – and your gentleman friend as well, if he wishes. When spring comes and the passes open and Fu attacks Tso-Lin – and the Whites in Harbin too if needs be – well, he will win those battles, for with all this gold he can buy more weapons from the Japanese, recruit more men. He'll have the strongest army in China then. We'll be in Pekin by summer.' She smiled. 'Fu on the Emperor's throne – and me the power behind it!' She laughed now outright. Anna couldn't decide whether Masha really believed all this, or whether she just loved the idea of it all. Either way

Anna enjoyed Masha's relish of it. 'I see you doubt it?' Masha looked at Anna seriously. 'You shouldn't. Fu is of a great Manchu warrior dynasty. The Manchus were emperors of China for three hundred years, till the last of them, the child Emperor Pu-yi, was overthrown almost ten years ago. China's in chaos now. And Fu has as much right as any to be Emperor. More right – because he'll have the intelligence to set things in order. So you see, I could well be the power behind the throne.'

'Yes, I see that –'

'And I could make you – whatever you wanted. Mistress of the Bedchamber! Some Court title. Or medical work. You could run the new hospitals. You are a nurse, after all. And you have no family left in Russia.' Suddenly, seeing Masha's concerned face, Anna saw how entirely serious she was about all this. Whatever nonsense she was talking about Fu becoming Emperor, the woman genuinely liked her. It was a difficult situation. 'And your gentleman friend, as I said, he could come to Pekin as well. Russia is finished. You will neither of you ever go back there.'

'No, I suppose not. Thank you.'

Masha brightened then. 'Shall we play some cards? A bit too cold for a walk in the garden. I don't look forward to this evening's festivities in the open with Fu. I'm sorry you're not coming, but Fu – he insists that there are no foreigners present apart from me, and I must dress up in regal Manchu fashion, pretend to be his Empress. What nonsense! – the games men get up to.'

'No, I shall be perfectly happy.'

'I hope so. An evening alone with your friend. There's nothing like it!' she added enthusiastically, without a hint of prurience.

'No . . .' Anna agreed.

'But afterwards,' Masha went on in a businesslike fashion, 'Fu and I – we are having a little "modern" party for my birthday, here in my room. I would like it if you and your friend came, and I've asked the others, the two people who came in the aeroplane.'

'Yes, I'm sure we'd both love to.'

'Good.' Masha patted her arm. 'It'll be like old times.

Harbin and Shanghai.' She looked away, fingering her golden bracelets, then back at Anna. She smiled happily.

'A keen disciplinarian, Fu,' Johnny said. 'He knows how to run things – only issuing the men with *sake* now, and no *sake* for those up on the battlements.'

The celebrations started well after dusk, the square and the main street all lit up with paper lanterns. A freezing night, a starlit sky with a half-moon. Johnny and Yelena watched from the window of the Inn. Large jars of rice wine had been set up in the square. The men crowded round, taking their ration.

Behind them, down the central avenue, many of the old shops had been opened, made over as dining-rooms or offering hot snacks outside, cooked on wood-fired grills under the awnings. Soon the men, taking their *sake*, had gone down the avenue and were crowding round the food stalls and little restaurants. When they were fed – and many drunk – the procession started.

They could see most of it from the back window of the Inn. Hordes of men carrying banners, beating drums, surrounded the centrepiece, a long, snaking paper and papier-maché dragon, a beast with a huge scarlet head, yellow fangs and a rolling forked tongue, a score of undulating men inside it, just their feet visible, as the beast squirmed about, like a giant centipede, slowly approaching the square.

The noise increased – a wild shouting, roaring and drumming, with fire-crackers let off everywhere – as the dragon finally entered the square. Behind it came Fu and his mistress, carried aloft by a dozen men on two gilded palanquins, both of them dressed in regal Manchu fashion in richly coloured red and yellow robes, cut at the waist by wide scarlet cummerbunds; with elaborate headdresses, their faces heavily made up in a stark contrast of black and white, the slant of the eyebrows emphasized, cheeks dead white, faces like masks, already Emperor and Empress.

Johnny focused the field-glasses on them as they came into the brightly lit square, where the palanquins were set down on a raised dais facing the inside of the concealing wall. Then the firework display began. The fuses lit, a sudden crackling and run of fire, when one by one the patterned wooden trellises exploded in colour, to either side of the wall at first, illuminating the minor animals in this second Noah's Ark, the monkeys, bears and tigers, while Catherine wheels spun and sparkling candles exploded and *tourbillons* went off with a great whoosh and a trail of brilliant sparks and green powder, screeching high up into the night sky. Finally, the pair of mandarin ducks caught fire in a rainbow of colour, sheeny green necks and blue and red feathers.

Johnny and Yelena could hardly take their eyes away from it all. But they had to. 'Now's the moment, disguises and make-up.' Johnny started to put the yak blankets round his shoulders, the cap he'd made from the same material. But they were too late. They heard footsteps running down the corridor. The door burst open. Three of Fu's guards were there, with their carbines. They beckoned to them both, leading them downstairs, where they held them at the doorway of the Inn, waiting for the display to finish.

When it was over the guards led them to the dais. Fu, in his emperor's robes, leant down, speaking to Johnny in lordly good humour. 'Ah, there you are! My consort' – he used the Russian word, looking at Masha – 'is anxious to meet you both. You who fly the bird, and your friend. We are returning now to the Palace. She wishes that you both join us there, for a more "modern" celebration. A "party" . . . Be so good as to follow on behind us. My guards will accompany you.'

The fireworks over, the regal couple were held aloft, the procession formed again: the papier-maché dragon and the firecrackers, the drums and the gongs, and everyone, with great 'huzzahs!' and frantic timpani, went back down the avenue towards the temple, lit everywhere with tiny coloured lanterns now, the pagoda roofs glittering in the distance. The guards, to either side of Johnny and Yelena, moved them forward, following right behind Fu and his mistress. Yelena glanced at Johnny, mystified. 'A "modern" party?' she asked. He shrugged his shoulders. 'Search me.'

After passing the little motor car, the palanquins were set down in front of the temple. Fu and Masha disembarked, then walked with Johnny and Yelena up the steps, past the Manchu warrior guards into the great pillared hall. Fu went forward on his own, with several of his lieutenants, while Masha turned to them, taking off her elaborate headdress, sighing, smiling. 'I'm glad that's over.' She tossed her glossy dark hair about, freeing it. 'And I'm glad you're coming to my little party. I'm Masha.' She came towards them warmly. Johnny immediately responded in his most forthcoming American manner.

'This is the Princess Yelena Rumovsky – and I'm John William Michael Quince, from Charlottesville, Virginia. And pleased to meet you, Masha.' They shook hands, introducing themselves, all of them relaxing now, very much in a western manner.

'I'm so glad you're teaching Fu how to fly,' Masha said to Johnny, with just a hint of irony.

'Yes, he looks like being a good learner.' Johnny avoided any hint of irony in his own tone.

'Well, just give me a few minutes – to get out of these clothes . . . ' Masha led them forward, up the hall, towards the brightly lit silk-screened room at the top and showed them inside. 'I'll join you, with Fu, and my good friend – and her particular friend. Two other Russians who are . . . staying here,' she added diplomatically. 'So we can make a party of it!' Her smile was happy and anticipatory. 'Take a drink. Serve yourselves.' She pointed to the cocktail cabinet. 'I'll be with you in a minute.'

'"My good friend" – and *her* "particular friend" – what can she mean?' Yelena looked at Johnny after Masha had left.

'Well, Masha's "good friend" must be Anna. And her "particular friend" must be Sasha. What luck – to get to meet them this way.' He went over to the cocktail cabinet. 'I could do with a drink. What about you? There's gin, whisky, port.' He held up the bottles. But Yelena was thinking of something else.

'Yes,' she said, anxious now. 'One of them must be Sasha. But why would he be a "particular friend" of Anna's?'

'Well, they've been up here together quite a while, haven't they? Gin, whisky?'

Yelena didn't answer. Bemused and on tenterhooks now she started to pace the bright room, shivering though the big stove in the corner was roaring away.

Ten minutes later Fu and Masha returned, Fu in a smart

white gold-braided uniform, Russian-army style, with a Manchu sword and scabbard; Masha in dramatic and voluminous silks and satins spattered with gold ornaments. Walking behind them, coming in past the white silk screens as if making up the supporting cast of a play, were Sasha and Anna – clearly a pair, very much together, until they saw Johnny and Yelena.

Everything stopped suddenly – as the four of them looked at each other with varying degrees of awkwardness, astonishment and pleasure. Johnny, drink in hand, was pleased that he had brought brother and sister together – how he was to get Sasha and the other woman out of the fortress was another matter. He looked at the woman. He could see it – she and Sasha were clearly "particular friends".

Yelena, on the other hand, though she had expected to see Sasha and Anna, was utterly thrown when she recognized, as Johnny had, the nature of their friendship. Anna and Sasha looked even more stunned, expressions of guilty surprise frozen on their faces. Then everything moved again.

Yelena started to tremble. 'Sasha!' she managed to get the word out at last, rushing over to him, embracing him. 'Dear Sasha!' She saw Anna's face then, over his shoulder, embarrassed. 'And Anna . . .' Yelena, disengaging herself from her brother, turned to her. 'Dear Anna!' She embraced her, but less fervently, awkwardly indeed.

Yelena felt it in her bones now, what she had suspected from the start. She sensed it clearly now, all her worst fears confirmed: Sasha and Anna were lovers. So that after nearly eighteen months in abeyance all her irrational love for her brother returned – and with it jealousy, a hatred of Anna.

There was silence again, everyone except Masha thrown by this awkward turn of events. 'My goodness,' she said. 'It seems all you people know each other!'

'Yes, he's my brother.' Yelena wanted to stand next to Sasha, to confirm their old intimacy, but she couldn't. She saw that Sasha didn't want to be with her now in any intimate way, and certainly not in front of Anna.

Fu was worried by these developments. Everyone stood about awkwardly, until again Masha took charge. 'Well, so much the better – you all knowing each other. You must explain it all to me. But let's have a drink first. And music!' She went over to the horn gramophone and put a record on. The sound of 'Alexander's Ragtime Band' spread around the silk-screened spaces. Masha turned, her back against the bureau, looking at the frieze of startled, uneasy, immobile figures. 'Fu – don't just stand there; ask our guests what they'd like to have to drink.'

8

'Look! – the latest ragtime and tango records from the States. They only had them in Harbin a month ago.' Johnny, over by the gramophone, looking idly through Masha's collection, was able to talk to Yelena alone before the party got under way. 'Listen, Princess – we have to keep the party going till daylight at all costs. Another couple of hours, when I can get Masha with the gun at her back, take her down with us to the big gates and out to the plane. So tell your brother what we're doing. Dance with him, chatter, laugh. Get a real good party going. And I'll dance with your friend Anna and tell her what we're doing. We have to make things go with a real swing till dawn, else we'll have lost our last chance of getting out of here.' He turned back to her, whispering, 'Oh, and the other thing – we have to ply Fu and Masha gently with drink. But only pretend to drink ourselves. And Fu's sword – I'll have to get that away from him at some point. He'll take it off. He'll have to when he starts to dance.'

Johnny threw himself into the party spirit. Sinking another heavily watered whisky, with the ragtime music blaring, he went up to Masha in his most provocative manner, took her by the hands and started a racy jitterbug with her. 'Yes! The latest craze,' he shouted, 'back home in the States!' Wreathed in smiles, feet flying, throwing himself about, he showed Masha the dance. Silk skirts swishing, bangles jangling, she took to him at once, enchanted by his attentions thereafter.

Later she persuaded Fu to dance with Anna – when he had to take his Manchu sword and scabbard off, leaving it on the sofa cushions – which left Sasha alone with Yelena for the first time. They didn't dance together. He held an untouched glass of whisky awkwardly. She said to him, without rancour but with deadly irony, 'You and Anna – who could have thought it? – your ending up with her . . .'

He saw no point in denying his sister's correct intuitions. Just the opposite – he saw the opportunity of getting things straight with Yelena from the start. 'I've not "ended up" with Anna. We've hardly begun.'

'You might have waited.'

'For what, Linochka? That side of things between us is over. Has to be. Anna's told me of your journey across Siberia. The miracle is that you've all survived. And that I have – so far. So that's what we have to concentrate on now – surviving, getting out of here. What's the position? Why did you and Johnny come up here?

Yelena explained the situation briefly – the bargain Johnny had struck with Fu for their release, the impending attack on the fortress by General Suchitsky's troops.

'But Fu's never going to learn to fly in a few days,' Sasha commented.

'No. But Johnny has a gun with him. They don't know about it.' She told him of Johnny's plan with Masha.

'That's a mad idea. Fu has armed guards everywhere. He'd never make it. We'd all be killed if we touch his mistress. He's crazy about her.'

'That's just the point. They won't shoot, if we have Masha. Besides, Fu has the bullion, and Johnny's banking on the fact that that's all he really wants to keep. So listen –' She clutched him by the shoulder. 'We have to keep the party going till dawn. So dance with me, Sasha, for God's sake, and make things go with a swing.' She propelled him forward, forcing him to dance to the ragtime music. 'And smile, Sasha, *smile*! Make it look like you're having a wonderful time. Our lives depend on it.'

She forced him round the floor, beneath the bright hanging lanterns, the roar of the big stove behind them, the two of them bumping into the others, so that soon they were sweating. It wasn't easy for Yelena, holding Sasha, smelling the vague honey-and-oatmeal smell of his body, for the first time in years. It was painful.

Later Sasha danced with Anna. 'Linochka – she knows about us already, doesn't she?' Anna said. 'The way she looked at us.'

'Yes. I more or less told her anyway. But the real problem is Masha. Johnny Quince is going to take her with a gun. He told you?'

'Yes. And Fu will go off his head.'

'That's what I said. But what else is there?' He looked at Anna. Her face was pale, despite the heat, her brown eyes alarmed, loving. 'Yes, I know,' he went on. 'We could both be dead in an hour. But that's been true many times, for both of us, in the past year.'

'Yes. But not since we met each other.'

They danced on, before Sasha said lightly, 'I wonder, if we're not here in an hour, what sort of life we might have had together?'

'There's no answer to that,' Anna said, less lightly. 'All in the working out of it.' Then she shuddered for a moment before looking at him intently. 'But let's assume it would have been a good life. And if this is all there's going to be of it, well – you are much loved.'

'You, too.'

They kissed, without caring who saw them.

Yelena saw. It increased her feelings of turmoil – of envy and frustration. She, too, was well aware that this might be the last time she would be with Sasha. This could be the end of the long road for both of them – starting in the womb, with all their subsequent attachments and divisions. Having barely met him again, they might be lost to each other for ever in an hour or so.

This could be the last chance she would have to make things right and proper between them, to fulfil her better nature with him, all that learning about life she had come to with Harriet over the past year.

And yet, having danced with him, been in his arms, smelt that special odour of his, she knew all this good sense was gone in her. She wanted him once more, in every way, wanted him to herself, in love and music – and she would have him.

When she danced with him again she said, 'The last time we danced together was that evening at the Countess Shouvalov's ball . . .' She let the memory slide away nonchalantly.

'I was never much good at dancing.'

'You weren't bad. Not so good as Miki.'

'I wonder what happened to him.'

'I'll tell you later.'

'May not be a later. So all that counts is getting out of here safely. The rest – all that rubbish between you and me – it's of no consequence.'

This was an error. His last words were too obviously insensitive, too harsh.

'Damn you, Sasha,' she said to him quietly. 'I wish you were dead.'

She stopped in the middle of the dance and walked away from him.

Later still Johnny danced with Yelena. She was still in a fury, and he knew why. 'Come on, Princess, forget your old problems with your brother. You should have other things on your mind, like our getting out of here –'

'Oh, we'll get out all right. I'll see to that.' For the first time in years, born of a bitter fury, she felt a rising well of fire, a sure sense of all her old powers returning.

'Good,' Johnny said. 'That's the way to look at things. Now listen,' he went on, 'I want you to tell Anna and Sasha to dance between the sofa and the other two, Fu and Masha. I'm going to get rid of that sword . . .'

A few minutes later Johnny collapsed on the sofa, laughing, pretending exhaustion, mopping his brow with his huge handkerchief. Fu and Masha, dancing on the far side, were shielded from him by the other couple. He was half sitting on Fu's sword. He slipped it out of the scabbard quickly and hid it under the sofa, covering the top of the scabbard with a cushion.

In a break afterwards he chattered with everyone, plied Fu and Masha with whisky, regaled them with a stream of witty remarks and stories. His sense of fun was so infectious they would have had little trouble in prolonging the party until midday.

But the tension rose among the others as dawn approached, all of them knowing his plans, Johnny confirming them with Anna when he danced with her. 'When I make my move on Masha – and you'll know because I'll do a sort of fandango step towards her, get behind her and take the gun out – then keep in a complete circle around me and her as we walk out of here. That way they can't shoot at us from any direction without risk of hitting Masha. Though I hope to persuade Fu just to behave as if we're all friends, and that he's showing us back to the plane.'

'That plane you have – Yelena says it only has two seats. How can we all get in?'

'Squeeze,' he told her shortly, smiling. Anna looked at this extraordinary man. Of course, he must be the American Yelena had told her about, one of her lovers years before in Petersburg. 'Say, I'm going to have another dance with Masha. Daylight's not far away. Why don't you dance with Sasha again?'

Johnny turned away and moved towards the gramophone where the record had come to an end. Anna went after him. 'One thing. I'm fond of Masha. She's not a bad woman. You're not really going to kill her, are you?'

'I hope not. But I will if I have to.'

Ten minutes later, stretching his legs in the pillared hall of the temple, Johnny saw the dawn light shining through the clerestory windows high above him, a soft pearl-pink sky emerging from the night. In half an hour the sun would have risen completely on another bright frosty day. It was time to go.

He was only just in time when he returned to the others. Fu and Masha, both happily befuddled now with drink, were keen to make for bed, Fu about to call the guards to take Johnny and Yelena back to the Inn. 'Just one last turn, Masha!' Johnny put the tango record on again and danced towards her, arms on high, clicking his fingers. The other three, seeing this sign of impending action, tensed. Johnny circled round Masha provocatively, feet stamping, head arched back, every inch the cold suave gigolo. Masha couldn't resist him.

He circled her once as she prepared herself for him, tossing her head back proudly, shoulders shivering, eyes flashing, gold bracelets jangling, almost every inch the Carmen. Johnny circled her a second time, then suddenly stopped halfway round. He took the gun from his pocket and prodded it gently into her back. It tickled her.

'What are you doing to me, Johnny?' She wriggled suggestively.

'It's a gun, Masha.' He had to shout above the music. 'And it won't do anything to you if you do exactly as I say.'

Fu, his smart dress uniform now somewhat dishevelled, and expecting to leave, was standing over the far side of the screened space, near a gap which led to their quarters. At first, not seeing the gun, he thought Johnny was about to show his mistress some new steps. 'Masha,' he said. 'It's dawn. We must go –' Then he saw the gun pressed into Masha's back.

His reaction was instantaneous. He made a leap towards them, in a sudden bound of extraordinary animal energy, aiming to rush them before Johnny had a chance of doing anything. And he would have made it but for his tipsy condition. Instead, misjudging the distance in his sudden career towards them, he collided with the arm of the sofa, then tripped on the ruffled carpet beneath it, landing flat on his face.

This gave the other three the time they needed to gather round the couple, forming a protective circle. Fu stood up, staggering, dazed for a moment, looking wildly about for his rope-handled Manchu sword. He saw the scabbard poking out from among the sofa cushions, and went for it. But taking it up he found only the empty sheath.

'No, Fu.' Johnny had to shout over the tango music. 'The sword is gone. Just do as I say. Do anything foolish – and you and Masha will both be dead.'

Fu, holding the empty scabbard, was mad with fury. He made another move towards them. 'Don't, Fu,' Masha said. 'Do whatever he says. And let them go. We have the bullion. That's all that matters. Besides, there's no point – in spoiling the party . . .' She turned to Johnny, with a half smile, breathing heavily. 'Pity. You dance so well.' Then she looked at Anna less appreciatively. 'I'm surprised at you, though. I thought we had a future together, you and me, in Pekin.'

The record came to an end. 'Right, Fu.' Johnny's voice was loud in the silence. 'Over here, just in front of Masha.' Fu came over unwillingly and stood in front of her. 'Now here's what we're going to do. We're going to all leave here and walk down the avenue the best of friends, chattering, laughing. And before that, Fu, you'll have these sliding doors open at the end of the temple, with the guards outside, and you'll walk straight past them, not looking to left or right, quite casually, because you're showing us all out, leading us back to the gold bird. So when you get to the big main gates, you'll have them opened, and we'll all move out onto the plateau, where you'll come right up to the bird, to see us off, both of you. But if you make a wrong move, I'll have the gun in Masha's side, all the time. And your back, Fu, will only be a few feet in front of me. So let's move. And don't forget – everyone – chatter and laughter.' Fu started to strap on his scabbard belt, preparing to leave. 'You won't need that, Fu. It's empty and it's going to stay that way.'

'It's part of his dress uniform,' Masha said. 'He'll feel naked without it.'

'Okay.'

Fu strapped the belt on.

Johnny changed his mood then, his tone bright and cheerful. 'Say, that was a great party, thanks!' He spoke brightly to Masha. They started off, leaving the silk-screened space, and walked down the great temple hall with its pillars of hammered gold leaf. Fu opened one of the filigree wooden doors at the end and they went out, past the Manchu warrior guards, down the steps and into the clear morning light. The little motor car, parked directly ahead of them, covered in hoar frost, glittered in the bright sun that had risen over the fortress walls. Crossing the temple courtyard, they walked towards the avenue leading to the great square and the concealing wall at the other end.

At first there was almost nobody to be seen. But soon, with news of this strange procession, the avenue, to either side, began to fill up with Fu's bleary-eyed pigtailed troops – stumbling out from the narrow alleys, the small shops and restaurants, gathering in lines along the processional way, a few thin grey plumes of smoke from the house stoves rising in the crystal air.

The troops, the old women, the younger women camp followers, were at first simply intrigued with some of Fu's lieutenants joining the crowd now. Fu, walking a little ahead of the group while the others behind him chattered and laughed, made no untoward move or gesture. Yet halfway down the avenue one of Fu's officers, standing outside the old theatre with its gong, and peering at them closely, shouted out something after they'd passed. Almost at once there was a rising murmur of surprise and alarm from the troops behind them, who had gathered now in groups and were following the procession. The lieutenant shouted again. Johnny didn't understand the words. But Masha did.

'The Commander has no sword!' 'No sword?' 'No sword!' The cries were taken up by all the men as the news spread. 'The foreigners are taking him!'

Johnny heard the quickening steps of the men behind them. They all turned. The troops, in their padded jackets, some with their own swords out, were breaking into a run. The high concealing wall, with its remnants of firework trellises, and gateway to one side, was some hundred yards ahead of them across the square. 'Run!' Johnny shouted. 'Run!'

They ran, Johnny pushing Fu ahead of them, the mob at their heels, their feet clattering over the cobbles, veering off to the right then, making for the open gateway at the end of the concealing wall. A rifle cracked, and then a second, the bullets whining over their heads as they zigzagged across the square. Then Masha stumbled. And it was Anna who stopped to pick her up. 'Wait!' she shouted to the others ahead of her.

'Leave her! We have Fu,' Johnny shouted back.

But Anna wouldn't. Johnny had to turn, firing off several shots from his automatic at their pursuers, so that the troops, ducking, paused in their chase, giving Anna, and Sasha who had returned to help her, time to get Masha to her feet, to turn and run on. They made the gateway in the concealing wall some fifty yards ahead of Fu's troops, slamming the two big wooden doors behind them. But now they found they had no way of securing them, since the doors could only be locked from the other side by setting two big wooden crossbars into brackets.

They threw themselves against the doors instead as Johnny looked wildly around for something heavier to put against them. They were now in the smaller front courtyard leading to the main gates fifty yards away. There was no one about. But the battlements were manned with two machine-guns, at either side of the great gates, several men tending each of them. Seeing what was happening behind them they started to move the guns on their heavy tripods, so that they would face back into the smaller square. In a minute they would be under attack from both sides.

'Those carts!' Johnny saw the two heavy, high-wheeled carts parked farther along the wall. 'I'll try and wheel them.' He had his back to the doors, with Sasha and the two women pushing against them for all they were worth, the troops shoving behind them. If either man left to fetch the carts the doors would give way. It would be the end. It looked like the end anyway, Johnny thought, seeing the machine-gunners manoeuvring the guns to face them.

Then, above the shouts of the troops, they heard the drone of engines, the roaring throb of aero engines, the sounds approaching them quickly from the south out of the pale blue sky, the aeroplanes still invisible behind the high walls.

Fu, looking upwards, turned to Johnny. 'Your golden bird,' he said happily. 'Someone has taken it. You will not escape now. You will pay for your impudence!'

Johnny, straining to keep the gates shut, gasped out: 'No, Fu. Not my bird. Those are bigger, more dangerous birds and –'

Looking up then Johnny saw the first of the bombers coming straight towards the gates, about a hundred feet above them, with another behind it: two of the big single-engined De Havilland Nines with their open, rectangular radiators from the White Russian Air Corps at Harbin. The first bomb hit the wide battlements near the machine-gun nest to the east of the gates, knocking the men and the gun out completely. The second plane ran on, over the concealing wall, dropping its bomb on the large square behind, in the middle of Fu's troops, it seemed, all gathered there, crushed together, for there were cries of alarm, the shouts of wounded people. And suddenly there was not the same pressure on the doors.

'Quick! Before they circle round and come back at us – the carts. Sasha, help me with the carts.' Johnny and Sasha left the doors, running to the carts, each getting a wheel and turning it, pushing it furiously back towards the gates, where they wedged it against the wood. They returned for the other cart, wheeling it forward, ramming it against the other door in the gateway. This, at least, was secure.

But now they had to face the bombers again, and the second machine-gun, still untouched. The men beside it were uncertain now whether they should aim down into the yard or up at the bombers. The planes had circled the fortress and were making a second run in from the south, approaching the main gates again. Fu started to shout at the men beside the machine-gun. 'Shut up, Fu,' Johnny told him. 'They can't help you now. Those bombers are coming in again. Take cover, all of you, run, over to the main walls there.'

They saw the planes clearly as they ran across the courtyard – and the black cylinders with their white tail fins fall from beneath both planes some way out from the huge gates. There were two tremendous explosions as the bombs hit the ground, obviously just in front of the gates, for the great wooden doors shook and splintered, leaving a gaping hole at the bottom of one of them. The bombers flashed over their heads.

Now they had an exit. But it was a risky one. The second machine-gun, if they went out onto the plateau, would have an easy target, could pick them off as they ran to the Curtis Jenny. They stood transfixed for a moment in the middle of the courtyard, before the bombers droned away to the north and there was almost silence.

But before they ran on to the cover of the main walls they heard the sharper clattering tone of another lighter engine, coming towards them from the east, out of the rising sun.

Then they saw it. It was one of the smaller biplanes they kept at Harbin, Johnny saw, a Sopwith Camel with its nose-mounted machine-gun which fired through the propeller. It was making straight for them in a shallow dive. They saw the flash of fire and heard the 'rat-tat-tat' of the gun a moment later, then saw the bullets, coming in a line towards them, taking chips out of the cobbles.

'Run!' Johnny shouted. 'And separate, don't bunch together. Run, to the big wall!'

The six of them scattered. The bullets, kicking up spats of snow and stone chips, passed over the ground where they'd been standing. The Sopwith passed so close over their heads they could feel its turbulence, before it climbed steeply over the walls on the other side. They sprinted across the yard; Fu, with Johnny, Anna and Masha, making for one side of the main gates; Sasha and Yelena running for the other.

But they had not allowed for the sudden return of one of the bombers, coming at them again from the south. Sasha and Yelena, separated now from the others and over halfway across the yard, heard the roar of the engines approaching them. They ran now for all they were worth towards the cover of the wall. The bomber roared directly over their heads. The bomb exploded a second later, landing inside the courtyard, not far behind Sasha, who was trailing Yelena. He was picked up like a feather by the blast and thrown forward, landing on the snow-covered cobbles, just a few yards from where Yelena had fallen, hitting the ground as soon as she'd heard the engines.

The bomber disappeared to the north. Yelena got to her feet and ran back. Sasha was lying on his side. He seemed unharmed. There was no blood anywhere, or twisted limbs. His padded Manchu jacket was torn and blackened at the back. There was a small graze on his forehead. Yet he lay there, absolutely still, eyes closed, deathly pale, with no sign of life. Yelena's worst fears were realized. She had wished him dead an hour before. And now he was dead.

'Sasha!' she shouted. 'Sasha? Are you all right?' She bent over him, putting an ear to his chest. She heard nothing. She looked across the courtyard to where the others had gained the safety of the great walls, sheltering right beneath them. 'Johnny, help me. Help me pull him back!' She was some way out from the cover of the walls.

But Johnny couldn't help her then. And she saw why. Looking round at the smaller gateway in the concealing wall, she saw how Fu's men behind it were gradually breaking it down from the other side, hammering, pushing at it with some improvized battering ram, so that both the carts were slipping forwards. Johnny, having seen the same thing, automatic in hand, was climbing the narrow stone steps cut into the walls, making for the second machine-gun nest on the battlements. The two gunners, unaware that Johnny was coming up the steps behind them, were firing away, in bursts, at the bombers disappearing to the north, and then at the Sopwith, which was still with them.

Yelena looked up. The smaller plane was making straight towards her again. Gripping Sasha beneath his armpits, she tugged him violently across the cobbles towards the shelter of the wall. The flash of fire came again from the nose of the Sopwith. The 'rat-tat-tat' of the bullets spattering over the cobbles towards her. She pulled Sasha out of the way just in time again.

Johnny by now had climbed to a position just below the top of the wall. The two machine-gunners, firing at the disappearing Sopwith, were right in front of him. He shot them, one after the other, very quickly. Then he was up on the battlements, swinging the Vickers round on its heavy tripod, adjusting the ammunition belt, aiming the gun at the concealing wall where the doors were just about to give way. With a final splintering the carts overturned and Fu's troops, armed now with their carbines, piled through the opening.

Johnny opened fire with the Vickers. The hammer rattled. The ammunition belt, feeding through the breech, stammered. Crushed together as they ran through the gateway, half a dozen of Fu's men fell in the first burst, the same number in the second. The others, letting off a few random shots at Johnny, retreated behind the concealing wall.

There was silence again. The bombers droned away southwards. The higher engine note of the Sopwith faded. Johnny shouted down to where Anna, with Fu and Masha, were crouching at the bottom of the main wall. 'Anna! Get over and see if you can help Yelena. Get Sasha up and take him out of the big gates and over towards my plane. Quick, before Fu's men regroup and come again through the other gate. I'll keep you covered till you get across!'

In all this time Fu had been concerned only to protect Masha. But now with Johnny busy with the machine-gun, high above them, out of sight, and the bombing apparently over, Fu took his chance. He grabbed Anna from behind as she was about to move off, taking her in a stranglehold, one arm round her neck, the other gripping her wrist. He stayed in the shadow of the wall where Johnny couldn't see him, then shouted up at him. 'I have your friend by the throat. Leave the machine-gun. If you fire again, or come at me with your own gun, the woman will be dead.'

Anna couldn't begin to struggle. Fu had the inner edge of his wrist pressed fiercely against her windpipe. She could hardly breathe. Johnny heard the message. He left the machine-gun and leant over the battlements. He could just see the three of them, round a bulge in the wall, forty feet below. But he couldn't risk a shot at Fu with Anna and Masha so near. He looked up across the courtyard. Fu's troops, regrouped on the other side of the concealing wall, had started to fire at him again, more purposefully now, from either side of the smashed gateway, with some of them on top of the wall doing the same. A bullet ricocheted off the stone just to his right. Another whined over his head. He had little cover and less time to decide what to do.

Yelena, without help now, was still crouching over Sasha, beneath the wall on the far side of the main gates. She looked at his face, lolling over to one side. She set it straight, holding it upright in both hands. He wasn't breathing. His breath was gone. She had wished him dead not an hour before just as she had wished her uncle Dmitri and her brother Ivan dead, and Harriet, years before. And now he was dead. Her awful powers had returned, she knew, and she was suddenly stricken by them. But if she could kill by a wish, she could cure by a touch, she remembered. So she would give Sasha her own breath now. She would breathe back life into him.

She bent over and put her whole mouth to his, sealed her lips against his lips with a firm tight pressure. She started to breathe into him, pausing each time between long steady breaths. She tasted the taste in his mouth, felt his tongue, his teeth. She drew away, gulping air, then put her mouth back on his, repeating the process, propelling her breath, her whole spirit, into him.

She felt his chest rise slightly each time beneath her, muttering to herself in the moments apart, 'Make him live! *Make* him live.' Then back to his mouth again, in a fierce sort of frenzied kissing now, blowing, filling his lungs with air. 'Let him live . . .' Unaware of everything around her she concentrated every thought, every fibre of her body, on her brother.

After several minutes he stirred. His head twitched. He avoided her mouth when she put it on his again. Then suddenly he began to push forward, gasping. She lifted his head and shoulders off the ground, pulling him forward. His eyes were half open. Then he was sick, a spume of gummy mucus and vomit pouring over her as she held him. He was alive.

She looked up. Fu's troops, to either side of the gateway and on the top of the concealing wall, were firing at Johnny on the battlements. A bullet hit the wall right behind her. They were firing at her and Sasha as well. Sasha was alive. But there was every good chance that they would both be truly dead in a minute or so.

It was Masha who broke the impasse, still with Fu and Anna on the other side of the main gates. Anna, she saw, in Fu's grip, was close to death. Her eyes protruded. Her face was a livid colour. Masha was suddenly firm with Fu. 'Fu,' she said calmly. 'Let her go. It's no "modern" thing to kill an unarmed woman. Besides, she went back for me when I fell. Risked her life. Let her go.'

'Let her go?' Fu's eyes were wild. The veins stood out on his face, red with fury. His broad head swung from side to side, a bull enraged. Ever since Johnny had taken Masha he had had to suppress his old barbaric nature. But now he could give it full rein. 'Let her go? So that your American friend up there may continue to massacre all my men? – and then kill us?'

'He does that simply because you won't let them go.' Masha went to him, her deep hooded eyes gazing at him intently. 'Let the whole business with these people be finished with, Fu. You and your men have much more important things to do here now. Repair the gates. Replace the machine-guns. Get your troops in proper order. Don't you see? These aeroplanes with their bombs are just the start of a White Army attack, with troops from Harbin any moment now. If you don't get things in order here, you'll lose the gold bullion. And with it the chance of winning your battles with Chang Tso-Lin and the throne in Pekin. You'll lose everything just for the sake of these few people.'

'They are hostages. He's a Romanov prince –'

'The Whites don't care a damn about them, Fu. They're never going to get back to Petersburg now. But they care about the bullion. And they'll mount an attack for it at any minute.'

'The Whites won't attack in midwinter with all the passes closed.' Fu tightened his grip about Anna's neck. 'We have plenty of time for repairs.'

Masha was suddenly incensed. 'Let her go, Fu. Else you'll never touch me again.' Her tone was ominous, and Fu knew the validity of her threat. But he took no notice of her. It seemed indeed as if he might strike Masha with his free arm, his head moving dangerously again.

Masha stood her ground, quite unafraid. 'Fu, let them all go. Show me, show them, everyone, how you are an entirely "modern" man.'

The firing had stopped for a moment. There was silence. Fu dropped his wrist from Anna's throat. She coughed violently, gasping for air. Masha said to Fu, 'Now tell the American what you're going to do. Then go over to the wall and order your men to stop firing.'

The firing started again. Fu didn't move. He was doubtful once more. Masha came close to him and put her hand on his chest, her gold bracelets jangling. Then she smiled, looking at him proudly, the proud mistress of a great man. 'Yes, Fu, do it. Finish with it. It's the sensible thing to do.'

Seeing Masha's smile, Fu's expression changed. He looked at her now with that admiration and gratitude which he had shown her before, in return for the smallest evidence of her favour. He nodded, then walked out from the shadow of the wall and shouted up to Johnny. 'Come down, American! I will stop them firing. Come down and you all may go.'

Fu stepped out into the courtyard. The bright sun glittered on the gold braid of his uniform. He marched purposefully, walking towards the smashed gateway in the concealing wall. Fu, the great commander again, a "modern" man, full of pride, buoyed up not by the sensible advice he had just had from his mistress, but simply by the look of love and admiration she had just given him.

He raised his hand as he approached the gateway at the side of the wall. 'Stop firing!' he shouted in Manchu. 'Stop!'

The firing stopped. Johnny climbed down from the battlements, joining Masha and Anna in the shadow of the wall. 'All right?' Anna nodded. Both of them ran towards Sasha and Yelena. Sasha was sitting by the wall on the far side of the gateway, Yelena crouching over him, supporting him with her arm.

'Is he okay?' Johnny looked down at the couple. 'I thought he was gone – in that bomb blast.'

'He was gone. But he's recovered.'

'You seemed to be kissing him?' Johnny bent down, curious.

'Yes. Blowing air into him. He'd stopped breathing.' Yelena looked up at Anna, who had seen the same thing, and Sasha's recovery. She was equally mystified.

'Blowing air into him?' she asked.

'Yes. Breath of life. My life,' Yelena added, looking up at Anna, without malevolence or pride – just the flat look of someone who has taken a final victory. She tightened her grip on Sasha. Johnny saw Yelena's cold expression – and Anna's frustrated emotion. She would clearly have liked to have cradled Sasha then, her lover. Sasha, recovering now, looked from one woman to the other with a dull, undecided air. One battle was over, Johnny thought, another beginning.

'Come on, before someone changes their minds here,' Johnny told them all brusquely. They joined Fu and Masha again, in front of the broken main gates. The two groups stood apart, awkwardly, for a moment. 'What the hell,' Johnny suddenly said. He went forward and embraced Masha. 'Thank you for the party.' Anna followed him, doing the same. 'Thank you – for our talks,' she said. 'For everything. I hope you get to Pekin. When you do, I'll come and visit.'

'Yes. I hope you will. Here, take this –' Masha undid a large brooch at her neck and handed it to Anna. It was a huge domed emerald, surrounded by diamonds. 'No, not one of Fu's splendid presents.' She smiled at Fu. 'One I earned myself when I worked in – in that establishment in Shanghai. An old admirer. Remember, Anna – with men, independence and respect. Nothing else matters. Open it – the emerald opens.'

Anna slipped the catch. The emerald, hollowed beneath, hinged back. Inside were two tiny figures, a couple in eighteenth-century Court dress, finely wrought in gold, each holding an arm above their heads. They started to turn, in a dance, to the faint strains of a minuet, coming from the mechanism inside. 'It's wonderful,' Anna gasped.

'Fabergé. I hope it all goes like that for you, with him.' She looked over at Sasha, then back to Anna.

Johnny shook hands with Fu. 'I'm sorry I wasn't able to teach you to fly the golden bird. One day maybe . . .' Fu was suddenly disappointed at this reminder. 'I'll tell you what, though,' Johnny went on. 'When you get to Pekin, I'll come and show you. I promise.' Fu nodded, rather glumly.

Masha went over to him. She took his hand and put it to her cheek, then looked at Johnny. 'Fu won't fly in any of those damn birds. I want him with me safely, here on earth.' She turned to Fu and kissed his huge hand.

They left by the great gates, passing through the smashed wood, over the partly broken drawbridge, and out onto the snowy plateau, where the sun, risen now, glittered on the icy crystals. The Curtis Jenny, unharmed under its canopy of furs and yakskin blankets, stood some way to their left out on the snowy surface, the sheer drop to the valley of the Hulan river in the distance beyond.

The yakskins off, Johnny helped Yelena into the rear pilot's cockpit. He primed the engine, advanced the ignition and the throttle. 'As soon as the engine fires, push back this ignition lever,' he told her. He moved round the plane checking everything, then swung the propeller. Twice, a third and fourth time. Suddenly the motor started with a splutter, then roared. Back beside the fuselage he helped Sasha and Anna into the front observer's seat. 'Squeeze in, and keep your heads down,' he told them. Then he climbed up into the rear cockpit with Yelena. 'Christ, it's lucky all three of you are pretty small. Move over.' He pushed himself in, crushed next to her. He moved the throttle forward, warming the engine for several minutes, checking the fuel mix, oil pressure, flaps, tail rudder. He relaxed the throttle, the cylinders warbling, then advanced it slowly, almost up to its limit, the engine roaring. The plane began to move. He swung it round in a half circle so that it faced down the plateau, into the wind.

He gave it full throttle. The fuselage shook, vibrating fiercely. The plane started forward in a clattering roar. They skimmed along, the skis riding the hard crust of icy snow, faster, towards the edge of the plateau several hundred yards away, with the valley falling away sheer beyond.

The plane veered about. He kicked the rudder one way, then the other, keeping a straight momentum. But the plane, with its additional load, was still a dead weight, land-bound, as they neared the sheer drop.

'Rise up! Rise up, for Jesus!' Johnny sang out his version of the hymn above the roar, the icy searing wind. Yelena saw the canyon clearly now, looming up, the vast fall from the mountainside into the valley, the plane still swinging from side to side, straining to rise. They weren't going to make it, she thought. 'Rise,' she said to herself. '*Rise* . . .'

Twenty yards from the edge the plane rose. An inch. A foot. Two feet. They were off the plateau. Yelena could see straight down into the great valley, the bright morning sun casting harsh shadows on the western side of the crags, a dazzling whiteness blazing on their eastern flanks. Above her a line of pearly violet haze ran all along the horizon, cut through by towering snow-clad peaks thrusting into a vast, pale-blue arc of sky. 'We have won,' she thought. 'I have won. And Anna has no power like mine.'

9

When they got back to Harbin everyone rejoiced at the success of Johnny's daring mission. The newspapers made much of it, strangers congratulated him, while the three women and Sasha were hugely grateful. Johnny took it all with a shrug. Matty slept easy again. Everyone ignored for the moment the problems implicit in Sasha's having taken up with Anna.

Only Holly, unaware of the implications of this new relationship, found an unalloyed pleasure in the return of her father. They hugged and kissed each other, and played with Tomcat and the furless Teddy by the hour, on his first day in Harbin. Sasha suddenly became a true father. Yet he remained neither husband nor lover to Harriet and Yelena. His role with them was more ambiguous than ever.

His new circumstance with Anna upset the balance of affection and emotion between all three women, while the good resolutions which Harriet and Yelena had made about Sasha, by way of making things decent and proper with him, were put in complete jeopardy.

Anna was the bugbear in the matter. Had Sasha become involved with a stranger things would have been different. A quite fresh face would have clearly demarcated allegiances and made reconciliations easier. But in taking up with Anna, Sasha divided the three women, who before had come to see themselves as inseparable.

For Yelena the matter was quite simple. She was incensed with her brother, quite unable once more to come to terms with Sasha's involvement with another. And that this other should be Anna, her friend to whom she had confided many of her feelings for her brother, made it all the worse. Anna, like Harriet before, had betrayed her. Yelena brooded increasingly.

Harriet, although she never expected to live intimately with

Sasha again, found herself almost equally put out by the new situation, when she should have been pleased by it. Anna was a great friend. She expected to remain close to her. What better than that she and Sasha should come together, where in this friendly inclusiveness Sasha could be closely involved with Holly as a father. Yet Harriet saw how there were a number of obvious flaws in this happy equation.

There was Yelena for a start, furious already with this new situation. She would never take kindly to Sasha and Anna being together. There was a future of division here. And Sasha himself, Harriet thought – he could well now nurture fresh antagonisms towards her. He had long been cold and unfriendly, for he had never forgiven her for not marrying him. His intimacy with Anna up at the fortress would no doubt have included an account of some of her most intimate, not to say shaming, secrets in her long affair with him.

True, she herself had told Anna much, but not all, of what had happened between them. Anna had readily accepted her account of it at the time. Now she might well give more credit to Sasha's version of things. But then Anna, as regards Ivan, had behaved very badly. She had betrayed him. Harriet had thought not to tell Anna what she had seen of Ivan down in the Chinese town – Ivan gone to seed with his concubine and opium. Now – with an element of spite, no doubt – she thought she would tell her.

In the event she didn't have to tell Anna in any ill-natured way. The day after their arrival in Harbin Anna contrived a meeting privately with Harriet, in her bedroom next to Sasha's which Johnny had arranged for them, close to the suite he shared with Matty on the top floor of the Orient Hotel. Anna initiated enquiries about Ivan, so that Harriet quite naturally described her meeting with him in the ramshackle house, his living with a Chinese woman, pregnant, and with a year-old baby. She omitted the opium.

Anna was duly shocked. 'I can't believe it. It's so unlike him. It's astonishing . . .' She returned from the window, looking at Harriet, who was sitting on the bed in the over-stuffed room, filled with reproduced Second Empire furniture, and with narrow striped brown and cream wallpaper which made Harriet dizzy, so that she had intermittently to screw up her eyes. Anna stared at her now as if searching for an answer to this unexpected behaviour. Finding none she changed tack suddenly. 'Yelena is furious. About me and Sasha. You, too, by your expression,' she went on, as if anticipating a rebuke.

'No. It's just my eyes – I'm dizzy – the wallpaper. And no, I'm not put out by your taking up with Sasha.' The lie hurt her, so that she suddenly felt annoyed and bitter at Anna.

'Good. I'm glad.' Anna was enthusiastic. 'Because it should really make things better. Between all of us.'

Anna was standing with her back to her now, against a wide expanse of the dreadful wallpaper. Harriet's eyes began to waver and lose focus, the stripes to mingle. She felt dizzy again and angry at the whole situation. 'I'm simply surprised,' she said in harsher tones than she'd intended. 'It would be unwise of you to rush into anything with Sasha. You can hardly know him – the difficulties there.' Anna swung round, equally surprised, not expecting comments of this nature. 'You should be careful. He's like Yelena. Though it's not so obvious. Moody, unreliable. I told you on the train.'

Anna moved towards her, no longer puzzled but very slightly venomous. 'You didn't give quite the full picture, though. Just to speak of facts. For example – that at Ladoga, up at the Rumovsky castle, when you got together for a second time. That Sasha asked to marry you. A second time. And you agreed. But later said no. Again.'

'Yes, I did.' Harriet stood up from the bed where she felt vulnerable. She realized she must stop this confrontation at once. It would do her no good. But the wallpaper dizzied her and she wavered, steadying herself with her hand on the back of a coarsely gilded chair, so that Anna continued.

'Rather convenient? So easily to break your word like that.'

'It wasn't easy at all. But it was honest. I soon saw – again – how things wouldn't work out for us, in marriage.'

'*Dis*honest. Surely.' Anna was more forceful now, while maintaining a perfectly reasonable tone. 'You led Sasha on. Then broke your word. He wanted to marry you. And be a proper father to Holly. You turned him down on both counts. That won't be our problem. Because we're going to marry. As soon as possible. Here in Harbin.'

Harriet didn't even try to hide her amazement. 'Anna, that's nonsense, a completely childish idea. You've only known each other a few weeks. Marriage between Sasha and me wouldn't have worked, Anna. And it won't work between you two either. I know you both. The differences between you – temperament, needs, outlook –'

'How do you really know? No one does.' Anna went to the window and looked down at the traffic. 'We're never ideally suited to anyone. One has to work at it. You might have taken the risk with Sasha. I'm going to.'

Harriet almost laughed then, at the idea of Anna marrying Sasha – and, in her anguish, at the memory of her unhappiness, her incompetence over the whole business. Her weakness. This thought gave her a cue into another aspect of the matter. 'Of course there's one thing in all this which I doubt Sasha's dwelt on with you, or even mentioned, since he's never faced it himself. He's always loved and wanted Yelena almost as much as she has him. I was an excuse, a way out of his temptations there. A very willing decoy, I admit. And Sandy, the Englishman, was just the same sort of distraction for Yelena, when she took up with him. Both of us were small part players in the twins' drama. They really only want each other,' Harriet said, suddenly vicious. 'As you too may find to your cost.'

'I won't.' Anna moved towards her calmly. 'I won't let things slide that far. Because I'm actually *going* to marry Sasha.'

'Do you think, after a few weeks, you know Sasha so well – to be sure that his demanding and difficult nature wouldn't sink your boat with him? – as it did mine?'

'I don't think it will.' She looked at Harriet, summing her up. 'We are almost the same age, he and I. You are twelve years older. His nature and mine are more in tune, I think. More things in common. Both Russian. Same background. Born and brought up in Petersburg.'

'Yes, I'm sure.' Harriet lost control again. 'All the things you had with Ivan, who you have so lightly abandoned!'

'We were talking of suitability, not fault, Harriet –'

'It's simply not like you, Anna!' Harriet burst out. 'On the hospital train you were realistic, even cynical, about men. Now you're blind about them. You can't see that now you're *really* barking up the wrong tree. You've lost your head with Sasha. Just as I did!'

'No.' Anna walked away, thinking.

'Tell me, Anna,' Harriet said after a moment. 'What would you have done if you'd found Ivan here, without his Chinese woman, all loving and loyal and waiting for you?'

'I'd have told him the truth.' Anna spoke firmly, brown eyes wide with honesty. 'If you're parted from someone for a long time, and given fate, opportunity, you can fall in love with someone else. Which is exactly what I assume Ivan's done. And more than a year ago at least. Without waiting very long for me. Though I don't pretend I'm not relieved. In the circumstances it would have been an awkward meeting with him. To put it mildly.'

'Yes. It's been very convenient for you, hasn't it? Ivan's taking up with his Chinese woman.' Harriet could now look at Anna circumspectly and critically.

Yet they parted fairly amicably. Harriet had to admit that Anna had made some reasonable points so far as she and Sasha were concerned. They did have some things in common – more than she had ever had with him. They might make a go of it.

Yet, no – the truth was that they had made a fantasy with each other, Harriet thought, after she left the hotel. A pact against the devils of disruption, a snatching at the heels of love, in a sudden hunger for a stranger, where passion could be mistaken for real suitability and affection. Homeless and in peril they'd invented love, as a home in the heart at least, as a stay against the nightmare journeys they had both made across Russia, during the years of terror, deprivation and murder.

But who was she to undermine their hopes? She would have so wished for what they had with Sandy. Some, at least, in all these failures and mismatchings might find a happy ending. Yet again, in her heart, Harriet felt this would not be so for Anna and Sasha. The odds of right thinking were against them. She walked on down the street with a strong sense of foreboding.

Harriet and Yelena, some time before, had taken help in the restaurant, employing a young Russian couple to assist in the kitchen and wait at the tables. This help proved all the more necessary on Yelena's return from Shanyang since, sunk in a surly depression, she'd now lost all her enthusiasm for running the restaurant.

'I just don't care any more,' Yelena told Harriet that same evening, after Harriet had seen Anna, when they were tidying things up after everyone had left, with Holly asleep upstairs. 'All the efforts Johnny made – and me – all for nothing.'

'No, Linochka. Not the way to look at it. Now is when we have to make an even bigger effort, about Sasha and Anna. You simply can't stop people becoming fond of each other.'

'But Anna has another man waiting for her, Ivan. How can she throw him over so readily? She doesn't know he's living with a Chinese woman – and a baby.'

'She does. I told her. I saw her this afternoon in the hotel.'

'You *told* her?' Yelena slammed the cutlery drawer shut, glaring at Harriet.

'Yes. She asked me directly. I had to. And why not? You don't suppose I could have lied about it indefinitely, do you?'

Yelena hesitated. 'No. But you might have reminded her – how she took up with Sasha before she knew anything about Ivan –'

'I did.'

'So she had betrayed Ivan, in any case.'

'Yes. I told her that.'

'And what was her answer?'

'That such things happen. The usual thing. And it's difficult to contradict.' Harriet sighed, concentrating now on collecting the dirty napkins.

'You're not wild about their being together either, Harriet.' Yelena followed her from table to table.

'Me?'

'Don't pretend. I can feel it.'

'Not at all. I was just very surprised, that's all. Things don't usually work out so happily, between one's friends. I'm pleased –'

'You're not. You're pretending. You're playing the goody-goody governess again. "Doing the right thing", when in fact you're almost as upset as I am. Sasha was yours as well as mine. Besides, you can't think for a moment they're suited to each other. It's a spur-of-the-moment business, alone together up in the fortress. The whole thing's nonsense. And you know it as well as I do.'

Harriet stopped gathering up the napkins. 'Yes,' she said

quietly. She turned to Yelena. 'Yes, you're right. I do feel upset. And it is nonsense. But you're right as well when you say I'm doing the "right thing". I am – because there's nothing else to do. We have to keep our heads now more than ever, and try and face them both reasonably, with none of the old high drama.'

'Easier said than done.' Yelena spoke curtly.

'Of course. Nearly everything is.'

'Sasha's only alive because of me, my breathing into him.'

'But you gave him life to live his way, not yours.' Yelena continued her scowling expression. 'Your good powers came back to you, Linochka, in doing that. Why lose them now in this hopeless surliness?' Yelena said nothing. Harriet took pity on her. 'Do cheer up, Linochka. Now that we have help in the restaurant, we'll all go out and do something nice. There's Chaplin at the picture theatre in New Town. Or the circus.'

That same evening, downstairs at the Hotel Orient, Johnny talked to Matty, having dinner together in the potted-palm dining-room – where Johnny, the hero in all the papers that morning, was the centre of attention. Friends and complete strangers came up to congratulate him. He took the compliments graciously, relinguishing his little caviar spoon, lifting his glass of champagne, returning their toasts and commendations. He was in his element again. He had much to be pleased with. Even Matty had praised him warmly. But now Matty was more circumspect, even critical. He put down his fork – he was eating ham and eggs – and looked at Johnny through his thick spectacles.

'So, home is the hero. And the stockholders can sleep easy again. But what now, Johnny?'

'Well, my sister Ida's coming over for a visit. Be in Harbin the day after tomorrow. I told you.' Johnny leant back in his chair. 'And after that it's home, Matty. You saw the telegram from Colonel Stevens. They're winding up our US Advisory Railroad Commission here. The wars are finally over, Matty. Then it's back to Philadelphia for both of us!'

'Yes, I know all that. I meant the Princess. She must be plenty grateful to you for saving her brother. And her brother's new girlfriend.'

'Yes.' Johnny leant forward, speaking slowly. 'Yes, she is grateful. But she's furious, too, Matty.' He smiled, licked his lips, applied himself to the caviar once more. 'She's in a real state, in fact, because of that other woman, Anna.'

'Of course she is. Because she's crazy. And she'll never change. You make another play for her now, and she finds out you're married, she'll really explode.'

'I'm not making another play for her. I told her once, on that train to Dvinsk, that I'd never ask her again to marry me. And I won't.'

'What'll you do then?'

'Wait and see.' Johnny sipped his champagne. 'My, this is good. Roederer Brut. They've not had it here for a while.'

'What do you mean, "wait and see"?'

'It's been my experience with women that when they really get worked up emotionally, in a real sweat, that's when they do the least expected things.'

'You seem pretty confident that whatever she does will favour you.'

'Yes! Yes, I am.' He took the bottle from the ice bucket and poured them both another glass. 'Here's to us, Matty. Just you and me. As for the Princess, I don't really have any worries there.'

'You don't?'

'No. Give a woman enough rope, Matty, that's the secret.'

Mary Woodrow, that same evening, spoke to Sandy over another of Hu's attempts at a proper English dinner: some tough pork chops cooked in what Sandy thought might have been engine grease.

'It's in all the papers today,' Mary said brightly. 'Natasha was translating them for me. Extraordinary exploits with that warlord up in the mountains. With this American and Princess Yelena Rumovsky, the great friend of your friend Miss Boulting down the road at The Firebird.' She smiled at Sandy nicely. 'Of course you must have known the Princess well in Petersburg in the old days. She lived next door to the Embassy too.'

'Yes. Yes, I did know her. And her parents. And their head doorman.' Sandy struggled with his chop. 'I met the Princess now and then, socially. Met a lot of other Russian people then, as well, before the war. One long social round in those days. . .'

'Of course. All the same, since these two old friends of yours are just down the road, it seems strange you've never asked them round here. And especially now to congratulate them. You must have known her brother, too, this Prince Alexander Rumovsky they rescued.'

'Yes, I did. I went to their concerts then. Brother and sister. They were a greatly gifted pair, piano and violin –'

'Oh, then we *must* have them round! They could play here. There's a good piano here. We could have it tuned. We could have a musical soirée. You have such an interest in music, don't you?'

'Yes,' he said brightly. 'We could . . .' He left the remains of his chop, head on one side, eyeing it sourly. He wiped his moustache delicately with his napkin.

'You liar, Sandy,' she said to him lightly: so lightly that he thought, with his bad ear, that he had misheard her. 'I'm sorry?'

'You liar!' She shouted this time, throwing down her fork with a clatter, continuing loudly, so that he heard every syllable. 'You bloody liar!' He was astonished. He had never heard her swear before. 'You know those two women down the road at The Firebird *very well*. And you've been hiding it all from me. You went down there the other afternoon in the snowstorm, under the excuse of getting some tobacco, when you had some in your desk here all the time. So I followed you. There must be some very good reason for your hiding it all from me. You had an affair with this Miss Boulting' – she spat the name – 'in St Petersburg, four or five years ago. And that child of hers, who's just the same age, she's your child, isn't she?'

Sandy remained calm. 'No. You are quite wrong, Mary. The little girl is not my child and I have never had an affair with Miss Boulting.'

'Liar.'

'It's the truth.' But Sandy was talking to thin air. His wife had stormed out of the room. After a minute he leant forward and rang the little bell on the table. Hu appeared. 'Hu,' he told him nicely, 'the chops were delicious. Just I wasn't feeling quite up to them tonight, that's all.'

Hu nodded understandingly. 'I no much good – with this English food,' he said in his pidgin Russian. 'Mr Sly, he very like the Chinese food I do.'

'Yes, Hu. I'd like it, too.' Sandy smiled at him. After he'd left, Sandy said to himself, 'But I fancy I may have to eat out from now on. Start with The Firebird, perhaps. It's only just down the road.'

10

Iazko's Big Top in New Town. The smell of warm greasepaint and resiny sawdust. The cheap perfume of salesgirls, a musky attar of roses. The sour odour of stables and horses. The rank air beyond the curtain of wild animals in cages. Tiger's dung. Elephant's urine. All the fevered airs of the circus.

They were in the front row, Holly with her mother and Yelena. The interval approaching. The troupe of dwarf jugglers, the bare-backed riders, acrobats, ballerinas and the two wrestlers, gleaming with sweat, taking their bows and leaving. The next act coming. The little orchestra, trombones and horns blaring, cymbals crashing. Then fading. Just the drums rolling. The house lights darkening.

The shadows suddenly split by a single dazzling limelight. Pinpointing a slender girl in a leotard of glittering sequins. Dangling from a swinging trapeze high above them. A great Imperial eagle perched on the bar above her. Swinging through space, girl and bird together. The bird with wings outstretched, huge scimitar beak and talons, the limelight following. Swinging to and fro, ever faster. The bird carrying the girl away into the shadows. The girl struggling. Twisting and turning. Trying to escape the bird's clutches.

The drums rising in a frenzy. Suddenly stopping. Another trapeze, a man hanging by his legs, swinging into view. A split second later the girl somersaulting in empty space. Her hands meeting the man's outstretched wrists with a resounding slap. Swinging from his arms then. Tumultuous applause. Both swinging back to the high platform, sliding down the rope, taking their bows in the ring.

The clown rushing in from the curtained doorway. Red-nosed, baggy-trousered. Falling flat on his face, then mimicking the trapeze artistes. Somersaulting across the ring, looking up into the big top. A white dove flying down, perching on his head. The clown arms high, holding an imaginary bar. Making hopeless little jumps, trying to get airborne. Another four doves swooping down, perching on either shoulder. Dancing with them all, as if on horseback. Cantering round the ring, arms ahead of him, attached to reins, mimicking both horse and rider. His long gangly arms and legs in perfect rhythm. The effect of horse and rider together uncanny.

Passing close to Yelena. His cheeks puffing in and out under a bright white make-up. A face so mobile, like indiarubber. The dark eyes skittering. The intense concentration of nervous performance, so that everything would look utterly relaxed and easy. The applause increasing, cantering away through the curtain.

Yelena turned to Harriet, who faced her at the same moment, both saying together, 'It's Miki!'

The doorman let them go round afterwards, upstairs in the circular building, to the corridor which gave onto the artistes' dressing-rooms. The troupe of juggling dwarves, half costumed now, ran to and fro, like little serious animals, from a doorway halfway down. Yelena peered quickly inside as they went past. The room was filled with acrobats, trapeze men, some other clowns and animal tamers, sitting at mirrors, wiping their faces, in various states of undress. But no sign of Miki.

A couple passed them, in a hurry, already dressed. It was the small dark-haired slender girl they'd seen on the trapeze with the eagle and the man, her partner, who'd caught her. They'd done another act, more sensational still, without the eagle and with double somersaults, towards the end of the second half. A vital sinewy woman with black eyes, small and beautiful, her partner – her husband, Yelena assumed – rather like her, compact and wiry, equally good-looking.

In the next dressing-room, they saw Miki, sitting near the door, at the nearest mirror. Yelena peered round the edge of the doorway. 'Miki,' she said softly. He didn't hear her. 'Miki!' she sang out, louder.

He looked up. There was a moment's complete unrecognition, then sheer disbelief. 'Yelena!' He jumped to his feet, his face half smeared, half cleaned, a mess, his wispy hair dank and sweaty, his eyes flickering now. 'And Harriet! And Holly!'

On his feet he hesitated, still holding a wad of dirty cotton wool, paralysed, speechless, awkward. He looked at Yelena intently, eyes no longer skittering, sadly, as if, in this moment of confirming her existence – and from this all the possibilities of a future with her – he had already lost her again.

Then he embraced them, each one, slowly, lifting Holly off her feet, high up, like a trophy, hugging her.

'Can you come back with us? A late supper?' Yelena asked a few minutes later, the incredulous rejoicing over in the corridor. 'You see, we have this restaurant down at The Wharf in Harbin.'

'Yes. But . . .' He looked at his watch.

'But you must! And tell us all, dear Miki. And we'll tell you. All of us – all risen from the dead!' Yelena was sparklingly happy, her glooms quite forgotten. So was Harriet – and Holly was in seventh heaven, joining in the clamour, fascinated that they should meet this clown, whom she had not forgotten. 'Oh, please come back!' Holly asked him. 'And tell us how you do it, with those doves.'

'We have a droshky coming to pick us up –'

'Right,' Miki said, confirming something in his mind. 'I have an hour.'

They gave him supper in the inner room, at the big table next to the kitchen, the restaurant closed. They hardly knew where to begin with their chatter. 'Start with the ambush of the train,' Yelena said. 'Start with that horror Drushov, when he caught up with us. And that anarchist gang or whoever they were. Those bandits, they must have taken you. Why? How did you ever escape them alive?'

Miki picked at the *zakuski*, lifted a pickled herring, ogled Holly with his great brown eyes an instant, then dispatched the herring in a mouthful, magically, like a pelican.

'Yes, the bandit. He was called Lekovich. Andrei Lekovich. Just a crook, a robber. Plausible, though. And clever. He'd had an education at a seminary of all places. He'd wanted to be a priest. Anyway, he wanted Drushov, the commissar from Kharkov. Lekovich needed Drushov, you see, as a bargaining counter with the Bolsheviks in Kharkov. They'd taken his brother sometime before, his companion-in-arms. Lekovich thought he could do a deal with the Bolsheviks.' Miki took another herring and a gulp of vodka.

'Yes, but how? Then what?'

'After he'd ambushed Drushov's train, Lekovich lined us all up – the survivors, there were twenty or thirty of us, from both trains. He was looking for Drushov, but Drushov had managed to escape down the line, with some of his men, before Lekovich's final assault. Drushov wasn't there. Lekovich was furious. He went down the line, looking at each of us men – his own men going through our pockets afterwards, and taking anything valuable. When they got to me they found my Commissar's identity card. And the special order authorizing my Agit-Prop train signed by the General Secretary himself, Comrade Lenin in the Kremlin. This made a tremendous impression on Lekovich. He'd found another Commissar – much more important than Drushov, he thought: a friend of Lenin's. Well, he took me. And shot all the others . . .' Miki's face was suddenly still again. He cocked his head to one side and fiddled with his fork.

'Yes. We heard the shooting. We were hiding up the line in the railwayman's hut. And we looked for you afterwards, among the . . .' Yelena didn't go on. Holly was there.

Miki looked up. 'So, with me, an intimate of Lenin's as Lekovich supposed, he thought he could do a better and quicker deal with the Reds. Lekovich didn't know that Drushov was after me, didn't understand that I was of no importance at all among the Bolsheviks in Kharkov. I knew they wouldn't swap his brother for me. I knew what the message from Kharkov would be: "Go ahead and kill Commissar Ostrovsky. He's nothing to us." So I hadn't a lot of time.'

'How did you get away?'

Miki took another herring. 'You remember my ventriloquist's act – that day you came to the watchmaker's shop?'

'Yes –'

'And the way I can imitate people's voices?'

'Yes! Yes! So, how –?'

'I studied Lekovich's voice, practised it. They had me shut up in a room of an old tannery by a river. There was a guard outside the door. But there was an iron grille in it and I could see out, across the corridor, to a door opposite, which was the room where Lekovich was sleeping. The guard – a big dolt of a man – I waited till he was asleep. Then I shouted out in Lekovich's voice, "Wake up, you lazy oaf! Let the prisoner Ostrovsky out. Bring him to me, here, in my room." All this coming from the door opposite. The man jumped to his feet in a panic. "Go on," I shouted. "Let him out. And next time you fall asleep on duty I'll have you shot!" The fellow unlocked my door in a hurry, holding me by the arm as I came out. But he let me go, so he could knock on Lekovich's door. I picked up the chair and hit him hard over the head with it. The rest was fairly easy. I took his fur coat, hat and rifle, ran down the passage and escaped out onto the frozen river. I ran and ran. . .'

Miki paused. He shook his head, fiddling with a slice of pork sausage.

'All the way to Harbin?'

'It felt like it, often enough. It went on and on, the journey. Every sort of scrape and odd bits of good luck. I got down to the Volga a few days later. I knew I was finished with the Bolsheviks by then. Drushov had escaped the ambush. But he knew how I was involved with you people, White reactionaries. He'd kill me if I ever turned up with the Bolsheviks again. Besides, with people like Drushov as Commissars with the Bolsheviks, and some others like him I'd met, I realized the cause was becoming corrupt, involved in every sort of brutality and murder. I decided I had to get up the Volga, cross over the lines somehow, and get into White territory. It took me months, one way and another, before I finally reached Omsk. Oh, nearly six months ago now. And another two months on trains and carts and sledges and foot before I got here. I went straight to Iazko'a circus, and asked for a job. It was easy enough. Several of the people here, including the ringmaster, had worked in Ciniselli's in Petrograd. I knew them. I was doing my clown act within a week, for matinées. Then they gave me the evening shows. Where you saw me tonight. So that's my story. And yours?' He looked at the two women, sighing, shaking his head. 'I can still hardly believe it.' He speared a piece of sausage. 'All of us getting to Harbin in the end. When we were all making for Moscow last time we were together.' He looked at Yelena. 'Remember?'

'Yes.' Yelena said no more. She remembered well how she'd

told Miki that she would come with him to Moscow, would take up and work with him, do everything with him, only a day before their train had been caught in the snowdrift. She would have gone with him, she wanted to persuade herself now. The snowdrift and Drushov had stopped them. She would have gone with him, into another life.

And looking at him then, this loved figure from the past, the gifted, nervous Miki who had first brought her the 'new' at the Countess Shouvalov's ball, who had teased and loved her dearly upstairs that snowy morning in the watchmaker's shop – suddenly, seeing him resurrected from the dead, her own love for him revived, and she would have gone anywhere with him at that moment.

'Yes, Moscow,' he went on, still looking at her. 'We – you and I – we rather lost our chances there. Though I doubt you would have made a life with me!' He laughed, taking the memory lightly.

'I would.' Yelena was serious.

Miki picked up a plate and spun it on top of his index finger, playing a trick for Holly, who had been listening, and looking at him wide-eyed throughout his account. 'I wonder . . .' he said, looking at Yelena, over the spinning plate. 'I wonder if we ever would have worked together? Perhaps we were too good at teasing and fooling each other . . .'

Yelena took her life in her hands then. 'I'll come with you *now*,' she said. 'I'll do now what I promised then.'

Miki saw how completely serious she was. He was astonished. He lost his concentration and the spinning plate fell to the floor, smashing in pieces. There was silence. He didn't move. He looked at her. His eyes were angry in a way she'd never seen them. Angry and then full of frustrated passion. 'We're a little too late,' he said at last. 'I'm with Galina. A month ago. We're together.'

'Galina?' Yelena was dead still.

'Galina Viktorovna. The trapeze girl, with the eagle. I knew her in Ciniselli's. She was here when I arrived in Harbin, at the circus.' He shook his head, turning away from Yelena.

'But I saw her tonight, rushing away, with her partner, the man who does the act with her. Her husband surely?'

'No. No, that's her brother, Andrei. They've always done the act together. Survived the crossing of Siberia. That was her brother, Yelena.'

Looking at his watch again, Miki didn't stay to hear the story of their own crossing of Siberia. 'I have to meet Galina and Andrei. We have a chance of a decent flat at last. Out in Modianko. A railway engineer who's leaving for America. He was due in off the late train from Hulan Ergi. That's why Andrei and Galina were hurrying.'

Miki stood up, hugged Holly again, kissed the other two briefly, then bent down and picked up the pieces of the broken plate, putting them in one of the big ashtrays on the table. He rubbed his hands, looking for specks of broken china. 'Another time,' he said calmly, his normally mobile face a mask now, eyes no longer focusing on either woman – looking into a lost world: the dawn of a Bolshevik millennium and a life with Yelena, where the political and the personal would have come together, one supporting the other in a bright new era. 'Another time,' he said dully. 'I'll come round and hear your story.' He put on his long green serge overcoat and a wide-brimmed sombrero-style hat and, without turning back, walked out into the night.

Later, with Holly in bed, the two women made a final tidying of the restaurant. Harriet was folding the red check tablecloths, the napkins and towels, putting them in a bundle. 'Washing day tomorrow. Bin-tao's coming, the laundry –'

'But don't you think it's extraordinary?' Yelena was boiling. 'First all these old friends of ours turn up in Harbin. And then we find them all married or spoken for or taken up with mistresses and concubines. Sandy, Sasha, Ivan – and now Miki.'

'No. Not surprising. Two, three years, we've been apart from them. We've been out of things for a long time, Linochka.'

'But so have they.'

Harriet shrugged. 'Well, they've had more luck than us then, in that department.' She went into the kitchen and took out the ledger in which they planned and wrote the menus for the coming week. 'I'd like to do the lake bream again this week. And there's been a lot of those small powan fish again. We could fry them in batter –'

'But Harriet!' Yelena shouted into the kitchen. 'Now that everyone's got themselves so unsuitably paired –'

'We don't know that.' Harriet had come round to the serving hatch with the ledger and was peering through it at Yelena.

'Yes we do! Sandy's wife's a horror, by your account. Sasha and Anna are nonsense together. Commander Ivan Rayevsky can have no real future smoking opium with his Manchu concubine. And as for Miki, well, I can tell you – the way he looked at me.'

'Critically?'

'No. Lovingly, at first. And I *would* have gone off with him – now. I meant it.'

Harriet, stooping down at the hatch, looked across at her carefully. 'Yes . . . All right. So you would have done. But it's not to be. And we have to get on with our own lives now. You and me.' Harriet started to write in the ledger. 'Lake bream, then. And the fish in batter.'

'What life?'

Harriet went on writing. 'Holly's my first concern. She'll need to go to school soon. And back in England if it can be managed. So that's where she and I have to go. My friends in Chiswick, the Dewhursts – I've written to them, I told you. I'm sure they'll have me to stay for a bit, with Holly. Then I'll rent something in London.' She looked across at Yelena, sucking the top of the pencil. 'And you? Wouldn't you come with me? If you wanted to?'

'Yes. Yes, but . . .' She stopped.

'But what? There'd be musical work for you in London, I'm sure. And I'd hope to teach the piano. I'd need the income. That's my plan, when we've sold up here, to someone suitable, which will take a week or two or more.'

'But what about Sasha and Anna?' Yelena looked through the hatch at Harriet urgently. 'Will they – do you think they'll marry?'

'No.' Harriet lied too quickly and emphatically.

Yelena saw the lie. 'So, they *are* going to marry.'

'No. I've just told you –'

'How do you know "No" – unless they spoke to you about it? Of course! That's what Anna told you, when you saw her the other day, that they were going to marry, and not to tell me.'

'No . . .' Harriet said weakly. She could say no more on the subject. So she changed it. 'Linochka, just forget Anna and Sasha. You'll meet lots of new people in London. You'll think and feel quite differently there. And so will I. Don't think that I don't feel quite a bit like you – having lost any chance I might have had with Sandy.'

'Yes,' Yelena said dully.

'Linochka.' Now Harriet leant right forward into the serving hatch. 'You must see, how all these plans we're talking about and sensible feelings – this is the only way for us to survive *and* to get things on a decent civilized level with Sasha. So let him be happy with Anna, if he can. And let's all of us be friends together, in London or wherever. It's the only attitude to take, Linochka. The rest is a waste of spirit. Your spirit.' She put her hand on Yelena's. But Yelena made no response, so that Harriet became impatient. 'Now's the last chance, Linochka, for both of us with Sasha. To make amends there. And if you don't change your feelings about him – the old selfish, hurt, jealous side of you – you'll be finished. You won't be worth living with. With anyone. Or with yourself. Do come and help me decide what we're going to have on the menus next week.'

Yelena, unwillingly, came into the kitchen and joined her. Of course, she thought, there was one name they'd both omitted in all this talk of men and change and betrayal – Johnny. Johnny hadn't changed in his feelings towards her. She could sense that clearly. Johnny hadn't taken up with anybody else. And he wasn't married.

Ivan Rayevsky was not so far gone in the decrepit house in the Chinese Town that he did not read the newspapers. He read them every day, from cover to cover. In his vacant, unhappy state he had little else to occupy himself with.

So, to his astonishment that morning, he had read the account in the *Manchurian Herald* of Anna's dramatic rescue from the mountain fortress city – and seen her name, 'Anna Denisovna', so that it was clear she was still unattached, and her photograph, with the Rumovsky Prince and Princess and the American, all of them standing outside the Orient Hotel.

Overjoyed, he could hardly believe it. They'd had their differences. It hadn't all been plain sailing: rows about his preoccupied moods, his supposed indifference to children and music; his criticism of her contrariness – smug and unyielding one moment, abandoned the next. But by the end of their three months together in Petrograd, after her husband had left her and before he'd had to leave suddenly to join the Black Sea Fleet, they'd come to terms with most of their problems, agreed to differ, or to change, or compromise, and loved each other the better. They would marry on his next leave, or when the war was over, whichever was the sooner.

Two months later, with the revolution, and unable to get in touch with each other, it seemed they had lost each other for ever. Yet he had never become reconciled to her loss, never finally accepted that she was dead. He'd been desolate for months, years. Different in character and temperament, they had surmounted this hurdle and come to benefit from the other's differences. They felt they had a future because they would never be quite certain of the other: a future of surprises, which would revive the mundane in marriage, like sudden rain or sun on flowers. A future which, whatever else it was filled with, would contain jokes and fun and bed and chatter.

With her loss, as the months turned into years, he'd gone into a decline. He knew it. There'd been other reasons for this. The severe wounds he'd received commanding the gunboat against the Reds nearly two years before on the Upper Volga, his being invalided out of the service he'd loved, his time in brutal hospitals, the pain he still suffered – for which opium, and vodka, had proved the only readily available palliatives.

But the main reason for his decline had been the loss of Anna. He had seen a future with her, and she with him. Now, out of the blue, life seemed to have given him a second chance. It was incredible! Anna! There she was, not a mile away from him, at the Hotel Orient. He would go round and see her at once.

His great friend, Commander Leonid Basikov, with whom he shared the lodging in the house, came in then. Leonid, an old shipmate, less badly wounded than him on the Volga, who now held a minor position in the naval section of the *Stavka* in New Town.

Ivan jumped up from his quilted bed. 'Leonid, you won't believe it!' He showed him the front page of the *Herald*. Leonid read it, shaking his head in astonishment. Then he embraced Ivan. 'My dear fellow. I couldn't be better pleased. Fuong!' He turned to his wife Fuong, who was coming down the stairs with their year-old baby. He spoke to her in Russian which both he and Ivan had been teaching her over the last year and which she spoke almost fluently now. 'Fuong, listen to the great news! Anna is alive. Ivan's dear Anna! What luck! It couldn't have happened to a better person.' He showed her the newspaper.

Fuong came up, her baby cradled in one arm, embracing Ivan with the other. 'You . . .' she said slowly in her careful Russian. 'Leonid is right. No better person. All this time, two years and more, you have been loyal to her, still believing, hoping she was alive. Such men are made in heaven.' The baby gurgled at him, seemingly in equal appreciation.

'Come, Ivan,' Leonid said. 'We must get you suitably dressed to meet her. Your medals – and your old naval uniform – I'll have it pressed by Bin-tao round the corner. And your hair, your beard, my dear chap – they need trimming. I'll arrange for Lu-min to come round. What a day! What a day!'

They all scurried round, in and out of the house and kitchen, for the next hour – Fuong and Leonid, Lu-min and Bin-tao, the barber and clothes presser, helping Ivan to prepare himself. His old naval Commander's uniform was made ready, medals and boots polished, hair and beard trimmed. Leonid put a twenty-rouble note in his pocket, then inspected him, straightening his tie, picking fluff from his shoulder. 'My dear fellow,' he said, standing back, admiring. 'Topsails, amidships, stern and high rigging – all shipshape and gleaming! Cast off, fore and aft – you're ready . . .' They saluted each other, smiling, and Ivan set off, a new man, to see Anna.

That same morning Johnny met his younger sister Ida at the station off the Vladivostok train. 'So you finally made it!' He kissed her quickly. 'What you always wanted – Holy Mother Russia!'

'Yes!' she screamed joyously. 'Russia – and Russians. I can't wait to meet some real Russians. Balalaikas and onion-domed churches!'

'Trouble is, you're in China. Though it's fair to say you won't know it when you get into town. There are more Russians and balalaikas and onion-domed churches here than you could shake a stick at. And you've come at just the right time. The Railroad Commission work is over. I can show you the sights. Meet all my new Russian friends here. And some old ones. The Princess Yelena . . .'

'That beautiful crazy Russian pianist you were always on about at home – before you married Louisa . . .'

'Louisa ran out on me. The hell with Louisa,' he said grimly. Then he returned to his happiest mood. 'Yes! – you'll meet the Princess and her brother. They don't come more Russian than the two of them. The Princess runs a restaurant here. She's coming round after lunch. But come on.' He picked up her two small suitcases, leaving the two trunks behind. 'Porter!' he shouted out, striding on ahead.

Ida ran after him. 'Hey, wait, Johnny!' She rushed up to him. 'Give me a *proper* kiss, for God's sake – all this damn talk of Princess Yelena. What about me?'

Johnny put her cases down and gave her a great bear hug, then kissed her more attentively. 'Dear sister, dear Ida.' At arm's length, shaking his head, he looked in happy wonder at this loved younger sister.

Ida was a smaller, feminine version of Johnny: a slightly, nicely plump woman of twenty-six, with a mop of springy fair hair, big blue eyes, a cheeky nose and turned-out lips in a round, happy face. And just like Johnny in temperament: quick, tough, impatient, energetic, exuberant, tart, intelligently scatty, scathing, decidedly outspoken, interested in everything, alive to every nuance, an outrageous fibber, joker, storyteller. A whole rag-bag of indiscreet qualities. But a woman in essence who knew what was what, took quiet counsel with herself and whose heart was always in the right place.

'Dear Ida,' Johnny went on, 'I've missed you.' He let her go. 'You better tell me everything first, since I know as sure as dammit you won't listen to me until you have. How are things? The boyfriend – might as well start with him, the serious stuff–'

'Oh Gawd,' she said drolly, rolling her eyes. 'Yes, get him out of the way first. Like I had to.'

'No?' Johnny was worried for an instant.

'Yes. I knew I had to chuck him, a few days before I got the train from New York to 'Frisco. So I contrived a damn great row with him at the Commodore. This gave him the chance of chucking me. Which he did. So we both felt much better afterwards. Why, we damn nearly parted as friends we were so pleased with ourselves. Trouble was, Johnny . . .' She looked at him plaintively. 'He was a slowcoach –' Johnny had resumed his walk some way ahead of her. 'Couldn't keep pace with me.' She had to raise her voice now. 'Pedantic at heart, you know – sparks all on the surface but no fire underneath.' Johnny was several yards ahead of her now, striding up the platform. 'Hey! – wait for me, godammit!' She ran after him as fast as she could in her hobbled skirt and quite unsuitable new shoes, waving her tiny umbrella at him. 'Wait for me, Johnny!' she wailed. When she caught up with him she dotted him one on his astrakhan hat with her brolly.

'Sister,' he said, taking the little umbrella from her, then standing away, looking at her fashionably skimpy Fifth Avenue outfit. 'You know something? You've come perfectly dressed – and equipped – for Russia and China in midwinter.' He picked her up, and swung her round and round like a conker on a string, so that her neat legs and ankles showed, and one smart shoe fell off, and people all over the platform looked at them askance. He set her down. 'Come on. We can talk later. I've fixed lunch for us, just you and me, in my suite at the Orient. Your first taste of real caviar. I love you . . .'

Some hours later Yelena set out to meet Johnny and Ida at the Orient Hotel. She looked forward to the meeting. A whole new life for her, perhaps, in America – with Johnny? She didn't care for the idea of rented accommodation with Harriet, in some dreary London suburb, teaching the piano.

When she got upstairs to the suite there was a mood of almost boisterous conviviality, an empty champagne bottle, a debris of caviar. Yelena was at her most winning. Ida was enchanted by her. Johnny – proud host and brother – pleased to show off the Princess, this exotic and secretly loved friend.

They had coffee and chocolates. There was an account of the daring mountain-top rescue at Shanyang, then talk of holiday jaunts in the Harbin area, a possible trip to America for Yelena later. After an hour Yelena went to the bathroom, down a thick carpeted corridor, then through Johnny's bedroom. On her way back along the corridor, the drawing-room door ahead of her just ajar, she heard Ida talking, quite loudly, the last few words of an enthusiastic sentence. '. . . she's wonderful, Johnny – *much* better and more your sort than Louisa. Louisa's no wife at all for you.'

Yelena didn't quite take in what she'd heard for a moment. Then she understood, and a feeling of swirling giddiness came over her, a complete blackness where she seemed to be falling through an endless black void.

But suddenly she recovered her balance. She felt a quite different person – alert, purposeful, decided. She knew exactly what she must do. Not kill Johnny – he was nothing to her now, no more than Miki or Sandy had ever been. They were all just weak men – and there could be no other men for her in the future. No, she must kill the one person who deserved her, the real object of her love and now the source of all her ills – Sasha, who had so finally and completely betrayed her. Kill Anna, too, collaborator with Sasha in this ultimate betrayal. Sasha would never marry. She would kill him to make sure that he didn't, and to ensure by his death that he would never escape her again, for then she would kill herself. So that what had always been meant between them would come irrevocably to pass: they would be together forever. She had made a pact with herself years before at Orlov that she would always be with Sasha. She would confirm that promise now, ensuring by his death that he would too.

She went back to the bedroom, looking about her quickly. Where would Johnny keep his automatic? Near the bed, she thought. She tried the drawer in the bedside table. There it was, the black muzzle sticking out from beneath a pile of his great white handkerchiefs. The gun and a spare clip of ammunition. She took both, stuffing the gun inside the waistband of her skirt, putting the spare clip in the small pocket there.

She returned to the drawing-room and resumed her lively chatter with Johnny and Ida. She waited until she was saying goodbye to Johnny, alone with him, when he came down with her to the foyer. 'I couldn't help hearing,' she said to him nicely, in the bustle of the hall, 'that I'm "much better and more your sort than Lousia". I'm glad. Louisa – a nice name. Your wife, of course.' She smiled at him harshly. 'You never told me you were married,' she went on quickly, before suddenly turning away.

'Say, wait a minute!' he shouted after her. 'There's nothing between me and Louisa. We're getting a divorce –' But by then Yelena had disappeared through the swing doors out into the crowded street.

Johnny would have followed her. But at the same moment there were sounds of a fierce altercation right behind him in the lobby. He turned. A young bearded Russian naval officer, in the full dress uniform of a Commander, was being manhandled by a waiter, with much shouted argument, out of the bar. The officer seemed somewhat drunk.

This was not an unusual occurrence at the Hotel Orient. Drunken oafs or hapless, hopeless officers from the White Army or Naval services, wounded, invalided out, often had nothing better to do than walk the streets of Harbin and drink their small pensions away in the Orient or some other bar.

Johnny watched the officer being frogmarched across the lobby. He hated to see this, even when these officers were badly in their cups, or clearly stupid oafs. This man was neither. He had 'drink taken' in Matty's tactful Irish description, but was clearly a man of distinction. He walked with a slight limp and his shoulder obviously hurt him, the waiter gripping him there. 'Let go my arm!' the officer shouted. 'My shoulder's gone, you bloody fool.' The waiter gripped him there all the harder.

As the officer approached Johnny saw the medals in a line over his breast pocket. He recognized the first of them – the Cross of St George, the supreme Imperial award for bravery in battle. The waiter continued to bully and badger the officer. The others in the lobby turned their backs on the distasteful scene. Johnny didn't hesitate. He went up to them, halting their progress.

'What's the matter, Commander?' he asked the officer in Russian.

The man turned his bushy face to him, wild-eyed, flushed. 'My shoulder, an old war wound –'

Johnny turned to the waiter, a big, tactless fool, he knew. 'Let him go, Kyril,' he said ominously. 'Let him go – *now*,' he snapped viciously. 'This instant.'

'But he's been drinking, Mr Quince. Spent all his money. And now he won't pay the rest of the bill.'

'I'll pay it.' He turned to the officer. 'How much do you owe?'

'I don't know,' the man said hopelessly. He wiped his eyes, breathing heavily, utterly downcast. He was clearly in a state of shock.

'Put whatever he owes to my account,' Johnny told the waiter. 'And don't ever treat a Russian serviceman like that again. Drunk or sober they've most of them faced more trouble and danger than you'll ever know.' He turned back to the officer. 'Apart from the shoulder, Commander, is anything else the matter? Can I help? I'm Johnny Quince, with the US Railroad Commission here.'

The man looked at him, his eyes focusing more clearly now. 'Yes. Yes, I know you now – from the photograph in the *Herald* this morning. You're the American who rescued Prince Rumovsky and – and Anna Denisovna from that warlord's fortress a few days ago.'

'Why, yes, I am. Is that some sort of a problem for you?' The man shrugged, impatient to say something, yet unwilling to come out with it. 'No, go ahead. You can tell me. You won't embarrass me in the least. I've heard everything,' he added jovially.

'I was Anna Denisovna's . . . great friend, in Petrograd, three years ago . . . The woman you rescued.' He spoke hesitantly, as if being tortured for the information. 'I thought she was dead.' He pulled himself together and spoke more fluently. 'But I saw she wasn't, in the newspaper this morning, her name and photograph. So I came straight round to see her, only to find, when she told me . . .' He turned away, biting his lips.

'I see.' Johnny saw everything. 'Only to find she'd taken up with the Prince, Sasha Rumovsky?'

The officer nodded, still looking away.

Johnny took the initiative at once, quickly, brightly. 'Hey, come up to my room, tell me about it. We'll see if we can't sort something out.'

With Ida resting in her own bedroom then, Johnny plied Ivan Rayevsky with tea and listened to his story. He had to quizz him often enough to get a clear picture, for the man didn't wear his heart on his sleeve. But drink had loosened his tongue, and his emotions. Johnny was appalled by the Commander's account of things. Johnny barely knew Anna. But he'd seen enough of her and Sasha together to think it was a flash-in-the-pan affair, brought about by the perils and confines of the fortress. Sexual lightning.

'I'll tell you what, Commander,' he said finally. 'It won't last between them.'

'How do you know?'

'I know Sasha Rumovsky. He's like his sister – they're twins, you see – and I know her even better.' Johnny smiled.

'So?'

'They neither of them know what they want. They take up with other people just because they're desperate to run away from each other. You'll see. Sasha and Anna – just a passing phase.'

'I don't follow you. You mean the Prince and Princess – brother and sister – they'll end up with each other?'

'No! Not if I can help it.' Johnny stood up. 'Give it a week or less. I'll be in touch with you. And I'm pretty certain I'll have better news for you.'

Yelena, after she'd left Johnny half an hour before, had gone across New Trade Street to the other pavement, and walked up and down, looking in shop windows, generally dawdling, while keeping an eye on the hotel entrance, waiting for Sasha and Anna to emerge. She knew they were in their rooms. She'd gone back into the hotel and checked with the desk clerk.

The little black dog had come up beside her while she'd been standing outside Filipov's *piroshki* shop – a hungry dog, smelling the meat inside. She'd bought a meat pastie, and shared it with the animal, which had kept at her heels thereafter.

Before, when she'd seen the dog scuttling round the corner of the covered market or at the end of the railway bridge, she'd been terrified of what it might portend. Now she welcomed it.

Then she saw them, Anna and Sasha. They were dressed in smart new *shubas* and squirrel-tail hats, walking out of the hotel arm in arm. They turned right into River Road, among a great crowd of people. But Yelena was on their tail at once, following them on the broad pavement down the long avenue leading to the river a mile away, never losing sight of them, the black dog at her heels as she moved forward among the throng making for the Butterweek carnival.

After Ivan Rayevsky had gone, Johnny stood at the window, looking out over the city, the blue dome of St Nikolayev's Cathedral set against a paler blue sky, a slanting sun from the west, every detail vividly clear in the freezing afternoon air. With the same clarity he knew something crazy was going to happen with Yelena. He didn't know what.

Yelena had gone through his bedroom on her way to the bathroom. The gun – his automatic? Was she crazy enough for that? He went to the drawer in his bedside table where he kept it. It wasn't there, nor was the spare clip of ammunition. Yes, in finding out he was married, she'd gone over some edge in her mind, as she had before in Ladoga, and taken his gun. But why hadn't she shot him when she'd had the easy opportunity, returning to the drawing-room? Who was she out to get? It could only be Anna – and Sasha.

He'd speak to Harriet. He put a call in to The Firebird. There was no reply. Matty came into the suite then, taking his gloves off, in a hurry.

'Hey, Johnny – things go okay with the Princess?'

'So-so, Matty.'

'Because I just saw her out on New Trade Street as I was coming by. She looked straight through me, passed me like a ghost.'

'She did? Which way was she going?'

'Walking up the far pavement, next Filipov's pie shop, with a little black dog at her heels. I didn't know she had a dog.'

'She didn't when she left here.'

Johnny told Matty what had happened.

'Christ, she has your automatic! Is this what you meant by

"giving her enough rope"? Her doing the "least expected thing" – which'll be to shoot you all. Great, Johnny. You've really done it this time.' Matty was incensed. 'That crazy bitch was always going to be nothing but trouble for you. I told you from the start – and now she's trouble for everyone! We'd better find her, if she's not at the restaurant. Get the police.'

Johnny was quite calm. 'No, not yet, Matty.'

Matty was incredulous. 'You mean, you'll wait around for her – you and the Prince and this girlfriend of his – wait for her to get you? Any one or all of you? She's crazy, Johnny. You're playing with real fire this time.'

'Not yet, Matty. I'll find her first. And warn Sasha and Anna in the meantime. I'm not going to give up on her.' He looked at Matty steadily. 'She's worth it, Matty. She and all the other godammed Russian friends of ours – and Harriet and Holly. All been through more trouble than you or I could ever dream of. They've survived till now. And by God I'll see they all survive some more. I'll settle things right for all of them, once and for all, if it's the last thing I do.'

Johnny hurried out of the room, down the corridor to the next bedroom, which was Sasha's, and beyond that Anna's. He knocked on the first door, then the second. No reply from either. He ran downstairs to the lobby and spoke to the hall porter. Yes, the man told him, the couple had gone out together ten minutes before. They'd turned right, down River Road, among the great crowd – all of them making for the carnival city built on the river ice. It was the first day of *Maslenitsa*, the hall porter reminded him – Butterweek, the week-long celebrations before Lent. 'And your other friend, Mr Quince, the Princess Rumovsky, she came back in here asking for the couple at reception. Then she waited for them outside – I saw her – and when they came out she followed them. They've all gone to the carnival, Mr Quince!'

Johnny, rushing out of the hotel and turning down River Road, was soon enveloped in a vast throng of people. But he had no sight of Yelena or the other two ahead. He skipped and ran and dodged through the crowd, jumping up now and then to get a better view, like a springer dog, his straw-coloured hair gold-tinted in the dazzling afternoon light, the sun slanting straight up the avenue from the river. He saw the yellow cupola and pillared façade of the railway station coming into view at the end of the avenue, and beyond that the great latticework railway bridge. He ran on, pushing and shoving.

Yelena, nearing the end of the avenue, kept Sasha and Anna in sight a dozen yards ahead of her among the crowds passing the station, before they turned left along the ramparts above the river which gave over the carnival city. She would find her opportunity, somewhere out on the ice, among the crowds, on some street corner or alleyway.

Anna and Sasha stood on the high river bank, looking down on the fantastic city. The sun slanted through the latticework of the railway bridge, patterning the ice with a long filigree of shadow. The crystal air was plumed with fingers of white smoke rising from a hundred little food and tea stall chimneys. A whole town in miniature had been built on the ice. Small squares and arcades, streets and passages, elaborately decorated, vividly coloured wooden buildings, with theatres, shops, ice slides, merry-go-rounds, swings and a skating rink, with gramophone music, out in the centre of the river.

Bright log braziers at every corner warmed the blue air. Odours of many varieties came from ovens and hot-chestnut stands – the smell of hot gingerbread and chocolate almond cake, of oranges and lemons stacked in huge pyramids. And everywhere the sizzling *blini* stoves, the straw-covered ice around them smeared with butter, reeking of sugar.

Yelena, down on the ice, moving through the carnival city, the little black dog at her heels, never lost sight of her quarry. Walking, running, hiding, watching, waiting – she was their avenging shadow. On just such a day in the same tingling bright air, years before, Sasha had taken her out to the Butterweek carnival in St Petersburg. Sasha had cheered and loved her then. Now he was doing the same for Anna. Hand in her sable coat pocket, Yelena tightened her grip on the automatic.

Johnny, finding no sign of Yelena or the other two on the long avenue, knew they must all have gone to the carnival. Now he was out on the ice himself, struggling among the crowds, looking everywhere. A sleigh swept past him, red ribbons flying, harness bells ringing. A bear tamer cracked his whip. He smelt the tart lemon and burnt butter from a *blini* stall. He longed for one, but couldn't stop, looking at every face, his head swinging from side to side, in the ever thickening mass of people.

Yelena saw Anna and Sasha waiting their turn at one of the street corner *kacheli*, beribboned swings in rows that were everywhere about the city. Then they were sharing a seat together, rising higher and higher, Anna's petticoats flying. Yelena watched them. She had done just the same with Sasha, at that last great Butterweek carnival in Petersburg before the war. Watching them now made her stomach churn. She felt the weight of the automatic in her pocket. She would have used it there and then if they hadn't been on the swing.

Johnny got held up by a big crowd watching two clowns on stilts fighting a boxing match high above him, the crowd roaring, laughing. He stood there looking round, bemused. A troupe of dwarves was turning somersaults and forming a human pyramid on a small stage in one direction – people lining up with little toboggans to take the huge ice slide on the other. Where the hell were they?

Anna and Sasha gambled with a few kopeks, putting money on an orange, a pear and finally a pineapple, as the arrow spun round the circular board. Finally he won. Anna kissed him as he took his ruble. Then, gazing at him, she took her glove off and touched his lips with her index finger. 'See, you won at last! It's all going to be all right, Sasha,' she told him, smiling.

Yelena watched them playing the same game which she had won at the Petersburg carnival, seeing the winning fruit beforehand with her strange gifts. Those gifts had returned. She looked down at the little black dog. It looked up at her encouragingly. Again she put her hand on the automatic in her pocket. But Sasha and Anna had moved on.

*

Johnny was caught in another crowd, blocking his path across a passageway. They were watching two women in white smocks and caps making fudge, stirring a huge cauldron, one of them taking great dollops of it, putting it onto a slab of ice-cold marble, then rolling it into a long brown carpet, throwing nuts into it, letting it chill, while a third woman was cutting up another hardened slab and selling it in tiny ribboned packages. The air smelt of warm caramel, vanilla, hazelnuts. He licked his lips. But finally he managed to push through the crowd.

The sun was beginning to set, slanting over the ice, the air full of strange tints – carmine, cobalt, vermilion. Sparks from the log braziers leapt up, little gold fireflies against the darkening, crimson-streaked sky. Chinese lanterns had been lit everywhere. Music came from the ice rink nearby, Strauss's 'Gold and Silver'. The air chilled further, vibrating with colour. In the dazzle of lanterns there was light and laughter. Johnny moved on, grim-faced. Time was running out.

Yelena, half hidden to the side of the Punchinello Theatre, watched Anna and Sasha. Two children, a brother and sister obviously, with fur muffs and squirrel-tail hats, roared and shouted in the audience beside her. She smiled down at them. She was suddenly touched by them. Anna and Sasha were just across the street from her, at the entrance kiosk, choosing papier-mâché masks for the 'Animals' Masked Ball'. Beyond them was an open-sided tent with a wooden floor, where a crowd were dancing to balalaikas and accordions, in various grotesque, terrifying or ridiculous animal and bird masks.

'What fun!' Anna said, fingering through the choice of masks at the kiosk. 'A lion? An eagle? Or here – a toad's head!'

'I'll take this Russian brown bear. We had a pet bear like it once in Petersburg, called Ivan.'

Anna chose the mask of a tiger.

Johnny, coming to the Punchinello Theatre, saw Yelena suddenly. She was across the street from him with the little dog, choosing a mask. He watched her pick one out and put it on, the mask of a fat, merry-faced pig. Leaving the little dog at the edge of the tent she joined the dancers.

He'd found her at last. And she had obviously found Anna and Sasha. They were somewhere beyond her, out on the dance floor. And that was the problem. He couldn't warn them, for he wouldn't know them. They would be masked already, in the guise of some different animals. But at least he could now identify Yelena, in the mask of the happy-faced porker.

He chose a mask himself, so that he could close with Yelena without her recognizing him. He hurried now, taking the first mask that came to hand, which turned out to be a rabbit with large ears and long whiskers. Tying it round his face he pushed out into the throng. The dancing was informal. Some danced together, arms about each other. Others danced in groups, in the traditional Russian manner, arms linked over one another's shoulders, down on their haunches, boots kicking, the balalaikas and concertinas rising to a crescendo.

Yelena saw the bear and the tiger dancing together, holding each other, rubbing muzzles together. In her merry pig's mask she danced and cavorted about the floor alone, joining one group for a moment, leaving them, alone again, joining another, using each group as cover, stalking her prey across the dance floor.

Johnny looked everywhere for Yelena in her pig's mask. Suddenly he saw her, on the far side of the floor near the orchestra. In her sable coat she was dancing among a group, all happily bouncing about together. He pushed his way towards her, circling her at first before coming right up to her. He gripped her firmly by the arm.

'Yelena! It's me, Johnny. Stop it, whatever you have in mind. Give me the gun.' She started to wrestle with him. 'For God's sake stop it!' He was sweating. He tried to take his rabbit's mask off with one hand, but he couldn't. She was resisting furiously. He needed both hands to hold her. 'Just forget it, Princess. There's plenty else for you in life besides Anna and Sasha. Me, for example. Louisa's nothing. She ran out on me.' Yelena was struggling fiercely now, shouting at him in a strange, hard voice he didn't recognize.

'Let me go, you fool! Let me go –'

Another mask, of a lion, loomed up in front of him. A man gripped him fiercely by the arm, pulling him away. Yelena kept on shouting. 'How dare you! You brute –' She pulled her pig's mask off. Johnny saw the face of a total stranger – another woman, fair-haired, outraged, not Yelena.

A moment later he heard the shots, the sharp crack of his own automatic, from the far side of the tent. Once, twice. A pause. Then a third shot. Everyone spun round, dozens of birds and animals, lions and tigers, parrots, porkers and rabbits. The music died, all the masks quite still now, alert, looking questioningly, sensing danger, like birds and beasts in a jungle.

EPILOGUE

Christmas 1920

1

It was towards midday, the Saturday before Christmas, nine months later. The Reverend Harold Woodrow, a tall figure in Wellington boots and an old tweed overcoat, with wisps of rust hair and handsome features, stood behind the rectory on the hill above the long meadow, by the sheep pens with his shepherd William. Hearing the sound of the train in the still air he turned, looking down the wide valley beneath them, the sun flooding over the bare, frost-covered trees round the rectory, glinting on the stone of the church steeple, brightening the white pasture beyond, touching the snow-dusted Malverns with silver twenty miles away.

He saw the plumes of white smoke, spurting intermittently, straight up in the crystal air, and a moment later heard the equally irregular sound, a series of thunderous whooshes from the engine as it laboured up the gradient.

'There they are, Bill.' He turned to the blunt old man, shepherd with him and his father before him for over fifty years. 'I must be off. They'll be at the station in ten minutes. Let me know if you want the vet for that ewe.'

The old man humphed. 'There's nothing that man could do that I couldn't – and better.' He looked at the Reverend, gazing up at him sourly from beneath his old cap. 'Good luck to you, Reverend, you and Mrs Woodrow – with your Russian crew.' He turned and went in among the ewes in the pen, starting to sort them out vigorously with his crook. 'Russians,' he muttered. 'And Americans as well . . .'

They sat in two compartments of the carriage. After their journey from the Southampton boat, changing trains at Cheltenham, they were tired. They looked out of the windows silently, absorbing what for most of them was an utterly strange landscape, so far from the vast steppes and prairies of their own lands: a world of neat fields and stone cottages, barns and small farms and bare beech coppices. A world enclosed, an immemorial peace, the Cotswolds.

The Reverend Woodrow took his new bull-nosed Morris to the station three miles away to meet them. George, the local taxi driver, would be there as well, for there were a number of them, all coming to the big rectory for Christmas.

The train pulled into the station, steaming furiously. Some local people with parcels got off first after a morning's Christmas shopping in Cheltenham. And then the others, rather different, burdened with larger bags and suitcases, in great coats and furs, bright scarves and strange hats, emerged. Harold went forward to meet them, while Charlie the porter walked down to the guard's van where he'd been advised there was heavier luggage. There were greetings and introductions on the platform. Ten minutes later all of them were crammed into the two cars, with their trunks and suitcases, driving up the hill, along a twisting road, so arched over by huge beech and chestnut trees that even now, in the bright day and with the trees quite bare, the light was pale and shadowy.

They turned left by the new war memorial, a gilded bronze statue of St George vanquishing the Dragon, and drove along a narrower road that led to the elaborate Jacobean gateway and lodge of the Manor. Skirting the Manor wall for a hundred yards they swung round to the right and took the road through the parkland, the cricket pitch and pavilion on one side, vast old oak and beech alleys on the other. Soon they were in the village of Saunderton, with its thatched houses and cottages, going up the narrow main street and then into an even narrower lane which led to the church, and beyond that to the white gates of the rectory, the house covered in the leafless tendrils of an old wisteria, with its latticed shutters, French-looking, the winter sun on the stone turning it yellow.

Mrs Woodrow and Holly were in the hall, by the tall Christmas tree, with the two terriers, Sammy and Dodo, to greet them. For ten minutes there was mild pandemonium. A lot of barking and shouting and laughter – pushing and shoving and unloading, before the hall door was finally closed on the sharp air outside. The two terriers relaxed and the guests were shown to their rooms by Harold and Mrs Woodrow – and Sally, the talkative and inquisitive Irish housemaid in attendance, with warm towels, much advice and instructions.

Half an hour later the guests came downstairs in dribs and drabs, singly, sometimes in pairs, past the Christmas tree in the hall, into the bright drawing-room, where the Woodrows and the terriers waited for them, all grouped round the big log fire, the mantelpiece above laden with holly and Christmas cards.

Sandy arrived first and warmed his hands at the crackling logs.

'You met them all right, then?' his father asked, raising his voice, for Sandy was still hard of hearing.

'In the end, yes. Boat was late, as Harriet phoned you. We had an awful cold time lurking in Southampton overnight. Atlantic storms. Half of them were seasick.'

Harriet came in then, with a bouncing Holly, still excited at seeing her mother again, though she had been away for only twenty-four hours. 'They've brought lots of strange presents!' Holly looked up at Mrs Woodrow, wide-eyed. 'Big boxes, from America!'

'Have they indeed!'

'Yes! I never had a proper Christmas in Russia.'

'No . . . Well, we'll have one here, Holly, you'll see.'

The others arrived soon after. Johnny clattered down the broad stairs with his sister Ida, the two of them coming into the drawing-room like a hurricane, so that the terriers started barking again.

'Mrs Woodrow!' He strode over to her and took both her hands in his. 'I'm so pleased to be here. It's really very good of you.' He pumped her hands, smiling hugely. She looked up at this cherubic, energetic figure with some astonishment. With her delicate face and gentle grey eyes Alice Woodrow was a shy woman. She knew how Americans were less formal – stood less on ceremony. But this man, in his strange lounge suit, rather loud tie, and hair like a straw bale – well, she wasn't quite certain. 'It's all right,' he went on, seeing something of her surprise. 'I'm really quite tame. I won't steal the silver. My family – we're Methodist.'

Ida burst in on them then. 'Don't let him bother you, Mrs Woodrow, with his blather. Here, let me talk to Mrs

Woodrow.' She pushed forward. 'And you talk to the vicar, if you're such a Methodist.'

Ida, in a smart corduroy dress with a lace collar and velvet trimmings, engaged Mrs Woodrow in vivid talk about the boat trip. 'We were seasick! Third evening out, mid-Atlantic, waves like mountains! The waiters falling about like tenpins! An old dame at the next table, she was crossing herself. Looked like it was all over. Let me tell you!'

Mrs Woodrow looked at this similiarly cherub-faced young woman, her bright blue eyes blazing with childish excitement and fervour. She liked her. She was perhaps even more astonishing than her brother.

A minute later there was Yelena and Sasha together; then Anna and Miki came into the room, and finally, talking animatedly in Russian, Galina and Ivan arrived. At last, among an increasing hubbub, with glasses of sherry, everyone was in the drawing-room.

'Welcome! – all of you.' Harold raised his glass in the big bright room, with its flowered wallpaper, chintz-covered chairs and sofas, family portraits, hunting prints, grand piano, and two large windows looking over the frost-covered drive. 'Welcome to England – to Saunderton.'

All of them raised their glasses. Holly had orange squash. Half an hour later they had lunch.

'Oh yes, they're all a great lot of people,' Mrs Woodrow agreed, taking coffee with her husband by the drawing-room fire after lunch – the others having gone for a walk over the hills – while Harold made notes for his sermon the following day in an exercise book on his lap. Holly was out in the kitchen, with Hazel, the cook, and Sally, the maid, both of whom she had immediately made friends with when she'd arrived at the rectory six months before. 'Though I'm still somewhat puzzled . . .' Mrs Woodrow said.

'Yes, a puzzling people, the Russians.' Harold wrote quickly then crossed out what he had written. 'No, won't do. Too "devotional" . . .'

'Of course you learnt more about it all from Sandy, when he came back and I was away, with poor Aunt Sarah. But I've never entirely understood what happened in that Chinese town. The Princess – I gathered from Sandy's early letters – she took a gun to her brother.'

'And her brother's girlfriend at the time. The girl Anna, who's now married to that nice naval chap Ivan.' Harold returned to his sermon.

'Confusing . . .'

'Somewhat – since Anna, apparently, had been much involved before that with Ivan. And before that he – the Prince, that is – was involved with Harriet, of course. Hence we have Holly.'

Mrs Woodrow nodded vaguely. 'Well, she at any rate is quite straightforward. Delicious. Such a self-possessed little girl. But not pushy. She'd be a sort of step granddaughter to us, wouldn't she? – when Sandy and Harriet marry.'

'Yes . . .' Harold picked up a prayer book, consulted it. 'What an extraordinary coincidence! The Epistle for tomorrow couldn't be better suited to the circumstances. I'll use it as my text.' He put down the prayer book next to his coffee cup. 'Is there a piece of that walnut cake we had yesterday?'

'That's for tea. It's not teatime yet.'

'Oh. Pity . . .' He went on writing.

There was silence. The winter sun streamed through the big windows. Dodo, the old terrier by the fire, woke from some nightmare, growled throatily, then went to sleep again. Sammy, the younger dog, woke in turn and scratched himself furiously, then subsided.

'Harold?'

'Yes?' He didn't look up.

'I don't want to harp. But the Princess – that tiny woman. I take it she was trying to murder her brother?'

'Yes. And his girlfriend Anna. Then kill herself, I gather.'

'Suicide?' Mrs Woodrow found this idea more difficult than murder.

A log fell off the fire. Both dogs woke up with a yelp. Harold took the tongs and manoeuvred the log back on again. Smoke filled the air, the sun shining on a cloud of white motes now.

'Yes. Suicide, and murder. Both common over there.' Harold sat down and returned to his sermon.

'But where exactly, Harold? And how?' Mrs Woodrow was more insistent now.

'They were all at some sort of carnival, in Harbin. A big pre-Lenten do the Russians go in for. Sandy told me about it. I've forgotten . . . Butter? . . .' He looked up, thinking. 'Something to do with butter. A whole week of it, yes. Tons of butter. They pile it on pancakes. With jam and sugar. We do the same, of course, on Shrove Tuesday.'

'Yes, Harold, so we do. But what actually happened? – when she shot them. Or didn't she shoot them? The two of them look all right to me. Or have they recovered?'

'Oh? Didn't Sandy tell you?'

'No.'

'They were all wearing animal masks, for some reason. They were dancing . . .'

'*Animal* masks?'

'Yes. The Princess had one of a pig over her face.'

'A pig?'

'A *pig*. And the other two – a bear and a tiger.'

Mrs Woodrow shook her head, perplexed. 'And?'

'Well, the other two were out on the dance floor as well, I gather.'

'What other two?'

'You've just met them, Alice. Don't be so vague.'

'There were so many of them –'

'The two circus people, the Ostrovskys. Michael and Galina. Tall, gangly man, wearing a sombrero hat when he came in. And his wife who's a trapeze artist. And he's a clown.'

'But this wasn't at the circus, was it?'

'*No*. A carnival.'

'What were they doing there?'

'The Ostrovskys had gone out dancing there as well.' Harold was anxious to return to his sermon. Sammy woke up again, fretful, wanting to be let out. Harold got up and opened the door, then closed it.

'And?' Mrs Woodrow was impatient when he sat down again.

'And what?'

'What happened? Did the Princess try to kill these two circus people as well?'

'*No*. The Ostrovskys, who were dancing nearby, stopped her killing her brother and Anna. The Princess had taken her mask off, apparently, before she started with the gun. They saw her. Or Michael did. He's called Miki –'

'Yes, I know, with the sombrero – do get on with it!'

'All right, no need to get ratty. I wasn't there, you know.'

'Sorry.'

'Yes, Miki saw her. He jumped at her, grappled with her. She let the gun off several times, but missed. Or she may have winged one of them. Or in the air, or something. I don't know. Anyway they disarmed her. Then Johnny – the American, you surely know him, the stout gentleman –'

'Yes, yes, I know him. The man to do with railways. He was telling me some long and improbable story about bison and the Wild West before lunch.'

'Bison?' Harold was puzzled. 'I thought he was in railways. At any rate he was there, too, on the dance floor.'

'What was he doing there?'

'Alice, I've *no* idea. I wasn't there. They were all out dancing. People do, you know . . .'

'With guns and animal masks?'

Harold sighed, put down his pencil. 'At any rate, the whole thing seems to have been a storm in a teacup. And everyone settled their differences afterwards.'

'Quite a lot of differences to settle, by all accounts.'

'Yes, but then you see they're Russian. Murder, revolvers, plum-pudding bombs, unsuitable liaisons, throwing themselves under trains. All commonplace in Russia. They like to make a drama of things. I don't think they really mean it. Quick to temper, quick to forgive. A fine people.'

He picked up the prayer book again, making notes, returning to his sermon. Sammy, pawing at the door furiously, wanted in again. 'I'll let him in,' Mrs Woodrow said. Halfway across the room she stopped and turned. 'Harold?'

'Yes?'

'Those bison and the Wild West – do you think we've got it all wrong, and the American is really a cowboy?'

Harold considered this, taking off his spectacles. 'I think that's stretching things too far, Alice. We mustn't be entirely carried away by these – by these imaginative people.'

After lunch all five couples had gone for a walk, out behind the rectory, climbing the long meadow on the frosty grass, up on to the hills, with their sheep flocks and high beech coppices. They walked in groups, sometimes all together, sometimes in pairs apart, striding out in an assortment of boots and coloured scarves and astrakhan hats, in the cold sunshine under a pale blue sky.

Harriet walked with Sasha. 'So, what do you think – seeing Holly? She's well, isn't she? And so happy to see you.'

'Yes – yes, she's well. It's wonderful to see her.' His tone was distant. He didn't look at her. Instead he turned round, gazing intently behind him as if searching for something, looking for some landmark he'd missed.

He'd been unsettled and awkward ever since he'd arrived. Harriet had not seen him for nearly nine months. A week after the fracas at the Butterweek carnival Johnny had taken most of them – Yelena, Sasha, Anna, Ivan, Miki and Galina – with him to America, to San Francisco and then to his big house in Philadelphia, where they had begun to set their lives in some sort of order. Harriet and Holly had stayed on in Harbin.

Mary Woodrow, after several more storming rows with Sandy, still certain that he'd had an affair with Harriet and was Holly's father, that he was nothing but a liar – an accusation which, in the new circumstances of his having met Harriet again, he then ceased to deny – Mary had soon returned to England. Harriet had first to settle her business with the restaurant, which she eventually sold to the owner of Rogozinsky's wine bar farther down The Wharf. Then, after Mary's departure, she stayed for another three months, to be with Sandy while he settled his affairs at the Consulate, resigning from the service, but waiting until his replacement arrived, when all three of them had returned to England and the rectory.

In Harbin, during that week before the others had left for America, Harriet had had little opportunity to talk to Sasha alone. He had been distant with her. But he had made no objections to Holly's staying on in Harbin. At that point it had been assumed by everyone that he still would marry Anna. Then, on Johnny's persuasion – Johnny who, in a flurry of organization, had taken charge of everything and everybody – the others had all left.

Harriet had written to Sasha from Harbin, and later from the rectory, keeping him in touch with Holly's developments. But these had been familial letters, and what few very brief replies she'd had from him had been impersonal, so far as she herself was concerned. Now, for the first time, she had an opportunity of talking to him in calmer circumstances, alone.

She and Yelena had crossed Siberia in search of him, hoping, if they found him, to make things right between them all. And it was clear that, insofar as they were doing their music again together – as she'd heard from Johnny – Yelena had managed this while they had been in America. But she was not at all certain how she stood with him.

She spoke to him again, warmly, trying to catch his attention. 'She goes to the village school here – I wrote you – since September, with the little ones. Mrs Taylor takes them. And I do the piano with her, of course. She's getting on very well.'

'Yes, that's good.' Sasha turned back, but looked straight ahead now, still not looking at her.

'She's very happy here,' Harriet continued easily. 'Alice and Harold love her. And Hazel and Sally. She gets on with everyone.'

Sasha turned to her at last, abruptly. 'I'm sure you and Sandy look after her very well,' he said tartly. 'But you ought to see that you and I could have been looking after her – even better. Because *I'm* her father, and Sandy isn't. You seem to conveniently forget this –'

'No, I don't. But what's the point –?'

'The point is that I'm an absent father, when I could have been a full-time one. And I don't jump up and down for joy at seeing Sandy take over my role.'

Harriet didn't want to make an argument of anything. 'No, I see that,' she said reasonably. 'But all the same – you and I – we should try and get on. And not just for Holly's sake, but for *ours*, as friends. I've wanted that so much, all these years.'

'As a salve for your conscience? For the way you behaved towards me?' He was ironic.

Harriet was aghast at the way things were going. 'No. Because it's the reasonable, decent, civilized thing to do.'

'In the circumstances, with Holly here as evidence all the time, you ask rather too much.'

'No, it's very difficult for you. I see that. But we have to put it behind us, Sasha. Everyone makes asses of themselves, with others, at some point or another. I've done that, Linochka, Anna – we all have. The thing is to get over it, and we have –'

'I don't know that I have. So easy for you, just to say you made an ass of yourself – with me obviously. But there was more to it than that, between us.'

'Yes, but one can't undo the past. Why not make the best of it? Or do you want to punish me forever for my not marrying you?'

They had fallen behind the others, walking slowly up the steep sheep track towards the top of the hill. Sasha, wrapping his muffler more securely round his neck, then thrusting his hands deep in his overcoat pockets, said nothing.

'Well?' she asked, walking behind him. Silence. She knew he could make no sensible answer. She came up beside him, walking on the frozen pasture. 'You can't go on bearing grudges, Sasha,' she said quietly. 'Everyone close hurts the other at some point – and you and I especially have done that. And I'm sorry, truly sorry, for the way things happened between us – most of which was my fault. Now we should try again, as friends.' She looked at him. He stared straight ahead.

Finally he said, 'Yes,' but without conviction. Then he turned to her. 'It's all rather easier for you – and Anna, and Linochka. You all got what you wanted – with Sandy, Ivan and Johnny.' He was petulant now.

'But, Sasha, you have Ida. You haven't told me. But it's obvious. And when Johnny wrote he clearly hinted –'

'Oh, yes, I have Ida. But I'm not certain of anything there.' He strode on ahead of her. 'The fact is,' he turned, 'yes, I made a great ass of myself – with you, Linochka and not least Anna. I'm none too keen to start it all over again with another woman.'

'I see that. But you've nothing to reproach yourself for there. We all make mistakes in that department. You, too. But it's not the end. Ida's wonderful.'

They had stopped by some trees halfway up the hill. Sasha examined the smooth, still slightly frosted bark of a beech.

Harriet looked at him, hatless in his red muffler – saw his face brightly caught in the slanting sunlight. The curiously divided features – severe jaw and chin, taut lips. Something cruel there. Distant, adult, arrogant. But then the upper half, so different – sensitive, the confiding eyes, generous brow, the casual thatch of tousled hair. Touched with poetry. A divided face, half man, half child. Anxious to hurt, so readily hurt. Petulant, gloomy, sometimes insufferable, sometimes wonderful.

He looked surprisingly young in the freezing afternoon light. Adolescent. Almost a boy. The boy she'd practically brought up, whom she had taught, and later seduced – as much as made no difference; whose child she had borne, whom she'd refused to marry; but had made love with, so happily, with such fulfilment, for so long afterwards; whom she'd kept by cowardice, when they'd finally parted so coldly, meeting again just as coldly, in Ladoga after the revolution, the same in Harbin and now here at the rectory. What a catalogue of pain and error.

And yet, as he'd said, there was more to it than that. She simply didn't know what to do, how to make things up with him, now at this moment, which might be their last chance of coming to some sort of decent terms.

But seeing such youth in his face then, she was suddenly taken back to that time before the war in Petersburg when she'd first realized how overwhelmingly attracted she was to him. She felt the same thing now, irrationally, a physical passion for him striking her out of the blue. Yet this no longer seemed anything like the obsession, the illness, she had once felt it to be. She saw that her feelings for him – then and now – were not perverse but had a rightful place in all the many ways of loving. There had been great pain and hurt between them. But there had been a brightness, too – a wonderful light which had permeated their affair and which she felt again between them now, recreated, as the low sun on his face seemed to recreate his youth; so that she forgot their arguments, his continued coldness and spoke at once, all in a rush, with quiet urgency.

'Sasha, if we weren't made for marrying, we were perfectly made for everything else we did, almost from the beginning. Feeding you golden syrup sandwiches as a child, teaching you music – loving, making love, having Holly. And it was the first time, for both of us, doing all these things. Only you and me. And two people who've had so much, and done these things – perhaps they have to lose something. Permanency, marriage. I'll marry Sandy. But I'll never have with him what we had together.'

He turned at last and nodded. 'Yes. Yes . . .'

Yelena, with Johnny, strode ahead of the others, up the winding sheep tracks. 'How clever of you . . .' She looked at him pertly. 'To get us all together here. To get us all together anyway, after Harbin.' She was more serious in this.

'Nothing too clever – just a bit of energy and common sense. Besides, the only reason you're here – that we're all here for that matter – is due to Miki and Galina, who stopped you at the masked ball.'

'Yes . . . But you cemented everything, in taking us all to America. So that we were able to sort things out sensibly. Great gift you have, dear Johnny – sorting people out.'

'Princess – Mrs Quince – as I told you before, I'd have done the same for any friend. And you, all of you – you're all my good friends. That's what counts.'

'We were lovers, though. Before we were friends. On the train to Dvinsk . . .'

'That was no trouble. Except you wouldn't marry me, when I asked you that night.'

'Why didn't you ask me again, in Harbin or up at Shanyang? Or when we got to Philadelphia? I still wonder. And not telling me you had married.'

'That was a mistake. But as for marrying you – I told you: I'd never ask you twice. It was your turn, if you wanted it.'

'I did in the end. But I'd never have had it – you, anybody – without Father Byrne.'

'No . . .'

Johnny remembered Father Byrne, remembered all that had happened after Yelena had tried to kill Sasha and Anna on the dance floor, and then herself.

The police had come. She'd been locked up and charged with attempted murder. Johnny had at once got in touch with General Horvath. Given Johnny's standing in the city and with the Governor, and with an undertaking that he would at once remove Yelena from the city, she was released.

He had brought her first to the Orient Hotel. Sandy had arranged for the Consular doctor to come and see her. She had been numb, vacant-faced, silent to begin with – then restless, violent, shouting obscenities at Johnny and the doctor. Apart from giving her sleeping draughts, which she largely spat out, the doctor could do little for her. Her bedroom door was kept locked. Johnny, Sandy or Harriet kept a constant watch – waiting for her wakings-up. And then the stream of abuse and foul language again, the attacks.

Her condition remained much the same on the long journey to Philadelphia, by boat across the Pacific to San Francisco, and then across America, during which Johnny had hired a series of nurses to look after her. The doctors, for Johnny brought several to see her, all diagnosed a case of severe depression, with what went with this by way of periods of unnatural elation and paranoia, which accounted for her foul oaths, her shouts and screaming.

Sandy, at least, had seen just the same behaviour in her five years before, at the castle on Lake Ladoga, when he had found her similarly afflicted, dressed in medieval clothes, with her evil little pug dog. And Sandy had told Johnny all that happened at Ladoga, with Yelena, and between them, that first evening of sheer nightmare, when she had miscarried the child, and the dog, supposedly dead, had come for them both in the tower bedroom.

'I didn't believe it,' Sandy had said to Johnny. 'Until I saw her then, her behaviour. I wasn't the sort to believe – but I was forced to then – that she was possessed by something, some evil – Satan, the devil, call it what you will.'

Johnny hadn't wanted to believe it either. But when he got her home to Philadelphia, and there was still no real improvement, he'd gone to see a Catholic priest he'd been put in touch with, who he'd been told dealt in these matters of Satanic possession, a Jesuit attached to the Cathedral, Father Byrne. He'd told him the whole story. 'Is it possible, Father, that this woman is possessed by . . . by the devil? I mean – is there such a person, as a reality?'

They were talking in a small bleak room upstairs in the

Presbytery, sparsely furnished, with a white crucifix and a picture of Our Lady of Sorrows over the desk. The priest, a white-haired, middle-aged man, strongly built, dressed in black, with an alert, intelligent face, had automatically, it seemed, put his hand out on his white breviary before replying.

'Yes,' he said quietly. 'The answer is yes, to both your questions. St Ignatius calls him "the enemy of human nature". And the scriptures certainly present him as a personal being, without a body but with free will and great intelligence – ready to act in any number of evil ways, in and against individuals. Though the individuals themselves have largely to encourage this, to ask him in . . .'

'But how do you tell if a person is possessed in this way?'

The priest was silent for a moment. Then he'd leant forward, still keeping his hand on the breviary on the desk in front of him. 'One can't exactly *tell*. It's a matter of experience. One can feel it, in the presence of the person. And from all that you have told me of this unfortunate woman – it seems possible – if all medical means have failed to effect a cure – that she may indeed be possessed of the devil.' He gripped the breviary in his powerful hands, before looking back at Johnny. 'I take it that you have come to see me because you want the church to consider an exorcism.'

'Yes. Yes, I do.'

'It's a serious matter, Mr Quince. The church does not practise this except as a last resort. We would hope for improvement first through administering the Rite of Deliverance, in which we ask Christ to order the devil to depart. Exorcism is quite another matter. Here the priest must confront the devil himself without any guarantee of divine intervention. There are certain dangers for the exorcist, which is one reason why it is very rarely done. It would have to be with the authority of the Bishop.'

'Yes. Yes, I see that. But will you ask the Bishop? Will you consider it? I see no other answer to her condition.'

The priest stood up, letting his breviary go at last. 'Yes, it will be considered. If there is agreement, I would need to see the woman first. I gather, from what you say, that Miss Rumovsky can be violent.'

'Yes, sometimes, if contradicted, forced in anything, put upon.'

Father Byrne nodded. 'Yes . . . You see the difficulties.' He turned and looked out of the window at the cherry trees blossoming in the Cathedral garden. '"The devil is as a roaring lion, seeking whom he may devour" . . .' he said, more or less to himself, before he turned and showed Johnny out.

Father Byrne, when he'd come a week later, had asked Johnny to be present at what he intended to be a Rite of Deliverance, in the room above the old coachhouse at the back of the tall house on Delancey Place which Johnny had made over as quarters for Yelena, where she was looked after by a nurse.

It had been a spring evening, the pink and white cherry blossom out all over the city, covering the two cherry trees in Johnny's small garden which led to the coachhouse. They had gone upstairs. The nurse had left them. Yelena had been lying on the divan bed, in a dressing-gown, face firmly to the wall, emaciated, silent.

'I've brought Father Byrne to see you.'

Father Byrne, in his black soutane, with the white crucifix round his neck, stood some distance from the bed, his hands folded over his white breviary. After a few moments, as if sensing the priest and these holy objects, Yelena had suddenly twisted round. She saw the crucifix which he held up now in front of her. The effect was immediate. She reacted like an animal, a bull to a red rag. Eyes widening, she'd jumped to her feet and started to shout. Father Byrne began to intone a prayer.

'Lord God, through our Saviour Jesus Christ, intercede in this Rite of Deliverance with this woman, that the devil and all his works may be cast out from her . . .'

She had started to scream at him then, in a gathering fury, every sort of blasphemy and obscenity, her eyes soon so risen in their sockets that only the whites were properly visible.

There was a sudden foul stench in the room, the air filled with an aura which Johnny couldn't account for – a darkening of the spring light through the open window, a heaviness which coursed through his limbs, a thickening in his mind, so that he seemed befuddled, confused. The room, he realized, was suddenly very hot.

She screamed. She talked in some strange tongue now, moving towards Father Byrne, shaking her fists. He raised his voice. '. . . intercede, with Thy might, and with Thy holy spirit, that this evil presence . . .' His voice died, as he continued the Rite. He stepped backwards as Yelena approached him threateningly. It was clear that no Rite of Deliverance would be effective here. He changed his prayer, speaking in Latin now.

But he'd hardly begun this new and more formal Rite of Exorcism, when she attacked him. She launched herself at him, furiously, starting to grapple with him, to bite him, like a dog.

Johnny had leapt forward, trying to separate them. But now he found he had no strength. And her own strength was incredible. She had easily thrown him aside, lunging again at Father Byrne. Big man though he was, she nearly felled him. She would have done so but for the wind that came then, through the open window, a sudden furious wind that blew a snow of cherry blossom into the room, whipped the curtains aside, a tablecloth, threw the chairs about, a fierce wind that had rammed him back against the door, and Father Byrne against the wall. Only Yelena was untouched by it, standing in the middle of the room, triumphant.

Father Byrne got to his feet at once, holding up the crucifix again. He started another prayer now, urgently. '"Christ beside me, Christ to win me . . ."'

Reaching into her dressing-gown pocket she took out a pair of scissors, held them like a dagger and moved towards Father Byrne again.

'"Christ behind me, Christ before me . . ."'

Closer to him now, the blades raised.

'"Christ to comfort and restore me . . ."' A yard away now, as Johnny had watched them, wanting to stop her, to try and separate them, as he had before. But this time he found he couldn't move. He was paralysed.

'"Christ beneath me, Christ above me . . ."'

Father Byrne's voice had been quite steady, holding the crucifix up in front of her, inches from the raised scissors.

She wavered. She started to shake, as if suddenly touched by an electric current. Her eyes flickered. Her face was suffused with pain. She was wrestling with something, her body beginning to contort obscenely. She sank to her knees, on all fours then, pawing and growling like a dog, menacing, about to attack.

'"Christ in quiet, Christ in danger . . ."'

Then, after a minute or two, she was a beaten dog. A dog trying to rise from the floor, foam at her mouth, trying to rise, a scalded dog, whimpering, dying. Then she vomited, voiding everything inside her, a frantic retching, gulping, spurts of bilious yellow liquid. Then, at the end, she spewed out a black matted substance, successive gobbets of congealed black hair, it seemed, all over the floor.

Father Byrne had continued his prayer over her now, sweating. '"Christ in hearts of all that love me, Christ in mouth of friend and stranger . . ."'

She lay on the floor, curled up, motionless. The wind had gone. And the stench. The spring light was there again, the floor littered with white cherry blossom. Father Byrne had knelt over her. 'Lord God, through Thy only son Jesus Christ, grant perpetual deliverance to this Thy servant, from all the wiles and spites of the devil, now and forever more. In the name of the Father, Son and Holy Ghost, Amen.'

Now, nine months later, on the Cotswold hill, in the chilly December sunlight, Johnny looked at Yelena and remembered all this. But he didn't take up the theme of Father Byrne which she had just introduced. He didn't comment on the matter then, as he hadn't before, after once talking about it to Yelena a few days later. Yelena herself remembered very little of the whole business, describing simply a feeling of great light, and of lightness in her body afterwards. She didn't remember much. But he would never forget.

They'd come to the top of the first hill. 'What do you think that is?' Johnny asked. There was an ancient stone, an angular slab of limestone, set up as a post on the crown of the hill.

Sandy joined them. 'Part of a stone from a long barrow near here. Place where they buried Iron Age Britons. Now the animals use it to scratch themselves.'

Johnny, turning round, scratched his back on it. 'I see . . .'

Harriet and Sandy walked on ahead now, arm in arm, down the gentle slope on the far side of the hill towards another higher rise ahead of them. 'Any news from her solicitors?' Harriet asked him. 'I saw you had some letters when we got back.'

'Yes, a letter from Mary's solicitors, via mine. She's still trying to fight it.'

'But she has no grounds. She "deserted" you.'

Sandy nearly slipped on the steep and now muddy sheep path, the frost melting in the afternoon sun. 'Yes,' he said simply.

'Nor did you ever have an "affair" with me – as she's contending.'

'Not then. But I have since.' He looked at Harriet's freckled face and cornflower-blue eyes, wisps of reddish hair sticking out from beneath her fur hat: the high-cheeked pre-Raphaelite profile which he'd always loved.

'Yes . . . Yes, you have, dear Sandy.' She smiled at him, laughed. 'All rather like Elinor Glyn isn't it? *Three Weeks* – remember, you brought the book to me in the English Hospital in Petrograd.'

'Yes. Both of us so keen, then, on Shilling Shockers . . .'

'Living them now, though. Living "in sin" –'

'"Or would you like to sin, with Elinor Glyn, on a tiger skin?"'

'I would! But where's the tiger skin? None in the rectory. Do your parents mind, do you think? Us. They must know; though we have separate rooms, we sleep together here.'

'I'm sure they know. They're not fuddy-duddies. Papa's thought to be a dangerously liberal churchman. And he is. And Mama, she's shy and a bit vague. But not prudish. Don't worry. The Mary business will be settled very soon.'

Anna walked with the bearded Ivan farther down the line, slipping and slithering on the thawing track. The affair between Anna and Sasha had died on the long boat journey to San Francisco. It had died quite suddenly for Anna, one morning in mid-Pacific, when she'd been playing deck-quoits alone with Johnny. She had said to him suddenly, off-handedly, 'Sasha doesn't love me.'

'Oh?' Johnny had thrown his quoit nonchalantly.

'No.' She'd been ironic. 'Harriet was right when she told me

– the thing between him and Yelena. Still strong. Even though she tried to kill him. He's divided over it. Her and me.'

'I'm not surprised. I could have told you that. It's an old story.' He threw another quoit, just missing the central peg. 'Damn.'

'I suppose that's why you brought Ivan with us. For me. Your knowing so much about the twins' nature.'

'That was one reason why I *asked* Ivan if he'd *like* to come to the States – where I thought I could get him some work.' He'd turned then, holding the last quoit. 'And getting to know something of your nature, too, Anna. I'm really pretty good at Russian nature.' He fiddled with his quoit, smiling. 'How you people blow hot and cold. Rush around looking for the wrong thing, when the real thing is staring you in the face. That's why I asked Ivan along. He's the real thing. You know that.'

'Yes, I do.'

'Lucky you still had a chance with him then.'

'Yes. Not luck. You. Thank you.'

Johnny threw his last quoit. It landed perfectly, over the central peg.

In Philadelphia Johnny had got Ivan a temporary job in the offices of the Philly–Reading Railroad Company, helping Matty plan schedules, where he moved cardboard trains about on a big wallboard, like ships, with great skill. Ivan had taken an apartment in the suburbs, near the offices. Soon afterwards Anna had moved in with him. And soon after that they had been married in the small Russian Orthodox church there. Now they walked together, in the middle of England.

'What do you think?' Ivan asked her. 'Of England?'

'I've only been here twenty-four hours.'

'Impressions, though?'

'I like it. The tiny fields. Like pocket handkerchiefs. And each of them walled or hedged off, so neatly, carefully. It's extraordinary. Such an enclosed, cosy life the English lead. Everything so *small*. Tiny fields and roads. And those minute straw-covered houses in the village.'

'They're called "cottages".' Ivan used the English word.

'Yes, of course.' She looked at him, frustrated, half annoyed, teasingly. She wanted to kiss him – and smack him. 'Oh, you're so very knowledgeable about the English!'

'I am quite. Though naval matters mostly. All the reading I did at the Naval College. The Battle of the Nile. Lord Nelson . . .'

'And Lady Hamilton –'

He slipped on the path then, went sprawling on his backside. She tried to pull him up, but couldn't. He just lay there laughing. 'What fun, what good talk we had in Petrograd then, before the revolution,' he said, hands behind his head, gazing up at her.

'Don't we now?'

'Oh, now we're married,' he said with mock solemnity. 'It's all quite different. Isn't it? Serious business. No jokes. No suddenly jumping into bed together. No chatter. Me, the wicked dominating husband, not interested in music or children –'

'Get up, you bizarre man! . . . You *untidy* man. You Gogol, you, with your big ears. Your coat's ruined.' She managed to pull him up then, brushing the back of his coat. 'You'd better be interested in children,' she told him. 'Given my condition. And as for music – we'll just have to differ about that, won't we?'

'I'll come to concerts with you – now and then.'

'So long as you don't tap your foot to what you imagine to be the tempo – you can come with me. So long as you don't tap your foot *at all*!'

'Yes, Lady Hamilton.'

She looked at him, her expression suddenly changing, from tease to one of astonished tenderness, looking at this big gruff gentle funny man – so brave, and nearly lost, first in the civil war, and then by her.

'Yes, Lord Nelson . . .' She paused. Then kissed him, quite fiercely. 'Let's always keep us like that. Like them.'

'Yes,' he said slowly, looking at her with an equally surprised expression. 'We'll try.'

Ida was walking with Sasha now. They had fallen behind the others, Sasha dawdling, looking ahead to the succession of small hills still to negotiate; then turning, gazing at the bare beech coppice behind him, on the other hilltop, the branches silhouetted against the crimson-streaked sky where the sun was falling.

Ida was bossy. 'Come on, Sasha! If we're to get to this brewery –'

'I don't want any beer. Not thirsty.'

'Be polite, at least. It's Sandy's uncle's brewery. He's expecting us. And don't be *difficult*.'

He joined her. 'God, you're so bossy sometimes.'

'And you're sometimes so bloody.'

They looked at each other, challengingly. Sasha was sweating slightly, his cheeks flushed. She touched his forehead. 'You're all hot,' she said. 'Too warmly dressed. Take your scarf off. You're not in Siberia now.'

'Well, you're dressed – in that skimpy fur-trimmed outfit – like some tart out on the Nevsky Prospekt. You must be freezing. Here, take my coat.'

'I'm fine. I'm not cold – I'm *fat*,' she told him shortly.

'No. "Plump" is the better word. I've told you – nicely *plump*.' He looked at her appraisingly, nodding. 'With competent paws, tiny pretty ears, opinionated hair – and a delicious little belly.' He kissed her, low down, about the latter area.

'Thank you,' she said very formally.

'If only you weren't such a nanny –'

'And if you weren't sometimes so bloody *contrary*!'

'Ah,' he said, mock ponderous. 'It's the Russian in me, the Slav soul . . .' He drew the last words out lugubriously. 'But that's what you want, isn't it?' he went on brightly. 'A full-blooded Russian. Romantic, voracious, negligent, passionate, difficult. You can't complain.'

'I'm not complaining. Only commenting,' she said equally brightly. She kissed him briefly. 'Anyway, don't worry. I can handle you.'

'Yes, I can handle you, too.' He looked her up and down again. 'Tonight? We will, won't we?'

'No. We're not married. And not in England anyway. Very stuffy about that sort of thing here. And *certainly* not in a rectory.' She stuck her tongue out at him and ran away.

'You little brute!' He ran after her. 'How did you and I ever get together?'

She turned to him, excited, all red in the face. 'Gawd knows,' she said, exaggerating her southern accent. She ran away down the hill, helter-skelter, in her unsuitable fur boots.

'Hey, wait for me!' he shouted, chasing her.

'Look at those two!' Miki said. 'Surprising, they're getting together. They're never done arguing and fighting and chasing each other.'

'And touching each other,' Galina said. 'Never done with that either'.

'Yes . . . A full-time, fascinated occupation for both of them. Like two animals together, of a quite different species.'

'They are.'

They walked on, slipping down the track. The others were ahead now, walking up a rise, on sheep's tracks that wound in and out through a beech coppice, cut into the side of the hill. 'What do you think of England?' Miki asked her.

'Only quite like it. It's all so small. You could put it up your sleeve and do a conjuring trick with it.'

'There are good circuses in England, Chipperfield's and Bertram Mills. Not so good as ours –'

'As ours used to be.'

'Yes. But we could get work here, if we wanted. When your brother Andrei comes over – all three of us. The act we did.'

She looked at his mobile features, the eyes that were flickering now, as they did whenever he thought of performance. She knew how he had so little real life outside a performance of some sort. It wasn't quite the same with her.

'I don't know. You know I want to give the trapeze act up. Too dangerous – I'm not so supple, or young. And you don't want to be a circus clown and conjurer all your life.'

'No.'

'You want to do something in the moving-picture business. In Hollywood. Chaplin, Buster Keaton, Fatty Arbuckle. Like them.'

'Buster Keaton – yes.'

'Well, why not? Your mime, your glum-funny face, so mobile. Legs and arms – throwing them all over the place, yet so controlled. You'd be very good in moving-pictures.

'All right. Let's try it. Together. Do a two-reel comedy. With Andrei. Make a moving picture.'

'Money?'

'Wouldn't take much. Anyway . . .' He paused. 'I asked Johnny on the boat over. Talked to him, about doing a story I have in mind – making a short picture. He said he'd put up the money for it any day.'

'He *did*? You never told me. What about?'

'About a crazy postman – me – in a small village, and all the trouble he gets into delivering letters. Dogs – and irate husbands who think he's seducing their wives. He has this old bicycle; bees sting him; he gets drunk; everything goes wrong for him. The fat wife ends up clobbering him –'

'And I'm the fat wife, I suppose!'

'No. Well, you could pretend –' He backed away.

She started to chase him. They ran down the rest of the hill, shouting and laughing when she ran around the trunks of the beech trees, playing hide-and-seek with him.

'Look at those two,' Harriet said to Sandy, watching them from higher up the hill. 'Never done chasing and acting out little dramas together.'

'Yes. They like each other.'

Anna, dropping back, left Ivan and walked with Sasha. They had not come to any decent new terms with each other, after their separation in Philadelphia when she had gone to live with Ivan in the suburbs, and Sasha had taken a room alone above a bookshop, round the corner from Johnny's big brownstone house on Delancey Place.

They had both made asses of themselves, they knew, and were still pretty ashamed of this. But she had recovered her life with Ivan, and Sasha hadn't, deciding to live alone after Yelena had married Johnny. True, he had taken up with Ida, but without commitment. He remained the outsider: brooding, unsettled, unforgiving, sometimes angry.

'Hello!' She came up to him, warmly.

'Hi,' he said dully.

'Sasha,' Anna said to him at once. 'We have to be better friends – than this.'

'Just what Harriet was saying to me ten minutes ago. Everyone wants to be better friends with me.'

Anna couldn't hide her impatience at this childish remark. 'Sasha, stop feeling sorry for yourself! Good God, you've more talent in your little finger than – than . . . *And* you have Ida. She's more than fond of you. And you of her. So all this gloom is just a show you put on for us. For me and Harriet particularly. It's not really you. And you don't have to hurt us that way, or yourself with this sulky performance –' He turned to her, about to contest all this. 'No,' she said. 'Don't start. I know what you're going to say – that it's my fault because I hurt you, because I left you. Well, I did that because I saw you were still divided, between me and Yelena, that you'd probably taken up with me as a way of avoiding her. Even though she'd tried to kill you. And me. Still stuck with her. So that when she got married to Johnny, you acted as if you'd been deserted, with a face like an abandoned lover at their wedding –'

'No –'

'Yes! And it's all damn nonsense. Yelena got out of it. And so can you. What did you think you were ever going to do with Yelena? *Live* with her? Sleep with her? You couldn't have –'

'No. But I owe her – a lot. It was she who made all the efforts, with Harriet, in looking for me, following me all the way across Siberia. And it was because of Yelena that Johnny came and rescued us up at Shanyang. Rescued *us*, Anna. And it was Yelena who breathed life back into me, when that bomb winded me. I owe her plenty. I owe her my life. You seem conveniently to forget all this.'

'Yes. Yes, all right. I see all that. But it's always been more than something of all that, between you both. And you've never come to terms with it – in yourself now, like she has.'

'Yes.' He looked at her with an element of triumph. 'By marrying Johnny.'

'You think she doesn't love him?'

He said nothing for a moment. Then he said abruptly, 'You make up your own mind on that.' He walked on ahead of her.

'None of which alters the fact that you and I ought to try and get on properly,' she shouted after him, then catching up with him.

'Just like Harriet,' he said, looking straight ahead, frowning, hands stuffed deep in his pockets. 'The two of you on about doing the "decent, civilized thing". You both find that conveniently easy. I don't.' He strode on.

She stopped in her tracks, looking after him, frowning. Then she laughed, running to keep up with him again. 'All right, Sasha. But I'm not going to behave like that – with you. You're far too valuable a person, did you but know it. You should like yourself a bit more.' They walked on together, in silence.

They had all reached the highest point in the hills now. The land flattened out ahead of them, in ploughed earth and pasture, dropping gently down to another valley, where the brewery lay, a mile away in the distance. They could just see the tall chimney rising from the mist which was creeping up towards them. But where they stood there was clear brightness, the sun still behind them as they paused on the heights, looking both ways, to their misty destination, and behind, admiring the sunset, a blood-red orb sinking over the Malvern hills to the west.

They moved down the slope, past a shepherd's stone hut, through a beech plantation and along a fenced farm lane, where the going was easier. Sheep gazed curiously at them in the fading light as they sank out of the sunset towards the mists, the air quite still. Harriet walked with Anna.

'I talked with Sasha,' Harriet told her. 'Still hurt. And angry.'

'Same with me, just now. You were right, Harriet – all you told me that day in the Orient Hotel. It would never have worked, me and Sasha. But I told him just now – that he couldn't go on and on blaming me, for leaving him.'

Harriet smiled a fraction. 'I told him just the same thing half an hour ago. Whatever mistakes we made – and we all did.'

'Yes. He has this obsession with marriage.'

Harriet wrapped herself up more warmly. The sun had disappeared. They were walking now in an eerie, yellow light. 'It's security. The difficult childhood – no proper mother. And wanting to get away from Yelena. Funny – when most men are usually so anxious *not* to marry!'

'But he could so easily marry Ida.'

'Feels that's too easy, I expect. He's so stubborn. And a need to punish people. Just like Yelena before she married Johnny.'

'Well, Sasha's right, of course. Marriage is the answer, isn't it? Awful risk, even with the most suitable type. But it is the best answer. Anything less than that – well, it's just a pencil sketch, which one should either tear up, or go on and paint the full picture.'

'You and Ivan – are you managing that?'

Anna nodded. 'Yes. Yes, so far. Except the navy thing. I

know he wants to go to sea again. And I don't know how we'll manage that. And you? With Sandy?'

'Like you. So far, it's absolutely fine.'

'So far?'

'Sandy's not the countryman his father is. I don't know that he'll want to immerse himself completely in a rural life. He hankers after Russia, his books, translating. He'd like to do that full time, in some way, writing about Russia. Or go back to the Foreign Office. But his deafness would prevent him getting any decent posting. A mercy in a way, because I've done enough travelling . . . And I love it here.'

'Yes, it *is* lovely.'

Harriet turned to her, more urgently, happy to further confide in this great friend, with whom she'd experienced so much and survived such dangers, a friend lost in Harbin, but now clearly regained. 'So you see, with Sandy, there's this professional frustration in the background. And also – children. We'd love to have them. But until the divorce, it's difficult, all that side of things. Being careful all the time. But otherwise, so far it's marvellous.'

'"So far" . . .' Anna pondered the words. 'So far, each day. That's as much as we can hope for. And work at it, every day. Love *doesn't* grow on trees, like leaves.' Anna looked at her. Harriet smiled.

'All right, you needn't remind me. I know that now. And any sort of reconciliation with Sasha – no easier. I'd like that so much.'

'Me, too.'

'What can we do?'

'Nothing,' Anna said firmly. 'Nothing that we haven't tried already. Sasha – and Yelena – they're both in a special category. Their artistry. Makes them impossible, quite often. You either have to chuck them – which I'm not going to do – or accept them. They're in another world a lot of the time. I've seen them playing, these last months, in Philadelphia. Living on a knife edge – of ambition, perfection, obsession, love and hatred for each other. Nothing to do with real life or ordinary people, who they'll ride over roughshod, given half the chance. Except with Johnny – Yelena can't quite do this with him, because he's equally ruthless!'

'Like Ida?'

'Yes. She and Sasha would be well matched.'

They'd come down the lane and had reached the outskirts of the brewery, an arched gateway rearing out of the mist. There was a smell of malt and hops. Johnny sniffed the air. 'Why, that's better,' he said eagerly. 'The wonderful smell!' He turned to Yelena.

'Yes,' she said. She came up and sniffed at him. 'A bit like you. You have a smell of warm barley corn and woodsmoke about you. That's the *real* reason I like you. Humans, like animals, did I tell you? – it's how they smell for each other that *really* counts, that brings and keeps them together.'

'Why thank you, Princess. I'm honoured. And yes, you smell pretty damn good, too.'

2

At the small brewery, in the wood-panelled taproom, Sandy's uncle Willie, a big man in tweeds and gaiters, was lavish with a specially brewed Christmas ale. It came in small bottles, dark, frothy, a touch of sweetness, very strong.

'It's a bit like that black Russian beer,' Ivan said to Miki. 'That Kron's used to make in Petersburg.' He remarked on this later to Willie.

'Oh, yes,' he told Ivan slowly. 'Same sort of beer, I should think. This is sometimes known as "Russian Stout" in England.'

They all got quite tipsy in the lamplit room, with its wooden benches and coloured advertisements for 'Saunderton's Best XXX Ale'.

'I think I'd like to live in England,' Ivan said to Anna later. 'Join the British Navy.'

'What about your old wounds?'

'I'm as fit as ever now. And only thirty-two. And plenty of experience. Second Officer on the *Kiev* – as big a battleship as any the British have.'

'All right,' she said. 'I'm not being honest. Best seaman going, highest honour for valour – I'm sure they'd take you. It's just that I'd miss you. Away for months.'

He looked at her seriously. 'I would too. We'll see.' He brightened then. 'Perhaps they'd take me on in the Admiralty in London. Knowing so much about Nelson. But seriously, as a Staff Officer – for my knowledge of the Red Navy. They're going to need people who know about that. A landbound sailor!'

'You wouldn't be happy. It's the sea you love.'

'True.' He drank some more of the strong ale. 'Perhaps I could join a passenger boat, and you could come with me.'

'They don't let wives come. And officers on passenger ships are supposed to chat and flirt with the women. And I wouldn't much like that.'

'No. But I'll have to do something to earn a proper living. You with the child coming. Besides paying Johnny back the money he's lent us.'

'Yes.' She looked at him for a moment, incredulously, as if she'd only just met him. Then she kissed him. 'Ivan, I'm sorry.'

'For what?'

'You know what. That I could ever have – done what I did – to you.'

'We've been through all that,' he said easily, taking some more beer. 'None of us were ourselves then. How could we have been? What we'd lived through. I was smoking opium like a chimney. And drinking. All of us then – up to something crazy.'

'You waited, though. And I didn't –'

'We've talked of that. Have some more beer –'

'I have. And the beer makes me say it –'

'You don't owe me any apologies now. If it hadn't been opium or drink with me, it might well have been another woman.'

'But it wasn't, that's the big difference.'

'All right,' he said brightly. 'I was strong and loyal and noble. And you lost your head and made an ass of yourself with Sasha. That make you feel better?'

'Yes,' she said. 'The truth always makes me feel better.' She kissed him again. 'Thank you.'

At the other end of the taproom Yelena talked to Sandy, raising her voice, for his deafness, over the babble. 'So – here is your "cosy Cotswolds"! At last. "The house that goes yellow, with latticed shutters, lilac outside the church door, dozy farmers, the long meadow, and here' – she raised her glass – 'here's "the beer over the hill". I've longed to see it all, Sandy, and I love it. What a time, what a journey, since you told me all about it – at that lunch party nearly seven years ago, on the battleship in the Gulf off Petersburg, when they played Gilbert *and* Sullivan.'

Sandy nodded, holding his glass diffidently. 'Well, we'll have Gilbert and Sullivan at last as well. They're doing *Pinafore* after Christmas at the Savoy and I've booked seats for us all. You'll have to wait till spring for the lilac. Though you'll see the dozy farmers in church tomorrow.'

'We'll come back in the spring.' Yelena was enthusiastic, the beer going to her head. 'Of course we will, come over often. Johnny loves England – has a thing about it now, like he had about Russia. Keeps talking about English kings and queens, and his Quince ancestors up in Yorkshire, and the Magna Carta. And I'd like to play here – concerts, with Sasha. We've done well with that, so far, in America.'

'And you've been settling in? What about that great castle of Johnny's in Virginia?'

'Yes, you've never seen anything so phony in your life. All turrets and battlements – put up thirty years ago.'

'Do you like it, Yelena?'

She smiled. 'I love Johnny. So it doesn't matter.' She took another sip of beer. 'Don't tell him, but if you want to know, I'd prefer to live here.'

'In England –'

'Here, in Saunderton.'

They looked at each other. 'Yes,' she went on, in a great bright flow of words, so that he didn't know if it was the beer talking in her or the truth. 'I went into the library after lunch. Saw all those Russian books of yours. Gogol and Pushkin and Lermontov and Chekhov. And all your Russian dictionaries and the lecterns you use – that we said we'd use together, translating. Remember?'

'Yes. Yes, I do,' he said lightly.

'One can't have everything.'

'No.'

Later she talked to Sasha. 'So?' she said. 'What are you thinking about?' He rocked on his feet, pensively, the glass of beer almost untouched in his thin fingers. 'You're looking glum – again.'

'Tired, that's all. A long day.'

'Gloomy. And not touching your beer. It's deliciously warming. Go on, have some. And stop looking *farouche* and poetic. Else I'll get Ida over to deal with you . . .' She smiled wickedly. Ida was on the other side of the taproom. They could hear her, chattering vividly with Willie the Brewer, fascinating him. 'You're so luky to have her,' Yelena went on. 'Why don't you marry her?'

'Not certain she wants it.'

'Good God, you could ask her, though.'

'We – we haven't got round to it.'

Yelena stood back, and looked at him, amazed. 'Sasha, you're as mad as I was. Marry her. She'd like that. I know she would.'

'How?'

'Johnny told me.'

'Oh, did he?'

'Yes. But don't tell Ida.'

'I wasn't certain –'

'You can be. You're a pair. Though quite opposite, like Johnny and me. Which is why things work for us. And it'd work with you and Ida for the same reason.'

'Perhaps.'

'You and I – so alike. That's always been our trouble. But that doesn't trouble us any more,' she added firmly.

'No.' He looked at her – carefully, but uncertainly. 'No, it doesn't trouble us any more.' He looked at her with a moment's impatient frustration then. 'No,' he said at last, quickly.

'No.' There was an edge of sadness in her voice. The drink had suddenly left her. 'So,' she said brightly. 'Have some of that beer. And marry her, you idiot. Don't look this gift horse in the mouth. I did that, for years. It's fatal.'

'Yes, I know. It nearly was.'

'Don't remind me. That's all over, too.' She put her hand on his, rubbing his long fingers for an instant, feeling the fine hair running along the top of them. Fingers she'd first properly touched in their grand-uncle's house at Orlov, years before, the two of them playing Tchaikovsky on the terrace; looking at his fingers so carefully then, suddenly wanting him. She put his hand down. 'Yes, that's all done with, as well, the madness. Marry her, Sasha.' There was an urgency in her voice now. She wanted him to be taken away from her in this way, as she had been taken away from him by Johnny.

Ida came over then. 'Hey,' she said brightly. 'I like it here.

And this beer.' She lifted her glass. 'What have you two been up to? Nothing serious, I hope.'

'No, no, nothing of that sort.' Sasha had started to quaff his own beer now, taking big gulps of it.

Ida looked at him. 'You said you weren't thirsty! The beer's improved you. Got you out of your gloom.'

'Yes,' he said off-handedly. 'I was just thinking . . . Whether you'd care to marry me,' he added even more casually.

She stood back from him. 'My, that beer has done you some good.' She was equally matter of fact. She looked at her own glass, half empty. 'I'll take some more. I'll think about it.' She tipped the glass right up to her mouth and finished it in one gulp. 'Yes,' she said finally.

'Yes, what?'

'*Yes*. I've thought about it. I will.' She glared at him, fair hair all askew, scatty and cheeky, round face flushed, and somehow a little more beautiful than she had been a few moments before. She looked at her empty glass. 'We'd better bring a few boxes of this back home with us, Sasha. For when we have problems . . .' She kissed him.

Miki talked to Johnny, savouring the beer, looking round the hop-smelling taproom full of lively chatter. 'It's pleasant, isn't it?' Johnny said. He was sweating slightly. 'The beer's quite something,' he added, licking his lips. 'Keel you over pretty quickly. Need some food with it. I talked to Cook at the rectory after lunch, good woman called Hazel, had quite a chatter with her. She's doing what she calls "roast" lamb for supper. I suppose she means "broiled". Looking forward to it. I told her I'd show her how to cook a proper ham, a Virginia ham. How's Galina liking things here?'

'So-so, I think. She misses the great open spaces, Russia and America. Says everything here is like a pocket handkerchief.'

'That's what I like about England.'

'Yes –'

'No matter. If you're going to make moving pictures, I suppose it'll have to be America. And, hey!' He turned to him, taking him by the shoulder. 'That's what you have to do, Miki, because you're good. The mime and the acting. Good as Buster Keaton.'

'Thank you.'

'You know, Miki, it's great magic, what all of us do. We're so lucky. Playing with trains, sailing ships, clowning, flying on trapezes, making moving pictures, the music those two do.' He looked over to Sasha and Yelena, talking with Ida. 'Damn magic!'

'Yes –'

'And you know something?' He looked round the taproom. 'The most of us – we'd never have made it, had a future in all these fine things, if it hadn't been for you on that dance floor.'

'Or you – afterwards.'

'No, I just did my stuff. A bit of bullying and high-handedness. You people . . .' He looked round the room. 'Every one of you Russians, and half-Russian Holly, and Harriet – survivors, against the worst. Things we'll never know. More to admire there than anything I've ever admired in anybody.'

Johnny raised his glass to him, then waved it round the room, encompassing the others, then drank. Then he belched a fraction. 'I tell you something else. My old Methodist aunt in Lynchburg, the one who threw her alcoholic husband down the embankment into the James river – did I tell you about her? – no, I will – she'd have liked this sweet beer. She was "partial to a drop", as Matty says. On the quiet.'

Yelena came up to Anna. Some time after her recovery at the hands of Father Byrne she had made what apologies she could for the horror on the dance floor in Harbin. Subsequently she had seen little of her and Ivan until after her marriage to Johnny, two months before, at the Methodist church in Philadelphia. She had seen Anna more often after that. They had regained something, but not very much, of their old friendship. Anna was wary of Yelena now. And Yelena continued to feel deeply ashamed of what she had tried to do to her. So that in her company Yelena overreacted being either too jolly or too offhand towards her. They had, in truth, lost each other.

But now, more affected by the strong ale than they realized, they were less inhibited. Yelena lifted her glass.

' "Saunderton's Best Triple X" – I think I've drunk too much of it!'

'Yes, me too. But why not? You said once, Yelena – don't

settle for anything but the best!' Anna raised her glass. 'And I said one could never get that. But you were right. Go for the best man, you said. No compromise. Wholeheartedly. And I didn't agree. Saw it far more as a matter of compromise. And settling for less. I was wrong. Because we've got the best men now.' She looked away. 'And I went for the wrong man, with Sasha. And I'm sorry. When the right man was always there – for both of us. We've survived everything, Linochka,' she went on urgently. 'So for God's sake, whatever we do – let's neither of us throw away a fraction of what we've finally got now.'

'No.' Yelena swayed a bit, glassy-eyed. Yet it wasn't entirely the drink. The horror of her life – images of pain, terror, cruelty, stupidity – swept across her mind's eye. So that she said at once, almost fearfully, shaking her head, 'Such terrible things I've done. And whether it was me or some devil I was born with, I don't know. But I never wanted what I had, from the very beginning, when that old Lapp woman told me I had these special powers. Good or bad – it was all a curse from the start.'

Anna nodded. She saw the pain in Yelena's face now. She knew of Father Byrne's exorcism. Before she had never wanted to believe in Yelena's supernatural gifts. She had wanted to see her behaviour as simply malign, on her own account. Since then she had had to revise her opinion. Now she did so to Yelena herself. 'I never believed in your strange powers. I'm so far from being that kind, or any other kind, of believer. But now I'm convinced you had them, that you were cursed in some way. So I don't think you should blame yourself.'

'Thank you.' Yelena looked at her, less baneful now. 'I hope not. It's so good to be free of it all, to be an ordinary person –'

'You'll never be that, with your music –'

'Though Father Byrne told me afterwards,' she interrupted, 'always to be on my guard. The devil knows his own, he said. So he gave me a card, a small prayer-card. It's an Irish prayer, called "The Breastplate of St Patrick" – "Christ be with me, Christ within me . . ." It's funny, isn't it? But I keep it with me all the time, round my neck.' She fingered beneath her collar.

Anna looked at her, bemused, as if at some object that encapsulated all the mysteries of the world. 'No, not funny,' she said at last. 'It's good.' Then she changed her tone. 'I'm glad we got a bit drunk here.'

'So am I.'

They raised their glasses and smiled at each other properly for the first time in nearly a year.

The church was packed to the doors next morning. News had spread of the rector's exotic house guests. Dozy farmers, nosy parkers, some of the county gentry – everyone had their eyes out on stalks as the visitors filed in, all ten of them, in their outlandish clothes, with Mrs Woodrow and Holly. They took up two whole pews, behind that of the Cottesloes, the lords of the manor, who alone among the congregation took no notice of them. For the others it was a different matter.

The rector's foreign visitors! – My word, they thought. A Russian Prince and Princess, they'd heard; actors, circus people, an American railway magnate. This was heady Christmas fare indeed for the sober, isolated community. Most hoped to gather further material for gossip – malicious, very likely – from a direct viewing of these bizarre strangers. They were certain to be surprised by them. They hoped to be shocked. Foreigners of this sort – mummers and millionaires, unmarried couples, royal twins (the Princess, it was rumoured, had had to do with Rasputin); Bohemians all: such people were quite unpredictable – and dangerous, a threat to the status quo, so that barely concealed enmity vied with curiosity among many in the congregation. There was a distinct *frisson* of bad motive in the air.

After loud singings of the Advent carols – Ida much to the fore, so forward, indeed, that she outpaced Mrs Woolston on the organ, who had to pedal frantically to keep up with her – Harold climbed the steps to the pulpit, took off his spectacles and began his sermon. He had no notes. He knew what he had to say.

' "Now therefore ye are no more strangers and foreigners, but fellow citizens with the saints, and of the household of God . . ." The epistle of St Paul to the Ephesians has perhaps more than usual relevance – today . . .' He looked round the congregation, at his exotic house guests and then at the local parishioners with just the smallest hint of a smile. 'I had intended those words to be my text this morning. I thought about the sermon yesterday – thought much about it, how it should go and what I should say. I made copious notes. But the more I thought and wrote – and you all know how long-winded I like to be – the more I realized how little I could add to St Paul's words here. St Paul says it all in this epistle – all that I wanted to say and all that we need know. Because this is the essential Christian message – for all of us in this small church, and for everyone else, to the furthest corners of the earth: "Now therefore ye are no more strangers and foreigners, but fellow citizens with the saints, and of the household of God . . ." '

He paused. People settled themselves for a long sermon. But there was none. 'In the name of the Father, the Son and the Holy Spirit, Amen.' The congregation was astonished. Then he started again in a lighter tone. 'You'll all be delighted to hear – I hope – that among our guests today we have two very fine musicians, Alexander and Yelena Rumovsky. They have kindly agreed to give a short recital after the service, at the rectory. There will be light refreshments.' He glanced at Johnny. 'You will all be very welcome.'

There was quite a rush after the final blessing, from the church to the rectory. Even the Cottesloes came.

The terriers had been put in the stables. The big drawing-room had been cleared of all armchairs and sofas, replaced by other smaller chairs from all over the house, some forty of them set in rows. They were not sufficient. People had to stand. They overflowed through the large double doors into the hall. The room became hot. The fire was banked up. A window was opened. There was some unseemly pushing for advantage among the guests, for seats in the front row. The dozy farmers were awkward. Most stood in the hall. They would not have been there at all but for their wives, who had insisted.

There was a murmur of chatter, a scraping of clumpy boots, a settling of heavy women, among an audience most of whom had never attended an occasion of this nature. But this didn't matter. Their purpose here was social, not musical. At last there was silence, an air of the keenest expectation.

Sasha and Yelena walked into the bright sunlight of the

drawing-room, Yelena stopping briefly to kiss Sandy, standing alone by the doorway, as she passed through. She was dressed in a long blue velvet skirt, white blouse and brightly patterned Cossack waistcoat. Sasha looked uncomfortable in a formal suit. Both looked small and vulnerable, Sandy thought, as he watched them walk away. There was polite applause, which gathered some strength as they made their way to the far end of the room.

Yelena sat at the Blüthner grand. Sasha, with his Amati violin, standing by the curve of the piano, faced her. She gave him a note. He made a final tuning. There was absolute silence, except for the faint sound of the terriers complaining. Then they began: Tchaikovsky's *Souvenir d'un lieu cher*.

It was music they had often played. They needed no score. They knew it by heart. Tchaikovsky's Opus 42 in three parts, Méditation, Scherzo and Mélodie – music which was for them now a memory of a lost Russia.

Sandy was frustrated when they started to play. It was the old problem, of course, but most especially annoying now – that he couldn't hear their music properly, with his bad ear. Just muffled sounds, dull echoes – one-dimensional hearing in which their music was tinny, without body or resonance.

He was astonished therefore when after a few minutes there was a sudden change, as if a vacuum had been realeased in his bad ear. Now their music rushed through the freed passage in all its glorious vivacity and attack, flooding both ears now, in its every dimension, high notes and low, and all that lay between, in sharply struck harmonies, dissonances and rushing arpeggios.

Now he could hear their playing in all its uncanny, instinctual accord, just as he'd heard them in the first concert of theirs which he'd attended at the Petersburg Conservatoire almost seven years before: a wonderful mix of the unexpected, often quite opposite qualities – detachment suddenly turning to passion, serenity quickly becoming ecstasy; passages of soft legato, a studied quiet, broken by explosive tumult. It was magic. Magic indeed, since the doctors years before had told him that he would never regain proper hearing in this ear. And then he remembered how Yelena, as she'd passed him on her way into the drawing-room, had kissed him briefly, on the side of his face, just next that ear. He left it at that, shaking his head, giving himself to the music, in wonder.

Before, when he had heard them, that first time at the Conservatoire, he'd felt they were making love to each other in their music. Now he didn't feel this. Nor did Harriet, standing by the fireplace, who before had often felt just the same thing. She thought now how they had gone beyond themselves and were making love to the music; that their eyes meeting briefly, their similar expressions and shared emotions had nothing to do with their own lives or feelings for each other, with any of the old fevers or disagreements there: now they were giving themselves to Tchaikovsky. Now they agreed, co-operated without a shadow of dissent. They lived only in the music. They were free.

But Harriet was forced drastically to review her opinion of the twins' relationship in the next piece they played – Cesar Franck's Sonata in A Major, his turbulent portrait of a marriage, its loves and bitter furies, its struggles for possession, dominance, its perfections and follies.

Here the twins played in quite a different manner, returning, in their combative style and expression, to a partnership filled with all their old antagonism and passion for each other. Now their looks, their love and anger, were for each other, not given to the music, as they moved into the story cannonade of the sonata.

Yelena's fingers rippled over the keys in a frenzy, Sasha's dancing about the upper strings, his bow darting in a blur lower down, the music pouring forth, flooding the bounds of the drawing-room with what was still unreconciled between them, what they still harboured for each other; a mix of fierce love and resentment. It was superb. They were not so much interpreting the sonata – they were living it, creating it there and then, in all its love and fury, for each other.

Things were not over between them in that way, Harriet realized. But then, she came to think that, so long as they played music together like this, they never would be. It was the nature of their musical partnership that they should use their love and hatred – what was unreconciled there – as the well-spring of their playing.

Yelena, through Johnny, had vanquished the birth curse of

the bad fairy and her own later self-destructive impulses. She had come clear of the nets of folly. With Johnny, with her and everyone else, she had become the full glorious person. But not with Sasha. Such a bounty, a balance, would always elude her there. Yelena would never make things entirely 'right and proper' with him.

And nor would she. She would never quite make things up with him, as she so wanted, in a decent civilized manner. Such a scheme was not in his nature, which demanded all or nothing. His, in the Russian mode, was a nature of uncompromising passion. And so in her forthright American way, was Ida's. They were likely, in this, to make a go of things.

But between Sasha and Yelena it was a different matter. The same sort of utter fulfillment which they wanted with each other they could not now have. It would hang over them, as stark light and shadow, for the rest of their lives – the unachieved, the unbrought-together.

True, the Sonata, when they came to the last movement, resolved its earlier furies. And no doubt, in the same way, they would resolve things from time to time between themselves. But it would be temporary, Harriet felt. There would always be something of Sonata's earlier tensions, its passion and anger, between them as people. There would be no end to their musical art, no final interpretation or statement. It would always be subject to the powerful vagaries of their hearts, to what was forbidden in their feelings for each other. There would always be this provocative excitement in their playing. There could be no final reconciliation. If there was, there would be no music.

The applause was loud and sustained. Even the quite unmusical appreciated the fervour of the performance, while the few who knew about music were stunned. Their friends – they, too, saw something of what Harriet had seen – how in some crucial ways they would never impinge on these twins. Sasha and Yelena had a secret world together, like children, with its own codes and passwords, a magic castle in their music where they would always be inviolate.

After they'd finished playing, and taken their bows, both of them left the drawing-room hurriedly. On their way through the hall, among the awkward farmers gathering round the coffee table, Holly left Harriet and rushed up to her father. 'Papa!' she yelled. He picked her up, gazed at her a moment, then held her high up in the air, before sitting her round his neck, on his shoulders.

All three of them went out through the front door alone, into the frosty sunshine. They stood on the drive looking out over the hills, dusted again with a smattering of overnight snow. 'Papa,' Holly said. 'Could I learn to play the fiddle like that?' She turned to Yelena. 'Or the piano? I can play scales, and chopsticks already – with Mama.'

'Yes,' Yelena said. We'll teach you.'

'We'll teach you the piano – and the fiddle,' Sasha added. 'And your Mama – well, she does already, doesn't she? – she'll go on teaching you, when we're away.'

'You won't be away for long, though, will you? – like you were in Russia.' Holly looked down over his brow, her arms clasped round his neck.

'No, I won't.'

He did a little jig with her then on the crunchy gravel, dancing round and round, so that they both had a turning view of the sun-touched house, the frosty hills. 'I like this!' Holly said between her gasps of laughter. 'I like you here!'

That evening, when Holly had gone up to bed, where she slept in the bedroom which had been Sandy's as a child, filled with his old toys and books, all the guests came, successively, to see her – troops of strolling players, mummers, rogues, vagabonds and millionaires, paying court to her, magi bearing gifts.

Her father played her the Russian 'Pedlar's Dance' on his fiddle and did another jig with her afterwards, while her mother took up the music on the upright piano in the room.

Johnny and Ida came in, boisterously – Johnny finding an old rattle of Sandy's on a shelf, swinging it about and making a fearful racket. 'You're like Tweedledum,' Holly told him. 'And Tweedledee,' she added, more softly, thinking of the equally plump Ida, but not looking at her.

'Who are they?' Johnny asked.

Holly thought it better not to explain that they were two fat boys. She simply said, 'Twins, in *Alice Through the Looking-Glass*. One of them spoilt the other's nice new rattle.'

'Oh, I see.' Johnny put down the rattle. He spotted an old tin train set on another shelf, with a circular track. 'Here, this is better,' he said. 'Can we play with this?' She nodded. She and Ida and Johnny played with the train set. Johnny insisted that he had to be the engine driver.

Ivan came with Anna. He saw a model yacht of Sandy's on top of the cupboard. He took it down and showed her how the sails worked, the rudder, how it tacked into the wind in a zig-zag fashion. Then he took her for an imaginary voyage in it, all three of them, holding the boat in front of her. 'You take the tiller,' he told Holly. 'And I'll show you – we'll go to the Happy Isles.'

'Is that where the Owl and the Pussycat went? – the island where the bong tree grows?'

Ivan didn't know about these creatures, or about the tree, so Holly explained. ' "The Owl and the Pussycat went to sea, in a beautiful pea-green boat. They took some honey, and *plenty* of money, wrapped up in a five-pound note . . ." '

'That was wise of them. Well provisioned –'

'Yes, I'll show you.' Holly picked out, from among the scores of Sandy's old children's books, packed on shelves and scattered all over the floor, Lear's *Book of Nonsense Songs*.

Ivan inspected the picture of the Owl and the Pussycat, with a guitar and a pot of honey, adrift, under the moon, in their fragile pea-green boat. He was fascinated. 'Very brave of them,' he said. 'Yes, that's certainly where they went, the Happy Isles. That's where the bong trees grow.'

'Have you been there? – on all your boats. Have you *seen* the bong trees?'

'No. It's not an easy voyage. Storms and things. The Owl and the Pussycat – they must have been better sailors than me.'

'Yes . . .' Holly thought about this. 'Better even than you!'

Anna then read the whole rhyme, and more of them, and they laughed a lot.

Miki and Galina came next, and there was no doubt, so far as Holly was concerned, as to what she expected him to do, so that he'd come prepared. He took out a big handkerchief, opened it up, then put a seed in the middle of it, a tiny hard seed. Then he folded the handkerchief round it, lifting it up, saying magic words over it. Then he opened it again. Inside was a whole ear of corn. He did this successively, with other seeds, taken from his pocket, each time unfolding a different growth in the handkerchief – a carrot, a small parsnip, an apple, a pear, an orange, a lemon. Holly shook her head in wonder. 'How do you do it?'

'Ah,' he said slowly. 'That's a secret . . .'

'Will you show me?'

'Yes. Not now though. It's a long business, this sort of magic.'

'Oh, yes, I know – I *know* it is,' she said earnestly.

When Yelena came last to see her, Holly was tucked up in bed clutching her furless Teddy. Yelena looked round the chaos of books. She picked several up – all Sandy's old books, many of which were the same books that Harriet had read to her as a child, in Petersburg and at Ladoga. They were all here. Caldecott's illustrated edition of *John Gilpin* which she and Sandy had argued about buying in Watkins's English bookshop in Petersburg, and others which she knew equally well, from earlier times in Russia: *Treasure Island*, *Little Women*, Henty's Books for Boys, *John Dough and the Cherub*, *The Wizard of Oz* and *The Phoenix and the Carpet*, with Cook and the savages on the desert island, and the 'oggery-doggery' words with which she'd frightened the wolves off when their *troika* had tipped over on the ice. And there, too, was Afanasiev's collection of *Russian Fairy Tales*, of the witch Baba Yaga and *The Firebird* and *Alenoushka*.

So many of the same books which had been hers, which Harriet had read to her and Sasha, which she had thought lost for ever, long since destroyed in the Palace in Petersburg or in the great castle at Ladoga – all of them had turned up here, like homing pigeons.

Of course, they couldn't ever be finally lost. These sort of books were indestructible, magic books, proof against evil, against the worst adversity.

Yelena picked up Afanasiev's *Fairy Tales*. 'One of these?' she asked. 'Or these?' She picked up Doyle's *Red Book of Fairy Tales*. ' "Little Red Riding Hood"?'

'And the Big Bad Wolf!' Holly laughed. 'That's just soppy. We had *real* wolves in Russia, didn't we?' She leant forward eagerly, fascinated by the memory.

'Yes, we did.'

Yelena saw how Holly had no fear of wolves, just as she herself had had none as a child. Holly – for all that she knew of them, in gobbling up Red Riding Hood and huffing and puffing the little pigs' houses down – for Holly wolves had no wicked reputation. For Holly, as with her years before, they were creatures of an enchanted kingdom, where Holly herself was now part of that wonderful company – of wolves, firebirds, hobgoblins, witches, fairies. Holly shared their magic.

'So which book shall we have?'

Holly couldn't decide. She hummed, putting a finger to her lips, looking round. 'Hummm . . .' she said. Then she pointed to the end of the bed. Yelena turned, seeing the much battered copy of *The Tailor of Gloucester* which they had taken with them through two years of peril, all the way from Pestersburg, to Ladoga, right across Russia and Siberia, to Harbin – and now here, to the final safety of the rectory. It had been her own book originaly. She opened it, looking at the inscription. 'For Linochka, on her sixth birthday, with love from Miss Harriet'.

'Sandy reads it to me sometimes,' Holly said.

'Yes, he read it to me once, when I was ill.'

'Did it make you better?'

'Yes. Yes, it did.'

Holly gazed at her intently. There was silence. 'Books can do that,' Holly said suddenly. 'Can't they? Make you better.'

'Yes, they can.'

There was silence again. Yelena gazed at the child now. 'What are you thinking?'

'Tomcat,' Holly said at once. She leant forward. 'Do you think he's all right? Mama says he is. But do *you* think he is?'

'Yes, I do think he's all right. The man who bought the restaurant, Mr Rogozinsky who owned the wine shop up the road – he promised to look after him, and –'

'And the black pigs? Molly and Mary – and Timmy the fat porker. Mr Rogo – I can't say it – he won't ever eat them, will he?'

'No, he won't. That was part of the agreement your Mama made with him, too. Tomcat and the pigs – they'll just eat scraps from the restaurant for the rest of their lives.'

They'll all get terribly fat, even fatter!'

'Yes, they will. But it's nice to be fat. It's a happy thing.'

'Yes, it is, isn't it? Like Uncle Johnny and Ida. They're terribly happy.' Holly considered this point for a moment, frowning. 'I'm *quite* fat, aren't I?'

'Yes, quite. Just about right.'

They gazed at each other now, intently, saying nothing, just nodding their heads together, mute evidence that they agreed about more or less everything. Then Yelena picked up the small book and began to read.

' "In the time of swords and periwigs and full-skirted coats with flowered lappets – when gentlemen wore ruffles and gold-laced waistcoats of paduasoy and taffeta – there lived a tailor in Gloucester . . ." '

Holly, quite exhausted with the evening's magic, and before Yelena got to the end of the second page, fell asleep sitting up, the furless Teddy slipping from her grasp. Her aunt put the animal back in her arms, settled her down, kissed her, and closed the book.